The Wild Highway

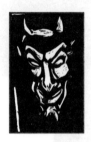

The Wild Highway
Bill Drummond & Mark Manning
ISBN 1-84068-116-0
9781840681161
Published 2005 by Creation Books
www.creationbooks.com

Contents

PART ONE
THEY RAPE NUNS HERE

Chapter 1	*The Bumming Of Gimpo*	005
Chapter 2	*They Rape Nuns Here*	060
Chapter 3	*The Strange Man In The Disturbing White Bell-Bottoms*	104
Chapter 4	*Larium*	122
Chapter 5	*Boneyard Earth*	145
Chapter 6	*Soft Cargo*	150
Chapter 7	*Colin Wilson, The Genius Of Crime*	169
Chapter 8	*The Secret Plot*	176
Chapter 9	*For Us Queers, Love Is All*	198
Chapter 10	*Oscar Wilde, Nonce*	221
Chapter 11	*The Jungle Chooses Sides*	248
Chapter 12	*Feasting With Panthers*	253
Chapter 13	*Steel, Honour And Sodomy*	259
Chapter 14	*Sodomistic Justice, Bummed By Friends*	272
Chapter 15	*The Greek*	279

PART TWO
ALL THE SCUM OF THE JUNGLE

Chapter 1	*Underneath God*	315
Chapter 2	*The Wankers Of Paris*	320
Chapter 3	*All The Scum Of The Jungle*	334
Chapter 4	*Logarithms Of Murder*	356
Chapter 5	*The Wild Highway*	374
Chapter 6	*Dreamstorm*	386
Chapter 7	*Kisangani Mayhem And Sleaze*	393
Chapter 8	*Meatloaf Electric Sexy Boy (Sockets Ahoy!)*	404
Chapter 9	*Wipe Out*	409

Part One
THEY RAPE NUNS HERE

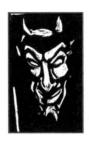

Chapter One
THE BUMMING OF GIMPO

Delirium tremens was not a problem. The drunken French mercenaries pissing around with their handguns behind me were. We were eight miles high. Way above the Zairean rainforest, juddering around the clouds in a scrap metal jigsaw puzzle held together by prayers and rust. I peered through the dirty window. One of the propellers had fallen off.

I didn't give a fuck. My alcoholic sidewinder withdrawal shit was chewing itself up into a full-blown rattler double fast.

I needed a drink.

Jean-Paul Bonehead and Pierre Fellatio were the only fuckers on board Suicide Airlines who had any medication.

Blam!

Well, well. It seemed like those two poodles of war behind me couldn't wait till they reached jungle to bag a bush nigger and had started early. Black blood, bone and crinkly hair splattered across the ceiling. Small ragged pieces of brain matter, like baby's teeth, hung in the mess.

Man, was I pissed off.

Frenchy and his pal were in the employ of some major multinational that wanted to suppress a popular people's revolution in a small republic. The usual cosmosodomistic machinations of the black gas.

I didn't give a fuck. My pants were ruined.

I grabbed muscle-faggot Pierre's Glock 9mm and jabbed it hard into the cocksucker's face. The small bone at the bridge of his nose collapsed into his brain, killing him instantly. Jean-Paul went for his piece. Too late. The brandy had slowed him down. My bullet hit him in the heart, spinning him into the aisle, spraying blood and brandy all over the back of Gimpo's head.

King Scat removed his headphones to find out what all the fuss was about. He flicked a piece of grey gloop from his chartreuse safari suit and replaced his cans.

Just violence. He didn't give a fuck.

Bill looked up from his book, checked that his shocking-pink number was still pristine – it was – and carried on reading.

What kind of fucking airline was this anyway? I strode purposefully down the aisle. A couple of French hostesses tried to stop me. I kicked one in the cunt and hurt my hand on the other one's teeth.

What was this shit?

I entered the flight deck: shiny black arses pumping hard into slick French gash. Laughter, cocaine and liquor.

'Who's flying this fucking thing?' I demanded.

A shit-faced spade with a skinny Somalian chick sucking on his dick laughed.

'No one, man.' he answered and handed me a half bottle of Johnny Walker. 'Plane, she flies herself!'

Fat boy thought this was hilarious. His pilot's hat was on backwards, his shirt undone revealing his jiggling gut. The Somalian cocksucker slurped her guppie lips off laughing boy's wood.

'Autopilot,' she dribbled through spunk and saliva. 'Plane flies itself.'

I chugged a large hit on the whisky and laughed. Nigger Biggles gave me a high five, said something appreciative about the powder-blue Roger Moore number and told me to grab a wife.

I apologised to the cute hostess I'd assaulted earlier and waded into the gash, buggering with abandon.

DRUMMOND'S LOG, WEDNESDAY 5 JUNE 1996
RACISM AND HOW TO HANDLE IT

Racism is based on fear and I am frightened. Very frightened. In fact shit scared. The smell inside this 747 is unbearable. Apart from Gimpo, Z, two French mercenaries and myself, this jumbo is crammed with Africans. The stench is of that acrid body odour that only the black man seems to be able to produce with ease. We are on the final descent into Kinshasa International Airport, after a turbulent eight-hour flight from Brussels. My fear shows no signs of subsiding.

Throughout my life I have steadfastly refused to use any sort of deodorant. A man should smell like a man, not a perfume counter assistant. That's my rule. Sallie, my partner, is pretty handy with the barbed comment. After one particular hard day pushing the pencil across the open page, she passed a remark about my honest sweat: 'If I'd wanted to live with a man who smells like you do today, I'd have married an African.'

Within the privacy of their own homes most consenting adults feel free to be as racist as they need to be. As long as it's out of earshot of the children, what's the harm? Living in a modern multicultural society, most of us have learnt to curb our racist tendencies. On the surface our society has been reasonably successful at this suppression. I mean, we even find black men to act *Othello* these days.

In fact, as the 'fasten safety belt' sign comes on and we start our final descent into the post-colonial and thoroughly modern African state of Zaire, I've got my notebook open on my knees, a pencil in hand and I'm trying my best to neutralise all those inclinations towards racism by freely expressing my thoughts on to the virgin white and willing page. It's an old trick I learnt from the marriage guidance counsellor the last time I needed to go for a top up.

We're hitting the runway, my pencil goes flying from my hand, and a massive cheer goes up from my fellow passengers before they break into song. As the plane shudders and skids to a halt, all the black passengers are on their feet trying to drag their bulging bags from the overhead lockers. All the women are that large type, swathed in yards of brightly printed cotton with matching head-dresses. It is the women who seem to be less able to control their impulses to drag their now splitting bags from the overhead lockers and push their way to the front. And the 'unfasten safety belt' lights have yet to come on.

As I said before, it's a jumbo we are on, and our three seats are in the central block. From this position we have not been able to see out of the windows, so none of the descent, let alone the thousands of miles of the African continent we have already crossed over.

With my seat belt still fastened, I'm straining my neck and I've just had my first glimpse of Africa. What I see is the charred remains of a burnt-out propeller-driven troop carrier sitting on the runway about 50 yards from where the jumbo has finally ground to a halt. As yet, I've not been able to rid myself of my fear by sharing it with this page. The 'unfasten safety belt' lights finally come on. Z, Gimpo, the two French mercenaries and myself are the only passengers left at the back of the plane. The rear door opens and we are beckoned by the slim and beautiful air hostess, the one who Z had suggested earlier we should bugger in the toilets. As I put on my broad-brimmed bush hat and brush out the creases of my sand-coloured safari suit, I notice Z's is already looking a tad soiled. His crotch is stained with spillage of whatever it was he was so liberally spending our daily allowance on from the in-flight drinks trolley. I was obviously already winning in the Roger Moore lookalike contest.

Gimpo had refused to wear or even try on a safari suit, insisting on his pale purple muscle-hugging T-shirt, lightweight military fatigues and Caterpillar boots. Z and I had both invested in pairs of Clark's sandals as endorsed by Ranulf Fiennes. Ranulf Fiennes seemed to be the sort of arrogant, stuck-up and useless English explorer-tosser type that we most wanted to identify ourselves with, in a twisted ironic sort of way. Clark's campaign to sell their sandals had worked on us. I don't like wearing sandals but Z had insisted it was *de rigueur*.

Gimpo is ignoring us and is obviously infatuated with the two Frenchmen. Somehow he has discovered they are in the employment of a company called Executive Outcomes. It has long been one of Gimpo's great regrets that he has not put his experience in the Falklands war to good use and made his killing as a soldier of fortune. My mean little mind is thinking that Gimpo is probably hoping that this pair of muscle-bound snail crunchers think that Gimpo is also a mercenary off to another small mess that needs sorting out by highly trained professional white men.

We are just about to step out of the door on to the top of the staircase-on-wheels thing, I take a glance back down the cabin of the 747. What I see is a surge of angry black women in their robes raging up the aisles towards our just opened rear exit.

*

Katie Blade slings back her sixteenth large gin and tonic. The ice clatters against her perfect teeth. She slams the bucket glass on the shiny walnut bar and orders another. It's 10.30am at the Memling Hotel.

Katie is pissed and her cunt hurts. She's sitting alone waiting for room service to clean up last night's weirdness. Things had gotten a little out of hand. Even for her.

Katie is the BBC's fearless number-one war correspondent. Wherever in the world the locals could take no more of that eternal jackboot stomping down on their faces and had decided to do something about it, Katie and her camera crew were always there. She'd be booked into the nearest five-star hotel colour co-ordinating 'it' into whatever hue her cosmosodomistic employers required. In the theatre of war, Katie always had champagne and the best seats.

But the accolades and endless awards the khaki-clad sex bomb received didn't reveal the whole truth. Katie of course lives the whole truth and the alcohol helps her deal with it.

Katie was a blood slut. A war-whore violence-junkie. The only way this daughter of a privileged education could juice her cunt up was by getting down in the dirt beneath the black clouds of war-torn skies. Down with the poor and their suffering and despair. Down with the blood, guts and soldier-boy tube steak. Sucking in the smell of cordite, fresh death and warm torture curling off GI Joe's Yankee bell end. These days however, it took a hell of a lot of death to whip Katie's cream.

Of course none of this was entirely Kate's fault. A lot of the blame could be placed at the staunch feet of her parents and their choice of school. But there again, Katie's parents could almost be excused – after all, wasn't this the way that the good and the great always chose to educate their precious sprogs? The mores and attitudes instilled within these hallowed halls were defined at a time when territorial and domestic rape was the order of the day. Unfortunately these whispered attitudes exploded sideways in poor sensitive Kate and instead of manifesting themselves in her social and political orientation decided to take a hike south and curl like a perverted leper around her fermenting libido.

This would explain the mess up in suite 17.

TWO WEE DARKY BOYS

As I look down at my right toe sticking out of its sandal, as I'm lifting that foot to step out of the cabin door into the African sunshine, I remember something that happened when I was six, back in small-town Scotland circa 1959. Sam, my best pal and I were on our way back from Dash Wood Square via the graveyard when we bumped into the bogeyman. Now, he wasn't a real bogeyman, just a man who lived alone with his black dog up the hill. We didn't know his real name but what we did know was that he liked to scare us young lads. He wasn't averse to chasing us with his stick and threatening to lock us up in his coal hole. I suppose in this day and age he would be chased out of town by the paedophile-fearing proletariat, but back then I assume that every town needed one of these men so our mums could threaten us with him to get us back home before bedtime. They performed a social function. Anyway, Sam and I were taking the short cut across the graveyard when up popped the bogeyman with his stick.

'Hallo there lads, off for a spot of grave robbing today?'

'No sir, we're just off home.'

'Past your bedtimes?'

'No sir, we've not had tea yet.'

'Well, why not come round to my house for tea. Do you fancy a fish supper? And it's not even Friday.'

'No sir, our dads are coming to meet us,' says Sam.

'Is that so?'

'Yes,' we answered in unison.

'Well, there is something I want to tell you before you run along. I've just come down from the railway station. Do you know what I saw getting off the train?'

'No sir.'

'I saw two wee darky boys. Black as the devil's boots. About your age they were, with bones through their noses. I heard they were going to be living here. In fact, they were going to be in your class at school. Primary two isn't it?'

'Yes sir.'

'Well, if I was you I'd run off home. A graveyard is not place to be if there are darkies about. You know how they like the taste of human flesh.'

We ran.

And that night, sleep was a long time coming and when it did it was filled with bad dreams. The only knowledge I had back then about black boys was the bad golliwogs that lived in the wood outside of Noddy's Toy Town and from the black and white photos in the pre-war edition of Arthur Mee's *Children's Encyclopaedia* we had at home.

The next morning I trudged to school at a slower rate than the lad in Shakespeare's second age of man. Of course, when we got there, there were no two wee darky boys. Nor the next day, or the next. In fact, if those two lads ever moved to our town I never got to see them.

Things have moved on since the dismal days in the late 1950s. The golliwogs have been banished from the woods in Noddy books to be replaced by Robbo and Gobbo, the goblins and in the modern-day children's encyclopaedia that my kids have, the civilising exploits of the British Empire are hardly mentioned at all.

But what I did learn as I grew up is that every white woman I'd ever known would apparently rather be shagged by a muscle-bound black man from dusk to dawn and back again than spend a night with the likes of me.

*

Lovely Kate had been entertaining three studs from the local army barracks when her guests' cocaine and whisky acrobatics had spiralled weirdwards. Katie loved it at the time. What passionate public school-educated gel wouldn't?

 Airtight African style: one black cock jammed to the nuts in her lathering cunt; jungle-stud number two ripping up her stretched jacksie. The pièce de resistence at this exotic banquet spumed into overdrive when powerful Sergeant Rastus castrated the shoe-shine boy into Madame's gibbering mouth.

Sweet meat indeed.

The kid's howling screams sent Katie oscillating into multiple-orgasm mode and when sexy little Sambo unloaded his terrified bowels all over her juddering mams, why scat heaven itself just upped and farted its way down to earth.

But that was hours ago. Right now Kate felt used. Her laughing paramours had left her unconscious among the flanged gore. And, to add insult to injury, those low-rent Lotharios had cleaned out our heroine's purse.

'Bastards,' hissed the sexy splanchophiliac through gritted teeth. 'Black bastards.' 'If they didn't all look the fucking same...' she lit another Gauloise. 'I'd have them publicly sodomised.' The commanding officer of the local regiment, the charming sadist fond of dildoing Katie's fudge bullet hole with his Browning 9mm would have seen to that.

'For fuck's sake,' exclaimed the pretty pervert to no one in particular. 'It's a gentleman's duty to dispose of the garbage.'

Katie threw back her seventeenth G&T. The ice cracked angrily against her white teeth.

KEEP YOUR CHIN UP

So I put my right foot down on the top of the staircase on wheels and just as my left foot is following, I look up to take my first proper look at Africa. What I see is 1,000 black faces screaming, waving and surging towards the bottom of this flight of stairs that we are about to descend.

The two men from Executive Outcomes lead the way down the stairs to Africa, us three following behind them. I'm happy to hide in their shadow. I kinda hope they can protect us from whatever is yet to happen but as soon as they step on the tarmac a Jeep appears from nowhere and whisks them off to wherever it is that men like them have to go. There is now nothing between us and the sea (OK, boating lake) of black faces, waving arms and yelling voices.

'Bill, shall we just kiss the ground then get back on the plane and demand they fly us home?'

'What?'

'Well, we have actually been to Africa now. We can just go home and make the rest up.'

Z has a talent, one I'm envious of. A talent to make everything up and so that it still sounds believable, whereas I have to rely on telling the factual truth and even then it sounds like a pack of lies. Z's suggestion to get straight back on the plane is the sensible course of action, especially if we had any sense of responsibility towards our families. The trouble is, it's already too late, and Gimpo is striding out towards what I assume are the airport terminal buildings, directly into the oncoming surge of unbridled humanity.

Gimpo has that sense of confidence that only the white man with an empire to build can display but due to Gimpo's diminutive stature, the first wave of blackness swallows him up whole. It's now only me and Z.

'Z, do you think we should hold hands?'

'Fuck off Bill, we bought these safari suits for moments like this. Just keep your chin up at a prepossessing and jutting angle and stride.'

With that, Z is off, his head tilted upwards, his eyes scouring the horizon, his cheeks sucked in, his lips pursed and his chin jutting out. All that stuff he learnt on 100 scuzzy rock tours. It may have convinced a goth-metal chick in Crapsville, Idaho of his rock-legend status but I don't think it's going to work here.

But I'm not going to be out-fuckin'-macho'd by Z at this early stage of our quest. I jut my chin out further than he could ever dream of and stride past him into the blackness.

The Negroid faces scream 'passport', 'taxi', 'luggage', 'hotel'. I'm being pushed and pulled this way and that and, as I am swallowed into the mass of dark humanity, I try to draw some comfort from the fact that most of these screaming faces are beaming with huge smiles, and looking genuinely pleased to see us. A few are wearing white uniforms that may lend them some form of official authority but, as they too are jostling with each other for our attention, I'm assuming it's best to ignore the lot and keep wading towards the terminal. The trouble is, as I keep wading I get no further through the pushing and pulling and smiling and screaming crowd. It moves with us. Are we honey pots or lumps of shite?

*

I surfaced from my blackout surrounded by fire. It seems like the autopilot was pretty good at flying aeroplanes, but he sure as shit didn't know how to land the fuckers.

Bill and Gimpo had made it out of the carnage and were standing dazed on the boiling tarmac. Their safari suits hung in tatters. Somehow, despite the blood stains, my elegant outfit remained remarkably dashing.

Welcome to Kinshasa. A colonial meltdown, kleptocratic, apocalyptic, human-shit hell hole, where President Joe Mobutu is permanent top sausage and apart from his favourite frankfurters of the month, everyone else eats shit.

The aeroplane we crash-landed on explodes in the distance.

Idi Amin with bulbous eyeballs and Niagara saliva grabs my passport and smashes me in the face. I fall to the tarmac. Fatso kicks me in the balls. Pain like a giant intestinal parasite eats the air from my lungs and shits in my stomach.

From the corner of my bloodshot eye I see Gimpo buckle beneath the blows of a messy pistol whipping. His face looks like a broken pomegranate. Two skinny soldiers in mismatched uniforms drag me to my feet and throw me into a small room buzzing with flies and ghosts.

Slashed arcs of shit and blood are smeared across the cement walls, a single dim light bulb the only witness. Heavy boots thunder and bones crack in adjacent rooms. Idi enters the cell carrying my empty snakeskin wallet. His big melon-head face shines gun-metal blue, white teeth smiling like a washing powder advert. He pats my shoulder and embraces me fraternally. 'Ha ha. Airport tax,' he laughs, suddenly my long-lost friend. 'American dollar, yes? Ha ha. Zaire is good for you, ha ha.'

And that's it. Idi disappears to kick the fuck out of someone else.

I'm left $200 lighter in the derelict space that's supposed to be Kinshasha airport. Ebola-ridden refugees cling to the walls, puking blood.

Flies and yellow-eyed old men are everywhere, wanking and shitting in the dirt. Skinny child whores with xylophone ribs are pulling at the front of my pants: 'Suck meestah, suck. Yeah, Jesus is coming.'

Fuck knows what the missionaries out here were up to. A nine-year-old girl bends over and pulls her arse cheeks apart

'You fuck my bum hole, meestah? Like Virgin Mary, yes?'

It didn't take too much imagination.

A LITERARY WORK OF MERIT

I've just seen a tall black man loping out of the buildings. He is holding a card up with the names Goodrick, Manning and Drummond, felt-tipped on to it. Our names. I wave. He waves back.

'Z,' I shout, 'head for that man over there.'

We wade on through the quagmire of black humanity.

'Welcome to Kinshasa. My name is Mr Oliver Banga Bonga, you can call me Bongo, and I'm here to look after you and drive you to the hotel. Follow me.'

Bongo had an aura about him, an amiable authority that said, 'I'm a nigga that even a white man can trust'. Z and I are only too happy to lend him our trust. Gimpo trusts no one. The three of us are now sitting in an air-conditioned people carrier outside the terminal buildings. Bongo has our passports and $300 of our limited float, which he tells us is to sort out airport tax and a few other minor trivialities.

The travel agency in London had promised us that our air fares covered all such costs. When Gimpo tries to explain this to Bongo he only smiled. A benevolent smile. A 'you will learn' smile. A smile that ensured we hand over the $300 anyway and are grateful to do so, as long as we can sit in this air-conditioned people carrier for a few minutes longer.

While we wait for Bongo to return, I'll try to explain to you why Z, Gimpo and myself are here. As will be revealed to you in the following pages, Z and I realised that we had sold our souls to the devil and that if we wanted to retrieve them we should head for darkest Africa, confront Satan and demand our souls back and if that didn't work, nick them back off him while he wasn't looking. As for why Gimpo is here, I've no idea. He's obviously never been stupid enough to have lent his soul to anyone, let alone sell it to the devil.

Of course this is a preposterous proposition for any modern man to put forward. We are more likely to be taken for attention-seeking fools, jesters, or just plain liars. We freely admit that is what we are. We also believe that in making this ludicrous and somewhat foolhardy jest we may retrieve something of what we call our souls from Satan, Lucifer, the Fallen Angel, however legend and literature has titled him. We also think the tale of this venture may have the makings of a literary work of merit.

This, you should know, is not the first time the three of us have set out on a wildly illogical voyage of recovery [sic]. Back in late 1992, we had set off for the North Pole bearing an icon of Elvis Presley, convinced that once we had placed it at the very summit of the earth it would leak love, happiness and good vibes down the longitudes and out across the latitudes, bringing about an outbreak of world peace and general grace to mankind.

We not only failed to reach what is usually accepted as the North Pole, we also failed to write a book that changed the course of literary history and make our names as major men of letters. Z has since suggested to me that the true reason for our exploits as Arctic explorers was more an attempt to place Elvis, in a symbolic sense, as far away from us as possible. In this way we would somehow rid our lives of the havoc and devastation that the sordid world of rock 'n' roll had brought about in our own domestic arenas. This may be the case. But if so, this too has failed, to judge by the trail of broken marriages and fatherless children we continue to leave in our wake.

Actually, I do know why Gimpo is here. We asked him to come and he knew if he didn't come we would either not ever get it together to catch our flight or if we did manage that we would be dead within hours of our arrival. Either way he felt a responsibility towards us that goes deeper than we could fathom. There is also the small matter of narcotics. Z had told Gimpo about some substance to be found in the rainforests of the Congo Basin that is supposedly more wildly hallucinogenic than anything to be found in the jungles of the entire Amazon Basin.

Whatever the reason, I'm glad he's here. Z might be my bosom buddy, soul mate of dark disorder etc. but I can't stand being in his company for any more than 60 consecutive minutes without wanting to twat the arrogant vain cunt. Gimpo seems, in some way, to bring an equilibrium to our joint proceedings. He usually knows which way to go to get safely to morning. Third star on the left and all that.

*

The Hotel Memling courtesy bus shone dazzlingly white in the liver-scraping stench.

Gimpo sits in the back nursing his head injuries.

Bill is wearing the poached expression of someone wishing they were somewhere else, anywhere but right here, right now.

My traveller's hubris had led me to believe that Zaire would be pretty much the same as all the other third world countries I'd visited. Barefoot raggy-arse kids laughing and bathing in open sewers deflecting the poverty, flies and disease with their natural *joi de vivre*.

I couldn't have been more wrong.

There was no soul asylum of spiritual self sufficiency here.

This place was sick, jaundiced. Poisoned from within. Those dry-cunt Christians with their anaemic faith had sucked the energy out of the place, bled its animist soul dry.

Joe fucking Mobutu and his insane supernatural greed had taken care of the rest.

GIMPO THE AUTEUR

What landscape that we can see from the safety of our people carrier looks pretty much what you'd expect in any shitty corner of Africa: nothing spectacular, just a bit of scrub, a few knackered sheds, ragged black people milling about with nothing much to do. The only time most of us ever get to hear about Africa is when there is a war, a famine or a flood. What they do the rest of the time I've no fuckin' clue. From the looks of this they just seem to be sitting around waiting for a disaster to happen so the Western media can turn up and start filming them.

The more enterprising of these raggedy people tap on the windows and attempt to engage us in conversation. We try to ignore them. Is Africa still the white man's burden or is it our birthright to ignore the plight of our black brothers? I don't know the answer to either of these two questions. I do know that I don't want to do anything to upset the mild sense of security I'm now feeling.

'What the fuck are you doing, Gimpo?' asks Z.

'Getting my video camera out.'

'I thought I told you not to bring that.'

'It's not down to you to fuckin' tell me what I can or can't bring. You've brought your pen and notebook so you can write a book. I've brought my camera so I can make a film.'

Two things you should know that have happened to Gimpo since our first recorded adventure to the North Pole: he's got married to a Serbian refugee and he's become a film maker. First, the marriage thing. He somehow thinks that being married makes him a normal human being. He isn't. He never will be. Secondly, the filmmaking thing. Ever since Jimmy (Cauty, my fellow trustee in the K Foundation) handed him his camcorder and told him to film us burning our money and the subsequent footage became an underground cult classic, known as *Watch The K Foundation Burn A Million Quid*, Gimpo has believed his future is that of an avant-garde filmmaker. Gimpo the auteur now takes his video camera everywhere with him. Filming anything, anything at all.

He seems to use no critical faculty when choosing what to film and what not to film. His favourite stunt is to engineer a bit of road rage then jump out of the car he is driving, camera rolling in his left hand, leaving his right fist free to cause trouble. He then shows us the footage. He thinks it's very funny. The sad truth is, it is. In fact, *Road Rage the Movie* is a classic, as is *Concrete Enema* and *You Cunt*. In fact, Z and I are rather concerned – and maybe feel somewhat threatened – that Gimpo is about to be taken up by those art house-film types as the great filmmaker of our times, a primitive genius like Rousseau or Alfred Wallace. They'll be falling over each other to heap praise on him. As far as Z and I are concerned it is us who are the creative geniuses. Gimpo is our entertaining side-kick who provides us with protection and light relief and adds a bit of colour to our tales.

'Bill, tell him to put that camera away. They'll think we're a film crew.'

'So?' snaps Gimpo.

'Gimpo, Z has a point. If the niggers think we are a film crew they will think there's about to be a famine or a flood, or a war or something and they will think we are responsible...'

'You're just fuckin' scared Bill, aren't you?'

'Yes!'

*

The smiling driver and his enthusiastic buddy introduce themselves with loose friendly handshakes. They don't speak much English and their French is too weird to understand but we manage to find out each other's names. Theirs are Tombo Bamba and JC.

They will save our lives several times.

Tombo Bamba stomped the van into gear and we sped into the potholed suburbs of Hell. Almost everywhere across the garbage-strewn landscape mean-looking soldiers in skinny mirror shades wandered around purposefully. Machine gun bullet belts draped across lean shoulders, black berets pulled down low over their shades.

One of the many cool things young black guys know how to do really well is to look totally fucking evil. These cats looked totally fucking evil. A lot of them were wearing scraggy leopard skin scarves tied around their arms or hanging from their belts, fingerless black leather mittens and, bizarrely, gold faucets on heavy gold chains worn around their necks. They looked more like a bunch of heavily armed LA gangbangers than an organised military outfit. Small shoals of these exotic dandies of violence roamed the ruined streets firing at random at anyone who seemed to vaguely annoy them.

The van ground on into the casual insanity. JC, the driver's mate turns around from the front seat and smiles. He says something in French and pulls out a massive handcannon. He casually winds down the side window and shoots a young woman full in the face. The baby she is carrying falls from her arms and gets tangled in the wheels of the speeding bus. I can feel the tiny bones grinding around the rear axle. The driver laughs and gives his psychotic buddy a high five. He swerves to mow down another small kid whose head comes clean off and splatters across the windscreen. Tombo Bamba curses good-naturedly and the wipers smear the pink viscera across the glass.

Gimpo laughs.

THE RETURN OF BONGO

As Gimpo is putting his camera back in his bag there is a rap on the window. It's a black man in what I assume is a police uniform. Gimpo unwinds the window. The policeman is jabbering in French. We don't speak French. In fact, Z and I don't speak any language but English. We smile at him and point to the terminal building where Bongo disappeared over 20 minutes ago and where we are praying he's going to return from in the next 20 seconds.

The cop is smiling but carries on jabbering in French. His right hand is resting on his revolver. He leans his head through the open window.

'You boys speak English?'

'Yes we do. In fact, we are British,' says Z in a rather camp 1940s Ealing comedy upper-class English accent.

Does he think that speaking like this will gain us respect and protection? What a fuckin' wanker.

'Welcome to Zaire, boys. My name is Sergeant Charles. I'm here to help you. But first you must help me. $20 to feed my family and I will be your friend.'

'We don't need friends,' says Gimpo.

'Just give him the fuckin' money, Gimp,' says Z.

On cue Bongo arrives back, a smile on his face, brandishing our passports in one hand and a wad of dollar bills in the other. Sergeant Charles stands to attention. The ragged hoardes and millers-about gather around. Bongo hands the passports back through the open window to us then starts to hand out dollar bills to each and every one of the small crowd.

'Merci, Monsieur Bongo, merci.'

He jumps in the front seat, turns the key and we are off.

Bill is changing into a new safari suit. He throws the scorched rags of the shocking pink number out of the window and struggles into a new brown outfit. I don't think he thought pink was really him. He seems much more at ease in his new choice of leisure wear. Suddenly the bus skids to a squealing halt.

'Hey Meestah Scottish,' it's Tombo Bamba in barely comprehensible English. 'You see this?' He's smiling cheerfully. 'Ha ha, is good Zaire sport yes?'

For some weird reason I get the feeling that Tombo Bamba thinks we are on holiday.

He leaps excitedly from the bus and slides open the door for us. A small crowd a few yards away had gathered around three scared-looking teenagers, all three are naked, their hands lashed behind their backs. A cheerful fat woman is laughing and dancing, she starts singing, the crowd join in, the woman is shaking something above her head. A hi-life soca band is banging out happy tunes, their electric instruments powered by a noisy old petrol generator. The crowd dance along to the syncopated rhythms. Gimpo starts to join in, dancing at the edge of the colourful throng. It's only when the car tyres go over the teenagers heads that I realise what's going on.

The crowd start jumping high off the ground screaming hysterically and snapping into violent tribal moonstomping, chanting a scary chorus. The jolly fat woman pours petrol over the kids' heads and torches all three of them. The small crowd goes apeshit. Whooping and hollering, a couple of little kids start moonwalking and bodypopping. Machetes appear from nowhere and start chopping into the flaming kids who are screaming and trying to struggle out of the burning tyres.

Death by Dunlop man. Radical.

This was the first time I noticed the bucket kids, scrabbling little motherfuckers in raggy bare-arse shorts and nothing else. When chunks of flesh and burning limbs were hacked off the flaming martyrs the agile little fuckers, like wiry scrum halves from some grammar school team in hell would scoop up their gory trophies, slam them in brightly coloured buckets and disappear beneath the legs of the hysterical crowd. Tombo Bamba and JC had joined in and were dancing enthusiastically, Gimpo had found a beer from somewhere and was dancing along whitely.

Bill too seemed to be enjoying the spectacle, a creepy masturbator's smile spread across his twitching face. His left hand was moving furtively in his trouser pocket. A familiar stink like rotten airline food and sour milk oozed from him, a halo of blowflies gathered around his brown trousers and a bad feeling of *déjà vu* started trying to suck its own dick.

ON THE ROAD TO KINSHASA

The road from the airport into Kinshasa is what I'd expect any road into any African capital to look like. Potholes in bigger potholes, kids playing in the gutters, women walking along with baskets balanced on their heads. We've all seen it before on 1,000 news reports. There is nothing new for us to describe, nothing left unfilmed. I know that you know that but Z went to India last year for a two-week package holiday and he now thinks he's an expert on the third world. I've never been to the third world. They didn't do gap years when I was a teenager but I've listened to From our own Correspondent on Radio 4 for the last 25 years. I know everything there is to know about places like this. Fergal Keene and Kate Adie have told me the lot. But Z keeps going on and on about India. When Z starts on a subject there is no stopping him. It's as if a mania is creeping up on him and the only way to keep it at bay is for him to keep going deeper and further into his topic for the day. It could be anything: the design of door handles, the shape of clouds, how painting is about to make a comeback. Today it's India. Gimpo is ignoring him completely. He is totally engrossed in unpacking and repacking his bag, then unpacking it again. I just want to stare out of the window at the passing sights. But out of politeness I feel I should at least nod every few seconds at whatever Z is going on about.

'You see, Bill, they are like little children. Their attitude to religion is childlike, their faith is not troubled by doubt. That's why it works. They like things that sparkle, colourful clothes, and shiny shoes. They like to smile and laugh and make you happy. Bill, I just want to make people happy.'

'Z, this is fuckin' Africa, not India.'

'But I can see they are the same. Did I tell you about the time Sally and I visited a temple in the desert we…'

My mind has just drifted off into a blank space where nothing is going on, no thoughts, no worries, whatever happens now we have no control over. It feels good. Is this what it's like being on heroin? Outside, the vast majority of the other traffic on this six-lane dirt track are Volkswagen Dormobiles. They are all battered and bashed, doors missing, tyres bald. Each Dormie is carrying a cargo of at least 20 humans. Africans seem to love hanging off the side of them, screaming, shouting and laughing at other passengers hanging on to the outside of other passing Dormies.

I've never understood why people want to be so happy. What's with all this laughing? Haven't they got any dark psyches to explore? Fuck it. Fuck it. Fuck it. My mind's drifting off into those dark lagoons again. There will be plenty of time for that when we get up river.

'… So I said to Sally when we were staying in this colonial hotel in the Rajhastan desert, that you and I should become sadhus. What do you think, Bill? Let's jack it all in, leave our wives, kids, everything and becomes sadhus?'

'Sorry, Z, I didn't hear you. I was wondering if any of these BBC foreign correspondents might be staying at our hotel. The one with the white suit, what's his name? Or Kate Adie.' And that was it. At the mention of Kate Adie's name Z was off on one of his towering monologues. I can only wonder at where it all comes from: the immeasurable depths of his imagination, the limitless volumes of adjectives just waiting to be invented to describe things that have never in the entire history of mankind been thought about before, let alone written down for others to read.

*

The bus approached the Memling Hotel. A huge white obelisk, its confident geometry towered arrogantly above the mad angles of the bombed-out buildings. These remains were peppered with so many bullet holes they resembled strange hallucinogenic coral at the bottom of a deeply weird ocean. Its bleached-bone dignity was protected behind a lethal skirt of electrified fencing decorated with razor wire and the broken bodies of small children bobbing gently like the grisly supper of a giant spider.

Stoned soldiers in Chanel sunglasses packing serious heat lounged around the gates smoking jungle weed and slugging easy on cold bottles of beer.

The inevitable orphans, barefoot and raggy-arsed, hung around in the shadows peering in at the ridiculous opulence of whitey's sinister palace. The guards took occasional pot shots at the kids to scare them off and relieve their own intoxicated boredom, the children's skinny bodies would dance like rag dolls and disintegrate in a shower of guts.

The guards stuck these same guns into our bus, checked our passports through narrowed eyes and copped a seriously disturbing homosexual feel before waving us through the electric gates.

I HATE HEAT

Me, I don't trust adjectives. I think the English language would be better off without them. They only encourage writers to wallow in their overindulgences. I'm sure the entire history of English literature could be condensed and strengthened if all the adjectives were cut from the canon, dumped in the river and never allowed back into the British Library.

Take, as an example, the end of our hour-long journey from Kinshasa International Airport to the Hotel Memling. We have just climbed out of the people carrier to walk the few yards it takes to get to the smoked plate-glass doors of the Memling and a wall of heat has hit us. Now I could indulge myself for the next two pages describing the intensity of this heat, the pungency of the heat, the almost weighable quality of the heat. But what would be the point? It's Africa for fuck's sake, near enough on the Equator and not up Mount Kilimanjaro. 'Course it's fuckin' hot. You know that, I know that and everybody knows that Africa's hot and the kind of rotting-vegetable heat it's going to be. So there is no point in wasting words to describe it. So all I need to say is, 'It's hot, Z'.

'Course it is Bill, it's Africa. Mind you it was hotter in India. A different kind of heat there, it was more...'

'I don't care about the fuckin' heat in India. We are in Africa and I hate heat.'

'Well, you knew it was going to be hot.'

'Yeah, but…'

'Shut up, the pair of you,' says Gimpo, 'and give me a hand getting the bags out of the back.'

*

We stepped into the recycled air of the Memelin reception lounge to be confronted by acres of cool Italian marble and polished jungle woods decorated with intricate gold inlay. Carved ivory pillars supported a fantastic mosaic ceiling. Sleek black panthers with shining yellow eyes wearing jewelled collars were restrained by gold chains bolted to palm trees. The elegant animals lazily eyed a giant tortoise, its shell studded with diamonds and precious stones as it inched its way across a beautiful Persian carpet.

Far out.

An elderly Belgian man dressed in a white suit dripping elemental succubi is beating a young porter to death with the silver handle of his ebony walking stick. The man's small grandson laughs at his relative's apopleptic splutterings.

'What's this damn place coming to,' shouts the demented pensioner, the heavy cane cutting the boy's head to the bone, 'When the bloody guests have to beat the niggers themselves!'

A senior member of staff races to his assistance, plying the disgruntled old man with a monster G&T and somehow managing to slit the wounded boy's throat at the same time.

'Wild,' mutters the Gimp.

MANICURED NAILS PAINTED A VIOLENT CRIMSON

'Welcome to the Memling, the finest hotel in Central Africa.'

Standing at the marble-topped check-in desk I can almost believe the third world nightmare outside doesn't exist. The Memling is the only building that we had seen on our drive into the city centre that seems to be putting up any kind of fight with the equatorial elements intent in dragging everything back to some primordial state. A white-helmeted, razor-pressed uniformed armed guard stands blocking the entry to the hotel to anybody that wasn't white or who didn't look like they were black multimillionaires. We liked this. Even Z would find it difficult to hype his appearance in his prose beyond the reality.

The elegant black receptionist can speak English perfectly with just a hint of a stuck-up Parisian accent. I hand over my letter of confirmation, she accepts the credit card. It's as if we had only popped over to France for a couple of days to check out a new show at the Louvre.

She has long manicured nails painted a violent crimson. I would never want to have a girlfriend who either grew or painted her nails. But on a strange woman whom I don't need to know, they always work in the way they are supposed to. I imagine bending each of her nails back in turn until they are all broken, suppressing my thoughts or am I indulging them?

'Gentlemen, your rooms are not quite ready yet. Would you care to retire to the bar where we can offer you a complimentary drink?'

The Memling Hotel is internationally famous for its ridiculously opulent style. Journalists love it. Built during the reign of the Belgian King Leopold by the legendary Arab sodomite Fat Miguel it was originally a fantastically elegant brothel. Prosperous Arab slavers, wealthy European industrialists, perverted aristocrats and their wasted heirs, men of fortune, Sultans and rich adventurers from every corner of the spunky Earth would come to milk their spongy jizzbags there in days gone by.

Nowadays the hotel caters for foreign journalists reporting on the perpetual wars and the rich businessmen and sodomocrats whose businesses and political buggery cause them. Strictly speaking, nothing has really changed. Spermifadous desires and bloody lucre spin on the same rigged roulette table.

The indoor gardens of the reception area are themed around the grim history of the Congo/Zaire state. I noticed severed hands and ears preserved and arranged in floral patterns on the walls. A small explanatory note informs us that during the Belgian and later the French administration, soldiers working the rubber plantations were required by their senior officers to account for each bullet dispensed by presenting a human hand to prove that there was no unnecessary wastage. The canny soldiers of course didn't care whether the hands came from live or dead natives and kept a large back-up supply of gory extremities to excuse any genuine wastage. The surplus hands became popular with the soldiers' wives back in Europe and along with other curios from the exotic continent were used to make fashionable displays around the home.

SHIT LIKE THIS

Z is at the bar ordering a cocktail. Gimpo and I are, so I think, putting our passports into the hotel safe deposit box.

'I thought you said we had a room each, Bill.'

'So did I but...'

'Well I'm not sharing with Z, you know what the cunt's like.'

'Yeah Gimpo, but I'm not sharing with him either, I've just had to do that for three weeks in Europe.'

'So what are you saying? We have to share and he gets his own room. Typical. He acts like an arsehole, unable to do anything for himself so he gets his own room.'

'But...'

'Never mind three weeks in Europe, I've had to put up with years of this on the road with him getting away with shit like this.'

*

Not much surprises Katie Blade. The BBC war reporter sex bomb has pretty much seen it all. The gas-blown horrors of war and the spermy monstrosities of her own debauched sexuality made jaunty Kate pretty much unshockable. Not that the BBC lesbo pin-up is shocked by the sight before her. On the contrary, a shudder of queasy delight limbos beneath the emotional Antipodes of her depraved sensuality.

'How unusual,' she squeals coquettishly, clapping her hands tight beneath her chin.

Kendo Nagasaki Wankamoto smiles and bows, pleased that his offering had met with such enthusiastic appreciation.

Kendo Nagasaki and his camera crew had recognised the internationally famous Ms Blade in the hotel foyer earlier in the day and had extended an invitation to the demure broadcaster to join Nagasaki and his team for a traditional Japanese banquet in her honour. The Japanese had brought their own chef, an esteemed professional about to serve the first course of a very special meal.

The 13-year-old Tutsi girl, heavily sedated, yet fully aware of her situation, lies naked, eyes open, on the white silk tablecloth. She is surrounded by beautifully prepared parcels of tiny vegetables, infant prawns and pale fish. The chef, with the precision of a master surgeon, carefully and without spilling one single drop of blood removes the child's voice box. A gentle ripple of admiration passes around the hushed table in respectful awe at the chef's consummate skill.

Kendo Nagasaki leans towards his guest and whispers quietly by way of explanation: 'To prevent the food from talking and spoiling the ambience.' Scented candles flicker gold on the pink walls. 'Although the natural sedatives prevents our meal from moving,' continues Kendo Nagasaki, 'It does not dull the pain and because it can become so intense, especially around the seventh or eighth courses, sometimes the food has been known to gasp or exhale a strangulated cry.'

Katie nods, fascinated by the exquisite terror dancing in the girl's bulging eyes.

Artistically, with breathtaking skill the chef removes the girl's eyelids and arranges them with a few leaves of rare fruit on a small plate and offers them to Katie.

'The eyes of the lover,' explains her Japanese host. 'The soft eyelids of a nubile girl are considered the greatest delicacy of all.'

Katie places the tiny sliver of flesh on the tip of her tongue

'It is the highest honour a gentleman can offer his noble guest,' continues Kendo Nagasaki, his penis jigging slightly within his traditional yellow silk boxer shorts. The rest of the diners hold their breath as Katie closes her eyes and purses her lips savouring the morsel.

'Delicious,' she purrs, acutely aware of the erotic tension humming beneath the table.

Her pink English cunt slicks up, she feels gooey between her legs.

The chef serves the other diners their lesser portions, strings of optic muscle from around the eyes and strips of soft facial skin. Next the girl's lips are gently removed and presented to the sexually aroused Ms Blade.

'The kiss of the lover,' adds Kendo Nagasaki, feeding her with his fingers. 'Second only to the eyelids for sweetness and symbolic of the wisdom of the Buddha.'

When the chef hands Katie the thin scalpel she knows instinctively what to do, parting the wet purple velvet of the young woman's vagina, she removes the glistening pearl and, tossing back her head, swallows it like a tiny oyster.

TROPICAL COCKTAILS AND THE DEVIL INCARNATE

It's just past 11.00am The three of us are sitting in deep leather armchairs, sipping on ludicrous tropical cocktails. Z and I are surveying the scene while Gimpo unscrews the zoom from his video camera to polish the lenses one more time. Z, for once, is silent, no doubt relieved to have a drink in his hand and nothing mildly threatening in sight.

The scene we survey is a large, open-plan, split-level lounge bar with a restaurant. Tame jungle plants in pots. The air conditioning works. There are no insects and the sound of Dire Straits playing 'Money for Nothing' wafts at a mild volume from invisible speakers. I'm unwinding and my general pissed-offness with my travelling companions has abated.

'Is that you that's farted, Bill?' asks Z.

'No it fuckin' isn't.'

'It wasn't me,' adds Gimpo.

'Why lie about it, Bill? We all know it's you.'

'It wasn't.'

'OK. Have it your own way.'

The three of us return to our own thoughts. I let another one I've been holding slip out. The only other customers in the lounge are a wealthy looking African family. Both parents and their two children are all dressed in those brightly coloured robes you see African premiers and their first ladies wearing when doing state visits or standing up to talk at the UN. The central motif of the brightly printed robe worn by the man, is of a large black face with a leopard skin hat perched on its head. This face features heavy specs and a broad smile. The woman's robe is of a similar print but the face in the pattern is of a beaming black woman. It looks fantastic and I promise to give myself a belated birthday present of a set of these robes.

I have no interest in modern African history or politics. Of course I suffer from the required amount of post-colonial guilt that a modern white Western man should. I always support the rebel cause in any struggle for independence that may pop up on the Nine O'Clock News. I know that Rhodesia is now Zimbabwe; Mandela has done his long march and found the rainbow's end; the Portuguese got kicked out of Angola and Mozambique; and Africa is run by blacks for blacks. It's what they wanted. They are even beginning to field sides in the World Cup that turn in an inspiring 90 minutes. Other than the odd natural disaster, what have they got to complain about?

OK, you see through my fake cynicism but you know what I mean. That said, my ignorance is almost genuine. Until a couple of months ago I had no idea that what I thought was the Congo was called the Belgian Congo and for the last 30-odd years had been known as Zaire.

All my research for this expedition had been invested in reading and thinking about Satan. What was the history of this fallen angel? How had he sneaked his way so thoroughly into the lot of mankind? Why did we need him? And what was the precise hold he had over my soul? Of course I wasn't expecting, even in the most irrational zones of my brain, to meet the horned one in person. I hope to use this journey to focus my mind.

What I've learnt from this reading and thinking is that I'm not interested in wars in heaven. I'm not interested in the nature of evil made manifest in man's history or even in wondering if evil is real or imagined. I've no interest in the unfairness of our global society or if politics can be used to resolve those unfairnesses. And, lastly, I'm certainly not interested in becoming a better person.

My interests are purely selfish. All the days, weeks and months spent sitting in the British Library, reading anything vaguely connected to Satan, Lucifer, the Serpent or the 40,000 other names we have concocted for the Dark One have led to nought. The one thing I have learnt is that for me it all begins and ends with the story of Adam and Eve in the Garden of Eden. The Fall of mankind. Dante's *Inferno*, the various tellings of the Faust tale; all just great minds wanking off into the laptops of the day compared to that original tale of Adam and Eve sent packing from the Eastern Gate.

The fact that the tale was originally conceived with misogynist tendencies and somehow Eve gets the blame for the apple business is irrelevant to me. As far as I'm concerned it could have been Adam tempting Eve with the fruit and the story would just be as powerful. What matters to me is that we (the human corporate we) allowed ourselves to be tempted by knowledge. Allowed ourselves to evolve away from all other forms of life. With knowledge came doubt and indecision. Have you ever seen an oak tree wracked with doubt or indecision. It just gets on with being an oak tree, growing, breeding and dying. Dealing with the hand it has been dealt with no introspection, no buts and if onlys. And before you say, 'Yeah of course he wants to see himself as an oak tree standing tall and proud for 400 years or more, not just a nettle in the back yard', I would use the same argument if I'd picked a common cold germ whose individual life span lasts for no more than a couple of hours. That germ just gets on doing what it has always done in the Garden of Eden without having to think about it.

All other forms of life are truly themselves. We humans are always trying to become ourselves and no amount of knowledge is going to get us there. This is what I rage against. This is why I stamp my feet like Violet Elizabeth screaming 'I want to be me, truly me and not the me I already am.'

Do you understand what I'm on about? Yeah, of course you do. But you might be thinking, 'We all know that, so what's the big deal? That's part of the package we get when we enter this world. We grow up, we accept it and get on with being humans and do the best we can. We don't go stomping off to Africa to demand some vague thing we term as our soul from some bogus symbolic concept of evil made flesh.'

Well I am and it's too late to stop me now with rational argument. This has got nothing to do with rationality, it goes way beyond that.

I have decided to use this time while waiting for our rooms to be readied to start writing up the story of the visit to Ireland that Z and I made some weeks ago.

The Japanese applaud Katie's deep understanding of the refined cruelty at the heart of their culture, and Kendo Nagasaki enthusiastically reveals more about the banquet's history. The chef, learns Kate, is from a long line that traditionally would serve only the Emperor. His skill is such that he can remove all the edible parts from a human body completely avoiding all the arteries and larger veins. This fine art takes many years of practice – usually upon jailed convicts held in obscure prisons – to learn. Most of these Canniwosa chefs are well into their 60s before they are considered adept enough to prepare and serve a human meal.

As you can imagine, any slip of the knife could cause serious trauma to the fine sensibilities of those privileged to attend this special feast. The culinary artists spend many years studying human anatomy, each successive chef imparting new lore to the canon of this refined art.

THIS FUTILE ESCAPADE
Shit! I've just knocked my cocktail over my notebook.

'For fuck's sake Bill, watch what you're doing. You nearly got some of your drink on my safari suit.'

'Sorry.'

'Fuck his safari suit, you've just flicked the fruit off your notebook and into my camera case now.'

'Sorry, Gimpo.'

'For that get another round in.'

'OK.'

'Make mine a double.'

'You don't get double cocktails, Z.'

The barman brings over a tray of fresh cocktails. The three of us settle back down, waiting for our rooms to be readied, Gimpo polishing his lenses, Z and myself tending to our notebooks. So what was I saying? Ah yes, the Fall of mankind, my own vain attempt at regaining my soul and our proposed journey into the interior. It was some months ago that Z and I came to the conclusion that we had to make this mission to Africa. Since then we've been on a grand tour of Europe together in the hope that we would learn something more about the arch-adversary. I have already learnt too much. I know there is nothing to be gained from this futile escapade. The most that I can practicably achieve is some time away from my family responsibilities, to write up my notes about a visit Z and I made to Ireland, our jaunt around Europe and why we are packing a set of Punch and Judy puppets and then to frame these notes within whatever happens as we head for the interior. Of course I hope something terrible happens to us so I can have a dark night of the soul. This would give my tale some gravitas, make it more than just the shallow jottings from the diary of a student doing a gap year in somebody else's poverty. As you will learn, Z's interpretation of Lucifer is quite markedly different from mine. He seems to still be charmed by the charismatic figure drawn by the Romantics and their progeny, the French poets, that to me is mere literature, a thinking man's holiday read. As Z knows everything there is to know about all that 'sympathy for the devil' shite and had done a couple of seasons in hell himself, his research at the British Library took him in a different direction altogether.

Z wholeheartedly immersed himself into the concept of Africa as the white man's burden. Starting with *Boy's Own* adventures, wrestling with crocodiles, evil Arab slave traders and tales about the sun never setting on the glorious Empire, to in-depth tomes on the hidden motives of Livingstone and Stanley. In fact, of late, he has become fixated by the notion of Stanley, his identification with the low-down liar, conman and cheat almost complete. Of course, he has me down as the suppressed, fucked-up and arrogant tosser, Livingstone.

*

Kendo Nagasaki explains that the meal is kept alive so as to ensure that the body's adrenaline flow remains at its highest level, thus ensuring that the meat is extra sweet and retains the buttery texture that Japanese bon viveurs covet. Only when every one has eaten their fill is the meal humanely killed.

This honour is reserved for the guest. A thin blade is thrust into the heart, usually through the third and fourth ribs which are considered lucky.

Towards the end of the meal as Katie takes the knife and is about to despatch the unfortunate food Kendo Nagasaki suddenly interjects:

'Ah, one moment Ms Blade, you are indeed fortunate, please look.'

Katie peers at the peeled meal. Unsure of what she is supposed to be looking for until Kursaro indicates that the chef's immaculate cruelty has revealed that the young girl was pregnant. The tiny foetus, perfectly formed within the placenta is old enough to determine its sex. The tiny boy's pea-sized heart can clearly be seen beating beneath his thin wet skin. The chef with a few snips carefully removes the infant from the girl's womb and hands it to an assistant.

'It will be poached in tiger's milk, flavoured with rose petals and served with a few cumin seeds. You are most fortunate Ms Kate, this is a very good omen, our wise Buddhist monks believe that the discovery of an unexpected foetus usually foretells of an important and unexpected meeting, a new lover perhaps?' Kendo Nagasaki immediately realises his flirtatious manner is inappropriate and adds quickly, 'Or perhaps an old and esteemed friend?'

TWO PINTS OF PORTER PLEASE

'You tight-arsed cunt, Drummond. Just 'cause you thought it would save us 20 quid. I'm about to spew my ring instead of enjoying the in-flight entertainment on the London to Belfast shuttle.'

It was a rough crossing. Z and I sat in the bar nursing our pints of badly poured porter and tried to ignore the ever-increasing swell of the Irish Sea. Holyhead to Dun Laoghaire, according to the timetable, was only supposed to take three and a quarter hours. We had already been at sea for three and a half and according to the Assistant Purser's Assistant we were only halfway there. There was a bodhrán-bashing ceilidh band at the back end of the saloon bar, the fiddler sawing away for all his worth. Or at least for whatever he is getting from his paymasters to create an on-tap Irish parlour knees-up in this heaving and tossing supermarket selling all that can be construed as Irish.

'Can't the Irish fuckin' ever stop trying to sell themselves and their dead culture?'

Z and I had driven up from London to Holyhead, made the 15.45 ferry in good time. Docking at Dun Laoghaire the plan had been to take the big road north from Dublin, cross the border between Dundalk and Newry, bypass Belfast, then up and over the Antrim hills and down into the glens and be in Cushendall in time for last orders at Johnny Joe's bar before turning in for the night in our newly acquired Curfew Tower. But even if the ship didn't go down, the soonest we were going to make dock according to the Assistant Purser's Assistant was 9.00pm.

'Fuck it Bill, let's just head into Dublin, find a b&b then hit the bars,' suggested Z. It sounded like the right thing to do in a Brendan Behan sort of way, seeing as we were trying to model ourselves into world-famous Literary Arseholes.

The only problem was that neither of us knew anybody or anywhere in Dublin. It's one thing reading *The Gingerbread Man* and thinking 'I could do that', or imagining that we will bump into Bloom on his 24-hour odyssey and we'll just tag along for the porter, but in reality we both already knew the evening would be spent in a quiet bar, us retelling our threadbare anecdotes about our sordid lives to each other before turning into a net-curtained and nylon-sheeted b&b. And I'm only using the word porter instead of Guinness or Irish Stout because J P Donleavy did in his books.

'It's your round, Bill and tell them not to do that shamrock thing in the head of my Guinness.'

'No it's not.'

Then I remembered that a London-based Irish acquaintance of mine had told me she was going to be spending some time in Dublin while she worked on her book on the trials and tribulations of the rock band Nirvana. But I only knew her first name – Victoria – and had no idea where she was staying.

As Z went up to the bar to get another couple of pints of porter in, I found a pay phone that took cards and made some calls. After the third I was talking to a young lady whose flat Victoria was staying in.

'No, I'm sorry I've not seen Victoria all day.'

'Any idea when she'll be back?'

'You can never tell with Victoria.'

'Or where she may be going this evening?'

'Oh yes, I remember now, she did say something about meeting up with the others at the Shamrock Pizza Parlour.'

'Any idea of a time?'

'No.'

*

I decked my sixth bottle of Primus beer, lifted my left arse cheek and let rip an industrial-strength pig shitter. It warmed up the leopard-skin bar stool real nice.

I was feeling a little more relaxed after the heart-stopping journey from the airport. The beer was working just fine.

We'd changed into fresh safari suits. Bill already had on his subtle brown number, Gimps was swanking in lurid canary yellow, mine was a sublime mauve creation with mother of pearl buttons and slightly flared trousers. Jason King would have been proud. Our Ranulph Fiennes-endorsed sandals completed our elegant outfits beautifully.

Gimps and Bill were skeezing with the hotel tramps while I worked on my alcohol. The whores were fine looking with those stupendous jutting backsides all black chicks have. The Gimp was laughing, trying to balance his beer on one of them.

I sighed resignedly, ten years of rock and roll had disenamoured me of the charms of whores. I ordered up another beer. Don't get me wrong I still have time for a good slut.

I was still powerless beneath my criminal libido, it just demanded a more exotic stimulation than your average working girl could provide these days.

I checked out the foxy gaggle of cocksuckers. It was going to be purple gash from here on in I guessed. Those cute little Belgian air hostesses and their pink slits were locked up tight and safe in their rooms, guarded by a couple of hotel soldiers.

Shame. Not that I have any objections to purple gash, but it would have been nice to get nasty with a couple of pink slits before we sailed up into Mau Mau land.

HAVE YOU SEEN HER?

The Holyhead to Dun Laoghaire ferry didn't sink and it finally docked some time around 9.30pm. We didn't bother with finding a b&b and went straight for finding the Shamrock Pizza Parlour which we did just as it was closing. No Victoria, but I challenged a gaggle of likely-looking youngsters.

'Do you know Victoria?'

'Yes, I do that.'

'Have you seen her?'

'Now, let me think. I did see her leaving the Black River Bar about 2.30 this morning and then sipping Russian tea at the Waters of Athlone Oyster Bar just after 3.00 this afternoon. But since then not a sighting. But if you be looking for her try the Horseshoe Bar at the Shelbourne Hotel, Victoria is often there of an evening.'

The affected dialogue above is more down to my bad pastiche of caricatured Irish than in any way a true record of the way the young lady at the Shamrock Pizza Parlour spoke to me.

We were now on a mission to find Victoria. Which is strange, because I hardly know her and Z had never met her, but it had somehow given the night a purpose: 'We must find Victoria at all costs.'

Twenty minutes later Z and I are pushing the revolving doors of the Shelbourne Hotel and stepping on to the thick green carpet. We check the Horseshoe Bar. Deep, worn leather seats. Prints of hunting scenes on the wall, cigar smoke. Not the sort of place that Z and I should be. No sign of Victoria.

'This is fucking stupid Bill. Let's just check into this hotel and have a quiet drink and an early night. Sod trying to find this Victoria girl.'

'No Z, you don't understand, we must find her.'

We were just leaving the Horseshoe Bar when Z whispered, 'Do you see who is sitting over there by the fire?'

'No. Who?'

Now, as you may know I'm not a drinking man but I had been drinking pints of porter since we first got on the Irish ferry at Holyhead. So by the time I saw the corpulent and rotund figure of the world famous rock 'n' roll genius snug in an armchair over by the blazing hearth I've got a full supply of Dutch courage. I'm over there immediately.

'Excuse me sir, have you seen Victoria in here this evening?'

'Urr, wharr did ya say? Victoria?'

'Yes, sir. Have you seen her?'

'What's Victoria to you? Are you with her? I thought she was with me. Where is she? Why do you want to see her? She's got a man you know.'

'I'm just a friend and I'm told she often comes in the Shelbourne for a quiet mid-evening drink.'

'I've been waiting for her for over two hours. She said she'd be here by 8.00pm. You can't trust her. Anyway what's your name? Speak up man.'

'Bill.'

'Bill what?'

'Bill Drummond.'

'What, *the* Bill Drummond?'

Now I'm obviously going to have to stop the telling of this tale here to confess that one of the main motivations for wanting to include this anecdote as we risk every known tropical disease and death by machete is to flaunt the fact that this most famous son of Belfast said 'What, *the* Bill Drummond?' and seemed to mean it.

'Bill Drummond of The KLF?'

'Yeah.'

'Pull yourself up a chair, friend. What are you drinking?'

Z might not be impressed by this – he's had more practice out there hob-nobbing with the good and great of rock 'n' roll – but I am. Z and I pull up a pair of chairs. I introduce Z. The Man (I take it you know who I'm talking about? As he has something of a litigious reputation, I'm chickening out of using his name.) is not drinking alone, he has two companions of similar age and similar stature. But instead of wearing the M&S-style brown leather jacket and casual slacks of The Man, they are dressed in identical black satin bomber jackets with The Man's latest album title embroidered across the back, black jeans, cowboy boots and what remains of what were once feather-cut hairdos. The Man introduces us to the pair of good ol' boys who it turns out are also from Belfast and have been on the crew payroll since those far-off 'Gloria' days, the only consistency in his otherwise meandering life.

The two good ol' boys have obviously never heard of Bill Drummond or the KLF or anything else that The Man seems to know all about in detail. They are giving me suspicious looks. They've obviously had a lifetime of steering their wayward charge through a minefield of hangers-on, chancers, corrupt managers, bent accountants, crooked promoters and ex-wives. Also with The Man's reputation for turning nasty, and his diminutive stature, I guess this pair have to sort out the dirty work.

'How did you do it, Bill?'

'Do what?

'Get out the music business. What else?'

'We just stopped making records, that's all.'

'But they don't let you. They just keep you making another one, then another one, then another one. They don't let go of you.'

'I don't know what you mean. You mean you want to stop, but you don't know how?'

'Yeah, I've been wanting to stop for years, but I can't, they won't let me. Who's your solicitor?'

'It's got nothing to do with our solicitor. We just wanted to stop, so we did.'

The Man has obviously been tucking into the brandy and cokes. He turns to the two good ol' boys.

'This man here was one half of a band and they were selling more fucking records in the world than any other fucker and they just said 'stop' and they did. I want you to find out the name of his solicitor and his accountant then get on to them and get them to get me out of the music business.'

Orders dispatched, he turns his unfocused gaze on me.

'You all right, Bill? You want another drink?

He pulls out a pen and a bit of paper from the inside of his brown leather jacket.

'Just write down your solicitor's name there.'

I knew there was no point in arguing with him. He was obviously not the sort of man you could say no to. I obliged for all I was worth.

'You see Bill, I've thought about this a lot over the years and I've tried every fucking religion going, but I reckon I must have done a deal with the devil, a long time back. Back when I was still cleaning windows. The thing is, the devil has kept his side of the bargain all the way along. I've still got the best voice in the world, still sell a shitload of records. Still get all the money I can spend, even get the ladies when I need them. But I want off. I want out. I want to stop.'

You can tell that the last thing the two good ol' boys want their man to do is stop. What future would they have if our hero packed it in and settled down to a spot of fly-fishing and gentleman-farming somewhere out in Wicklow?

'We all do deals with the devil, us lot. Even if we don't know, we sell him our souls. For what? So I can sit in the Shelbourne sipping Napoleon brandy and make the same fucking record over and over again? Waiter, get my friends here another drink. Are you going to the club? It must be time to go. Waiter, get us two taxis.'

I was just sliding towards maudlin when she glided into the room.

Her long hair swept across her face like Lauren Bacall. She perched herself on a bar stool a few yards away. I studied her silhouette in the smoked mirror behind the bar. Gabriel, the barman, lit her cigarette. Her heady scent drifted across the dust motes suspended in the small spotlights beneath the bar, I could detect the slightest hint of gun oil in there with the Gauloise and the Chanel.

'Katie!' I turned towards her, smiling.

'Z darling!' We embraced.

Katie and I had had a brief thing once, somewhere else. It was pretty intense while it lasted. I'd just finished a soul-frying tour of America, rocking the nation's idiot children with some bad heavy metal.

I was cross-addicted to more substances than I care to remember and mighty sick of women, well, groupies, which don't really qualify. Those skanky vagina zombies aren't even human, just a collection of diseased suppurating holes occupying roughly the same space. They're amusing at first, but after the first ten billion... I mean, they only have so many gummy holes.

That is until Katie showed me that they had as many holes as you cared to carve. Heh, heh, Katie, Katie... what a gal, with her smoking irons, her dripping blades and her chewing gum. Katie was the nearest I ever came close to love on the road. She was one wild fucking psycho bitch, and I mean that in the nicest possible way.

She'd been in Los Angeles covering some race riots. I remember at the time there was some real fear that this was going to be it, the big one, major civil insurrection, some kind of civil war. But as usual the local niggers just torched a few liquor stores, looted some TVs and that was it. Helter Skelter never came down again.

Katie's sleazy camera crew was holed up at The Sheridan while she went on the prowl looking for some fat negroid tubesteak. But instead she met me, and that's when the fun started. Like I said, I was getting bored of all the little Yank sluts and their shitty blow jobs. I ran into Katie at The Showtime bar opposite the Chinese Theatre in Hollywood. The Showtime was a real sleazoid place and I liked it just fine.

The rest of the band and their diseases were headed back home to their various detox clinics. I wasn't quite finished, I still had a yard or so of liver left and a few braincells that weren't completely fried. I'd been in the Showtime most of the morning, a nice little stream of gin and juice constantly filling up my bucket glass, when in walked the BBC überbabe.

The drinks that morning blurred into an extremely far-out six months.

GIMPO'S LONELY PLANET

As for Gimpo, he has no interest in all this Satan stuff or what the white man did or didn't do in the dash for Africa.

Gimpo did the sensible thing and went out a week ago and bought a copy of the Central Africa edition of the Lonely Planet Travel Survival Kit. In this book are 102 densely printed pages about Zaire: history, geography, climate, politics, how to get about, all that kind of stuff. I was all for Gimpo having the book if it meant we could find Satan more easily but I wasn't interested in reading the kind of garbage that any two-bit back-packer could shove in his rucksack.

Gimpo is good with practical things, like remembering to bring a first-aid kit and a bag of beads to trade with. The trouble began last Friday when Z started reading Gimpo's Lonely Planet. At 2.00am Saturday morning, Z phoned me and forced me to listen as he read paragraph after paragraph. Z is never without an infatuation and it seemed he'd just got himself a new one. Its name was Mobutu. According to Z this Mobutu had been and still was the president of the country for the last 30 years. It was him who had changed the country's name from the Congo to Zaire at the same time as changing the colonial place names back to African names. He decreed that all Zairians replace their Christian names with African ones. He changed his from Joseph Mobutu to Mobutu Sese Seko Koko Ngbendu Wa Za Banga. This, Z took great delight in telling me, meant 'the all-powerful warrior who, because of his endurance and inflexible will to win, will go from conquest to conquest, leaving fire in his wake'.

*

I'd never really contemplated the idea of being a serial killer, too much hassle, but Katie made it sound like so much fun.

She told me that although it wasn't exactly legal in America, the cops were so lazy and involved in their own scams that unless there was any shakedown money to be had, they pretty much turned a blind eye to it. As long as your hits were low profile and you didn't make too many in one particular state you pretty much had *carte blanche* to slice and dice your way all across the country.

The guy in the army surplus store was really helpful. He had signed photos of all the most famous serial killers pinned on the wall behind the counter: Ted Bundy (the serial killer's killer); The Gainseville maniac, Ed Gein; Jeff Dahmer; Charlie, Peter and a few I didn't recognise.

He was a creepy fucker and smelled of way too much masturbation.

He sure knew his stuff though, advising us on the best hardware for bipedal quarry and all the rest. He must have taken a fancy to Kate because he threw in a few free extras: gaffer tape, strong nylon cord, handcuffs, red pepper spray, a couple of black ski masks and some beautiful Finnish flensing knives. The guns were the latest models, ridiculously powerful with laser sights and ergonomic designs.

They looked more like ray guns than the real thing, light too, only a couple of pounds each. Katie insisted on some old-fashioned revolvers for reliability, she thought that the automatics and semi-automatics were too prone to jam for serious death work. During her work as a war reporter she'd seen many times how important those few seconds can be.

'Nice guy,' said Katie, caressing her blue steel on the motel bed.

THE BADDEST MAN ON EARTH

'So you see, Bill, Mobutu is obviously the baddest man on earth. He is evil personified. He is the closest thing to the devil we are ever to come across. If he is not Satan made flesh, he has got to be one of his higher-ranking aides. We have to meet him and anyway, hanging out with Mobutu sounds like a whole lot more fun than hacking our way through the jungle catching malaria then giving up on the third day.'

'Look Z, it's the middle of the night, I'll talk to you about it on Monday.'

By Monday, which was four days later, Z had tracked down a character called Mr Arthur Malu-Malu. Now Mr Malu-Malu is the Reuters correspondent in Zaire. His base of operations is the Intercontinental Hotel in Kinshasa. According to Z's sources it is only through Mr Malu-Malu that anybody from the Western media stands any chance of meeting up with Mobutu himself. Sally Agarwal, Z's partner and our editor, had already made telephone contact with Malu-Malu as had Hugh Barnes, our executive editor at our publishers, Penguin Books. These are the faxes sent by Agarwal and Barnes to Mr Malu-Malu:

Dear Mr Malu-Malu

I hope you are well. It was good to speak to you this afternoon and thank you so much for all your assistance. As discussed, here are a few lines to describe the work of Mr Bill Drummond and Mr Mark Manning.

Messrs Drummond and Manning are fictional novelists. They travel widely to gain an appreciation of interesting cultures, which they then use as a springboard for their imaginations and their writing. As I have mentioned to you, they have no interest in politics.

They are very interested in the culture of Zaire and hope to learn more about it during their forthcoming visit. They will be bringing with them a traditional form of English entertainment, a comedy puppet show called 'Punch and Judy' for the amusement of the people of Zaire and, they most sincerely hope, for the enjoyment of the President himself. I will fax you a letter from their publishers, Penguin Books UK, to confirm the above. If you need any further information, please do not hesitate to contact me on the London numbers above. For your information, Mr Drummond and Mr Manning and their travelling companion, Mr Alan Goodrick, will arrive in Kinshasa on the 5 June at 8.30am on the Air France flight. They will be staying at the Hotel Memling.

We do hope that the President will grant Mr Manning and Mr Drummond the honour of permitting them to perform their Punch and Judy show for his entertainment. We sincerely believe that he would enjoy the performance.

I do look forward to speaking to you next Tuesday, Arthur. I will try and call after I have sent the fax from Penguin Books to ensure that you have received this correspondence. Thank you once more for all your help.

Kind regards

Sally Agarwal

Penguin UK, 27 Wrights Lane, London W8 5TZ

Mr Arthur Malu-Malu

C/o The Curfew Press

Dear Mr Malu-Malu

I am writing to confirm that Bill Drummond and Mark Manning are internationally respected writers of fiction whose work is contracted to be published by Penguin Books, and that they are not at all interested in the politics of modern-day Zaire, but rather in the rich tradition of literature and culture in that country.

In October 1996 Penguin Books is very proud to be publishing the first volume in a

projected trilogy of novels by Bill Drummond and Mark Manning. I will be delighted to send you a few complimentary copies as soon as we have the finished book from the printers, and thank you in advance for your co-operation and assistance.
With best wishes
Yours sincerely
Hugh Barnes
Executive Editor

This was a *fait accompli* on Z's part but I was able to put my foot down when he suggested that we fake up a letter of introduction to Mobutu from the Queen of England. My vision of the three of us hitching, hacking and paddling our way to the source of the mighty Congo River where we would confront Satan in whatever way he chose to manifest himself seemed to be fast slipping away into Z's vision instead, where Mobutu had become some kind of stand-in. There was nothing I could do about it.

Over the past four days I've had to twist things around in my head and somehow see our quest to have an audience with the all-powerful warrior who, because of his endurance and inflexible will to win, will go from conquest to conquest leaving fire in his wake as in some way relevant to my inner and, dare I say, selfish needs.

I now accept that on a surface and practical level we are here, sitting in the Memling Hotel, Kinshasa, Zaire on our way to meet the baddest man in the world. At a deeper level, I'm on my own journey to sort out why I'm not an oak tree or common cold germ. Sometimes I think it was easier making pop records.

*

The next six months were exhilarating to say the least.

But even the strangling, murdering thrills of sexy lustmord can't keep the suffocating toad of existential ennui at bay forever.

I left when she was sleeping.

'Why, Z?' she asked, lighting two cigarettes and handing one to me. 'Why did you just up and leave like that?' Her eyes looked uncommonly watery. 'You never even said goodbye, just left in the middle of the night, we hadn't even started working on little Mary. There she was when I woke up, spinning from the ceiling.'

'Oh Katie, you know,' I replied, remembering the look of unholy terror on the pretty teenager's face as I packed away my knives and guns. 'I guess I didn't have the stomach for it anymore.'

'But baby, you were getting real good, *we* were getting real good. Shit, we were starting to get write-ups in the local newspapers, it was only a matter of time till the FBI linked up the slayings. The National Enquirer had already started picking up on us, all we had to do was start taunting them with cryptic letters, send some weird cyphers to national newspapers... and those fantastic knots you used to tie, what a superb MO that was.'

I laughed, that little detail was pretty classy.

After we'd had our fun with little Mary Jane and Katie had done her thing with the cigarettes, I'd truss up what was still left hanging together of our little playmate using some fancy sea knots. A tomfool was always really good for cuffs, then I'd throw in a few running nooses, rogues knots, some swabs hitches and if Katie was in the mood for a long torture session I'd even start working on some serious splicing.

The Feds thought they were dealing with some kind of sexually insane sailor. She was right though, it had been fun at the time but to really make it in the serial game, get the movie offers rolling in and stuff, you have to get caught. And I couldn't dig that. No way was I gonna ride the lightning for something as trivial as murder.

'I guess it was all that downside stuff to deathwork,' I told her. 'Cleaning the blood and piss out of the car, getting rid of the body, avoiding detection, moving around all the time.'

'Yeah, yeah I know what you mean,' said Kate resignedly, lighting me another cigarette. 'That's what's so great about this place – Zaire or whatever it's called now. Nobody gives a fuck. You just call room service and they clean all the shit up!'

Katie was laughing at the simplicity of it all.

'The Army guys and the cops here are the biggest killers around. I'm serious Z if you ever get the urge again, along with Liberia, Zaire is the only place sex killers serious about their work should be.'

WIPE YOUR ARSE

Thirty minutes and a lot more barking of instructions later, Z and I were being squeezed into the star-bar room of what must be Dublin's top night spot. The walls were oak panelled, the furniture was padded leather and the place was packed with people you assume must be the most despicable people on earth, but in reality and in daylight are probably OK.

To be honest, I can't remember what Z and I were talking about now. If anything, maybe we were just accepting this is what happens in a night out with Dangerfield Bloom, Behan and the boys. I found myself squashed on one end of a settee. At the other end was a young northern lad (as in English northern) and between us a lass. There was something vaguely familiar about her. She too had a northern accent, one of those sing-song Lancashire accents. The pair of them were arguing. It was getting heated, the lass got up and started demonstrating something, while Z was over at the bar with The Man talking about the big things. Singers have a tendency to gravitate towards each other.

'Which way do *you* do it? You do it from the front don't you?' This was the Lancashire lass talking to me. It's then that I placed her face, she was none other than the Rochdale songbird and I'm not talking about 'Sally Pride of our Alley', I'm talking 'All Around The World' and all that, but yet again I am too cowardly to mention names because what she was asking me was not the sort of thing that multimillion-selling hip MOR artists should be asking complete strangers.

'What do you mean?'

'You wipe your arse from the front don't you? Everybody does.'

While she was saying this she was giving me a demonstration of how she wipes her arse.

'He tells me he does it from the back. If I'd known that before, I'd never have married him.'

I didn't know what to say. I've only ever wiped mine from the back. Wiping from the front would seem to encourage smearing your balls or your cunt with shit. Before I got further embroiled in this arse-wiping domestic tiff, The Man stumbled over clutching a bottle of champagne. I removed myself from the settee to make way for the gifted one. And I thought how 'Astral Weekend' or whatever it's called would never sound the same again. He demanded a snog from the Rochdale songbird and just as she was beginning to whack him about the head with her handbag, Victoria turned up. She looked fabulous. The sweaty heaving throng of Dublin's degenerate elite parted as she glided through. The Man, already well into his cups, recognised her, or at least thought he did. He tried to lift himself off the settee. In one hand he had a clutch of 50-quid notes. In the other he had the now-empty bottle of champagne.

'Victoria, Victoria, do you want some champagne? Take some of these. Get some champagne.'
Victoria smiled benignly and ignored the invitation. Her gaze swept the room, passing me by before disappearing once again into the parting throng of coke-sniffing, champagne-swilling trash.

The Man collapsed on to the low table in front of the settee and broke down, his tears rolling, his sobs audible over the nightclub din.

*

'You haven't changed a bit baby,' I said, leaning over and pulling on one of her fantastic tits. I squeezed till she winced and bit her on the lip. I could smell her English mott juicing up, sweating like the jungle itself.

She reached over and grabbed at my dick boning up in my safari pants like a flaming zeppelin. I pulled her hand off my knob and grabbed a hank of her long blonde hair. 'Later baby,' I said, 'First I gotta shift gear. The beer's OK, but it's too slow for seriously insane sex action.'

'Whatever you say, stud,' replied the BBC sexbomb. 'Only you know how to rake my fire.'
She threw back her whisky like a man and ordered up some more.

'Your two geeky pals over in the corner with the whores...' she pointed at Laurel and Hardy.

Bill was sweating, his hands thrust deep and nervous in his pockets, a forced grin on his insane face. Gimpo, ever the life and soul of the party was doing handstands and balancing pints of Primus on his boner. The whores were hysterical with laughter, they thought Gimpo was great.

'The tall one that looks like a spastic, that's Bill. The ugly little fucker with his cock out, that's Gimpo. They're cool.'

'Yeah?' Kate sounded as if she didn't believe me.

'Seriously,' I persisted. 'Bill, you'd like him, you two are similar in a lot of ways.'
The BBC sex bomb looked horrified.

'Well, maybe not exactly. I mean he's a splanchnophiliac like you, but I don't think it's entirely sexual with him, it's something else.'

'Like what?' The gorgeous pervert was intrigued.

'I'm not really sure, it's a religious thing. His father was a Presbyterian minister. Bill doesn't like to talk about it much. His father was really strict, no vegetables – sinful or something, decadent. All the minerals needed to support life can be found in the soil. Poor little bastard was given a plate of dirt at mealtimes, can you believe it? Had his hands strapped to his bed during the night, the maniac even made him go to school with a cork sewn into his butt, though how can anyone think farting is sinful? Anyway he's made up for that one that's for sure. You'll see what I mean in a minute.'

Bill's expression had changed.

The tight-lipped look of prurient pleasure told me he'd just set a slow bubbler loose. Like an evil invisible faerie, the brown gas was circling the room in our direction. Several drinkers were making fanning gestures in front of their faces, the whores were laughing loudly and holding their noses.

'Fuck me!' gasped Kate incredulously, eyes watering, straining not to be sick. 'The concentration camps in Bosnia were bad. How does he manage it? What does he eat?'

Bill looked smug, several people had left the bar clutching handkerchiefs in front of their faces, eyes streaming as if exposed to mustard gas. It has to be said, when it comes to arse thunder, Bill is the guv'nor.

Gimpo, seemingly undisturbed by the flatulent disturbance, was still performing tricks with his scarred knob, smashing beer glasses and using it like a cricket bat sending ashtrays for six. The laughing whores were singing loudly and pulling him towards the elevator.

Bill followed, holding a newspaper over his behind: a follow through. Even experts are not infallible.

'Would you like to see something funny?' I asked her, pointing at Bill and Gimpo.

'What do you mean?'

Katie was intrigued, I think the blind intensity of Bill's rotten guts had secretly impressed her.

'Leave it for ten minutes or so and I'll show you.'

I ordered a bottle of Black Bush Irish whisky and we sauntered casually to the elevator. The pinging brass cabin descended slowly, like a beautiful space ship. Its glass doors opened silently.

A cloud of cheap whore stink, cologne and gummy gash, wafted into the lobby.

I wasn't sure of the exact number of our suite, but I was pretty sure we were on the twenty-third floor.

'Believe me, you'll like this,' I said as the elevator door closed. Then opened on a gutted whore, ripped from cunt to throat, intestines unravelling like angry serpents flailed around wildly. Screaming in her gore, she was desperately trying to shove her guts back in.

'Well, it looks like we've got the right floor. Excuse me,' I said, stepping around the dying slut, trying to avoid getting any blood on my safari suit.

'Quite amazing isn't it?' I observed, 'It never fails to astound me just how long the human intestine actually is.'

The trail of blood and shredded viscera was easy enough to follow. It led straight to our suite of luxurious rooms. The sound of an electric motor whined loudly inside, almost drowning out the sound of MTV and screaming. I banged loudly on the door.

No answer.

I tried again, harder. Gimpo appeared, his beautiful safari suit absolutely ruined, drenched in black blood, tattered brains, bits of liver and all kinds of other unidentifiable shit.

'Sorry, Z,' said the grimy clown, 'I didn't hear you. Bill's got a chainsaw.'

Katie and I entered the room. What a fucking mess, these boys didn't waste much time that's for sure. The place was like a fucking abattoir. I turned the TV down, Guns and Roses' 'Welcome to the Jungle', what else?

There were three whores bound and gagged, struggling in the corner.

Bill with his back to us, was working on the fourth, cackling insanely, farting like a fucked Harley. Sheets of blood and skin, like the wake of a speedboat sprayed the room.

'For fuck's sake, Bill!' I shouted. The Scottish nut turned around, an idiotic look on his monged-out face. He pushed his blood-spattered specs back up his nose and screwed up his eyes. 'What?' he asked innocently.

'Look, you dumb fucking psychopath, you may not give a flying one about your appearance.'

The retard looked down at his gory suit. 'But I fucking do.' I dabbed away at the stray drops of shit on my stylish flared suit. 'I fucking hate those things,' I shouted, pointing at the bloody chainsaws. 'How did you get them through customs anyway?'

'They're not mine, I got them from room service,' he answered.

The petrol-powered Stihl chainsaws sat like evil beavers on Bill's bed.

'Who's the bird?' he asked, pointing at Katie, pulling on the spluttering starter cable. 'Anyway you've got loads of safari suits,' he added petulantly.

Katie was laughing at our altercation, covering her face when she spotted Gimpo.

The Choc King had dropped his pants and was squeezing out black turds on to one of the trussed-up shagbags.

The poor whore was screaming trying to avoid the legion of faecal rats fleeing his evil arse.

'Gimpo!' I shouted. I don't know what it is, but I really can't stand Gimpo's scat stuff, it turns my guts big time.

'What?' shouts the innocent dumper, nipping off a massive peanut log and smearing it into the tear-strewn woman's face. 'It's not quite as good with black women, you don't get the contrast,' comments artist boy.

Katie tittered. Taking this as a sign of approval, scatboy strained hard producing a long shiny turd, which he coiled on the whore's head like a Danish pastry.

MY LITTLE SWAGGER

'Gentlemen, your rooms are ready. Would you like a boy to help with your bags?'

'We can do it ourselves,' snaps Gimpo.

I swing my large kit bag on to my left shoulder and head for the lift. I like having a kit bag perched on my shoulder, it makes me feel like a seasoned sailor. I indulge in a bit of a sailor's swagger, a little affectation that doesn't escape Z's radar for minor detail.

'Well hello sailor,' he says in his best Julian and Sandy voice. (You do know who Julian and Sandy are, don't you darling?) Z gets up leaving his bag behind for someone else to deal with.

'I'm not carrying your fuckin' bag, Z,' says Gimpo.

'OK Gimpo, just cool it.'

Z returns to the table and picks up his bag. Z is unused to having to carry his own bag. This bickering between the pair of them does not seem to be abating and we've only been in Africa a couple of hours. What's it going to be like when we are up-river with or without paddles? At least this little bout of bickering has put paid to Z's continuing his 'Hello sailor' jibe but somehow I don't think he will forget it. Once Z has spied a minor affectation in a character he has the talent and tenacity to build it up and up to ludicrous and frightening proportions. There is no escape. I will pay for that little swagger.

*

'Bill, meet Katie Blade, the famous BBC war reporter sex bomb,' I said proudly. Bill wiped the gore from his hand and reached out as if to shake her hand but grabbed her right tit and twisted it viciously.

'Yeah whatever, you gonna fuck her or kill her first?' He was addressing me but staring straight at Katie, a slight trickle of drool forming on his bottom lip.

'No man,' I replied, 'She's cool.'

'Yeah?' said Bill, incredulous. 'You sure?'

Kate reached inside her purse and pulled out an evil-looking blade.

She walked over to the stack of whores and stabbed one of them straight through the eye. Bill laughed goofily.

'Yeah, studmuffin,' she said to Bill, placing a defiant hand on her hip, 'I'm cool.'

Spaz-boy Bill was gash struck, he started laughing like a schoolboy, embarrassed.

'You gonna skin these bitches?' asked Katie casually stripping down to her white bra and pants. The trim sporty ones. Katie was comfortable with her raw sexiness and knew that it didn't need the pathetic scraps of satin and lace her lesser sisters employed to try and snare the dumber sex.

I felt old Cyclops limbo dancing in my Jockeys.

'Erm,' began Bill nervously. Gimps had unlocked his pud and was twanging away.

'I usually just mess them up till there's nothing left, skinning's a bit technical for me.'

Katie smiled and wiped her knife on her pants, a delicate pink stain blossomed at her hip.

'Right! You! Wanking boy!' she barked at tugging Gimp. 'Gimpo isn't it?' Surprised, the tugger nodded. 'Put that down and help me over here, we need to string one of these ladies up. Over there.' The bossy school ma'am pointed at the bathroom door. 'Between the jambs.'

The Gimp bowed to her natural authority and after quickly throwing off a shank into the carpet, locked up his pud and grabbed hold of the shitty whore, obviously his favourite, and dragged her over to the bathroom door.

I noticed the pathetic collection of grannies and half hitches the fat-fingered fools had secured her with, it was a wonder she hadn't escaped. I stepped in and rearranged her bondage with a couple of blood knots and some nice slippery hitches.

Gimpo positioned her securely, upside down between the jambs, and Katie went to work.

'OK tuggers, first things first,' barked the confident Kate. 'If we want a nice clean hide, first we have to bleed little lady here.'

Bill was impressed, his hand was back in his crusty pocket.

Katie carried on, 'We need to cut the jugular or carotid artery in the neck. You can see here, they bulge quite clearly, make the cut either behind the ears or lower down in the v of the neck. Don't cut the throat ear to ear or you'll get contamination with the stomach contents.'

Katie pricked the whore twice behind each ear, two thick gouts of arterial blood spouted about 18 feet from the body on to the white-tiled bathroom floor which was angled towards a central drain.

'Cutie pie here should take about an hour to drain and then we can get working on the gutting and the skinning.'

MR MALU-MALU?

The rooms are regular international-style, all the usual fittings, well stocked mini bar, CNN on the TV, no pubes in the sheets, no shit skids in the bog, no used condoms under the bed. Gimpo is happy. Z is happy. I'm happy, although not happy with what we are having to pay to stay here. Three hundred fuckin' US dollars a night. If we stay here any more than a few days we will have blown our float.

I put in a call to Malu-Malu.

'Hallo Mr Malu-Malu?'

'Yes.'

'Good morning. My name is Bill Drummond, I've...'

'Ah, good morning, Bill. You have arrived?'

'Yes, but...'

'Welcome to Kinshasa. You still want to meet our president?'

'Well, yes but...'

'I'm afraid he is at present at his palace in Gbadolite. If you want to meet him you will have to travel there yourselves. I don't think he will come to meet you in Kinshasa, a busy man is our president.'

'So how do we get there?'

'You can either fly, but there is not a commercial flight until next week, or you get a boat up-river then drive from Lisala or Kisangani. I'm a bit tied up today, I've a BBC World Service report I have to finish. What do you say to you coming over here to the Intercontinental in the morning? Will 10.00am be fine?'

'Fine.'

'Have an enjoyable day in Kinshasa, there is plenty here to see.'

He had that dark rich African but well educated type of voice. A voice that inspires confidence. Like Bongo, a man to trust. I like trusting people.

Things are looking good, it seems we can combine Z's desire for us to hang out with the baddest man in the world with my need to travel up the mighty Congo River all the way to the inner station and beyond.

*

Bill was impressed, he'd taken out his notebook and was scribbling notes and making cackhanded sketches at a furious rate. Gimps was twanging his gash hammer like a maniac in the remaining whores' faces. Katie had got herself all juiced up, the bloody carnage was having its usual effect on the BBC sexbomb. I fucked her slow, her fat tongue slobbering in my ear as I felt her judder towards her seventeenth orgasm.

I flipped her on her belly and whacked the baby gravy considerably up her khyber. Katie reckoned that was the most natural and effective method of birth control. I wiped my dick on one of the prostitute's blonde wigs, the little cash slag looked so scared I almost felt sorry for her.

'Katie, quickly!' It was Bill, he was crouched next to the draining corpse. 'I think she's finished, the blood's stopped dripping.'

'Yep, looks that way,' answered Kate pulling on her white pants and lighting a cigarette. 'OK studmuffin, let's get to work.'

Kate grabbed a hold of the girl's heel.

'Cut a circle around the leg, just below the ankle, here like this.' The flensing knife sliced into her black skin. 'Do the same to the other leg and the arms, around the wrists.'

Katie was performing her butchery with an impressive detachment, no wonder the bosses at the BBC found her irresistible, all that public-school matron-wanking shit. 'Then,' grunted the ice queen, placing the knife back into the left leg, 'Slice down inside the legs to the vagina, cut a circle around it, like so, and then down to the stomach and neck. Make sure the knife doesn't penetrate the stomach or digestive organs, lift the skin as you go, slip the knife in.' Katie made it look so easy. 'Sharp edge outwards and cut along. Draw the knife slowly down, cutting away from the body.'

Bill was scribbling away, an eager student. 'Now,' continued Katie, her hands barely blooded, 'Cut down the inside of the arms and start to ease the skin from the legs, use the knife as little as possible, roll the skin outwards, as you can see it's very elastic at this stage, and pull it downwards. When the legs are clear, cut a hole around the anus, insert your hand down the back of the body and use your fingers to separate the flesh from the skin.'

Katie stuck her hand down the whore's butt, Bill and Gimps were battering the old turkey necks like madmen.

'Finally,' she continued, 'Peel the skin from the arms and separate it from the neck with a strong twist of the head, and...' Kate snapped the knife, 'Cut.' She threw the human hide above her head triumphantly, 'Voila!'

I applauded, genuinely impressed. Katie hadn't been idle since we'd last met. Bill and Gimps demonstrated their appreciation in their own inimitable ways: Spaz-gnome Gimps jizzed off a barrage at the ceiling and Bill squeezed out a winning room-clearer.

'The reason I'm showing you all this, jungle boys, is because if you two are as useless as Z over there and you're going up river,' Kate pinched the purple stomach bag together and made a small hole, cutting up and down, her hands preventing the guts from falling out. 'Chances are,' she continued as she cut down to the breast bone letting the guts spill and hang down loosely, 'You're gonna get mighty hungry.' She whipped out the kidneys and liver then cut through the membrane to the chest cavity. 'So you're going to need to know how to catch and prepare your own food. The bush niggers up river would rather see you starve than give you a single groundnut.' She removed the heart, lungs and windpipe. I could see the other whores through the gutted woman's butthole. For some reason this seemed really amusing at the time.

'And believe me jungle studs, humans are a lot easier to catch than animals.'

It was Bill's turn to spurt, he jazzed off a shiny blob of nadjam which hit a light bulb and fizzled to steam.

'Don't these two guys ever stop?' she asked, incredulously.

'Only when we're asleep,' answered Gimps, stringing up another whore with his free hand.

Bill was poking around with the remains of Katie's impressive lesson, comparing his notes and diagrams with the mess in the bathroom.

'Loverboy,' Katie exhaled in my ear, 'Me so horny.'

MAN IS HAPPIER IN A STATE OF POVERTY

We step out of the hotel into the midday heat, walk a couple of blocks, find a street bar, get three beers, sit and watch, try not to judge, just take it in. My fear-inspired racism of earlier today seems to have evaporated. The three of us are sitting here with smiles on our faces, sipping our cold beer. The beer is called Primus. I love the label on the bottles. Z likes the fact that it has an alcohol content above the average. One of Z's biggest fears about travelling to foreign countries is the possibility of being cut off from a regular supply of strong lager.

Gimpo is polishing his camera lenses. Men are dealing diamonds on the table next to us. Young, healthy-looking lads with smiles on their faces walk past with what I can only describe as miniature shop counters balanced on their heads. They all seem to be selling the same range of goods. Lucky Strike cigarettes, toothbrushes and hard-boiled eggs.

Z buys a pack of fags, me a toothbrush and Gimpo an egg. The egg comes with a pinch of chilli powder in a twist of blue paper like you used to get in crisp bags with salt in.

Z leans back in his chair.

'You see Bill, man is happier in a state of poverty. We have everything in the West but our souls are sick. We have no room for religion. That is our downfall.'

'Yes we have. But it's...'

'Our version of Christianity is a dried-up religion. It's worthless. It is we who are in poverty. They should be sending missionaries to us and not the other way round. When I was in India they had no shoes on their feet, slept on the streets, but they always smiled. They were happy all the time. No hang-ups about sex or work or drugs. This was because they had the Hindu religion. A religion thousands of years older than ours, far richer, deeper and more meaningful. A religion that meant you could find a god in it to relate to whoever you were in society.'

'But Z, this isn't India.'

'Bill, as I sit here and watch the people pass by I can see they too, like the Indians, are happy. I don't know what religion they have but it works. Look at them, Bill. They don't look malnourished, depressed or angry and they don't look like they want to kill us.'

Z is partially right, in his pompous way. The blacks here are not walking around trying to look like the meanest motherfuckers on the planet, none of that 'Cooler than Cool J and tougher than Tyson' business, to quote myself. They're not trying to look like they want to mug you or rape your woman. They don't have any of the chips on their shoulders that the blacks in Britain or America have.

'The trouble with blacks in the West is that they've never forgiven us for the slave thing. What they don't understand is that it was their own kind that sold them into slavery in the first place.'

'Z, if you go around saying things like that it will get you in trouble.'

'But it's true.'

Gimpo is ignoring our conversation, he is lost in his *Lonely Planet*.

'Z, I spoke to Malu-Malu on the phone before we came out.'

'So has he sorted out when we can meet up with Jo Mobutu?'

'No, it seems if we want to meet up with him we have to travel to his palace at Gbadolite.'

'Far fuckin' out. I've read about that place, it's his Versailles in the jungle. He's got his own private Concorde there and a motorway built for only him to use between the runway and the palace. So when do we go?'

'We have to travel up the Congo on a ferry first. That will take a couple of weeks, then we hire a car and drive the rest.'

Gimpo looks up from his *Lonely Planet*.

'What did you say Bill? We've got to travel up-river? I've just been reading about it here. *"One of the great African adventures is taking the steam boat up the famous Zaire (formerly Congo) River from Kinshasa or vice versa – a 1,734-kilometre trip. You'll pass by numerous villages and through some of the thickest rainforests in Africa. However, this trip is not for everyone. It's hot and muggy and far from tranquil. Over 1,000 people will be floating along with you, most of them on the three or more barges tied to the steamer's bow.*

The place is a floating zoo, with chickens cackling, pigs squealing, goats tied up anywhere and everywhere, and live crocodiles. There are also loads of dead monkeys and other wild animals piled on the deck along the way, waiting to be put under ice or dried. You'll find the smell of smoked fish everywhere, people sprawled all over the deck, radios blasting away, people joking, babies crying and Primus beer flowing – a good opportunity to make some Zairois friends.

Those travelling deck class will find that little 'quarters' develop and that you will become fast friends with those in your section. They will also guard your belongings when you want to wander about. In addition to sleeping gear, you should bring all of your food and cooking utensils unless you expect to live off the food provided. You should not have any problem finding someone in your section to cook you a meal but it'll cost double. All day women are pounding manioc into meal, and frying bananas and doughnuts for their families. On the more exotic side, chicks, baby crocodiles and snails are sometimes cooked and eaten as snacks; stewed monkey is also popular.

The prime entertainment on board is the thriving commerce. For many passengers, the trip is not a journey but a job, as many of them are actually merchants who have miniature stalls on the deck and sell soap, matches, beer, black-market penicillin, malaria pills, etc. The barges are moving so slowly that there's commerce going on constantly during the trip. Day and night, men and women from villages along the river paddle out to the barge in dugout canoes (pirogues) filled with bananas, avocados, baskets of fish, monkeys, and sometimes live parrots for sale. At times as many as 100 canoes may be tied up to the barge. Once the villagers sell their goods, they come on board to purchase goods from the bazaars.

The main boats are operated by..."'

'OK Gimpo we've heard enough. So Bill, did he tell you about flights? I reckon we should fly straight there. None of this pissing about playing sailors.'

'There are no flights.'

'There fuckin' must be!'

'Well no scheduled ones.'

'So we charter one.'

'We ain't got the money.'

'I thought you said we've got $3,000 in cash?'

'That's for emergencies.'

'Z, listen to this,' and Gimpo starts reading again.

'"*The main boats are operated by the government agency, ONATRA, and each has three classes of cabins. First class includes two small bunk beds, a cabinet, private toilet and shower and a large padlock. Each steamer also has one or two first-class deluxe cabins which are about 50% more expensive and have air-con; meals are served in the air-con dining room or your room.*"'

'What do you think?'

'It sounds OK,' says Z, 'bit like *Death on the Nile* or a Mississippi river boat steamer. This could be good.'

'OK, let's sup up, head back to the hotel and see if we can sort out tickets for the next sailing,' says me.

*

The next morning, Katie was still down there slobbering away having orgasms. She crawled up my belly, I could smell my balls on her breath.

'Hey stud, I'd almost forgotten how fantastic you are at being sucked off.'

I smiled. She wasn't the first to have made that observation.

I selected a beautiful lime-white safari suit with short sleeves while Kate washed her cunt.

Down in the breakfast bar Bill and Gimps were attacking their fried sausages, bacon, dozens of fried eggs and fields of mushrooms. Both were battering themselves bog eyed under the table

'There's something wrong with those guys Z, it's not normal,' said my cocksucking bird.

'Ah, you get used to it,' I answered, unconcerned about the wankers.

The tug brothers were wearing cute little Ed Gein Texas Chainsaw-style waistcoats of human skin. Bill, who's quite handy with a needle and thread, must have knocked them up after we had left the party last night. We sat down and Bill presented Katie with a similar waistcoat.

'Oh, Bill, you shouldn't have!'

Fucking right he shouldn't have, it radiated insanity, but I guess Kate was just being diplomatic. Bill obviously had a crush on her. The thought of those two as an item didn't bear thinking about.

Over breakfast Kate wanted to know what we were doing in Zaire. She assumed, naturally, that we were just here to groove on the lawlessness and mayhem, which of course was partly true. When I told her we were here to reclaim our souls she didn't bat an eyelid. She knew all about the maleficent machinations of the Fallen One, how at certain pivotal moments in an individual's life the usually innocuous arch fiend arrives with his honeyed temptations. Some succumb, some tough it out, remaining faithful to their youthful dreams and ideals. Some even manage to strike a half decent deal. Not many, but it is possible.

Not us literary arseholes however.

Katie nearly fell out of her chair when she found out the chump deal me and Bill had suckered ourselves into. I'd gone for the gash, Bill had weighed in for a lump sum. Cash and Gash, what a couple of fucking idiots.

I WILL BE YOUR DRIVER

Back at the Memling's travel desk, they are horrified that we want to go up river by steamer. They don't sell boat tickets. It seems if we insist on using this form of transport we will have to buy our tickets down at the docks.

We get in a taxi waiting outside the hotel. We explain to the driver using a mixture of hand signals and the ten words in French we know between us that we want to get to the ONATRA ticket office down by the docks.

The taxi driver is a young man with a warm smile.

'I speak English little. My name is Jean Claude and I will be your driver for your stay in Kinshasa. I can show you around. Plenty of places to see. What do you want to buy?'

'We just wanna get tickets for the steamer up river. We're not tourists.'

'Ah, missionaries?'

'No, not missionaries, just...'

'Please, please, climb in my taxi and I will take you wherever you want to go. You can call me JC and what are your names?'

'You do realise this place is about to blow don't you?' asked Katie sucking on a chipolata.

We didn't, but seeing Katie out here it was pretty obvious some major badness was about to go down. She doesn't piss around with trivial domestics, she only deals with big-time international fuck-ups. She passed a pitying look over my subnormal companions.

'Do you know how dangerously weird it gets out here when shit goes down?'

Of course we fucking knew, why else would we be here? We sure as shit weren't going to find the devil at EuroDisney.

Anyway what's wrong with weird? For a long time now weird had been our meat and bread.

BILL, IT'S OBVIOUS WE JUST HAVE TO BRIBE THEM...

About an hour later, after visiting two sets of ONATRA offices in government buildings and various docks, which turn out to be the wrong ones, the three of us with JC, now serving as our translator, are standing in a dark office. On the wall is a framed portrait of Mobutu. On the desk is an old manual typewriter. There is a dark-green filing cabinet with paper spilling out from its open drawers. The one window to the office has no glass in it. It is filled with dark faces, all staring in at us. Everything is dark. Is this why it is called the dark continent?

There is a steamer leaving on the day after tomorrow, Friday. This is good, as there is now only one steamer travelling between Kinshasa and Kisangani and it won't be back again for three weeks, at the earliest. What is not so good is that there are no deluxe cabins left or first class, or even second class. We are going to have to travel third class with the dead monkeys and live crocodiles. Gimpo is loving all this. Z isn't.

'Bill, it's obvious, we just have to bribe them a few dollars and we can get the deluxe.'

We have a few words with JC. JC has a few words with the all-powerful man behind the desk who, up until now, has not even deigned to look in our direction, turns his large head to face us. The corners of his mouth turn up. A faint smile.

'You think your Yankee dollar can buy you whatever you want? Well, here it can't. You will have to travel third class. Not because I want you to offer me a bribe or because I want to punish you but because there are no other cabins available. If you are stupid enough to try and book tickets just two days before the steamer leaves, what do you expect? Everybody else buys their tickets weeks in advance. You are lucky to get a cabin at all. It is only because I have just had a cancellation that this one has come up.'

'Sorry sir, we didn't mean to offend you.'

'You didn't.'

He shifts his gaze back to JC and negotiations continue between them in French.

It turns out that it's going to cost $200 for each of our three tickets. And that includes two meals a day for 14 days. This is cheap. This is good. Even Z is smiling. But the man behind the desk won't accept our dirty US dollars. He wants good, clean Zaire – the currency has the same name as the country.

'OK Z, Gimpo, Bill, we go get Zaire and then we come back get ticket, then I show you sightseeing. OK? Only $10 an hour. OK?'

'OK JC, you're our man' says Z.

We like JC. Even Gimpo seems to trust his judgement.

DRUMMOND'S SECRET LOG, MEMLING HOTEL, KINSHASA, ZAIRE

Oh Jesus Christ, fuck. God, please help me. The insane drinking and the blackouts have started again. And now I fear the sodomy is once more upon me. I thought all of this was behind me in Toledo.

Toledo!.

God curse its name.

Toledo, Toledo, TOLEDO!

And that damned Arab boy, tear out my heart and feed it to the vultures, damn his brown eyes! KIKI! There, I've said it! his name, damn him. But how can I say that, how can I, my desert flower? I loved him. And if he were here again now, I would love him with every fibre of my being once more.

Oh tainted, tainted love that whispers its name beneath sacrilegious idols in the dark churches of Sodom. Where is the source of this black river shame? And why does my love fear to speak its name?!

Ah, beautiful boy Kiki, come to me now in this sweet oasis of memory and dream! With his soft black hair, his honey-coloured skin. The light fragrance of jasmine and cherry blossom that eddied around us, the scent of melting wax and coconut butter as we lay in each other's arms in the private rooms of Fat Miguel's Catamite club.

In all the shining of Heaven and all the freezing fires of black Hell, no one knows the depth of my pain, my howling anguish. How I miss my precious boy.

I'll never forget the night he died. Stabbed through the heart on that dirty Spanish street, he died cradled in my arms. I cursed Heaven as my tears mingled with his blood on that blasted pavement beneath midnight stars. Rolo, the assassin, disappeared into the eldritch labyrinth of the medieval city.

In all the time spent within the heady atmosphere of The Catamite I never suspected the depth of my true feelings. That damned place. How many men have lost their souls in that temple of decadence, that perfumed den of hopeless boy love?

I remember that first night there.

Z and I were playing an increasingly perilous cat-and-mouse game with the elemental agents when the bacchanalian Miguel himself welcomed us into his blasphemous grotto.

The Catamite Club is famous in some form or other to those in the know throughout the world, its location shifting like the colours on a map. Yet somewhere, somehow, The Catamite has always existed. A place where the bittersweet pleasures of longing and loss, the songs of love and her intricate dances can be rented by the hour.

The fat Arab, like a perfumed spider, showed us to a fine table dressed in crystal and silver. Fat Miguel, a ludicrous character anywhere else but here at his perverted court, he possessed the supernatural gravitas of Wagnerian opera.

His thick orange makeup, like the grease paint of a perverted clown imitating a grand dame, glowed eerily in the candlelight. Small beads of sweat hung on the sebaceous paint above his thick red lips. His kohl-black eyes were like tarantulas. The fat fuck flounced away in his flowing white robes and disappeared into the blue clouds of hashish smoke.

This was where I first met my love boy.

Oh Kiki, Kiki, Kiki!

Damn the stars! I would kill God himself to have him back for just one hour out of all eternity. Those soft purple nights drifting upon the lagoons of forever when, lounging upon a scented litter of hyacinth and rose petals, we made heaven with our love.

Kiki! My true love! Those languid hours we spent delirious beneath the crescent moon, our lungs heavy, hearts adrift, high over the enchanted back streets of the city.

I remember the night my boy, with tears in his soft brown eyes told me his pale history, his life as a citizen of a gilded world. Orphaned on the streets of Cairo with nothing but his beauty, fallen men from the West would worship at his secret temple. His tender years were lost in a mad symphony of dark emotions, suicide and desperation. And shame.

How little I, macho Bill, know of that dirty little world. Stranger, the shame I confess to you now in this damp closet of my soul. Poor Kiki, raised in the city of the dead, among the pious meditators and malevolent buggers, among the crumbling monuments, sweet Kiki would read comic books. As we lay among our foolish dream Kiki told me of the dangerous sphinx and the Sultan of thieves. Of the mysterious Futuwwa lodges and the sodomy ranches of Babylon where first he met his nemesis, the boy, his brother, Rolo.

WE ARE THE NIGGERS HERE

Thirty minutes driving around tree-lined, potholed boulevards in JC's taxi, stopping off at various money changers. These are one-man operations. They sit at the side of the roads with huge bundles of Zaire notes. Each bundle is the size of a house brick. We have learnt that all cash in Zaire is paper money, coins do not exist – a byproduct of hyperinflation.

JC is looking for the best exchange rate he can get on our behalf. Gimpo is not so sure. 'I reckon he is just wanting to find the one who will give him the best backhander.'

'Trust him Gimpo, he's a good bloke.'

'He's a nigger.'

'Look, Gimpo,' says Z, 'We are the niggers here. We are the ones not to be trusted. It's us that filched them for everything they had, then dumped them leaving them to sort out the mess.'

It never fails to surprise me how Z can seemingly shift his world view, political leaning and moral standpoint at 180° in less time than it takes for him to order a beer.

JC has finally found a money changer he is happy to do business with. We change $1,000, by my reckoning enough for the tickets and see us through to Kisangani. This means we are now squillionaires in Zaire and even though each note has at least half-a-dozen zeroes on it, none are worth more than ten pence each. There is no way we can secrete this amount of money in my cash belt, we've got ourselves a pile of cash two house bricks' high. Nigger rich indeed.

*

'Just fuck off Z, all right?'

Gimpo was pissed off and limping.

'Watch your backs, lads,' quipped Bill.

'You as well, cunt, it's not funny.'

Gimpo was furious and with good reason. He'd just been raped by armed police and was not amused by the cruel taunts of his so-called friends.

'Where's your handbag?' started Bill again.

We'd just been out with our friend JC, the driver, checking out a few of the downtown Kinshasha sights. Bombed-out buildings, crusty lepers, whores, public hangings. The usual third world shit, when four agitated cops in a beaten-up Mercedes forced our car off the road. JC told us to be cool and do as we were told. Cops don't like killing white guys, it's too much hassle. I wasn't worried, I knew they just wanted money.

We were taken off the main drag and told to kneel down with our hands behind our heads. I was pissed off with the brutality, all this fucking pistol-whipping shit and shouting. The boss cop was another body odour Idi Amin character, fat eyeballs about to pop, shiny sweating face, ranting and swearing, kicking and punching.

One of them was paler than the rest, skinny, North African. There was something supernaturally creepy about the guy, he had a high-pitched laugh and was searching our pockets with his skinny fingers digging into our groins copping horrible queer feels.

This was what probably made Gimpo turn all heterosexual. The dumb bastard gets to his feet and does his low-IQ Manchester hard-nut routine, refusing to hand over his money, calling them niggers and black bastards. Idi had Gimpo's pants down in four seconds flat and slammed him face down on the Merc bonnet.

He was up his dirtbox even quicker.

Gimpo howled like a bear in a trap. A small group of school kids had gathered around and were laughing at the silly white man getting his arse reamed out by the head of Kinshasha's finest. I have to admit it did look funny, but then again I didn't have Donkey Kong up my arsehole.

Bill was trying hard not to laugh and failing.

Idi wasn't laughing, he was obviously taking his buggering duties seriously, thrusting savagely and battering poor Gimps around the back of his head with his revolver.

The other cops had taken mine and Bill's cash with no problem and let us on to our feet to see our friend's humiliation. The gathering crowd of children thought it was hilarious and were wiping tears of laughter from their eyes.

The tension was dissipating somewhat and one of the cops got a cold six-pack of Primus from the boot of the car and handed one each to me, Bill and JC. A hi-life band had wandered by and started accompanying Gimpo's bumming with some jangling happy rhythms. Idi had started laughing and was banging up Gimpo's arse in time to the music.

It seemed like the only person who didn't find the whole thing hilarious was poor old Gimps, his face was as black as thunder, murder bleaching his blue eyes white.

'Fucking hell, Gimps, come on,' chipped in Bill, dancing to the music, 'Where's your sense of humour?'

Gimps simply glowered. Idi jizzed and took out his knob, it was pretty fucking big. Gimpo trembling, remained prone. Idi walked around and pointed a stern finger at Gimpo's face.

'And remember, my friend,' he admonished in a mock serious, heavily accented English, 'To be showing the proper respect in a black man's country. You are not the Queen of Hingerland here.'

One of the little kids had jumped on to Gimpo's arse and was banging away with his little pencil dick. Idi smacked him around the head and shooed him away.

'Better be pulling up your trousers my friend or they will be thinking it is a free ride.' His tone was conciliatory. 'No hard feelings friend, I see you are a military man, no?'

Gimpo, surprised, answered in the affirmative.

'I thought so, you took your punishment bumming well. Anyway, we must go, enjoy Zaire, soldier, it is good for you.'

The fat sodomite and his pals fired up the Merc and screeched off downtown. Gimpo pulled up his pants and punched one of the little kids hard in the face, the rest of them laughing and making mocking buggery motions ran after him.

ZAIRE WIVES

We're back in JC's cab and heading back to the docks to buy our ferry tickets.

'So boys, you want Zaire wives?'

'No thanks, we have wives back at home.'

'No! No! No! But you must have Zaire wives. She very good. You will like. She not sleep. I can get. All night long.'

There is nothing seedy in JC's proposition. It's very matter of fact, open, friendly, as if he is proud of Zairese womenfolk's talents at not sleeping.

Z tries to explain to him.

'Thanks for the offer but your Zaire women would be wasted on us, we just like to put it in, cum and then go to sleep. We can't be doing with all that other stuff.'

I added, 'Don't get us wrong, JC, we think your Zaire women are very attractive.'

'What are you talking about?' blurts Gimpo.

Have I mentioned before – Gimpo is deaf and he hasn't brought his hearing aids with him. It's a war wound of sorts, him having been a gunner in the Falklands.

'Nothing, Gimpo,' says Z.

The thing is, Gimpo is not like me and Z in the love-making department. He likes to keep going all night, all through the following day and all the next night. There is no stopping him. We didn't want Gimpo to start shagging all over the jungle. He is supposed to be looking after us. And, anyway, he's just got married.

*

'How come he knew you were a squaddie, Gimps?' I asked, confused about how he knew from just looking at his arse.

'Punishment bumming,' he replied, 'It's an army thing.'

I was still no wiser. Gimpo explained that in the military, especially in the British and American forces, sodomy was a common form of discipline. Squaddies, for obvious reasons, like to keep quiet about it.

'Yeah well, you shouldn't have called him a nigger anyway, it is his fucking country.'

'Yeah,' added Bill, 'Because now you're a faggot.'

'Don't be fucking stupid!' spat angry Gimps, obviously still sensitive about his painful ordeal. 'Being a fag's not contagious, you don't turn queer just because you've been fucked up the arse! Half the fucking armies in the world would be bent if that were true!'

Gimpo's overstated denials made me feel that his conviction was not quite as secure as he would have us believe.

'Yep every one knows that, Gimps,' taunted Bill.

'Well you had better sleep with your back to the wall tonight then, hadn't you sailor,' minced Gimp half-heartedly. The seed had been sown.

'Oooh, is that a promise?' rotten Bill again.

ROGER MOORE'S BROTHER

Back at the ONATRA ticket office, JC buys our tickets. We stand around being a freak-show attraction. One young man sporting a Neil Diamond tour t-shirt is taking a special interest in my safari suit.

'So tell me sir, you look like Roger Moore. Are you his brother?'

'No, it's just the safari suit. We got them from the same place that he gets his.'

'Can I buy it from you?'

'I'm afraid not, it's the only suit of clothes I have with me.'

'You give me the address of the shop in England where you got it from. I have a brother in Brussels, he can go and get it for me.'

Now there is no punchline to this short tale, the only reason for documenting it is that Z and I had been trying to affect a style that was the ultimate 'white-man chump' look. A style that no black man would ever want to have anything to do with, or so I thought up until now. And, of course, I must now be way ahead in our 'who can be the most like Roger Moore' game.

DRUMMOND'S SECRET LOG, HOTEL MEMELIN, KINSHASHA, ZAIRE

Here beneath this equatorial blanket of damp sin I continue my squalid confessions.

But within this sordid opera, *mon lecteur, mon frère*, perhaps a little sympathy?

Kiki, mon amour, how you haunt my fevered dreams dear ghost.

Let this short history of your brief time upon this cruel Earth be my memorial to you till we meet again little one.

Kiki was born less than 17 years ago to a family of beggars. When he was seven years old his father sold him to one of the notorious sodomy ranches popular in the more wealthy suburbs of the teeming metropolis. It was there, in that university of depravity that Kiki met his first lover, brother and eventual killer, the bastard Rolo. After four years of enslaved homosexual education at the hands of some of Cairo's most cruel queers the two boys killed a man and escaped. They fled north like their Moorish ancestors to Spain and Toledo where they dreamed of becoming great matadors.

Toledo, on the hill, that fantastic city of cold steel and hot blood. The twists and turns of its mysterious streets, the rat-blind alleys leading to dark cul-de-sacs and dummy staircases, the atmosphere of danger and dreadful secrets reminded them of Cairo and the terrible city of the dead where they once lived. The boys wallowed a while in their new-found freedom. Opium offered sweet release from the grotesque reality of their situation.

But not for long.

It was inevitable that they would eventually have to turn to the shameful trade they had been forcefully pressed into if they were not to starve.

Toledo is famous for three things. The magisterial beauty of its many churches – so many it is said that the devil cannot cast his shadow within the city wall; its magnificent swords and knives, hand-made for centuries by families of master swordsmiths; and of course that nefarious cellar of buggery and evil, The Catamite Club and its patron, the globular monster, Fat Miguel.

The Catamite Club, a place whose very name whispered on absinthe breath has the power either to stop hearts or speed them; where men's souls are lost, sold or gambled; where the wicked caprices of Fat Miguel are law. Within the invisible walls of this neverland of boy love and sin there is only one law. Miguel is Dark God within the poisoned confines of The Catamite. The velvet grotto flickers chiaroscuro, Caravaggio's ghost shades the ambience. Writhing boys sweating beneath yellow candlelight undulate in and out of the deliciously sinister shadows.

They are dressed simply, in jewellery. Diamond cat collars studded with blood-red rubies, sapphire and silver tiaras rest upon their oiled black curls. Thin chains of gold, loose around their hips swing with the rhythms of their blasphemous couplings.

The sweet mind-heavy aroma of hashish and the deep tones of boy musk mingle in the slow motion air. Falling upon impossible luxury amid rose petals and exotic down one notices the breathtaking ceiling swirling above the opium smoke.

It's the legendary lost masterpiece, 'The Sodomy of Christ' by Toledo's most lauded son, El Greco, The Greek. Believed to have been smuggled out of Spain by those occult dandies, the Nazis, by others believed to be a wicked symbolist joke. But no, painted upon the low ceiling of the world's most notorious club, here is the world's most notorious masterpiece. My Presbyterian heart shudders at its mere recollection.

Beautifully executed in the elongated visionary style of the master, the breathtaking painting depicts the Nazarene at the thirteenth station of the cross. After the Saviour has been lifted from his crucified agony he is held down by the Roman soldier, Longinus while the betrayer Judas, a look of hideous gratification on his face, buggers the tormented son of God. The pieces of silver can clearly be seen falling from his robe.

I think this painting was why Z liked the Catamite so much. He would spend hours attached to his opium pipe staring at the dreadful masterpiece.

'Far fucking out,' he would mumble glassy-eyed, to no one in particular.

It was here beneath this blasphemous ceiling that the sick flower of dark romance first blossomed for Kiki and I. The saponaceous shadow of Fat Miguel slithered from a cloud of blue smoke leading a veiled boy by a thin silver chain.

'Meester Beelee,' he said, his breath smelling of sperm and icing sugar. 'Someone I think you will enjoy.' His red lips were like wet liver. 'A friend of mine.'

Miguel pulled away the boy's chiffon veil and handed me the chain. The clouds of heaven caressed my ballbag. There he stood, the love boy, in a pink thong, oiled and lithe in his little diamond cat collar. Blue black curls framed his shy face. His charms had attracted the admiring glances of some of the older buggers lying around the central fountain.

The breathtaking beauty flashed me a coy glance. I caught the ghost of a smile dance upon his gorgeous mouth. Pomaded Miguel, whose spectacular degeneracy seemed to escalate when contrasted beside Kiki's seraphic beauty, laughed throatily. The fat slug disappeared back into the blue smoke, the ripe odour of corruption trailing in his wake.

Kiki's black eyelashes like iridescent butterflies fluttered as I led him by the ridiculous chain to a private alcove behind muslin curtains. His plump lips parted as he whispered softly to me on lavender-scented breath, 'Mr Billee.' I trembled on my litter of purple cushions and clumsily made room for him, the elegant teenager gracefully arranged himself like a cat.

He was wearing the standard uniform of the Catamite love boys: bejewelled collar, tiara, sapphire earrings, a garland of rare orchids around his long neck.

'You want for to bugger me now or later?' So unashamed, so natural, so beautiful. 'Or maybe first I will be smoking your horn?'

The language of lovers rarely transfers well to the printed page: the whispered nuances, the inflection, tone, even the smell of lovers' words, like jasmine and tangerine, sweet and gentle like a child's prayer. How can our clumsy alphabets convey such emotions?

We loved among the rose petals, they were fresh and moist. I drew a veil across the small candlelit alcove. We smoked hashish and drank fine red wines by the bowlful drifting deliriously to an intoxicated paradise wrapped in each other's arms, our souls entangled with eternity.

BANDY LEGGED RUNTS

Z and I have wandered out of the ONATRA offices leaving Gimpo with JC to get on with the form-filling that has to be done before we get our tickets. We are standing in the rusting and rotting docks, staring north out across the huge sweep of the Congo river. On the far shore is the low outline of Brazzaville, capital of some other central African state. Huge lumps of vegetation are floating down the river.

'You know, Bill, I was reading about the slave trade last week in the British Library. The vast majority of blacks in America are descended from slaves taken from the Congo Basin.'

'I suppose that explains why the blacks here look far more like the niggers in America. They are far better looking, finer features than those from Nigeria or Ghana. Their skin is more rich chestnut than the blue/black of those further north.'

'Yeah, but have you noticed the slave traders must have taken all the best ones out of the breeding pool and just left behind all the bandy-legged runts behind? These lot they left behind are the equivalent to the weasely Liverpool inner-city scallies whereas what they took were their equivalent of the strapping rugby-playing, public schoolboy types.'

'You're right. I can't say I've seen too many Mohammed Ali or Will Smith types here.'

THE BOOK OF GIMPO, BY GIMPO

What is it with all this bumming business? Yesterday this fat fucking copper had me over the bonnet of his fucking cop car and he banged the technifuckingcoloured shit right out of my fucking arse. I pretended to be, but I wasn't really that bothered. Stuff like that goes on all the time in the army. The fucking SAS, Special Arse Service as they're known as by the regulars, are turd burglars to a man. I bummed a few of the new lads meself once or twice. You get used to it, it doesn't mean you're a puff or anything, it's just like being in jail, sort of.

Anyway it freaked Bill and Z right out. Well, Bill mainly, Z just thought it was funny.

I know Bill can be well weird when he wants to. Those fucking whores the other night, it was a laugh at the time but I don't know, I never really thought about Bill's pathological hatred of women before. Most blokes can't stand women really. Some times I get so mad with my missus I just want to pull her head off and kick it down the road.

Maybe it's just me but after I got bummed by the cop, that night Bill asked me if I wanted him to rub Germolene on my ring piece. He'd waited until Z were out of the room as well. He had a really weird look on his face too. No, it doesn't bear thinking about, I must be imagining things. Bill a sneaky fudge packer? No way.

Anyway where was I? Yeah, this bumming business. Today right, we had our hair cut. After that stuff with the cops yesterday JC the driver said that if we wanted we could get a soldier from the hotel, only $25 a day with a gun and everything, so if anybody tried to bum us or rob us we could kill them. Sounded pretty good to me, so we got Golf.

We went to the barbers' with Golf and his AK47. I couldn't fucking believe it, these hairdressers, right they were just standing around combing each other's hair and like just bumming each other, dead casual. As if it was just a normal everyday thing, about 20 of 'em just thrusting away and not taking any notice. I thought it was a wind up. Fucking hell, anything for the weekend, sir? You know what I mean? I didn't say fuck all, they weren't going near my arse that's for sure. Golf said something in African and they all stopped, thank god.

I didn't really want my hair doing, but Bill said that we would get ringworm if we didn't. When the guy had finished doing mine I looked like a fucking pineapple. I asked the cunt if he'd ever cut a white man's hair before. He said no but he'd been bummed by a few and asked if I wanted to bum him. I told him to fuck off.

Bill sneaked off into one of the back rooms with a big jar of snake oil and one of the junior assistants.

Z just sat there with his beer. That's all he ever fucking does, just sits around with his beer. People say he's cosmic and stuff but I can't see it myself, just looks like a grumpy pisshead to me.

The guy was just finishing my pineapple, smearing it down with snake oil when I heard all this gunfire and shouting. It was fucking Golf, he'd shot the shit out of all the hairdressers. They were splattered all over the place, some of them not quite dead, moaning and stuff. Golf started going through all their pockets getting their money and watches and stuff.

The little assistant Bill had taken into the back room came running out with no pants on, snake oil all down the back of his legs and Golf let him have it with his revolver straight in the face.

What a fucking country. And then right, Golf has his cock out and he's bumming one of the dead hairdressers. Smiling as well he was.

Fucking Africans man you think that you know 'em and that they're OK and stuff, then they go and pull a stunt like this, shooting people and bumming them.

Fuck it , I'm starting to wish I'd never fucking come here. I thought I might get to see loads of animals, monkeys and elephants, giraffes and what have you. But all that's happened so far is I got my arse shagged and them two, just turning fucking psycho as usual. And my fucking arse is killing me as well.

IT'S A FUCKIN' STITCH-UP

JC has just called Z and I back into the ticket office. It seems that although we are now the proud owners of three tickets to take us from Kinshasa to Kisangani and a cabin with three vacant bunks has been reserved for us, there is a problem.

'It's a fuckin' stitch-up Bill,' blurts out Gimpo. 'He's trying to tell us we need a special visa to travel out of Kinshasa.'

I turn my attention to the big man behind the desk.

'But excuse me, sir,' I start, as I pull my passport from my back pocket, 'You see here we have our visas stamped in the back of our passports. It was done at the Zairean Embassy in London. We were told this allows us to travel wherever we please in your great country.'

A warm and friendly smile spreads across his large face.

'Don't come the white man with me. That stamp in your passport that you got in London means nothing here. Here in Zaire no foreign national is allowed to travel outside the capital without the right papers signed by the right government officials.'

'So what do we do?'

He doesn't answer me, instead he turns his gaze to JC and starts jabbering in French. A debate ensues between the two black men. JC seems to be holding his own. But finally he looks resigned. He beckons the three of us to follow him outside.

'I'm sorry, gentlemen. He says if you don't get the right papers by this time tomorrow then your tickets become invalid.'

'Let's just get a refund now. What do you think, Bill?' says Z.

'I'm afraid, gentlemen, refunds are not allowed.'

Gimpo cuts in, 'You mean that cunt has just got us to hand over $600 for three tickets he knows we cannot use?'

'I'm sorry, it is my fault but everything will be OK. I've a friend in government. Everything will be OK. I will have your visas by this time tomorrow. It may cost a few dollars but not much. But let's forget about all that and I will show you the sights of my lovely city.'

JC is a good man.

*

I'm back at my usual place. The bar, alone.

Gabriel smiles at me and polishes a sparkling glass, busying himself, arranging bottles neatly so that all the labels face forward. Tidying up his small world. His barman uniform is immaculately clean. Crisply ironed white jacket, black trousers with a military crease. It's the heels of his shoes that touch me though. Worn down almost to the leather, but polished to a shine way beyond any hotel regulation. There's a pride to the man that somehow shames me. I instinctively understand that in paying attention to the small details of everyday life, he has his priorities right.

I order another cold bottle of Primus, Gabriel smiles once more and places a small bowl of salted almonds in front of me. I catch a strange whiff of gasolene and madness, a nervous tic flickers across Gabriel's face. An obsidian chip glitters in the black man's handsome eyes and I catch his thoughts. I can hear machetes being sharpened in distant shanty towns, eyes stinging in the kerosene half-light, spears and assegai being honed on the anvils of revenge and sharpened on the unforgiving flint of revolution.

WE ARE ALL HIS CHILDREN

The three of us are willing victims to the subtle charms of JC's personality and for $10 per hour we are more than happy to be driven around the sites of Kinshasa for the rest of the afternoon. I also have complete confidence that JC will sort out our visa difficulties.

'I will show you where the rich men live.'

It turns out to be a wide tree-lined avenue with large, colonial houses on one side and 1960s' style luxury apartment blocks on the other, but the place is a mess. Wild dogs roam, potholes breed, everything's in a state of dilapidation. My theory for the moment is that it's not the black man's innate laziness that prevents him from bettering himself, whichever race of humans was out here would be beaten by this sweltering and humid climate and this is the dry season when supposedly work can get done.

'Now I show you the national stadium where they had the famous Rumble in the Jungle... Are you sure you don't want Zaire wife, only $20 for all night long... Zaire has best football team in all Africa. People think it's Nigeria or Cameroon but we have beat them both. One day we will win World Cup, you wait and see... $20 for very beautiful lady... Mobutu is a good man. A great man. It is the men that advise him that are bad. We love Mobutu and he loves us. We are all his children...'

*

Gabriel knows with the knowledge of a fellow sensitive that I had caught his thoughts. Spooked, he throws an olive in my beer. Unfortunately the head barman caught this unforgivable blunder and started battering Gabriel around the head with a heavy crystal soda fountain, apologising profusely in English to me and cursing Gabriel in French. Gabriel whimpers and makes things worse by trying to fish the olive out of my beer with his fingers. The head barman, incensed by the naïveté of his ignorant country man, whipped out a small barman's handgun and stuck it in poor Gabriel's face.

'No, no,' I protested, 'It's OK. I like olives in my beer, really, it's what I ordered.'

I fished out the offending article and popped it in my mouth.

Gabriel laughs nervously, still unsure if this is a cruel white man's joke.

'Relax, Papa,' I say to the head barman, 'Take a beer.'

The last thing I want now is more fucking blood on my canary-yellow safari suit. For fuck's sake doesn't this violence shit ever end, all I wanted was a quiet drink, Fatso pours himself a beer and wanders off behind the alcohol.

Gabriel eyes me suspiciously, my telepathy had spooked him.

'How you do that thing, Mr Z?' he whispered, keeping a wary look out for his violent boss.

'It just happens occasionally,' I told him honestly, 'I can't turn it on at will, if that's what you're worried about. The psychic frequencies have to be aligned and all sorts of other variables.' The gentle soul seemed relieved and carried on with his simple chores.

'I think you are a good man,' he said thoughtfully. 'Alphonso would have killed me, you stopped him, you are a good man. My daughter is very young, it would be an honour for me if you would sex her.'

I laughed and reluctantly turned down his generous offer.

'Mr Z,' he continued, pouring me another drink, 'You and the other white men, you are not priests?'

I coughed on my beer.

'No Gabriel, we're not priests.'

'You are not diamond men, no?'

'No.'

'Missionary bugger men?'

'No Gabriel, we're not soul poachers.'

'Why for you in Zaire then? You like boys? My cousin is very young.'

What could I tell him? The truth I guess.

'My colleague, the tall one,' Gabriel made a fanning gesture in front of his face.

'Yes, the one that farts a lot,' I continued, 'Mr Bill and myself are here in your country to find the Devil, we believe he has our souls and we want them back. We sold them to some of his freelance agents some time ago and well, we've changed our minds, we reckon we got a bad deal.'

'And the small man with the penis?' asked Gabriel.

'Gimpo? He's a bullet catcher, very good at violence, karate and stuff.'

Gabriel found nothing unusual at all about my explanation, he possessed the emotional intelligence of illiterates and poets. He carried on cleaning his bar and mopping the floor.

'The freelance agents, they were known to you?'

'I don't know who bamboozled Bill,' I said. 'But the wormy cocksucker that hit me up for six was an unpleasant little fellow by the name of Balfe. I kind of felt sorry for him at the time, he didn't have any friends. I didn't realise the reason for that till too late.'

'So you would not say he was in league with the Devil?'

'No Gabe, the poor idiot was in the same boat as the rest of us, just another regular fool.'

'The Gash and the Cash I think I have heard the diamond men say.'

'That's about the measure of it, friend,' I laughed.

'Mr Z, I think you are a good man, I wish you luck. My daughter's bum hole is always open for you.'

GIMPO'S VISION

Z and Gimpo are bickering again. I'm in the front passenger seat and will use this opportunity to tell you about one of the underlying problems between the estranged brothers-in-not-quite-law.

Gimpo had taken over the management of Z's band, Zodiac Mindwarp and the Love Reaction. The band had had their 15 minutes and they were on the slippery slope downwards, that all scuzzy rock bands find themselves on. The only hope of salvation that any band has is that once they have reached the bottom and have been forgotten by all but the most die-hard fans, is that those long-gone 15 minutes will begin to take on mythical proportions.

As for Zodiac Mindwarp and the Love Reaction, they reached the bottom of their helter-skelter descent some time last year in 1995, the band split up and now they are having to wait it out for a future generation of trash rock fans to rediscover the Love Reaction and judge them to be the greatest lost rock 'n' roll band of the West. These things take time.

Gimpo had boldly taken the reins of the band's management, just as they were beginning their descent. Gimpo has many gifts but he hasn't got a fuckin' clue when it comes to managing a band. I think he thought it was just about trying to realise the band's vision by treating record companies, promoters and agents like a bunch of cunts. Instead he should have had his own vision, treated the band like a bunch of cunts and somehow inspired the record company, promoters and agents to go along with him in realising his vision. Actually, Gimpo did have a vision. He planned to buy a horsebox, convert the horsebox into a tour bus and thus save the band having to shell out a fortune on hiring tour buses when they went out on tour. This was a bad vision.

Gimpo had an assistant, a cute little rock chick, from somewhere in the Midlands. Although she was more than willing to work for nothing, her ambitions lay way beyond shagging the odd bass player. She reckoned she could do a better job than Gimpo.

One day a band and management meeting was called for 3.00pm by the band. Gimpo went around to the bank, emptied the band's account and put the cash in his own, then went to the meeting where he was duly sacked. Gimpo then explained to them that because the band owed him a few thousand in unpaid commission, he had taken the liberty of helping himself to what they could afford and as he was a big-hearted kind of bloke would let them off with the rest.

Sadly, the rock chick from the Midlands was unable to do a better job than Gimpo and within months the band was no more. I have a sneaky feeling she will yet make her mark as I believe a future generation will venerate Zodiac Mindwarp and the Love Reaction's burgeoning mythical status. Distance in time will justly magnify their legend.

Anyway, the upshot of all this was that Z was left with a load of back tax and accountant's bills to pay and Gimpo was never able to get his horsebox. So that is why there is a certain amount of niggling going on in the back of the cab between Gimpo and Z.

THE BOOK OF GIMPO, BY GIMPO

Shitting hell. Whose fucking idea was it to come to this fucking place? I can't believe what's just happened. Golf is a fucking maniac.

Killing a load of fag hairdressers is one thing, everybody's scared of queers. But these were just ordinary whores. OK there was all that business in the hotel, but we were all drunk and it was that Katie bird's idea, we just went along with it, as you do when you've had a few. It started out a normal day, just walking around downtown Kinshasha, not a lot to see really, a couple of bodies hanging from lampposts with little kids throwing stones at them. Golf shot a beggar kid who was hassling us, but only in the leg. Seeing as how I was an ex-squaddie I thought I might have something in common with Golf. He spoke a little bit of English and I was getting OK with the Lingala so I was asking him about the army and stuff.

I fucking tell you man, these fucking African wars, they're not like our wars, long-distance guns, bombs and shit, these fuckers are still into hand-to-hand liver-ripping stuff. Golf's been fighting in one war or another since he was 11.

Most African soldiers are mercenaries. The names of countries, boundaries and shit, they're changing all the time. Most of the guys fighting in the wars don't even know whose side they're on, they're constantly switching allegiance to whoever is paying out most American dollars.

They're fucking weird wars as well, especially the smaller jungle conflicts. As if the AKs and machetes aren't enough these fuckers have to deal with all the black magic voodoo stuff as well. Golf says it works because every body believes in it. They bang up all kind of weird jungle drugs before they start fighting so I can believe it as well.

So anyway, where was I? Yeah I remember, we were having this normal day out, had a burger and some bananas when JC wanted to know if we wanted to go to any music clubs that night.

Fucking music clubs, my arse. It was a totally skeezo whorehouse with just loud disco music, pitch fucking black as well, except for the candles. All the tarts were wearing these tags with their names on, not their real names, stupid prozzy ones like Candy and Roxanne. I had a go on one called Mercedes. You just do it in the disco, it's really dark and has mattresses in the corner with like a little curtain you can pull across.

These fucking black birds they can fucking go some as well, I can tell you. It was like riding a rubber shark, them big muscly legs squeezing your breath out, finger up your arse, the works. I've porked some women in my time but fucking ball-crusher Mercedes, she could fucking hide the banana with the best of them. Only five quid as well, didn't have to wear a johnny or nothing.

I could see Z getting sucked off under his table while he drank his beer. JC was in the next tent to mine making a right fucking noise with Candida.

I don't know how it all started, but it must have had something to do with Bill and his big skinning knife, he must have tried skinning one of the girls. He hadn't talked about anything else since that session with Katie. Tiffany's stood there crying, covered in blood with one of her tits lopped off. Laughing-boy Drummond, he's covered in blood as well with a black fucking tit in his hand and his fucking knob sticking out of his trousers. And then fucking Golf kicks in with that fucking gun of his, he's got it on automatic and its ripping the shit out of everything, whores and bouncers jerking around like dolls, bullets flying everywhere, wood splintering, glasses and bottles smashing.

I saw the DJ go spinning across his decks records smashing all around him. He was a real pro though, I'll give him that, I don't think I've seen anyone reload as quick as Golf. Z's just sitting there, he hasn't moved a muscle, the mashed-up body of the bird that was sucking him off laying in a pool of blood at his feet. Nutter Bill of course, he doesn't miss a trick, he's wading in there with his big fucking skinning knife like there's no tomorrow. He's forgotten all Katie's lessons and was making a right fucking mess. Then Golf starts mopping up, blasting anyone that wasn't dead. He stands there when he's finished, covered in glass and bloodstains in his cool shades with his gun smoking, smiling.

It was spooky, like a film or something. The needle had caught on a record, it was just clicking away dead loud. Golf shot it and made me jump. Z said something first, he was pissed off because he hadn't jizzed and Golf had shot his whore.

I mean what was it all about?

Bill was quite willing to pay for any damage to the whores. It was only when I saw the opportunist soldier frisking all the corpses for money and shit I realised what he was up to. Can't blame a man for making a living I suppose. I must admit though I am getting a bit pissed off with all this buggery and killing. I mean, if I'd wanted all of that shit I would still be in the army. I just want to see some zebras and stuff.

MANKY DOG SAUNTERS

JC's cab is a beat-up beige-coloured Opel Rekord. The engine sounds fine, the gearbox doesn't grind, the brakes don't squeal but I had noticed when we first got in that all his tyres were completely bald. No grip whatsoever. I assumed that this didn't matter here, as the roads were so knackered that any tyre grip would be irrelevant and it's not as if they ever have to watch out for black ice on a February morning.

A manky dog saunters out into the road. JC swerves in an attempt to miss the African mutt and hits a stray lump of concrete. The dog saunters on its way.

'Excuse me gentlemen.'

JC climbs out, kicks his front left wheel and swears in what I assume to be African. His composure regained, he gets back in. We drive a couple of blocks on the flat tyre. Pull in at a yard piled high with knackered and bald tyres. We wait and watch. A suitable replacement is found from the mountain of tyres. All look equally as knackered as the one that is being replaced.

'Have you noticed JC's club foot?' I ask Z.

'Yeah, he hobbles like Dustin Hoffman in *Midnight Cowboy*. I like him. He's one of the good guys. It must be really hard to keep your morals together in a society where corruption is so endemic.'

'What the fuck are you saying? He'll be just as corrupt as the rest of them. You watch, he thinks he's got us, he's going to try and rip us off rotten before we get out of this place,' says Gimpo. New tyre in place. JC opens the car door, pulls a wad of notes from under his seat, peels off 100 or so of the almost worthless notes, hands them over to the man who is king of the rubber.

'OK boys, we go have good times.'

DRUMMOND'S SECRET LOG, MEMELIN HOTEL, KINSHASA, ZAIRE

These memories of my Arab love boy are distressing my soul, I cannot continue, it is too painful. But continue I must, if only to cherish and immortalise his brief existence on this unkind planet.

But I am distracted. Oh weak fool that I am.

Today Golf and I... it cannot be, I swore to the homosexual Gods that after Kiki there would never be another.

Golf with his gun, gunning down the whores. My soul trembled in awe at his savage grace, his powerful arms. His fierce, primal being, the purity of the man, his raw connection to the forest. Ah Golf, perhaps in another life as comrades in arms. Beneath an African moon, in your village home, sharing a simple meal.

Kiki and Rolo had been lovers since childhood. Rolo suspected nothing at first. It was only when Z and I overstayed our sanity at The Catamite, not leaving its drugged walls for over a month that the one-eyed Rolo became suspicious.

We were eventually asked to leave when our credit ran out. We left the place penniless. Our entire fortunes blown in the mammoth debauch. The fees Miguel charges, while guaranteeing discretion, are also usurious.

Z, it seemed, was as fond of the place as myself, dreaming his way through thousands of dollars' worth of opium and vintage wines. Our money squandered, we had to leave our debauch and take squalid rooms in the filthiest corner of Toledo's Arab quarter.

We both suffered terrible withdrawal symptoms. Z from the opium, myself from Kiki. Z puked and dosed himself with cheap rum until the sickness eventually receded. I mooned over my lost love like a schoolgirl. Like a fool I wandered the winding streets of the city hoping to catch a glimpse of my beloved. I would spend hours concealed in the shadows outside the entrance to The Catamite hoping to catch sight of him slipping out for baguettes or couscous. The food served in the Catamite was too rich for Kiki's simple tastes, he preferred the peasant food served at the street markets near Montmartre.

I knew I was only fooling myself by thinking Kiki could possibly feel anything for me. After all, he was being paid to drip his honey in my ear. But somehow I couldn't help myself. Within those bewitched hours sliding on those languorous dreams I had believed every sweet word. My head told me I was paying for beautiful lies but my idiot heart refused to listen. I knew that Kiki was probably in another man's arms right then, whispering the same sweet everythings. The thought was killing me.

That night I got violently drunk and told Z everything. He just laughed and made tasteless jokes. Damn him, I know he's right. I should have got all this confused sexuality business out of my system at art school.

That night as I lay tossing and turning, unable to sleep, my entire being consumed with longing for Kiki there was a frantic banging at the door. Kiki's voice, desperate and breathless ripped me from my tormented slumber.

'Billee! Billee!' There was panic in his voice. 'Come quickly please!' Could it be possible, had my love searched for me? I charged to the door in my underpants and flung it open.

Kiki, with a black eye, fell into my arms, huge sobs wracked his delicate frame. Somehow even his black eye looked beautiful. He was wearing strange clothes – it occurred to me that I had never seen him fully dressed – the uniform of a French sailor, blue and white horizontally striped shirt with white trousers ridiculously snug around the crotch flaring into huge baggy bellbottoms. A scarlet neckerchief knotted to one side set off his tragic attire artlessly.

Tears welling in my own eyes, I held his wet face close to mine and brushed away a salty jewel of his pain and confusion. I ignored Z's derisive laughter behind me and ushered the distraught boy into our rude apartment.

'Sit down, Kiki. What is it? Tell me, what's the matter?' I tried to calm him down, he was trembling, like a flower.

'Oh Billee, I am so frightened,' he blubbed, 'I searched everywhere. Fat Miguel, he refused to let me leave, there was a terrible fight. Oh Billee, Billee what am I going to do, what will become of me?'

Kiki started crying once more.

I sat him down on my bed and poured him a tumbler of the cheap rum Z had used to stave of the sickness.

*

GIMP'S CLOCK WATCHING

Gimpo is now in the front of the cab with JC, keeping his eye on the clock that has been left ticking. He is convinced that the $10 an hour deal is a rip-off and that the clock rate would be considerably cheaper. But as we have no idea what the exchange rate is I don't know what he thinks we're going to gain from staring at the clock.

'For fuck's sake Gimps, we agreed the $10 deal. Just be pleased for him, he has a decent job with us for the day. Have some humanity,' says Z.

Gimps mutters something.

'I take you boys to biggest market in all of Africa then we go for cold beer.'

'Sounds fine to me, JC. You're our man.'

Z is into one of his expansive and generous moods. He has his window down and is waving and smiling at the passers-by. Who the fuck does he think he is? He's behaving like some minor movie star out on location patronising the natives.

'I like it here Bill and they like us.'

I don't reply and instead pull out my notebook, decide to get on with the next part of my Irish story.

*

'Start at the beginning, child. What is all this, what's the matter?'

The fragile boy forced down the foul gut rot and pulled a face like piss and raw lemons, coughing violently. The rancid liquor seemed to work, Kiki composed himself momentarily and continued.

'It's Rolo, Billee, He knows everything.'

His shoulders shook as the tears once more began to flow.

'What do you mean Kiki? I don't understand.'

'Oh Billee, about all our love! Oh please Billee, please don't say you don't. Oh no please no...'

I was confused. 'But Kiki, I thought, I mean...' My heart was racing like a runaway train. 'Weren't you just saying those things because...'

I hesitated, hope and fear clashed in my stomach, 'Because you were paid, because I paid you to?'

'Oh no Billee,' he blurted, 'No, a thousand times no. Even a whore such as me has a heart, even a tramp like I can love!'

'Oh Kiki!' I took him in my arms, our tears ran together like two lonely rivers.

Z made his distaste obvious. He farted loudly, laughed derisively and with a few curt homophobic expletives left the room.

I fell starving upon Kiki's soft mouth, ravishing him with kisses, our tongues twisted together like hungry serpents. We spent the next rapturous hours wrapped in each others arms. After the intensity of our ardour calmed, Kiki slept a while and I ran to the nearest florist. Kiki adores making love on the moist petals of fresh flowers, one of the many small idiosyncrasies I adored about the boy.

Later I closed the dusty curtains against the fierce Spanish sun and we siesta'd well into the evening making drowsy plans and smoking hashish. We would live together in a house in the English countryside. We would wear moleskin trousers and frolic in the garden. Somewhere deep in Gloucestershire where Fat Miguel, Rolo and all the other ghosts of Kiki's past could never find us.

For a few short hours we were happy, love buoyed us on impossible dreams. We would travel the world, be married in San Francisco, visit Acapulco. Kiki wanted to dive from the famous cliffs like Elvis.

Then Z came back. He was hideously drunk and made Kiki cry. Poor Kiki, his fragile North African sense of manliness was no match for Z's Yorkshire belligerence.

He left to buy baguettes and couscous. And never returned.

Rolo was waiting for him. Skulking in the cankerous shadows. With his knife.

I heard a scream. It was Kiki.

My heart banged in my chest as I ran down the worn stairs and into the street. There in the yellow pool of light from a solitary street lamp, supporting himself on his elbow, clutching at his bloody breast, Kiki lay bleeding. A black pool of blood slowly spreading around him. His frightened eyes confused, he reached out for me as I ran to him. I cradled him in my arms as if in some black dream, I felt light-headed as if I wasn't really there.

'Billee.' Kiki's voice seemed to be coming from somewhere else, I shook myself into the now of the situation.'

'Billee.' With his last breaths. 'Please don't forget me.' He tried to smile and closed his eyes as if falling asleep.

The assassin had stabbed him through the heart.

He died in my arms.

I stayed there a while watching my tears mingle with his blood on that dusty street, beneath the cold stars.

I howled like an animal at that callous moon.

'Why! Why! Why!' I screamed. 'Why now?! When happiness seemed so close.'

My insane cries echoed around the narrow streets

'Damn you, stars! Damn you, God! If there is a God, then I denounce him. I abandon him as he has abandoned me. To hell with you, Christian God of bastards. To Hell with your pale mercy! Fuck your Heaven and all your scabrous angels!'

I fell to the ground, squeezing the bones of my beloved on that rat-stinking pavement, bereaved more completely than any man had ever been before.

Z picked me up and hurried me into the apartment before the arrival of the police. Any witness to a murder in this part of the city would be more than suspicious. Z stank of rum. He laughed at me, his callousness quite unbelievable.

During the days that followed I searched every inch of that evil city. It was as if Rolo had simply vanished into thin air.

One of the boys from the Catamite told me that there had been some kind of quarrel between Rolo and Kiki on the day that Kiki died but that it was not unusual, the two of them often argued. They both had left at about four o'clock to buy some baguettes and couscous, and that was the last he had seen of either of them.

SKID MARKS AND BREAKFAST

George Graham (the then Arsenal manager) was asking me how my problem was and I can't quite remember what my problem is. Then I'm running along the side of the A37 somewhere past Dagenham. It's night-time, I can see the eyes of a fox caught in headlights. I run past the freshly killed corpse of a beautiful badger and I remember there is some organisation or other that you are supposed to phone to report the sighting of a dead badger – something to do with the spread of TB. The phone is ringing. It keeps ringing. It's getting louder. My arm reaches out and after some fumbling is clutching a phone. I hold the receiver to my ear.

'Good morning, Mr Drummond. This is your eight o'clock call.'

The receiver dropped to the floor beside my bed. Something stinks. I pulled back the bed covers to discover skid marks on the Irish linen sheets.

'I've shit myself,' I said aloud which wakes me up and George Graham was gone so I suppose I'll never find out what that particular problem was.

Z was asleep on the other bed, daylight struggled through a crack in the heavy curtains. I bundled the evidence of my nocturnal bowel movements up into one of the at least half a dozen carrier bags I carry around with me in case of emergencies. Found the bathroom, filled the bath, sunk in and washed away my sins. My head started to clear and I tried to work out where I was. Moments of memory came back to me from the previous night. We must have gone back to the Shelbourne Hotel with The Man and checked ourselves in.

Washed, shaved and born again.

'Z, I'm going down for breakfast.'

'What? Where are we? OK. I'll be down in a while. What time is it?'

Down in the breakfast room with a freshly squeezed orange juice and a full Irish breakfast in front of me, I was beginning to feel better. I looked around the room, besuited business men and retired couples doing Dublin. Then I noticed a very familiar face sitting at a table set for one. After last night I should have been ready for anybody. But I wasn't and certainly not the king of the one-liner. The wittiest man in Manhattan. The ultimate Jewish creep – Woody Allen.

Chapter Two
THEY RAPE NUNS HERE

The sonic beatitudes of the BBC World Service bathe the earth with soporific lullabies. All is not madness, it coos dovelike from behind the clouds, all is not chaos. The BBC World Service with its soothing Received Pronunciation English acts as a kind of global existential-fear filter.

Don't worry citizen of the sane world, shit may look bad now beneath that Orwellian jackboot but eventually order will be restored, everything will be as soothing as the familiar colours of the topographical map of the London underground.

The world, it tells us, is not a severely fucked-up patchwork of interrelated megalomaniac power trips and savage gardens. Reality does not revolve around autodidactic perversions of grand narratives and year-zero fundamentalism.

No, these sane vowels murmur us as they caress the various constructs under which we all nullified, everything's fine.

Big Mother proffers a sweet lactating tit.

Arthur Malu-Malu knows this is all a crock of shit. He is contractually obliged to the cosmosodomistic tower of lies. The cocksucking little bastard works for them. An agent of the beast.

But who in all honesty can blame him in this vile sodomocracy of an excuse for a nation where the gooks on both sides don't kill him. Within the focused insanity of war the main players know the scintillating value of spin. The BBC World Service is the dizzy conduit of countless sodomocratic governments' clumsy attempts at spin and outright propaganda.

Arthur leads us across the charred mezzanine of the Kinshasha Intercontinental where naked Mai Mai are taking it in turns to rape a nun

'I must apologise for the mess,' he says.

The powerful black magic of the BBC has convinced him that the clipped tones of his beautiful accent can keep out even this dreadful reality.

'Things are getting a little hairy out here.'

Gimpo and the satanic blowflies linger. The scatalogical Earth elemental fiddles nervously with the front of his pants.

'They rape nuns here,' runs his feral logic, suppurating evil, dripping shite.

'They rape nuns here,' echoes Bill's bog-eyed insanity. He farts warmly, enjoying the sensation of the brown gas as it chugs pleasantly between his legs and swirls sensually around his greasy nads.

OPEN SEWER

JC has just spent 30 minutes driving us through mile after mile of shantytown. Everywhere there are people swarming this way and that. African pop music blaring from every shack, the sun streaming and a cool breeze from the wound-down windows. This feels good. Z keeps shifting the tilt of his bush hat in an attempt to affect the most raffish of slants.

'Gentlemen, here we are at the largest market of all Africa.'

We climb out, the heat hits and the place stinks. We have to step over what appears to be an open sewer. How far the market sprawls I have no idea. JC might be right in his innocent boast. 'Fuck!'

Z has just soaked his right foot in the open sewer, totally soiling a sandal and the bottom six inches of one safari-suit leg. He was obviously still concerning himself with the right way to alight from a stretch limo when attending the Oscars. That's once Scorcese has discovered him and given him the leading role in his back-to-form movie now that De Niro is shite. Gimpo laughs loudly. I smirk at the antics of my vanity-infested friend.

'Serves you fuckin' right for wearing that jessie drag,' shouts Gimpo over the blaring Afro pop.

*

Bill and I join Arthur in the elevator. A drunken Mai Mai is crashed out in the corner, dressed in a bizarre combination of garments looted from the smashed hotel shops and three pairs of designer sunglasses one on top of the other. His cock hangs wet from his Burberry slacks, a string of ball snot stretching from eye to fist.

'They came out of the jungle yesterday,' says Arthur nonchalantly as the lift glided to the top floor. The totalled masturbator farted in his drunken sleep.

'They're from the Llualaba, cannibals. See his pointed teeth, they file them like that to frighten their enemies. Works, doesn't it?'

The lift door swishes open, Arthur leads us down the corridor of what was obviously once a very beautiful hotel.

Dead bodies lay scattered all over the place. The naked Mai Mai lurch from room to room ransacking the mini bars. We pass another nun being gang raped

'Those silly women.'

He points at the semi-conscious nun, her face badly beaten. She appears to be mumbling some kind of prayer through smashed teeth.

'They could have got out weeks ago.'

He shakes his head and carries on down the corridor.

'What is it with Catholics, always trying to suffer more than the idiot on the cross. Oh well,' sighs Arthur, 'I hope their heaven is worth it.'

We reach Arthur's suite of rooms. Two of the naked warriors, the first sober ones I've seen, stand sentry at his door. Arthur says something to them in Lingala and the sinister guards step aside.

Gimpo has disappeared.

SOAP

I hate going to foreign places, especially foreign shops or markets. Everything looks different. I like things to look the same. Every day, everywhere, the same. It's only when everything looks the same that you begin not to notice it's there and that you begin to notice all the things that are going on inside your head. The danger with going to foreign places is that you end up being seduced by all the different ways they package things, the cheap printing, the crap but endearing graphics, the charm of the primitive use of advertising. I fuckin' hate the lot. Of course Z loves it. Shallow.

'Look Bill, have you seen the way the hippopotamus is printed on the wrapping of this soap?'
Z seems to be ignoring his sewer exploits and is now being seduced by the cheap charms of all the basic wares being displayed on the first market stall. I now briefly take in that half the stall is piled high with bars of soap. The majority are unwrapped, chipped and are of those faded pastel colours that foreign soaps come in. There are a couple of African women with babies strapped to their backs rummaging in this great heap of soap searching for the perfect bar. The other half of the stall, the half that has captured Z's malformed imagination has rack upon rack of soap bars all wrapped in these crudely printed wrappers.

'Look Bill, this one's got a reindeer on it. Why the fuck would they choose to put a reindeer on the wrapper of soap? It's great. And this one here's got Michael Jackson on it. What do you reckon, Bill? What's with this one? You can smell like a reindeer, wash with this one and your skin whitens up like Michael Jackson.'

I'm trying not to listen to what Z is on about. I'm more concerned with the fact the skin between my bollocks and my arse is beginning to itch and I'm wondering if it would be considered the wrong things to do for a white man to put his hand down the front of his trousers and have a scratch in a place like this.

'Look Bill, they've got one called Rambo. It's got Sylvester Stallone on it.'

I suppose I should address what Z is on about, so...

'Didn't you bring any soap with you? I never go anywhere without my carbolic.'

'Well you fuckin' wouldn't, would you Bill? Your personal soap regime is irrelevant to me. What intrigues me here is the creativity, the thought process, the wonder that has gone into the packaging of these bars of soap here.'

'Z, it's just advertising, primitive maybe, but capitalist con-tricking advertising all the same. You don't wash yourself with wrapping. The soap is probably shit anyway. That's why I bring my carbolic. You can trust that.'

I decide to go for it and shove my left fist down the front of my safari slacks and have a scratch. One of the African mothers, the pretty one, gives me a withering look.

'Control yourself Bill. Just 'cause we're in some primitive land, you can't go openly wanking all over the place.'

'I wasn't, I was...'

'Just give us some of that African money, I'm going to buy some of this soap.'

Z is now cradling about a dozen various bars of this soap.

'No!'

'What do you mean "no"? What petty high horse are you on now?'

'OK. But I don't want this soap thing getting out of hand.'

'What the fuck are you talking about, "out of hand"? I just want to buy some cheap soap 'cause the wrappers look great.'

'OK, OK.'

I pull a wad of notes out and hand it over. Z knew exactly what I meant. He has an habitual need to collect things, must be something to do with his addictive nature. During the past year it has been bottles of chilli sauce. It started after he had made his aforementioned visit to India, when he came back with a couple of dozen of these small bottles of chilli sauce with their crude but brightly coloured labels. I had tried to reason with him then as I have done just now regarding the soap.

'Z, it's all just the same chilli sauce inside the bottles.'

But he was having none of it. He is now unable to pass a deli or other ethnic-type shop without slipping in to see if they have any small bottles of chilli that he hasn't got. His collection has now expanded from the original 24 to more than a couple of hundred. All lovingly lined up like tin soldiers on a high, purpose-built nick-nack shelf, around the wall of his kitchen. Cute but irrelevant.

'Look Bill, I don't go on at you about squandering thousands on shit art or, come to that, you burning...'

'Shut the fuck up. We agreed not to talk about that. Anyway, where's Gimpo and JC?'

THE BOOK OF GIMPO, BY GIMPO

I know I shouldn't have really, but I couldn't help myself.

I think it must have something to do with those Athena posters I remember from when I was a little kid. There was one with a tennis bird scratching her arse and another with a nun fastening her suspender belt. That was the one that really used to shock my monkey. I used to wank myself into the carpet over that one. That and Pan's People, they were like our generation's Baywatch. Because of censorship and all that I think we were a lot more perverted in them days, at least I think we were , but maybe that's just another illusion that comes with the roll of time's creeping amnesia.

Yeah, anyway the nun.

It was the 1970s and like I said wanking was a lot more perverted, it was just before feminism caught up with all us liberated tuggers and banged down on all that free-love shit we were trying to trick women with. The fucking bitches never went for it anyway, did they? And of course there was the lesbian movement, all them nice birds cutting their hair off and turning into tuppence lickers. I know there's a point I'm trying to make here but like most mental prisons that you need structured argument to escape from, I'm fucked if I can be arsed.

All right I admit I'm trying to find a weasling justification as to why I had a go on the nun. Well at least it wasn't rape. You can't rape a dead body, can you?

Anyway like I said, she was dead. Fucked to death by the weird soldiers. I asked one of them if it was OK to have a go on the nun. He grunted and said that it was fine. Of course I would have rather shagged a live nun but at least she was still warm. I wiped all the soldier's spunk out of her cunt and her arse, I never was one for stirring the porridge, and then I gave the little sister of the poor a right fucking seeing to.

I didn't mind the soldiers laughing at my arse banging away either, I was used to this sort of thing. We shagged quite a few dead bodies in the Falklands. You get bored of just wanking and buggering enemy prisoners. The officers all had first bagsies on any captured women and by the time it was the men's turn they're usually dead anyway.

I didn't reckon we'd be getting any white gash up-river so I thought fuck it, the nun wasn't going to complain, was she?

BATTERIES

Z and I make our way between the tightly packed market stalls. I won't waste my time or yours on description. You've got an imagination so use it. What you may come up with is probably more interesting than what is here.

'White man go that way,' a friendly stallholder points down the darkening path between the covered stalls. We soon find Gimpo and JC. He is haggling with an aged man over the prices of some EverReady batteries. The stall is piled high, like the soap one, with batteries.

'What the fuck are you haggling for? Just pay what he's asking and let's go and get that beer.'

'I'm not haggling. He's selling these batteries loose. They are not in sealed packaging. How do I know they are not used? How much power is in each of them? They could be almost completely flat and just because he can show me that each one he is trying to sell me lights a torch bulb, he thinks I should be satisfied.'

'Well, what can you do about it? For that matter what can he do about it? You either trust him or don't buy them,' I say.

Gimpo reluctantly buys the batteries. We make our way back to the edge of the market.

'If these batteries go flat when we are only halfway up the Congo then I will blame you two.'

'What the fuck do you need batteries for anyway, Gimps?'

'For my video camera.'

'Then I hope you've been ripped off and they go flat within the hour.'

Silence, except for the cacophony of African pop music blaring out from the blaster on each and every one of the market stalls.

TOWELS

'Hang on a minute.'

We are just about to climb back into JC's cab but Gimpo has just spied a stall selling towels.

'Gimpo, you won't need a towel here, the heat will have dried you before you've even washed.'

'But they are Man U' towels.'

Anyone who lives in England will already know that everybody that isn't a fan loathes everything about Manchester United. Everything that can be hated about the modern corporate industry that the beautiful game has become can be focused on Man U and their exploits.

The 1990s will forever be remembered for being, among other things, the decade when local football clubs sought to create a fan base on a global scale. It was bad enough when I was a kid and you supported a team just 'cause they got to the cup final instead of your struggling local lower league side. But now, kids across Europe are supporting clubs like Man U, Inter Milan or Real Madrid and they don't even know where these cities are!

Now there is a lot I respect about Gimpo. He can usually see through the crap of any situation. But I've long since held the view that any self-respecting Manc supports Manchester City. Forever the underdogs of the city of rain. I can't believe here where not even Western pop music, Hollywood films, foreign lager or News International can make any sort of impression, they are selling Manchester United bath towels with giant-size prints of Ryan Giggs and David Beckham to dry your black face on. How and why does this happen? Because it does. And I suppose I should not even bother asking such stupid and facile questions.

'But Gimpo, why do you have to support Man U? They don't need you. They don't give a fuck about you. They just want your cash.'

'Fuck off, Bill. I wasn't going to buy the towel. I've never bought any Man U merchandising. I was just pointing it out.'

'Just cool it, Bill,' says Z. 'Why do you have to get so worked up about football? A game for bazzers, played by bazzers and run by bazzers.'

'Bazzer' is Z's general term of mild abuse for all white working-class and would-be working-class males who aspire to nothing more than the lowest common denominator with a few macho eccentricities on the side.

'And anyway Bill, you never complained when all those kids around the world were buying the mindless pop manufactured by the KLF.'

'All right, Z. Let's just get in the cab and go for this beer.'

I'm sitting in the front. Outside the endless shantytown bumps by. I do know why Gimpo supports United. He told me a couple of years back. When his mum left his dad and left Manchester, taking the kids with her to live in a caravan in North Wales, Gimpo had a hard time of it. In those days Gimpo was just a skinny little runt. He was sent to the local school. The local lads were Welsh speakers to a boyo. And they hated the English. They took it out on Gimpo and Gimpo was homesick for the grey days of Manchester. So he focused on the all-conquering exploits of Bobby Charlton, Georgie Best, Dennis Law and the rest, it gave him something to hold on to. And, as we all know, once you've nailed your colours to a team's mast it is impossible to ever shift, however much an embarrassment in later life it becomes. As someone once said, 'You can change your wife but not your team.'

DRUMMOND'S LOG, THURSDAY 6 JUNE 1996
THE LESS STIMULATION THE BETTER

I've just woken up. Gimpo is asleep in the foetal position with his bedding pulled tightly around him. The trouble is he is not on the other twin bed, he is in the corner of the room. I'm not surprised. This is typical behaviour.

I fell asleep last night with notebook on lap and pen in hand and did not hear Gimpo come up. I've no idea if he had put himself to bed in the corner of the room out of drunken ineptitude or out of design.

I get up and look out of the window. What I can see is a grey dreary day. What I expect from Africa is blistering sun or torrential, tropical storms, not grey dreary days. I have a suspicion the greyness and dreariness has followed me here to keep me company. There's no sparrows or starlings, not even any feral pigeons. Just these rather large crow-like birds swirling about making a very uncrow-like din.

The horizon is flat and featureless. There is nothing to inspire the imagination. It's the way I like it. The less stimulation the better. I hate the 'Oh my God, look at that' effect that travelling to foreign parts can sometimes have on you.

I've decided to run myself a bath and write some more of the Irish stuff while having a soak.

*

Arthur sits by the towering collection of antique BBC broadcasting equipment. He flicks a few switches, turns a couple of dials and talks into a microphone. He sounds authoritative, like he is in control. He signs off and turns towards us.

'Are you quite sure about all of this?' splaying his fingers and placing them together as he leans back in his chair. 'I'm afraid I need to know a little more.'

That was the only excuse Bill needed. He was off, a grandiloquent soliloquy about metaphor, allegory and occidental tradition, Blake, Byron and countless other Byzantine theories and irrelevancies as to why we were here.

The real truth, I'm sorry to say, was much more along the lines of grooving on the weird, sliding piss-close to death and shitting into its bony mouth, throw in cross-dressing, buggery and serious sex-death action and you've got yourself a cigar. I kept quiet though, I'm not really into bucking other people's trips.

Bill rationalised for a good three hours, his theories oscillating between Whitmanesqe metaphysics and Melville-like doubts on the nature of the reality of transcendence. And of course the usual music flobber.

Arthur stretched out on his desk and took a nap. I wandered down to the bar to find Gimpo fucking a dead nun. Wild.

The funky bollock-naked warriors are well trashed, sprawling all over the wrecked foyer. One or two of them are trying on some looted Gucci and Versace. Unaccustomed to wearing clothes, they are wearing the colourful shirts and leather trousers back to front. Some have on women's blonde wigs, others are wearing bras like hats.

The place is piled high with corpses, some of them have been skilfully butchered, presumably for the warriors' evening meal. Nearly all the alcohol has been drunk, the liquor they didn't like the taste of, they smashed. I managed to find a bottle of Primus and waited while Gimpo had finished on his new girlfriend.

TURNLY'S TOWER

The Curfew Tower, or Turnly's Tower as some locals call it, deserves some explaining. The tower was built in 1820 by local landowner Francis Turnly, a man of mystery and imagination with the funds to realise a number of his whims. One of these whims was to bring about world peace via his philosophies; another was to build a tower affecting medieval origins, 'as a place of confinement for idlers and rioters'. As the Irish had made a name for themselves for being good at idling and rioting, it seemed like a worthwhile project. The tower is five floors high, with a windowless dungeon on the ground floor and parapets to its flat roof. There is a four-inch-thick, iron-studded front door. The walls are thick enough to withstand cannon balls. There is a well in case of a lengthy siege. And a bell with a rope. The bell is hung between two of the parapets. Turnly left instructions that the bell was to be rung at 9.00 each evening, the curfew hour. If anybody was caught out in the locality after the bell had been rung, they were to be thrown in the dungeon until their debt to society had been paid. One of Turnly's other instructions was that the tower had to be guarded night and day by a permanent 'garrison of one man' – initially a veteran of Waterloo named Dan McBride. Wild Dan was given enough provisions for a year and was armed with a musket, a bayonet, a case of pistols and a 13-foot-long pike with a cross at the end 'so that it could not be pulled through the hole guarding the doorway' by rioters.

I'm quoting most of this information directly from the particulars we got from the estate agent when we bought the place, not from some broad historical knowledge I have of Ulster.

*

We went back up to Arthur's room, Bill was still pontificating grandly, gesturing expansively and banging his fist on the table to emphasise one point or another. He'd been ranting for a good four-and-a-half hours now and was winding up on one of his more familiar themes, how he had invented homosexual music, punk rock, the Beatles and acid house.

Arthur was startled from his slumber as Bill slammed his fist on the table.

'And that,' he shouted, 'Is why I am a genius!'

'Yes, yes, fascinating, centre of the universe, your arse, Rupert Bear, Liverchester, burning a hundred pounds...' said Arthur helping himself to a bottle of Primus from beneath his desk. 'You really have no idea what you are getting yourself into do you?'

FAULT LINES

You may be asking how Z and I came to be the owners of a tower in the wilds of County Antrim and plenty have been the times we have asked ourselves the same question. It all started back when we were heading for the North Pole with our icon of Elvis Presley to place at the summit of the earth. It was a time when everybody was eagerly talking about the influence that the internet was going to have on culture, a popular theory being that books would become redundant as all text would be available free on the internet. This seemed like a good idea, something democratic society had been working towards for the last couple of hundred years. Very hard to argue a case against it, but there was something I didn't like. I loved books as objects, I loved the feel of them, the smell of them, new ones with their virgin pages, old ones, worn and thumbed from generations of past seekers of knowledge.

I had a puritanical notion that knowledge that wasn't struggled for wasn't worth having. To be able to download the sum total of man's learning for nowt seemed to reduce it in some way. I knew these were mere prejudices and didn't stand up to any critical analysis. But still I wouldn't let go of my notion. I had always been attracted to the idea of a pre-Caxton golden age of learning when all books were handwritten, decorated in the margin by dedicated monks and scholars going blind with concentration and a little self abuse on the side. The rumour of learned books spreading slowly across Europe from abbey to monastery to royal court and down the Danube filled me with a romantic longing to be one of those learned monks tramping across Europe in search of them.

So, come the dawning of the age of the net, I saw my chance. The books that Z and I wrote either together or separately we would write out by hand in large leather-bound editions of one. We would find ourselves a secure and sound building and that would become our library. If people wanted to read the wisdom we were going to impart, they would have to seek it out, track it down and make a pilgrimage out of it.

We were on the lookout for a small but distinctive building. A Second World War pillbox or a retired signal box that BR were flogging off or a tiny Methodist chapel no longer ringing to the good Wesleyan call – something like that would do fine. Whatever it was, we didn't expect to find it in the property pages of *The Independent On Sunday*. Z phoned me up one Sunday evening to tell me he had found the place. There was a small box advert with a picture of a tower, a price and a phone number, but no letting on where the tower was situated. I phoned up immediately, not only to find out that the offices of the estate agent were closed of a Sunday evening, but they were in Ballymena, Northern Ireland.

This was an obvious sign. I remember thinking, 'Of course, where else in the world should we have our library other than in Northern Ireland?' I had one of my highly subjective theories to hand. It went like this. We all know about the geological fault lines on the skin of the world where the continental plates push and shove and sometimes the earth's thin crust can't take the strain any more and we get our fissures, earthquakes and volcanoes. Like the San Andreas Fault in California, a mega-disaster waiting to happen. Well, my theory goes that these geological fault lines are not the only ones on the surface of the earth, there are fault lines of our human soul stretched and stretching across the skin of our magic blue ball as it spins noisily through space. The most obvious place is down the Valley of Jordan where the continental plates of Islam, Judaism and Christianity and all that they symbolise are grinding up against each other.

Then we, out on the western edges of the old world, have our own local fault line on our collective soul pulled tight across the ancient Irish kingdom of Ulster. To understand this you first have to strip away all that tribal loyalty stuff and the political whatsits and ignore the sash that someone's father once wore and any post-colonial guilt that might be hanging around to get to what's really going on.

Aside from a bit of fornicating and feeding which we as a species do along with all the other animals in the garden, the one thing that marks us out as a distinct species is our fallen state. From that morning when we got kicked out of that eastern gate, we have been trying to find our way back. You as an individual might not think this is your big concern – maybe just getting enough cash together for the rent or a ticket for Glastonbury or your personal vendetta against global capitalism is enough for you to be dealing with. But for us lot as a kind, all we ever do, aside from the fornicating and feeding bit, is trudge these various paths, some more worn than others, each of us reaching out while trudging along in an attempt to catch the hand of God, hoping he will give us a yank up and we can scramble over the wall and back into the garden. Even those sad nihilists are playing the same game, they just can't see it from where they are moping about.

Of course, I'm using the language of the religious nutter for literary effect, but that's the way I like it. In those six counties that make up Northern Ireland two certain well-worn paths cross each other and the travellers on each of these two paths can't accept that there is more than one path to take.

One path, we are told, leads directly to the Chief himself. If you are on that path, however humble, ignorant, fucked up or evil you are, you can deal direct with the big one, no intermediaries. If you are on the other path, it is plain to see that a mere scrap of mortal flesh like yourself is going to need a few more learned intermediaries to even start getting a channel of communication going between you and the one that's in charge.

From this overtly biased description, I'm obviously on the former path or at least that's the one my folks were dragging me along before I got kinda lost and decided I would try and trample a more idiosyncratic path of my own.

Is any of this making sense? Good! I knew you would understand. Nothing like a bit of equatorial heat to get the mind banging into the less logical quarters enabling me to dig up these nuggets of flawed wisdom.

CLICK

A couple of hours after breakfast in the Shelbourne Hotel, Dublin, Z and I were on the road north heading for the border. We stopped to get a paper and supplies. Z was reading aloud from the front page, putting his own spin on the news of the day.

'New York funny man Woody Allen flew into Dublin yesterday with no luggage but a bag of toys. His estranged movie star wife, Mia Farrow, is currently filming on location in County Sligo. It is assumed by Hollywood insiders that Woody Allen is here to try and patch things up with Farrow and their adopted children.'

We crossed the border, we bypassed Belfast. We made it up over the hills, down into the glens, but instead of heading straight for Cushendall and the Curfew Tower we stopped off at Glenarm.

'Auction today,' proclaimed the poster on farm gates and telegraph poles. 'House clearance, antiques, furniture, art, etc. O'Boyle's Auction Rooms Glenarm.'

'Let's go and get some stuff for the tower,' urged Z. 'Maybe we can get some cheap furniture.'

A stuffed eagle, a box of turning chisels, a pair of broken muskets and a basket of assorted cutlery to our name and we were still bidding for the useless and unwanted.

Forty-five minutes later the back of the truck was piled high with broken furniture – enough to furnish the tower and all for less than 50 quid. We were heading up the coast road. The sea was mirror calm, the gorse on the hillside burning gold and Z and I were happier than eight-year-old lads on their birthdays with brand new Johnny Sevens to take on the world. Z had the passenger window down. We were passing the heavily fortified Royal Ulster Constabulary police station in Carlough. He cocked the flintlock, took aim, then pulled the trigger. Click.

'Did you get him?'

Z didn't reply. He was too engrossed in reloading the eighteenth-century musket with imaginary powder and shot before priming the flint and finding another passing human target to practice his lethal markmanship on. Click.

'One less Paddy to run around causing trouble.'

'Oscar was a Paddy.'

'Yeah, but he wasn't stirred enough to run around trying to kill someone just 'cause their grandpappy said something nasty to his grandpappy.'

I probably should have been concerned that Z playing this game in a part of the world like Northern Ireland could get the both of us into serious trouble, but I was not. What concerned me was that Z is going to baggsy the best of the two muskets we got in the auction as part of a tea-chest job lot. We pulled up at the tower. As the weak sun was sinking behind Lurigethan, the strangely shaped hill that looms over Cushendall where fairies dance come mid-summer's eve.

*

His refined voice was resigned, he knew that we were determined to go up river and that nothing he could say would make us change our minds.

'I suppose the least I can do is warn you about a few of the things you might come across up there.'

He lit a Marlboro and watched as the blue smoke made its way through a shaft of sunlight and dissipated around the ceiling.

'First of all, what do you think all this is, this carnage here in the hotel?'

'Civil war?' said Gimpo, a wild guess. I noticed the necrophile's pants were bloodied around the crotch.

'Zaire and most of central Africa is and always has been in a state of perpetual war. The modern uniforms and mock politics make it appear to the outside world that eventually there will be some form of an outcome, that these people know what they are doing, that the conflicts will be resolved, a stable government established. This, my friend, is crap.

Zaire was never a country to begin with. A tawdry collection of warring cannibal fiefdoms, yes, but not by any means a country. You Europeans dropped that tidy little concept upon us. It's a fucking jungle for God's sake, no roads, no real cities or towns, only concentrations of people gathered together to exploit natural resources.

In terms of diamond and mineral wealth this country is one of the richest in the world, but its people are some of the poorest on the planet, why is that do you think?'

Arthur pops the top of another Primus.

'Because it's fucked?' profound Gimpo once more

'Zaire has always been fucked, you idiot. It had been fucked for centuries before that cocksucker Leopold and his tame Yankee Stanley claimed it for themselves.'

This wasn't the BBC version of Zaire's history.

LAVATORY PAPER

So, not only was this building of ours in Cushendall, County Antrim our library where we could stash our knowledge built precariously on a fault line of the human soul, it was a tower too. There were a lot of reasons why a bloke would like a tower. The obvious ones being its phallic nature, bigger and tougher than an electric guitar, more gnarled than a car, more erect than a wad of notes. Just the job. Then there was all that 'getting our own Rapunzel to lock up in the dungeon and do what we want with her' side of things. 'It's no good dear, nobody can hear you scream.' For Z, a dab hand at the Tarot, it had rather deliciously sinister connotations. For me, who likes to celebrate man's many weaknesses and vanities, my own included, it was like having your very own Tower of Babel. I long to be standing on top of the tower one starry and cloudless night calling out in a whisper hoping to catch the ear of God himself, only to discover he doesn't understand a word of my rather debased version of English preferring to stick with an ancient form of Hebrew that he learnt many thousands of years ago when men were willing to slaughter their own sons in his honour.

Anyway, we unloaded the truck of all the rubbish that we had got at the auction. As this rubbish included a rickety kitchen table, two chairs, pots, pans, cutlery, the remnants of a dinner service and a Calor Gas cooker. We thought we would try to survive without relying on a staple diet of Chinese takeaways.

We inspected each floor for broken windows and break-ins. We climbed through the trap door in the ceiling of the top room (Z's) and on to the lead-lined roof. We leant on the battlements and stared up towards the spooky looking flat-topped summit of Lurigethan. No wonder the fairies like to dance in a big circle up there. If I was a pixie, it would be my first choice for a mid-summer ball. The stars were coming out and twinkling down at us pair of unreality seekers. Below us the teenage tearaways were congregating for another evening of fag smoking, dirty joking and engine revving.

Back down through the trap door into Z's blue room, down the first flight of narrow stairs to my maroon-ceilinged and magnolia-walled room. In each of our rooms we have had small wooden beds made, almost seven dwarfesque in cuteness. The staircase up the tower being too narrow to take up anything bigger than an aspidistra and a portmanteau, every stick of furniture in the rooms above the ground floor had to be built in situ.

The next floor down is the living room. It has an empty bar, a sack of peat and a bookcase heaving with secret and/or discarded knowledge only valued by the likes of us two heroes in our own books. There is a hearth. I dream of spending long winter evenings sitting in front of the comforting glow and enveloping fragrance of the burning peat, reading forgotten texts about lost civilisations and anti-Arthurian chivalry.

The next floor down is the bathroom. All mod cons – hot and cold running water, even soft lavatory paper.

'Long before the French and the Americans were bleeding the rubber and diamonds out of the place those great Babylonian sodomites from the north, the Arabs, were buttfucking the area for its other great natural cash crop, human beings.'

At some deep level it seemed that Arthur actually cared.

'Those hook-nosed semitic bastards have been slave-raiding the forest for centuries. The forest people are generally a trusting naïve people. They live in a natural Eden for fuck's sake. The Arab however, a son of the infertile harsh desert, is naturally mendacious and cruel. In a De Sadean universe you could almost call their relationship natural.

However I am no philosopher and the complex issue of slavery and who sold who is not one I would like to get into here. I will point out though that black men had black slaves long before whitey needed cotton for his satanic mills and sugar for his millworkers' tea. Capital not colour was the meaning behind that sticky patch of multicultural history, my friends.'

The African was starting to get agitated, his monologue was becoming more confused. I hoped he would wrap it up soon. The thought of that other rambling soliloquist, Drummond and Arthur somehow symbiotically spiralling into a self-perpetuating vortex of wordy swordplay worried me. We might never get out of here.

'I've no idea,' I attempted.

'Exactly!' spat Arthur, 'And neither do they!' His eyes were wild, he pointed at the two naked Mai Mai standing by the door with their AK47s.

'Yeah, but that's normal,' butted in the Gimp. 'They're soldiers, soldiers just do what they're told, they're not supposed to even think about why they're killing and buggering and torturing. If they stopped to start thinking about why they were doing it, then they wouldn't do it. And what's the point of having soldiers that don't mindlessly kill, torture, rape and die?'

Gimpo's logic was flawless.

'Think you're really smart don't you, blue eyes!' snapped Arthur pouring himself a monster shot of Johnny Walker. 'Are you the one that Sammy the cop popped down on Fuckhead Street?' Gimpo's face blackened, he bit his bottom lip.

'I thought so, you wise-ass little fag, now shut the fuck up. Believe me, soldier boy you'll appreciate what I'm telling you when you're out there in that wild bumfuck jungle.'

THE DOG'S BOLLOCKS

'I suppose this is suburbia,' I've just heard myself remark.

The others didn't hear me. We are sitting at one of a number of white plastic tables on the porch outside an empty bar. It's late afternoon. The street is a quiet one. No hordes of tramping Africans. Nobody trying to sell us stuff we don't want. No blaring African pop music and no stench of open sewers. Just the four of us and four large glasses of ice-cool Primus beer. The other buildings in the street look like dilapidated American-style white weatherboard bungalows. Definitely not shanty. If they have a middle class in Kinshasa this must be where they live. Gimpo is filming a stray dog that is sitting in the middle of the dirt road trying to chew its bollocks off. Z is giggling his little girl's giggle to himself as he fills the pages of his notebook with his tiny hand. He once told me about the aesthetic perfection of the minuscule handwriting in the original manuscripts of the Brontë sisters. I think it is one of his new aspirations. The genius of the Brontës is one of Z's favourite subjects. That and the antics of their wayward brother, Bramwell.

'Bill, if I ever move back to Leeds, I'm going to call my house Wuthering Depths,' he once said to me. I think he thought it was a very funny thing to say.

But right now he is happy to sip his Primus, giggle and scribble. JC has that look on his face of a man who has just come up in the world. If that last sentence has racist overtones in it, I'm sorry. But not sorry enough to cross it out.

The dog with the itchy bollocks has just let out the most painful of yelps and skittered off between a couple of the bungalows opposite, one of his legs, a dragging and useless thing.

'Well, that's another one,' announced Gimpo to no one in particular.

'Another what?'

'Classic film.'

'What's it called?'

'*The Dog's Bollocks.*'

I'll get on with telling you more about our Irish trip.

*

Arthur was drunk. How much of the wild information he was giving us was true was anyone's guess. Weird scary shit it was as well. Stuff about brutal cannibalistic arse-raping river pirates, the great Congo whale, the sinister Order Of The Black Eel, sodomy barges and the inscrutable quiddity of the Black Gas.

I listened with a twist of delicious fear and excitement to Arthur's terrible litany.

'The Order Of The Black Eel,' he hissed, 'You must understand.'

He coughed and refilled his whisky glass. 'The ONATRA company, they own the barges. They're about the only thing in this country of sliding meaning that actually means anything. They control the freight, the food from out of the jungle, the villagers, who grow and gather the food trade it for shiny plastic shit that they can't make out of grass and wood, skins and shit.' Arthur drained his glass.

'It's not just food though, the barges also transport diamonds from station to station. The Black Eel have all sworn allegiance to Mobutu. Their main job, apart from being a bunch of vicious Gestapo security thugs for is to make sure Mobutu gets his fat cut of everything worth anything found within Zaire's legal borders.

A lot of The Eel are from the same villages as these Mai Mai characters, cannibals. They probably won't bother you if you behave yourselves and pay for any of the women you damage. Killing a white man is bad luck so you would have to really piss them off before they killed you. Saying that though, whatever you do, don't lose your ticket. This they take personally. Because there's so much petty crime and constant scams going down, forging and stealing tickets, the Eel take it as an insult.

The Eel will simply assume that you have sold it on to forgers and are in effect making a statement that you regard them and their company's reputation and honour with contempt. Believe me, the punishment Mr Gimpo received from Sammy the cop is nothing compared to the anal justice meted out by The Order Of The Black Eel.'

Arthur topped up his glass and lit a cigarette.

Gimpo looked worried. I noticed him gingerly feeling his violated jacksie.

'Death by sodomy.' said Arthur gravely staring at the light dancing through his whisky.

'A horrible, horrible fate, one I would not wish even upon my worst enemy.' Arthur shakes his head and swallows hard on his drink. 'Have you any idea how long it takes to die by having an endless procession of young jungle studs batter the living hell out of your ring piece?'

Gimps had turned a ghostly shade of vomit, shifting nervously from foot to foot.

'Some of the poor bastards die quickly within the first week,' continued Arthur, getting no pleasure from relaying this information. 'Most people though they think maybe somehow they'll be pardoned or a relative might spring them. These hopeful idiots, some of them hang on for nearly a month. That's the real cruel thing see, you get plenty of food and water when you're trussed up in the sphincter stocks, nobody's died of starvation up there on the quarter deck.

It's purely the horror and physical exhaustion of having your arse continually battered 24 hours a day. I've seen a couple of guys die up their. Believe me, it ain't pretty. A continuous line of young studs dumping their bollock porridge in your backside. Soon as one's finished, up steps the next in line. Most of the condemned go mad of course before they die, providing additional entertainment for the rest of the bored passengers.'

Arthur allows himself a cruel smile, savouring Gimpo's petrified expression. 'So blondie,' he laughs, 'Hang on to your ticket, my friend.'

*

'You mentioned pirates.' It was Bill, all this talk of buggery and death seemed to have agitated him somewhat, he'd floated off a sexy one. 'They're after the diamonds I presume?'

'And the gold, women and boys, yes. They rarely succeed in capturing the diamonds or the gold. The Eel are far too formidable a force of fighting men to let the cut-throats escape with anything of real value. They usually make do with the slaves, human life is of no concern to the Eel. They take the women and girls to cook and keep their vessels shipshape. The boys, depending on their age and quality are sold to the sodomy barges.'

Arthur was referring to the floating chicken ranches that are run by Arabs for the international paedophile trade. Rich Germans mainly, but a considerable number of Jewish American and Japanese perverts who seem to have developed a recent taste for black meat since the Philippines started taxing the brothels at such ludicrous rates.

Taxing brothels, man. Cool. At least their government makes no bones about being a disgusting bunch of pimps, unlike a few others I can't be arsed to name.

'It's very likely that you will be boarded by all variety of desperadoes and river pirates, the Eel will not interfere. Unless of course the treasure hoard is threatened. They will more than likely find white men something of a novelty and invite you to drink with them. By all means be companionable with them, but make sure you take a drink only from bottles you have opened yourself. Try not to get drunk with them and I advise you in the strongest terms possible not to gamble with them. They are very, very bad losers.'

Arthur pours another whiskey. Each drink I notice has been larger than the previous one.

'When all the alcohol has been finished, that's usually when the fireworks start. Don't interfere with the rape and pillage. If you annoy any of them, there's a chance you'll be taken as a novelty for the sodomy barge.'

Arthur has reached the last two inches of whiskey, his eyes are glassy, his speech theatrical.

'And of course there is the quiddity of the black gas. The cosmosodomistic nature of evil itself. My friends, this you will taste with your very souls as you slide up that greasy river into the ventricles and chambers of the forest's primeval heart. You will hear it whisper your name in the arboreal gloom. The pale ghosts of missionaries hovering in the oppressive verdure will call you into their dead arms. The wild spirits and djinn of long-forgotten slavers will screech across the black waters, the howls of dead slaves and tortured miners.

Cannibals chattering their filed and pointed teeth silently boarding your barge at midnight stealing among the sleeping passengers looking for a little fat one.

The casual brutality of The Black Eel, the stellar evil of the Moorish slavers. The inhumanity and feral sexuality of the river pirates and of course somewhere in the centre of this green Hell you may meet the great frozen soul of the all-conquering mighty prima-sodomisticus himself, President Sese Soko Joe Mobutu.

I don't know whether I should pray for you or laugh at your stupidity.

The closer you get the more you will feel the slow vibrations humming on the strings of your diaphragm, maybe the low bass throb of absolute incandescent evil will make you void your bowels.

That is of course if the biggest killer of the whole area, that tiny winged angel of death, the mosquito, doesn't send you sweating, shitting and screaming into the ground first.'

Arthur drains the last of the Scotch and falls off of his chair. One of his naked Mai Mai guards helps him back up. The inebriated BBC professional cracks open another bottle and tries to pour himself a drink, missing his glass completely and spilling Scotch all down the front of his white shirt. He adjusts his heavy-framed glasses and swigs a large chug from the bottle.

'Cheers,' he says slamming down the bottle. 'You're fucking insane, excuse me.' Arthur reaches for a bucket and hurls.

ONE MORE TALE TO TELL

'I fuckin' didn't get a wink of sleep on the plane over. I wouldn't mind getting back to the hotel and making an early night of it.'

For Z to make a statement like this is highly unusual. He is usually one of those people who keeps putting off that final decision to switch off the lights and let the night take control. He always has one more tale to tell or drink to drain.

'OK, JC, back to the Memling.'

We settle our bar tab and climb in his cab, I'm in the back. Gimpo is in the front passenger seat. We've been bumping along for a couple of minutes, still in low-key African suburbia, a mild haze in my head from the Primus and heat. A car overtakes. A man is leaning out the window waving us down. JC pulls his cab up to where a kerb would normally be in a civilised country. A large man climbs out and saunters up to us, leans his face into JC's open window. They start talking in French, then jabbering in African. Nothing threatening, nothing untoward. Maybe a friend, a colleague from the taxi rank. The large man points down the road to a small turning to the right. JC nods, then the man gets back in his car.

'What's up, JC?' asks Z.

'It's OK, boys. They are the police. They just want to check your passports. Everything is fine.'

JC follows orders, drives the cab the 100 or so yards down the road, turns to the right and pulls up on the verge. We are silent. The police – plain-clothes – have already parked up. This time all three of them climb out. There's the big one, shaved head, sweaty face. A skinny, mean-looking, motherfucker one. Actually he isn't mean-looking and probably not a motherfucker, I'm just letting the clichés slip from my pen, out of slackness on my part. But he is skinny. Then there is a kid, no more than 15 years old. The mean-looking motherfucker one starts jabbering to JC. JC is keeping his cool, not looking nervous. He turns to us.

'So boys, can the police inspect your passports and then we head back to Memling. Everything OK.'

'But JC, our passports are in the hotel safe.'

More jabbering between JC and the fat cop.

'Boys, it seems that you are breaking the law. It is illegal for a white man to be without his passport at any time. They will have to fine you.'

'Not fucking likely' says Gimpo. 'I've read about this sort of thing in the *Lonely Planet*. They're just trying it on.' It is only then that I realise that Gimpo has his video camera out and is filming everything that is going on.

'For fuck's sake Gimpo, you arsehole. Switch the sodding camera off.'

'I can use it as evidence.'

'This is jungle justice Gimpo, learn to respect it!'

JC is explaining about our passports, taking it easy back in the Memling safe. The skinny motherfucker has just opened Gimpo's door. He yanks him out. Climbs in himself, turns off the engine that JC has left ticking over, pulls the keys out and puts them in his pocket.

The young lad is up the road a bit, standing lookout. He has an Uzi, a real one. This is getting heavy. Time to go home for tea, I don't want to play anymore.

The fat cop wants to know what Gimpo's video camera is for. Gimpo obliges. It seems the Japanese never thought it worthwhile trying to exploit the Central African market with their toys and gadgets.

Gimpo shows him a rerun of the action that has just been occurring. Fat cop thinks this amusing. He gets Gimpo to rerun the footage to the skinny motherfucker one. He too is now smiling. I wonder if they've got an equivalent of a Starsky & Hutch or The Sweeney out here for them to fantasise themselves into the roles or maybe they don't need to watch the programmes, seeing as they can play out the reality with this much ease. But the bonhomie evaporates as they throw Gimpo's camera on to the verge and slam him over the bonnet.

Actually they don't slam him over the bonnet, it's just me letting the Starsky & Hutch thing slip in. But they do get him to turn out all his pockets. Gimpo is carrying only some loose sterling change and a couple of Belgian notes. This is instantly confiscated. JC explains that it is illegal to carry foreign currency in Zaire.

'But why is it then that everywhere in Kinshasa they are more than willing to trade in US dollars?' is a question I do not think worth asking right now.

Z is silent. I'm trying to suppress panic by scribbling in this notebook. I have no reference points for this sort of situation and how to deal with it. What with no lawyer to call, no common language, no common anything.

And now they have fuckin' found Gimpo's passport on him after all. And they look furious that they have been lied to. There's lots of jabbering going on between JC and the two cops. JC, for all him being a lowly cab driver with a gammy leg, is going at it in our defence.

'What's happenin',' JC?' says Z.

'They say they want to take Gimpo's passport back to the police station to check that it hasn't been stolen.'

'But it hasn't, they know it hasn't. They're just trying to trump something up. How much do they want?'

JC ignores Z's last question as he is back jabbering with the fat cop. I keep writing.

'Boys, they want to know what drugs you are carrying. They think you must be drug dealers. They want you to hand over all your drugs or they search you.'

It seems the skinny, mean, motherfucker one isn't waiting for me to hand over the stash of tea bags that I've got secreted up my arse. He's got the back door open and is getting me to shove up as he climbs in beside me and starts to go through my pockets. He finds a loose bundle of dollar bills which he instantly confiscates. It's weird, as all this is going on he has not once tried to stop me writing. I suppose they don't feel threatened by the word. Take note: in darkest Africa the pen is not mightier than the machete.

He's now working Z over. Z has nothing on him. Royalty don't carry cash. And that's it, they are off.

'You arsehole Gimpo. I told you to leave your fuckin' passport at the hotel.'

'I always think it best to carry your passport with you at all times. You can't trust those hotel safes.'

'Yeah well, look what's happened now. They've got your passport. We haven't got our visas to go up river, the whole point of this journey is fucked 'cause you didn't trust the hotel staff.'

The police car sweeps by us and Gimpo's passport is thrown from the open window.

'You lucky cunt, Gimpo.' Z turns to me, 'How much cash did they get?'

'About 30 to 40 dollars. My only concern is whether they divided it up fairly with the Uzi-toting lad.'

In fact, I'm feeling mightily relieved. My safari suit trousers are held up by a canvas belt. If the cops had taken my belt off, they would have noticed a zip that runs all the way along the inside of the belt. If they had unzipped it they would have got themselves more than $2,000 in neatly folded greenbacks. And then we would have been truly fucked. I don't mention this to the other two.

'Well boys, I'm truly sorry about that incident. I feel ashamed of my fellow countrymen. Tomorrow I get a soldier. He will guard you.'

'With a gun?' asks Z.

'Yes, of course, with a gun.'

'Wow! An armed guard. I've always wanted one of them.'

Z seems to instantly have forgotten about the incident that has just happened. He didn't lose any money or have his passport almost confiscated so he's OK. Typical.

'We drive back to hotel now. Everything be OK. You just take it easy. No more trouble.'

I like JC, he just deals with whatever shit he has to. Keeps calm and does his job.

We trundle on into the city centre.

'Hey Gimpo, I thought they were going to give you a punishment buggering.'

'Ya what?'

'Punishment buggering. Doesn't it tell you about that in your *Lonely Planet* book?'

'No.'

'It's a standard on the spot punishment in places like this. They drag the suspect down the police station and the top dog gets to bugger the lucky victim while all the other cops watch.'

'Fuck off, Z.'

'It's true Gimp.'

Turning to me and giving me one of his sly winks, he says, 'Tell him, Bill, you've heard about punishment buggering.'

Now this is a typical Z stunt to pull. He knows that Gimpo won't believe him but if I go along with it he might believe me.

'I don't know Z, but I wouldn't be surprised. Anyway, I think we are lucky to get off so lightly. I mean, being white is a pretty heinous crime and I'm sure we deserve life.'

We pull up outside the Memling.

'OK boys, see you tomorrow 10.00am I will have soldier for you, then no more trouble from police. Police frightened of soldiers. You still not want Zaire wife?'

I'm sitting in the Memling lounge bar, the other two are off in their rooms sorting themselves out in whatever way they find necessary. I've got a large pot of tea in front of me. I'm trying to pretend the rest of the world doesn't exist. I've wiped from my memory banks all that police stuff that happened at some distant time in my earlier life (45 minutes ago). The tea is shit but at least it's tea and by the way, I don't have any teabags shoved up my arse. That was supposed to be humour. And now my equilibrium is sorted I will try and tell you more of what I can remember about our trip to Ireland.

*

The whisky seems to have dissolved Arthur's immaculate BBC British accent, a strong French one is surfacing, punctuated with swearing on the Gimpo level.

'But what's it got to fucking do with me anyway, I don't give a fuck if all three of you get your fucking arses shagged off, I just want to get out of this fucking hole before the whole fucking thing implodes into machete blood bath fucking insanity. These fucking cannibal cock-biting bastards won't let me though will they?'

He gestures at the impassive guards, blacker than space, inscrutable and silent with cold reptile eyes.

'Not these two, obviously, but whoever's in charge, and that, my pink little friends, could be just about fucking anybody. One thing I do know though, it isn't Joe fucking Mobutu that's for sure, all the bogus short-wave shit coming out of the jungle all seem to be setting the fat idiot up for some kind of coup.'

The guards are eyeing him warily.

I assumed they couldn't speak English, maybe I was wrong.

'But who then!?'

Arthur's pissed out of his skull, ranting.

'It could be any-fucking-one. The fucking jungle, do you know what those trees are sitting on. The place is pregnant fit to bust with money, my friends. Diamonds. Gold. Copper. And my favourite, fucking uranium! The only source in the world, nuclear fucking uranium. Can you believe it?'

Arthur was right of course, that kind of raw money and naked violence attracts big fish.

Someone somewhere, an agent of the black gas and the global cosmosodomistic conspiracy was sitting on top of all this out-of-control madness.

It smelled of the CIA, all that destabilising shit that was cooking up in Kinshasha. Classic CIA. Whoever the nefarious gonorrhoea-bag, secret-service pus-licking shitheaps shafting this piece of the pie were, they'd obviously decided our increasingly dislocated presence was of no threat. If they did we'd be dead by now. Bummed and bleeding, face down in Monkeyshit Alley feeding the rats.

Uranium, I couldn't stop turning the word over in my head. Raw mega-death.

You couldn't invent that kind of black poignancy. Oppenheimer's destroyer of worlds, a sliver of apocalypse buried warm and radioactive here at the end of the world.

I grabbed a blast of Arthur's Johnny Walker. An old Depeche Mode song started playing in my head, something about God having a sick sense of humour. Sitting on top of all those uncooked atom bombs, it seemed appropriate.

'You'll need these,' Arthur lifted a bag full of Duracell batteries on to his desk. 'The currency is devaluing so quickly, by the time you reach Mbandanka all exchanges including bribes and ransoms will be conducted in barter. There's no electricity outside of Kinshasha, these things will be worth their weight in gold, you've seen how much they love their ghetto blaster music.' He was right you couldn't escape the jangling racket blasting at distortion-level frequencies everywhere.

'You can have these for $800. Believe me, that paper money shit won't mean fuck all up river.' I could see his point.

'Kiyamo over there will get you on the barge, you'll need to bribe the port officer, a few packs of Duracell should do it. Don't try it without Kiyamo, the bastard will just take all your batteries and deny that he knows what you're talking about. Once you're on the boat that's it I'm afraid, if you get ill or break a limb you're pretty much fucked. I think there's a doctor up in Kisangani.' Kiyamo interrupts him, speaking in Lingala. 'Sorry, Kiyamo says the doctor got himself eaten last month by a bunch of drunken Mai Mai.'

Arthur was right about the cash situation, it was way beyond Weimar-wheelbarrow proportions. You needed a couple of carrier bags full of the useless crap just to buy a packet of dried-out Marlboros.

Those little black and gold batteries of Arthur's were probably worth about ten carrier bags each of the Zairese spunkdollars.

Bill, ever the purser, did the deal quickly, bartering badly with Arthur and ending up paying twice the original asking price.

JOHNNY JOE'S

After unloading our tea chests of treasure and inspecting the tower, we were thirsty and for Z a pot of tea wouldn't do, so we hid our muskets, locked up and headed down to Johnny Joe's bar. Now, if you ever visit Cushendall, you should drop in at Johnny Joe's for a drink. It's not officially called Johnny Joe's – on the sign outside is the name Macullam's. But everybody knows it as Johnny Joe's. The front bar is minute and on that particular night was crammed with the local hill farmers celebrating a good day at the market. Some farmer who had done better than expected had filled a silver cup won by the village hurling club with Bushmills whisky and was passing it round for all to sup at.

Z and I, not being of gregarious nature, squeezed our way through to the kitchen bar. It was empty. The kitchen bar had an ancient and very magnificent cooking range. Its door was open and a fair blaze was churning out the heat. We ordered our pints through the hatch in the wall in to the front bar and we were told that it was our job to keep the range stoked.

Z and I, pints of expertly poured Guinness in hand (no shamrocks), got to talking. What we talked about may have sounded like a load of rubbish to eavesdroppers, but to us it was the most vital conversation that two men could have.

'The Man was right. We've got to get our souls back.'

'But how? That is the question.'

'And where and when did we hawk them?'

'And why?'

'Don't be stupid Bill, anybody would hawk their soul given half a chance for a tenth of what we got for ours.'

'But how do we find Satan to renegotiate?'

'Satan? He's not called Satan, Bill. His name is Lucifer, so much more in keeping, much more regal.'

'Fuck regal, Z. In the Book of Job his name is Satan. Lucifer is just some comparatively modern literary name used to dandy the dark one up.'

'If you're going to be pedantic about it Bill, in Genesis he is known simply as the serpent.'

The conversation took some ludicrous twists and turns and luckily we didn't come to blows. On reflection it must have had something to do with that fault line on the human soul thing I was going on about before and not the well poured Guinness. One of the good things about Northern Ireland is they don't try and sell you all that bogus Celtic myth shit.

The kitchen bar filled with about a dozen laughing, joking women. Their ages spread evenly across the adult end of the three score and ten years allotted and all finding much more in common they attempted to draw us outsiders into their party spirits, but Z and I had more important and manly things on our minds. What we did discover was that they had been having a stripping party.

'What in God's name is that?' I asked the loudest one, presumably the ringleader of the party.

'You've never heard of a stripping party? You hear that, girls? This young man has never been to or even heard of a stripping party.' Turning back to me but loud enough for all to hear. 'When your house is in need of wallpapering, you get all your sisters and aunties, your mum, your daughters and all your friends around. You pack off your men folk and you get stripping. A job, if done alone, that would take a few long dreary weeks, but this way in a couple of hours your walls are stripped bare while you sing, dance and tell stories. And as you've told your men folk to not come back until midnight or else, it leaves us all with two hours down Johnny Joe's to have a celebration.'

I remember being impressed by this woman's sage wisdom and trying to work out if there was any connection between the most expensive wallpaper book in the world and what these women had been up to, but I couldn't find any. A meaning too far perhaps.

*

President Joe was way up river, beyond the inner station. Paranoia and dictatorships go hand in hand, it goes with the territory.

But here in another of his white palaces, protected by his loyal cannibal guard, Joe felt reasonably safe and was able to chill fairly medium.

The self-styled king of sex, a title that was passed on to him by his old friend Idi Amin, is entertaining a beautiful 14-year-old *Vogue* model flown in from Paris that morning. The young girl laughs more through fear than amusement as the sophisticated head of state sets fire to one of his huge flapping black farts.

The other guests at the great man's table, more knowledgeable about their Napoleonic despot's ways, laugh heartily, none daring to stop until with a quick wave of his hand the President indicates that it is required. Death is always just a whim away in the capricious court of this mighty black Caesar.

The poor girl is completely unaware of the origins of the highly toothsome sweetmeats she is eating. Just as well, if she was, the sublime creature would no doubt have puked her pretty little guts up.

The President is known for his fine table. Many Western heads of state have enjoyed his sumptuous hospitality. The former Prime Minister of Great Britain, the first and probably the last woman to hold such a position complimented the President on his exquisite table. Her particular favourite was the African fois gras made from the livers of small Ugandan children, about three or four years old, force-fed a diet of sugar, almonds and double cream.

The wine works its magic and sexy Joe runs his hand along the inside of the pretty Parisienne's thigh and inserts a sharp nailed finger into her virgin cunt. It hurts, little Nicole bites her top lip and starts to cry. The other girls at the model agency had never told her about this. She turns towards her chaperone, a stern woman from one of the top agencies. The young girl's watery eyes plead for help. The frigid ex-model glares and tightens her lip, shaking her head. The sexy President is greasily tumescent beneath his stiff military trousers, his big old blutwurst about to burst a blood vessel.

The following morning the smart chaperone collects the government cheque for one million dollars and what was left of little Nicole made a tasty breakfast for the President's favourite crocodiles.

A BLACK STREAK OF URINE

As Z and I stumbled back down the road from Johnny Joe's towards the tower, we stopped off at the Chinese takeaway. Yes, even at that far outpost of civilisation, there is the Chinese takeaway. On ordering our chicken chow mein and fried rice, we were culturally shocked to discover that Jackie Chan's fat brother had a hard Ulster accent.

Back at our new kitchen table, we were tucking into the contents of the aluminium foil containers trying to ignore the taste and wishing we had gone hungry, I started to stare at the map of Africa on the wall. Z was telling me some tale about his mate Kirky, the champion gardener and Armley poet, but it wasn't making any sense. What was making sense was the river Congo. There at the centre of that innocent schoolroom wall map was this black serpent of a river uncoiling itself from the heart of this darkest of continents. Vague buried memories of having read a novella in an untender teenage year were obviously taking effect. For some kids it may be *Catcher In The Rye* and for those hitting 17 in the first half of the 1990s it may have been *Less Than Zero* but that spoilt-brat nihilist rubbish just left me cold. At the age of 17, if I needed a literary hero to identify with it was Marlow in *Heart of Darkness*. And there, as Z was reciting one of Kirky's poems – the one about catching our reflection in the TV screen after the porn video has ended, your trousers round your ankles, your limp cock still in your hands and your spilt semen going cold as it dribbles down your thigh towards the mushroom velvet of the settee – it all fell into place. It was so simple. We've all been told at some time or another that man as a species distinct from his fellow apes came from Africa. This is scientific fact not my usual sort of mumbo jumbo fact. If man came out of Africa that is where the Garden of Eden must have been. From the look of that map on that kitchen wall of the Curfew Tower whose foundations were built right on that most precarious fault line of the human soul, the Garden of Eden had to be that dark green throbbing blob of colour that represented the equatorial rainforest that filled the Congo basin.

All that Z and I had to do was start at its mouth and keep going up it until we got to its source. Its source wouldn't be a burbling spring flowing pure and clear from the rock. No, it would be the serpent still coiled and clinging to the Tree of Knowledge, still handing out rosy but rotten apples and pissing and pissing and pissing his black streak of urine. This is the source, a festering streak dribbling along the ground darker than sump oil, more putrid than the bottom of your dustbin. It is this that becomes the wide ark of the Congo river heading on its way to the not so boundless ocean. Contaminating all man's aspiration, polluting our doings more successfully than any former Soviet Union nuclear power plant leaking its wares.

Of course I have a tendency to wantonly confuse symbolic fact with the real sort and all the above may be a case in point.

But that night I climbed the narrow stairs of the tower to my bed knowing that Satan, even if he wasn't to be defeated, was going to have to accept my bite of the apple back.

I remember waking at some dark hour of that long night to hear a voice shouting and hollering at some unknown foe. It was Z.

✻

Kendo Nagasaki Yamaha is wanking himself bog eyed.

The Japanese film maker sits in his Memling hotel suite battering the fuck out of himself in front of the VCR.

A great wad of nad jam explodes from the end of his juddering yellow dick and splatters across the screen. The snuff classic, *Sex Murder Bloodbath Fury* fizzes to its sado-scat climax. Kendo Nagasaki wipes the screen clean, checks for any loose jizz and zips up his Burberry slacks.

Kendo Nagasaki and his crew of Nipponese pornographers are also intending to go up river.

Within the cloistered world of pornography and serious masturbation three nations stand a good purple bell end above the rest of the world for sheer trouser-sliming depravity. The Germans of course with their Wagnerian S/M guignol: Valkyries, Rhine maidens, Nazis and German Shepherds all grooving down at crazy animal farm, flinging the fudge at each other and getting sexy with the stinkhorns.

Israel probably has the worst racist crap of the lot, plenty of chicks with dicks and paedophile mongol shit. But I better not say that in case those intellectual Bible-tugging dickheads call me a Nazi and hurl that anti-Semite shit at me. Heil Hitler, Hymie. Fuck you and your miserable state that isn't even yours. I tell you, man, someone should erect a statue in Tel Aviv of Adolf Hitler, the founding father of that shitty bit of desert excuse for a country.

But the kings of wild weird wanking have got to be those crazy, laughing knights of bashing Bushido, the Japanese. The Japs, when it comes to extreme masturbation are initially a little more refined, lots of setting up the scene, bowing and drinking of tea. But when the pants are off and the knives are out, boy, do those skanky slope bitches know how to grind. Not much in the way of scatdumping but more than enough slash and fuck than even your ginkiest Broadmoor wrist expert could get off on.

Those three losers of world war two, allies once more in the debased toilets of the sexual underworld. The funky torture gardens of Belsen and Auschwitz and that wild outdoor happening, the Burma Railroad didn't end when the bad guys got their butts kicked, they just went underground, straight to video.

THE RED BUDDHA OF ULSTER

Driving down the Antrim coast bright and early the morning after our night in the tower, hoping to catch the 7.30am ferry from Larne to Stranraer, Z unloaded some of his vodka-fuelled wisdom.

'After we've tricked the Dark One and got back from Africa, I think we should start a new religion and we can be its founding fathers.'

There was nothing surprising in this, Z had always been full of ideas of how to start new religions, his primary motive was usually to abuse and exploit the followers. I put it down to him reading, at an early age, the literary works of the good Marquis.

What I did find comforting was that it seemed we were both in agreement with what our next epic voyage was to be and what purpose it would serve. We could now dump all notions of travelling on foot to the Holy Land dressed in white robes with a big red cross on them to rescue Jerusalem from the Mohammedans and their dirty cousins, the Christ-killing Yids. I had never seen that vision of Z's as practical and also didn't relish trying to reason it out with my multicultural associates. What with the trouble we'd already had in the twentieth century trying to sort that one out it did seem a bit of a non-starter.

'A new religion! About time, Z.'

'Yes Bill, exactly, and no better place to start a new religion than in Northern Ireland. Firstly, they seem to be a religious lot and the ones they've got don't seem to work particularly well. It was last night, you may have heard me. I was swinging on the battlements when I found myself laughing in tongues. They like flags, this lot. So I thought we could take the Ulster flag and replace the red hand, 'cause the Catholics don't seem to like that, and replace it with a Buddha. The Red Buddha Of Ulster, what do you think Bill?'

'Sounds good, but what does the religion stand for, Z?'

'I haven't worked that out, some sort of hard-line Buddhism I suppose. They like things hard-line over here. A kind of no-surrender Buddhism but very republican.'

*

Kendo Nagasaki regards himself as a serious filmmaker and not just a pornographer. He is in Africa trying to secure passage on board the ferry. Kendo Nagasaki has heard of the sodomistic death penalty and is keen to record it for posterity. The sphincteral execution has never been filmed before, only one other Westerner has ever seen this barbarous form of capital punishment (no prizes for guessing her identity), and Kendo Nagasaki is determined to capture this remnant of a dying culture for future generations. Similar in many ways to the Steven

Spielberg Shoah archives.

Obviously, because of his reputation in the extreme masturbation world there is a chance that his motives may be misconstrued. This is a chance Kendo Nagasaki is willing to take. For too long he has denied himself expression as a serious artist, churning out the highly popular slash and fuck films for the domestic audience in order to finance his more serious pieces.

He quickly rewinds *Sex Murder Bloodbath Fury* back to his favourite scene, the one with the pigs and the knives where the great British actor/director Gimpo shits in the baby's cot while a Princess Diana lookalike wipes his arse on a copy of the British *Sun* tabloid newspaper.

Kendo Nagasaki cannot rate the work of the auteur Gimpo highly enough.

IN THE LIFT WITH A WHORE

In the lift going down for my first African breakfast, it stops at the third floor. The door slides open. It's the upper-class black whore that had been cruising the bar the previous evening. She still looks stunning. Extra long legs, tight, brightly patterned, shiny dress with a slit up the side, high heels and cleavage. The only trouble was her overpowering black odour that even a dousing of Chanel No5 couldn't get rid of. That said, I wished I hadn't farted just before the lift arrived at the floor she had been working on. I smile at her. She looks the other way. I try to empathise with her life. I can't. The gulf seems too wide. I try to remind myself we are just two human beings making our way through life's little difficulties and great unknowns. I notice that one of her heels has been broken off. I try to think of her acrid body odour as a sexual turn-on. It doesn't work. The lift arrives at the ground floor. The doors slide open. I act the gentleman and let the lady alight first. She's got a great arse, one of those firm, sticky-out ones that you so much want to touch. She looks over her shoulder and smiles at me as we go our separate ways. I feel ashamed that I was ever born a man.

∗

Maybe it was the weird heat.

Rainforest heat. Hot as hell and perpetually overcast. Slimy heat. Like New York in the summer turned up to a thousand.

Whatever it was, it was getting to me. Or maybe it was those giant gobstopping horse tablet malaria pills. Larium.

Bad news to anyone with a history of mental instability. So it shouldn't be a problem for us regular guys.

The lesbian doctor at the hospital for tropical diseases at Kings Cross warned us that one of the new drug's side effects was a tendency in highly strung individuals to hallucinate. But that was only in extreme circumstances. There had been no recorded cases of complete mental breakdowns and attempted suicide whatsoever. The cunt-sucker doc was quoting directly from the promotional guff sent by the drug company supplying this absolutely safe medication with the new batches. She made psychotic possession sound like some pesky little cold virus. A mild inconvenience.

The fist-fucking bitch didn't have to deal with the oscillating psychosis I was having to live with on a day-to-day basis.

It was the final night before we went up river. Whatever flesh-eating horror was waiting for us up there surely it couldn't be worse than the demented crap singeing my eyebrows on an hourly rota down here. Could it?

A LITERARY CONVERSATION

The breakfast room is empty. That's the way I like it. I'm just heading for the furthest table in the far corner when I hear:

'Hey Bill, over here.'

It's Z. He's at a table under one of the giant pot plants that I hadn't noticed. He's obviously been on one of his all-night vodka binges.

'So Bill, you did that whore?'

'What you talking about?'

'The one who just got out the lift with you. She was the same one who was in the bar here last night. She went and got the lift about 30 seconds after you went off to bed last night. I saw the way she smiled at you just now.'

'Fuck off.'

'Bill, are you spending our float on expensive AIDS-infested harpies?'

I know Z doesn't really think this. He's just trying to wind me up. The fact is he doesn't have to say any of this to wind me up, just the fact that he is down here at all is enough – any thought of a quiet introspective breakfast is buggered.

'So Z, get any sleep?'

'Yeah. But I was woken up a couple of hours ago by what I thought was gunfire but was probably just a car exhaust backfiring, so I came down here to get myself an eye-opener and get on with the writing.'

'How's it going?'

And without answering, Z launches into reading me all this stuff about me and Kate Adie chopping up some black whores right here in the Memling Hotel. I just hope that my daughters never get to read it.

'What about Kate Adie? She won't be too pleased about her inclusion in our work of fiction.'

'I'll change the names. Happens all the time in literature. It's the price she has to pay for being a public figure. Anyway, read me some of your stuff.'

So I read him the opening page about the smell inside the plane and the landing.

'You can't have that in. Nobody will publish it.'

'Why?'

'It's just out-and-out racism. No proper publisher would dare print that kinda stuff. It sounds like you are some NF nutter.'

'What, and you going on about chopping up black whores and little black sambos wanking in the gutter doesn't?'

'The difference is, Bill, my stuff is literature. Any intelligent reader would be able to tell that what I write is an allegory for the world at large. It's about the corruption and deceit that lies at the heart of all human transactions.'

'I thought you wrote what you write because it makes you laugh.'

'It does, but that doesn't change the fact that it is above all else a tale about the fate of mankind like Dickens or John Steinbeck.'

'Maybe what I'm writing will be interpreted in the same way.'

'No Bill, it can't be. You're writing what purports to be no more than the factual truth as you see it. It reads that way. It is that way.'

'So are you trying to tell me what I can and can't write Z.'

'No, but you have to accept there will have to be some heavy editing before anybody will be willing to publish it.'

'Well thanks for the show of confidence.'

'Ah fuck it, Bill. Write what the fuck you want. I'm sure there will be some two-bit publisher willing to go with it as it is. But I don't think it will be Penguin. It was hard enough with all those cock-sucking six-year-olds we had to change into teenagers above the age of consent.'

'The cock-sucking six-year-olds were in your writing not in mine.'

'Yeah I know. I'm just saying we may as well accept we won't get any sort of reasonable advance for this lot.'

We fall into glum silence.

'Excuse me sir, would you like to order your breakfast?'

'Yeah, full English please.'

'Pardon?'

'Oh sorry, I mean whatever the African equivalent is.'

Sexy Bill saunters into the Memelin bar in a shimmering green cocktail dress, black Cleopatra wig, full tart's make up, smoking a menthol cigarette through a 12-inch holder.

What was I supposed to say?

'Those fucking malaria pills, man,' I said.

'I am the Lady Mantis,' he replied. His left eye was twitching, three-day stubble poked through his oily foundation cream. He looked as if he had just stepped out of a Diane Arbus photograph.

'Lady Mantis, yeah, groovy, whatever.'

I tried to keep the situation non-confrontational, as normal as possible, the best tactic to adopt when dealing with someone surfing the Antipodes.

'Bill Drummond is dead,' he answered in a weird voice I'd never heard before, a strange kind of Scotch-German hybrid.

Those fucking Larium pills. They weren't like the kind of disorientating seven-dimensional crap that you get with the usual synthetics, the cosmic search for cosmic truth baloney. This crap was medieval, like demonic possession.

The small part of your everyday consciousness that directs you safely through life and its inherent dangers gets squashed into some tiny box at the back of your brain and forced to watch as some completely alien vampire elemental takes over and parties recklessly in your fragile body, completely unconcerned for its well-being. Like piped-up council estate kids joy riding a stolen Ferrari.

One of the weird things about these psychedelic hijackers is how they're all into this cross-dressing thing. At some time, some place on that splintered fast-forward, weirded-up road you can bet that Johnny wants to turn into scary Mary.

This shit can get heavy if Johnny's tripping on knives when the urge to explore his feminine side kicks in. My old buddy Evil tells me Broadmoor has entire choirs of these cosmic DIY castrati.

It seemed like I was just going to have to humour Bill's spooky anima for a while.

GIMPO GETS

Ten o'clock on the dot, JC shimmies across the breakfast room. Actually he hobbles.

'Mornin', JC.'

'Good morning, boys.'

'Got the armed guard?'

'He will be here soon and then I will take you to the Intercontinental to meet your friend Mr Malu-Malu. He very big man, friend of our president and your Margaret Thatcher. He can sort out your visa problems.'

Obviously JC had been doing some research on Arthur Malu-Malu.

'Let's hope so.'

'Bill, I'm going back up to my room for a dump. I'll see you outside in a couple of minutes.'

'Give Gimpo a shout while you are up there. Anyway, what happened to him last night?'

'Got totally bladdered. I had to almost carry him up the stairs. Just shoved him through your door which, by the way, you had left open.'

'What was up with him?'

'All the usual stuff. Terrible stories about his miserable childhood, being abused, learning not to be an abuser. Paranoia about Ana shagging around and wanting to beat the shit out of some cunt.'

'I blame it on all the crack he's been doing lately.'

'Yeah, it was OK when it was just amphetamines and a couple of grams of coke for the weekend. But freebasing on a Tuesday night is no good for anybody's health.'

In walks Gimpo. Looking better slept and healthier than the pair of us could ever have done. Z disappears for his dump and probably for a slug or two on his duty free before we hit the streets of Kinshasa. Gimpo gets himself a freshly squeezed orange juice. I follow JC out to his car.

*

'So, Lady Mantis, how is shit?'

I made like a nice friendly black man in a seedy but convivial bar.

'Rolo is here.'

Bill was stony faced beneath his make-up, that scary detuned violin and brain-damaged piano playing started spiralling in from the twilight zone. I had a bad feeling.

'Who the fuck's Rolo?'

Things were hitting a crisis point, I was familiar with Bill's mercurial nature, all the signs were there for his open paranoia to descend into random slaughter and liver-flanging psychosis.

'Rolo!' he barked.

His eyes had that weird gleam, the one you see in proselytising religious nuts and photographs of serial killers.

'The one-eyed Arab!'

His face cracked and he started crying. His mascara left two black rivers down his quivering cheeks. I ordered him a large whisky from a terrified Gabriel.

'The assassin!' he shouted, gripping me by the shoulders and staring insanely into my eyes.
Fuck man, I think I'd rather take my chances with the mosquitoes than chew down on the Larium if this is what it was going to do to us.
'And his white dogs.'
Bill was becoming incoherent, he collapsed on to the bar and threw me a screwed-up piece of paper.
'It was waiting at reception for me.'
I looked at the stubby pencil scrawl: 'BiLLE i aM HERE in the afriCAn,' it began,
My wOrk sHE iS onlY HALF OF it done. for the QuEERS LIkE US LOVE IS ALL,
MY knife She IS thirsty for your BLoods. You stOLE THE heaRt OF MY kiki ANd now hE IS with the FLOWERS'
It looked like some kind of weird arse-bandit poetry. It had affected Bill badly.
'What is all this shit, Bill?' I said, authoritative but compassionate, the concerned English teacher routine.

$100 A DAY
Leaning on JC's cab is the meanest looking motherfucker of a nigger I've ever seen in my life. Totally the real thing. Maroon military beret pulled tightly down to one side. Loose jungle fatigues, the trousers tucked into brilliant white spats over highly polished black boots. Aviator mirror shades and an AK47 slung over his shoulder. Z will cum in his pants when he sees this. Goodness knows what fuckin' stories are going to start spiralling off in Z's imagination and into the pages of this book once Z has checked him out.
'Bill, this is Golf.'
Obviously Golf is too cool to say anything, he just nods. Well, not actually a nod, just a minimum fraction of a nod. I can't see anything of his eye movements but it seems Golf is already at work shifting his gaze to check all directions from the hotel every few seconds like some programmed security camera.
'Wow! Is he fuckin' ours?'
Z has arrived. He's changed into an open-necked Hawaiian shirt which I'm sure Roger Moore would never wear with a safari suit. He's obviously going for that Al Pacino in *Scarface* look and failing.
Gimpo arrives. He doesn't look so impressed with Golf.
'How much is he fuckin' costing us?'
'$100 a day.'
'It's a rip off. That must be what they earn in a year over here.'
'Shut up Gimpo. He looks fuckin' brilliant. Bill, do you reckon he would kill somebody for us as part of the daily rate?'
'I dunno. Ask JC.'
Of course I know that Z wouldn't dare.

*

I was going to have to talk him down from the mountains of this evil Larium madness.
Talking people down from bum trips is a real pain in the arse, sitting there for hours as the

hideous creatures from the grimiest corners of the subconscious enjoy their brief drug-assisted freedom and slime all around their host's scrambled head. Freed from the dark lands of nightmare to scare the living crap out of the uptight jailers over on the conscious side of the mind.

Like I said, it was a shitty detail, but if us psychonauts don't look after each other we'd all end up pumped full of Largactyl stoning around in run-down NHS mental hospitals. I looked at the note again, it seemed to be in Bill's own spastic scrawl. His malaria trip was scooting around frighteningly homosexual latitudes.

'Rolo!' he spluttered, jerking his head from the bar sending the black Cleopatra wig flying. 'He murdered Kiki!'

The crazy jock has lost me, I haven't a clue what he's talking about.

'Oh God!' He places the back of his hand against his forehead 'You were drunk! Toledo! You fucking alcoholic!'

I smarted at this, I could quit drinking whenever I WANTED!

'The murder!' He carried on shouting, 'Outside in the street! Baguettes! Couscous!' I was still no wiser. 'Kiki! Rolo! Oh What's the use?'

Z IS TRANSFIXED

The three of us climb in the back of the cab. Golf is in the front passenger seat. We head out into the downtown traffic. His AK47 is cradled in his lap, the barrel is casually protruding from his wound-down window. Every time we stop at a junction he coolly leans his head out the window to check what might be coming up behind us. Z is transfixed. Gimpo looks grumpy.

'What's up Gimpo?' I ask.

'Nothin', why?'

'I know what's up with him. He's jealous.'

'What have I got to be fuckin' jealous of?'

'Golf.'

'What?'

'Yeah. It's because Golf is a real soldier with a real gun and you're just an old soldier and everybody knows there is nothing as uncool as an old soldier living off his war stories. And the Falklands wasn't even a real war, it only lasted a couple of weeks. I mean did you actually kill anybody and see them die, real hand to hand, Gimpo?'

'I was a gunner on the gun that sank the Belgrano. I pressed the button. I'm probably single-handedly responsible for more deaths than any living person in Britain since the Second World War and that's more than even your Yorkshire Ripper.'

'Is that a boast?'

'No but it's something I have to live with every day of my fuckin' life. They were lads just like me. Had no fuckin' idea what we were doing there.'

'Yeah, but you didn't see them die. You never sunk a bayonet in.'

'Shut the fuck up Z. You don't know what you're fuckin' talking about.'

'It doesn't change the fact that you are jealous of Golf. He's the one with the AK47. You think that we think that now we've got Golf that we think we don't need you to protect us.'

'I don't know what you're fuckin' saying.'

'Yes you do and I just want to let you know it's not the case. We value you for what you really are, not what you think you are.'

'So what am I?'

'A Manc' half wit who is probably going to wank himself to death.'

'Shut up the pair of you' is something I don't say but have just written it down because it is something I should say.

'JC, can Golf speak English?' asks Z.

'No.'

'Good. Can you tell him that Gimpo was once a soldier in a real war.'

JC then gets jabbering with Golf. He then turns back to us.

'Golf has been in five wars.' Golf turns his head in the direction of Gimpo and smiles a full-on 'black man, white teeth' smile. But a warm, friendly smile, not one of those 'by the time this day's out you will be dead' smile.

*

Bill seemed to be peaking, he tucked his cocktail dress into his stained yellow Y fronts and leapt across the bar, he started trying to tango with a terrified Gabriel. The poor man was nearly in tears.

'Mr Z, Mr Z, please do something, I am very frightened.'

Bill was sailing real close to a full-blown psychotic incident. He grabbed Gabriel by the balls and started to kiss him. Gabriel was trying to push him away, white-eyed with fear

'No, no please Mr Bill, not the sodomy please, I have a wife!'

Bill's attention suddenly shifted, his brain seemed to be working like American TV, zapping from channel to channel. His body was twitching and snapping into weird electricity spasms, his dick had boned up in his dirty pants, scaring the shit out of poor Gabriel.

Bill leapt back over the bar and made his way to the grand piano where he started battering out old Shirley Bassey numbers, screaming about big spenders and diamonds. The scariest bit of all this Larium craziness was when he grabbed a tablecloth and wrapped it around his arm and started circling around as if he was in some 1950s juvenile delinquent flick, knife fighting an invisible foe.

'I fookeen kheel you,' he spat, parrying, slashing and stabbing.

'Hi curt of your beeg scorteesh bohlls, il bastardo! Si! si!'

He stabbed at thin air and then twirling like a matador delivered his phantom *coup de grace*, laughing in Spanish. Arrogantly he pissed on the body of his non-existent foe. Poor Gabriel hurried over with his mop and bucket, eyeing the potential sodomite warily.

NOT EVEN SCHOOLBOYS

The Intercontinental is a massive hotel. Set back from the road among trees, high 1970s' aspirational architecture. It's already falling to bits, being reclaimed by jungle. It doesn't matter how many life forms we push over the edge into extinction, man will never win his war with nature. Nature will just keep on coming at us, evolving new species faster than we can kill off the Siberian tigers or the Tasmanian devils.

For all the tacky grandeur of the foyer and the in-house arcade of shops selling gold nick-nacks and glittery junk that rich blacks seem to favour, the nauseating odour of rotting life forms is all pervasive. No amount of air freshener can mask it.

None of the hotel staff bat an eyelid as the three of us saunter in with Golf brandishing his hardware. Imagine walking in to a London hotel with an AK47 primed and ready to rock. I could get used to this. I have to admit it feels quite good. We can do what the fuck we like 'cause we've got Golf.

Arthur Malu-Malu has his suite on the seventh floor. I'm expecting the lift to be out of order. The lift door opens. A large fat African, swathed in robes, breezes out. He is accompanied by two armed guards. I feel slightly deflated. It seems the measure of a man round here is the size of his private army and we are not even schoolboys.

*

Bill seemed to have flipped channels again, he came over to the bar looking confused.

'Rolo,' he mumbled, 'The guy who killed Kiki.'

His eyes were darting wildly from side to side, he had his hand in his underpants and was masturbating nervously. I decided to take advantage of the lull in his malarial cyclone to try and figure out what nutso boy was talking about

'Who's Kiki, Bill? What's all this mad shit all about?'

The absent-minded masturbator looked confused, he shook his head trying to rectify the chemical imbalance that was snowing up his reality.

'Kiki, the Arab boy. You remember, in Toledo.'

'You mean the Paki shirtlifter you were buggering at Fat Miguels?'

I vaguely remembered some creepy little bummer always hanging around Bill, but there were so many of the little fags nancing around in their rhinestone cat collars you couldn't tell one from the other. Plus I was so fucking bombed on all the brown and the wine I didn't know my own name half the bleeding time.

'Yes, Z, the little Paki shirtlifter I was buggering. God how can you be so insensitive! The boy's dead. I was in love!'

'Just shut up, Bill, you'll regret saying any of this crap when the malaria pills wear off,' I cautioned my over-emotional friend. I knew he should have stuck to the heroin and liquor. That fucking snake oil, it's deadly.

'He was murdered. Don't you remember anything at all?'

'Bill, I was totalled, that shit at Miguel's, it was pretty heavy duty.'

I scoured my brain trying to recall any fizzled memories of Bill's little snake charmer. 'Didn't he run off or something when I kept grabbing his arse and calling him Shirley?'

'Straight to his death. A knife to the heart from Rolo.'

Bill was shaking with emotion, the only other time I've ever seen him in this sort of state is when he's blading his way through some tart's reproductive system

'OK Bill, so you might have been attached to little Kookoo. I remember when my dad stamped on my pet rabbit when I was a kid, horrible. But you have to face it Bill, homos kill each other, that's what they do, it's part of their culture, all those queeny passions, crying and Paris and Shirley Bassey and sailors and shit.'

GIMPO SMILES AT GOLF

'Well, good morning men. It is so good to meet you. You must be Mr Drummond, you Mr Manning and you Gimpo. I'm Arthur Malu-Malu. This is my assistant, Mr Tombo Bamba.'

'My name is Mr Goodrick,' interjects Gimpo.

'Ah yes, Mr Goodrick. I understand you like to be called by the name Gimpo, a term of endearment I was informed. But never mind. Please come in. Take a seat. Would you like a Coca-Cola or a Seven-Up?'

'Any chance of a Primus?' asks Z with a practised smile that makes it hard for our guest to decline, let alone question his request. 'I mean, the sun is almost over the yard arm,' adds my brother-in-prose.

Arthur turns to Tombo, a small but solid man. 'Can you go down to the bar and get Mr Manning a Primus. Tell them to put it on my bill.' Turning to us, he says, 'I only keep Coke and Seven-Up in the fridge here.'

'Keeping temptation at arm's length?' asks Z.

'No, beer is too expensive.'

The suite is crammed with filing cabinets and large old BBC-style recording and broadcasting gear.

'You seem to have all you need here Arthur, very impressive.'

Z is trying to flatter him.

'Ah yes. There is a satellite dish on the roof of the Intercontinental. I can broadcast to the world from here. No problem. But I'm so ashamed.'

'Of what?' I ask.

'Our city. Our Kinshasa. Our country. What must you think? You come from wonderful London. You must think we are savages. Sometimes I think so myself. Some days, while I'm despatching another report, another minor atrocity, to the world I ask myself, can't we do anything properly? Can't we treat each other with the humanity that every man deserves? Instead we embroil ourselves in little tribal wars like primitives. You have lent us so much money to invest in our future and we squander it on weapons of destruction, on vain follies like our national stadium. But oh, I do love Zaire and one day I hope you will return and it will be a place I can be proud of, like a true western democracy.'

OK reader, I've kind of embroidered what Arthur has been saying, turned it up a bit, but that was the overall vibe.

Tombo has just arrived back with Z's Primus on a tray and a small bowl of groundnuts. Z takes a sip and looks up at our hosts.

'Well Arthur, I think you do your nation down. I always find the best way to judge a civilisation is by the standard of the beer they are able to manufacture. If a nation can make a good beer there is nothing they can't do.'

He stops to take a second draught.

'This Primus of yours is a fine beer. Up with some of the best in the world.'

A third draught.

'Let me tell you I have toured extensively in Eastern Europe and the beer there can be of the lowest order. No wonder they have no culture and collapsed economies if they can't brew a good beer. What do they expect? A working man deserves the reward of a long, cool beer at the end of his day. If it's not up to scratch, what's the point of putting in the hours, getting the job done, working up a sweat?'

Stopping momentarily to take another slow draught.

'What you have here with Primus is a fine beer. A beer to build a successful nation on.'

And on that note Z downs the rest of his glass and helps himself to a handful of the nuts. I take a sip from my Coca-Cola and Gimpo gives Golf a withering look. Golf has been hovering by the open door in case we get rushed by a rival band of hired hands. JC is keeping his council in the corner. By the look on his face I think he must be very much in awe of our host, Mr Malu-Malu.

'Well I cannot deny that Primus is a fine beer but gentlemen – to business. We have some difficulties with our President Mobutu. I have been on the phone with his private secretary in Gbadolite. It seems the President is on a wine-tasting tour of the chateaux of the Loire Valley. Our President prides himself in having not only the most extensively stocked wine cellars in all Africa, but a most refined nose. His secretary, a good friend of mine, assures me our leader will be back in his palace within the fortnight.'

Malu-Malu has an odd way of stringing his words together and there's an almost imperceptible irony in the tone of his voice. This is a country where political satire of even the mildest variety would undoubtedly land you in the hottest water that cannibals could cook, but he seems to be attempting to communicate to us a lot more than what is contained in the mere words, or that's what I guess.

Is this what comes of feeling he has a responsibility to his fellow countrymen to communicate to the rest of the world what is really going on in his beloved land? And to do this without ever giving the authorities and henchmen of Mobutu any cause for alarm. This must be what it was like for all those artists, writers and composers working in Stalinist Russia. It somehow gave their work so much more strength. I can say what the fuck I like and it doesn't concern anybody, change anything, or threaten my life. I think I'm being a bit radical by playing with the whole race thing and Z is out to shock you with chopping up whores and Gimpo's bad behaviour, but so what? It is nothing more than sticking out our tongue at the teacher when her back is turned.

'So boys, when you get to Kisangani – you got your tickets yes? – well at Kisangani you give me a call and I will give you the precise time and date that our president will give you an audience.

'Great Arthur.' It's Z. 'And did you talk to him about us performing a Punch & Judy show for him?'

'Ah yes. This is your marionettes that you mentioned in the letter? No, I can't say that I did. One thing at a time. First we arrange the meeting with the great man. Now, is there anything else you need to know?

JC jumps in. In French, no African jabbering with a man of the standing of Arthur. Arthur replies in English.

'Ah, so you have a problem with your travel permits. That is only natural with the way things are here. Let me have a look at your papers.'

JC hands over some forms that the man from gave him.

'Ah yes, what this needs is the signature of a government minister.'

'A government minister? Sounds like an impossibility Arthur.'

'No, no Bill. It is my job to have friends who are government ministers. Well they are my friends until Mobutu decides it is time to let a younger crop have a go. Our leader holds with the view that it is best to regularly call on a fresh pack instead of reshuffling the old one. Something he learnt at the poker table. Anyway I digress, let me make a little tinkle.'

He dials. No push buttons. We sit around and stare and say nothing as Malu-Malu does his thing on the phone. He switches from speaking in French to African, depending on who he has been passed on to on the chain of command. When he finally gets through to the minister – well that's what I assume to understand from the nod and the smile he is giving us – he switches to a language I've not heard before. It sounds more chattery than the African language that my ears have got accustomed to over the last couple of days. More like the sound that chimps make at the zoo.

He smiles, he beams, he laughs at the unseen minister's witty asides. His confident charm pours down the phone line. I sip my Coke nervously, try to make these notes. Notice that Gimpo is smiling at Golf and that I have just eaten all the peanuts.

'Well, men, that seems to have been sorted. My man Tombo Bamba will go with you to the government buildings. He will explain the little details of how much this will cost.'

Unsure of the etiquette of this situation, I blurt out, 'Well Arthur thank you very much and how much would you accept as a show of our respect and appreciation?'

'Now now, don't insult me. I have done nothing for you that a friend would not do. As for Tombo, I think $30 should see him fine. Now gentlemen, you must excuse me. I have to go to the airport.'

'Are you flying somewhere?'

'No, no, more's the pity. No, just before you arrived I was informed that there has been an air disaster. A military plane burst into flames on landing and ploughed into a crowd of airport workers.'

'And you will be filing this as story for Reuters to sell around the world?'

'Not exactly. Maybe my job will be to make sure that no journalists file this as a story anywhere. Some things are too sensitive to be reduced to a mere news story for the Western world to consume. Gentlemen, it has been an honour to meet you. I hope your journey up the big river is all that it wasn't for Mr Conrad. And don't forget to phone me as soon as you get to Kisangani. I hate to think you would have gone all that way without meeting the President.'

We shake hands. I almost bow. We leave with Tombo Bamba, leading the way.

*

It was coming back to me now, Bill had taken up with some little snake-oil jockey down at the Catamite, totally out of character for the staunch son of the glens, but then again, so's cross-dressing and hanging out with cissies. There's obviously some flower-arranging aspects of the macho misogynist's personality that he likes to keep well hidden.

Yes, I remember it perfectly now. Bill's little bitch got stabbed by his ugly boyfriend and Bill brought the stiff into our room and got blood all over the carpet.

'Well he's here, in Zaire!'

It was Bill again staring hard at his scribbled little poem.

'Bill, that note is in your handwriting, look. I pointed at the distinctive spaz scrawl. 'It's just the malaria pills man, you'll be fine when they wear off.'

'Z, that is not my handwriting. The one-eyed bastard, Rolo, he's here'

'What one-eyed bastard?' It was Gimpo. 'And why is Bill wearing a dress?'

I explained to our heterosexual friend about the malaria pills. 'And what was that about the one-eyed bastard?' Gimpo wanted to know.

'Bill thinks there's a one-eyed Arab following us. He wants to kill Bill to avenge the death of his lover, who he killed himself in the first place. It's some demented fag thing Bill's got himself involved in. The best thing we can do is get him shitfaced drunk so he can sleep off the effects of the Larium.'

MORE AND MORE IRRITABLE

Z, Gimpo and myself are sitting at a table of a street bar sipping from our glasses of ice cold Primus. Golf is sitting on the table next to us with a Coke. He hardly drinks it at all, every couple of minutes he lifts the bottle (the classic one) and takes a very small sip from the straw. Sipping from a straw seems quite incongruous with his sublime cool. He has yet to remove his reflector shades. His hidden gaze continually scans the street for suspect activity. His AK47 is still cradled in his lap. Z is playing with his yo-yo, hoping that his technique will impress a bunch of young lads sauntering past. It doesn't. Gimpo is polishing the lenses of his video camera and I'm trying to resist scratching that bit of skin between my bollocks and my arsehole, which gets more and more irritable.

We are waiting for JC and Tombo Bamba to come back from their meeting with the government minister.

JC has gone from being our taxi cab driver – by chance at the head of the queue outside the Memling – to being our representative in all areas of our life, in not much more than 24 African hours.

I pull out my notebook in the hope I'm left in peace by the other two long enough for me to tell you some more of our visit to Ireland.

*

'Actually Z, I don't think all of this is just the drugs,' said the Gimp nervously.

The brain-damaged piano and the melting furniture edged their way into my peripheral vision.

'On one of my wanking diary videos, the one I did last night...' he began.

Back in the UK Gimpo is a respected avant-garde film maker, one of his government-sponsored projects over the past four years has been to film himself every time he masturbates. Gimps has collected thousands of hours of footage of himself choking the chicken all over the world.

'I think both of you had better take a look, ' continued the world's greatest masturbator.

'No fucking way Gimps, the last time I saw one of your fucking tapes it put me off murdering my own monkey for months. Those horrible faces you pull and the intensity, I'm surprised you haven't fucking pulled it out by the root,' I said holding back a hurl.

'I'm serious. When I played the footage, I didn't notice at first but on second viewing, something appears in the corner outside the window. I thought it was a bird or something since we're so high up but when I freeze framed, there was a....'

'One-eyed Arab,' finished Bill, stony faced.

'We're on the twenty-third floor, Gimps. Was he on a flying fucking carpet or something?' I added, not nearly as confident as I sounded.

The film judders to a start with Gimps backing away from the camera and then rustling through his rucksack for a jar of industrial-strength snake oil. That was a new development in itself, the ace fist artist usually yanked himself off raw. He anoints the baby maker with the green ichorous jelly and starts battering the hell out of himself, eyes rolling into the back of his head, teeth grinding, horrible animal noises ginching through his nose as a timpani roll of baggy wet farts splatters from his uncontrollable sphinc.

It starts getting weirder, the priapic lunatic starts doing a little jig for the camera spinning in circles yet never once losing the rhythm and pneumatic intensity of his expert stroke. Eventually he lets out a blood-curdling scream and unloads his bollocks like an Uzi; shattering furniture and taking out the light bulb.

'Look! there!' shouts Gimpo stabbing the pause button.

'Fuck!' It's Bill, flobbering off a rank one like rubbish dumps and spoiled mayonnaise. There in the grainy left-hand corner of the TV screen, leering satanically in the static, outside the twenty-third floor of the Memling hotel, was the unmistakable face of the one-eyed Arab, Rolo. The ugly scar that stretches from his forehead across his ruined eye and on to his left cheek is vivid even on video. His thick purple lips are parted, white teeth bared in a feral grimace.

FEMALE BONDING WITH THE COLERAINE LADIES HOCKEY CLUB

Z and I made the Larne to Stranraer ferry. After a breakfast that featured some very tasty Ulster fry, we retired to the bar for the rest of the short two-hour crossing to Scotland. The bar was already full of thirsty and somewhat unruly Irish. Don't they ever give it a rest? There was one gang of young women with exceptionally stout legs who kept singing some verses of what I wrongly assumed was a rebel song. Between each verse they would all tumble off their seats on to the floor. There they'd be on their backs, waving their legs and arms in the air like a swarm/pack of useless ladybirds struggling against their upturned fate. Their ringleader would give a cry and they would all leap to their seats and take another deep draught of their Guinness before banging into the next verse of the song and the cycle would begin again. They kept this up for the whole crossing, much to their own amusement. I learnt they were the Coleraine Ladies Hockey Club and they were off somewhere to take part in a tournament. I never knew that ladies' hockey required such disciplined training.

All over the rest of the ferry were families in a state of stress. In each family the focus of their stress was the youngest female member. These young girls whose ages ranged between four and eight were all having rags removed from their hair. As each rag was removed, a lock of hair would spring into life. Once all were undone a whole Shirley Temple mop of curls would flounce and bounce. This undeniably added an eye-catching precociousness to every move they made. And the moves they made were dazzling even to my jaded eye. At the behest of their fretting mothers, aunties and grannies these girls were all being made to sharpen their dance steps. All in that hands-behind-your-back Irish-style we've all seen used as a focus of ridicule and which has latterly been exploited in that *Riverdance* thing.

'It should be banned, Bill. That sort of behaviour only encourages the latent paedophile in any red-blooded male. I can control myself but with the likes of you, Bill, free to roam the streets they should be warned.'

'Fuck off, Z.'

Where all these dancing Sineads and Nualas were off to I had no idea and hadn't the steel to ask. So, anyway, there were all these little girls dancing away with no music other than what they can hear in their heads; there were the ladies from Coleraine on their backs waving their hands and legs in the air and there was that lot from the wallpapering party last night. And I wondered what it was all about. Why had I been confronted with three versions of female bonding and togetherness in the space of 12 hours? Had it got anything to do with the great undertaking that Z and I were about to embark upon?

Is there a link between this and Peter making his denial thrice before the cock crowing? Any time something happens in triplicate I take it as a sign that some sort of denial has been going on.

*

'Z! Gimps! Quick, over here, look!' Bill was over by the window, he had opened it and was pointing at the ledge that ran around the building just beneath the windows. 'The bastard's been sleeping here, right outside our window!'

There on the ledge were the crumbs from a half-eaten baguette, a few grains of couscous, a copy of *Buttered Buns* and a small tube of snake oil.

Bill was hysterical, screaming about the Arab Cosa Nostra and snake oil. His arse had rumbled into adrenalised overdrive, Gimpo opened a window and fanned the door.

Bill was raving about baguettes and the occult significance of fish oil and couscous. It was obvious that the malaria pills were still splicing his wiring, he'd started doing his weird crab-like circling again, fighting the phantom Rolo.

'I fockin keel you,' he said over and over to himself. 'Your ass ees mine, Scottish, I fockin weel keel you.'

GOLF SUCKS UP HIS COKE

JC and Tombo Bamba are back.

'OK boys, we have it all sorted. $300 and the Minister will sign your papers. He wanted $3,000 but we did good negotiating, yes?'

'Three hundred fuckin' dollars? Surely it's his job to sign these things, not something to be negotiated about?' says Gimpo.

'Don't be so fuckin' naïve Gimpo. Just hand over the cash, Bill, and let's get back to the Memling.'

I remove the required sum of greenbacks from my cash belt and hand it over to JC. He smiles. 'Back in a short while, boys.'

He and Tombo Bamba disappear from whence they came.

'It's a fuckin' set up.' It's Gimpo again. 'That's the last we see of the pair of them, our $300 and our passports.'

'Don't be fuckin' stupid Gimpo. For a start JC's cab is right here as is Golf and it isn't in JC's nature to behave like that. He is one of the good guys in life.'

'And you think I'm naïve? So even if he comes back with our passports and the papers signed, this minister bloke, whom I very much doubt is somebody of such high ranking, that was just Arthur Malu-Malu trying to impress us with his influence, the three of them will have split the money three ways. JC and that other nigger have just made themselves a $100 a piece. If I...'

And before Gimpo has time to express any more of his paranoid minefield of a mind, JC is back. 'OK boys, business taken care of. I now show you the sights of Kinshasa and then later I take you a nightclub.'

Tombo Bamba has to get out to the airport with recording equipment to meet up with Arthur Malu-Malu. We shake hands and go our separate ways, Tombo to count the dead and to find out if it's a news story to be suppressed from the global gaze or one that can be translated into an item with a cash value that can be sold to our ever-hungry appetite for international atrocity news. As you have probably learnt elsewhere, 1,000 slaughtered black Africans only equals the same as about ten white Western Europeans in news-item value.

One thing that we can be certain of, that begging cop and raggedy bunch of alms seekers will have had their suspicions confirmed – a bunch of white media types turning up must mean a disaster is about to happen.

'Hey JC, take us to wherever and whatever you want. You are our leader.'

For the moment I'm at one with Z's sentiments and only wish for once Gimpo could give his all-encompassing paranoia a rest. Golf sucks up the rest of his Coke with the most uncool and childish of last drop sounds through his straw. We all climb back in the cab and set off to find out whatever it is that Kinshasa can offer three white men when they have the security of an armed guard. I feel good.

DRUMMOND'S SECRET LOG, MEMELIN HOTEL, KINSHASHA, ZAIRE.

Vigilance is the key word.

Rolo is here in Zaire. Z and Gimpo have no idea how much danger we are in. Rolo is a blood member of the dread Cthulu Lodge, the most lethal, highly trained secret order of homosexual assassins in the entire world. Those Japanese knife queens, the Ninja pale into Barbie pink compared to these satanic bastards.

Kiki was a member of the Rainbow Lodge, a non-violent sect dedicated to the composition of love poetry and the gentle art of rearing the precious oil snakes. Rolo is an Ipissimus Dagon, the highest rank afforded to members of the Cthulu Lodge. A master of covert death. One of the many things that makes the Ipissimus Dagons so feared even among members of their own sect is the mystical significance they attach to the act of murder itself. Master Dagons are supposed to achieve some form of transcendental ecstasy during their bloody work.

This explains why Rolo has not despatched me to the stars already. To initiates of Cthulu the murder of another human being is a religious act, all manner of ritual and secret significance has to accompany this black ceremony. Planets and stars have to be in their correct houses, specific occult ley angles of latitude and longitude calculated, the sun must strike certain pyramids at certain times, the swords of the master assassin anointed with semen of virgins.

To try and find Rolo would be pointless, Dagons are masters of stealth and disguise, in Iraq they are known as the brotherhood of the Black Chameleon because of their uncanny abilities to avoid detection.

I remember once on a trip to Cairo I was visiting the city of the dead with little Pooti when I accidentally witnessed one of these mystic slayings. Pooti and I were smoking opium by the Nile when a bluish spinning blur appeared from behind one of the broken headstones. The strange light came to a standstill, the high-pitched humming noise quietened and there in front of us stood the tall dark Dagon. He was wearing immaculate white sailor's bellbottoms, his fly was undone and his blood-gorged dick pointed at the moon.

In his left hand he was carrying a 16-inch butcher's knife, the pale moonlight danced upon its razor edge. In his other hand the limp body of a young sodomite on the run from the Catamite. The Dagon smiled dreamily and then started working on the boy's eyes.

Little Pooti dragged me away telling me that some of the secrets of Arabia are not meant to be seen by occidentals. I didn't argue but from the little I did manage to see it was obvious that the Dagon are consummate experts with sharpened steel. A part of me is almost grateful that my death should be at the hands of such a skilled artist. To even pretend that I had any hope of eluding the Dagon, one of death's black masters would be futile.

STICKY-OUT EARS

'Wow! Look at that place. What do you reckon it is, Bill?'

'A barber's or hairdresser's or something.'

'Let's get a haircut then.'

Now this barber's does look fantastic. We've been driving through a kind of shantytown version of suburbia, heading for some location or other. We are just passing a beat-up parade of shops when we are blinded by the reflected sunlight from 1,000 fractured mirrors. Outside one of these shops is a large mural map of Africa made from shards of mirror. At the centre of this map the outline of Zaire is picked out in red and the interior of the country is in what I guess is broken black crockery.

I know that post-Picasso Western man has had to acknowledge the creative genius of the native, but other than the bars of soap that Z was buying we've seen very little of any sort of visual self-expression since we got here. Not even any graffiti. I've always assumed the creative urge in man is almost as strong as the urge to procreate. But not so here, most everything looks stunningly dull. That's why this large broken mirror mural has such an impact on us.

'JC, pull up. We want to check this out.'

It is, in fact, a barber's and as you probably know from observing the black community in our own country, barber shops act as a big cultural focus for the negro. You have to assume that the black man spends many more of his vanity units on what his hair looks like than white men do. Maybe that's where all his creative urge is channelled.

A bunch of lads in their late teens or early 20s are lounging about outside. There are no customers inside.

'Looks fuckin' brilliant what they've done with the mirrors, don't you think Bill? It reminds me of an Indian barber I...'

'Yeah Z, but should we get our hair cut?'

'Why not?'

Now Z as I've explained on numerous occasions and probably will do on numerous more, suffers from an overabundance of vanity. His moustache and goatee can never seem to grow fast enough for all the trimming he gives it. But as for his hair, it's been the same lank, greasy mane for the last ten years. The only time he does anything with it is when the roots need doing black again.

'What do you reckon Gimps, a bit of a short back and sides before we head up river?'

'No fuckin' way am I going to let one of them near me with a pair of scissors, let alone a razor.'

Sixty seconds later the three of us are sitting in a line in the African equivalent to barber's chairs staring at ourselves in the wall mirrors. We've got the white towels tied around the back of our necks and the three young barbers are off. Snip, snip, snip. Snip, snip, snip. Snip, snip, snip. I like this. This is the best thing that's happened since we got here. I make an instant vow to always get my hair cut whenever I'm away from home. I've always liked barber's shops and this one is no letdown. The lads with scissors and combs seem to be having a fine old time. They can't seem to stop laughing at the texture of our hair. The way it flops about, unable to hold its own.

'Z, I bet they've never touched a white man's hair before.'

'Yeah, I remember when I was shagging this black model once in London. I couldn't get over the feel of her hair. You ever shagged a black girl Bill?'

'Nah.'

'Not worth it. They ain't what you expect them to be.'

'Bit of a generalisation.'

'Maybe. Maybe it was that I just couldn't get over the weirdness of her hair. Put me completely off the job in hand.'

'I remember my barber back in Aylesbury, Luigi telling me once about cutting black men's hair. He said it was like trimming a hedge. All you had to do was cut out the shape you thought they wanted and that was that.'

On the wall to the side of the mirror in front of me is one of those posters you see in black men's hairdressers back in the UK. It features all the varieties of intricate braidings and razorings that the more fashion-conscious black man goes in for, which is a bit weird because over here all the men have the standard radical short cut, not a braiding in sight. As for the Afro, did anybody in Africa ever actually have an Afro or was it just a fashion accessory of the American black power movement of the early 1970s.

They seem to be having major difficulties with our hair. We've been here for over half an hour and still their scissors snip, just taking away the most minuscule of fractions of hair at a time. They are obviously dumbfounded by the fact that our hair has no body and refuses to hold any position whatsoever.

In the mirror I can see Golf lounging against the doorframe, his beloved AK47 nestling loosely in his arms.

'I've had e-fuckin'-nough of this, we've been here for almost an hour and they show no signs of getting any closer to getting the job done.'

'OK Gimpo, just 'cause you can't handle it.'

'Handle it? We're just getting our hair cut but I bet they think they can charge us by the minute. These chairs will have meters ticking away on them somewhere.'

'Hey JC, do you think you can wind things up for us?'

He gets jabbering. We settle our bill, give a generous tip, shake hands. Z tries to praise them for the big Africa in broken mirrors thing and something about it pissing all over the has-been *enfant terrible* Julian Schnabel with his broken plates. We are just climbing back into the cab when I notice that Golf is getting heavy with the hairdressers. It looks like he is trying to exert some kind of levy from them for having brought us here. Z has clocked it as well.

'Hey, JC, can you get Golf to cool it?'

And JC does and Golf is back in the cab. I don't know if he got any of what he was after but it has somehow tarnished the respect I was directing his way.

'Z, should we ask JC to explain to Golf that we would rather he didn't behave that way?'

'Bill, it's the natural order. We all abuse our positions of power. It's what fuels the cogs that keeps culture ticking. It's just that over here it's naked in the raw and we don't like to acknowledge it. Britain has one of the most highly trained and well equipped armies in the world. We don't have to be seen going around throwing our weight about 'cause we...'

To be honest I don't know if Z has a point or not and, if he has, whether he is making it in any rational way. What is now filling my thoughts is nothing to do with the lot of man but the state of Z's haircut. He looks like a total buffoon. This, of course, I'm very pleased with.

'Anyway, I can see they've given you a pretty radical trim.'

'What do you mean? What's wrong with it?'

'Well, I never knew you had sticky-out ears.'

'So?'

'So that explains why you've always had long hair, to cover them up.'

'They don't stick out that much.'

'They stick out enough that you should have a complex about them.'

'Fuck off Bill, and anyway have you seen what they've done to you? You look even more like the archetypal child abuser than you usually do.'

Gimpo has to get his two pence-worth in.

'Shut up the pair of you. You both looked like idiots before you had your hair cut and you still look like idiots now.'

I would like to have a withering reply on hand to send in Gimpo's direction but the truth of the matter is that he is probably right and to make matters worse his hair cut looks good.

We climb back into JC's cab and get going.

After the haircut incident, JC took us to the National Zoo. It was closed. The idea of having a zoo in the middle of Africa seems ridiculous. Surely they have no need of one. They can just go out into the countryside if they want to see lions, elephants, zebras, giraffes etc. can't they? OK, I suppose it's not a living Tarzan movie out there but still a zoo in Africa does seem a strange notion.

Heading back to the hotel, JC says, 'So tonight I take you to nightclub. Eight o'clock I be here to pick you up. Golf be here to. No trouble. Lots of fun, girls, girls, girls.'

JC has just dropped us off at the Memling, now for a couple of hours stretched out on my bed to finish off the Irish notes.

*

The only thing I can wonder now is which cut Rolo will use to send me to the next life. The Dagon, like their spiritual brothers, the Samurai of Japan, have many ways to speed us on the last few turns of our mortal coils. Because many necro cults consider murder to be to be an act of sublime contemplation, the thrusts, stabs, slashes and cuts used in their murderous ecstasies are given rather beautiful names. For instance will I be sent to my maker by the 'whistling angel', so called because when the throat is cut at a specific angle to a specific depth, the air rushing into the severed trachea is said to sound like the call of a distressed curlew with a broken wing.

I am fairly certain it will not be the 'death of the lover', a quick single rapier cut to the heart, the method Rolo used on Kiki. If all of this has affected Rolo as much as it has me, I imagine Rolo wants to savour my death.

If that is the case then I can probably expect the 'death of seven hundred red flowers'. Many believe this spectacularly artful form of torturous execution to be of Chinese origin but the Arabs had perfected this slow death centuries before the sadistic mandarins of the East. The victim is hung by his feet and then 700 precise cuts are slowly peeled into his flesh.

The Dagon demonstrates his remarkable skill by insuring that the last drop of blood draining the victim's very essence drips a few seconds after the final cut. If the suspended victim dies before or a considerable time after the last cut great shame is brought upon the Dagon and an unspoken rule decrees that the Dagon should take the 'monk's cut'. That is to say he must castrate himself and enter a monastery. Or prison, call it what you will.

From what Kiki told me of his friend and lover Rolo I have a very good idea that the 700 blades are waiting for me whenever the lunar mysticism of the Cthulu Dagon decides. Being no stranger to death work myself I can appreciate the sanguine poetry of the Cthulu and a noble part of me almost welcomes this elegant death.

Maybe I should confront Rolo and ask that we face our entwined destiny without the heat of passion to disturb its cool dignity. The only real choice I have is whether to face it with the grace and honour of a noble homosexual facing the blade like Yukio Mishima or like a whimpering puff unlocking his baggy dirtbox on the killing-room floor. There is no choice.

WE'RE NIGHTCLUBBING

'This ain't a nightclub, it's a whorehouse.'

'Shut up Gimpo and get the drinks in.'

'There's no bar.'

'What do ya mean no bar? 'Course it's got a bar. How else do you think they think they are going to get us pissed enough to want to shag one of these black prozzies. JC, where's the bar?'

Z is in a truculent mood. Must be something to do with his ears sticking out.

The place is an ill-lit shack. Ill-lit? It's in almost complete darkness. There are no windows, there are some of those bendy tubes of coloured fluorescent lighting. The type that shows up your dandruff and bad teeth. There are a few low Formica tables with even lower leatherette settees. There is a DJ booth in the corner. As soon as the man on the decks saw us come in he whipped off the Afro pop and slipped on a Phil Collins album. I suppose he must think it makes us feel at home and in the words of Paul Simon, home is where I want to be.

Now that my eyes are accustomed to the gloom, I realise that Golf, JC, Z, Gimpo and myself are the only customers. We are outnumbered by girls three to one, but it's obvious they are all in the employ of some unseen whoremeister. They don't look high class like the ones working the Memling. These look more desperate, more skanky, like they're probably going to die of AIDs but not before they let their children inherit it. What a birthright.

Golf is in his usual position, leaning against the doorframe, AK47 ready, willing and able. JC is sitting at a table sipping his Primus, tapping his toe to Phil and looking very pleased with himself. Us three are sat around a table in the far corner.

'Don't look any of them in the eye.'

'Why? What they gonna do Gimpo, cast a spell on you?'

'I know what I'm talking about, Z. You so much as look at one of them and they will be over stroking your thigh and before you know some nigger will be out of the woodwork looking for his $20 and you will be expecting me to sort it out.'

'No I won't, Golf can do it.'

'Fuck off.'

'Gimpo, just cool it. Drink your Primus and relax.'

I move to a table on my own, get my notebook out and try and catch up with the passing moments. My eyes are getting accustomed to the darkness. Two of the girls have decided to dance with each other right in front of my table. Their arses packed tightly into what used to be called hot pants, are grinding away at my eye level. I'm pleased to report none of their efforts are having any effect on me. Such libido as I have can't be bothered to take any notice, however much they shake their moneymakers.

You remember when I was talking about sharing the lift with the whore in the Memling and I was going on about empathy? Well, I've just made a decision. I'm no longer going to entertain the concept of empathy while we are on this trip in search of Satan. It's obviously a highly dangerous indulgence. You start dabbling with a thing like empathy in a place like this or in any of the other situations we are likely to get into and we will be done for.

Empathy only works when there are a few thousand miles between you and the focus of your Western liberal sentimentalities. If I was watching these booty-shaking harlots on the TV in my living room and it was a programme about the tragedy of AIDs-riven Africa and the lot of those with nothing to look forward to but a short brutish life and an early grave, then I could afford to let empathy have its reign. But while here I should try and think of my brothers and sisters as mere two-dimensional extras in my own private biopic.

I'd like to tell you that the DJ is now playing Sting's song 'Roxanne', but you probably don't know the lyrics to it so the perverted irony of listening to a song about a whore while surrounded by Roxanne's African sisters would be wasted and I would be lying anyway, so I won't.

The dancing girls have decided to take a breather from their exertions and relax either side of me on the low-slung leatherette settee. One of them is about to place her hand on my thigh. My pen keeps going, my libido still happy to languish in its sick bed. But what do I do? Do I call on Golf to sort the hussies out? Or do I make my excuses and move table? The thing is, this is the only table in the dismal place that has enough light for me to carry on writing.

Above the din of Phil Collins I'm hearing Z raging at Gimpo.

'What the fuck are you doing, Gimpo? Do you want us all killed or what?'

The stylus on the Phil Collins record has taken a short cut across the grooves just as he was reaching the high point of sussudio right to the end of the album.

'Put it fuckin' away.'

Now dear reader, if this was Z's prose that you were chuckling your way through you would rightly assume that Gimpo had been bashing his bishop out in some sort of onanistic display of perverted bravado. In fact, what Gimpo was doing is ignoring Z's admonishments and crawling around the floor of the club, video camera in hand, filming the antics of the desperate whores. He still is.

'Desperate? Who says they are desperate?' asks a voice somewhere.

Well I did. There are 15 of them here at the last count; nobody else has entered the club since we got here about 40 minutes ago. JC and Golf are on duty so they are out the running and the three spooks (do American Negroes still call white men spooks?) have no interest whatsoever in tasting and trying whatever it is they have on offer.

'Gimpo, get off the floor and, for the last time, put that camera away. Bill, let's get going back to the hotel and what the fuck are you doing with those two black prossies either side of you?'

'Nothing. I was just about to...'

But before I could explain to Z the innocence of my situation and how I was just about to extract myself, the DJ dropped the needle back into the groove. Relief. It was no longer poor old Phil but Jimmy Cliff with his 'Many Rivers to Cross' song.

*

I was sucking down hard on my breakfast beer. Today we were headed up river and there was no way on Earth I was sailing up into Mau Mau land without at least half a serious drunk tied on.

Gimpo was buggering around as usual, packing things, unpacking them, swearing, kicking things, stealing stuff that he thought nobody would notice, unscrewing cameras, rescrewing cameras and generally creating a flustered air around himself.

I whacked back a large gin, I got the feeling we weren't going to be able to get hard liquor in the jungle so I was getting in my camel rations, sorting out my hump as the band used to call it.

'Z,' Gimpo whispered, 'Check Bill out. He was trying hard not to laugh.

Bill was over in the reception area sorting out our hotel shit. He was wearing a blue and white striped shirt with a scarlet neckerchief and a pair of snug white bellbottoms that clung obscenely to his generous Scottish arse. Scarlet ballet pumps completed his gay attire. Stern faced, he threw his kit bag across his shoulder and strode manfully to the bar. The sailor pants were pulled up painfully tight revealing that the strange man dressed to the left.

READ KIERKEGAARD

Five minutes later in the back of JC's cab heading for the Memling.

'So boys, you didn't want fun? Some pretty girls there, no?'

'Yes JC, very pretty girls, but not for us. We just want a quiet drink, some music to tap our toes to and maybe some chicks to check out, but that's as far as it goes.'

'You crazy guys. Don't you want fun?'

'No. We don't like fun.'

'Everybody want fun. All around the world man want fun. Woman there to give man fun. Man life bad enough as it is without a little fun. You got dollars, you could have fun all night long. What wrong?'

Where do you begin? Is the cultural gap too wide? Do I recommend he start reading Kierkegaard's classic *Fear and Trembling*?' I'm sure Z would have it that he should start on Nietzsche's *Beyond Good and Evil*. I'm not quite with Z on his quest for the ultimate moment of existential ennui but I'd rather have that than this fun, fun, fun thing that the ever-present sound of Afro pop seems to be bludgeoning us into.

'I'm sorry JC, we just ain't cut out for fun.'

We pull up at the Memling.

'OK boys, I be here 10.00 in morning with Golf. Take you to the ferry. Get you on board. Nice cabin. OK? Goodnight. Sleep well.'

'Goodnight JC. See you later Golf.'

I would like to take this opportunity to state that Golf did not say more than half a dozen words all day and not once were his shades allowed to lower their guard. Coolness above and beyond the call of duty.

Z heads for the bar. I head for bed and Gimpo heads out into the night with his camera. He won't learn.

Chapter Three
THE STRANGE MAN IN THE DISTURBING WHITE BELL-BOTTOMS

An eminent ethnologist once proclaimed that the oriental mind was generally predisposed towards a meditative state of being, that the occidental nature was one of a searching questing type and that the African was an instinctive observer.

Whatever any of this means and whether it's true or just another piece of irrelevance floating around in the wordy ether, a forgotten ghost haunting a closed-down library, who knows? who cares? What is true is the fact that black guys are not big on stress.

To the average funk soul brother on whatever street corner of the world he finds himself hanging out on, his natural instinct is to chill, to let the world slide by, to enjoy his life and to mind his own business. An admirable philosophy, any Zen master would agree.

Cities however are built from reinforced concrete and steel forged in furnaces fired with intolerable stress and hardened with urban paranoia. Cities send citizens insane.

You only have to walk half a mile in any direction in any major Western city in the world to see this quivering truth babbling bug-eyed in your face. Wild-haired lunatics screaming at the invisible tormentors of their own private hells. The ragged phantoms of housewives mugged by useless dreams pushing their broken shopping trolleys full of stinking garbage around magical circuits of invisible supermarkets. Immaculately groomed dollar slaves riding Sisyphean elevators inside the glass cathedrals of capital. Millions of people in their own homes sucking on the poisonous cathode tit of Mammon, dripping flammable mendacity on to the smouldering fires of consumer anxiety.

I AWAKE

I awake. And I know where this is. I don't know who you are but I know who I am. The grey net curtains billow in the breeze. The bed cover has slipped to the floor. I ban any thoughts from entering my head, especially ones like 'I wish I wasn't here'. The din of the day is making its way up from the street below, over the windowsill around the still billowing net curtain and on to my eardrums. I ignore this din.

What I can't ignore anymore is the noise coming from the bathroom. Gimpo is in there muttering. His muttering rises and falls then rises again. It is no longer just muttering. His words are measured. He is repeating the same line two, three, eight times. Each time he tries a different emphasis. Is he playing at being Travis Bickell in that mirror scene? I think not, that's more Z's line of play. Gimpo is secure enough in his own identity to never have to resort to playing out the role of a movie character. No, Gimpo is only interested in being more Gimpoesque.

I lift my head from the pillow. The bathroom door is ajar. I can see Gimpo sitting in the bath. He is still in his one-way conversation. I slip from the bed. Tiptoe over the scattered belongings. Gimpo cannot see me. I spy on him through the crack between the door and the frame. He has his video camera strung up with fishing line, hanging from the shower-curtain rail. The camera is pointing at its master and it is rolling, capturing all that the Gimp has to say.

I listen.

'So I told them, as far as I'm concerned Golf is a fraud. Anybody can buy a uniform from an army surplus store. As for the AK47, I bet it's not even loaded. I mean you've seen his bullet belt? Empty. Well, apart from the two spent cartridges. The pair of them think they are safe 'cause they are squandering $200 a day on a boy playing at soldiers...'

Gimpo carries on with his video diary performance.

At moments like this, it helps that Gimpo suffers from deafness. It means I'm able to get dressed and get out of the room without having to disturb his privacy.

*

Kinshasha is one of the most stressful cities on earth. The river port where the barge waits to ferry people away from the insane metropolis is stress from another planet. JC and Kivaru drove us to there. We edged our way into the Dantesque mêlée of boiling black flesh. Fat women in technicolour sarongs wobbled through the crowds with baskets of maggots on their heads, shaking carrier bags full of money and shouting at each other. Stinking beggars are knocked down by sadistic Ray Ban soldiers, abandoned babies cry in the dust.

On the back seat of the car Bill sits like a perspiring stone while Gimpo twists nervously with his rucksack. Contorted black faces start banging on the window when they see the pale freaks trying to blend in with the upholstery. A skeletal hand clutching a fat writhing grub pokes in through Gimpo's window. He quickly winds it up trapping the hand and the bug.

The bottle of Primus knocks nervously on my teeth every time I lift it to my mouth. I sit there tense and quiet, working on my nervous breakdown. Whenever I visit intense places, some form of mental derangement usually comes with me. It can happen at any time. The bizarre cultural differences, the isolation afforded by language difficulties, the profusion or complete lack of strange drugs and alcohol all conspire to produce some form of dysphoriastic mental breakdown. Fortunately my nervous system usually grinds down and I am reduced to a few days of catatonia. Saying that of course, in one or two more extreme places like Iceland and that shimmering hallucination in the desert, Las Vegas, I have experienced full-blown psychotic incidents.

Right there, right then I could feel my madness live and wired creeping up on me. A black banshee with electric hair festooned with finger bones, grinning with filed pointed teeth. Livid purple skin writhing with pulsating Maori designs dancing among fires fuelled by dead babies. I swallowed hard and consoled myself with the thought that at least I was getting the incident over with quickly. Both Gimpo and Bill had witnessed these manifestations of my cracked psyche many times before and knew how to deal with them promptly and efficiently.

Occasionally calling me by my original Christian name could snap me out of whatever paranoid cyclone I was windsurfing. Or a stiff dressing down in the military 'get a grip of yourself man' stiff-upper-lip vibe.

I had no idea what form the shifting perspectives of hallucination and the gurgling reverb of deep mindfuck would take. I held on whiteknuckle-tight and prayed to whatever benign jungle spirits that may have been tuned in. With drug-induced madness a simple 'none of this is real' mantra can do the trick. When the actual reality of the situation that you find yourself in is so monstrously alien that reality itself acts as the trigger that kicks in the psychosis then, my psychedelic friends, you're in trouble. Unless friendly catatonia steps in to smooth you down and out of this monster bummer, you had better hold on real fucking close to your sanity because there's usually something freaky out there that wants it a whole lot badder than you.

ON ROCK 'N' ROLL

'White Rabbit' sung by Grace Slick is one of the high points of my personal edition of *The History of American Popular Music*. If you didn't know that Grace Slick was the singer in the leading mid- to late-1960s hippy band Jefferson Airplane, you do now! And if you have ever read *Fear and Loathing in Las Vegas* you may remember the scene in the hotel bathroom where the attorney character is sitting in the tub holding a radio that is plugged into the mains. 'White Rabbit' by Jefferson Airplane is playing out of the radio. Now 'White Rabbit' is one of those classic building songs. From its sparse beginnings and opening line of 'One pill makes you larger' Grace Slick leads the way as the band take it up and up. Her inspiration for the lyrics comes from the innocent work of Lewis Carroll, she twists the tale of *Alice in Wonderland* into an out-and-out sermon to all us school kids around the Western world about the glories of taking acid. The attorney clutching the radio while sitting in the bath had a plan. When Grace reaches her climax repeating the line 'Feed your head', he's going to drop the radio into the bath so he can get himself an added fix of 240 volts through his body. I can't remember what was the actual outcome and I can't say I care. But seeing Gimpo sitting in the tub in his crazed drug-fried way reminded me of that scene.

So while in the lift going down for my breakfast, I'm singing 'White Rabbit' to myself and thinking what a brilliant song it is and why didn't I ever write such a brilliant song. When the lift doors open at the ground floor and out I step feeling grateful that even if I didn't, at least Grace Slick did, in the secure knowledge that my life would be a fraction the poorer if she hadn't.

And what I hear coming over the hidden sound system to make me feel far away from all that is Africa is not 'Money for Nothing' by Dire Straits, but 'We Built This City on Rock 'n' Roll' by Starship. This record, according to that same edition of *The History of American Popular Music* is probably one of the worst ever made.

I suppose the main reason for having an idol is to watch them fall, anytime I hear Grace Slick sing 'White Rabbit' (or 'Somebody to Love'). She is the ultimate strong, towering, 1960s female icon. There she is in total control of all her faculties and looking splendid while she's at it. In 1986, Grace Slick had her only British No.1. It was not a song written by herself but by songsmith hack Bernie 'Candle on the Wind' Taupin. By now, our Grace was a bloated, recovering alcoholic dressed in the worst possible $10,000 tat. Her No.1 is what I'm hearing right now: *We Built This City On...*' What city she is referring to I've no idea. San Francisco? LA? London? Surely not Kinshasa? All that plodding production and meaningless emotion, why do people bother to make such shit?

And just as I'm about to start going on about why blokes love to be rock bores, Z sees me.

'Hey, Bill, over here. You got some stuff for me to read?'

'What?'

'We agreed to get together each morning for a literary breakfast. Compare prose sizes. Make sure what we are doing is travelling in the same direction. That the tales we are telling weave together. Remember?'

'Oh yeah.'

'So, let's see what you've been doing.'

I hand Z over my notebook, order breakfast and start writing up the tale of Gimpo in the bath, Grace Slick and what you're reading now, on a white paper napkin. It's one of those porous napkins. I like writing on them. I like watching the ink from my pen soaking in, blurring and blotching the line. Looks arty.

Z's been reading for about ten minutes. It gets the odd chuckle from him, which is a bit of a relief. Nothing's as nerve-racking as somebody reading your stuff for the first time.

'Bill, I don't know how to tell you this.'

'What?'

'It's rubbish.'

'What do you mean?'

'Well, none of it's true. At least that racist stuff I read yesterday morning was expressing your genuine fear about arriving in Africa. It was making a point. But all of this is just made up. It's nearly all in dialogue – the reader will think it's what we actually said.'

'But...'

'I mean that could be all right if you had just condensed what was actually said.'

'I thought you...'

'You've reduced us to these cardboard cut-out characters who spend all their time bickering. Nobody in reality relates like that.'

'So what were you chuckling at while you were reading it?'

'Yeah well, some of it's funny but that's not the point.'

'So what is the point? Am I supposed to be the stooge, the boring straight man to your flights of fantasy? I'm just Ernie to your Eric. Well fuck that. Look, I can turn my specs upside down as well as you can.'

'No, Bill, you don't understand. For this to work we have to keep hold of the trust of the reader. It is only with the strong foundations that your prose can bring to the work that the reader will believe in the seriousness of our mission and the precariousness of our situation. The reader knows my stuff is rubbish. It only works if there is that bedrock of reality that your stuff brings to it. The reader will be able to tell that I only write what I do as a defence mechanism to deal with the reality of us being literally stuck up-river without a paddle.'

'We are not up-river yet.'

'Yeah, but you fuckin' know what I mean.'

'So what you are saying, I've got to be the bass player plodding away while you widdle away all over your Les Paul?'

'If that's the analogy you want to use, yes. You know more than most that a band of lead guitarists would fall to bits at the first rehearsal.'

My breakfast arrives. We fall into silence. Z carries on reading my stuff and he carries on chuckling at it. Maybe he is just jealous that my humour works in a way that people will be able to identify with. Like it does in a classic TV sitcom, Dad's Army or whatever.

'What's this, Bill?'

'What?'

'Us in that joint last night. Those two whores never came over and sat either side of you stroking your leg.'

'Well?'

'Just fantasy on your part. You wish they had.'

'Look Z, yesterday morning you were wanting me to slip into my notes that Gimpo had actually been buggered by the police. It seems you want me to bend the rules when it suits you.'

'That would work as long as you keep the reader's trust.'

'And what about this now?'

'What do you mean?'

'This conversation we are having now. Does this encourage the trust of the reader? Does the reader think we are actually having this conversation or am I just making it up at some later date?'

'This is irrelevant.'

'No it's not. What track was playing over the PA when I came in?'

'What's that got to do with anything.'

'Just tell me.'

'OK, calm down Bill. It was *We Built This City On Rock'n'Roll* by Starship.'

'And is it one of the worst records ever made?'

'Of course it is. A complete travesty to the whole genre of rock 'n' roll. Bonn Scot didn't die so records like that could be made.'

'Thank you, that was perfect.'

'Why?'

'You have just strengthened my bond of trust with the reader. For the last couple of pages I thought it was slipping.'

With my bond of trust between you, the reader, and me, the writer, stronger than ever I can tell you that things settle down between Z and myself. We get on with our own versions of breakfast, his more liquid than mine, and tending to our note-making. At some point Gimpo joined us, though neither Z or I acknowledged his presence. He busies himself once more with taking apart his zooms and polishing his lenses.

I have to note that Gimpo smelled fresh. His t-shirt and lightweight fatigues washed and freshly pressed. It made me feel grubby. Z doesn't notice things like that.

*

The car inched its way slowly into the forest of swirling limbs, eventually pulling to a dead stop. Endless people crammed together with their animals, dead and alive, some with giant fish tied to their backs and buckets of scorpions balanced on their heads made it impossible to get any further. It was like trying to swim in tapioca. I could see the huge barge towering above the ramshackle shanty towns and corrugated iron warehouses hulking in the distance. It was a monster of a vessel.

JC decides to hire a couple of soldiers to escort us to the ticket office, he gets out of the car and makes his way into the black stew. Ordinarily the thought of being left in a car surrounded by desperado cannibals would have sent me thrashing into some kind of hyperactive overdrive pretty quickly but fortunately there seemed to be something mellow mandraxing its way down on me. I sat still like lead.

The interior of the car was becoming suffocating, Zyklon Bill was sat on a constant leakage of pigshit ferocity. Gimpo gagging, risked opening the window a fraction. It really says something about the stellar intensity of Bill's apopleptic bowel syndrome that his rotten arse could cut through the unholy effluvium of an African river port.

An hour or so later JC returns with a couple of bad-ass soldiers wearing the usual mean shades and mismatched fatigues. I noticed they had affixed bayonets to their rifles. Bill paid them $20 each and they fired a couple of volleys into the air to clear the mob away from in front of us. The people there were packed so solid that no matter how hard they shoved it was impossible for them to make a path for us. This didn't seem to deter the two soldiers who started scything into the crowd with their bayonets, gouging and stabbing, creating a bumpy road of human bodies which the car nervously negotiated. The two army devils kept on slashing and cutting their way into the screaming butchered crowd laughing joyously at their handiwork.

WIGS DON'T WORK

At 10.00am sharp, JC did his shimmy across the breakfast room's swirly carpet.

'OK boys, time to leave for the big river. I've got Mr Arthur Malu-Malu's man Tombo Bamba with me in the cab. If we have any problems at the ferry we will be able to sort them out. You all packed?'

'Give us a couple of minutes to get our stuff.'

Thirty minutes later we are in reception trying to check out. The same woman is on duty as when we first checked in.

'I hope you enjoyed your stay with us and that we see you again the next time you pass through Kinshasa.'

I refrain from telling her that I hope never to pass through this city again in my life.

Outside a group of schoolgirls in neatly ironed, navy blue pinafore dresses and starched white blouses pass by. On their heads are perched their books. I make a mental note that this is the sort of thing that I should be writing about if I was making a proper travel book. But I'm not, so instead I will remind you about the fingernails on the Memling receptionist's hands. The ones that I described as being painted a violent crimson. The ones that I would have liked to have bent back until each and every one had broken.

Well, this morning I didn't feel that way. This morning nothing about her worked as a symbol of womankind put on earth to make my life miserable. In fact, her fingernails were no longer violent or crimson. They were painted in rainbow colours. Well I suppose they weren't painted. Two of them were missing – alerting me to the fact that they were false ones just stuck on. False nails, however long or garishly coloured, have no power to destabilise my equilibrium. Looking at the two naked stubby little brown fingernails where the rainbow talons should be just fuelled some sort of pity for her.

What didn't fuel any pity was her wig. One of my more righteous theories is: the Afro-American's struggle for equality in all areas of life and culture will not be realised until black women stop wearing those ludicrous wigs. Those arguments that may be put forward that everybody has the right to express themselves in whatever way they want as long as it doesn't harm anyone else don't cut it with me. Those wigs are symbols of denial of who and what they are and not a celebration of self-expression.

'I say to all you black women around the world, throw away your wigs and embrace your true and beautiful blackness.'

'Shut up Bill and just get in the cab.'

'OK, yeah, all right Z.'

I climb in the cab.

'What the fuck were you on about anyway, Bill?'

'It was just something going through my head. I didn't realise it was coming out my mouth. Something to do with her two missing fingernails. You know?'

'No.'

Of course he didn't. I hate it when all that internal stuff starts leaking out. That's what writing is for, not reality.

*

JC turned on the windscreen wipers, there was so much blood covering the front of the vehicle it was difficult to see where we were going. Out of the side windows I managed to make out those weird little bucket kids we'd seen on our journey from the airport. There they were again, horrible little fuckers, their raggy shorts caked with dried black blood, scooping up the severed limbs and the tangled sloppy viscera and banging it into their buckets. I asked JC who the kids were.

'Lualaba orphans,' he said casually, 'Little cannibals.'

The crowd in its panic, trying to avoid the psychotic soldiers eventually managed to clear a road for us to the ticket office.

Maybe its some weird requirement of the job. Maybe all officials in Zaire have to look like Idi Amin. The fat fuck, sweat beading on his bald held checked our passports and looked us up and down sussing out how much he could realistically rob us of. He is over-optimistic and wants $10,000 each.

Arthur's man enters into negotiation with Fatso, shouting in Lingala. Several times Idi punched his desk and tried to wave us away. Arthur's man persisted screeching like an animal and pointing at Gimpo's arse. Idi got his dick out and started to fuck his desk. Gimpo looked very worried at this altercation and made a mental note to learn Lingala as soon as possible. Idi's armed assistants laughed loudly at their boss's joke. Our soldiers watched with keen interest checking out the port officials' office layout. Eventually Idi screamed something and one of his men went for his piece. Luckily our guys were faster, Idi's man took a burst full in the face. His head exploded as his body spasticated backwards splattering us all in warm blood and shit. The other soldier skewered the second assistant to the floor through his groin, removing his weapon and pricking the screaming fucker like you'd prepare sausages for frying.

After this Idi was a lot more generous in his negotiations, smiling and gesticulating fraternally. We got three first-class tickets for $100 each, a 3000 per cent reduction in the original asking price, I think. Bill generously gave the soldiers an extra $20 each. They smiled and enthusiastically saluted the strange man in the disturbing white bellbottoms.

THEY LOVE IT

Now I'm frightened. Z is obviously shit scared and even Gimpo is a little unsure. The drive from the Memling to the docks was uneventful. My theories on the struggle for black liberation and wigs on women has been safely stored away.

What is now troubling us is the reality that surrounds us. JC is trying to drive his cab through a sea of blackness. There are literally thousands of living, breathing individuals all pushing and shoving into the bottleneck of a road that is heading down to the waterfront. We've not moved an inch in the last 20 minutes. The ferry was scheduled to leave at 11.00am It is now past noon. Every so often we hear a ship's horn blow. This sets a panic off in the crowd and the surging and heaving and pushing and shoving lifts a gear. Nobody gets anywhere. Tombo Bamba is in the front with JC. The three of us are crammed on the back seat. I'm in the middle. JC has his hand almost continually on his horn. Up until now JC has seemed like an island of calm rationality in this continent of base instinct. Of the hundreds of bodies packed solidly around his cab not one is taking a blind bit of notice of his horn blowing.

Maybe he is only doing it so we think he is at least trying. Z is sitting to the left of me. He has his notebook out and is furtively scribbling away, sniggering to himself as he goes. The right-hand side of his notebook is turned up. He obviously doesn't want me to see what he is writing. This is rather unusual for Z. He is usually so cocksure about what he writes that he is more than happy for the world to watch as he spews forth his genius prose.

I know this should get my paranoia going, nourished with questions like: what nasty little truths is he revealing about my core being for you to read? Whatever it is, don't believe him. He just makes it up to cover for his own inadequacies. But my petty paranoia is left untroubled. What is troubling me though is the fact that Gimpo has his video camera out again and is filming the heaving and pushing sea of black humanity that has engulfed our tin can of a cab.

What's playing in my head is that news footage filmed from a helicopter at an IRA funeral somewhere in Northern Ireland. It's the one where the mourners drag people from a car that has somehow got caught up in the cortege, two men who they then kill in hot blood and slow motion as the news camera innocently keeps rolling above capturing it all for us to watch on the Nine O'clock News. The two men were plain-clothes cops, so I suppose they were as guilty as Z and myself are right now. Don't ask me to define the cause of our guilt. Just being white right here, right now and in JC's cab is enough to be going on with.

'Put that fuckin' camera away Gimpo.'

It's Z. At least he is given up his furtive scribbling and sniggering.

'You'll get us all fuckin' killed.'

'You pair of jessies. Nobody is going to kill us, they love it.'

And to prove his point he unwinds his window, sticks the camera out and starts filming. Instantly the crowd that had been pushing and shoving around his side of the cab start to wave and smile at the camera. Some even go as far as singing and dancing for the all-seeing and freshly cleansed lens. Gimpo then replays the 30 or so seconds he has just filmed for the performers to watch on the small in-camera viewing screen. This brings squeals of delight and shrieks of laughter from the instant stars. Turning to us Gimpo looks satisfied with the power of his demonstration. 'See, they love it. Why would they want to kill us? We are all just people waiting to get on a boat. They just do it different here.'

To be fair to Gimpo, if I look closely at this surging black mob, I see it is mainly made up of happy, smiling and chattering mothers, babies strapped to their backs and barefoot kids having as much fun as they can cram into a day waiting to board the ferry. I mean, this is a big deal occasion, something to be savoured for a long time to come. They are not going to waste it killing two or three worthless whites. Well, not actually worthless, as the kids who were such eager and willing performers for Gimpo's camera are now demanding payment for their efforts. Should I act as their agent? Do Equity rates apply here?

The ship's horn has just gone off again, mightier and louder than before. Two short bursts and one long one. The crowd surge forward. The brief lifting of my paranoia is over. The terror is back blacker than before. This time it's not the IRA funeral footage but the disaster when all those Liverpool supporters got crushed to death against the old terrace barriers and security fencing in Sheffield. It's not so much our death I'm fearing, but those of the babies strapped to mother's backs and the toddlers at their feet. I've got no fuckin' clue what to do with crushed babies and kids with collapsed lungs. And don't you get AIDs from giving an African mouth-to-mouth?

'I fuckin' told you Bill. We should have kept Golf on for an extra day. He would have cut a swathe through this lot in a couple of minutes. You were being your usual skinflint self of course.'

'No I wasn't. He had a prior engagement.'

'Africans don't have prior engagements, well not ones that they feel any obligation to honour. A few dollars could have sorted it.'

DRUMMOND'S SECRET LOG, SS MKONGO, 8 JUNE 1996

It is decided, I will accept my fate and die here in the primeval forest. My eternal soul shall join with Kiki in whatever afterworld awaits. I shall make arrangements with Rolo who I am sure is also on board.

Never in all of my life and travels, not even in the slums of Cairo, the homosexual ghettos of Tangiers and Toledo have I come across such depredation as on board this floating barrio. The port master swindled us. We were promised and paid for first-class passage only to find that the usurous toad had allocated us some hellish third-class box cabin.

A metal windowless hole, ten by six foot, with just enough room to stand. There is no electricity so we have no light. We are also sharing with a cannibal, a veritable Queequeg lurks beneath Z's bunk.

Some how death almost seems to be the easier option.

I have decided to confess all my sins and meet my God as pure as any papist dog. This dreadful sodomy business. Kiki was not the only one. There was the German, Fruitus at his grandmother's castle in the mountains of Tyrol. He was the great-grandson of the Nazi Luftwaffe commander and homosexual morphine addict, First World War fighter ace Herman Goering.

Goering was one of the more interesting characters of the Nazi elite. Although he didn't share Himmler and Hitler's interest in the occult sciences his caprices were just as fascinating. A great admirer of art, he looted the private and national galleries of all the Nazi-occupied countries and had amassed an incredible collection of classical and modern masterpieces. His speciality interest, unsurprisingly for a notorious sensualist, were pieces of an erotic nature.

One suspects that many of the national galleries would have been quite relieved to rid themselves of the more difficult works from their underground vaults. Picasso's 'Buggering of the Nazarene' for instance. The infamous thirteenth station of the cross, the missing act from Christ's Passion that the church has managed to conceal for so many centuries. The depiction of Jesus' final indignity has fascinated artists down the centuries.

The church in an Orwellian conceit has managed by coercion of nearly all the governments of the past 2000 years to keep the terrible fudge packing of the Lord a hushed secret known only to a select few. Many artists however seem to have a supernatural gift, a visionary connection to the truths of the universe and have revealed this despoliation.

A SECRET AGENDA

I didn't argue the case with Z about Africans not having prior engagements. He was probably right. Instead I got on with making these notes. In fact I buried myself so deep in them I didn't notice the minutes slip by and the fact that now we are parked up on the quayside and almost ready to board.

'Bill, we have to do something about Gimpo and we have to do it now. We've got to get that camera off him. If it's not confiscated before we board, he will have all three of us in deep shit.' I don't know if Z is correct in his interpretation of the situation but he does seem pretty convinced.

'Gimpo knows it's illegal to film from the boat. But that illegality just acts as a provocation. The only way to stop him is if he doesn't have the camera. I think you should get it off him and throw it in the river.'

'Why me?'

'I couldn't do it.'

'No, of course you couldn't. What can you fuckin' do other than get other people to do things for you?'

OK, I didn't say that but Z had been doing more of his furtive scribbling and sniggering again while hiding behind the covers of his notebook. He's obviously up to something in his writing that he doesn't want me to know about and it's got to be more than that *Book of Gimpo by Gimpo* stuff.

'OK Z, where is he?'

'He's off filming down at the other end of the dock.'

'Look, when he gets back we'll talk to him. I'll get something sorted.'

'He'll listen to you, Bill.'

In reality I don't give a fuck about Gimpo and his camera. I'm sure Gimpo can look after himself. I know what I should be doing right now is describing this whole ramshackle dock scenario, what this towering rusting heap of paddle-steaming ferry looks like. The fact is that it's a whole flotilla of 'its' of various sizes, design and in various stages of dilapidation, all tied together with rusted and frayed lengths of steel ropes. These are all sights and scenes you will never have seen before on film let alone experienced in real life. I'm here experiencing it for you first-hand so that you can experience it vicariously in the safety of your bedsit, or hall of residence, or squat, or bus to work. Well fuck you, I ain't here to make your dull days and meaningless life more bearable.

It's not Gimpo's camera that I want to throw in the river, it's Z's notebook. There is something going on those pages covered with his tiny effeminate hand and flowery prose that he is wanting to keep hidden from me. A secret agenda.

∗

Fruitus had many of these visionary depictions of the thirteenth station of the cross hanging in the salon of his great-grandfather's mountain hideaway. The other favourite subject depicted in the salon was of course the prickly martyrdom of St Sebastian, the patron saint of cultured bummers the world over.

It was young Bobby Sockett, a member of my cub scout pack back in Aylesbury who had drawn my attention to this descendant of the notorious Nazi libertine. Bobby, though only 11 years old, was extremely advanced for his years and possessed a stunning intellect. Through his expert knowledge of the internet young Bobby had tracked down the Goering heir's current address here at his grandmother's Tyrolean castle.

Research both Bobby and myself had been carrying out – young Bob on his internet, myself in the more obscure corners of the British library – had led us to believe that the Nazi Goering was on intimate terms with the devil. Bobby had little need of persuading me that a visit to the Tyrolean castle and Goering's great grandson was in order.

Z and myself took the first train from Toledo. Kiki was with the flowers, there was nothing to keep me there now. How one so ethereally beautiful could possess such a cancerous disease of the soul is beyond my reckoning.

I was reminded of the malevolent capriciousness of that other nemesis of literary greatness, Lord Alfred Douglas. Bosie, the ruin of dear Oscar Wilde.

Young Bobby had been in touch with Herr Fruitus and informed him of our visit and despite the lateness of our arrival, a black limousine was waiting for us at the deserted railway station. There was thunder lurking among the black clouds. I could smell the ozone fried sweetness of sheet lightning and, I swear, a wolf howled in the distance. Our limo was driven at high speed by an unseen driver through towering black pine forests along the winding roads of the forbidding mountain. The castle atop the summit occasionally revealed its gothic silhouette against the frequent stabs of white lightning. The rain came lashing down like a slaver's whip. Eventually our limousine pulled up at the castle gatehouse, the electric doors slid open letting in the pelting rain and the deafening sound of the storm. We dashed across the cobbled yard to the large oak door. Z pulled the bell and swore. I could hear the bell echoing around the bizarre castle perched like an eagle's nest atop one of the Tyrol district's more obscure peaks.

ME THE GOOD SAMARITAN?

Tombo Bamba had greased the right palms to get JC's cab and us parked up on the waterfront on the other side of some barbed-wire barriers from the heaving throng of our fellow would-be passengers. He's on board right now seeing if he can get us upgraded.

I would like to tell you that I hope he fails, that I want us to travel in the cheapest conditions possible but that isn't how I feel. I want to stamp my feet and scream, 'But do you know who we are? World famous, retired rock stars and Arctic explorers. We deserve the best you have. You should be honoured to have men like us on board. After we've written our book about our adventures on your shitty boat, legions of white and wealthy tourists will start pouring in wanting to travel and spend good Yankee dollar on whatever you have to offer. So...' No, I'm not thinking that. I don't know what I'm thinking. I suppose I'm trying to suppress thought and just be.

A young lad has just brought my introversion to an end. He's about eight or nine. He's got a couple of baguettes wrapped up in a tea towel. He's wanting to sell them to me. He's trying to unroll them from the tea towel when he drops them. A big black woman appears from somewhere and starts screaming, and slapping and kicking him. Is this because he dropped the baguettes or for some previous misdemeanour? Whatever it was, it reminds me of a scene from *Alice in Wonderland*. A scene not reflected upon by Grace Slick.

I decide that looking the other way is the best tactic. Clearly all those Sunday School teachers who attempted to drum the parable of the Good Samaritan into me at an impressionable age had not quite achieved their aim.

While looking the other way and ignoring the screams of the young lad as he gets his beating, I enjoy the wide vista across the mighty Congo River. On the low horizon of the far shore, ten miles distant at a guess, lies Brazzaville, the capital city of somewhere else. On the river three ferry boats are plying their way to and fro. These don't hold my interest, but the large clumps of vegetation floating on the river do. There are bright green, egret-type birds perched on some of them. Some have chunky pink flowers. Maybe they are called river hyacinths but as I have no Central African or any other kind of natural history reference books with me I will never know.

Maybe you could make yourself useful here by doing a bit of research: find out exactly what kind of pink flowering vegetation it is, and send the information to whoever ends up publishing this book. The address should be at the front somewhere. Then, if the editor is willing, your research could be added to future editions of this text. Right here...

So, the parable of the Good Samaritan may not have had the desired impact on my better self, but at least my diversion from that scene has lead to offering you, the reader, a small way of interacting with the evolving text of this tome. The screams of the lad who dropped the baguettes have diminished. I turn from admiring the view. In the distance I see the boy being led away by the large woman using that ear-pulling method so beloved by teachers in my youth but now, I understand, outlawed in these modern and liberal times. But not here.

*

My pedestrian imagination had prepared me for some RKO dwarf lurching from the shadows but it was the master himself, Herr Fruitus who greeted us. The massive hallway smelled of neglect, damp and woodworm. Fruitus held a hurricane lamp aloft and explained that most of the castle was shut down and that his mother and himself occupied only a few rooms in the eastern tower. Young Bobby, Herr Fruitus informed us had arrived a little earlier in the day and was resting at the moment.

'A charming young fellow,' commented Fruitus, his English tinged with a slight American accent. 'And so erudite, a virtue unusual in one so young.'

I felt a fatherly pride swell in my breast for my young protégé.

I felt myself strangely attracted to the somewhat fey Mr Fruitus. We made our way up a wide spiral stone staircase and then through a maze of corridors towards the eastern tower

'Grandmama has retired for the night,' said Fruitus. 'She is 97 next October. Dear Granny, I don't think she will see another spring.'

I watched Fruitus's lithe shadow flutter in front of me, there was a feminine sway to his gait, his voice was soft, musical.

'Mother and Grandmama loved London in the spring – the crocuses, so beautiful. We often spend a month or so in Kensington between the end of March and the beginning of May.'

We arrived at another oak door, Fruitus pushed it open and beckoned us in. A warm yellow light bathed the luxurious apartment creating a cosy intimacy one would never have believed possible from outside.

Our host turned to us. 'Welcome. Now does anyone need a drink, I certainly do,' he said moving towards a well stocked drinks cabinet.

FILMING THE NIGGERS

For a few moments I was almost able to hold on to a calmness, alone with my thoughts about future readers in far-off places raiding equatorial natural history shelves of their local reference libraries. This fantasy has now dissolved as I see Z heading in my direction.

'Bill, you've got to fuckin' tell him now.'

'What?'

'His fuckin' video camera. Get it off him, hand it over to JC. I've tried reasoning with him, he won't listen. Just go and take it and hand it over to JC. I've already arranged it, JC's willing to look after it until our return to Kinshasa. Bill, do it now!'

There is a hysteria about Z's current demeanour that I've seen before. Its root cause I don't know. What I do know is that it is often brought on by either a sudden lack or an over-abundance of alcohol. I want to tell Z that I don't give a shit if Gimpo has his video camera or not but somehow Z's state persuades me that something should be done.

'OK Z, where is he?'

'Over there, on the other side of those sheds, filming the niggers trying to lift a taxi from the dockside on to the deck using nothing but bamboo poles and bits of string.'

'You stay here. I'll sort it out.'

'Yeah, I'll stay here, get on with writing. And Bill, if you have to, throw it in the river.'

*

Fruitus was beautiful. Thick flaxen hair with a floppy fringe that covered one eye, full red lips, long aristocratic neck and eyes as blue as a Caribbean lagoon. The blonde Adonis wore a powder-blue jacket many sizes too large for him draped across his shoulders. He noticed Z paying close attention to the braiding and insignia that decorated the jacket.

'You like Great-granpa's jacket?' he tittered, 'I have all of Grandaddy Goering's old uniforms. Of course they're all far too large for me to wear, Granpa was rather a large Nazi, but they do make lovely dressing gowns, don't you think?'

Fruitus was feeling playful, he pointed one of his elegant feet towards us. He was wearing ruby slippers.

'Grandaddy loved that movie, I think he identified with Dorothy. Now, can I get anybody anything? I'm having a large brandy. Bill? Z? We have an excellent cellar of vintage wines. Heroin? Morphine?'

Z's attention switched from examining the Third Reich needlework on Fruitus' jacket.

'It's excellent quality. Grandaddy and Mr Hitler liberated all the pharmaceutical opiates from the Parisian hospitals just after they had taken that divine city. I've still got sacks of the stuff down in the sick room.'

Z shamelessly grabbed several dozen bottles of vintage wine and a couple of bags of grade-A hospital smack and made his way down to the room Fruitus had provided for us. I didn't see him for a week. And what a week that was, sailors.

TRYING TO SOUND ASSERTIVE

I've just sauntered down the quayside, round the shed and found Gimpo helping a gang of black dockers load a beat-up Dormobile on to the one square inch of deck space not already crammed with baggage, tackle, goods and rubbish. I was going to say that Gimpo seemed to be in charge but that was not quite the case. Nobody seems to be in charge but the other hands are finding it jolly good sport watching the white man getting down to some backbreaking work. And, of course, Gimpo always loves the challenge of solving a practical problem which involves him displaying his physical strength.

I'd almost forgotten the video camera business when I noticed a young lad lying on the ground, the camera in hand, filming the whole loading the Dormobile scene. Here I am admiring Gimpo's skills at mucking in with the savages when in fact it's all just a display to be filmed by this lad so Gimpo can impress whoever he thinks might be impressed by his doings back in London.

'Hey Gimpo, I wanna talk to you.'

I'm trying to sound assertive.

'Yeah, what?'

'The video camera, I've decided you can't take it with you on the boat.'

'Why?'

'You know why. You know what we've been told. Laws of the land and all that. We've got to respect that, we are just guests here.'

'Bill, it's got fuck all to do with any of that and you know it. It's Z. For some reason he's jealous of me and my camera.'

'Jealous of what?'

'He's scared of the truth it may tell of him. And I know that you don't give a fuck but you're too weak to stand up to him.'

'Gimpo, I don't want to have to say this but we have paid for your ticket to be over here and provided a generous per diem for you. If it wasn't for us would you have ever had the chance of coming to a place like this?'

'Don't fuckin' start down that road, Bill. If I'm here as an employee I want top mercenary rates, full insurance and two grand up front and in the bank.'

'OK, OK.'

'So I'm here as an equal. You two are writing a book. I'm making a film.'

'I understand, Gimpo but...'

'No buts, Bill, that's the way it is or I'm off on my own. You go and tell Z that.'

And just before I have to think of a way of manoeuvring around my weakness of character I see JC, Tombo Bamba and some other man, who's dressed up in grubby Navy whites, coming down the gangplank and heading our way.

'Boys, everything is good. I have got you cabin. You don't share. It clean. Everything fine. We go. But first, Gimpo I must ask you to leave camera with me. It not allowed on board. It get stolen. I take it back to Memling. They keep it in safe. You get it on your return.'

Without hesitation and with no tone of resignation, Gimpo says 'That will be fine.' He then turns to the lad still lying on the ground and says 'cut'. Only now do I realise that all my negotiating with Gimpo has been caught on film.

The lad hands the camera to Gimpo who packs it carefully in its case, and hands the case over to JC. Then he smiles at me. Situation resolved.

*

The passions Fruitus unleashed within my staunch manly libido during that glorious semester from reason I am ashamed to admit temporarily blotted out all memory of dear Kiki. Fruitus was decadence incarnate. His demonic sensuality opened my eyes to vistas of nectareous pleasure I never would have believed existed. It was the beautifully damned Fruitus who enabled me to find the raped woman inside myself, that battered anima, whipped and beaten almost to death by the skinhead Christ of the Presbyterians.

I resisted at first but eventually I was camping around like a born-again drag queen. We raided Grandmama's old dressing-up trunk and laughed ourselves senseless, buggering and fellating wildly among the old frocks. Unfortunately our mad love affair was scintillatingly brief and again ended in tragedy.

The beautiful Fruitus revealed himself one mask too far. The free-spirited beauty truly was damned, he was possessed of a demon that was treacherous and consumed with self destructive evil. The legacy of those occult buffoons the Nazis perhaps ? Was the blood of the master chumps fucking up Fruitus's moral intelligence?

MY FATE

I go to get Z. I find him where I left him, tittering to himself as he fills his empty pages with more lies.

'Hey Z, time to board. We got a cabin.'

'Yeah but did you get Gimpo to hand over the camera?'

'Yeah, no problem.'

'Knew he would listen to you, Bill.'

Z packs his journal away and we head back to Gimpo, JC and the other two. Z is whistling Colonel Bogey. I hate people whistling. He is yo-yoing his yo-yo. I hate that as well. We get to the gangplank.

I'm looking up at what we are about to board. I recognise that I will never have the literary skills to describe what I'm feeling now. Maybe other writers would be able to put on paper for you what it feels like to face certain death. Not me.

Right now I'm more than willing to accept that my soul has long since been sold. Eternity in hell is my just desserts and the rest of my life will be spent evading this fate as long as I don't have to board this, this, this... whatever it fuckin' is.

'Come on, Bill get a move on. I say we dump our bags in the cabin and head for the bar.'

Sometimes I wish that Z's alcoholism had killed him before things had got this far.

*

Openly I confess that my own morality is considered wicked and debased by the unenlightened masses. This has always been the price paid by those cursed and blessed with genius. I do however have certain ethical standpoints, one of these being that if a chap can't wait till a child has reached the age of at least 12 or 13 before schooling him in the ways of Sodom then he's nothing but a degenerate and deserves all that the tabloids fling at him.

I was taking a rest from our breathless love, washing the shit off my bollocks when I heard a familiar whimper from one of the rooms in the tower. I raced up a few stairs and kicked down a locked door and there he was. Young Bobby, chained to a radiator, his cub scout uniform in tatters, his eyes red from tears, blood and fecal matter leaking from his torn rectum. I slew Fruitus generously, a single stiletto to the heart, he deserved much worse.

I am beginning to understand the poetry of Rolo. He is right of course. For us queers love *is* all. I felt a hot tear sting my cheek as I pulled my sucking steel from Fruitus's breast.

THE JAPANESE SCULPTOR

As Z and I drove off the Larne to Stranraer ferry and out across the bleak landscape of the ancient and now forgotten county of Wigtonshire, I remembered that it was at times like these when my mind starts to lose its moorings in mundane reality (read 'forgets real life responsibilities') that some great internal shift in my mental make-up was trying to happen. This seeking of mystical interpretations in the mere coincidental is the sound of the subconscious rummaging about.

Along the A47 we flew in silence, bypassing the haunts of my boyhood. When we got to the granite quarry a mile or so past Creetown, we turned off the road for a slash – those early morning pints of Guinness needed releasing. Although I had passed the entrance to this quarry thousands of times as a boy, I had never entered it. At primary school we would hear the far-off boom of the quarrymen at work with their sticks of dynamite. Back then I was always too afraid to enter this quarry. I would cycle the few miles out of Newton Stewart and stand at the quarry gates by the big red sign that said 'DANGER OF DEATH – KEEP OUT', wait to hear one of the great booms then feel the rush of air and dust followed by the rumbling and crashing as the granite rocks fell. In my boyhood imagination one of the gates to hell could possibly be found behind that red 'DANGER OF DEATH' sign. But not any longer. What Z and I found was a huge silence, a large, clear, deep, deep pool of water. If we were kids, we would have stripped off and dived into it. The walls of the quarry towered over us, white quartz granite glittering with flecks of mica. The quarry men had obviously long since left with their sticks of dynamite and their sandwiches wrapped in greaseproof paper. A muffled echo followed each of our footsteps. We came across some large granite boulders that had been fashioned into what I supposed must be a type of sculpture. The sort of stuff that Henry Moore might have done when he wasn't doing reclining Madonnas with holes in. The sort of thing that large corporations in the 1960s would like to have displayed in front of their administrative HQ. The sort of thing that bores us these days. But here these large rounded lumps of granite looked fine. In place. Serene. I can remember admiring their rounded fullness, like the belly of a pregnant woman. Each of these works of art were mounted on rough and ready cairns made from smaller rocks and railway sleepers. On the ground around them were flakes and chips of granite where they landed as the artists, chisel in one hand and mallet the other, sought the shape that he needed. Z was silenced, a rare occasion.

We had assumed we were alone until, 'Excuse me, gentlemen, can I help you?' Z and I turned to find an Asian man in his late youth dressed in working clothes approaching us.

'Are these yours?' asked Z.

'Yes, I live here in the hut and out here I make my art.'

His accent was heavy.

'We too are artists. We are on our way to the dark continent where we are going to find the Fallen Angel and trick him into giving us back our souls.'

I don't recall how this Japanese sculptor responded to Z's proclamation. What I do remember is that it was the first time that either of us had told anyone what we were off to do.

*

Poor Bobby, his incredible intellect was his undoing. The occasional advantage of a type of divine ignorance is not to be overlooked on our perilous quest towards selfhood. I freed him from his bondage, he was delirious at first and didn't recognise me. I gave him a small injection of morphine to calm him down.

'Oh Arcaler, it's you.'

His weak voice indicated he was coming to his senses.

I took a needle and some surgical cotton and fixed the little tyke's arse.

That poor bastard Fruitus, I should have known that the unhinged nature of his aristocratic sexuality would never stop at pederasty. I found passage home for young Bobby and set about detoxing Z.

Z's sensual appetites seem to be completely selfish, the idea of involving another human being in his gargantuan excesses seems to strike my friend as being absolutely ludicrous. He resents giving perverse pleasure even to the comeliest of submissives.

WHEN I WAS 19

When I was 19 I wanted to jump out of an aeroplane. I'd seen an ad on the pinboard in the art school canteen. Twelve quid for one day's training and then a parachute jump from 3,000 feet. So one Friday evening me and my mate John Mears hitched down to Penny Farthing airstrip, somewhere in the West Midlands, handed over our respective 12 quids. Spent the Saturday learning how to roll over on hitting the ground, and all the things not to do. On the Sunday morning us two and about half-a-dozen other minor thrill-seekers folded up the parachutes given to us, put on white flying suits and orange helmets and clambered aboard a six-seater biplane. It was made from canvas stretched over a wooden frame and painted grey. Up until then I didn't know that planes could be built from such flimsy materials as canvas and lengths of 2 x 1 pine. This concerned me, as did the information that our instructor imparted to us that it had been built in 1934. I tried to comfort myself with the idea that since it was made from canvas stretched across a wooden frame, like an oil painting, what we were about to do might be in some way connected to art. Dying in the name of art seemed more noble than dying in the pursuit of adrenline-thrills.

Other than the one for the pilot, there were no seats. We all had to crouch on the floor, one behind the other, the instructor at the front facing us. The engine started. It roared louder than anything I'd ever heard. The biplane headed down the runway and lurched into the air. There were no portholes, I could see little more than the helmet in front of me. We kept climbing, being buffeted this way and that. After about 20 minutes the instructor started with his hand signals, ones we had learnt to read, understand and follow the day before. There were three other idiots in front of me. One by one they obeyed his hand-signalled instructions and were off and out the plane heading for whatever destiny had in store for them. Then it was my turn. The instructor gave signal one, which meant I had to move forward. It was then that something happened to me. The thinking, decision-making part of my mind made a statement: 'I'm out of here Drummond, anything you do from here on in is nothing to do with me'.

I did move forward to the open door. I was following orders. The second hand signal was given. This meant I had to climb out of the door on to the lower wing, holding on to the struts between the lower and upper wings. I was now just a lump of meat following orders. My mind had well and truly scarpered. If the next instruction had been to decapitate my mother, kill my first born or press the red button, I would have done so without hesitation. The instructor then gave his third and final hand signal. This one meant I was to let go of the struts and leap backwards into the void.

This is when I lost consciousness. The parachute was on a fixed line, so I didn't have to pull a rip cord to open it. I came to, not knowing where or who the fuck I was. Then I remembered and I enjoyed the next couple of minutes drifting earthwards before smashing to the ground like a sack of potatoes, having totally ignored all the landing techniques I'd been taught the previous day. Nothing was broken. And John Mears and I hitched back to Liverpool and got on with putting paint on canvas that had been stretched over wooden frames.

The reasons for relating this anecdote now are various. First and foremost my purpose is to take my mind off the reality I find myself in. Second, that after doing this jump I arrived at the position that I thought it pathetic to ever get your adrenaline kicks in life from prepackaged, dangerous sport pursuits. In my elitist mind they are the sort of thing that men on middle-management ladders to success do at weekends to make their lives feel more vital. So no hang-gliding, skiing, white-water rafting etc. The working reality of one life should produce all the adrenaline rushes that a man needs. Third, what I witnessed in myself for those few seconds above the fields of Avalon is what I suppose every well trained infantry man should achieve – a state of mind where you automatically follow orders without ever considering their implications for yourself or others.

In the past 20 or so minutes I may have broken with both of these life-governing tenets that I've held on to for the past 25 years. At the very moment I put my foot on the gangplank that leads us on to this heap of rusting, dilapidated and certainly not MOT-passing, heap of just-about-floating metal, my free and proud mind repeated that statement it made in 1973: 'I'm out of here, Drummond, anything you do from here on in is nothing to do with me.'

And so it went, for the time it took for Gimpo, Z and me to clamber over sacks of maize, screaming babies, squealing pigs; for the time it took to squeeze through heaving and throbbing, pushing and shoving black humanity; the time it took to leap from one barge to the next; the time it took to climb a broken ladder above the flowing Congo; the time it took for us to pass along the narrow walkway to an unlit, metal cubicle containing a pair of bunks that was to be our home for the next three weeks or so; the time it took for JC and Tombo Bambo to shake our hands and say their farewells; the time it took for Gimpo and Z to tell me they were going in search of the bar; and for the time it took me to climb up on to one of the top bunks, open my bag, get my notebook and pencil out. That was the point when my mind came back and said, 'What the fuck are you doing Drummond?' I didn't answer. It then said, 'This escapade is nothing more than one of those dangerous sport experiences they have on middle-management bonding weekends that you have spent your life decrying. This is nothing more than trying to make up for the fact that you have never done anything in your life that...'

'Ah fuck off and leave me alone. If you don't like it here, go back home. I don't give a shit for any of the real motivation that has brought me, us, you or the fuckin' puppets in the bag here. We are here and we have to deal with it.'

So I am dealing with it in the only way I know how, by filling empty pages with words.

Chapter Four
LARIUM

Imagine the most bumhole, shite-infested, death-trap, electrocution, Satan's sphinctoid shanty town wankpit on earth. Take three of them and pile them on top of each other, float them on a black river of shit and, just maybe, you might get an idea of what, for the next month or so, we were going to call home.

Arthur's man bullied his way through the heaving masses slashing around with one of the soldiers bayonets and showed us our cabin: a fetid steel box with no windows and no lights. Two fucked-up rusty bunk beds hung off the slime dripping walls. The floor is two inches deep with some kind of fecal slurry from the single latrine next door to our cabin. This single shitter had to suffice for more than 3,000 passengers.

There were five barges in all lashed together by lethal-looking steel ropes to the main motorised pusher barge, the *Colonel Ebeya*.

My insanity was creeping up fast , I could feel its hot dogshit breath wet in my ear. Johnny Panic, a lascivious demon the alcohol usually kept at bay, was jerking off in my other ear. The horror was deafening.

I didn't think I was going to last long on this floating Gomorrah. There were so many people all jammed together it was a struggle to breathe. Although I didn't know it at the time we were incredibly lucky to have any form of private accommodation at all. Most of the other passengers were travelling deck class, which meant trying to find the least shite-covered piece of deck available among all the swirling insanity, screaming babies on the tit, wild pigs being clumsily butchered and those creepy little Lualaba bucket kids hanging around sick people and unhealthy babies.

STOICS UNITED

'Wake up Bill.'

'Ya what?'

It's Gimpo. I'd fallen asleep in my bunk after writing all that stuff about jumpin' out of a plane. 'It's fuckin' brilliant isn't it?'

'Where's Z?'

'I've left him at the bar, happy as a sandboy, on to his third bottle of Primus and already storming into his writing, something about calling him Ishmael. Come on, the boat's going to be leaving soon. Don't you want to wave goodbye to Kinshasa?' Gimpo seems happier than I've seen him since that time he took those six Es.

Time to stiffen my upper lip. Time to renew my membership to Stoics United. Time to put my introspection away and follow Gimpo to wherever the bar is.

Truly we had arrived in Hell. The fat fuck at the river port had shafted us. A bunch of sleazy looking Japs had commandeered all the first-class accommodation, they'd even hired themselves a tame nigger, a ridiculous looking idiot in a red tracksuit festooned with big zoom lens 1970s cameras and other electronic crap he'd blagged off the Japs. House boy liked nothing more than strutting around and looking important, unaware that the little kids up on the roof laughed at his ridiculous pomposity behind his weird snob-retard back.

We stood a while in our prison cell like cabin, dazed.

An irascible barefoot African with a shiny bald head, vicious looking tribal scars, big wiry muscles and filed pointed teeth stomped into the room splashing my safari suit with the slurry on the cabin floor. He was carrying three feculent slabs of foam rubber which he thrust angrily at us. It took a while to realise that these lice-infested pieces of industrial packaging were to be our mattresses.

What's more, the bald-headed cannibal was sharing our cabin.

Call me fucking Ishmael.

CALL ME FUCKING ISHMAEL

'"Call me fucking Ishmael."'

'Ya what Bill?'

'"Call me fucking Ishmael."' Have you used that as the opening line of your on-ship text?'

'No, why?'

'Well Gimpo said you were writing something about calling yourself Ishmael.'

'Yeah but not as the opening line.'

'So what is your opening line?'

Z picks up his black journal, adjusts his specs and reads, '"Imagine the most bumhole, shite-infested, death trap, electrocuting, Satan's sphinctoid shantytown, wankpit on earth." That's it. Do you have a problem with it?'

'No.'

'So what's your problem?'

I don't answer. I sit down and sip my Coca Cola through a straw and start writing. I followed Gimpo all the way from our cabin, clambering over all we had clambered over when we first boarded ship an hour or so ago. The three of us are now sitting in the spacious but severely functional lounge bar, at the rear upper deck of the diesel-driven pusher whose job it is to push the flotilla all the way up the Congo to Kisangani. I've just learnt from Gimpo that it's called the *Colonel Ebeya*. Whoever *Colonel Ebeya* is or what he did to have this ferry-cum-barge-cum-rust bucket named after him I don't know, probably killed a load of white colonial oppressors. As for my outburst with Z about who gets to be called Ishmael, you may already have guessed the explanation. Most people who are addicted to high literature, as Z and myself are, have a favourite opening line. For many a woman it is 'a truth universally acknowledged that a single man in possession of a good fortune, must be in want of a wife.'

My favourite opening line is from the greatest piece of nineteenth-century American literature, *Moby Dick*. Some weeks ago I lent Z my worn and treasured edition of the book and suggested he might read it before we headed out on our voyage to harpoon Satan. Z fell instantly in love with the book and decided it should be used as the blueprint for our own epic tale, the one you're now this far into, and then proclaimed that its opening line was also his favourite.

That's when the jealousy started to burn in me. If anybody is going to be Ishmael on this journey it's going to be fucking me.

*

The lithe man-eater slung himself on one of the lower bunks, claiming his berth. Gimpo and Bill, obviously more alert than myself, leapt on to the top and bottom of the other bunk, leaving me to sleep directly above cannibal fucking Joe.

The nervous breakdown was racing hard on the inside, catching up fast. My heartbeat was hitting fours on the floor and someone had turned on the flashing lights. My legs were the first to go, wobbling like rubber, then my arms wanted some of that shaky action and pretty soon my whole body was rocking big time to the dypso boogaloo. Fortunately Doc Gimp saw the signs of imminent alcoholic calamity and poured me a half pint of rum and fed it to me just in time.

Johnny Panic and his ugly buddy madness retreated for a while, but I knew the rum wouldn't keep them at bay forever. That's the really shitty thing about being an addict, your medicine is also your poison. The shit that gets rid of the symptoms is also the shit that's causing them, the chump's dilemma. Believe me sick junkies, your cold turkeys are as nothing compared to the torched buzzards of an alcoholic's withdrawals.

I made my way to the bar which was no mean feat believe me. The length of the flotilla was the size of two football pitches. We were up on the front barge and the bar was way at the back on the first-class section of the *Colonel Ebeya*.

To reach this oasis of comparative cleanliness and white paint you had to traverse about 3,000 other people by climbing up and down rusting broken ladders, balancing across treacherous rooftops, squeezing through thumping, deafening engine rooms, avoiding the knives in the dark sweltering kitchens, making the four-foot leap from barge to barge, negotiating the live crocodiles tied beneath the benches, not to mention the monster turtles, wild pigs and the crazy butchers preparing still groaning monkeys.

The whole flotilla was basically a huge floating supermarket, a drifting bazaar that sold shiny plastic shit: mirrors, razors, batteries, plastic buckets and Jerry cans, T shirts. In fact anything that couldn't be made from jungle shit: bamboo, vines, dried mud etc.

The villagers up river sold the stallholders fresh meat, monkeys, pineapples, coconuts, fish, peanuts, fruits of the rainforest-kind of vibe and with the money they got from the stallholders they would buy the plastic shit.

The stallholders sold all the rainforest stuff in Kisangani and Kinshasha and then restocked with the shiny shit and got back on the boat and did it all again.

A lot of the traders had been making this journey for upwards of 20 years and actually lived on the barges.

ABRAHAM'S TRUE SON

'Look Z, sorry about my outburst, it's just that I...'

'That's OK, sailor boy. Do you want to read my opening paragraph to this chapter?'

I read it. You've probably already read it 'cause I imagine that the way this chapter will be edited together it will appear at the beginning.

'It's fucking brilliant Z, other than the bit about soldiers and bayonets you've not exaggerated it at all. What with that description of what these barges are like in Gimpo's *Lonely Planet* guide and your opening paragraph it alleviates any need on my part to try and describe the overall vibe of the place.'

'Your round, Bill.'

'OK. What do you want?'

'I want a triple vodka but all the bar stocks is Primus and Coke.'

Reading this banter between me and Z regarding Ishmael, you'd think I was the edgier one but there's something about Z that is definitely more unhinged than usual. He is displaying an ever-growing collection of nervous tics, the most noticeable of which is that he keeps looking over his shoulder every ten seconds or so, as if he thinks somebody is coming up behind him.

Gimpo has been sitting silently sipping his beer and staring up at the large ceiling fan that is turning lazily and making no difference to the hot and heavy air. Then he turns to the both of us.

'So, who the fuck is Ishmael?'

'Well, he is the bastard son of Abraham. His mother was Hagar the beautiful, handmaiden to Abraham's wife, Sarah. He and his mother were banished to wander the southern desert by the understandably jealous...'

'Well Bill, you seem to be sticking to the strictly biblical telling of the tale,' interjects Z. 'In the Koran there is no mention of him being a bastard, he is Abraham's true son and heir and Isaac with his Israelite offspring was very much the second and minor brother.'

'So what's this got to do with calling yourself Ishmael and that book about whaling that you've both been going on about?'

And before either of us can muster the energy to answer Gimpo's enquiry we are shaken to our very souls by a mighty and lengthy blast of the ship's horn. Then a huge shuddering of the engines from somewhere deep below us, followed by a great shunting. Z is jolted from his seat and his bottle lands on the floor and rolls across it to the open door. I laugh heartily at my good friend. We are on our way and, oh yeah, you can call me Ishmael. William Ishmael Drummond.

THE BOOK OF GiMPO BY GiMPO

Z fucking lost it. I knew he would. At least Bill got his over with quickly, dressing like a tart, poncing around in the bar singing Shirley Bassey songs.

He seems all right this morning though, well, apart from his bummer's sailor suit. The bellbottoms are obscene, they make his arse look massive and squash his bollocks all up against his leg like a perverted ballet dancer.

But Z, man, he went totally loco. A bloke came running into our cabin yelling about some white guy up on the quarterdeck, he'd stolen the barman's handgun and was shooting the fuck out of everyone, ranting in Bible language. Bill jumped down from his top bunk splashing me with shit.

'I'll handle this, Gimp,' he said in some kind of war-film hero voice.

'It's probably the Larium,' he quickly rummaged through his kit bag for his cocktail dress and high heels.

It wasn't the Larium, I've seen Z pull this shit before. It used to happen all the time when we did long tours with the band. He'd be dead normal one minute, reading one of his weird books and then for no reason he'd just flip into psycho mode, torturing and murdering groupies in his bunk with pliers and electricity and stuff. I wouldn't have minded but he used to use all the stuff out of my tool box. I'd get them back in the morning and they'd be covered in dried fanny batter, blood, spunk, snake oil and shit. Fucking horrible.

The twat usually couldn't remember what had happened and then me and the lighting guy, Stevie McBastard would have to go and get rid of the stupid slag's body. Fuck it man, we were on good wages in them days and if the tour got cancelled because of some stupid murder trial we would have lost fucking thousands.

FAREWELL TO KINSHASA

Gimpo, Z and myself are leaning on the white painted railings of the small deck outside the lounge bar. What we are watching is probably the wildest mass outpouring of human emotion that any of us has ever witnessed. The flotilla is edging its way from the dockside. Below is what must be more than a thousand Africans going stark staring crazy as they leap up and down, waving both arms in the air. Those that have space are running in circles. Foolhardy teenage lads are leaping the widening gap from dock to deck. Except there is no deck space for them to land on 'cause it's already crammed with passengers going stark-staring crazy, leaping up and down, waving every arm they have at those on the dockside. So these foolhardy, teenage lads are either being grabbed by the more concerned or quick-witted and are drawn into the mass of deck passengers or they fall into the swirling and sucking water below. This everybody finds incredibly joyous, even those in the water with their bobbing heads and spaz-style doggy paddle. The one thing that the black man is truly crap at is swimming. His lack of gold, silver or even bronze medals for any kind of water event in the Olympics is in some way indicative of his lack of swimming prowess.

The horn goes off again. We head steadily away from the shore and at an angle against the mighty flow. I've got over all that stuff when I was going on about jumping out of planes. The inner station here we come. Satan, you better be ready. Feet won't fail me now.

It's late afternoon. A large orange sun is dropping vertically towards the western horizon. The sky is turning a thousand shades of pink and purple and still kids are leaping from the barges to swim the 200, 300, 400 yards to the darkening shore.

'Hey Bill. Let's get back to the cabin. I don't fancy trying to make it in the dark.'

*

America was the worst, Z reckoned that killing groupies was legal in the states. God knows how many sluts we buried in that Arizona dessert. Finland as well, that was pretty awful. There's a lot of dead girlies beneath that frozen tundra.

I followed Bill up the stairs, through the engine rooms where the gasolene made your eyes sting, leapt from barge to barge, through the sweaty kitchen, across the roof, past the witch doctor and finally got to the bar.

There were only four bodies, maybe he threw the rest overboard. Z was sat in the corner with the gun in his mouth, shaking and ranting, you couldn't hear what he was saying properly because of the gun. His eyes had rolled up into the back of his head, he looked fucking horrible.

'Z,' said Bill, quiet but firm

'It's me, Bill. Bill and Gimpo, your friends.'

Z pulled the gun out of his mouth and started firing at us. The bullets missed by inches, splintering into the wood behind us. He was ranting all this bible shit about the Devil, deserts, temptation and stuff like some mental preacher.

I've seen him do this bollocks before. We were on a tour bus on our way to Italy from Switzerland up in some mountains when he started doing this scary preacher stuff. The bus crashed into the side of the road when Z decided to baptise the driver by pissing on him from the front lounge. That was when Slam left the band. He didn't mind all the dead groupies, in fact I think he killed a few himself, but as soon as the grim reaper started sniffing around his underpants that was it, he was out of there.

'Hail Satan! Hail horror!' shouted Z and started firing the gun at Bill. The gun clicked, it was either out of bullets or jammed.

I leapt at him and slammed him to the deck.

'Bill!' I shouted. 'Rum!'

Bill knew exactly what to do, he jumped over the bar past the dead barman and started scrabbling around manicly, smashing shit and opening draws.

'There's no rum! No hard liquor at all, just fucking beer, Primus!' he shouted.

'Bring as much as you can carry.'

I knew Z was having withdrawals, torched buzzards we called them.

There was no hard liquor so we had to feed him fuck loads of beer to try and get his blood/alcohol level up to its normal mix.

A FAILED AHAB

In the cabin Gimpo is sorting out his mosquito net, Z is rubbing himself down with huge dollops of some sort of lime-green cream, I'm on my bunk feeling good.

'What the fuck are you doing, Z?'

'Malaria cream. Got to protect yourself.'

'What with Gimpo and his net and you and your cream, what kind of example is that to set the natives?'

'Bill, that kinda talk may have been faintly humorous in a bar back in Clerkenwell but here it's just stupidity. If you get malaria you're dead. We ain't built up the immunities that the locals have.'

'Yeah but would Stanley or Livingstone have used cream? Next you'll be advocating water-purifying pills and that's it, you'll be on the slippery slope down to underarm deodorant and the rest.'

'Ah fuck off. And anyway I've just thought of something. You're not Ishmael, you're a failed Ahab. Ahab without the strength of character.'

I don't reply. We fall silent. A black man has just entered our cabin and climbed on to the one free bottom bunk. I've never slept in the same room as a black man.

Z tries to whisper something across to me.

'Ya wha'?'

'Queequeg, Bill. It's Queequeg.'

Why didn't I make that observation first? It's always crap when an associate makes a witty observation and you say 'I was thinking the same thing myself', as if anyone the fuck cares if you were thinking the same thing. You never said it, never acted upon the thought. It's as if Martin Luther is up there giving it 'I had a dream' and you are down there going, 'Funny you should say that Martin, I had the same dream, just that I...' did fuck all about it other than tell the readers that I've never slept in the same room as a black man. Not quite the same thing as telling the world about a little white boy walking along hand-in-hand with a little black girl down in Alabama, now is it Bill?

I'd like to report that I drift off to my slumbers but I don't. I've now been lying here for a couple of hours. It's the non-stop music. I'm having to listen to seven different ghetto blasters simultaneously pumping out non-stop Afro pop. The nearest of the blasters is in the cabin next door to ours. From there on they seem to be dotted around the barge we are on and the neighbouring one. Up until these past few days I've totally associated this sort of music with Andy Kershaw, the radio presenter. I keep expecting his Lancashire tones to cut in with something like, 'So that's a track from the fabulous new long player from the ever-wonderful Bhundu Boys.' It never crossed my mind that Africans would actually listen to it themselves. I just assumed they would go for all that aspirational R&B shit and gangsta-rap shite that the rest of the world has to accept as modern black music.

There are now only six blasters going. Lying here, eyes closed, I keep counting them, testing my spatial hearing judgement thing. I'm now working out which key the various tracks are in. Then the chord structures and then how many bars make up a verse and how the chorus is built. It is this uncontrollable habit of mine that made me never want to listen to another pop record again in my life. This total addiction to deconstructing everything I ever heard destroyed any appreciation I ever had for the glories of pop. All had been reduced to meaningless figures, facts, sums and calculations.

And I'm doing it now. Deciphering these confusing, conflicting, competing Afro-pop tunes that are conspiring to take over my brain. All with their skipping snare patterns and intricate but melodic guitar lines.

What I've learnt so far is that African musicians' favourite key to play in is C Major. They never play anything in a minor key. All their tunes are happy ones. They never write songs about heartbreak or anger or betrayal.

They never flatten their thirds or sevenths. And this is the confusing thing, all recorded black music that has ever come out of North America from the earliest ragtime to the latest R&B anthems is based on the flattening of the third and the seventh. It's what makes it sound black and non-European. It's what gives it attitude.

So how did this come about? Did something happen on the slave ships crossing the Atlantic to the New World that caused this evolution in music?

Ah fuck it. I don't want to be thinking this. I just want to sleep, and I do.

*

The fucking shit you learn tour-managing bands, fucking unbelievable. I've tour-managed dozens and believe me they're all the same. Every sad last one of them has some kind of primate wanking away on their backs, drugs, booze, women.

Z's got a whole fucking zoo of them up there and all of them carry knives. If those ugly bastards don't get what they want when they want, they start tearing the shit out of Z and whoever else is in the room with him.

It took us 47 bottles of beer to sober him down. That's the weird thing about alcoholics, I mean if you or I, or any other normal person drank 47 bottles of beer we'd be pretty fucked up, right? But with alkies it just makes them fucking normal. It's when they don't get their drink that the monkeys start hacking into them with their knives, wanking madness into their ears, and the voices telling them to kill everyone. When they're not drinking, that's when they're dangerous. I could tell when Z was back to normal because he started laughing at Bill's cocktail dress. I won't even try to work out what the dress shit was about.

'For God's sake man,' he said sternly to Z, 'Get a grip of yourself!'

And teetered away out of the bar in his size 11 stilettos. I noticed that he'd left one of his lingering ones, high putrescent eggs and milk on the turn.

MY FIRST SHIT

'Wake up Bill. Wake up.'

'Wha'? Wha'? Where are we? Are we there yet?'

'It's breakfast time. Come on.'

'Where's Z?'

'He's already there.'

'What, eating my breakfast?'

'No, getting on with his writing.'

That's enough to banish the sleep from my mind and bring the new day into focus. Z is already writing. What is he writing? What lies is he telling you? Don't listen to him, listen to me! But I'm already missing the day, missing the passing moments to be understood, explained, interpreted by me for you, for posterity.

I pull on my trousers, slip on my sandals and climb down from my bunk. The blasters are already blasting. The narrow walkway outside our cabin is already busy with morning washers, men shaving in hand-held pocket mirrors and women cooking on little portable stoves. Hives of activity buzzing all around. People with lives to live, stories to tell and I'm missing it.

I follow Gimpo. Breakfast. I wonder if they do black pudding or maybe kippers? Oh fuck, I'm about to shit myself. I'm clenching my flabby buttocks, trying to hold in the torrent of diarrhoea.

'Gimpo. Where's the shitter?'

'Just at the end here before we get to the ladder.'

There is a door, but no light. I shut the door. I'm in a cubicle of pitch black. There is no lav, no lock, no sink, no nothing, just a hole in the floor. I undo my belt, keeping one hand on the back of the door to prevent any would-be intruders from intruding. The other hand lowers my kegs and underpants making sure they don't slip too far and touch the sloppy floor. I loosen the clench on my buttocks, letting a Niagara of loose stools cascade. There is no point in trying to take aim. I have no idea how big the hole, I have no control of my motions or, come to that, my emotions.

I can feel splats that have bounced off the metal floor on to my calves, dribbling down to my ankles. Oh no! No bog paper. I'm dripping in my own diarrhoea and I've got nothing to wash it off or wipe it up with. Ah fuck it. Pull my pants and kegs up. Face the world like a man. If I smell of shit at least it's white-man shit. I wonder if there is any difference between white-man and black-man shit?

*

Bill and Gimpo told me that I flipped out yesterday. I didn't believe them at first, I couldn't remember a thing. Then they showed me the bloodstains and bullet holes up in the bar. They even showed me a couple of corpses, but that could have been anyone's doing. There were a lot of trigger-happy desperados in this jungle. Playing cards were scattered all over the floor, it must have been a card game that got out of hand.

I dismissed their accusations and wandered up to the quarterdeck to get some damp air. Up there by the silent captain, who apparently never spoke a word to anyone the whole journey, just kept his gaze laser beamed on to the black river, there was a small escape from the boiling intensity of sprawling life that busied itself all over the rest of the barge. I felt much calmer. I'd managed to locate a supply of jungle whiskey.

I noticed a nervous respect from the traders and an excited fear from the roofboys. Gimpo told me that the guys I had shot had been leaning on the stallholders for the past six months, and they were nervous because they thought that I would now start demanding money in return. I told Gimpo, who had become completely fluent in Lingala in just two days, to tell them that they had nothing to worry about. I wandered off to the back of the barges and climbed up on to the roof to be alone with myself.

IMPRESSING THE WOMENFOLK

'You stink of shit, Bill.'

'No I don't, Z.'

'Bill, you do.'

'It must be somebody else. Maybe one of those piccaninny kids or something.'

'Whatever you want Bill, but just sit down the other end of the table.'

So I sit down at the far end of the table, open my book to get on with these notes. I can still feel my trousers sticking to the back of my legs and I'm thinking these last few minutes of my life that have now been documented should well and truly put paid to any chance of me being able to impress the womenfolk with my star status as a risk-taking, hit-making, money-burning polymath of a man.

Ah well, maybe you think I'm just making it up to impress the more fucked-up of the readership. So I suppose I should move the story along from this rather distasteful topic and try to describe where we are sitting and waiting for our breakfast.

*

Our first night aboard I had been dreamily aware of the strange life forms dancing beneath my pillow, herds of graceful hippopotami, shoals of bizarre fish, undulating crocodile and eels.

And Queequeg of course, banging away on one of his concubines, she was moaning away and screeching like a panther on heat. Strange gurgling grunts, breathless words urging Queequeg to unload his giant junglenads. In the bunk opposite mine, shuffling madly beneath his mosquito net Basher Bill was murdering his fowl, one beady eye bulging out through a gap in the green netting spying on the frugging couple, the other rolled up into his head. Gimpo was making no attempt whatsoever to conceal his joyous appraisal of the lovers' vigorous coupling, sat on the edge of his bunk bopping his salami in time with Queequeg's smooth-stud wiggles as if Queequeg and his woman weren't actually there and he was just watching some skeezy vid he'd rented.

The shaggers knew Gimpo was sat there with his unabashed masturbation but didn't seem to mind. The ace fist artist jizzed politely into a piece of bog roll and turned in. Psycho tugger let rip an excitable one from the top bunk and soon snored off into whatever hell he visits in his troubled sleep.

It was about 3.00am when it hit me. The thing I'd dreaded since setting foot on the barge.

My stomach was tight, stabbing pains like low-voltage electricity throbbing around my lower abdomen quickly escalating into hot rapiers slicing through my guts.

The shits. Jungle shits.

I leapt from my bunk. Gimpo cussed, I'd splashed him with floor slurry.

I borrowed his Maglite and made my way to the khazi of horror. The decks were full of sleeping families you had to step over carefully in the small gaps of deck between them. My guts were burning up, cramps kicking in like an electric donkey. I finally located the rusting door, propped against the wall, its hinges broken and forgotten about long ago.

I decided that I didn't really want to see where I was going to stick my bare arse and turned off the torch.

I stepped into the carpet of burping soup, dark formless shapes snapped at my ankles. God and all his holy angels only know what kind of disgusting sub-species lived and fed in this shitter of Beelzebub.

A DESCRIPTIVE PASSAGE

The dining room is about 25 feet square with a low ceiling. As with our cabin, the floors, the walls and the ceiling are made from sheet metal. All dark, dark brown from years of rust and neglect. One wall is open to the passing river. On this side is a broken rail, not one that would prevent an infant or a drunken Z from tumbling into the waters below.

There are a couple of trestle tables and attendant benches. As with everything else in Zaire, excepting the mirror thing outside the barber's back in Kinshasa, there has been no attempt at decoration and everything is in a state of disrepair. And of course me being post-ironic, post-Duchampian, post-contemporary and post-everything else you can think of, love is just the way it is.

In the corner of this room are huddles of mothers with all their worldly goods tied up in dirty bundles. Babies are strapped to their backs, naked toddlers with distended bellies are staggering about. Older kids, but kids still young enough to be in some way under their mother's control, racing and screaming about. All the girls have plaits up to about eight inches long that spring out from their heads and bounce about as they run around.

The mothers show no concern about the likelihood of their offspring taking a tumble over the open side of the canteen into the river. Is this because they are bad mothers? Is this because mothers in the UK are over-protective? Is this because the mothers in Africa have so many kids that the odd kid falling to certain death into the swirling waters below is just a form of natural selection, ensuring the stupid, slow-learning, less sure-footed children get weeded out early, allowing only the fast-thinking, fleet-footed ones to grow and deal with the bad hand that fate has dealt them?

'And who are you to say that being born black in this continent is a bad hand?'

Well, I'm here right now and you're not and my subjectivity feels pretty objective to me.

*

The Central African ethnographically is known to be the world's speediest dumpsters, only taking a shit when it is absolutely necessary. The reason for this is the African faecal cockroach (*Blattodea excretus*), a large winged insect about two and a half inches long with a flattened body, usually brown in colour and with a hard exoskeleton. The insect feeds exclusively on human excreta.

Of course I knew none of this when I was squatting over that black hole unlocking a massive barrage of beer shit. I had no idea that the grim thing laid its eggs in the lower intestine of human beings; that the tiny arse demon was known to leap from the bottom of rank latrines and settle itself comfortably in the upper anal cavity; that it could only be removed with pliers and a blowtorch; that the monster slowly eats its way up the colon into the lower gut where it lays its eggs, 70.000 of them in a hardened capsule called an ooetheca; and that after depositing its young in the stomach of the host it dies immediately and is passed in the unfortunate victim's next tough shit.

The eggs hatch slowly over the next two months causing the unfortunate host untold agonies as the larvae literally eat him alive. Constant amounts of food are required to keep the poor fucker alive as the larvae will quite happily continue to dine on the faecal matter. Only when there is no faeces left do the larvae start to feed on the living tissue. Eating vast amounts of food to sustain a supply of excrement is only prolonging the agony however because as the larvae begin to grow their appetites become insatiable and they start eating into the living tissue anyway. This can take as little as three or four days. It is important at this stage that the victim, who remains fully compos mentis throughout the whole ordeal leaves the vicinity of human habitation and heads into the bush as far as possible.

Eventually the larvae consume certain vital organs and the host will lay down and die. In another two days the body will be reduced to mere bones.

On exposure to sunlight the larvae, clinging to the skeleton enter the chrysalis stage, eventually entering the imago or perfect state when as one the fully formed faecal cockroaches take to the wing and swarm. Fortunately most are taken by birds but one or more will make it to village latrines where the whole ghastly business begins over.

BREAKFAST

A kindly looking old man with a still fit and muscled body, baggy shorts, string vest, flip-flops and an apron that obviously took pride in the knowledge it had never been washed, enters the room with a tray. He smiles and laughs. Puts the tray down on the table. He shakes our hands in turn, babbles away in French. The fact that we make it clear to him we don't understand a word he says makes no difference. He grabs my pen, writes the word 'TREFOR' in my notebook, then pats his chest, then invites us to write down and then pronounce our names.

I have decided I like Trefor. Trefor is going to be our friend.

On the tray is a bowl piled high with golf ball-size deep-fried lumps of dough. And three large plastic mugs filled to the brim with a hot milky brew. These mugs are almost pint-sized. My mug is a pale, faded blue. I lift it and take a sip. I think it's tea but as I take my tea both black and unsweetened any tea flavour there may be is masked by the milk and sugar.

I put my prejudices to one side and decide that this beverage is something else altogether. There is obviously no choice. The menu is decidedly short so I make a decision to love this drink. I take a second sip, put the mug down, pick up one of the dough balls and take a bite. It's made from slightly sweetened maize flour. I like this too. If this is to be the way our fast is broken each morning on our cruise up-river, then I will look forward to it.

Trefor is still with us managing to make small talk with Gimpo. Gimpo has his *Lonely Planet* out and opened at a map of Zaire, showing him the planned route of our journey and, using a mixture of sign language, Jamaican patois and that sub-language that only Gimpo knows, is explaining how the three of us are on our way to Gbadolite to have an audience with their great President. Trefor laughs in a good-natured way. I catch his eye and with a smile and a thumbs-up, show my appreciation of what Trefor has prepared for me. Trefor disappears through the door to his kitchen.

'I can't eat this fuckin' shit, Bill.'

'What's wrong with it Z? I think it's fantastic.'

'You would, but I can't take much more of this shit. You can have mine, I'm heading up to the bar. At least their beer is OK.'

Z packs up his journal and heads off.

'What the fuck's up with him Gimpo?'

'You know what he gets like on tour. Always has to be the first to throw a wobbler.'

'Well I like it. Mind you when we first boarded yesterday I thought this was the biggest mistake of my life but now I'm beginning to relax.'

To be vaguely honest with you dear reader, I always feel better in myself when I know that Z is having a shite time. Something to do with the fucked-up nature of our friendship or maybe all friendships are like that. Gimpo and I divvy up Z's dough balls and enjoy them at our leisure while a bevvy of the feral kids that have been running around the room pluck up courage and close in on us watching us pop the succulent belly fillers into our mouths.

'I'm going for an exploration, Bill. Fancy coming?'

'Nah, Gimpo, I'm heading back to the cabin. Going to get on with writing up some of my notes from that jaunt Z and I had in Europe.'

'OK. See you later.'

*

Luckily I didn't take on board any of the stowaways and made it back to Queequeg and the masturbators pretty OK. Their frantic activities seemed to have calmed down and they were all lost in the fields of their dreams. Queequeg and his ladylove slept soundly, not a murmur or a movement from either of them.

Not so the tug brothers. Bill was sweating and grinding his teeth to dust, whimpering and barking like a dreaming dog. Squintering whines and belches of passing gas were blowing his mosquito net around like curtains in a haunted house. Gimpo was thrashing from side to side, punching the steel walls and beating his somnambulistic pork half to death.

I lay awake unable to sleep – the slimy heat, Bill and Gimpo's nocturnal racket, the 24-hour ghetto blasters – it was fucking impossible.

Eventually I slid into a waking dream-like state, It may have been the Larium, who knows. I remember lying there listening to strange howling spirits, old as the jungle itself. I could hear them moaning among the lower frequencies of the perpetual blaster racket when suddenly the barge hit a sand dune, shorting the electricity and cutting the jangling ghetto blasters dead.

Immediately the shrill symphony of cicadas rushed in to fill the sudden vacuum of noise. It was a high flat plane of sound, a constant pitch which all the other keys of nightmare could swoop in and out of. Deep sonorous whoops and deafening shrieks, fat blood-gorged bats flapping leather wings on the sweating night, chasing fist-sized bugs clamouring around the lights on the barge.

That's when I realised the reason for the constant ghetto blaster chorus. There's no such thing as silence in the jungle, better the rhythmic sounds of hi-life than this prehistoric soundtrack to nightmare. The sounds of predator and prey, weird featherless jungle owls ripping the living fuck out of saucer-eyed marmosets, warring tribes of carnivorous apes waging surprise midnight raids upon their simian rivals, smashing skulls to feast on the protein-rich brain matter. Paeolithic bloodlust reverberating across the jungle's dark malevolence. Species after endless species devouring each other at some savage banquet. The razor-sharp mandibles of monster insects chewing each other to paste down in their mulch, carnivore rending carnivore into bloody shreds. The heated fuck songs of jaguar and panther caterwauling like tortured infants, echoing into the swirling arboreal acoustics, adding their hellish voices to the corybantic cacophony of the jungle at night.

Without the jingle-jangle happy African music to drown out all this metaphysical terror, men would go mad. The pulse of distant drums floats on warm plateaus of rising vegetable heat beating out sick blasphemous rhythms. The tattered ghosts of missionaries sent spinning into fevered insanity and winding up as cannibal shit moan in the rolling mist spilling across the black water.

CROSSING THE BAY OF BISCAY
'Look Bill, this one's called "Walk the Dog". What do you think?'

Z's latest fad was yo-yoing. He'd got himself a top of the range yo-yo and a book called *Zen and the Art of Yo-Yoing*.

'Very impressive, Z, but is it relevant?'

'Relevant? Why does everything have to be fuckin' relevant in your world?'

Late January 1996.

Z and I were at sea on a ship out of Portsmouth heading for the Spanish port of Santander on the northern coast. We had rail tickets that were going to take us on a nine-day journey around some supposedly important places in Europe. We had set out on this not-so-Grand Tour for research purposes. We wanted to learn more about what Satan had been up to in Europe these past couple of millennia. We were seeking information about tricks he had used in the past and ones he might try again. In reality, my main concern wasn't what tricks old Hornie might play on us, but whether Z and I could put up with each other's company for nine days straight without Gimpo there as a human release valve and buffer zone between the two of us.

Both Z and I are too comfortable with our own miserable company to get along with any other human being for any length of time. We may be bosom buddies, but to have to deal with the reality of the only person who is a bigger arsehole than me for more than a week was going to be hard going. A couple of days earlier, my long-time sparring partner, Balfey had wanted some sort of rational explanation for our plans. 'Balfey, each century has to redefine Satan for its own times. In the twentieth, the responsibility for this job has fallen on the shoulders of Z and myself. I would rather it hadn't, but that's the way it goes.'

I had also told him that the artist is next to the saint in communicating with God. Balfey gave me one of his knowing looks as if to say, 'Bill, when you've blown all your cash, you'll be on

the plane back here to me to find out if there are any bands on my label that you can produce.'
What Z and I hadn't done was discuss what we were up to in any sort of rational way before we had set sail on what in reality may have been a self-indulgent jaunt around Europe. It was only halfway across the Bay Of Biscay as the ship began to roll and the cabaret band started to play 'Tie A Yellow Ribbon' and the bar was almost empty, that Z and I got to talking about Satan. That was when I realised we both had complete different takes on what or who Satan was, is and will always be. The conversation went something like this:

Z: 'You don't like the devil do you?'

Me: 'Of course I don't.'

Z: 'I quite like him.

Me: 'How can you, he's a cunt?'

One of the main problems with Z and myself is that we are unable to discuss anything in even vaguely rational ways. As far as I was concerned Satan was the ultimate cunt, the total fucker-upper, the one who takes all the blame. For Z he is... well, more of that later. As for Z's yo-yoing, it was already beginning to piss me off.

*

I must have drifted off at some time during that evil night because I remember been jerked into consciousness by the clattering liturgy of the demented witch doctor outside our cabin. Queequeg's woman had placed a thin piece of decorative cloth across the door to our cabin to allow a little privacy and to allow the cool air from the river to circulate and get rid of Sailor Bill's squawking gas. I could see the witch doctor's shadow silhouetted against the greasy Congo dawn. He had some kind of skull shaker on a stick in one hand and a lethal spear decorated with feathers and strips of skin in the other. He was bollock naked, the shadow of his monster jungle tackle flobbering up and down in time to his hectic voodoo stomp.

He started throwing monkey bones all over the place and then ripped a chicken's head off, a jet of blood splashed across the thin cotton sheeting. His hyperventilating voice was shouting some kind of animist recital. His ranting and raving weren't exactly what they seemed, there was something almost comforting about his prayer, he seemed to be mispronouncing odd words and then correcting himself. A maniac never fluffs his lines, let alone corrects them.

'Zombie! Zombie! Zombie!' he chanted, throwing bones and rice into our cabin and then moving on to the next one and repeating his incantations.

THE SERPENT BEGUILED ME

We arrived in the port of Santander at 17.00 hours on the Sunday evening. We had time for a couple of hours of bar hopping on the seedy side of town watching the local prozzies ply their trade before we had to get the night train down to Madrid at 23.00 hours, if I remember correctly.

I woke early the next morning and from my top bunk I could just see the moon-lit Spanish plain out of a crack in the blind as we trundled south. My mind got to wondering what the fuck we thought we were doing. Was all this some far-fetched excuse to give ourselves the outline of a story to hang our follow-up to volume one of the *Bad Wisdom* trilogy? Just another vehicle in which to air our perverted prejudices? Just something to do to get us out of the house? What was it about the notion of the devil that I kept coming back to?

Don't get me wrong. I'm not some born-again religious nutter hiding behind a load of ludicrous arcane beliefs. I know as well as the next modern man that Satan is just a name we give to some internal shadow of the imagination. I don't fear the reality of him like a medieval peasant. I would be a liar to let you think I was the holder of some fundamental beliefs just to make me look like a seriously deranged but interesting character. And yet and yet… I keep coming back to him, old Hornie, the Fallen Angel, the Morning Star, the Great Enemy, the Prince of Darkness, the Father of Lies, his Satanic Majesty, the Eternal Adversary, Lucifer, the Serpent, Nickie-Ben, the fiend, the demon, the lord of this earth, the rebel – a thousand different names I've enjoyed using and tasting and trying out over the years. But those are just names to entertain us. Names for the weavers of myths to use. For poets who like to play at being bad boys. But over the decades since childhood, my mind, when at a loose end, often drifts back to the story of Adam and Eve. It's as if I want to try and unlock something from it but never can find the right combination of numbers. I'd even gone as far as to learn it word for word. Well, *Genesis*, Chapter three verses one to seven:

"Now the Serpent was more subtle than any beast of the field which the Lord God had made. And He said unto the woman, 'Yea, that God said, "ye shall not eat of every tree of the garden."' And the woman said unto the serpent, 'We may eat of the fruit of the trees of the garden: But of the fruit of the tree which is in the midst of the garden, God hath said, ye shall not eat of it, neither shall ye touch it, lest ye die.' And the serpent said unto the woman: 'Ye shall not surely die: For God doth know that in the day ye eat thereof, then your eyes shall be opened, and ye shall be as God's knowing good and evil'. And when the woman saw that the tree was good for food, and that it was pleasant to the eyes, and a tree was to be desired to make one wise, she took of the fruit thereof, and did eat and gave also until her husband with her; and he did eat. And the eyes of them both were opened, and they knew that they were naked; and they sewed fig leaves together, and made themselves aprons."

I'm not very good at blaming. I have a tendency to always blame myself, and not only for the things that happen in my own life but for all that war and famine stuff that gets fed through to us via the TV screen and newspaper. I sit there watching the news as another would-be Pol Pot brings about misery and death to his people and I think I should do something about this instead of poncing about spending my days reading poetry and humming tunes.

But I can't take all the blame. There is just too much of it for me to lug around as I go about my daily business. So I unload some. But not on the government of the day or the tax man or the commies or the cops, but on that serpent in the tree. It's his fault our lives are filled with misery and wretchedness, that futility hangs like a pall over our existence. I'd spent years wishing I wasn't laden down with this knowledge thing that I could be like the beasts of the forest or even a scabby feral tom cat just getting on with life instinctively doing whatever it is, eating, fucking, pissing, shitting and sunning myself when the days are warm. None of this doubt and guilt and trying-to-work-it-all-out stuff. None of the why, where, what and when. Just getting on with dealing with life as it is. No big questions. No writing books or making records. Just to be like the birds of the air, even if it's just a squabbling cock sparrow in my backyard with a couple of summers of life before he gets pounced on by a cat or swooped down on by a hawk.

I knew that a more rational and, dare I say it, modern reading of chapter three of Genesis would have me seeing it all in a different light. Yes, of course I could say to myself, 'Hang on a moment, Bible Bill, it's the Chief who stuck the tree in the middle of the garden in the first place and told Adam and Eve not to partake of its fruit. He in all his wisdom knew that serpent or no serpent to do a bit of tempting, it was only a matter of time before one of them or their seven billion offspring took a bite. And he lied to them as well. He told them that they would die if they even as much as touched the fruit. He didn't mention anything about having one's eyes opened and being as gods.

And it wasn't the serpent that kicked them out of the eastern gate and handed down the awful sentence that we are still doing the porridge for, it was that prime-moving thug, that maker of heaven and earth – even the subtle serpent with his beguiling ways – the jealous god himself. But with my pick-and-mix approach to all things unworldly I've never really gone for that Old Testament version of God. Mine is a more forgiving New Testament model with a pinch of Zen, Sikh and even at times the Allah of our Mohammedan brothers, kind of vague and friendly, at times a bit hardline, but ultimately unknowable. It works for me. Especially on a spring day when I spy a bank of blooming primroses that make me feel good to be alive and I'm looking for something or someone to thank.

But as for the serpent, it's just those few brief lines in the King James that defines him forever more to me. There they are, etched deep in my psyche. All that eternal damnation stuff that kept our medieval forebears in fear meant nothing to me. *Dante's Inferno* is just so much over-written poetry. I dig Milton as much as the next consumer of verse but it's the language and imagery that soothes my soul, not the threat. As for that decadent bunch of nineteenth-century French bum boys who entertained us with their absinthe and opium-fuelled tales of sympathy for the dandy with the club foot. They were as revealing as a night down the Bat Cave club circa 1982. But more of that later when I tell you about our days spent wandering through Père Lachaise cemetery and hanging out with Charles and Gussy.

So as I trudged my way through life and at times got bored with pointing the finger at myself I pointed it at the serpent in the tree instead. It was him I blamed for me not truly being me, not saying what I want, doing what I want and all that other eternal adolescent 'I just wanna be free' stuff.

To overturn the fall of mankind had always been the only worthwhile thing to do with your life. To that end I've left a trail of half-baked and unrealised schemes and dreams that vaguely fall under that broad church known as late Western art. Pop records, grand gestures, secret musings, both published and diminished scribblings all kicking at the gates of Eden while I screamed and stamped my feet like Violet Brown.

For fuck's sake, God, are you listening? Can you see me? Are you gonna let us back in or what? Just one bite of the apple and we gotta suffer this for evermore? Open the sodding door and I'll rip the tongue right out of the serpent before I chop the tree down, build a bonfire with the logs, tie the dumb serpent to a stake and use a whole can of kerosene to get it going and watch as he writhes in pain as his scales blister and pop, as his flesh splutters and falls away. As his black bones bleach to a white dust.

So that is why I'm on this infernal boat risking sanity, safety and the use of my big toe. It has very little to do with some post-modern literary nods and winks to Faust and the like. I wasn't just interested in getting my soul out of hock, I wanted to bring the whole lot down and this was the only way I knew how.

*

It seemed Bill, Gimps and the Queequegs had slept through the whole thing and I was left wondering if I had dreamt the entire incident. A twanging flapper echoed off the metal walls. Bill had resurfaced, arse blazing, from his spermy dreams. The rat-a-tat-tat from Gimpo's pop-gun sphincter indicated he too had returned from wanking wonderland.

The methane kid jumped down from his bunk covering poor Gimps once more in fecal slop from the floor. He changed quickly into his sailor outfit, struggling hard to get into the ridiculously tight bellbottoms, he adjusted his scarlet neckerchief and started buggering around with the huge bollock parcel in the front of his pants, shifting it from one leg to the other, holding a small hand mirror at crotch level admiring his powerful nads.

Gimpo tried mopping up the shit from the floor but it was hopeless. I quickly made my ablutions using a bucket of Congo river water — bollocks, bell end, arsehole, face, armpits — and threw on a colourful pillarbox red safari suit with a gorgeous sunflower yellow cravat. My sunny outfit cheered me no end and I started singing breakfast cereal jingles.

In this buoyant mood I made my way to breakfast whistling 'I'd rather have a bowl of Coco Pops'.

QUALIFIED COLONIC IRRIGATORS

The train pulled into Madrid. As usual, Z and I were the last up and off. We retired to the station café for morning coffee and to stare at a bunch of Gucci-clad young women.

Z had taken an interest in colonic irrigation at the time. He suggested that these three young ladies might be the type who would go for it and that we should head over and say to them, 'We are qualified colonic irrigators. Would you like to bend over so we can give you a free estimate?' In fact, I was no expert, the only thing I knew about it was that Princess Di and Fergie had it done.

Z was wearing his balaclava and an old man's coat that he got from a charity shop and I was sporting a dustbin man's fluorescent yellow coat with reflective strips and the Aylesbury Vale District Council logo on the back. I think our attire if nothing else would have undermined any notion of us being colonic irrigation experts. Z insisted on strutting past the three of them doing his 'Walk the Dog' yo-yoing trick. Not one of them turned their head.

Now that I've got all that Crossing the Bay of Biscay devil stuff and the bit about us being colonic irrigators out of my head and into my notebook, I think I deserve a little reward. Maybe a Coca Cola up at the bar. See how Z's getting on.

*

Of course my mood couldn't stay that way, not when I saw the dining room. This Calcutta-like hole was probably the hottest place on board. A dark window-less purgatory. Perspiring mothers with bone-bag babies hanging on to wasted tits skulked in the shadowed corners. The squalid heat and its attendant torpor made the place feel more like a sick room than somewhere to take your victuals.

The cook. Trefor, a wiry septuagenarian with salt and pepper hair and the yellow rheuminess about the whites of the eyes that bibulous Africans acquire in old age, bounded into the room, naked but for a pair of dirty string Y-fronts.

He was babbling away good-naturedly and kicking the roof orphans out of the way. He carried a tray of fried round things that looked like donuts and three steaming plastic pint pots of over-sweetened tea. The donuts of course weren't doughnuts, they were made from dried termite flour. They didn't taste unpleasant, they just didn't taste of anything.

The blasting turbulence from the hi-life soca music made it impossible to talk, the reverb bouncing off the metal walls was making me feel perturbed. The hangover from the last dislocated incident had not fully disappeared and I knew I had to get out of there fast.

I gave the roof kids my bugnuts.

I expected them to fall upon them like starving wolves but to my surprise the eldest, a handsome little chap called Serge, cut the donuts into small pieces and shared them equally with his raggedy little family of lost boys.

Gimpo was licking his plate clean and demanding more while Bill was grumbling about bacon and sausages. He pumped a disgruntled one to indicate his disappointment. Smokey, Trefor's assistant, a muscular bald headed fellow dressed in nothing but a pale blue Tesco cashier's overall popped me a bottle of Primus with his teeth.

I thanked the beaming Smokey and knocked it back in one.

I needed to get up to the quarterback bar, I could feel my alcoholic urgency creeping up on me, the Primus had woken the monkeys.

ZOMBIE ZOMBIE ZOMBIE

It takes about 20 minutes to get from our cabin to the bar. I will leave off describing any more of the sights and sounds that are confronting my senses and just cut straight to my conversation with Z.

'How's it going, Z?'

'I'm fuckin' bored out my skull.'

'Wha' do you mean?'

'Bored, Bill. Fuckin' bored. Don't you understand English?'

'But most of life is boring. That's the way things are. It can't be dancing, girls and fairground rides all the time.'

'Ah, fuck off. Look Bill, this boat contains everything that I hate in life. Number one, blacks. I hate blacks. Number two, African pop. It's mindless drivel and there's no let-up from it. They play it non-stop. Even up here in this bar I can hear their stupid blasters. It all sounds the fuckin' same. It may as well be the same song they're playing over and over again. Three, heat. I fuckin' hate heat. The idea of having a holiday in a hot country is, well... Four, bugs. I fuckin' hate bugs more than I hate anything. Last night while I was lying in my bunk and you two were snoring, there was this bug crawling across the ceiling above me. A fuckin' big, huge thing and I thought...'

Ten seconds silence. That's apart from the rumbling engines of the *Colonel Ebeya* and the ever-present but for the time being distant cacophony of Afro pop.

'Well Z, what did you think?'

'You wouldn't understand even if I told you.'

'Go on, try.'

'While I was watching this bug, I started hearing this voice going 'zombie, zombie, zombie'. I assumed it was just in my head. But it kept getting louder, closer. Then I thought it was the bug that was going 'zombie, zombie, zombie'. Total Kafka. And it's like when you're on acid and you know it's not real but all your senses are screaming at you that it is and...'

'Yeah but what is…?'

'Shut up and let me tell you. While I realise that this "zombie, zombie, zombie" voice is getting real close and is nothing to do with the bug or an acid flashback, it's still dark outside and you two fuckers are still asleep. Then, suddenly, a hand lifts the curtain in the window of the door of our cabin and there are these white teeth and whites of eyes set in the blackness. And he says 'zombie, zombie, zombie' right at me and you two fuckers are still asleep and it's fuckin' real.'

'What do you think it means, Z?'

'Zombie? You know what zombies are.'

'No.'

'The living dead. They come to get you. You must have seen the films. The fucker was a witch doctor and he was after me.'

'Z, there ain't no witch doctors. It's just 'cause it was our first night on the boat and your over-active imagination. You must have been dreaming or that thing that happens when you have been dreaming and then you're awake but the reality and logic of the dream is still going.'

'No, Bill. This was real. Look, I wanna be left alone. I gotta work some things out.'

'Yeah, fine Z, whatever. I'll go off and see if I can buy one of those tin cans that they use.'

'What?'

'You know. They've all got these tins attached to rope that they sling over the side to scoop up water that they use to wash themselves and their clothes and their pots and pans.'

'What? You want to wash yourself in the river water? That river is just a fuckin' huge open sewer for half of this continent. Wash yourself in that and you're just smearing shit on your face.'

'Yeah well, I'll see you later.'

*

I had worked out the quickest route to the bar. Up the rusty ladders, behind the pitch black corridors, underneath the blistering heat of the lower deck past the chained prisoners wretched in their own slop, up a couple of flights and through the makeshift charismatic voodoo evangelical church. I lingered a while there because I recognised the voice of the unhinged bone-slinging chicken slayer who had put the fear of God into me earlier that morning. He was dressed in a spunk-stained quasi-Catholic purple robe with a stained dog collar, preaching excitedly.

His wild congregation of about 200 ecstatic Africans were hollering and shaking, falling to the ground pissing themselves and rending their own flesh. Two young boys naked save for their white dog collars were writhing around like greased weasels banging frenziedly on their bongos. The entranced throng danced fiercely. Women were thrashing from the hip, aggressive spleen-crushing fuck movements, the long-gone men spaz jived insanely in sympathetic coitus.

MY TIN CAN

As I had made my way along the barge, numerous individuals were swinging these ropes over the side. Attached to each rope was a large tin can. These cans are about the same size as Party Seven cans from the 1970s. If you're not old enough to remember that far back, a Party Seven can contained Watneys Red Barrel or some other type of shite beer, stood 30 cm or so high and had a diameter of about 20 cm. I was very impressed with this swinging of rope, catching of water and pulling it back up. The water was then poured into a plastic bucket. In the buckets, pots and pans were washed, t-shirts rubbed, babies bathed. I wanted a go. I'm obviously acting upon instinct, an instinct that helpfully made part of me want to be part of this society that we now have to be part of for the next few weeks.

So I've just done my first deal with one of the many stallholders whose establishments are springing up all over the narrow walkways of the barges. And I'm now the proud owner of a pale blue plastic bucket, a ten-metre length of rope and a tin can. The rope has been handmade using some kind of raffia material. Straight out of the jungle kind of stuff.

But it's the tin can that I'm proudest of. I'm sitting in my bunk now with it in front of me and I'm going to describe it to you in detail.

It stands about 25 cm high and 15 cm in diameter. It has the same image on the front and the back. Down the sides is information in various languages, none of which are English. First the front/back image: it's printed straight on to the tin and uses the colours blue, green, orange, black and white. The product logo is white letters out of a blue plaque. The product name is Bella Holandesa, with a little 'R' in a circle to tell us that's its registered trade mark. This plaque is about 10 cm x 8 cm and takes up the top third of the front and back of the can. The bottom of the can has the words 'Leche Entera en Polvo & Leite Em po Intero' which may mean something to you but doesn't to me. These words are white out of a block of orange. Dipping into this orange is a blue ellipse. Out of the blue is a word in white letters. This word is 'Instantanea' which we may guess means instant. As in 'no waiting until the cows come home.' Between the Bella Holandesa logo and the text at the bottom is a very simplified graphic interpretation of what we must assume to be a Dutch landscape. From left to right there is a canal. On the canal is a sailing boat. On the far side of the canal is an avenue of trees, some farm buildings and a windmill. The nearside of the canal is rich green pasture. On the pasture are two black and white Friesian cows. One is lying down and probably enjoying a few spare hours cud chewing, the other is up on her feet grazing.

I was going to say that this pleasant scene would be immediately recognisable as a Dutch landscape but maybe here on this wild highway, on this shanty town on water, the percentage of people likely to instantly recognise this scene as one from Holland would be pretty low. We have no idea if the artist who was commissioned to produce this work of art had first consulted the sublime paintings of Aelbert Cuyp who is Dutch and is considered not only by me but all of those that make these kind of decisions to be the greatest painter of cows to have ever lived. I hope he did. But this pleasant landscape is as nothing compared with what the anonymous artist has placed in the immediate foreground for us to feast our eyes on. Standing with her shoulders back and a pail brimming with milk in each hand is a Dutch maiden who is herself brimming with everything we would hope for from a young Dutch milkmaid. She is dressed in what we have grown up to recognise as their national costume, although because the picture doesn't go below what may be her knees we don't know if she is sporting a pair of wooden clogs with the turned-up pointy-toe bits. But she does have that head gear with turned-up pointy flaps over each ear.

So now you have a picture of what she is wearing. What you don't know is about the ultimate 'come on boys' vibe she is projecting. Her neckline plunges to reveal a cleavage fit for a Wonderbra campaign and that portion of her breasts left to our imagination snuggle into her national costume like a pair of warm rabbits. Her face is wide and open. She looks more pleased to see me than I think any woman ever has. High cheekbones, big blue eyes, a little turned-up nose and a mouth – oh what a mouth – a mouth to make Julia Roberts sour with envy. Her full lips parted and waiting like those on the more up-market blow-up dolls.

If you have ever wandered the streets of Amsterdam's red light district, gaping at the women in their windows bathed in their light, nothing there touches the promise that this young milkmaid has on display. Yes, I'm smitten, there is no denying it.

To calm myself down I will try to describe the text down the side of the can. It's in four languages. Three European ones and the other Arabic. There is a little diagram that I understand to mean you have to mix one part of the powder that was once contained in this tin to three parts water. I try to read the text beside the diagram 'DILYA 1 parte de leche en polvo en 4 partes de agua' which is a bit confusing. So I look at the bar code at the bottom of the column of text in four languages. I suppose bar codes are the international language of commerce. I can't imagine that there is one place in all of Zaire that has one of those check-out counter laser beam things that could read this bar code. If you work in a retail outlet, tap in these numbers and see what comes up on your screen: 8 716200 140584.

On the strip of text on the other side of the tin as well as all the text on the four optional languages is a royal-looking seal in red with a couple of lions rampant, holding up a crown and shield. Around this coat of arms are the only words in English to be found on the can 'Netherlands Controlling Authority for Milk and Milk Products'. Why someone has judged that this information should be imparted in English I have no idea.

Below the shield are the words 'Friesland Fricodomo, P Stuyves Antweg 1, 8937 AC Leeuwarden Holland'. And in red lettering 1800g.

Gimpo sticks his head in the cabin and brings to an end my blossoming affair with a tin can. I will endeavour to tell you more about it later.

'Z wants to talk to you.'

'So where is he?'

'Up in the bar. Where do you think?'

'And he's sent you to get me? Who the fuck does he think he is? If he wants to fuckin' talk to me he can come here.'

'Look, Bill, this is serious. There's something wrong with him. I've never seen him like this before. It's scary stuff.'

'OK. OK. I'll fuckin' come.'

*

The drums suddenly stopped dead. It was time for the preacher to smack his bitch up.

He grabbed a ragged well-thumbed Bible and started punching it hard repeating the zombie! zombie! zombie! chant that had browned my underpants a few hours ago. He locked into his flock with inspired eyes focusing on a voluptuous young woman, instructing his greased weasels to bring her to him and then started rubbing her head and shaking her violently back and forth all the time bawling out his apocalyptic sermon at the top of his voice.

His two stripped vicars whaled into their bongos knocking out the tribal craziness even louder. Dozens of chickens panicking in clouds of feathers, some of them headless, sprayed blood across the possessed worshippers.

Father Zombie threw off his purple robe, his pulsating blue veined chopper stabbed at heaven straining to uproot itself and take flight. The throbbing monster was letting loose sparks and spiral thunderbolts, the shiny purple bell end changing colour like some over-charged electric cuttlefish.

The charismatic maniac juddered spasmodically, gyrating around an epileptic vortex of primitive rapture. He was ripping pages out of his untamed Bible and throwing the spooked confetti over his voodoo funky worshippers, without warning he grabbed one of his bare-assed vicars, jack-knifed him over his forearm and punched his ugly distended rainbow torpedo, slam right up his surprised padre's claggy bunghole.

'Hallelujah!' screamed the speared vicar.

More chickens were flung, beheaded and gushing into the ecstatic melee. I noticed Bill swept up in the religious fervour, his white bellbottoms around his ankles, up to his nuts in one of the sacrificial poultry. Taking advantage of the twisting hysteria, Gimps was squatting, a scat-crazy sumo laying black eggs on a catatonic female worshipper.

Blowflies and pointed teeth, vibrating in and out of some evil universe to which only he had access.

I picked up one of the tattered Bibles scattered around everywhere. It was in English and Lingala. The word for Christ in the Lingala language is N'zambe.

'Zombie! Zombie! Zombie!'

'N'zambe! N'zambe! N'zambe!'

I felt foolish and slipped quietly out of the berserk tabernacle.

IN THE BAR

'So what the fuck is it now, Z?'

'Bill, I've made up my mind. I've fuckin' got to get off this fuckin' boat.'

I sort of laugh nervously.

'You don't know how fuckin' serious I am, Bill. I keep looking at the shore to see how far it is to swim. I'm gonna jump. I'm not leavin' this bar. I'm not gonna go back to that cabin. Ever. If you two don't sort somethin' out, I'll jump.'

'Don't talk fuckin' shite, Z. You're not going to jump. You'd be dead long before you made the shore anyway.'

'Yeah Bill, what you don't realise is, I don't give a shit. I've gotta get off here. However slim my chances of making it to the shore are, they're better odds than me surviving on board.'

'What do you reckon, Gimpo?'

That's me trying to deflect any responsibility for the situation.

'It's Saturday today. On Tuesday we are supposed to reach Mbandaka. Maybe you could get a flight back to Kinshasa from there.'

'Tuesday. That's three fuckin' days away. I want a helicopter now to lift me off or I jump.'

'You're still talking shite, Z.'

'I'm not. Look, I'll try and be rational. I know this is just me. I know you think I'm a nutter but that's just 'cause you two are too thick to see…'

'Thick? I'm not fucking thick.'

'Sorry, Gimpo, I didn't mean thick. I mean, I know I'm a nutter but you see...'

'What?'

'You two can carry on without me. I've got all the information I need to get my half of the book written. Anyway me jumping ship, even if it's just metaphorical, will make your story all the more interesting. I don't give a shit how much of an arsehole you portray me as.'

In fact Z could look no more of an arsehole if he had spent three years at RADA learning how. His twat haircut is squiffed. His nonce specs smudged. The bottoms of what were his once pristine safari suit trousers have been turned up to just below his knees. But his fashion statement of total arseholedom is a long-sleeved T-shirt. It's sky blue with a big yellow smiley face on it. Z sporting a smiley face? That ubiquitous icon of the acid house boom of 1988 is far-fetched enough but him wearing it stuck up the Congo while having a full-on nervous breakdown in 1996 is so completely mind-blowing I'm almost jealous.

(Note: If somebody has been foolish, fucked-up or astute enough to try to turn this story into a major motion picture and you are in charge of the wardrobe, please make sure the character playing Z is wearing one of these smiley t-shirts as described above.)

'Z, if you are going to jump, can I buy your t-shirt off you before you go?'

'You what?'

'Your t-shirt. I want it.'

'Fuck off. I'm being serious. I'm not leaving this bar until a helicopter picks me up and flies me straight to Kinshasa Airport where I can get a plane back to London.'

'Just get a grip man.'

'"Just get a fuckin' grip?" What the fuck do you mean Bill? This is not some old black and white film. You're not Kenneth More acting Douglas Bader. We ain't sittin' in some pub in Clerkenwell making up stories about what we're going to do. This is reality. We are going to die.'

'We're artists, Z. We're supposed to die. Die for our art. That's what the punters want.'

'Well you can. I want to live.'

'I'm heading back up front. That Trefor guy is supposed to be making us some sort of meal. You may as well wait here for your helicopter to come and get you. What you doing, Gimpo?'

'I'll hang on here with Z.'

Chapter Five
BONEYARD EARTH

I left the barbarous church and its two new converts and made my way to the roof of one of the smaller barges. It was still early morning. A sliding mist unfurled across the water. I could hear the broken-glass mating calls of alien birds shrieking in the canopy half a mile away. Dozing orphans lay dotted here and there across the roof covered by thin blankets. There was a slight headwind escorting the violent stench of 3,000 morning dumps down river and bringing in its wake the heady perfumes of the rainforest and all its mysterious blooms.

We were passing close by to one of the many islands dotted along the meandering trajectory of this part of the river. I could see human forms within the verdure, corporeal shadows, like bipedial anti-matter leaping from fallen tree to fallen tree, running alongside the boat, occasionally cupping their hands to form loudhailers and shouting. One or two of the roof boys were shouting back and laughing, performing little dances and slapping their knees. We eventually cleared the island and made our way back to the centre of the black river.

SQUIGGLING

Back on my bunk. I had a meal. I'll go into detail about Trefor and his cooking methods later on. Just now I want to blot out my paranoia about what Z may or may not do by describing the light switch in our cabin.

Each of the five cabins along the upper deck of our side of our barge has a single bare low-wattage light bulb in the centre of its ceiling. Each of the cabins has a door with a small window, no glass but a metal grill. Our grill is missing. Each has a light switch just to the left of the door frame, except ours. Our cabin has two plastic-coated loose wires where the switch should be. These are live wires, just waiting to be casually shorted by Z staggering into them. One is red and the other is blue. Neither more than a couple of inches long with about half an inch of dulled copper wire protruding from each. These red and blue bits of plastic coating are the only coloured things in the cabin. I mean proper colours as opposed to the grey of the sponge mattress and the dark brown, dirt-ingrained, rusted vibe of the walls, floor, ceiling and bunks. Although these two bits of wire are squiggling out in different directions, they are desperately begging to be brought together so they can complete the circuit. They want sparks to fly. They want fuses to blow and they want me to officiate at the ceremony. The destination they long for is in my hands. 'Anyone who knows of any reason why these two... forever hold thy peace.' And just as I'm leaning forward to play my little part in the drama of their lives by bringing together these two souls, Queequeg opens the door to the cabin. He smiles at me. A big white-toothed smile. He's maybe in his late 30s. He's wearing the regulation shorts and flip-flops. No t-shirt, just taut muscles. A body waiting for a woman to stroke and to make me think, 'Yeah well, I bet you've never had a number one in the official UK charts.' He taps his chest and says something that sounds like Quamba but as far as these notes go, I think I'll keep referring to him as Queequeg. From my position on my bunk above his I tap my chest and say 'Bill. My name is Bill'. He stretches out his hand and we shake. I notice that none of his teeth are filed to a point. If you have a passing knowledge of British popular culture in the very late twentieth century, I could describe him having a bit of a resemblance to the footballer Ian Wright but friendlier looking.

In his other hand he has a light bulb, a roll of black plastic tape and a screwdriver. He gets to work with the wires. I watch. Ten minutes later he screws the bulb into the ceiling then he tries out his makeshift switch.

Let there be light and there is.

Queequeg looks pleased with himself. I warm to him even though I know every one of my ex-girlfriends would lust after him. He shows me how to work his makeshift switch. It won't pass any safety standards that we may have in the civilised world but it works.

*

Sometimes it appears as if the river is a mighty heathen king lording over all his creation. A fat spunky sovereign and his green queen, the jungle. There are no seasons at the equator. The elements are constantly engaged in a massive act of reproduction. Life thrives perpetually here, there is no dying autumn, no dead winter. All year round, life orgies away in this savage Eden, slowly grinding away at its mysterious work. Water in abundance, pouring from the sky, rolls through the skirts of the forest. When the storms lash down, rocking the barges from side to side, the river swelling in inches per minute, it is as if two titans, river and forest are engaged in some almighty monster Godzilla giant jungle fuck. Trees bending and snapping. Like a 50-foot flooze bucking away on top of her watersport stud groaning and screaming, smashing shit all over the fucking place. Nature's majesterial composure lost for an instant during the unbridled passion of her cosmic rut. The spermifidous river, like boiling water, spunking up into the air, the calm mirror of its surface shattered by ancient passion as all around is transformed, swirling insanely among the violent ecstasies of wild nature.

Then as quickly as it all began, the rains stop after maybe ten minutes or so and the river and the forest regain their regal composure. The river rolls on downstream as if nothing had happened, the forest continues its mysterious alchemy, cooking up new species from old recipes.

THE SOUND OF SEX

Queequeg disappears. I lie back on my bunk and listen to the seven ghetto blasters that are simultaneously blasting out from various points around our barge.

I don't know if I've ever consciously listened to seven pieces of music at the same time. In a weird way they all weave in and out of each other. Ducking and diving, careering and colliding to make a complete and unified whole. There are even snatches of this constant, evolving soundtrack to our journey that I'm beginning to recognise. I drift off to sleep. At some time I'm woken by Z stumbling in and Gimpo trying to lever him on to his bunk. The music is still twisting and weaving its intricate pattern then sleep drags me under again.

But I wake up again. This time there is no music. I listen. I can hear the river. The constant thrum of the ship's engines. A baby crying on a distant barge. Z snoring. And... I listen and I don't want to hear the sounds I'm listening to. It's coming from the bunk below me. Queequeg's bunk.

It's the sound of sex. The restrained moaning of a woman and the rhythmic creak of the springs. I feel my top half of the bunk move involuntarily in time to this age-old rhythm. I bury my head under the bundle I've made for a pillow. I can blot out the sound but I can't blot out the picture in my head. These pictures are of my Sallie being satisfied by the lithe body and expert touch of Queequeg. It goes on and on. The moaning rising and falling. I must have fallen asleep again at some point because I awoke to the sounds of chanting. The chanting was getting closer, 'zombie, zombie, zombie' and closer 'zombie, zombie, zombie' The grey light of dawn is forcing its way into our cabin. I see the silhouette of a man through the curtain. So Z was not making this whole voodoo shit up. The silhouetted witch doctor man is holding something in his hand that he is shaking. Yes, this is scary stuff but not as bad as all that sexual paranoia stuff that was going on in the night. I look over to Z's bunk. He's asleep with his mouth wide open. I poke my head over the side. Gimpo's bunk is empty, off for an early morning prowl no doubt. I take a peek down at Queequeg's bunk below mine. All I can see is the long, lithe limb of a female African's leg. Well at least I can allay my nocturnal fears that it was Sallie down there being satisfied good, long and proper. On this satisfying news I slide back into my slumbers.

*

It was late in the evening when warm melancholia arrived. I slipped out of my bunk and went up on deck. Sleeping families snored quietly in the darkness, I tip-toed between them and found a place at the front of the barge, lit a cigarette and stared at the orange ash a while. Sweet air breathed over me from upriver – hyacinth, orchids, gardenia – the redolence of the lost orchard. I waited for night's cloak of stars to wrap and comfort me. The searchlight from the *Colonel Ebeya* scanned across the water in slow elegant arcs. Bats and their gory suppers caught in the prying beam.

Little Serge lays down next to me and gazes at the night sky, he's 15 but he looks about nine. Dreamily awake and at ease with himself, he lounges, wearing the only thing he owns: raggy shorts and a faded and torn Oxfam Duran Duran t-shirt. He sails up and down this vast waterway day after day, year after year wanting nothing.

It is during these small epiphanies that I am made most aware of the non-sequential nature of everything and the limited vistas of human consciousness. That concepts such as past present and future are the feeble vanities of termites looking down the wrong end of a telescope, when I know in the atoms of my bones that everything is always now.

Sweet melancholia sings me lullabies on this boneyard Earth. The Almighty Unknowable who knew me when I was but a speck of dust hitching rides on cosmic winds. Her presence so silent, so inscrutable, watches even now on this doomed rivercraft sailing from nowhere to nowhere.

I light another cigarette, little Serge turns his head, I offer him one. His bright smile lights up in the darkness resting his head on his hand exhaling the blue smoke into the mysterious night. There is futile war somewhere in that black jungle. And futile peace, There never was an Eden. The Angel with the flaming sword that guards the eastern gate is there to prevent our return for the very opposite of all the reasons we all suppose. That was no Paradise lost, it was a Hell escaped. Our status as Lords of the Creation we managed to turn into a curse.

Rarely do I comprehend the murmurings of the sullen muse, but I appreciate the icy warmth.

Like the nectar of the red flowers appeasing the scorching agony of ridiculous rage. Melting cold futility with ambidextrous riddles so impossible that surrender yields its weary comfort. Slack release from the endless questions rattling around the black shaft of a dry well.

DRUMMOND'S SECRET LOG, 9 JUNE 1996
SUNDAY MORNING

'Bill, are you awake?'

'Wha? Yeah, yeah, course I am, Gimpo, just thinking. What is it?'

'Sunday morning, Bill. Time for church.'

'What? Where?'

'In the canteen. It's already started. Rocking. Fucking great. Like a jungle rave. You coming?'

'Yeah. Just wait while I get my kegs on. What about Z?'

'Fuck him. Anyway it's never worth waking him up, he'll just have a hangover. Behave like a cunt.'

The canteen is packed. Kids, women, men, all ages, swaying, singing, clapping hands. Not that hysterical black American gospel shit we like to see in pop videos or TV documentaries about Harlem or the Deep South. There are no instruments to accompany the singing. No need for a choir. Every member of this ragtag congregation is hitting rich and tingling harmonies. As for all that singing from the same hymn sheet stuff, there are none. Who needs them?

'It's fuckin' great, innit Bill?'

'Real.'

Yeah, I know it sounds like a totally pretentious thing to say but it is real. This is true religion. This is how I want it to be. Always. Forever. Now. And yeah, right now it is.

The singing comes to an end. There is a man up front, mid-40s, good looking, tall, black-framed specs and a Bible in his hand. He starts reading. It's not the King James, no Elizabethan cadences, and not the French of their colonial lords and masters. It sounds African, his voice rolling and tumbling through the verse. Between lines he lifts his head to beam good-naturedly at the congregation. They respond by chanting 'zombie, zombie, zombie'.

And whatever the literal meaning of 'zombie, zombie, zombie' is, it has obviously got nothing to do with voodoo. No, this is Christianity at its strongest, purest and best. Cutting through all the bullshit or rationality, the Reformation, the age of Enlightenment and all the other fuckin' bollocks that has ensured that history has left us with a dried-up, irrelevant form of Christianity. The reading done, we are all being swept up into the next song. Gimpo is swaying, clapping, grinning at all of those around him and they are even smiling at me. I never know what to do when people smile at me...

Look, yeah, of course I know Christianity only ever really works as a religion for the oppressed, the downtrodden and the rejected. That's what Jesus was all about. It may be shit now when your president, king or chief is a repressive cunt but grin and bear it, love thy neighbour, suffer the little children, turn your cheek, in the everafter you'll get your just desserts, sit at the right-hand side and hunger, pain, loneliness will be never more.

I want to clap my hands too. I want to sway. I want to hit a note and harmonise with my black brothers and sisters. The most my repressed soul can manage is the tapping of a toe.

Then I notice Z. He's entered the room. He's looking at me with cynical disdain. It's as if I've been caught out by my mum in possession of a smutty magazine. My toes stop tapping. I try and signal to him that it was somehow all Gimpo's doing. I just came along to accompany him while doing a bit of anthropology.

He pushes his way through my fellow believers, the mothers and kids and old men heading for the other door at the far side of the room. The door that takes him to the steps that lead to the next barge, that lead further back on his way to the *Colonel Ebeya* and the bar.

The fucker's now out of sight, I can deal with his cynicism and barbed bitter comments later on. As for now, the congregation have moved into another song. I recognise the thing but never sung like this, never with these harmonies, never with these spontaneous rhythms.

> *"The Lord is my shepherd;*
> *I shall not want.*
> *He makes me to lie down in green pastures;*
> *He leads me beside the still waters.*
> *He restores my soul;*
> *He leads me in the paths of righteousness*
> *For His name's sake.*
> *Yea, though I walk through the valley of the shadow of death,*
> *I will fear no evil;*
> *For You are with me;*
> *Your rod and Your staff, they comfort me.*
> *You prepare a table before me in the presence of my enemies;*
> *You anoint my head with oil;*
> *My cup runs over.*
> *Surely goodness and mercy shall follow me*
> *All the days of my life;*
> *And I will dwell in the house of the Lord forever".*

Well fuck the lot of you. If you've never felt what I've just experienced then it's your loss, and your life is all the more meaningless for it.

Chapter Six
SOFT CARGO

Because the seasons never change around the equatorial latitudes, no rainy season or dry season like the tropics or the four seasons of the northern and southern regions, perceptions of time and even direction seem to be affected. Rapid sunrises and sunsets clearly define day and night but somehow time seems stretched, like the equator itself. After three or four days I ceased registering the passing hours and seemed to connect to a more ancient calendar. This vicissitude was not unpleasant. I would take my journal up to the bar at the back of the *Colonel Ebeya*, order up my breakfast beers and take it easy on the canopied deck.

Most of the time I would be alone. People rarely visited this part of the flotilla, Bill and the Gimp would come by around 11.00am or so for their Coca Colas to sit around and grumble for a while. Bill would head off back to the shitty cabin to work on his earth-shattering theories. Gimpo would head on up to the roof to improve his fluency in the 326 dialects of the Congo.

UP TOP

After church Gimpo and I had breakfast. We banked on Z not turning up to claim his share so we divided up the dough balls and went halves on his mug of tea. I was going to give you a three-page description of my pale blue mug like I did of the tin can but Gimpo saved you from that by suggesting we climb up on to the roof of our barge. He'd seen the way some of the lads clambered up.

The pair of us are up there now and life feels good. I don't know if that's because of the spiritual lift the morning service gave me or the extra portion of dough balls or just because Z isn't here interfering with the equilibrium.

First to describe the rooftop. It's somewhat bigger than a tennis court and roughly the same proportions. It's gently arced from leeward to starboard. The ridge of the ark is a constant height from fore to aft. There is no railing or any other form of security around its edge so there is nothing to stop you taking a tumble from the side into the water below and it's made from the now-familiar sheets of steel riveted and rusted together. That's it. Nothing else. This rooftop, like the rooftop of the parallel barge to ours, is a world away from the cramped conditions below. There are no mothers with screaming babies, hectoring stallholders, no pushing and shoving. This place is the domain of young lads. Young lads with not much else to do than hang out, lounge about watching their world pass by. The youngest look about six or seven, none of them look older than mid-teens. All dressed in cast-off first-world t-shirts, ragged shorts and bare feet. The wearing of flip-flops must come with the responsibilities of adulthood. I've no idea if they have families below or for that matter families anywhere or whether this is their life, drifting through childhood, uneducated, unloved, nothing to protect them from all that we attempt to protect our youngsters from? No future, just the moment.

Gimpo and I make our way along the top of the arc to the very front of the barge and squat down on the still cool tin roof. I pull out my notebook, try to write but find it impossible to focus my mind on anything I could give a shit writing about.

This is the first time since arriving in Africa that I feel calm, nothing is bugging me. I don't feel threatened, worried, concerned about anything. There's a gentle breeze, the climbing sun is as yet not got high enough in the sky to overheat my system.

Three of the rooftop boys have plucked up courage and sat themselves down beside us. Warm open smiles, hands proffered to shake. They want to be friendly, learn who we are. Nothing seems forced. They have nothing to sell us, they are not on the scrounge. First they try French, then they realise that our French is no better than our Lingala. One of them pulls together a few words in English that he has learnt along the way in his short life. They want to know our names, our ages. They borrow my pencil and write theirs down in my notebook. Alain, Serge, Rachedi. Serge seems to be the ringleader or at least the one with the warmest smile and best grasp of English. They only look about ten or 11 but they tell us they are 15. They tell us they learnt English in the mission school. They don't bug us. They are quite happy to just sit here and watch the great vista.

A morning haze still sits on the water. The river a mile or so wide. Both shorelines are a featureless curtain of forest and beyond this curtain we can see nothing. No distant mountain range, in fact nothing to hint that there is anything else in creation other than the river and the first few feet of forest at either side. The weirdness of this is more pronounced as we are sitting up there in this privileged position 30-odd feet above the water level, where you would expect to see more of the landscape.

I say to myself, 'All is river'. I kinda hope I'm going to squeeze a minor epiphany from all this riverness thing, but nothing comes, just river, river, river. Big and wide and rolling and forever. I wanted to be confronted by a major unanswerable question that questions the whole meaning of everything but all that comes is 'So how much fuckin' water is there?' I suppose some bastard could sit here and turn their thoughts about what I'm looking at into powerful prose filled with the force and glory of creation but not me, not today. I'm just happy to be there. Then Gimpo breaks into my reverie.

'You better watch it. They're after what's in your bag.'

'What?'

'These lads. I've worked out what they are up to. While one of them has you distracted by writing his name in your book or something, the other is slipping a hand into your bag.'

'Gimpo, on a Sunday morning like this when all is well with creation, there is no way these lads are trying to pick our pockets.'

'Maybe not our pockets but if you leave your bag lying there open like that, of course that's what they're going to do.'

I steal a glance at Alain, Serge and Rachedi who are chatting away to each other beside us, not a care in the world, not listening to our conversation even if they were able to understand it, and I wonder at where Gimpo's paranoia comes from.

'Gimpo, somebody must of stole something pretty important off you when you were a child to make you this suspicious.'

'Yeah, they stole my life.'

*

Time seemed to dissolve up here with the beer and the weird heat. I wasn't sure whether we'd been gliding along this black water for a few days or a few months. The Primus, the Larium and the jungle skunk I'd been blasting on all contributed to this time-lag fog and when the fierce equatorial sun filtered its way through the thick banks of wet clouds, cooling down the heat it produced a unique sultry sluggishness that made every swig of beer a great effort. As I lay slack on that polished deck I found it difficult to resist the temptations of purple sleep and would gratefully slide into dreams.

One morning I was battered into consciousness by the ear-splitting klaxon of the *Colonel Ebeya*. There seemed to be much activity down on the main deck, stallholders belting around like flies, running from one side of the deck to the other, squealing with anticipatory delight. The roof boys were all gathered at the prow leaping up and down with noisy excitement pointing into the watery distance. There appeared to be another vessel miles up river perched on the horizon. The stallkeepers were busying themselves frantically with their wares, unbagging fresh cartons of cigarettes, rearranging their plastic trinkets, straightening their shaving mirrors, tubes of toothpaste, and razor blades. I joined Bill and Gimps up on the roof with their motley crew of urchins.

As the black speck on the horizon drew closer I detected a distinct drop in excitement from the jolly runaways. They hurried off below, dancing down the sides of the barge like mountain goats. The market traders too seemed to grow more subdued as the distant vessel edged closer. A sweet and sickly scent blew downwind from the mysterious barge causing even more trepidation from our shipmates.

Z APOLOGISES

Z, Gimpo and me in the canteen, waiting for Trefor to bring us our meal. The usual things going on around us. Kids, babies, mothers, Afro pop at max volume. Z is smiling and he says.

'This is OK.'

'What do you mean?'

'Being here, on this boat, travelling up the river.'

'So what happened to your mega breakdown?'

'It must have been lack of food. Once I'd got that chicken and rice in me yesterday I was all right. That and a good night's kip. I need my sleep and I got myself a bit of routine together. Yeah, and when I realised there weren't any zombies, just Jesus... I thought we were really travelling into the heart of darkness instead of just being on a ferry taking people from where they live to where they work. I can't get over the friendliness of them all.'

'Yeah, I know what you mean. It's as if they are niggers with no need for attitude, no need for all that bitter chip-on-their-shoulder stuff.'

'That would be 'cause nobody sold them into slavery,' says Gimpo.

'Yeah, but they still have a pretty shitty deal, post-colonial chaos, dictatorships, tribal wars, killer diseases, no doctors, no dole.'

'The thing is Bill, they don't need shades and stupid sports labels to be cool. They are cool, born cool without even trying.'

'So you won't be needing the helicopter then, Z?'

'What? Do you want me to apologise?'

'Well yes.'

'OK, I'm sorry and yeah, of course I knew there was no helicopter. You pair of cunts wouldn't have got it together even if I'd really needed one. I bet you never even sorted out that medical travel insurance anyway.'

'Yes I did.'

'So what does our insurance cover?'

'OK. I admit that whatever it says on paper is pretty irrelevant out here. I don't think they would understand the concept of insurance here.'

'Yeah, whatever. But I tell you what Bill, I'm going to write it up as if it was you that had the massive wobbler and couldn't cope with the reality of it all.'

'Fair enough. But before I finish this small prelunch section of dialogue, can Gimpo, me and all the readers hear you say 'I'm sorry' one more time?'

'I AM SORRY.'

'Thank you.'

'It doesn't count, Bill, 'cause the readers won't be reading this bit.'

'Why not?'

'They'll be skipping it to get to more of my stuff.'

'Fuck off.'

One of Gimpo's little language tutors explained the reason for the nervousness that seemed to have descended upon our happy ship.

'Is Arab sodomy barge, Mr Gimpo.'

It would seem that those enterprising sons of the desert, always quick to spot a hole in the market, had set up a special cruise for wealthy Westerners whose sexual appetites transgressed the laws of most of the civilised countries on Earth. Seeing as how for all intents and purposes there was no law in Zaire, save that which came from the barrel of a gun, and this sodomy barge of the Arabs was heavily armed indeed, the sexual tourists on this floating raft of degeneracy felt completely safe and at ease to pleasure themselves in whatever mode they fancied.

The roof boys were terrified of this dark craft of Sodom and scuttled into hiding, secreting themselves inside obsolete steam funnels, between metal roof supports, behind the dangerous fly wheels of the engine rooms. The sodomy barges apparently went through young boys at a furious rate. The barges' soft cargo was usually supplied by the poorest villagers on the more obscure tributaries off the main waterway. The Arabs however were not averse to capturing the odd attractive orphan boy that they came across. The traders while finding the very existence of this vessel repugnant and against every sacred taboo of their 800 religions were forced by economic necessity to trade with this horrific ship of arse bandits

Although the creepoid denizens of the barge were not all pederastic homosexuals they tended to outnumber the other sex weirdos by about 10 to 1. As the black barge drew nearer, a mute silence fell over the flotilla. The roofboys all seemed to have vanished. The stallholders were staring at the ground as if deeply ashamed to be in such close proximity to the depraved craft. But business was business, they started opening up some of their stored parcels and laying out more exotic items on their rickety tables – huge 18-foot dildos, black rubber buttplugs, hippopotamus-hide bullwhips, handcuffs. The usual bugger's arsenal along with even more extreme sex toys for the seasoned pervert: nitric acid, machetes, thumbscrews, caged rodents, baby pit bulls. One fellow was rolling out a huge barrel of industrial-strength snake oil and laying out his stall with all manner of perverted knick-knacks, gags, oversized stilettos, ropes, cut throat razors, scalpels. The little fucker even had a flat-pack rack.

THE FISHES' EYE VIEW

Trefor has just arrived, laughed good-naturedly as a form of greeting, placed three well piled plates in front of us and returned to his kitchen to get the utensils.

'I'm not fuckin' eating that.'

I will ignore Z's statement and concentrate on describing what is in front of me. First, the plate is that classic white enamel camping plate with a blue line around its rim. The enamel has been chipped at three separate places on the rim. After eating my meal I may turn it over to see if there is any information underneath that can tell us where it has come from, how many continents it has crossed to be sitting here on this table laden with grub just for me. On the plate is a heap of rice. Nondescript white rice. Nothing brown or carmargueish or basmati-ish or risottoish about it. Just standard white rice. I know they grow rice on the Nile Delta but I don't know if rice is grown anywhere else in Africa. So, if you have any better information than myself about where the rice consumed in Central Africa is grown, you can fill in my missing details.

On the rice, Trefor has ladled a dollop of sauce. This sauce looks identical to the sauce we had on the chicken and rice he served us as our two midday meals to date. Yesterday I plucked up courage to step into Trefor's kitchen and using sign language asked him to show me the secret of his sauce. I watched Trefor take onions from the sack in the corner, peel them and finely chop them. I watched him pour some corn oil from an oil drum into his frying pan. I watched him scrape the chopped onions from his wooden chopping board into the hot oil. I watched him open a small tin of tomato purée and scrape its contents out and into the now golden fried onions. I wanted to ask him why he used tinned tomato purée and not the fresh tomatoes that are sold on the stalls but I couldn't, so I didn't. I watched him take a tin can from his shelf, unscrew its lid and sprinkle a little of its contents into the tomato purée and onions. He screwed the lid back on the tin, returned it to its shelf and turned to me and said 'peeray peeray' and laughed. It may not be spelt like that but I'm sure from the letters I've used you can guess his pronunciation. I repeated 'peeray peeray' back at Trefor and smiled knowingly. Knowing that this peeray peeray is top-grade dried and ground chilli peppers. He added nothing else to the sauce, no salt, pepper, garlic, nothing. Back in my kitchen at home I'd be adding all sorts of herbs and spices to attempt to make a sauce that had the character that Trefor's has and still failing.

On the shelf beside the tin of peeray peeray with the screw-top lid is a cage about 18 inches square. The cage is handmade from bamboo and twine. In the cage is a small but very much alive cockerel. A few inches along the shelf from this cage and away from the tin is another similar-sized cage containing a similar-sized cockerel. Now these pair of cocks have not been taking any interest in what secret ingredients Trefor may put into his sauce. They don't even seem to show any interest in what fate might befall them. Their only interest is in expressing what they think of each other and from what I witnessed it was not a lot. They both were doing all in their powers to peck out the eye of their foe. Their rage knew no bounds and all their rage was focused on their one and only comrade in fate. Trefor looked up and smiles his good-natured smile and with his hands he mimed in no uncertain terms what this was to be. I wondered how many fowl have their necks wrung every day on earth and I thought how they had never sold their souls and I was about to wonder if I should feel anything in particular, me being a member of the RSPB. When Trefor repeated his little mime and pointed at the pot where both of these little strutting bundles of testosterone will have their flesh and bones spiced up a bit by his peeray peeray sauce.

But today, on the bed of rice and rich hot sauce, is no little red rooster. An eye is staring up at me. It's the eye of the most evil-looking fish I've seen served up as food in my life. It looks like something that even the Japanese wouldn't eat.

'What the fuck is it, Bill?'

'A catfish, Gimpo. Smoked catfish. Didn't you see them hung up on those bent bamboo tennis racket-shaped things that the stallholders were buying off the geezers in the pirogues?'

'Yeah but...'

Gimpo fell silent and, like Z, just stared down at the black fish lying on their plates. It's the face of the catfish festooned with at least half a dozen of his whiskery barbels, still seeming to twist and turn off the edge of the plate that makes him look like he's been sent as a messenger from Satan himself.

I know that I've got to somehow save face and be seen to take responsibility as leader when it comes to things culinary so I don't wait for Trefor to come back with the knives and forks. Instead, using my fingers, I peel back the charred black skin of the catfish. This reveals the white flesh underneath. I break off a morsel of this flesh and pop it in my mouth. It's fantastic.

'You fuckin' disgust me, Bill.'

'It's great.'

'Yeah,' as in 'no'.

'Honest. Try it.'

Trefor turns up with the cutlery and I set to work removing the tasty flesh from the bones. It is genuinely a fantastic meal. Gimpo is won over by my review of the dish but Z just pushes the fish aside with his fork and eats the rice and sauce.

What's now left on my plate is the classic cartoon fish skeleton with a tail at one end and a head at the other. The head is still complete, whiskers still twisting and turning, left eye still looking up at me from the plate. There is only one thing to do. I squeeze the eye out of his head. I hold it gently between my forefinger and thumb, wait until I know that both Z and Gimpo are watching me, then pop it in my mouth.

'Mmmm, tasty.'

Z throws up over his plate.

The Japanese film crew were not idle themselves, rushing around like piranha at feeding time, plugging things in, testing sound equipment, shouting at each other in the yapping toy-dog timbre of their barking language. The weird geometry of their faces was contorted behind thick-lensed spectacles, their short little legs were jerking them around urgently. As the dread sodomy barge hissed up close to us the perverted Japs in a flurry of fluffy mikes and digital chaos were the first to leap aboard, cameras clicking, LEDs flashing. They seemed to know exactly what they were after and immediately headed below deck.

A horrifically ugly Arab sailor, swarthy and cruel looking, threw a steel rope over to one of the *Colonel Ebeya*'s reluctant crew. As soon as the barges were secure the revolting anus freaks started mincing aboard. Two pale babyskinned Germans, naked except for leather face masks, multiple body piercings and garish tattoos were the first on board.

I thought I was pretty much *au fait* with the bum-shivering demimonde of dysfunctional sexual perversion, but these two...

One of the repulsive Deutsche fatherfuckers had his dick split in two, held together by numerous decorative clips and bolts. His straining nuts hung down to his knees, stretched by chromed weights which seemed to be stapled to his scarred ballbag. A massive silver buttplug like a giant baby's comforter stuck out of the back of his ruined khyber, across his belly the homosexual monster had tattooed the true confession 'I Am Shit' in 12-inch gothic lettering. Across the king of buggery's back was a remarkably accomplished piece of tattoo art depicting the cultured bummer's masochistic icon, St Sebastian.

The fag patron saint gazed up to heaven, his muscle-queen body nailed to a tree by the cruel arrows of an intolerant society that refuses to tolerate men's natural urges to bugger tattooed babies. Buggeryking's entire body was a web of scars and burns like some horrific contoured map of the antipodes of hell.

His boyfriend, Tweedledum was just as fucking bad, corpulent, somewhere around his middle years with grey pubic hair and slightly more muscular than his friend. The words 'Top Sausage' were tattooed across his fat gut along with all manner of pentagrams and black magic nonsense tattooed into the scar tissue. Top sausage was wearing a pair of shiny red PVC hotpants with a hole for his ugly cock to hang out from, which was also covered in tattoos and piercings.

ON THE ROAD TO TOLEDO

I'm back in my bunk. The other two are refusing to talk to me just because I ate the eye of a catfish. So instead, I will get back to where I left off with Z and me in Madrid station. But first I want to tell you I don't give a fuck about the notion of good and evil. Evil stalking this earth manifesting itself as ethnic cleansing, despot-style super cunts or just the teenage muggers of your granny doesn't wash with me. I'm sure it can all be explained by selfish genes, dysfunctional families, crap childhoods. That said, I'm totally up for complete responsibility for your own actions in life. Take the can like a man and help make the world a better place is what I preach.

We left the three young ladies unirrigated, took a taxi across Madrid, caught another train heading south. The timetable told us we would get to Toledo in 60 minutes. Toledo sounded like the right place to be heading. The name had a ring to it, like Reno. 'I shot a man in Reno just to watch him die,' sang Johnny Cash once upon a time. And we all like the idea of Johnny Cash.

I think the real motivation for us heading out on this jaunt around Europe was because we couldn't get up the Congo until the rainy season was over. And it wasn't over until May. So Z, easily bored, persuaded me we should do a bit of a satanic reconnaissance. The reason we were on the road to Toledo was because Z had read somewhere that it was the only place on earth where the devil casts a shadow. Now that to me sounded like a pretty attractive notion. Going looking for the serpent where his disguise may be most complete was one of those inverted things that often wins me over.

Toledo station was all Moroccan in style and, according to, Z the place where Take That filmed one of their video clips.

'So?'

'So Bill, you undervalue the value of boy bands. I think they are great.'

'They are shit Z.'

'No Bill, you are wrong, they are the modern Tamla Motown.'

This is a theory of Z's I've heard numerous times before. I'm having none of it. Boy bands are shite, Tamla was at times pop nirvana. We let the subject drop. We got a taxi into town. The place was a medieval walled city built on a rocky out-crop above a bend on the Rio Tajo. My tourist guide told me it had once been a mix of Jewish, Islamic and Christian cultures. A warren of narrow streets. All picturesque and stuff. Crawling with tourists in the summer months I imagine, but under a weak January sun, just the place for a pair of seekers like Z and myself to find something. Even if it's not what we were looking for. What we found is that the place has a history of armoury making. On every corner was a shop selling all manner of blades from seven-foot double-hander jobs to nifty little stilettos. And every other weird contraption with an expertly tempered piece of steel, ground to split the finest of hairs. There they all were, racked up in the shop windows waiting for the tourists to hand over their credit cards and buy a useless bit of merchandise to hang on the wall among their other tasteless and tacky trophies brought back from other holidays.

Of course Z was easily seduced by the tourist-guide rubbish in four languages telling us this was where the conquistadors had tooled up before they set off for Eldorado.

'You know you want one, Bill.'

It took all my limited powers of persuasion to convince him we shouldn't blow the rest of our 'Do Europe On A Tenner A Day' budget to invest in a pair of swashbuckling sabres.

'I don't. But you buy one if you want one.'

'What would the point be if only one of us had a sword? There'd be no fun in that. I'd be at an unfair advantage.'

I ignored him. He tried another tack.

'But look at the loving craftsmanship. That there is the groove where blood runs cleanly down. We must arm ourselves against Satan and his legion of warrior angels.'

Z may argue that these weren't his exact words, but he would know the sentiment of my accusation rings true.

'But I thought you liked knives?'

'I'm over 40 now. I've no need for the blade any longer.'

'What do you mean, Bill?'

'Well, Z, once you are over 40 you no longer feel the need to cut women up.'

'What, completely?'

'Yep. There was a time that I would argue that every woman had something of beauty about her. Maybe the turn of her ankle, the curve of her thigh, the swing of her breasts, the toss of her hair, and all I had to do was slice a good bit off, dispense with the rest and in no time at all I would have collected enough to build myself the perfect woman. You hit 40 and realise however many good bits you collect, you can never build that perfect woman.'

'So what have you done with your collection?'

'Donated it to a private museum.'

The rest of the day was spent bar-hopping and visiting every secluded chapel we could find. On our knees staring up into the stained glass-saints, seeking crumbs of redemption wherever we could find it. A miserable half an hour was spent reading some historical blurb (in four languages) on the interior walls of the citadel about the thousands who died in the Spanish Civil War defending this ancient city before it fell. I can't recall if it was Franco's men or the others. There was a week or so in my late teens when I wanted to be Laurie Lee walking out on a spring morning to do the right thing. But the Spanish Civil War was long over so I went to Portugal instead where they were in the process of throwing over their dictator. But I missed the action there as well. If there isn't a war for a young man to go and fight he feels a bit redundant so he goes and steals a car or joins a rock 'n' roll band. Either way it's a pretty useless second.

Z and I like painting. The tourist guide told us El Greco spent much of his working life in Toledo. We went looking for his work. We found it and it found us. Found us wanting in a certain department. And we studied the Greek's work for signs. Those little pointers that us seekers need along the way. Then we went looking for a cheap bed and breakfast, and we found that too.

*

They stepped aboard and started browsing among the perverted playthings as if they were a regular suburban couple performing their weekly shop at the local supermarket. More anal warriors stepped from the dark recesses of the sodomy barge to purchase tubs of snake oil, dildos, handcuffs, ropes, knives. One particularly gruesome brown-eye pirate bought himself a package of disposable baby's nappies and a tin of SMA formula milk.

The mind vomits.

Bill was trembling violently, he had to grab hold of the rail to steady himself. His hand was shuffling away again inside his crusty pocket.

I was curious, I'd never seen a sodomy barge before. I leapt on board. There was a familiar European sex-shop smell, perfumed disinfectant and bollock sweat. There was also the added brown odour of boy musk that clung to the walls.

I asked one of the perverts, a small Japanese guy crucified to one of the cabin walls if there was a bar on board. He couldn't talk much as he had hundreds of needles stuck into his neck like a dog collar. He gurgled politely and pointed with his eyes to the rear of the barge.

Bill and Gimps jumped on board. The decks were spotless compared to the sewage-swilled gangways of the *Colonel Ebeya*. We walked to the rear, past dozens of locked cabins with all kinds of weird noises and strangulated cries echoing from inside of them. It was dark in the bar area, a couple of furtive Arabs looked up as we entered and then returned to their task of filling up hessian sacks full of high-denomination American dollar bills. The place was sparse, painted black with the lighting all at crotch level, typical Urban Bummer Gothic. The lighting gave the place an edgy bad-trip vibe like a Fassbinder film. You expected Doc Caligari or some lowlife fag Jesus to wander in at any minute and order up a Bloody Mary.

TWIST AND GLIDE

It's dawn. Gimpo and I are up on the roof watching the sunrise almost vertically from the eternal jungle. We've already attended the early morning service. It being Monday morning it wasn't as full as the Sunday one. It seems these services are a daily occurrence and I think

Gimpo and I will become regulars. We've been taken to the bosom of the congregation. Well, at least Gimpo has, his twinkling blue eyes working their magic on some of the young mums. Some of the roof boys are still asleep – no blankets, curled up like stray cats – when there is this almighty roar of the ship's horn, followed a couple of seconds later by what seemed like a distant echo of it. The 20-odd roof boys are instantly up on their feet waving and pointing. The horn goes off again, and again there is an echo of it but this time the echo is a little louder. Gimpo and I get to our feet. Up river we can see what the boys are getting so excited about. Still a couple of miles away and coming around from a right-hand bend in the river is a similar flotilla of barges to ourselves but this one on its way downstream.

The horn goes off for a third time and again the same response. We are being joined up top by numerous fellow passengers. Even Z has dragged himself from his bunk and hauled his arse up on to the roof to see what all the commotion is about.

'What the fuck's going on, Bill?'

'Look, up-river, some more barges.'

'So how come all the stallholders are getting so excited by it?'

'Fuck knows.'

A couple of minutes pass. The other flotilla is only 100 yards or so away. The engines from the *Colonel Ebeya* have been cut. The rooftops of these new barges are packed with similar roof boys, waving and dancing, shouting and screaming at the roof boys on our barge who are behaving in a similar manner. The engines of the oncoming barges have also been cut and slowly, as I write these notes, the two flotillas twist and glide in the black waters closer and closer together. It seems as if even all the jungle blasters playing the infernal Afro pop have been turned down for the occasion.

Then bump and grind and scrape and then an almighty cheer from the thousands of witnesses of this strange coming together and coupling. Stallholders and assorted volunteers leap into action, binding the flotillas together into one being whatever lengths of rope or suitable material they have at hand. We, the big we, are now turning and twisting, slowly drifting downstream on our own combined axis. Our roof boys are leaping across the narrow abyss to the other roofs and their boys to ours.

I don't know if it's just because over these past few days I've got used to ours and I no longer notice the general filth and unseaworthiness of it, but this new lot are completely and utterly fuckin' rank, from their captain down to their roof boys. They all look of a lower order: worse dressed, dirtier, underfed and, it has to be admitted, there is a rotting flesh stench rising up from the flotilla.

'Shall we jump over, have a look around?'

'No fuckin' way, Gimps.'

'What about you, Bill?'

'You go, Gimpo. I'm happy just to stay here and watch.'

So that's what happens. Gimpo leaps the six feet. Z and I stay, make notes and watch the communal madness that arises out of this strange mating of two huge beasts out here on this wide expanse of the Congo, somewhere in that vast primeval blob on the side of the globe that is the Congo Basin.

I imagine it as if it's all been filmed from the air and they had dubbed on some ballet music and I was watching it on the telly at home, instead of sitting here on the roof making these notes.

*

The bar was lit in a more conventional style. The bartender himself seemed relatively normal, I expected some kind of toothless gorgonzola sex dwarf or at least someone with half-a-dozen bolts through their bell end. A bank of TV monitors above the bar itself was showing some grim bummer porn. Gimps was particularly fascinated by the sickening scat adventures splattering around on one screen.

'What the fuck are we doing aboard this abomination?' said Bill through gritted teeth, the muscles in his cheek were standing out like steel cables. He was trembling worse than before and had started farting even more than usual. He was muttering obscure bible references, Galations – something about the people of Christ being crucified for their lusts and desires.

The bar was happily well stocked. Row upon row of glittering optics, a shining rainbow of hard liquor. I ordered a giant Shit Sling cocktail and a rake of beers to wash it down with. The bartender seemed OK. He wasn't a bummer, he was an American backpacker trying to make a little money to support his wandering before settling down next year in Boston to study for his psychology degree.

THE CATAMITE CLUB

I couldn't take the hullabaloo anymore and have retired to my bunk. Z was mumbling something about evil Arabs, sodomy barges and some story he felt the urge to write so has headed to the bar. I'm happy to let my mind drift back to Toledo and let my pencil do the thinking.

After dark this city slips from its twentieth-century moorings back into its medieval self where it feels more at ease. Z and I made our way up the darkest of alleys looking for the bad side of town. Not only was Toledo the only place on earth where Satan cast a shadow, it was also known as the immortal home of magic. There was a green lamp hanging above a heavy door.

We pushed open the door and found ourselves in some ill-lit catacombs. There was a bar, above which smoked hams hung. We ordered wine, bread, olives and almonds, then found a recess where we could view the comings and goings and spin our tales.

And a story did start to spin and spin. The threads of which you may find holding together this book you have in your hands. It may have been the oily and over-weight proprietor of this cellar bar who set it off. It may have been the cigarette card-sized collection of sepia-tinted photos that hung on the walls. These pictures were not of pre-war cricketing heroes or even long forgotten matadors, but pretty little Arab boys. We knew with the certainty of holy liars that this must be the Catamite Club of sodomistic legend. The fat controller behind the bar was none other than Fat Miguel, the proprietor of the Catamite Club for at least the last three millennia. One of the ancient photos showed an Arab boy with a carnation behind his ears. He was the template for the now legendary Kiki. It only takes a whiff of homosexual decadence to fire Z's imagination and he is off on 1001 tales of far-fetched debauchery.

'Bill, this is where Mad Frankie Fraser first hit it off with Truman Capote.'

'What?'

'The last time I was here, Lord Mountbatten was canoodling with Francis Bacon.'

'The painter or that bloke in history?'

'The painter – don't be fuckin' stupid. The other Bacon has been dead hundreds of years. It wasn't the IRA that blew up Leggy Mountbatten, it was a jealous Francis Bacon. Word had got back from the Catamite to the Colony Room that Leggy had had a fling with a friend.'

I caught Z's wavelength.

'I remember, I was there. Bacon had just come in. He was raving about this latest screaming Bishop when in walked Boy George, sporting a Prussian-blue Nazi uniform. "Where did you get the threads, Fat Boy?" asked Fanny Bacon. Well, Fat Boy George had his answer: "I've just got back from spending a couple of weeks at the Catamite, powdering the bottom of that cuddly Nazi Himmler. And he told me that Leggy had checked in with Lucy Freud for a bit of a blitz and it wasn't just the Arab boys they were at, it was each other. So I nicked this uniform, got back to Soho fast 'cause I thought you should know." Fanny went ballistic. "I'll get the cunt" were his exact words and one week later Leggy's yacht was blown up and he was just dog food on the beach.'

'You're just makin' it up, Bill.'

'So?'

'So I was here last week. Dropped in for a late-night toddy and Oscar was snogging that teenage bum boy and genius Rimbaud and in walks Bosie. You should have seen the fireworks.'

Not to be outdone by Z's flights of fancy, I suggested that Brian Jones had been made a member and Mick Jagger was so pissed off and jealous he had him kicked out of the band, even had his death arranged. Mick has been trying to gain membership ever since, even wrote 'Sympathy For The devil' in an attempt to flatter his way past the hat check boy.

With the detail of the fanatic, Z described the large canvas painted by El Greco that we imagined hanging above us depicting the buggering of the still-warm Christ figure by the Roman soldier who had won the honour with the roll of dice at the foot of the cross.

So we came to Toledo in search of the true shadow of Satan, but what we uncovered in the dark recesses of our imaginations was the Catamite Club and its collection of art. To call this collection of art priceless would be to devalue it by bringing the notions of the marketplace too close in proximity. It seemed that every great painter with an unnatural tendency or two had reserved his greatest works to be admired by those select few who had gained entrance to the Catamite Club.

Sadly, my own unnatural tendencies were never of the Greek persuasion and it's so long since I felt the need to explore them I've almost forgotten what they were. But my passion for art has not diminished as my flesh has weakened. Since boyhood I've sought and found solace and inspiration in great paintings. My tastes are catholic and random as only a self-educated boy's can be.

Up until that day in Toledo, El Greco was just another name, one of at least 1000 others who had picked up the brush and I had stumbled into knowing a few irrelevant facts about. But that night after Z and I found our drunken way through the labyrinth of dark passages to our cheap hotel I fell into a dream-filled sleep. And I dreamt of El Greco's paintings with all their array of dissonant colours. Their bright yellows and ultramarines, their elongated and unnatural figures, their wonder and ecstasy. Their emotional power, their devotional intensity. All that Christian expressionism. *The Agony In The Garden. The Disrobing of Christ. The Assumption of the Virgin*. Late Renaissance on a roll, not overtly bogged down with all the classical stuff but kicking down the doors of mysticism using every trick of Saint John the Divine on the way. From the New York intensity of Rothko to the transcendental rush of Monet's lily pond to the kitsch of Dali's *Christ On The Cross* staring down at the Sea of Galilee, I'm a man for the power of paint to drag from the unconscious to the conscious world our deepest and darkest hopes and fears. Painting can tell us what it is like to be alive even this side of the Eastern Gate.

And by the way, Z's application to become a full member of the Catamite was turned down. They never tell you why, but I did hear a rumour it had something to do with him being a friend of that little snitch Marc Almond.

*

Gimps was still transfixed by the TV monitors, lost in some black wankzone hell. A small business-suited white guy wearing a Donald Duck mask was up on the screen beating the living crap out of a terrified Asian girl with a solid brass dildo. Business man of the year kept stopping to take a piss in the terrified teenager's face, doing weird little goose-step dances and throwing Nazi salutes. He had a big old pineapple and he was getting frustrated trying to stuff it up the screaming girl's cunt.

'Where the fuck did you get these videos?' asked Gimps, twanging away under the bar.

'Oh they're not videos,' said Ken, the barman helpfully. 'That's close circuit, a lot of these guys, you know the customers, they like to off the merchandise and not pay for a replacement. This way we always know who's killed who so we can charge it to their account. These Arabs, man, they're sharp. They don't miss a thing.'

'You mean that shit up there is live?' said sexy boy, a ripple of lust curdling his consonants and oscillating his vowels, 'It's happening right now, on the boat, here?'

Gimps was giving his turkey neck a double-fisted hammering. I moved out of the way in case he started shooting vinegar jizz all over the place.

'Shit, yeah man,' replied the nonplussed barman. 'Between you and me, I've worked some pretty fucking radical chutney ranches, far-out bars, man, New York, 42nd Street, and all that. I thought those East Coast faggots were pretty outer space, yeah? But man, I shit you not, the fags that ship aboard for this little cruise, they are like the crème de la shite of the crème de la shite, if you know what I mean.'

The Los Angeles man of the world threw Gimps the remote control.

'Check out cabin 23. Like I said, these guys consider themselves like kind of sexual gourmets, you know what I'm saying? They've pretty much used up all their options on the barking spider front so these cats like start partying with chicks, you know, for, like, the novelty-type thing. Shit man it ain't my business I just work here... yeah just push that 2 dot and then a 3.'

Gimps found his channel and started laughing. Bill was over in the corner with a beer, he had a glazed look on his face. He was scribbling in his book and muttering.

A couple of überperves peeped into the bar a little unnerved at seeing strangers on board their floating playpen. Eventually one or two pick up the courage to enter. They were a sorry looking bunch. I almost felt sorry for them. Nearly every school has one or two of these poor bastards. The nerdy weakling, constantly humiliated and bullied. In the better public schools they're usually referred to as the school tart. The older boys, under the cruel dictates of hormonal insanity and traditional toff codes of buggery and honour, would fuck the poor little sub senseless and then pass the bruised and bleeding little fellow on to his peers and occasionally some of the younger masters.

Is it any wonder then that after receiving their inheritance or having a lucky break in the world of computer science that these damaged individuals come out here to pass on the ritualistic sphincter-tightening horrors to another generation of doomed buggers? Ken said that it wasn't just the sexually crippled that came out here for the anal highjinks, that a lot of super-rich international businessmen from America, Japan and Germany paid premium dollar to get their funky monkeys stroked. The arse end of the English aristocracy, the lesser earls and druggy barons were also known to sell off a few heirlooms to spend a week or so in the scat rooms buggering away to their heart's content and eating shit.

Gimps was flipping through the channels laughing at some of the antics of the rich Westerners up on the monitors. One channel in particular was extremely funny, even grumpy Bill managed a chortle.

THREE OF US BEING POIGNANT

It's Monday evening I think. The three of us are sitting up top. The night sky is massive, filled with a million stars. No moon. The southern shore of the river is only a couple of hundred yards from the barges. In the daytime the shoreline is defined by the impenetrable-looking wall of rain forest. Massive trees standing a couple of hundred feet high stand guard along the river's edge. Where the geezers in the pirogues come from, I don't know. At night things are different.

'Seen those camp fires burning in the jungle?'

'Yeah look, there's a couple more burning up ahead.'

'Haven't you noticed them before? I've seen them every night since we left Kinshasa.'

'Nah.'

'You can see the silhouette of people dancing around that one. Kids and dogs as well.'

'Wonder what it's like to live in the jungle on the banks of the Congo with fuck-all but all of this?'

'That's very eloquently put, Gimps.'

'Fuck off, Z.'

'No, I mean it. People write whole books trying to say that and you've just captured it in half-a-dozen words.'

'Wonder what they talk about around those camp fires when they can't be talking about football and soaps? What they read in the newspaper, politics and shit?'

'Just the usual. Who's shagging who and made-up stories.'

'You noticed that some of the roof boys are smoking kif? Everywhere you go in the world and somebody is smoking hash.'

'This is how I thought it would be in Africa. I'm really getting to like it now. I've got used to all that stepping over sleeping babies. Yesterday I nearly stood on one's head, I'd have crushed its skull. But now I've got it all sussed. You just got to focus in on the small things, like this afternoon I was up here writing my story about your theory that Queen Victoria was Jack the Ripper and how you thought you should be the King of England.'

'Scotland. King of Scotland.'

'Yeah, Scotland. Whatever. Anyway, these lads saw my tattoos and came over and started asking me about them. They thought I was a kung fu expert, 'You kung fu man? You know Bruce Lee?' They wanted me to give them a demonstration.'

'How the fuck did they know who Bruce Lee is?'

'Bruce Lee is a god, everybody knows who Bruce Lee is.'

'Oh.'

'Have you written up that bit where I dared you to eat the catfish's eye?'

'Yeah but I changed it a bit. I didn't mention you daring me and I said that when I did you threw up all over your plate.'

'Why did you say that?'

'I didn't know how to finish the story. Me just eating a fish's eye didn't seem that big a deal, so I put you throwing up in your plate as a kinda full stop to it. You know, add some drama.'

'If you'd written the scene properly it wouldn't have needed any drama adding to it. By the time you ate the eye there must have been at least 25 kids standing around the three of us, silently watching us eat and when you popped that eye in your mouth they all screamed and ran away in horror.'

'Oh yeah but I forgot.'

'Forgot? How could you forget? You're supposed to be documenting what's going on not making things up about me throwing up in my dinner. If somebody used that scene in a film, it would look brilliant and if you don't get it in whoever writes the screenplay will have no idea that it happened.'

'Yeah but you throwing up could look good as well.'

'It wouldn't have the poignancy.'

And with that Z pulls out a mouth organ he has been harbouring and begins to improvise a strange, evocative lament. So in case a scriptwriter is looking for a poignant scene and can't use the one about the kids crowding round us in the canteen 'cause I forgot to write it up, this one can be used instead. The three of us, sitting here at one with it all: the campfires and dancing silhouettes; the massive sky, studded with strange stars; and our ragtag flotilla of barges, just a mere speck in this wilderness chugging up and further up river, hour after hour, day after day, forever.

＊

'Jeez,' said Ken, grabbing a can of snake oil from under the bar, 'That's the third time this week.'

He hurried out from behind the bar and left the room.

Up on one of the TVs a fat white guy was screaming trying to wrestle some poor black kid's head out of his arse. How the fuck he got it up there is anyone's guess. On the screen Ken enters and tries to calm the panicking white guy down and simultaneously applies huge dollops of snake oil around the thrashing black kid's neck. The poor little bastard, he could have suffocated up there. Ken grabs hold of the kid around his chest, puts his boot on Fatso's arse and wrenches the kid's head out. The kid falls to the ground gasping for air and wiping shit out of his eyes.

'Is there anything else up there, Mr O'Dowd?' enquires the helpful barman.

Fatboy squeals and points indicating that there is. Ken, used to this sort of crisis, stuffs his entire forearm, like a vet foaling a mare, up the blobbish degenerate's arse and pulls down not one, but two dead spider monkeys. He throws the dead primates into a black bin liner and bids a good evening to the wealthy guest.

Ken washes his hands and receives a standing ovation when he re-enters the bar. Gimpo is obviously impressed and buys him a drink.

JUST A THOUGHT

There are times when you realise you have not thoroughly thought things through. Your motivation is suspect and your ideas derived from a mish-mash of half-digested bits of information that you have either picked up in a haphazard fashion through your adult life or been force-fed as a juvenile by a bunch of narrow-minded bigots and occasional well-intentioned teachers.

You have a hunch that you have never applied rigorous and disciplined analytical thought to what you are about; that you are prepared to be swept this way and that by the winds of whim, always allowing for a bit of dilly-dallying on the way. And then you remember it's too late to stop now, so you just get on with it.

*

A steady trickle of weirdos slime their way into the darkened room. I started to get a little nervous as the brown bombers eyed us with a sinister curiosity over their garish cocktails. A spectacularly ugly transvestite with thick blue-frosted lips and eyes like tarantulas slurps on his stripy straw and with a flourish of his hideously long felching tongue licks up the icing sugar glazed around the rim of his glass.

I shuddered and switched my gaze to the bank of TVs. One of the screens shows a grim room somewhere in the rear of the barge. There's about 50 young boys aged about 7 to 15 huddled closely together shivering in chains.

'What's with the chained KFC?' I asked Ken.

'Spares,' he says. 'Some of these fuckers' – he derisively thumbs at his increasingly bold passengers – 'like to finish off their sexy torture games with a little death weirdness, so the Arab guys have to carry spares. It's sick shit, man, you know what I mean. If I didn't need the money... and Fat Miguel, man, he pays top dollar.'

Silence hits the room like Arctic winter. A glacier creaked at the South Pole, an orchestra in Bayreuth peeled down sliding spookiness, a choirboy is forced to smoke a verger's horn in the vault of a Hawksmoor church. Bill's glass of beer shatters in his clenched fist.

'Fat Miguel!'

He forced the words through gritted teeth. One of his incisors, long in need of dental attention snapped off and fell into Gimpo's cocktail.

'It's probably another Fat Miguel,' I said, hoping to avoid any more atrocities.

GIMPO COULD BE A GENIUS

In my bunk, trying to write a story about Z and myself in Madrid, when Z pokes his head around the open door.

'Bill, I've just seen Gimpo writing.'

'What are you doing here? You're supposed to be in the bar drinking and making shit up.'

'No Bill, I've just seen Gimpo writing in a notebook. Did you know that Gimpo could write?'

'I hadn't actually given it any thought but I suppose not. What, actual joined-up writing?'

'Yeah. I snuck up on him. He was down where they store all those sacks of grain. He's got a notebook. He's got pages and pages already written. This is serious.'

'What do you mean?'

'You know how Gimpo can't lie.'

'Yeah.'

'Well that means that whatever he is writing must be the truth.'

'Yeah.'

'The truth, Bill. The truth. Don't you get it? Who will want to read all the crap that we write if they can read the truth? People always want the truth.'

'Hang on a minute, Z. You're always telling me the opposite of that. That people want the poetry, the fantasy, the religion, anything but the hard facts.

'No, not that kinda truth. The truth that Vincent Van Gogh can tell, the truth of the real artist, the genuine poet, not what us jumped-up pair of jessies have to tell.'

'What, you reckon Gimpo could be a genius?'

'It's not worth taking the chance. I've had my suspicions before about him being the real thing. Up until now he's not been aware of it himself but as soon as the outside world or, God forbid, the literary establishment feast their eyes on it, the cat will be well and truly out the bag. Who the fuck will be interested in us? It will be Gimpo this and Gimpo that and we'll just be a couple of stooges in the background.'

'So what do you suggest?'

'We have to stop him.'

*

It was too late. Bill was up and making his way to the back of the barge, we followed his movements on the TV screens.

'What's with your buddy man, he looks real pissed.'

'Oh it's probably nothing,' I lied, knowing that ever since Toledo and that creepy little Arab kid there seemed to be an awful lot of bad blood flowing between here and old Espania.

Gimpo was up and dancing with a fine looking six-foot mulatto pre-op transsexual, a big parcel of beefsteak bulging beneath her cute red rubber miniskirt. Whether Gimpo knew or even gave a fuck, I don't know, but after a couple of slow grooves funky sex dwarf and his big old ladyboy headed off into some darkened alcove behind the bar.

'Oh fuck!' shouted Ken, 'Rambo alert!'

It was Bill up on the TV.

He was vibing in some Indiana Jones hero trip and had freed all the spares. The little arse slaves were running all over the place, a full-scale mutiny was kicking in. The little bumboys were freeing all their brothers and hacking into their sodomistic torturers with machetes and the surgical instruments they had been tortured with.

Gimpo, hearing all the chaotic pandemonium, came running out from his hideyhole stuffing his shit-stained tubegristle back in his pants. An angry transsexual with a black turd nestling in her platinum beehive and spunk on her false eyelashes came cursing and adjusting her bollocks after him.

Bill and the boys were fighting their way up to the deck scything into the Arabs and perverts indiscriminately. A fire was blazing in their wake. The freaks in the bar were hysterical, screaming and running around in high pitched circles.

A FEW MINUTES LATER

'Hi, Gimpo. How's it going?'

'OK.'

'What you up to?'

'Keeping a diary.'

'Why? What's the point?'

'I'm bored, Z, seeing as you confiscated my camera and seeing as you pair of fuckers are always writing so I thought I'd give it a go.'

'But we're the writers. It's our job.'

'Since when do you need qualifications to be a writer?'

'Penguin Books publish what we write so we are writers: that's the qualifications.'

'I don't give a fuck about that. I want to write because when I get home I want to be able to remember what happened, read it when I'm old, show my grandchildren. All that.'

'You can read what we've written. Show them that.'

'Yeah but it's not the same. And anyway what you write isn't what happened.'

'I've got an idea, Gimps. Maybe we could use some of your writing in the book that Bill and I are doing. What do you think?'

'Could be good. Would I get paid?'

'Maybe. If it's any good.'

'OK.'

'All right. See you later up at the bar.'

*

The little nip crucified on the wall was screaming for someone to unnail him. No one took any notice.

Any moment now it was payback. I can't say that I felt much sympathy.

Bill and his little gang of junior Spartacuses swarmed into the bar armed with high voltage dildos, surgical instruments, machetes, hippo whips and fell on to the freaks like a plague of locusts. A ragged limb would occasionally fly out from the black and red tornado of gristle and screams. The fire from the lower decks was spreading.

Bill rolled a drum of snake oil to the top of the stairway leading to the hold, he hacked a hole into it with a machete and kicked the highly flammable buggery lotion down the stairs. The drum exploded and the barge lurched sideways.

The Japanese film crew ran up the stairs coughing and shouting in their yappy voices. They moved like fast-forward Keystone Kops as they scrambled off the sinking barge and on to the *Colonel Ebeya*.

We followed the Japs and jumped on board just in time to watch the vile craft burn a bright orange on the black river.

It appeared that most of the young arse slaves made it safely to the river banks, you could see them finishing off the perverts as they too tried to struggle to safety. A few tried to follow the *Ebeya* but we were just a little too fast for them.

Their was a faint vibe of resentment floating around our barge, as if the three of us had broken some unknown rules of jungle etiquette. Gimpo discovered later that although the roof boys were more than pleased that there was one less sodomy barge floating on the river, the stallholders weren't. There wasn't much call for 18-inch vibrators, electric butt plugs and snake oil among the villagers.

In the end it turned out OK though, the dildos made ideal rolling pins and the snake oil was fine for cooking purposes. Africans from the Congo area don't bear grudges and pretty soon all was forgotten.

IN THE BAR

Z with a Primus. Me sipping a Coke.

'Z, I thought the plan was to stamp out Gimpo writing altogether and there you are encouraging him. Almost offering him a position as co-author. I'm not into dividing up the advance and royalties three ways.'

'No Bill, you don't get it. This is the plan. We let Gimpo write whatever he wants to write. Keeps him sweet, out of trouble. And when we get back to England he hands it over to us to be edited. In the meantime I write up my own version of Gimpo's diary and we use that.'

'But he'll notice.'

'We just tell him it's the editor that's done it. It's their job to tart up whatever we've written, make it readable. It's just his stuff needed a bit more tarting up than what is usual.'

'And the money?'

'We tell him that the editor's time is expensive and that they had to spend so much time in tarting up his writing, it used up the budget.'

'Do you think he'll go for it?'

'We have no choice. Have you got any alternatives?'

'No but...'

'So that's that. I'll get on with writing *Gimpo by Gimpo*.'

Chapter Seven
COLIN WILSON, THE GENIUS OF CRIME

After a while the nights became routine, though not entirely uneventful.

Our cannibal friend Queequeg appeared to have more than one wife, each one more enthusiastic than her immediate predecessor. So intense was their bouncy abandonment the grappling lovers never seemed to notice bug-eyed Gimpo's singlehanded steamhammer applause mere inches from their raw passion.

Bill though appeared to have seen enough after Queequeg's first performance. He was apparently working on more serious business. Inside the hermetically sealed world of his mosquito net by the light of a single candle, scholar Bill busied himself with scores of old books and papers. I could see his flickering silhouette shaking late into the morning, scratching away with his clumsy carpenter's pencil. Strange grunts, squeaks and stifled laughter, cries of 'yes! yes! of course!' echoed out across the river. I was pretty used to this kind of thing. Bill was often solving great mysteries, working hard to prove the unprovable.

Gimpo had managed to rig up a single light bulb in our cabin. The only problem was the lack of a light switch, instead there was an arrangement of Sellotape and bare wires. Personally I preferred it without the light. It was bad enough sharing a bed with four-inch cockroaches, I didn't want to see them as well. The light bulb was also a reminder of the night-time activities of the Eel. When they were frying some poor bastard's balls with their electricity tortures, the screams reverberating around the barges were accompanied by the dimming of the light bulb as all the boat's power was sent through the unfortunate's knackers.

This seemed to be about the only thing that put studboy Queequeg off his copulatory gymnastics. The spunk athlete would dismount sheepishly and tremble in fear for the rest of the night. At first light he would meet up with the rest of the terrified stallholders to find out which poor sucker had been dragged from his bunk and forced to trip the gonad electric.

DRUMMOND'S LOG, TUESDAY 11 JUNE 1996
A GREY DAWN

A grey dawn is creeping into our cabin... No! No! Fucking no more descriptions of dawn weather be they creeping, leaping or just walking. It's morning almost, the others are still asleep and I'm on my bunk and out of my bag I've pulled a brand-new minidisc recorder thing, a microphone, wires and an instruction manual. I'm trying to read the manual. I read the words. They mean nothing to me. I read them again. Still nothing. They are simple words, simple instructions but none of it stays in my head. I hate the fact that I have this thing at all. I hate having to come to terms with new technology. I love the idea of it in principle but hate having to learn how to deal with it myself. Some people, stupid people, read manuals and understand them. They enjoy reading them. They enjoy getting a brand-new piece of digital equipment, taking it all out of the box and polystyrene packing and then sitting down to read the manual. And they will understand what they are reading and will take pleasure in mastering how the digital thing they have just got works. Even thick people can do this. I can't. Even Z can do it. Now, if I had had my way, I wouldn't have this minidisc recorder thing with me.

'So why the fuck have you got it?'

Last week Sally – Z's Sally, not my Sallie – engineered some sort of arrangement with the BBC's Radio 4, for us to make some sort of documentary of our journey. We were each given one of these digital minidisc things, the idea being that we keep audio diaries. I thought this was a crap idea but I was outvoted. As far as I'm concerned, we are here to redeem our souls and to write great literature. Not piss around attempting to make a radio programme that if we are lucky will get aired once late on a Tuesday evening in February with three people listening to it. Great literature speaks down through the decades; a radio programme is forgotten the next day.

*

I woke up one morning and brushed the cockroaches out of my hair to find that Bill had been working the entire night. He was laughing triumphantly, packing away his library and his stack of blunt pencils. He pulled his mosquito net to one side and jumped down into the shit, splattering Gimps once again.

'So obvious!' he chirped to no one in particular. 'Oscar Wilde? ridiculous! Lewis Carrol? what nonsense!' he continued, lecturing an invisible audience. 'No gentlemen, my evidence is irrefutable! I am convinced!'

He was pointing at himself in the small cracked shaving mirror Queequeg had attached to the wall

'Mr Wilson, I propose that the identity of the Whitechapel murderer, the perpetrator of the so-called Jack the Ripper crimes was none other than the Queen of England her very self!'

'Fucking hell, Bill,' said Gimpo resignedly, wiping the sloppy shit from his eyes. Detective Bill was oblivious, fired up and ranting about his latest discovery

'Driven to despair by the death of her husband, Albert and his humungous memorial-sized penis, the sex-mad sovereign would steal from the palace and make her way to the eastern part of the city, her butcher's tools concealed beneath black petticoats.'

Bill left the cabin still pontificating. I caught up with him later in the bar. He was explaining everything to the confused bartender who hadn't the slightest idea of what it was that the cracked white man was so obviously excited about. I grabbed my breakfast and went outside to drink it. Bill collected his papers and books, his plastic carrier bag full of assorted crap and followed me outside. He tipped the contents on to my table, the usual obsessive's hoard: letters, pencils, rubbers, old Mars bar wrappers, pieces of string, yellowed newspaper cuttings, human ears.

I picked up one of the paperbacks and flipped through. It was heavily underlined in places with Bill's blunt pencil. Odd words scored across whole pages tearing into the paper. He had about 30 or 40 paperbacks on the Ripper and associated subjects, all of them containing the same demented annotations. Scruffy graphs, pie charts and scrawled lists of dates on curry-stained napkins and torn beermats. Ranting spiral-bound Silvine notebooks filled with 2B indecipherability.

TWENTY MINUTES LATER

The dawn's done most of its creeping but no sign of the sun yet. A new moon hangs in the clear sky. Gimpo and I are up top at the front. The roof boys are still asleep, curled up like stray cats, no blankets. Gimpo has his minidisc with him and he's showing me how to work mine.

'Look, Bill, all you've got to do is slide that, press this and hold it this way around. It's simple.'

'You're about to tell me any fucker could do it.'

'Yeah well, you know even these lads know how to do it.'

So I slide that, press this, and hold it the other way round and start.

'It's dawn. Day four. Gimpo and I are sitting up on top of our barge. The barge is at a standstill, moored to a small island in the centre of the mighty Congo. On the island is a village of no more than a half-a-dozen houses. Built on wooden stilts in the water and I don't give a fuck about what I'm doing, saying or for any purpose that it might be put to.'

I press the off switch. Rewind. Press play to listen back to what I've just recorded.

'I can't hear a fuckin' thing Gimpo.'

'That's 'cause you've just pressed record and not play. You've just wiped what you recorded.'

I gather up the minidisc Walkman thing, the wires, the microphone and the manual, put them all back in the Tesco bag that I had brought them in. Tie a tight knot in the top of the bag, making sure there's air trapped in the bag so that it might float even with its current cargo. I stand up and throw the bundle as far as I can towards the houses on stilts on the small island in the middle of the mighty Congo.

'What the fuck did you do that for, Bill?'

'Gimpo, there is no way I am going to do any more of this recording stuff.'

'But that was not yours to throw away. It was on loan. You're not in The K whatever-it-was with Jimmy now, thinking you can burn what you like, throw away what you don't own.'

'Gimpo, see that lad swimming out from the islands?'

'Yeah.'

'He saw me throwing the bag. The bag is still floating. He's got less than five yards to go before he gets it. He doesn't know what's in the bag. When he gets back to land he will open the bag and he won't know what the fuck any of it is.'

'So?'

'So, by tonight he'll have worked it all out and will have started to record stuff with it.'

'But what about the radio programme?'

'Whatever that lad does with it will be a thousand times better than anything I could do with it. And if anybody out there in Radio 4 land was to hear it, it would tell them 10,000 times more than I could tell them about an island in the middle of the Congo.'

'But they won't.'

'Won't what?'

'Hear it. Nobody who listens to Radio 4 will ever hear what he records.'

'You don't know that. And however long the odds are I'm willing to take the chance.'

'It's not the sort of thing I usually say but sometimes you are an arrogant tosser.'

'But I'm right.'

'No look. He's given up, the bag is floating faster downstream than he can swim.'

I look around, already feeling shit, knowing that whatever that minidisc thing cost could have provided all the cash that boy and his family would need for a year, living out on his island. What I see is not as Gimpo described. The boy is swimming back to the shacks on stilts using

only one hand, the other holding the Tesco bag aloft.
'Fooled you, Bill.'

＊

'It's so obvious I can't believe I didn't spot it earlier,' Bill laughed in a smug self-congratulatory manner. 'Of course I must give proper thanks to my friend, Mr Wilson.'
'Mr Wilson?' I said.
Bill seemed to think I knew who he was talking about.
'Why, the distinguished scholar and world famous genius of crime, Colin Wilson, who else?'
'Genius of crime?'
I had heard of him of course. An obsessive oddball with a thing about murderers. He had created a minor stir in the 1950s with his first book, *The Outsider* which the self-styled neo-existentialist had completed working in the British library by day and dossing out on Hampstead Heath at night. After the success of *The Outsider* the genius of crime started compiling lists of murderers and other assorted antisocial weirdos drawing particular attention to the links between creative genius and murderers. There is a kernel of truth in this of course but creative geniuses as a rule don't like to be reminded of it.
'Yes, the genius of crime, I can't wait to inform him that I have solved the greatest mystery in the annals of aberrant human behaviour, the true identity of saucy Jackie himself, the King of blades, pervert supreme, Jack the Ripper!'
Bill parped triumphantly and went on to explain his convoluted theory, explaining how he had been in correspondence with Colin Wilson since the early 1970s and had gained access to information only serious Ripperologists such as himself were privy to. How he had devoured every single book on the subject, cross-checked dates, visited sites, corresponded to living relatives of the victims, studied maps of the area, timed the walk from Buckingham Palace to the East End dressed in Victorian drag. How he had visited mental hospitals, interviewed and corresponded with Peter Sutcliffe, the Yorkshire Ripper, weighed small plastic bags of his own semen and so on and so forth. Bill's theory on the surface was like most of the autodidactic detectives theories and discoveries, very plausible. An extraordinary amount of research and fieldwork lent his work a weight many a sagacious new-age theorist would have been proud of. But like many of Bill's extravagant conclusions it was built upon a basic premise that seemed to have been plucked from thin air. Of course I never mentioned this. Although they were made from so much of the stuff that fills balloons, to prick Bill's theories would be to deny yourself the fantastic views to be seen riding in the baskets attached to those wonderful yarns.
Bill who ordinarily drinks little seemed to be celebrating, he ordered more beers and carried on with his tales of scholarly detection. As the drink flowed well into the early afternoon and Bill's intricate Victorian odyssey unwound, the motivating force behind all this detective work gradually revealed itself.
Bill, it seems, was convinced that in a previous life he himself had been The Ripper. Remembering his enthusiasm with the working girls back at the Memelin, I didn't doubt that in his own mind at least, this was most probably true.
'So you see!' Bill lurched. He was drunk, his eyes seemed to be focusing independently on different things altogether. 'That makes me...' He stood up, his legs were unstable, he knocked

our empty beer bottles from the table, they rolled across the deck and into the river. 'The rightful heir...' he paused, pulled an exaggerated pirate face and blutted out a tight one. 'To the throne of England!'

The small tight fart must have been one of the little Dutch boy's because when the excitable aristocrat sat down a torrent of splashing beershit blasted out of his arse like the giant belching of a smoking bog, breaching his waistband, skittering down his trouser legs and exploding across the deck, stinking out the entire bar. I noticed the barman covering his face with his t-shirt and trying not to vomit.

The rightful King of England fell face first from his chair into the lumpy dreck and passed out, blowing bubbles in the pools of diarrhoea..

TUG TOWN

We had given up on finding the true shadow of Satan in the back streets of Toledo so we took a train north back to Madrid then a metro to an area of the city called Anton Martin.

In the latter days of Z's pop metal combo Zodiac Mindwarp and the Love Reaction, they recorded an album in Madrid. The band had been holed up in a sleazy hotel Anton Martin. The studio was in a basement below a massage parlour. The album they recorded was never domestically released – it was seen fit only for the German market that truly appreciated the perverted.

As the boys in the band recorded the backing tracks and over-dubbed their guitar solos, Z, as the lead singer, had spent his loose hours attending run-down and poorly attended bull fights and adding to his collection of international porn.

As I may have explained in our last joint literary venture, *Bad Wisdom*, I have never understood Z's appreciation and appetite for porn. Not only does it seem to inspire his wayward libido, it also inspires his creative oeuvre.

Z had been like a kid on his way to Disneyland. With each telling, his tales of the biggest porn palace known to man got bigger, the wares that were going to be on offer got more debased. Z had assured me that the Spanish taste for porn was the most extreme he had ever come across in his extensive research. According to the expert, bestiality was their tipple. And if given a choice, donkey porn was their preference. Why donkeys? The fabled size of their cocks? Their big soft ears? Their sad eyes? Or the fact that one of their number bore Christ on both his first and last journeys on this earth?

Z skipped up the steps from the metro, his old man's coat flapping.

'Come on, Bill. This is Tug Town. I can smell the crispy Kleenex from here.'

I followed in silence.

'It's up this street on the right.'

We arrived at what looked like a boarded-up department store.

'They've fuckin' closed it down.'

Relief swept over me. It was good to know the God-fearing citizens of Madrid had seen fit to clean up this squalid side of their otherwise respectable city.

'Nah, that's it down there. I remember now. It was just the other side of the street from the Pizza Hut.'

If you have read *Bad Wisdom* volume one, you may think this whole Tug Town story is a rerun of that bit where I reluctantly follow Z around the streets of Helsinki while he is looking for some bracing Finnish porn. In one sense it is. But as in any riff, bad or good, only in repetition does it begin to make its impact felt.

I was confronted with the almost Harrods-sized emporium that Z had christened Tug Town. To enter you had to climb a broad sweep of steps and pass through a throbbing and flashing array of neon lights. These pink, red and purple lights had been designed to give the effect that you were entering a 50-foot-high labia.

We left our kit bags at the entrance kiosk and entered the tunnel. On both sides the walls were built from rows and rows of video cassettes. Z was pleased to note they had a whole stash of Sarah Young classics that he had only read about in specialist magazines but never actually seen for sale. Z informed me that Sarah Young came from Bristol and was now happily married to a German porn king. There was no sign of the much-heralded donkey porn, but still the dozens of videos featuring the acting abilities of Tabatha 'Cum In My Face' Cash was very impressive.

Z was eager to journey deeper. After the walls built from 10,000 video cassettes, the tunnel opened out. Around the outer walls were dozens of cubicle-style doors. By each door a red or a green light shone. There were many more red lights than green ones. Z explained, 'Bill, if the red light is on it means the cabin is engaged. I'm off to find a green one. See you later.'

I was left standing there with my reflective yellow dustbin man's coat on my back and my Aylesbury United bobble hat on my head. What to do? I found a green light, opened the door and entered the comparative safety of my chosen tug cabin.

I sat on the plastic chair provided. In front of me were two video screens, one above the other. There was a small shelf to my left, just the right size to support a man-size box of Kleenex. In the corner, to my right was a small waste bin lined with a pale-pink bin liner, the kind I use at home to put my youngest's used nappies in. There were a few freshly used Kleenex left by the previous inhabitants of my cabin.

Instructions came in four different languages. Easy to follow, even for a technophobe like myself. I dropped my 10-peseta coin into the slot and began flicking from channel to channel. You could use both video monitors simultaneously, mix and match your baser instincts as desired. Every perversion known to mankind in visual stereo. But still no donkeys. Was Z lying? Nothing caught my fancy, the ramming and rubber, the three-way air tight, not even the shitting so beloved of Gimpo could hold my flagging attention span long enough to get even the most minor of trouser twitches twitching. My 10 pesetas soon ran out and I didn't feel the urge to pump another into the slot.

Over the PA system, Queen's Greatest Hits Volume One was being pumped out to great effect. 'I want to ride my bicycle. I want to ride my bike,' implored Freddie. It successfully obliterated any festering introspection and shame about being in such a place. I wonder if Freddie could ever have guessed when he first sat down at his piano tinkling with a few notes, finding the right chords and finally coming up with the melody and lyrics dedicated to the innocent pursuit of pedal pushing, that his minor classic would end up being put to such a use.

I would have been quite happy to stand there lost in the wonder and pomp of Queen's mock-operatic splendour until Z reappeared ten cubic centimetres lighter. That is if it hadn't been for the truly sleazy and guttural voice that kept cutting through Freddie's over the PA informing all us citizens of Tug Town about what new products and pleasures were on offer. Each of his announcements began with 'Sexy, Sexy, Sexy', and the rest was in Spanish. But then, just as Freddie and the boys were getting into 'Fat Bottom Girls' came an announcement in English. 'Sexy, Sexy, Sexy, Blue Diamond's live sex show about to begin. Hurry, hurry, hurry for sexy, sexy, sexy.'

I had long since learnt from Z that in such places as this, you must never catch the eye of a fellow customer. We all had to act as if we were unaware of their very existence and they would return the favour. But after the Blue Diamond Live Sex Show announcement, I couldn't help but notice a general movement of my fellow citizens of Tug Town towards an island of tug cabins in the centre of this sea of depravity.

I followed and found a vacant cabin. I was pleased to note that the pink-lined waste bin was empty of tissues, and the man-sized Kleenex box was a fresh one. I dropped my 10 peseta coin in the box and, where the video screen had been in my previous cabin, an automatic shutter slid up. A narrow horizontal slot was revealed. I lent forward to look. The show had already begun. Blue Diamond, which I guess was the collective name for the troupe performing not more than six feet from my focused pupils, were two men and a woman. One man was tall, muscular, long haired and big of cock. The other was black, not so muscular, and gave the lie to the legend of black men being more than average in the size department. The woman left no lasting impression.

All three were naked and their performance took place on a large raised circular platform. They were bathed in a blue light which made all three look particularly unhealthy and cold.

They slid and rolled and pushed and gasped, all in slow motion and in time to the 'Power of Love' by Jennifer Warnes. White cock was inserted into KY'd cunt. Black cock was inserted into mouth. Some movements were made. Then they would change position. How much was choreographed, I do not know. There was nothing wild or abandoned, there was nothing funny or furious. Nobody came too soon. In fact, nobody came at all. The woman affected a few gasps and helped the black cock regain its erection when its attention seemed to wander. Then I noticed I was not alone. All around the raised circular platform that Blue Diamond practised their craft on were other horizontal slits, just like mine. Behind these slits I could see eyes. Eyes belonging to other men with lives and wives and children to feed. Were they too on a research mission, before heading up the Congo or the Amazon, the Orinocco or the Nile? Were they going to confront whichever particular version of the serpent they had locked up in their imagination and demand their souls back? Were they going to get back home and say, 'Sorry I'm late, love but I noticed that Blue Diamond were in town with a new show and I knew you'd think it foolish of me not to take the opportunity to pick up some love-making tips.'

Each pair of eyes with a different story to tell. Why were they there and where were they going? And then I got bored with all this wondering rubbish, left my tug cabin, man-sized box of Kleenex box still virgin, reclaimed my bag from the kiosk, left through the 50-foot pink, red and purple labia and went out into the cold light of a grey Spanish winter's day.

Chapter Eight
THE SECRET PILOT

I cleaned up the king's shit and laid him out in the bar, away from direct sunlight , placed a bucket next to him and told the barman to come and get me if his majesty's arse went ballistic again. Bill's bowel problem can be highly dangerous especially if the royal nutter is whacked off his head on too much beer and strange malaria pills. The last thing we needed now was for King Billy to shit himself to death half way up the Congo.

I decided to take a wander around the barge. The decomposing skunk stench of Bill's accident would take a while to clear and the smells of the rest of the barge were almost sweet in comparison.

DYING DAUGHTERS AND FLIP-FLOPS

Z is still asleep. Gimpo and I head off for our morning ablutions. We watch a pirogue desperately try and catch up with the barges.

'They wait five fuckin' weeks for this boat to come. Their only contact with the outside world. Their only chance to sell whatever they get from the jungle and buy medicine, flip-flops, razors. The bare necessities in life and they miss the boat. The train drivers might go on strike but you can always catch a bus or even hitch, but here you miss the boat and you are fucked. No flip-flops.'

'Yeah, and no medicine for your dying daughter.'

'Bill, there's no need to get real, let's just worry about the flip-flops.'

*

One of Gimpo's new-found friends is leaning over the railings beside us watching the entertainment provided by the man without this year's flip-flops and a dying daughter.

'Meesta Geempo, you think you can paddle a pirogue or you fall in?'

'I fall in.'

'Meesta Geempo, can you swim?'

'Yeah.' Gimpo then unzips his bum bag, which is hanging loosely around his neck. He is trying to pull out his inflatable neck rest. He had already tried to impress Z and I on the flight over with this life-saving device of his. I guess he is going to blow it up and demonstrate how it would keep his head above water even if he was unconscious. But as he is tugging it out, out come a couple of bits of paper that flutter over the side of the railings down towards the black water below. One of the bits of paper is yellow. Pale yellow, the same colour as our tickets.

'Fuck.'

'Was that your ticket?'

Gimpo doesn't answer, he's already climbing the railing as if to jump in after it. I go to restrain him but he thinks better of it. We both instantaneously know the mega implications of what has just happened. All thoughts of the entertainment provided by the man in need of flip-flops and medicine for his dying daughter are forgotten. There are ticket inspections at least twice a day. Without a ticket you are nothing. We have already seen a young man thrown over the side by the ticket inspectors for not having a ticket. Maybe he was a persistent offender, maybe he gave them some jip but over the side he went. I don't know why the roof boys seem to get away without having tickets. What do they have to do to keep on the right side of the only law that exists on these barges? Of course, they won't throw Gimpo over the side, he's too good a catch. They will shake him down until he has nothing left and then shake Z and myself down. This is bad, real bad. We both know this. Those around saw what happened. They know it's bad. You might not think it's that bad, nobody got hurt. It's not like the bloke with the dying daughter.

Look dear reader, there was no dying daughter – I just made that up to make a point. This is real. Gimpo has just fucking lost his ticket, taken by the mighty Congo, that in the end takes everything. You're just sitting there reading this book while Gimpo and I are standing and staring as a piece of yellow paper is floating away.

We have been travelling as illegal aliens on this barge. We bribed some corrupt official ('I thought you said all the officials were corrupt?') $300 to sign the papers to let us leave Kinshasa. I don't want to think about the consequences, let alone write about them. Gimpo laughs. Those around us laugh.

'Gimpo, maybe we should head for the ticket inspector's office, tell him what's happened. Better get it over and done with.'

'Yeah, maybe.'

So we do. Gimpo tries to explain.

*

Although I'd lost track of how long we'd been on board I knew we must have sailed quite a distance up-river because the stuff that the villagers were bringing alongside to trade with us was becoming more and more far out. Long gone were the domestic chickens, pineapples and cassava, the regular fish weren't seen much either, or the small smoke-blackened McCau McCau monkeys. The villagers were hauling out huge fucking catfish 15-feet long, scary looking smoked gorilla carcasses, monster turtles, foul smelling fruits and vegetables I'd never even seen on Brick Lane before. Fat insect grubs, baskets of them, still alive, writhing around in baskets of rich mulch from the forest floor.

The stallholders found our distaste at the sight of the grubs particularly amusing and were constantly playing tricks on us, putting them in our hair or down our backs as we made our way through the aisles of accelerating strangeness.

The thing that disturbed me most was the Tutsi monkeys. The stallholders never actually admitted it but some of the villagers were selling smoked human babies. Apparently these were infants who died accidental deaths. Rather than waste such a valuable source of protein they are sold to the stallholders who trade them for more palatable meats in the Llualaba and surrounding districts. Weird fowl as big as ostrich hung on the side of the cabin to dry. Only the most dangerous livestock is killed, the rest is kept alive till the barge reaches Kisangani. Alligators are securely bound.

I saw one of the larger 'gators get himself loose and take a couple of babies before it was battered to death by the mother of the kids. The local custom decreed that the alligator now belonged to her. The original owner cursed his luck and fastened the rest of his stock more securely.

WHORE SPOTTING

I paced the pavement outside the entrance to Tug Town waiting for Z. We had a train to catch, a place to get to, a mission to accomplish, a serpent to slay and he's just tossing himself off while some celluloid whore takes a donkey up her arse. Just as I was getting to seething point and about to find my own way to the station, leaving my fellow literary arsehole to his own sordid devices, I felt a tug on my arm. I turned around. A middle-aged woman, dressed in that smart Spanish way – shoulder pads, fur coat. She said something to me in Spanish.

'Sorry, senora, I don't speak Spanish.' It was then that I noticed her deep cleavage and smelled her heavy perfume.

'You look lonely young man, do you want some company?'

I'm slow at the best of times. It was only after I said, 'Nah, It's OK, I'm just waiting for a friend of mine' that I realised what her game was. Within seconds she was tapping the arm of another 'young man' as he descended the steps of Tug Town.

Whore-spotting is a hobby practised by many males, it's just they don't put it down on application forms when applying for new jobs. This street in Madrid was a prime site for a bit of spotting. You get five points for a spot. An extra point if she makes a move. Double points if she gets a catch. And bonus points if she gets beaten up by her pimp.

As I said, I'm a bit slow on the uptake, but I soon forgot all about what an arsehole Z was for keeping me waiting as I shot past 60 points in as many seconds and that was without any pimp violence to bump the figures up. The majority of these working girls had none of the clichéd outward signs of their trade. Dressed in stonewashed jeans and brown leather jackets, they stood around in pairs or threesomes chatting about the decline in standards since Franco passed away and how it was a shame that *Guernica* was no longer considered the greatest work of art of the twentieth century.

Within ten minutes I had beaten my personal best of 213 on the whore spotometer. Then my attention was caught by a desperate-looking individual – hardly in her teens, heroin addiction written all over her face and probably up her arms too. She paced up and down, turning her head this way and that. Desperate for a trick to make her next fix. She was approached by three separate males. Each time, a few lines were exchanged before they moved on. Was the price not right? Would she not perform whatever perversion was desired? Even in her desperate state she could still say no. Still hold out for the going rate.

I was saved from further deliberation on the fate of man's fallen state, by Z skipping down the steps of Tug Town. He seemed pleased with himself until I pointed out to him he had forgotten to deposit in the pink waste bin the incriminating evidence of his onanistic activities. Between the middle finger and thumb of his left hand he was carrying a less than virgin, man-sized Kleenex.

We made it to the station in time to catch the night train to Barcelona.

*

I found myself strangely drawn to the engine room for some reason. The thumping diesel monster that was the heart of the floating barrio. You could feel the omniscient presence of the engine no matter where you were, a gentle throb beneath your feet or in your hand as you took hold of a metal railing. The steel pulse of the *Colonel Ebeya* was one of those strange phantom-like things that you only really notice when it ceases to be there. Like an old clock that stops suddenly in a silent attic.

The engine room was a forbidding place deep in the bowels of the *Colonel Ebeya*. Grinding power and angry blue electricity flashed and sparked behind the iron grille that guarded the barge's internal workings. There seemed to be someone inside, the silhouette of a hunched old man occasionally lit by the strobing flashes of light that would explode sporadically from the antiquated machine. I was loitering around grooving on the raw power one evening when the steel gate to the engine room opened and the hunched figure I'd seen lurking inside the oily sanctum sanctorum stepped out on deck like some rare animal.

He was naked save for a pair of oil-stained shorts and had white hair and yellow eyes. His hands were enormous and covered in grease as thick as mud. He grunted and beckoned me into his sinister temple of antique machinery. The noise was deafening, the heat unbelievable. It was an eyeball-frying dry heat unlike the more tolerable wet heat everywhere else. Msomba Msomba doesn't even notice, he rarely leaves the engine room, his meagre meals are brought down to him by one of the roof boys. The overbearing, nostril-stinging stench of the superheated diesel is the air that he breathes.

The engine is the steel heart of the *Colonel Ebeya* and the spirits that live with him deep in the mysterious alcoves and chambers of this solitary place tell him all he needs to know. He has lived here some 60 years or so. He's seen the dreadful independence wars, witnessed Belgians being tortured on the massive fly wheels, seen the Mai Mai throwing screaming babies into the grinding gears, and the fearsome Congo machete reduce men to nothing but hamburger. Msomba Msomba didn't pay much attention to any of it. Life is cheap on this continent and anyway you can be born again, no big deal.

SUBMIT TO THE RIVER

Z is up and looking perky. Well over his breakdown.

'Bill, we got to talk about the book.'

'Why?'

'We need metaphors for the river.'

'What do you mean?'

'You know how Barns [Richard Barnes, our editor at Penguin] was going on at us about how all our descriptions of snow on the way to the North Pole, were bland and unimaginative?'

'Yeah.'

'The river here is like the snow was there. It's the one constant and as such we've got to be able to say more about it than how black it is.'

'But it is black.'

'Yeah I know, but to keep people interested, to keep them with us, we've got to build the river up into something else.'

'I've used the word "mighty".'

'But you called Echo & The Bunnymen "mighty". Nobody will believe you if you just use the word mighty.'

'Z, I'm not here to come up with different ways of describing a river. I'm here to get my soul back.'

'You're talking bollocks again, Bill. We are here to write a book. All that selling your soul stuff is just nonsense, poetry maybe, but we ain't fooling nobody if we don't write a half-decent book.'

'Look Z, it's you who's good at all that stuff. From now on whenever I mention the Congo I will either call it black or mighty. I won't go any further than that, the readers can imagine what they like about the river.'

'That's 'cause you can't.'

'OK. OK. Least I'll be able to remember what has happened.'

Silence.

'Bill, you know what's wrong with you?'

'No, well yes, but you're about to tell me something else that is wrong with me.'

'Yes.'

'Why?'

'For your own good.'

'Go on then.'

'When we went to the Pole we did it all in seven days. There and back, breakneck speed, mission accomplished.'

'We didn't actually get to the Pole.'

'Yeah but you know what I mean. It was non-stop, always something for you to be doing. You can't cope with this.'

'Cope with what?'

'The slowness. The lack of events, the lack of control we have over what happens. Bill, you have to let go. Just be part of it. Submit to the river. Drift among its islands. Everything will be all right and if it's not, Gimpo will sort it out.'

'I don't know what the fuck you're talking about Z. I'm fine.'

'Sure Bill, so get the beers in.'

∗

The smell of the engine to Msomba is like the delicate fragrance of a lover. What sounds like raging, grinding white noise to our ears is sweet music to Msomba Msomba. The sorcerer is intimate with every screw, every nut and brass bolt of this piston-pounding metal machine. He can detect the slightest aberrance in tone of his singing steel. An unusual tremour felt in one of his toes and Msomba knows exactly which screw, which washer, which nut or lever needs adjusting.

Msomba Msomba took out a small box of highly polished jeweller's screwdrivers from a small ledge inside one of the complex piston casings, his arm millimetres from being ripped from its sockets by one of the savage pneumatics. He opened the small wooden box to show me his tools, yellow rheumy eyes shining in the dry heat.

There was a loud hissing from one of the narrow gangways between the cylinders and pistons, I followed Msomba Msomba along the precarious ledge. Blood was leaking from above and boiling to steam on one of the brass casings. Msomba curses at the butcher on the deck above us clumsily slaughtering a pig and used an oily rag to clean the black stain from the engine casing. Msomba Msomba curses in Lingala, something to the effect of 'fucking savages!' He remembers when the Belgians were here and, after checking over his shoulder for the presence of any lurking Eel members, how much better things were. He concedes that the nation famous for paedophiles, chocolate and beer were mendacious and cruel, but then if Mobutu's reign wasn't equal or even worse in many respects at least the Belgians made sure that the rudiments of a state existed. Things worked, he complained.

Now nothing worked, even the diesel he receives to power his beloved *Colonel Ebeya* is cheap and substandard.

Msomba Msomba's beefs are rarely aired and seemed to have combined into one general stew of bitching irrationality. He sounds off about slavery and how it was all the overfed fat chiefs, like Mobutu himself, who instigated the foul trade and that the white man has unfairly been saddled with sole responsibility for one of history's most shameful chapters.

Mammon, he concludes sagely, is neither black nor white.

'The beast is grey,' points out a sombre Msomba Msomba. 'Gris gris,' he adds spookily.

BIG CAT FISH
Gimpo enters the bar.

'Seen the size of the catfish that they're hauling in off the dugouts?'

'They are not called dugouts, Gimpo, they are pirogues.'

'Whatever. But some of these catfish are more than eight-feet long, wanna come and have a look, Bill?'

'Don't bother, Bill, he's only trying to wind you up. You don't get freshwater fish that big.'

'How the fuck would you know?' Gimpo asks Z.

'Because if they were that big they would live in the sea, stands to reason.'

We follow Gimpo down to have a look. They may not be eight feet but one is certainly over six feet and still alive, its whiskers twitching.

'You see, the blokes that buy them off the blokes bringing them in carve their name on the side of the fish with their knives before turfing it into this refrigerated room here.'

Gimpo is entranced by the trading that's going on. The blokes on the boat have got the others from the jungle over a barrel. They keep refusing to trade and the longer this goes on the longer the ones from the jungle are away from their homes and after three or four hours they begin to panic and give in and sell for way below what they were wanting..

'So whose side are you on, Gimpo?'

'I'm not taking sides I'm just watching.'

'What about you Bill?'

'I'm just making my notes. I've decided its best not to have opinions about what's going on here.'

*

I spent many hours during the long journey towards the inner station with Msomba Msomba and even got used to the dry heat, preferring it eventually to the wet cock-rotting vegetable heat of the upper decks. I told him about our search for Mobutu and our attempt to claim back our mortal souls. He found nothing unusual about this but doubted if Mobutu would just hand them over. He also thought that we had been extremely stupid to sell them in the first place and that yes, we had got a lousy deal.

The Captain up on his proud bridge may have been the eyes and the cold intellect of the *Colonel Ebeya* but down here in the mysterious bowels of the freshwater juggernaut Msomba Msomba was the soul and steel balls guiding us along that terrible river. Down here it was Msomba Msomba who witnessed the day-to-day trials and tribulations, the quarrels and casual cruelty of the floating city's teeming population outside and above his dark engine room. The silent captain up on his bridge rarely if ever leaves his exalted position. Even when the rusting behemoth hauls up in Kisangani or Kinshasha the captain prefers to stay up on his lonely bridge. Like Msomba Msomba he takes his meals there and has a small berth curtained off to one side with a few possessions: a razor, some spare clothes, a Bible, nothing more.

He will occasionally greet a visiting dignitary, but this is done reluctantly and only at the express will of the ONATRA company HQ. He is the classic misanthrope. His thoughts are only of the river and the *Colonel Ebeya*. Like Msomba Msomba he has been with the *Ebeya* since it was built in Leopoldville, now Kinshasha in 1938.

He doesn't concern himself with the trivialities of the soft cargo that seethe with frenzied futility beneath his bridge day after vain day. His relationship is strictly with the river, the rain and the ever-shifting sand banks he has to negotiate. It is all-consuming. The lives of the passengers and crew depend upon his calculations and judgement concerning the fluctuating currents and shifting mud. Ten billion gallons of black water lurch beneath his fragile flotilla every second. He has no time for the petty squabbles, the divorces and marriages, the grinding poverty of the visiting villagers in their flimsy pirogues.

The captain keeps them alive, that is all. What they do with that life is of no concern to him. Lesser captains on lesser vessels have passed many judgements upon his icy detachment, the Captain closes his ears to such childish gossip. They say the roots of his strange obsession began with the death of his wife in 1956, since when the captain has not uttered a single unnecessary word. His sole communication concerns the navigation of the barges up and down this notoriously dangerous waterway.

Most people believe that when the captain dies the *Colonel Ebeya* will die too, joining the rusting wrecks that litter the banks of this steaming purgatory. Most people that is, apart from Msomba Msomba. For he like the captain knows every inch of the great Congo waterway intimately. The captain with his eyes, Msomba Msomba with his hypersensitive ears and his submarine soul. He knows its myriad cadences, tones and voices , its shifting guts, every belch, every gurgle and thump that echoes around the chambers and spaces of his precious engine reveals another jealously guarded secret of the black river.

None of the present crew are aware that during the frenzied rains of 1967 when the river was at its most dangerous that the captain was taken seriously ill with a potentially lethal strain of febrile malaria and that it was Msomba Msomba who piloted the *Ebeya* and all the other barges from Mbdanka all the way to Kisangani and safety. Msomba Msomba piloted entirely from the engine room using his unique human radar. Listening intently to the fly wheels and the echoes of the pistons straining against the added volume of torrential water, the sound and pull of the downpour echoing across from the tumbling sand banks. Msomba listened to the river and the river spoke to him.

Only the Captain and Msomba Msomba knew this. They agreed between themselves to keep it secret to assure order above decks and to maintain the crew's belief in the captain's supernatural powers of navigation. When the captain dies, which both men know will be soon, the boat, like the river, will belong to Msomba Msomba, the secret pilot.

BARCELONA, BHAGHAVAD AND BULLFIGHTS

Z and I pulled into Barcelona station at 8.00am. A long and empty day stretched ahead of us. There was no reason for being in Barcelona other than to catch a train leaving at 8.15pm that evening. A train that was going to take us all the way to Milan.

We wandered aimlessly from bar to bar, from church to church. Nothing satisfied us, nothing provided answers or even threw up fresh questions.

The topic for the day seemed to be Z's penchant for quoting the Bhaghavad Gita. It started with Z going on about how great bullfighting was. Now the sceptic in me put Z's professed love of bullfighting down to just wanting to be as un-PC as possible, his love of taking the outlaw position to make himself appear to have an interesting take on life. I had learnt, in our long association, that there was no point in confronting him with any of this. Instead I took a different tack.

'Z, what is the point of sitting there and watching somebody else perform for you, providing your emotional highs and lows, your sense of failure or achievement? This is a general argument I have used time and time again against the watcher of movies, the consumer of porn, the imbiber of narcotics, the football fanatic. Live one's own life, don't live it through the lives of others.'

'Don't be such an arrogant tosser, Bill. How come you think you are above the majority 'cause you've made a couple of records instead of just buying them?'

'I didn't say that .'

'But it's what you meant.'

'No, Z. What I mean is that it is fine to watch a film, buy porn, take a drug and even watch football if it inspires you as an individual to go out and do something yourself.'

'Fuck off, Bill. Are you ever going to stop crawling up your own arse with all your sanctimonious Presbyterian work-ethic shit?'

It was then that Z started to quote the Bhaghavad Gita at length. Now I like the idea of the Bhaghavad Gita. I'm a sucker for any ancient holy book. And if you have forgotten your Hindu studies, I will set the scene – the day is dawning, the hour of the great battle is fast approaching. Arjuna, the warrior leader is to confront his foes, many of whom are members of his family and long-standing friends. Arjuna is filled with doubt. He turns to his charioteer, Krishna, and asks him a load of questions about the nature of everything. Krishna proceeds to give him a load of complicated answers... I've dipped in and out of the Bhaghavad Gita a number of times in the past. A bit of a stand-by on rainy days in the library when the words won't flow from my pen. But it's all too long-winded for me.

At least when the Chief decided to give us a visit again as a carpenter instead of as a charioteer, he seemed to have got it all a bit more worked out, or at least simplified it for us to follow. The Sermon On The Mount only took a few short verses and that was it. No riddles, no intellectual shenanigans, just a straightforward 'this is how it is', in words that every fucker in the world could understand. But now as we sat in some sodding Barcelona bar, Z was quoting me chapter and verse of Krishna. Don't get me wrong, I love the all-embracingness of the many and varied strands of Hinduism as much as the next seeker, searcher and reacher for the unreachable but...

'Bill, there are many ways of reaching Him. Our conflicting views of the Holy Joke within all may be nothing more than the infinite aspects of the same supreme spirit that runs through all creation. To watch and appreciate the grace and artistry of a great matador is to appreciate one of God's many works. It's no different than you going on about how wonderful a bank of wild primroses are. It's learning to appreciate for appreciation's own sake God's work done well. There doesn't always have to be something in it for you to better yourself or get ahead with. Don't you know Bhakti is just as valid as Karma?'

'What the fuck's Bhakti?'

'Bhakti – devotion, worship, adulation. It is through devotion we learn to rise above the I, I, I, me, me, me egomania that seems to drive you on. Bill, you seem to be locked into karma as the only fuckin' way. And another thing, it's your round.'

As I've said before, when Z has had a couple of drinks there is no point in arguing with him and of course he may just be right. I doubt it though.

We watched the old men play boules. We wandered the streets until we found the Gaudi cathedral. You know, the one with the twisted towers you get on all the tourist pictures of Barcelona. Architecture on acid before Hoffman had made his first tab. I was disappointed to find they hadn't finished building it yet.

We sat on a hill and stared down at the blue of the Mediterranean sea and wondered at all the empires that had come and gone, risen and fallen while dreamers like me and Z had stared out over its waters, making up lines that rhymed and others that didn't quite.

Oh yeah, there is another thing I should tell you. That bit in my whore-spotting story about Z leaving Tug Town with his Kleenex still in hand isn't quite true. In fact it was based on a story Z told me about Tex Diablo, the Love Reaction's Mexican bass player who had played Tug Town a visit with Z back when they were recording their album in Madrid.

QUEEN KONG

Extracts from Z's dream log

Time has evaporated for me. I'm unsure who I am or why I'm here. My dreams are walking into my waking world. Huge snapping teeth. Giant turtles. I'm not sure if I'm writing this in a dream or if I'm dreaming that I'm awake. I'm lost in the dark, palpitating magic of the rainforest.

The soca and the sucking heat of the jungle conspire to hit me with dislocated rhythms, digitally destroyed and placed back together by a mad chimpanzee. When I try to sleep I can hear the puppets laughing and talking about me in Bill's rucksack. I daren't tell Bill or Gimpo. Maybe they can hear them too.

I can hear malevolent spirits, older than the forest. Reptile tongues flicker in and out catching passing insects. The mosquito and tsetse are on the wing. Corpuscular angels of death. Powers of the air.

The forest chatters and screeches. Those warring apes, don't they ever stop? Dashing flat skulls, spilling paeolithic brains. Ants troop across the skin of my eyeball pissing acid. Jungle drums bounce across the water. Tortured missionaries again, screaming in the mist above the canopy. The forest and the river conspire in bone-white dead of night and bring down voodoo. It stalks the deck of the boat, an invisible snake, sucking the air from babies' lungs, jangling talismans hang above cabin doors. I hear whispers and secrets. Several times in the night I wake to find everything covered in a pale grey ash left by a silent wind. Bill and Gimpo sleep fitfully, the ash makes them look like ghosts.

A giant mantid, the size of a small dog, perches at the bottom of Bill's bed, it turns its head towards me, black intelligent eyes focus on mine. It climbs down the bunk, stops halfway, turns around and stares at me, drinking my thoughts. Its three-foot antennae vibrate and reach out to touch Gimpo's mouth. It chirrups quietly like a bird, jumps into the effluvial carpet and swims out of the cabin beneath the curtain.

Gimpo wakes, yawns, wonders where all the ash came from, wanders outside for a crap. He returns and tells me that there was a croc in the latrine, thrashing around in the shit. Fucker nearly had his nuts. Vigilant Gimps managed to stamp on its head. Little known fact: Congo crocodile skulls are as fragile as eggshells. The locals call them flatdogs, they are considered more of a nuisance than any real threat to human life.

The word mosquito is afforded a much more reverent dread. Africans lower their voices when discussing the lord of the powers of the air. All the darkest deities of the Congo are winged. The Catholic natives converted by French missionaries know Satan only as the lord of the flies. No creature is as feared as the mosquito: the silent assassin. It strikes under cover of darkness with a painless bite. Twenty-four hours of sweating, shitting, delirious horror later your wormy corpse is ready to start pushing up mangoes.

One in four Africans die of malaria.

JUST OTHER PEOPLE

Back in the bar. Z reads me some of his stuff about the river being king and the jungle his consort or was it the other way round. I read him some dialogue from above.

'Z, I've given up trying to create any storyline out of all this. If I can just get snippets of conversation between us, I'll drop them into the shite you're going on about.'

'Shite? What do you mean shite?'

'Sodomy barges and the like. It keeps it real.'

'People don't want it real. We've come up the fucking Congo, risking everything. They want sodomy barges, they want catfish 20-feet long, they want all our fevered imaginations can deliver. If Vincent kept it real do you think anybody would have given a fuck how starry the night was?'

'But Z, I think if people read this stuff...'

'What, us bickering?'

'Yeah, well they'll be able to relate to it. They'll think it's just like them and their mates down the pub bickering.'

'Do you think when you and Jimmy were wearing rhino horns and singing about Mu Mu land they dug it 'cause they could relate to it?'

'No but...'

'No! It's our job to deliver what they can't relate to and I've got to give them what they didn't even know was possible to dream about. Let's have a look at some more of what you've got.'

'Hang on a minute Z. I ain't finished it yet, it's just notes.'

'Come on, what you got to hide?'

'No need to get belligerent.'

'OK. OK. Be precious.'

'All right, you can read this bit I wrote this morning.'

'It's like the dialogue from a sitcom. Did Gimpo really say that?'

'Sort of.'

'I never said that.'

'Yeah you did.'

'I didn't call them "fucking niggers" that was you.'

'No Z, you did.'

'But that makes me look racist.'

'We are racist.'

'Yeah but we can't say that or they won't publish the book.'

'What, and all the sexist stuff is OK?'

'It only sounds sexist if you're thick.'

'And it only sounds racist if you're thick. Z, I explained all that at the beginning about how the racism thing is only a natural reaction to us being scared, shit scared. Anyway, remember, we are not racist any more now that we don't even notice them being black. They're just other people.'

*

Just when you think you've seen the biggest catfish in the world, there is an even bigger monster blorping away in the narrow passageway outside your cabin, the next day. Still alive four hours out of water, lashing mouth antennae flailing blindly, sensitive tip flickering, curling around your thigh, probing your sphinc.

A weasly looking guy beckons me into his hole beneath some rusty stairs. It smells of fish and masturbation, a grey tangle of blankets moves uneasily in the corner. Wanker Sambo tries to sell me a four-foot catfish, pointing at its Naomi Campbell lips.

'Mermaid, Mermaid!' he says, miming thrusting movements. He unzips his raggedy-ass shorts and sticks his flaccid knob in the fish's mouth. I always thought this was a nautical tradition. When old salts were bored of buggering the cabin boy and each other they would often fuck large fish, hence the stories of mermaids. I didn't realise this happened on inland waterways, I thought it was strictly a mariners' hobby.

HAIL SATAN!

The night train from Barcelona to Milan, early February 1996. I was on the top bunk trying to get some sleep. Z was sitting on the bottom bunk reading *The Waste Land* out loud and giving me a running commentary about what it all meant and how great it was.

'"*In the mountains, there you feel free. I read, much of the night, and go south in the winter.*" Are you listening Bill? This is proper poetry. Hard-man poetry, none of that romantic rubbish.'

Z was trying to embroil me in a conversation. But Z was more than half-way through his bottle of vodka. I have a rule: no talking to Z once he is past the half-way mark. By that time his bitter demons are slithering through their bars and looking to spread their venom.

'"*Out of this stony rubbish? Son of man, you cannot say, or guess, for you*"... Bill do you think you are a poet?'

I was pretending to be asleep, hoping he would give up and just get on with his drinking before sliding into his coma.

'I'm a poet Bill. Do you know what it's like to be a poet? Do you know what poetry is?'

*

If I ever have to fill in forms – passport, driving licence, bank account, insurance-type forms – and there is that space to the right of the word 'occupation', I always put in the word 'publisher'. This started back in 1977 when I was the only one in the band I was in who was old enough to hire a van. The van-hire man's insurers wouldn't cover musicians, a bad risk. The van hire man wanted my money so he suggested I shouldn't put 'rhythm guitarist in a punk rock band' but 'publisher' instead. I didn't even know what a publisher was. Was he somebody who had a print workshop? Or was he Tiny Rowland? It all seemed a bit vague and that is why the van hire man suggested I put it down as my occupation. It sounded respectable but didn't actually mean anything too much. The strange thing is, over the years I have become a publisher of sorts. First, a publisher of posters, then a publisher of songs and latterly the publisher of a few books.

If the van-hire man had suggested that the space to the right of 'occupation' had been filled with 'knife grinder' would my life have followed a different path? I suppose I could have put down that I was a carpenter. Being a carpenter is the only proper job I ever had, the only one where I knew what I was doing and was able to take a healthy pride in my work. I've always held on to the notion that if everything goes badly wrong and the grocery bills need paying and shoes are needed for the kids' feet, I could always get my tools out. I have a habit of standing outside building sites watching the chippies at work just to check I could still do the job.

But back to poetry. As usual, Z knew how to prod the strained muscle. And seeing as his bitter demons were slithering about he felt the need to prod. You see the thing is, I've secretly come to the reluctant but vain conclusion that what I do is maybe a poetry of sorts. Not poetry as in short lines, slim volumes and all that. Not even putting any sort of words on any kind of paper. But poetry in another sense. Like this journey up the Congo, maybe that's a poem. Or Z, Gimpo and me trying to get to the North Pole, maybe that was a verse. And maybe all the things that Jimmy and I got up to together were in actual fact a bunch of poems. Even when I was supposedly managing Echo & The Bunnymen it was never about making them as big as possible and getting a pile of cash, there was always some weird story I was trying to weave. Some notion that I was trying to grasp the unknown, trying to order the unknowable. Like so many words arranged in short lines in a slim volume that you can read on the bus.

But calling yourself a poet, what kind of arsehole wants to be a poet? To have 'poet' down on your passport? To go down the pub and they all turn and say 'Mind your backs, lads, here he comes, the village poet. Seen any waving daffodils lately, Bill?' Not for me.

*

I could hear Z pour himself another tumbler from his duty-free supplies. The train pulled itself around the eastern end of the Pyrenees without falling into the sea.

'"With a wicked pack of cards. Here, said me, is your card, the Drowned Phoenician Sailor. The hanged man said "Fear death by water". Are you alive or not? Is there nothing in your head?

HURRY UP PLEASE IT'S TIME. Goodnight Bill. Goodnight Lou. Goodnight May. Goodnight."'

Then silence. I was lying there, hoping Z had finally given up trying to get me to respond and that he had slipped into his alcoholic coma. But just as I was beginning to think about the wide blue-black Mediterranean and Jonah being thrown to the whale out there again and again and again, Z started up again. But this time he seemed to be on a different tack.

'Just to wake up alive is enough for me, whatever else happens, I can deal with it. If I wake up alive I'm happy.'

Ten seconds of silence.

'I love people. I just want to make people laugh. You're like me Bill. We just laugh, that's why I like you. You make me laugh.'

Z almost successfully drew me into conversation then. I wanted to protest that I had never knowingly tried to make anybody laugh. I don't like laughter. People have laughed *at* me but that's a different matter. More silence but then he was off again.

'I know you are awake, Bill. I can hear you scribbling your little lies in that black book of yours. Those churches and cathedrals we've been visiting, I could spend hours in them. They make me feel strange. They fill me with a longing. Why can't I write about that? What's going on? What do you feel? Or are you too Presbyterian to appreciate them, Bill? You just think all those bleeding heart statues and stained-glass windows are kitsch rubbish. They're not kitsch, Bill. Those shrines are glorious, wonderful and true. You can kneel in front of one of those altars, look up into the eyes of our Lord and know he is dying for you. For all mankind. To die for what you believe is the ultimate. And Jesus did. To be nailed to a cross of wood. To hang there dying with your bleeding knees, with your mother below wailing. The Passion Play is all of life. Mankind without Jesus is fucked. In India they worship dogs, men with elephant heads and blue faces, even rats. Imagine worshipping a rat. Imagine going around with a rat on a chain around your neck. Man makes God in his own image. What kind of man are you if you make a frog your god? We made a man our god. The supreme man hanging there lean and filled with longing. With Jesus we took on the rest of the world and won. Are you getting all this written down, Bill? This is important. Without Jesus we are fucked.'

Of course I had to draw on all my reserve not to let myself be pulled into some late-night drunken theological debate. As far as I'm concerned all the Passion Play and empty tomb and Ascension Day stuff is just marketing. I've said it before and I'll say it next week: Jesus stands and falls with the Sermon on the Mount. Matthew, chapter five, verse one through to chapter seven, verse twenty-nine. That's what Jesus had to say. Plain and simple. If you dig it, fine; if you don't, fine, but all the rest is just mumbo jumbo for would-be idolaters.

GOATS, PIGS, CROCS, BUGS

I woke bleary eyed, in need of a shit.

I opened the cabin door, hooked on the loose piece of wire that that – BANG! – Gimpo keeps getting electric shocks from. Standing there in the mild chill of another Congo dawn is Mr Pitsu, one of our neighbours. He is eating a small bowl of very large, very live wriggling millipedes. The writhing brown things wrap themselves around his fingers which Pitsu then places in his mouth and sucks with smacking lips. He registers the abject horror blanching across my features and sticks the bowl under my nose laughing.

'Is good, Mr Z, you try.' I throw up over the side of the barge.

My nose is producing extra mucous, blocking up my sense of smell. An unconscious reaction from some body intelligence, like the build up of earwax when subjected to loud volumes of music for long periods of time. Obviously combined with the nuclear intensity of Nagasaki Drummond's rotting dirtbox and the daily ablutions of 3,000 Africans and their menagerie of swine and spoiling fish my body had decided to fend for itself. Quite remarkable, my sense of smell simply surrenders and closes down. It is impossible to describe the hellish stench the *Colonel Ebeya* leaves in its shit-dripping wake.

BACK IN THE CABIN

'Gimpo, what the fuck are all these people doing in our cabin?'

'It's OK, Z. I just stuck this map of Central Africa up on the wall and all the neighbours wanted to have a look and show us where they come from. And where we are and where we are going.'

'Yeah but what about our stuff?'

'They're going to nick it anyway if they want to. If we are going to all live this close to each other we have to trust each other.'

'Gimpo, you are the last person on earth to trust anybody.'

'Yeah well I'm trusting now. Mavuba, he's OK.'

'Who?'

'Mavuba, the bloke you call Que Ques or whatever.'

'He's written down his address here, says we can stay at his place if we are ever back in Kinshasa. And he's drawn this diagram of all the barges and what they are called. *Bangole*, that's our one. *Lokele*, that's the one opposite and beyond that, it's *Buluba*, behind us *Mukongo*, that's the one with the canteen and there's the *Bangal* and the *Bashielele*, the *Tifutu* and, of course, the *Colonel Ebeya* where the bar and engine room and bridge and first class is.'

'And is this one your girlfriend?'

'Anyway Z, where did you get the t-shirt?'

'Swapped it with one of the blokes who works on the bridge.'

'Z, can you describe the t-shirt you had before and the one you got now so I can put it in my notes as dialogue?'

'What, you trying to give up with description altogether?'

'Yeah, I'm going to see how far I can get up the Congo with only dialogue.'

'No internal monologue.'

'None. Anyway, describe the t-shirts.'

'This morning I was wearing a long-sleeved Buzz skateboard t-shirt. This afternoon I swapped it with our neighbour for an ONATRA 1935 to 1995, sixtieth anniversary t-shirt.'

'And what is ONATRA?'

'You know that.'

'Yeah but for the readers.'

'It's the shipping line.'

'I thought you swapped it with one of the blokes up on the bridge.'

'Yeah, but he lives next door.'

'One big happy family.'

'Right.'

Very small internal monologue bit coming up. I feel good. We feel good. All is good.

There is an almost constant high-pitched squeal of distressed jungle swine and, depending which barge you are standing upon, the equally high-pitched screams of human beings being tortured. The Order of the Black Eel are keeping a low profile, but they are here. The low hum of evil which vibrates sickeningly in the lower gut gives their presence away. I have heard the click of their jackboots as they prowl the decks at night when everyone sleeps. The wailing women in the morning indicate their nocturnal machinations; husbands seized under cover of darkness, eldest sons pressed into service.

Bill is spending more and more time on the roof with the young men. I can see him from the balcony of the bar practising naked karate with the shiny black athletes. He is showing them strange moves I have ever seen before. He is also spending inordinately long periods of time in the communal men's shower towards the rear of the barges.

PATHETIC DICTATOR
Back in the cabin trying to make sense of my Eurorailing notes. There is a problem: the unrelenting steamy heat has caused the glue that holds the binding to disintegrate and chunks of pages are now spilling on to the floor.

It seems Z and I arrived at Milan Central at 9.03am, that, as usual, we were the last off the train. We were scrabbling around for our soiled undergarments and holy trinkets as the cleaners were already trying to fumigate our sleeper cabin. The overnight train had taken us from Barcelona to Milan. Under the splendour and conceit of Milan Central, a monument to the vision of Il Duce, we were like a pair of woodlice exposed to the daylight, running around useless and frightened. Z in his old man's coat still flapping open. Me with my Aylesbury Vale District Council dustman's coat and my Aylesbury United bobble hat pulled down over my freezing ears.

A lot has been written about Benito, the playground bully with too many brains and too much charisma who found himself strung up on a lamp post, pathetic and dead. A lot has been written about the importance of major railway stations between the years 1850–1950 and their part in subjugating the proletariat. A lot has been written about Benito Mussolini and his railway stations, especially this one where Z and I found ourselves behaving like frightened woodlice. Milan Central is a great station even if it took Benito 'Il Duce' Mussolini, the most pathetic dictator of the last century, to build it.

According to my notes we went in search of bacon and eggs and all we found was a dried cheese roll. There are some lines that mention that the reality of Italy, as witnessed on a February morning in and around Milan Central, doesn't quite live up to the stylish myth we had presented to us in our mid-1990s British media.

'So Bill, who is your favourite dictator?'

'Haven't got one.'

'Course you fuckin' have. Spit it out.'

'No.'

'Mine is still Hitler.'

'Look Z, I'm not some rock chick who might be impressed by your made-to-shock opinions.'

'Bill, without dictators the world would be bereft of great buildings, no pyramids, no Great Wall of China, no Teotinhucán, no Parthenon and not this station.'

'So, what great buildings did Hitler leave behind?'

'His was conceptual architecture.'

'Fuck off.'

*

Today I discovered the roof hootch. Gimpo brought me a small bottle of it. It goes some way to explaining why the feral scamps have such husky voices. It possesses a distinctly odd aftertaste, not completely unpleasant, but best reserved for emergencies. The alcohol is fermented not from a vegetable source but from rotting human flesh. This is what the viscera and limbs left over from violent activity those pointy toothed bucket kids were collecting was used for.

Despite my earlier suspicions, cannibalism is not tolerated on the barges, but for some reason fermenting alcohol from human remains is not considered a cannibalistic practice per se. The boys rather disgustingly mix it with their own semen and the larvae of the giant millipedes Mr Pitsu was eating for breakfast.

THE STARS

Later. Three of us up top at the front lying on our backs staring up at the stars. The seven blasters are still battling it out below but kinda distant. Everything's all right. Gimpo has not been thrown overboard yet.

'You know what this is like?'

'No, Gimpo, tell us.'

'It's like we are on a space ghetto hurtling through the emptiness of eternity.'

'Gimpo, that's really good, I think I will use that.'

'You'll have to pay me.'

'Pay you for using a few words? Which one of those words do you own?'

'How much do you think they are worth?'

'That ONTARA t-shirt you got today.'

'Fuck off.'

'Did you actually invent any of them?'

'No but...'

'No but nothing. Words are in the public domain. I can use them, you can use them and I am using those ones you just said.'

Nobody says any more and we just stare at the stars again.

And so to bed.

*

Gimpo is becoming increasingly worried about a huge sexual mountain of a woman. Over the past few days this pagan Magdalene has made her dripping lascivious presence felt. A mastodon of untamed female desire, huge catfish lips painted lurid pink, shining like a wild vagina.

Black mascara'd eyelashes, dangerous butterflies fluttering in Gimpo's direction. She rolls past us in the bar her brightly coloured sarong pulled tightly across continental-shelf buttocks and man-killer thighs. Her sexy swollen belly as fecund as the jungle, resembles the curved earth itself. Thick strong arms for wanking off white men. Colossal tits to die between, bouncing in time to the lazy rhythm of her flip flops.

Every scintillating atom of this fantastic woman was created for fornication. Every carnal inch of her black arse suggests the fuck of a lifetime. She undulates past her rapt fiefdom of enthralled males quivering at the smell of her sex, a heavy ruttish musk visible like dust swirling in her wake.

Every man on the flotilla seems tremblingly excited and terrified in equal measures. She is main momma, the Queen Kongo and her cross-hair sights are set on the Gimp. Her thick pubic eyebrows arc enticingly towards the mesmerised studmuffin. He is utterly powerless against her putrid spell. Her massive presence stirs something far deeper than the confused worm writhing in his Jockeys.

Her colossal backside, as big as the moon, sways past like a gargantuan Russian bell. The Gimp's nostrils dilate, he can smell animal heat radiating from her dripping cunt. One of the many preachers on board trembles, drops his Bible and shaking like a leaf crosses himself. He knows that if Queen Kongo so desired him, his god would be powerless.

She stops at the entrance to the bar, Astarte Syriaca, a black Cleopatra, she fixes her supranatural gaze upon the bewitched Manchester boy, licks her gash-pink lips and is gone, leaving the shadow of her wild libido hovering in the doorway. Gimpo faints and tumbles tumescent to the deck.

DRUMMOND'S LOG, FOUNDAY JUNE 1996
INTROSPECTION
'Gimpo, are you awake?'
'Yeah.'
'What day is it?'
'Tuesday, I think.'
'Yesterday was Tuesday.'
'Well then maybe today is Tuesday as well. If you can have a month of Sundays the least you can have when you are heading up the Congo is a pair of Tuesdays.'
'Shut up, Gimpo, I'm trying to work something out.'
'When did you wake up, Z?'
'I've been awake all night.'
'Why?'
'I've been listening. I've worked it all out. At some point in the night one by one all the blasters stopped playing. As their owners fall asleep and the cassettes come to an end. It was then that I started to hear the sounds of the jungle. They were terrible. There is no point in me trying to describe it to you now, I will write it down later.'
'So what have you worked out?'
'What the African fears more than anything is introspection. That's why he has invented soca or hi-life or whatever their pop music is called. The music is invented to blot out the self. The music blots out the sounds of the African night until every last one of them has fallen asleep. The sound of the jungle at night is the sound of their own soul. For them to hear it is like us

staring down into the bottomless well of our own being. The African does not flinch from pain, can cope with hunger, can slaughter his brother, can deal with all the blows that this blighted continent throws at him on a daily basis but he can't deal with staring into the dark mirror at his own soul.'

'So what you are saying, introspection is a European invention?'

'Probably.'

'Z, can I borrow your minidisc recorder thing?'

'What's wrong with your own?'

'I threw it away.'

'You what?'

'Well I didn't throw it away. I threw it in the Congo so that this lad who lived on an island could have it.'

'What the fuck are you talking about? Those were just lent to us. They were proper professional ones not some cheap crap from Dixons. My Sally did a deal with the BBC for them. Promised them we would look after them. You're a fucking arsehole, Drummond.'

'Yeah, yeah I know, I'll explain it later but in the meantime can I borrow yours?'

'For fuck's sake, just take it but don't throw it away. What you going to do with it, anyway?'

'Gimpo and I are going to the morning service and I want to record it.'

'That's another thing I've worked out. That going to church thing they do every morning, it's not 'cause they want to be good Christians, it's not going to stop them killing each other. They use church to blot out any vestige of introspection that may be left over from the horror of the night.'

'And another thing, if they haven't got their happy-happy music at hand until they fall asleep they have to have sex. It's not that the African is more highly sexed than us, he just can't cope with lying in bed at night thinking about not only his own pointlessness in the grand scheme of things but that maybe there is no grand scheme. You'll never have an African asking the question, 'To be or not to be?' 'INTROSPECTION, THE WHITE MAN'S BURDEN', that could make a good chapter heading and yeah, you can borrow it. But be careful now, run along or you'll be late for Sunday School.'

*

Another day seems to have drifted into the glowing hues of another fleeting sunset. I slide around in my own grease beneath my tangled malaria net. Bill scribbles away in his tent. It is impossible to sleep, I light another cigarette and pray for land.

I'm woken by the mad sound of the jungle and the shrieking of the blasters.

Our cabin is in darkness, the rumbling permafarts Bill seems to exude like other people expel breath whines away in a continual wet drone. Gimp's grinding teeth confirm that he too is asleep. Slowly and mysteriously the ragged curtain at our door parts. My heart skips a faster beat.

A pristine spear of moonlight stabs into the warm darkness and falls upon Queequeg who mutters in terror, grabs his pants and skitters out between Mona Demonicus' stout legs, his latest wife follows chattering some unknown prayer.

The terrifying shadow of the sexual one frames herself in the doorway against the silver moonlight. Bill's flatulence shifts pitch. A whimpering whine petering nervously to silence, the wise Scot stuffs his finger up his arse and feigns sleep. I adopt the same strategy.

SAINT SEWARD

It was another crap day, filling the empty hours until Z and I caught another train at 3.10pm. A train that was to take us from Milan Central to Bolzano, a city up in the Italian Alps. The three and a half hours were spent in the buffet bar. Spent staring out at a miserable winter landscape. What my notes reveal is that as the grey Lombardy day retreated into darkness, our moods slid the same way.

"Stay out of church son. Don't let a priest near you when you are dying. The only key they've got is the one for the shit house." Do you know who said that, Bill?'

'Nope.'

'Well you should. That was Saint Seward. William Seward Burroughs. Patron saint to all low-life losers who have aspirations to make it to the high plains as well respected literary outlaws. That means you and me, Bill.'

'Does it?'

'Yep. And he also said there were innumerable gods. What we on earth call god is a little tribal god who has made an awful mess. I tend to agree with Burroughs.'

I sipped my red wine, stared through the window as we pulled out of Verona Station and thought, 'Why would I want a queer, drug-riddled, pathetic loser as a patron saint? One who needed to get his big-boy kicks by playing with guns. One who, if he hadn't accidentally shot his wife dead as a publicity stunt, none of us would never have heard of.' In reality, I knew what my problem was. If I had read *Junky* or *The Soft Machine* or *Nova Express* when I was 16 or 17, I would think he was one of the greatest writers of the twentieth century. But, as it is, I didn't. Not out of design but just 'cause my reading list was a purely random selection of whatever was in the second-hand boxes. And Burroughs never came my way. By the time you reach 21 you are pretty set in your ways. You've got your canon sorted and there is no room left on your parthenon for any more gods so Wild Bill Burroughs never made it. And the more I got told by would-be decadent doley layabouts that he was the king, the more I thought 'empty icon'.

'One day Bill, I will force-read you Burroughs.'

'Yeah.'

✳

'Meestah Geempo…' purrs the thick female baritone, ichorous vaginal mucous dripping from every syllable. 'Oh Meestah Geempo...'

She moves serpentine into the vegetable heat of our high cabin trailing her odour of sogging cunt. Like some hyperheated jungle cat she whips off her sarong revealing her shining junglebeaver. The sheer megawattage sex heat she radiates in tidal waves makes it hard to breathe. She bends over, legs apart her hands running down to her calves gripping her ankles and thrusts her flood warning gash into Gimpo's bunk.

'You lahv eet,' she purrs filthily.

The smell is unbelievable, a million rank vixen on heat, every small fishing vessel in the world all berthed at Grimsby. The heat threatens to melt the steel cabin. All this, the calm before the volcanic sexual apocalypse about to visit Earth right here right now.

Bill is torn from his bunk and crunched against the ceiling, a confused boner trying to hide up his own backside. The elemental sex force is blocking the door, Bill like a terrified squirrel scrambles up on to my bunk and hides with me beneath the mosquito net where we precariously observe the awesome force of nature. Bill has his pen out and is scribbling away, his smoking pen trying to keep track of the sexual corrida unfolding savagely beneath us.

Mama Kong is rubbing her huge purple pudenda up and down Gimpo's grinning chops, her piss flaps mashing his ears like some gargantuan killer butterfly, Gimpo's tongue is tangled up somewhere among the meshing wet flesh. Moonlight flashes on the cunt juice. She arcs her powerful back like rubber and lashing out with her muscular wanking arm grabs Bill's bunk and rips it from the wall and throws it through the door scattering the roof boys peeping in at the spectacle.

It reminds me of the beginning of the universe, the copulation of the Gods. The sex Titan is lashing around out of control, bawling and moaning, stammering and cursing. She blorps her catfish lips on to Gimpo's straining wood and slurps it up, bollocks and all. Gimpo gasps for air, he is drowning beneath a Niagara of slathering cunt liquor when he spots Bill cowering in my bunk near the roof.

'She laaahvvs it!' He grins.

There's no fucking doubt about that, Gimpo. Our happy friend, like a surfer finding his wave, smiles and gives the thumbs-up. The woman of all women starts sucking on Gimpo's tackle like a giant leech, trying to suck him inside out.

She leaps off his face with an audible pop, her big catfish lips surrender the object of her desire as she flips through 180 degrees faster than a hooked marlin and impales herself upon Gimpo's scraped boner screaming like Hammer Horror:

'OH MEESTAH GEEMPOH!' Louder than the *Colonel Ebeya* klaxon which farts out an acknowledging honk in respect at the titanic coupling.

'THE FAAACKING! THE FAAARCKING!' Mama Kongo starts with the steamhammer, pummelling Gimpo through his bed and down on to the shit-covered floor, banging away like a pneumatic city leveller.

'FFACKFACKFACKFACKFFFAAACCKK MEEE!' she wails before descending into some deep cavern of carnal guignol, her colossal breasts battering Gimps into semi-consciousness.

The poor bastard is slipping away, but still the insane sexual dervish bangs away on the drained white boy. He's popped the ball jam but she's not letting him off that easy. Her love talk switches into coquette mode

'Mist Gimpy,' a kittenish forefinger pointing at her bottom lip, 'You no love me baby?' Grinding away like a soft squelching medicine ball.

I take advantage of the temporary lull and try to get out, terrified that we'll be next on the African ballgrinder's menu. Gimps is obviously shot. Bill thinks otherwise.

'Don't worry, Z, you know sexboy. Give him another few seconds we're far safer here.'

He's right, an industrial slurp on the Moss Side Massive and his soldier is back standing rigid to attention, shafting for England. A thrusting banging pumping crunching twisting spunking six hours later the sexual miracle appears to be sated, for the time being at least. She wraps her sarong around herself, cracks off a couple of deafening fanny farts and steps out into the dawn.

I DON'T HUG GIMPO

The service this morning is in a different barge, we follow our fellow churchgoers clambering from barge to barge. It's on *Bashielele*. The service has already started. It's packed. The preacher, the same one that I've described before is wearing a faded Duran Duran t-shirt. He has a microphone, there is a small PA set up. He hands the mike over to a small guy with a bright green shirt on. He starts to sing. The congregation find their voices and join in. There are a couple of blokes down the front who begin to beat out a rhythm on two large carved jungle drums. Members of the congregation start to provide syncopated hand clapping. Some have small decorated maracas that give added cross rhythms. Gimpo gets the minidisc player working and I'm being the total white man there holding up the microphone, recording the lot. Look, I know how patronising it is doing this, even me just standing here experiencing this is some kinda crap voyeurism. I would throw the fuckin' machine away now but I promised Z I would look after it. I'm aware of Gimpo standing behind me. I turn round, he's got his big grin on and his pupils are dilated. I can feel it sweeping over me. There's nothing I can do to stop it, it's like five Es all coming on at once. Like it was when you went to your first rave. I can feel a big tear roll down the side of my face. I want to wave my hands in the air and move my body but I can't 'cause I'm holding the microphone in one and the minidisc thing in the other. The singing goes on and on building up and then emptying out to just the man with the green shirt and the drums then all build up one last time for a mighty crescendo of voices. After the hymn comes to an end the place erupts with cheers and clapping.

A short prayer from the main man again. If only Simon Le Bon could see this. I wonder what royalties he got from the sale of the t-shirt. He then passes the mike to a third man maybe in his late 20s who gets going with the sermon. Any time he looks like he is losing the concentration of the congregation he nails them with a stare, then lobs in a hallelujah and the crowd hallelujahs back as one. If you've got a mental picture of large West Indian ladies, dressed in their Sunday best hats, forget it. All the women have got on are gay cotton sarongs and a t-shirt or top. Some have their hair bundled into a cloth but most have just got short braids, nothing fancy. All have bare feet. The flip-flops seem to be for the men only.

The Congo drifts by. The sun has begun its almost vertical climb from the horizon. The lad standing next to me has his bible open, it's not in French, I guess its Lingala. I want to have one. I know it's crap Western materialism but I want one to take home as a souvenir. I was going to bring my dad's small khaki army one but I forgot. If I had one with me now, I could feel I belonged.

The sermon is over with much appreciative clapping from the congregation. The main man is back on the mike for the Lord's Prayer in Lingala. Didn't Duran Duran have a hit song with the word prayer in it? I try to remember the words to the Lord's Prayer in English. I must have said them every school day of my life at morning assembly. I can't even remember two consecutive lines. Fuck, what if I come back to Britain a born-again evangelical? Sallie couldn't be doing with that, I'd be kicked straight out the back door. The small man with the green shirt is back with the mike. I can now see that the shirt is in fact a Zaire national team shirt. He's kind of got that Toots – as in Toots and the Maytals – vibe about him. (And if you don't know what Toots is like you're missing out big time. *Timetough* is one of the all-time great reggae tunes.) He starts the melody and the crowd take it from there. He ducks, he dives, he uses the floor space available to him working the crowd all the way. At one point he stops and divides us all in two, right down the middle and gets us singing in parts. Everybody can sing – not a duff harmony in the house. *The bang, it folds.* When the singing is over a short prayer from the big guy with the Duran shirt and he tells us all where and when the service is tomorrow. Everybody hugs each other. I don't hug Gimpo and we head back to the cabin.

✳

Gallons of sperm, fanny slime, shit, piss, blood and fuck puke dribbles down the wall an inch thick in places. Gimpo has lost at least four stone, both his eyes are black, his mouth split and bleeding, he looks down at his shredded dick, smiles weakly and passes out. Bill and I jump down into the knee-deep mucous and wade out of the cabin.
Little kids are laughing and pointing at shrivelled Belsen-sexboy Gimpo floating around on the cunt slime. The little fuckers all have pencil hard-ons and are thrusting away at each others' legs. I shoved a couple of the little fuckers into the river as I forced my way past them and up to the bar for a beer and a confused tug.
I was a nervous wreck.

THE DEEP DARK WELL
After a long silence, but still on that train from Milan to Bolzano.
'You ever tried to kill yourself, Bill?'
'Nope.'
'What! Never? Never rolled a bullet round the palm of your hand and thought, "Why not?"' Never looked down the barrel of a gun with the catch off and your thumb on the trigger? Stared down that deep, dark well and wondered what it would be like to be dead? Not only wondered but longed to be dead when being dead seemed to make more sense than being alive?'
'Nope.'
'When we get back home I'm going to get you a gun and give you a bullet and a bottle of your favourite red wine and I'm going to ask you to go to the Tower and spend a night looking down the barrel of that gun. And if you come back I want you to tell me what you saw.'
'As far as I'm concerned, Z, guns are for killing the baddies and I'm not one of the baddies.'
'Fuck off. And before you do, it's your fuckin' round.'
A regular Bill and Z conversation.

Chapter Nine
FOR US QUEERS, LOVE IS ALL

Another greasy morning, the cabin stinks like a tramp's bell end. I leap down into the shit and make my way out on deck in search of clean air. Fat chance, a pigsty uppercut slams into my olfactory system and kicks it into mucous overdrive, only the most kidney-withering odours can breech my body's natural defence systems. Sailor Bill's rotting-corpse flatulence is naturally way beyond kidney withering.

Despite the perpetual horror of life on board and the sick geometry of evil that shapes the very air, occasional instances of sublime beauty would manifest themselves tantalisingly slowly then dissolve and float off down river in the *Ebeya*'s corkscrewing wake. We would drift into vast purple lagoons that stretched into the flat horizons encircling our barge.

Yellow hyacinths appeared like floating stars placed on the smooth surface of the water by a perfect hand. Our floating city of lights would drift by regardless, cutting through the shimmering stillness and into the dripping malarial arbours of another swamp. Impossibly tangled creepers and interlocking tendrils arched above like the complicated vault of a giant cathedral sending raw senses into queasy vertigo.

Occasionally I would hear my name sliding off the back of a sickly breeze, echoing in and out of the ventricles and chambers of the forest's black heart. The pulsating faces of dark forest elementals twisted and billowed in the canopy, leering down at my puny corporeality. Skittering phantom dogs, following the barge along the river's edge, flobbering pink tongues bouncing with the glooping rhythms of their gangling gait. My cautious reveries were more often than not brought back to Earth by the discordant sounds of arguing children or the dolloping splash of a large turd dumped from a looming arse hanging over from the deck above.

Z'S RIBBONS
Z is up and decorating the place.

'What the fuck are you going, Z?'

'Trying to brighten the place up. If we are going to spend the next two weeks in here then at least we should make it an attractive place to be.'

'But they're just the labels from the Primus beer bottles that you're sticking to the wall.'

'Well I happen to think they are things of beauty.'

He's also got some coloured ribbon that he is hanging up.

'Where did you get that stuff?'

'Bought it off one of the stalls yesterday. You got a problem?'

'No.'

What I'm telling you about Z and the ribbon is true. One of the great things about Z is that he can never stop himself from wanting to decorate things. A true artist in the proper sense. My art has always been about ideas and wouldn't it be great if we did this or that, it's never been about simple things like beauty.

'Anyway Z, enough housework, let's go and get some breakfast.'

'Stop fucking interrupting.'

✳

I wandered down through the markets. The things being bartered by the growing numbers of villagers in their dug-out canoes were starting to defy description. Strange animals I'd never seen even in the most far-out natural history programmes. River creatures that were neither fish nor reptile. A shining wet ribbed thing, a giant woodlouse the size of a cat shuffled along the deck being teased by small children. I often got the feeling that we had sailed out of Africa and into some Darwinian scientist's mad dream.

One of the stallholders was pulling up cages of what looked like feathered crayfish, some kind of flying lobster; another had hundreds of small six-inch box cages each with a solitary mantid clinging to a piece of branch. They were sold as pets in the cities and considered lucky. I bought one. The preying mantis is the only insect with a neck, which enables it to swivel its head on bony shoulders, a truly disturbing phenomenon that scares the living shite out of anyone not familiar with this rare and beautiful creature.

I bought some peanuts and a couple of dried kola grubs and snacked on them as I made my way below deck, past the wooden cages where the slaves were berthed, poor bastards who had broken some tribal taboo and were being sold into bondage by tribal elders. They considered themselves lucky too, they could have been sold on the Llualaba as food. I clambered up rusty ladders, over the roofs, across rickety gangplanks, back down into the bowels of SS *Mkongo*, waved at Msomba and climbed up to the bar at the rear of the *Ebeya*.

Bill was preoccupied so he didn't see me. But I saw him all right, dressed in that weird sailor's outfit. He was sharing a bottle of beer with some skinny black guy. They were drinking through separate straws, foreheads touching coyly, the skinny bumboy fluttering his long black eyelashes. The svelte sphincter pirate looked North African, a few shades lighter than the average Zairese passenger, hair less tightly velcro'ed. He kept fanning himself with long fingers like a tart drying her nails and jabbering excitedly to an entranced Bill. I didn't disturb their intimate little tête-à-tête, swallowed my disgust and got myself a beer. The bummers didn't even notice me.

Z, YOU ARE WRONG

Trefor looked pleased to see us. Bowls brimming with dough balls, mugs brimming with tea. He points at the dough balls, 'Mikatee.' He points at the tea, 'Tay'. Even Z tucks in.

'Bill, I've been thinking.'

'Yeah what?'

'I hate to disappoint you.'

'In what way?'

'I don't think we are going to meet Satan.'

'What do you mean?'

'You know Bill, face-to-face. There ain't going to be this bar we stumble into somewhere up-river and we have a drink with this guy, start playing cards with him and then he reveals himself to us. Or we just sus him out because of the way he deals the pack.'

'So what you saying, Z?'

'Bill, we got to make that happen for ourselves.'

'You mean we have to make him up?'

'You don't have to, I might. I don't know yet.'

'I'm not that thick. I didn't think we were actually going to, you know, get to the tree of knowledge and there he is.'

'Well I don't know with you, Bill. Sometimes you seem to take things so literal. But what I was meaning to say, maybe it's started happening already.'

'What?'

'Stop fucking interrupting me with your questions and let me tell you. I think us just being on this boat, on this river, in the heart of Africa. I mean it's not that dark, we are beginning to redeem ourselves. Bit by bit, I dunno.'

'Z, you are wrong, we haven't come all this way just to learn from our experiences.'

'Well, have it your own way. I'm off to the bar.'

DRUMMOND'S SECRET LOG, THE CABIN, SOMEWHERE ON THE CONGO

The pace and tempo on board the *Ebeya* is gradually shifting into some semblance of order. I am using intense will power and rigid Zen discipline to impose my own reality upon this floating Gomorrah. Z and Gimpo seem quite at ease flowing along with the alien ways of life on board this drifting world without boundaries.

I attend the voodoo church each morning intellectually transforming the scraps of gospel that these animists have corrupted and worship the rugged cross after my own fashion. The less-than-pious Gimps joins me in worship, I think the rhythms and drums reminds him of home, sweating and loved up at some cack-hole rave.

Z thinks the whole evangelical thing is a crock of shit, he reckons they're all better off with their animism and voodoo.

WE'RE LOADED

Z and I changed trains at Bolzano. We caught a local one that took us up to Merano. This was deeper into the Italian Alps, the Tyrol region where the locals speak German and don't have that pinched Italian look. It was raining, the snow turning to slush. Z had slept most of the way and was now suffering from his early-evening hangover. We were looking for somewhere to stay but the town looked closed down. No taxis. Hardly any cars. Just us unwashed two trudging along, pissed off.

'I want a hotel with cable TV. I need Meatloaf videos. I want a big bag of grass and five days doing nothing but watching MTV,' said Z.

I didn't give a shit where we stayed as long as it was cheap enough for us not to have to share a twin room. Twenty minutes of tramping later, a taxi light. We flagged it down.

'Guten abend. Ein hotel bitte.'

He replied, in English.

'Maybe the Europa in the centre of town but it cost much money.'

'We may look like tramps but we're loaded,' answered Z in a way the driver didn't hear.

*

I worry about Bill sometimes, he just seems to be one huge mine of contradictions.

How he manages to compromise the conundrums of his hydra-headed personality is beyond even me and Lord knows I'm not exactly Henry Wellbalanced. His long nights spent studying the King James, his pious attendance at the floating prayer meetings... how all this squares with his new-found rampant homosexuality is anybody's guess. Like most things on this meandering river I figured it was probably best not to scratch the surface too deep.

Bad spirits, I can feel them everywhere, hiding in coloured bottles waiting for some subnormal idiot to uncork them. I won't be popping any that's for sure, I've got enough monkeys riding gratis on my back without inviting a whole bunch more psycho primates on board.

BITS AND BOBS

'Bill, how many people do you think are on these barges?'

'I dunno.'

'Guess.'

'A thousand?'

'Three thousand, four hundred and fifty-one.'

'How do you know?'

'I was just talking to this bloke called Remi, he has one of the stalls. There are 96 stalls on the barges. Over a thousand of the people on the barges live on them all year round. Most of them are traders, well them and their families. Trading with the guys who come out of the jungle who sell all that jungle shit.'

'So, what's this Remi like?'

'He's a good guy. He used to trade diamonds but last year he went down to Angola to sell some diamonds and he got robbed. It was $3,000, everything he had in the world. So he started up his stall on the barges. He never leaves his stall the whole the time we are on the river. At night he sleeps on his goods.'

'Where's he shit?'

'In a bucket behind the stall.'

'What's he sell?'

'Marlboros, lighters, toothbrushes, razors, hair oil, bits and bobs.'

DRUMMOND'S SECRET LOG, THE CABIN, THE CONGO

Oh floating ghost of Kiki, tender baleful spirit please forgive me, I am but an imperfect man.

Who would have thought in this sweltering Hell that the fresh buds of love anew would stir in my ballbag. The Senegalese boy, Tally. We met quite by accident on the small promenade outside the bar on the *Colonel Ebeya*.

The decks up in the first-class areas are kept scrupulously clean. Small boys scrub them each morning with earwax and grease from the cracks of their arses. A handful of the richer merchants' wives lounge around eating bread and margarine. The fat proprietor is some kind of fiscal overlord to all the business conducted along the river, he saunters out occasionally to converse with his five wives. Although wealthy beyond the dreams of the average African, even the fat proprietor has to hand over a percentage of his money to the Black Eel.

The beautiful North African boy Tally was hired by the fat proprietor to entertain his wives, he was on board the Ebeya singing for his supper. Apart from possessing the beauty of a coffee-coloured angel he also has the voice of one. Always there was someone, a rich merchant, a general or some bewitched foreigner like myself who would pay to hear the silver notes of Tally's beautiful singing voice. It is hard to describe the honeyed cadence, the trilling delicato and elegant stanzas that tripped from the boy's untutored tongue. It was as if time had stood still and the lad was a conduit for the music of the spheres.

After many beers and bowls of hashish Tally told me a little of his life, how he was banished by his tribal elders because of his invert sexuality. Ah, this insane prejudice and persecution is universal for us men of the arse. The love that dare but sing its name is shunned everywhere but for the darkest corners of the demimonde.

Tally was travelling throughout Africa to try and understand a little more about his damned sexuality.

'Surely there must be somewhere?' the poor lad asked me. 'I have heard of the San Francisco in America where the marriage of men is looked on with the great happiness of every one,' he said to me.

Fortunately the merchant's wives were a philistine bunch and preferred instead to watch German pornography on the VCR machine they had hidden in their cabin. So while the fat proprietor thought the bonny homosexual lad was entertaining his wives they gave him many free unsupervised hours to while away on deck or at the rear of the barge where he had found a small alcove and had claimed it for himself. A patterned piece of cloth covered the doorway, inside there were cushions and a small oil lamp – once the cloth was drawn and the spluttering lamp lit we had the luxury of privacy.

Many lush hours I spent with the soft trilling sound of North African melodies swirling around my intoxicated senses, charged with heavy black hashish smoked through Tally's ivory pipe or sniffing a line of heroin from his long thin penis. At times we explored each others' bodies tenderly like butterflies, at others we rutted savagely, like elks skidding on Vaseline. Oh the amnesia of passion, the fragile memories of that other North African boy seemed to be drifting into time's dissolution like the dry sands of Libyan deserts stirred by the sirocco.

Occasionally a stab of grief would pull at my heart and Tally with the unique ESP sympathy of brown love would massage a little snake oil on to my bell end to evaporate my guilt into smooth lust. How long these orgiastic interludes in Tally's arms lasted I have no idea, it seemed but a brief eternity. At some stage along the trajectory of my intoxicated sojourn in buggery and fellatioland I decided to make my way back to my senses and refused any more hashish. Sensing that I needed a little time alone to mourn Kiki, the sensitive lad went to sing for the wives.

I pulled on my bellbottoms and arranged my parcel to the left before I took a walk across the rooftops. Most of the boys up there were sleeping beneath their thin blankets. One or two shared a joint, in the shadow of the boats large funnel I could see the undulating shadows of gentle buggerism.

A large silver moon hung full on the blue/black sky, stars twinkling like the sperm of god. The jungle was a black smudge off to starboard, magical lunar light danced on the corkscrewing wake of the barge. I could hear Tally's soft voice singing ancient tales of the desert and broken hearts. As the buggers continued their serpentine pleasures my attention was drawn to the muscular silhouette dragging on a cigarette in the same shadows. The orange tip drew a confident arc from hip to lip, the orange glow revealing a handsome, slightly cruel profile.

I respected the fellow's solitude and sat at the edge of the barge where I rolled a small single-skinned joint with Tally's strong hash. I drew the smoke deeply into my lungs, its flavour sweetened by the rare night-blooming perfumes of jungle orchids way across the silver water. I felt the pinprick of the dagger's point beneath my chin and heard the dry gnat's rattle of the assassin's voice at exactly the same time

'So, Billee,' I recognised the phlegmatic tones of Rolo's voice immediately, his strong odour too, brown Arab musk, tobacco and inferior quality snake oil. 'So quickly you forget eh?'

He pushed the point of the knife ever so slightly, just enough to break the skin, I felt a thin trickle of blood collect in the valley of my collarbone and throat. Rolo sheathed his weapon and sat down casually next to me as if we were old friends.

'The boy, the black one, he makes you forget, yes?'

Shame like a blunt razor sliced into my guts.

'No, Rolo , I will never forget Kiki.'

It wasn't a lie, but my dalliance with Tally had confused me. I passed Rolo my small spliff. 'You are not afraid, Billee? Just now, with my knife, I could have killed you, fed you to the crocodiles.'

He tossed his dagger in the air, it span a few times before he caught it expertly.

'You are Dagon, Rolo, I know the rules.'

I sounded a lot calmer than I felt. Rolo appeared surprised, his eyes narrowed as he calculated this new intelligence.

'Yes, I believe you do, Billee,' he eventually replied, 'But the correct alignment of the stars, the correct angles, Horus and the pyramids? This you do not know, yes Billee?'

'The exact time your steel will take me? No, Rolo, this I do not know.'

My death was so inevitable it seemed foolish to be afraid.

'You are not afraid, Scottish?' There was a tinge of admiration in the Arab's voice, inevitable really considering the all-pervasive machismo of the Arab world, even among its fairies.

'I will face your blade with dignity and honour, Mr Rolo, in memory of Kiki.'

Rolo clapped sarcastically.

'The noble Scottish, how brave.' And he laughed cruelly, he obviously considered me the lesser man. 'And this?' He waved his hand disdainfully around his crotch. 'This is how you remember Kiki, by playing the hiding of the salami with a nigger!'

His words stung me to the core of my being.

'Buggering your way through a gallon of snake oil while the corpse of Kiki still has its hair and teeth!'

I forgot, in my selfish grief that he too loved Kiki. Ignoring this I spat back at him like a queen Cobra.

'I doubt Kiki would have had me live the life of a nun! Is it not enough that we have both lost him to your ridiculous macho buggery culture! Each day I die, Rolo! Each day I die! Have you forgotten whose knife took his life, you idiotic sand fag! Have you?! It was you and your ridiculous desert-bumming religion that plunged the knife! God you make me sick!'

Tears of hot rage burned my eyes.

'You Scottish!' the one-eyed hornsmoker spat at me, 'It is you who has forgotten! Or did you never know, are you like your dirty Victorian Oscar Wilde, merely posing as a sodomite!'

Rolo grabbed me by the hair, his fierce eyes bright with righteous anger, his mouth pulled tight in a feral snarl.

'FOR US QUEERS...' he kissed me fiercely, his hard tongue like a serpent trying to choke me and then just as violently, pulled away and spat into the river, 'LOVE IS ALL!'

The proud young Arab got to his feet his electric eye piercing me to my very soul.

'Your death...' he spat again, the hot saliva landed on my cheek, 'Will not be quick.'

Then, grabbing me by my safari suit lapels and twisting them, he hissed, 'That I do swear.'

The Arab turned on his heel and strode like a toreador, haughty and aloof, to the rusty ladder. As he descended he stopped for a second and glowered at me, his scarlet neckerchief caught on a sudden gust from the jungle. In that frozen supernatural moment I knew my death had been written on the stars.

MY NAME IS TALLY

Heading up to the *Colonel Ebeya* for my midday Coca Cola.

'Excuse me, what is your name?'

'Bill.'

'My name is Tally. I am very pleased to meet you. Where are you from?'

'I'm from Britain, the United Kingdom.'

'Ah yes, you Englishman.'

'No, not English, Scottish.'

'Ah yes but you speak English, so you Englishman. But I'm very sorry my English is very bad. But can we talk? I like to talk to people. I like to learn English.'

'I'm on my way up to the bar for a Coke. Do you want a drink?'

'I just drink water. I got water in my bottle but I come with you and we talk.'

Tally is maybe about 30, but I find it hard to judge the age of Africans. He looks different to the others on the barges, same freshly washed and pressed t-shirts and flip-flops but his skin seems blacker, his features finer. Something very contained about him.

'So where you from? Kinshasa or Kisangani?'

'No, I'm from Senegal.'

'Is that up on the west coast by Gambia?'

'Yes.'

'So what are you doing here?'

'Travelling. I left Senegal three years ago. I want to see all of Africa, experience all of Africa. It is important for me to know Africa.'

'So when you are not on these barges how do you get about?'

'I walk.'

'What everywhere?'

'Yes, from one country to the next. It's not hard. Nobody stop me. I get to new country, I learn the language. Find work. Earn a little money. Then I walk. All the time meeting new people learning about their lives, learning about Africa.'

'What kind of work?'

'Any kind. I can type. Always work for a man who can type. And I can fish. My people are fishermen. The name of my tribe means fishermen.'

'You caught fish in the Congo?'

'No, no. I fish in the sea. Very different. I have some questions I need to ask you.'

'OK.' He pulls from his pocket a small piece of grey card about six inches by four inches. On it is some Arabic scrawl.

'These are the questions. Question one: What does Europe want from Africa?'

How the fuck does one start to answer a question like that? To stop having an AIDS epidemic, to stop killing each other, to stop having famine and droughts, to stop chopping down the rainforests, to stop killing the gorillas. I mean how the fuck do I answer that? Then I had the answer: for everybody in Africa to commit suicide so the whole place can be a big game nature reserve park. But I don't think that was the answer he wanted.

'Do you mean, what do we want Africa to do?'

'No. No. I mean what has Africa got that Europe needs to buy from us?'

I remember Z telling me something about a mineral that is mined somewhere in the Congo Basin. It's the only place in the world where this mineral is found. Without it nuclear bombs cannot be made. There are those in Europe that want that. There are those all over the world that want it. I don't mention this.

'I don't know, Tally.'

'It used to be, Beel, that Africa had so much that Europe wanted and now it doesn't want it any more. Tea, coffee, bananas, everything, but now it buys all this from other continents. Why?'

'I am afraid I don't know the answer to questions like that, Tally. Do you have another question?'

'Yes. My second question is, why does Africa have so many wars and Europe have none?'

'Well Europe has a war in the former Yugoslavia.'

'But that not a big war. A real war. In Africa lots of wars. All the time wars. Millions of people killed. I see thousands and thousands of people killed. Why do we do this? What does Europe think? Why we not stop? I used to be Muslim, my name was Kiladim. I go place and people want to kill me because I Muslim. I go somewhere else Muslim people want to kill me because they think I am Christian. So I change my name to Tally. Now I not Muslim, Christian or Senegal man. I am just African. I have another question. Should Africa be one country like the USA? Africa become United States of Africa.'

'But the USA is only one country in America. There are plenty of others in the north and south.'

Tally writes down my reply with a pencil in a very small, neat Arabic script.

'I have another question.'

'OK.'

'Should Africa have one President? Like President Clinton? He is a good man. Our Presidents are all bad. How do you get a good president?'

'I don't know, Tally. These are big questions. I don't know these sort of things. I know little things like how many weeks Rod Stewart was at number one with *Maggie May*.'

'Who is Rod Stewart? Can he be good president?'

'No, Rod Stewart could definitely not be good at any sort of thing other than himself.'

'How do you spell Rod Stewart?'

'Tally, forget about Rod Stewart. He is nothing to do with this. Do you have another question?'

'Yes. Should Africa have one money?'

What do you say? I can't even start to explain all the little Englander mentality back home, the pathetic need our nation seems to have to see the Queen's head on our currency. Bring on the Euro is what I say.

'Yes, Tally, Africa should have one money. The world should have one money.'

'One money, like American dollar?'

'No, definitely not American dollar.'

'But American dollar good. Wherever I go in Africa, American dollar good. Other money rubbish. Worth something one day, worth nothing next day. But American dollar always worth lots. I think Africa should have African dollar and it is good everywhere, every day.' Now I know I know fuck all about international economics and that Tally is fundamentally a very bright man, so how do I try to explain to him that there is this bigger picture out there? Or at least a different picture so that he would understand the naïveté of what he is hankering after. Mind you, my guess is Tally sees a massive picture, far bigger than I could ever hope to see. It's just our pictures are so different that we can't understand each other's. Like if you look at *Guernica* by Picasso and you'd never seen it before, had not heard about it, you'd think it was rubbish, not because you were thick but because you would need someone to explain to you what it all means and why it is the greatest work of art of the twentieth century. Of course they would be wrong but you know what I mean.

'Tally, I think American dollar bad, very bad but I don't know how to explain.'

And I think about the $3,000 inside the belt that's holding up my safari suit bottoms right now and I'm glad American dollars are good everywhere.

'I thank you, Beel. We talk some other time. I go now.'

'Yeah, see you later.'

We shake hands.

ANAL JUSTICE

'SHIT!' mumbled the Gimp, frantically searching through his wallet. Old bus tickets, receipts and prostitute phone cards tumbled like dirty blossom from his chewed-up Velcro-fastening wallet. 'Yes!' he shouted, finding the elusive receipt for our journey up-river.

For a brief moment the complicated viscera of his stomach seemed to detach itself and roll around in zero gravity behind his ribcage. The terrible fate of passengers discovered without adequate paperwork for the journey up river was razored behind his idiot blue eyes.

Death by sodomy.

The savage bumming he had received by the Kinshasha police still lingered in his memory and hurt him when he took a shit. He kissed the ticket and blessed his butt when suddenly a gust of wind from nowhere snatched the ticket from his hand and blew it down the gangway. Gimps chased after the spinning receipt, screaming at the top of his voice for someone to grab the elusive piece of paper.

The stallholders seemed confused, they couldn't understand what the overexcited white man was screaming about. The flimsy ticket stuck to the greasy back of a seven-foot catfish and fluttered in the breeze. Gimpo dived across a stall selling pineapples and disposable razors sending the merchandise flying in all directions, the irate stall owner screaming and waving her hands in the air. Desperate Gimps flung a wad of Zairean dollars at her, his blue eyes laser beaming down on the fluttering scrap of paper still stuck to the catfish's back.

He stalked the ticket as if it were nervous game, creeping up on the burping fish with his heart in his mouth, he whispered a prayer and grabbed at the fish-oil monster milliseconds too late. A breath of wind took the tissue-thin scrap of paper and deposited it in the corkscrewing wake of the barge where it disappeared instantly.

Gimps kicked off his shoes and was about to dive into the water when one of the stallholders, a big muscular buck grabbed hold of the panicking spunk gnome and stopped him. There was no way the barge would have stopped and this stretch of the Congo was notorious for homosexual headhunters, a depraved tribe of anal warriors known since the days of Stanley and Livingstone. The hardy explorers both lost several stout men to the jungle bummers' knives.

Gimpo's thoughts turned to his smarting ringpiece, it seemed to throb of its own accord, puckering and trying to hide inside his lower bowel. What was worse, trying to survive in the forest with the wild nancy boys or trying to explain to the Black Eel what had happened to his ticket? There were plenty of witnesses, surely they would believe him, wouldn't they?

THE INNER MAN

The taxi pulled up at the Europa. We checked in. Relatively cheap. Bang in the middle of whatever kinda town Merano was. Shower, shit and shave and I was down in the tea shop. Apple strudel and a pot of Assam. I was feeling fine. I'd got my long johns on. Wearing longjohns always makes me feel secure. There was even a good-looking hippy chick in the corner to brighten the place up.

Z arrived and ordered his vodka and soda. 'There's no fuckin' MTV. Had to watch cartoons.'

Z kicks off a conversation.

'I've always been shit at everything. Can't drive a car. Can't fit a carpet. There is no job that I'm qualified to do.'

The usual 'poor me but ain't I great really' stuff that I myself have come out with plenty of times in the past. And here comes the qualifier: 'The only thing I can do, Bill, is make women feel good. Make them feel the magic of childhood again. If you can do that they will do anything for you.'

'Z, I've never made a woman feel good. A couple of women have fallen in love with me. But I'm never able or willing to give anything back. They have had to put up with so much getting me, that once they do they begin to resent the amount of crap they have gone through to get that far. The resentment they feel towards me grows bigger than the love they have been professing. Mind you, I start from the premise that any woman who is attracted to me is attracted to the surface appeal of my supposed maverick antics and 'singular approach to life' vibe. It's only in time when the lack of charm, selective forgetfulness, the reluctance to socialise and the farting kick in do they realise they are now witnessing the real me, the inner man.'

'Bill, you've forgotten the bit about being an arrogant, lying wanker as well.'

'OK, Z, so you still can make them feel the magic of childhood when they realise they are waking up with an alkie who doesn't value the habits of personal hygiene.'

'Fuck off.'

'Yeah.'

＊

I'd been drinking some of the cannibal hooch up on the roof, grooving on the mellow fug. Shit, you didn't even notice the coppery menstrual aftertaste after a while. There's worse things than sangulfluous cunt, baby, that's for sure, especially up here in this increasingly butt-oriented jungle.

The roof boys were getting stoned on stinky jungle herb and chugging down on the bloody whisky. One or two of them were getting pretty lairy, their karate was all fucked up, a tall gangly kid got kicked in the balls and fell into the river. His friends thought this was hilarious. Gimpo had taught me the rudiments of Lingala so I could understand the pint-sized desperadoes pretty good. Nearly all of them were orphans, their parents bumped off in one fucked-up war or another. None of these little Huck Finns seemed too bothered. They ranged in age from around six or seven to about 13 years old. When they reach their early teens they usually joined up with what ever screwed-up army was around turning kids into fertiliser.

PENIS GOURDS
Enter Z.

'So Bill, who's your new bum chum? I saw the pair of you flirting.'

'Nah, Z. He's like the African Jack Kerouac, he's from Senegal, been on the road for the past three years.'

'Yeah well, he doesn't look that interesting to me. Have you noticed that there isn't one black chick on this whole caboodle that you'd want to shag?'

'I don't know, I've seen a couple...'

'Yeah Bill, but you're perverted. Don't take offence, not like Gimpo. I mean there are women whose features are fine, they're well built, nice tits and everything but you wouldn't want to shag them.'

'Z, that's about you.'

'What, you saying I'm queer?'

'No Z. I'm saying because of the heat the last thing us white blokes want to do is go shagging. We ain't made for shagging in this climate. Now the likes of me could shag behind the bus shelter in the middle of winter. There is no way your common or garden African would be thinking about shagging as soon as the temperature drops below... whatever.'

'You reckon so?'

'Yeah.'

'You're full of shit. Anyway there's something else I was wanting to tell you about. All these natives coming out of the jungle in their dugouts, with smoked monkeys and bunches of bananas to sell.'

'Yeah.'

'Well, they've all got tracksuit bottoms on, flip-flops and First Manhattan Bank t-shirts on.'

'Not all First Manhattan.'

'This morning I saw one with a U2 t-shirt. U-fucking-2. That one with the four faces.'

'So?'

'So I thought they'd be wearing leopard skins and have bones through their noses. I've not seen one penis gourd. I was hoping to get a couple of penis gourds so we could take them home then wear them on stage when we do readings from this book.'

You never know with Z when he says stuff like this how much is for real.

'Z, are you for real?'

'Yeah. Are you getting a round in?'

*

Little Serge is obviously the roofboys' leader. A funky little dude in a monkey-skin cloak stolen from a Mai Mai, the ubiquitous raggy-arse shorts and fur-lined washerwoman boots zipped up the middle. A dirty white vest with a picture of Starsky and Hutch on it completes the feral dandy's outfit. He sits in the orange twilight sharing my cigarettes and whisky and told me about the interbarge gangbanging. Each barge has a handful of young fighters protecting its turf, instead of streets they have barges. It's the same as any large city in the world, young studs following some biological imperative, locking horns and popping caps, trying to impress gum-chewing sluts so as to get a ride on the gene machine.

The roof boys look up to the fighters – these are young men who refrain from joining up with the armies that are constantly engaged in the surreal search-and-destroy wars of endless attrition. The average gangbanger is aged between 13 and about 17. Eventually when the bubbling nad juices simmer down they start families and take over a stall from a relative. The unfortunate ones die in the interbarge warfare.

Little Serge is filled with admiration for these teenage killers and already knows which barge he wants to fight with and hero worships its leader, a mean-looking kid called Snark. Snark is a weird motherfucker, older than all the rest of the gangbangers, he speaks English with an American accent. He was born and raised to the age of seven in New York when his parents upped from their stateside birthplace and came to Zaire on some ludicrous ethnocentricity trip. The dumb idiots were murdered up-river a couple of months after they arrived and young Snark was left to make it on his own with the rest of the continent's orphans. Snark developed a vicious rep – he had to be twice as bad as the rest of the funky little killers to earn their respect. Snark was particularly good with knives, getting an early name for stealth. Little Ninja, they called him. He could penetrate deep on to an enemy barge after nightfall and slit several sleeping throats which wouldn't be discovered until the next day.

There is no real reason for the interbarge warfare, no territorial or financial gain to be made. The whole thing seemed to be based around the testosterone-fuelled desire to display mucho cojones to each other and to the gum-chewing girlies.

SEW IT UP

Z had ordered his second vodka and soda and I poured my fourth cup of Assam. We tried being silent for a while but Z had a story to tell.

'Did I tell you about the time Kracks went on a date?'

Kracks is the one friend who has stuck by Z since childhood. One more than me. Kracks has never left the estate he grew up on in Leeds. Kracks is a hard-core bachelor. Always has been. Always will be.

'There was this bird that Kracks fancied. Fancied like mad. Had done for months. Courage had been plucked and he asked her out on a date. Kracks was desperate for a shag. He used whatever it is us Yorkshiremen use for snake oil and he managed to get her into bed. But once they had done it he was calling her a whore. "How could you have let me shag you on our first date, you fuckin' slag?" She was sent packing. A couple of days later he phoned her up to see if she wanted to come out on another date. He didn't understand why she didn't fancy it.'

I'm sure if I was to check the story with Kracks, his telling of it might not be as brutal or succinct as Z's. There have been plenty of other tales that Z has told over the years about Kracks and his life. These stories fulfill a function – they make the two of us feel, if only for a moment, that there is one other person in the world we both know who is slightly more socially dysfunctional than ourselves.

In Kracks' honour Z finished off his vodka and tonic and I sipped the last sip of my Assam tea and we went out into the street. We had noticed when we were entering the hotel that there was a lingerie shop next door. We stood in front of an exotic and tantalising window display and after a count of three we let rip with our howl of despair that even Ginsberg would have been proud of.

'Sew it up,' done in a slightly exaggerated estuary English.

If you're looking for an explanation for this rather questionable behaviour, it's got something to do with when in childhood you want to know what the rudest and baddest swearword in the world is. When you learn what it is whispered to be and you find yourself in a remote place, far from teachers and mums and big sisters, you shout it out as loud as you can to see what will happen. To see if you will be struck down by lightning or if teachers, mum or big sister will instinctively know you have been saying the word when you get back to civilisation.

And, as an adult the need to test the boundaries of what is acceptable and what is not has, somehow, yet to be fully explored. Don't ask why, it just has. Giving vent to homophobic fear isn't quite it, and screaming racial abuse to vent fear of those who are not as racially impure as yourself does not sit with your liberal-leaning self. So what is left? Only the war of the sexes. It is generally understood that the worst thing that mankind has ever done to womenkind is hack out their clits and sew up their cunts.

'Sew it up.

Sew it up.

Sew it fucking up.'

*

Little Serge has no idea why he wants to be like Snark and his massive knackers. He's like 11-year-old boys everywhere. A faint trickle of hormonal disturbance and testosterone is brewing in a small corner of his nuts; in a couple of years the trickle will have turned into a roaring deluge and poor Serge will be lost, adrift on a sea of macho machete violence proving some weird point for some weird reason to a similarly bollock-crazed teenage fuckhead. The only difference between this adolescent behaviour and the same dumb shit that goes down in the first world being that there is no law over here.

For these kids, with no parents, when the violence shit kicks off here it kicks off triple cannibal heavy. Here, spunking blood on his gory throne of bones, the Lord of the Flies reigns unchallenged.

I ask little Serge if a lot of kids get killed in these secret wars. He laughs at my naiveté and informs me that only the dumb ones lose their heads. He tells me why a lot of them join the army: two good meals a day, a uniform and a neat rifle. The downside however is that you don't last long, many don't even make it to their sixteenth birthday.

Serge reckons if he trains hard with his knives and hardens his heart even harder he could be the leader of the *Bashielle Eagle* (one of the smaller barges) before his fourteenth birthday.

Serge's long-term plan is to become a river pirate – probably the most dangerous and, for a 12-year-old boy at least, the most exciting prospect on offer out here at humanity's forgotten threshold. This means Serge has to build up a fearsome reputation and win extremely bloody spurs before he is even considered a prospect by the deeply satanic Congo river pirates.

The godless river dogs, merciless drunken bloodthirsty bastards all of them, resembled their seventeenth-century sea-going ancestors in more ways than one. The present day cutthroat's main trade is slavery, providing the Araby and Far East with breathing chattels. Serge tells me that the *Colonel Ebeya* has been raided four times already this year. The battles are ferocious with many stallholders killed but the Black Eel usually repel the pirates. Many times though it has been very close and it is only a matter of time before the pirates through sheer force of numbers manage to rout the Eel.

The pirates are cunning, joining the flotilla singly and in pairs mixing with the villagers and stallholders. The pirates never get their hands on Mobutu's diamonds and settle for the traditional black gold of human slaves, many of the youngsters taken end up on the Arab sodomy barges.

Serge has little sympathy for his captured comrades – if the laws of the jungle don't apply here, he reasons, then where the fuck do they apply? His logic is as usual flawless.

DYING OF MALARIA

Back in the cabin on my bunk, trying to catch up with European notes. It's getting fuckin' hot. No escape. Unbearable. I'm unable to focus my mind. I've got a couple of bites on my leg. The women next door to us pointed them out to me. Is this the beginning of malaria?

Z turns up: the last thing I need when I'm wanting to think about me dying, the romance of the white man's grave and all that.

'What's up, Z?'

'My nose won't stop running. I never get colds. I've been looking at my medical book.'

For those that don't know, Z always carries some sort of condensed medical book with him. At home he's got the full ten volumes of Black's Medical Dictionary.

'So what do you reckon you got?'

'Malaria.'

'Course you haven't.'

If I'm going to get malaria I don't want Z to get it as well.

'Have you got any bites?'

'No.'

'Well then, you haven't got malaria. See those two bites on my legs, that's malaria.'

'That's 'cause you're an arsehole, not putting cream on or sleeping in a net. You deserve to get malaria.'

Z is in his bunk with a runny nose and no note from his mum. Gimpo is learning to speak Lingala with one of our neighbours. I'm dying of malaria.

*

Gimpo's face crunches into the steel door frame. The sadistic guards twist spazboy's arms behind his back and start in with the kidney punches.

Now don't misunderstand me or anything but I must admit that there is a strange part of me that really does enjoy seeing the Gimp get a good kicking. It's something to do with the fact that tugging boy seems to be perpetually getting one over on Bill and me. Not things that matter of course, just petty stupid unimportant things like wiping the floor with us at pool or kicking our Mortal Combat giblets all over the death move screen and the smug smile he carries around with him after he wins the fourteenth game of Terminator pinball, as if the little cunt really thinks he is Arnold Schwarzenegger or something.

The sight of Bill and me grinning at bleeding Gimpo wounded in the fecal slurry seems to unnerve the guards so they start laying into him even harder. The steel-tipped jackboots start stomping, they hold his head beneath the raw sewage. Gimpo tries to protest, spitting out the piss and shit.

'Ticket ekuey na na!' he screeches in his cocky Lingala, 'My ticket is in the water!'

The Order Of The Black Eel couldn't give a shit, they kick him in the side of the head a few more times and leave. It seems lucky Gimpo might have just got away without the death-by-sodomy punishment. This was the first we had seen of the Black Eel, an impressive force.

'Great uniforms,' I comment to Bill who nods in agreement.

Gimpo groans through split lips, he spits out a couple of broken teeth.

'I think they've broken my fucking ribs.' He winces.

'Did you see the groovy hat badges, skull and crossed eels, fucking great!' I said, deliberately winding up the battered show-off, savouring his agony.

SHAKEDOWN TIME

'Tické, tické,' whack, whack.

'Tické, tické,' whack, whack.

I've written these eight words to try and alert you to the fact that there is a ticket inspection on the way. The first since Gimpo's ticket went missing. The 'tické tické' bit is what they shout as they get on to each deck on the barge. The 'whack whack' is supposed to represent the sound of the stick they use to whack the steel doors of each cabin they get to. They are two cabins away from ours. Z miraculously recovers.

'It's shakedown time for you, Gimps.'

'Tické tické,' whack whack.

'Tické tické,' whack whack.

That's them at our neighbours' to the left. Then it's 'tické tické' and no whack whack because our door is open. Every day it's the same two ticket inspectors. The same two that Gimpo and I went to yesterday to report his lost ticket. Z and I get our tickets out. They take them off us. Study them, stare at us as if there was a passport-style photo on the ticket they had to check the likeness with. They then compare the information on their clipboard to what's on the ticket. We sign something, they undersign it. They look at our tickets again, they look at us again. Then they hand the ticket back. I saw that in fact only the more senior one does all the signing and actual handling of the ticket bit. The other is younger but meaner looking. He's the one that carries the stick, shouts 'tické tické' and wacks the doors. They turn to Gimpo.

'Tické.'

They don't speak English, we don't speak French and as yet Gimpo isn't fully fluent in Lingala. Gimpo smiles, pats his chest as if to say 'Remember me? I'm the one that lost my ticket overboard that came to you yesterday and our friend, Remi, explained the situation.' 'Tické, tické,' the one with the stick commands.

One of our neighbours, a young lad of about 16 or 17, the son of the bloke he got the ONATRA t-shirt off, tries to explain. Z is loving this.

'They're not having any of this, Gimpo. They think you are making them look stupid in front of everybody else. Now that you've gone and lost your ticket they reckon every other fucker on the boat will be trying the same trick.'

'Dollar, dollar,' demands the young one. The older one just stares Gimpo in the eye.

'Now we are getting to the point. Shakedown time, Gimpo. You better pay them.'

Gimpo says nothing just this big wide open innocent smile. But I know he's thinking 'Will I fuck!'

The senior ticket inspector turns his gaze from Gimpo and moves on to the next cabin. The younger steps in, looks around, fingers Z's ribbon work. Looks at me and sniffs disdainfully. He steps out of the cabin, wacks the side of it twice before moving on to take up his responsibilities at the side of his boss. Above I can see a scurry of roof boys staring down at the entertainment.

'Meesta Geempo, you must have ticket. No ticket you have more trouble, big trouble. Trouble not go away.'

This is the lad from next door. He looks bright, intelligent, can speak some English and is concerned for Gimpo.

'My name is Pitsu. I be your friend. But I can't stop big trouble.'

Now I know you, as the reader, want big trouble. What is the point of reading about three arseholes heading up the Congo if big trouble doesn't happen. And I know there is no point in reminding you about all the garbage that Z writes his violence and carnage and stuff. No, you want real trouble not fantasy. You want at least one of us to die. Even better, all of us, and this book is just made up from the notebooks young Pitsu posted back in good faith to the Penguin Books' address that's on our letter of introduction to President Mobutu that I have in the front of my notebook. And all you've got so far is Gimpo losing his ticket and that bother we had in Kinshasa. Go and find your own trouble is what I say.

*

I was wrong about the sodomistic death penalty. Four members of the crack guard stomp into the cabin and start pummelling broken Gimp moaning in his bunk. One of them had an electric baton. An evil-looking thing, like one of Madonna's dildos. About 18-inches long, made of rubber with a leopard-skin handle. One of the mean bastards forces it into Gimpo's mouth and stabs it deep down his gagging throat before flicking the switch. The Gimp starts jerking around like some kind of marionette – sparks and fire, blood, teeth, fried vomit and smoke pour from his mouth as 400,000 volts of searing agony shatters through his bones.

Half dead, Gimpo kebab boy falls to the shitty floor. Bill is laughing loudly at Gimpo's torture until the guard with the baton whips him in the bollocks zapping him like a kick from a shire horse. I said fuck all.

TINA IS A SLAG

After listening to our distant cries of 'Sew it Up' hitting the unseen alpine mountain sides far above in the darkness and echoing back to us, Z was more than ready for the solitary pleasures that his hotel room could provide. As Z retired for the night, I decided to wander the empty streets of Merano. Cobblestones and renovated medieval buildings. This place must have been a tourist destination of sorts. All those obscenely picturesque buildings waiting to be admired, photographed and exploited to the max. But not that night. It was just the cobblestones, the stars and me. I passed a bar. I slipped in.

'Ein glas aus rot wein bitte.'

'It's cheaper to buy a small carafe.'

'OK. I'll have that, danke schön.'

Sipped my wine. Checked my notes. Checked the girls. Radio station somewhere in the background pumping out hits of yesteryear. 'Hey Carrie Ann what's your game now can anybody play?' I wonder if Carrie Ann is still playing out there somewhere.

Back out into the still, freezing night. A red-wine glow spread through my body from the tip of my nose to my distant toes. I heard a far church bell toll. For a moment, in my imagination, this was the village below Frankenstein's castle. At any moment the peasants would start streaming up the cobbled streets holding their flaming torches aloft, on their way to storm the castle and confront Frankenstein and his unholy goings-on that have been going on up there.

The moment passed. My thoughts were then caught by the crude graffiti that had been daubed on to the walls of some of the obscenely picturesque, medieval-looking buildings. Not the pseudo hip-hop style graffiti Z and I had witnessed as we had chugged into the arse end of Barcelona a day earlier. This wasn't the work of some trainer-clad, label-victim teenage tagger. This was work inspired by injustice and anger. Whoever the perpetrator was had worked fast with a pot of black paint in one hand and a brush in the other. Aesthetics had not been a consideration. Message was all. And they didn't give a shit about the loving work of long-dead master masons or civic pride or the upset they might cause down at the local tourist board.

I had no fuckin' idea what was bugging this local activist. But the work was everywhere. Words, phrases, whole paragraphs splashed and scrawled over these ancient walls. Street after street in the same angry and urgent hand, each statement punctuated with exclamation or question marks.

Was this work all completed in the boiling frenzy of one night when the anger just couldn't be contained anymore? Or was it a considered night-after-night campaign, carried out with a clinical preparation?

As for what it all meant, I hadn't got a fuckin' clue. I just hope that if the cause was a just one, that all the energy expressed had led to a positive outcome. And, if not, I hoped the perpetrator had discovered more rational and socially acceptable ways of bringing about the desperately desired changes in society. Of course, I may have misjudged the motivations of this unknown artist and all that was expressed in those hundreds of black, dribbling words were variations on 'Tina is a slag'.

*

The guards dragged unconscious Gimps from the cabin and up to the sweaty canteen. All the tables have been cleared save one. Sitting there, sinister in his mirror shades and black uniform is the leader of the Eel, top frankfurter in President Mobutu's private bodyguard, the man known only as The Leopard. A heavy set big man, compact and muscular although a good 70 pounds overweight. His peaked black cap with the skull and crossed eels badge is pulled down low over the mirrored shades making him tilt back his head in an arrogant, contemptuous fashion. A livid shiny scar disfigures the left-hand side of his jet-black face.

He stands slowly and places his hands behind his back. The uniform, complete with shining black jackboots, is obviously modelled on that of the Nazi SS. The leopard-skin trim on the collars and cuffs the only real stylistic difference, along with the cap badge. It has to be said, The Leopard cuts a fine if terrifying dash. An effete jungle dandy of marrow-shivering violence. He picks up his electric baton, the deluxe version with gold-braided handle strap, and points disdainfully at a worn wooden contraption with iron attachments not unlike a set of medieval stocks. The guards tear down Gimpo's pants and strap him in. The Leopard, silent and opaque in his mirror shades, walks around to the front of the stocks and peels back one of Gimpo's unconscious eyelids. He makes a silent order with a flick of the back of his hand and one of the guards jabs Gimpo in his battered ribs with his baton. Gimpo spasms, his dick jerks and he shits down the back of his legs.

A GENTLE KISS
Later, darkness. Z in his bunk sleeping off his afternoon intake of alcohol. Gimpo and I up top. The ship's horns give a full 30-second blast. Then another one. The ship's engines are switched off and the flotilla of barges just drifts. In the darkness we can see a dockside we are drifting towards. On the dockside there are a couple of bonfires burning. A searchlight that is affixed to the top of the bridge of the *Colonel Ebeya* is switched on. It sweeps the dockside. Hundreds of pairs of eager and expectant eyes are momentarily caught in its beam. Crewmen leap from the boat to the dock as the gap closes. A cheer goes up as the sides of the barges gently kiss the sides of the dock. Tens, hundreds of people are leaping ashore.

*

The Japanese film crew have appeared from their first-class hideyhole and are excitedly setting up their equipment, chattering and laughing in their yapping tongue.
Because of his nationality and because The Leopard miraculously actually believes his story it eventually transpires that Gimpo is to be spared the usual punishment of being buggered to death. The Leopard has reduced his punishment to the Black Eel equivalent of 40 lashes: four days and nights of constant jacksie-driving.
A small crowd soon made its way up to the canteen when word spread that there was to be a public bumming. Life on board the flotilla is repetitive and can be boring so anything out of the ordinary, anything with some semblance of ritual or ceremony, is a welcome diversion to the endless trade and gossip. The children gathered excitedly at the front of the small crowd, for many this was their first chance to witness a public arse-raping.
Some of the older traders were disappointed when they found out that this was not to be a capital shit-stabbing as they liked to make wagers on how long the prisoner would last before he expired. The younger men were not exactly pleased either as it was the fittest of their number who were forced to perform the actual sodomy. This in itself was a method of social control on the flotilla, any man refusing to perform his sodomistic duty was placed next to the prisoner and received the same form of anal justice.

VIVA LAS VEGAS
Twenty minutes later Z and I are on the dockside. The place is heaving with people. All the stalls on the barges are open and doing a brisk trade.

'Bill, over here.'

'What for?'

'Come and look at this.

It's a massive portrait of Mobutu painted on the wall of a warehouse.

'It must be 20-feet high. That would be my job if I had grown up here.'

'Why?'

''Cause I went to art school. I'm good at drawing.'

'So am I but I wouldn't be doing that, I'd be running the place.'

'Yeah.'

'Yeah Bill, but have you seen along here?'

Another humungous wall painting.

'It's the national emblem, a flaming torch held aloft, but what are the words painted underneath?'

'Viva La Zaire.'

'What, do you reckon it's a reference to Elvis's *Viva Las Vegas?*'

'Don't be fuckin' thick, Bill.'

*

Never has the phrase 'It's better to give than to receive' been more appropriate. About 50 or so young studs were ordered to dole out the punishment in a continuous rotation. This was not too bad as it meant that each of the reluctant buggers would only have to perform three or four times during the four-day punishment time. There were to be no fake orgasms either.

A member of the Eel was on hand to ensure that each lad deposited a full jizz load up Gimpo's dirtbox. This compounded both buggers' and buggeree's humiliation to the full. The Black Eel understood the psychology of power well.

There was nothing Bill and I could do. Fortunately we as his closest friends were not obliged to take part in this spectacle of oppression. The Eel knew where to draw the line.

The oppression, humiliation and cruelty required to break and subjugate a people is a carefully balanced machine. Joe Mobutu and his nadslime cronies had been in power in Zaire for close on a quarter of a century.

In modern times this is an achievement on a par with the barbarous autocracies of ancient Rome, a parallel not missed by Mobutu who insisted that his highest ranking officers referred to him as Caesar Mobutu.

The Gimp was shaking his head, gradually coming to his senses, he forced open his slit, puffy eyes. I remembered that Gimpo had lost consciousness before his sentence had been reduced, the poor bastard thought he was still to be fudgepacked to death. No wonder he started screaming so loud. The guard prodded Gimps with the electric baton and told him to shut up. Gimps breathed deeply, the baton had winded him.

THE MELODY FILLS MY REVELRY

Either s/he had run out of paint or s/he had said all s/he needed to say. Either way, the angry graffiti ended and anyway, from what I heard, Tina was not a slag.

All was silent, no footsteps of fellow late-night wanderers, not even the sound of distant traffic.

I moved across an empty square, drawn toward an archway lit by a single glass paned lantern. The kind that once Leerie? the lamp lighter would have lit but which has long since been replaced by the 100-watt bulb.

Under the archway on a roughly plastered wall and lit by the lamp, another artist has been at work. One who has chosen to use the more traditional medium of the graffiti artist – the spray can. As I may have written elsewhere, I'm not a fan of spray-can graffiti. All very worthy in a black-American ghetto sort of way, but not for me.

But this one, this more than held me, it sucked me in. It was a dot-by-dot spray-can copy of Roy Lichtenstein's pop art classic, *The Melody Fills my Revelry*. This had nothing to do with the fact Lichtenstein has long since passed into the also-rans of early 1960s' art history. But it may have something to do with the fact that he was the only one of his New York gang who wrung a pathos out of the then modern world and on to his primary coloured canvases. The perceived intent of Lichtenstein's work may have been an ironic celebration of American strip comics of the 1950s and 1960s but the effect always seemed to be that it heightened their real emotional impact. I'm going to get well pretentious here: it's almost like the way ludicrously overweight and middle-aged tenors can squeeze heartbreaking emotions out of the most trite librettos used in schmaltzy arias of Italian opera. I mean Rosenquist, Rauschenberg or Oldenberg never made you want to cry. They got your respect but never made you well up inside and want to weep for the lot of man and our own silly little insignificance in it all.

OK, I've got that out of the way. Back to this wall under the archway. Maybe I dug it because I liked the fact the same image had moved through three vastly different contexts. Ten-cent 1950s comic to million-dollar painting to spray-can graffiti on medieval alpine village wall. Why had the spray-can delinquent not picked *Girl with Hair Ribbon* or even *I know how you must feel Brad* but gone for this one, my favourite one? A lot of art hours had been invested into this bit of useless street graffiti and already the plaster was flaking away. It wouldn't take long for it to look like the recently uncovered faded and flaked painting on the interior walls of the Norman church near to where I live.

*

'Only four days, whitey man,' the guard taunted Gimps. 'It is nothing, you very lucky, whitey man,' he repeated in his odd English. 'I shit on your Queen of England and your Princess Diana, she lick my balls like bitchdog!'

The guard started laughing at his own weird insults. Gimpo hit him with a return barrage of obscenities before a man of about 40 approached the stocks and placed a black hood over his head. The buggers, all men in their prime were given similar black hoods, made from rough sacking. The hoods were of a symbolic nature: the customs and laws of The Congo decreed that the hoods conferred immunity from responsibility for any judicial punishments carried out while wearing them. The mask also provided a symbolic anonymity to the buggers – everyone on board the flotilla knew the identities of the men chosen for the distasteful task.

As Gimpo was impaled on the first black dick he started his unspeakable racial abuse. Obviously Gimpo's buggers took the abuse personally, seeing as there didn't appear to be any other black bastard nigger faggot rapists around and started ripping into his shitter extra violently. I called over to Gimpo to let him know that it was true that he only had to endure four days of this dreadful punishment, that he wasn't going to be buggered to death.

His apoplectic rage seemed to back off and unbelievably Gimpo, ringpiece of steel, started playing to the crowd, joking with the children in Lingala and flirting with the women. His comments on the buggers' penis size along with other camp asides even had those poor bastards in stitches. The sinister Eel guards, their authority somehow undermined by the cocky Brit's humour in the face of dreadful adversity, were not amused in the slightest.

One of them jabbed his electric baton deep into Gimpo's bowels and hit him up with ten thousand fizzing volts of stripped agony. Volt dancing Gimpo's turkey neck boned up and shot out a boiling wad of popping nadjam, Gimps managed to twist his body so that his bubbling spudwater splattered all over the guards' immaculate shining jackboots. The amazing Manchester boy even managed a triumphant smirk. The guard was stunned and didn't retaliate, secretly impressed by the Englishman's pluck.

THE EYE

'Hey, Beel. You not recognise me? I'm your friend.'

How do you tell an African that it's pretty hard for a European to recognise one black man out of two thousand, let alone when it's almost pitch black. I mean, you've seen one set of white teeth, you've seen them all.

'Hi, who are you? I mean, how are you?'

'I have some more question for you, Beel.'

'It's your bumchum, innit Bill?'

'Tally, this is Z. Z, this is Tally.'

'Happy to meet you.'

'Yeah.'

'Beel, there is a great misunderstanding in the world, it is the cause of much hatred and bitterness, and my feelings are that Africa must get over this hatred and bitterness before it can move on and unite and become strong.'

'Yeah, sounds good Tally. What's your plan?'

'Don't patronise him, Z. Let the man speak.'

'He not patron me, it OK, Beel. When the European man came to Africa looking for good, strong men who could work hard in the heat of their American colonies who would be resistant to tropical and sub-tropical diseases, he was willing to pay good wages to such workers. We Africans were willing to work. Then negotiations started between the white man and the chiefs. The chiefs were bad men. They said you do not pay men wages, you pay me gold and I give you the men. You take them away I never see them again, they work hard.'

'So Tally what you are saying is that it was not only the black man who sold his brother into slavery but it was his idea in the first place.'

'Yes.'

'Why are you telling us this?'

'You say you are writing a book about coming to Africa?'

'Yeah.'

'Well, in your book, will you write what I have just told you? Then the world will know. Then the people of Africa will know and they will overthrow their chiefs and corrupt presidents for selling them into slavery and will unite together and the feelings of hatred and bitterness towards the white man will disappear and Africa will be great.'

'Tally if we put that in our book they won't believe a black man said it. They will just think we, for some reason, want to be apologists for the white man's enslavement of the black man.'

'But they will believe you. You are good men and it is true.'

'Bill, will you tell him or shall you?'

'Whatever it is you may as well.'

'The people that read our books don't want to know about stuff like this. They don't give a shit about how slavery happened. When they see Will Smith in a movie they don't think about his great grandfather being born into slavery, they just see a dude that makes them laugh. The people that read our books just want things that make them laugh. Maybe we have weird shit and Bill likes to get his theories in but us two we are jokers, artists, clowns, we are here to make people happy. We like to make people feel happy. Don't we Bill?'

'Well Z, I don't know, maybe...'

'Tally, we want to make you happy as well. I think Bill could put your ideas into his bit of the book. He might be able to do it in a way that makes people laugh but still be your words. What do you think Bill?'

'I don't know, maybe...'

'Good.'

'Thank you Z and Beel, you are very good men. Now I want to show you something very important to me. You know I tell you I used to have another name, Khadim. If a Muslim stop being a Muslim it is punishable by death. I can be killed. Stoned to death. But I am me, Tally, there has never been another Tally before. I don't write my name in Arabic or in European script or Cyrillic. This is how I write my name.'

He pulls out his passport from his back pocket and opens it.

'See here, this how I write my name, it is my signature.'

He is pointing at a simple line drawing of an eye. Above, below, to the left and to the right of the eye are equally simple drawings of four stars.

'The star at the bottom is my life, the one to the left is yesterday, the one to the right tomorrow, the one above is today. And the eye is mine and with it I can see everything.'

'Everything?'

'Everything.'

Later, lying in my bunk, the other two asleep. I've got Z's minidisc recorder, the headphones on and I'm listening to the recording of the morning service.

Goodnight.

'Goodnight Bill,' says the African night.

*

The creepy Japanese film crew were beavering away with their fluffy mikes and flashing LEDs filming Gimpo and his reluctant buggers. They could not hide their disappointment when told that Gimpo's punishment was not to the death and started packing away their equipment sullenly. I recognised the look Gimpo flashed at them, revenge was in his eyes. When needs be the Falklands veteran was a competent and spectacularly cruel assassin.

The serial sodomy carried on through the night, Gimpo affecting a nonchalance I found hard to credit. The guards, tiring of their duties somewhat, allowed me to bring the brave ringpiece warrior a couple of beers and a cigarette. The crowd soon got bored of the novelty and drifted back to their cabins and spaces on the decks. Bill dropped by, still mumbling about Victorian London, and was relieved to find that it was only a punishment bumming and not a capital shafting.

We were going to dock in Mbdanka in a few hours, and the Gimp was well pissed off to be missing the brief shore leave. I gave little Serge a few dollars and told him to keep Gimps in beer and fags while we went ashore. Gimps wasn't going anywhere and I didn't want to miss an opportunity to check out the jungle.

'See if you can spot any wild animals and stuff!' called the ever-optimistic sperm dwarf as another black stud anointed his huge purple bellender with rancid snake oil.

DRUMMOND'S LOG, WEDNESDAY 12 JUNE 1996
NEVER LEAVE THE BOAT
'Wake up Bill, time for a bit of exploration.'
'What? What time is it Z?'
'How the fuck should I know? None of us carries a watch. There are no clocks. It's daylight, the cock's crowed, the barges are still tied up at the Mbandaka place. I've read all about it in Gimpo's *Lonely Planet*. Sounds groovy. Let's see if we can go and find a bar.'
'Yeah, hang on. What about you, Gimpo?'
'Never leave the boat. Never leave the boat.'
'What do you mean?'
'You know, *Apocalypse Now*. Never leave the boat.'
I didn't know what the fuck he was on about, maybe you do.

Chapter Ten

OSCAR WILDE, NONCE

We left Gimps with his beers and a bottle of piri piri hot sauce. He was planning some kind of intestinal revenge on his buggers.

'He who laughs last,' he quipped ambiguously before draining the volcanic chilli sauce and letting loose a sloppy fart of some other man's sloppy sperm all over his current anal tormentor.

The flotilla doesn't exactly dock, it just crunches up against the sandbank nearest the quay till it comes to a grinding halt. Hundreds of excited villagers were running around shouting and waving, the stallholders clutching bags of goods scrambled on to the shore and rushed all over the quay trying to find the best pitch. Bill and I were expecting Mbdanka to be a real town with buildings and maybe a road or two, no chance. Derelict steamers lay broken hanging half in and out of the river, the rusted skeletons of machines picked bare of any usable pieces of metal. Evidence of long-forgotten Western industry lies rusting and neglected, pieces of corrugated iron and palm leaves made up roofs of crumbling storerooms.

On one piece of wall a faded painting of Mobutu in his leopard-skin hat fades beneath the sun and rain. Mobutu was born here. Big deal, whispers the neglect. Families have colonised the wrecked steamers and are selling pieces of roast bush pig, black bubbling eyes peer blindly from a squealer's burnt face. We were wandering up and down the dockside when Bill spotted a white face in the crowd, then a small kid rumbled by on a knackered push bike and when he'd passed the white face had disappeared.

CHILD OF HAMBLIN

As I was standing there in the sub-zero night, still warm from the glow of the red wine, contemplating how the meaning of any work of art is always in a state of flux, a distant church bell rang the three-quarter hour. And then – and this is the only reason why I'm bothering to tell this story about angry graffiti and melodies filling my revelry – a band began to play somewhere. It was a coming-and-going, fading-in-and-fading-out sound, like a melody heard on an Eastern European radio station. The unseen band churned on regardless of their unseen audience of one. A drummer, a bass player, a rhythm guitar, no singer, and a lead guitar. On and on. From major chord down three semitones to the minor and somehow always ending up at the dominant seventh . The lead lines tumbled and twisted. Pulled and pulled again. It was like one of those never ending solos on 'Rust Never Sleeps' by Neil Young. But an Italian band sounding good, even one up here in the Tyrol sounding good – that's against all the rules of rock 'n' roll. Hands-in-the-air Italian piano house, yes. But not this stuff. Anybody who has ever picked up a Fender or Gibson know that Italians just do not have it in them to rock, especially not like Crazy Horse at their best.

I forgot the homage to early 1960s American pop art. Like the kids of Hamblin, I let this melody fill my revelry and I followed the unseen pipers. Down through narrow streets, across unlit courtyards I went. At times it was difficult to tell if the sound was getting closer or further away.

But on and on they played. No song. No singing. Just lead line on lead line. All over the same eight-bar chord structure.

After about 20 minutes I found myself standing outside a large, rather municipal building. Its large, heavy and studded door was firmly locked for the night but on the first-floor veranda windows were wide open. Light flooded out into the night. And the band played on. I stood below staring up like Romeo waiting to catch a glimpse of Juliet.

But finally it did end, with a clatter of drums and some ham-fisted twanging from the bass player. This was followed by raised voices. Musical differences were being had. Most probably the lead guitarist thought the drummer was at fault. It reminded me how crap it is to be in a band. The spell was broken. I found my way back to the hotel. It's only now, lying on this bunk trying to escape the sweltering heat, as these rusting barges slowly grind their way up the black river I realise why I wanted to relay this story of a solitary evening stroll.

It's as if the alpine medieval architecture, the angry black graphite, *The Melody Fills My Revelry* homage to Lichtenstein, the lure of a distant band, the need to follow it like the children of Hamblin and the final band row, all hang together as a piece. 'A piece of what?' A piece of art. But I don't know how they relate together or why. Or what should be done with emotions that were triggered by experiencing them one after the other. Is there a painting to be painted? A poem to be rhymed? Or is it enough to set it down as I have? To recognise that these things happen as we hack our way through life and when we stumble into them we should be grateful, learn to appreciate them as our own private masterpieces even if they have no importance outside our own little lives and even if they make little rational sense there either?.

*

Another small child, his face painted white with clay, mouth a bright cochineal red scampered towards us. The youngster was about seven or eight, he had a paste diamond choker around his neck and a dainty broken tiara in his hair, he handed us a small white card. I took the sweat-stained item from the smiling child and read the words written in a shaky old fashioned copperplate hand. It was hard to decipher, the card was mildewed and the handwriting infirm. I handed it to Bill who squinted and held it at an angle, 'Dinner, something something, the farm, ask something any of the boys,' he said. It was initialed A. D. A mystery indeed. The peculiar white-faced boy smiled and pointed to a dirt track that led into the jungle, 'You follow me.' He spoke in an odd English, aristocratic vowels mixing with guttural French undertones. 'Mr Douglas, him white man, excellent cuisine, wine jolly good yes? You follow Claudette.' He pointed to his bony chest and flashed a winning smile.

The barge wouldn't leave for hours and when it did the klaxon would give ample warning. Teams of jet black porters suddenly started pouring from the jungle in single file. Magnificent men well over six-feet tall with rangy muscles and sacks of produce balanced on their heads, they appeared so bereft of colour their blackness seemed to suck in the light around them.

The men carried on with their work as Bill and I followed little Claudette into the forest. The path narrowed and the heat hit us like a wall. It was different from the river heat, more sensual, a physical vegetable heat that closed in on us like sweat. The undergrowth teemed with life. Vast armies of ants negotiating fallen tree trunks devouring vegetation in their path, butterflies as big as birds, snapping lizards whipping into the undergrowth. Startled moon monkeys chattered in the canopy. Winged insects sensed the large source of sweating protein and descended in their droves, biting and stinging.

Claudette laughed and helped us swat them away with a small monkey-tail swat and told us to put our shirts back on. We were almost there he told us. One more kilometre.

'Listen,' he said, cupping his ear.

I could hear nothing out of the ordinary, just the usual cacophony of the rainforest raging ape wars, shrieking technicolour birds. I listened harder and could vaguely hear the sound of high-pitched singing and the excited voices of playing children.

'Mr Douglas, he is very kind to forest children.'

I assumed this Mr Douglas was some kind of missionary – apart from the diamond rapists, religious freaks were the only whites dumb enough to venture this far into the dangerous forest.

FUCKIN' HIPPY

The gangplank springs beneath our feet. The dockside is a hive of activity although nobody seems to be doing actual work, work that gets things done, makes the world a better place. There are no builders...

Fuck! Fuck! Fuck all this shite I'm writing. There is a six-foot eight-inch white man striding towards us. He has very long blond dreads. The last thing I want to meet here is a hippy. I don't want to be confronted with the fact we are just on some hippy trail, like going to an alternative Goa or something. I want to know that me, Gimpo and Z are the only white men within a 1,000-mile radius of Mbandaka. OK maybe an octogenarian missionary or a whisky-soaked ivory trader but not a fuckin' hippy.

I run back up the gangplank to leave Z to deal with him. I watch them laugh, talk, swap travellers' anecdotes. It's disgusting. Around them is a circle of black men standing watching them admiringly as if they are Stanley and Livingstone. I wanna puke.

'I thought you didn't want to have an ego-driven internal monologue going on.'

'You can fuck off as well.'

'Swallow your pride, just go walk that plank. Shake the guy's hand and say "Hi".'

*

Claudette, like the forest sprite that he was, bounded quickly down the path and disappeared behind a clump of spiky bushes. Bill and I hurried after our guide, the thought of getting lost in this man-eating wilderness was not a comforting one.

The forest eventually thinned and we came to what appeared to be a missionary school of some kind, high stucco walls stained green from the dry and wet seasons that occurred together all year round. It was Portuguese in appearance, the walls topped with broken terracotta tiles. A large arched gate opened on to a courtyard where more youngsters daubed in white clay and weird jewellery played happily.

Not knowing what to expect in this increasingly strange jungle we entered gingerly. There were 40 or so kids mainly about Claudette's age, some younger. Most of them were wearing a kind of straw skirt, others frolicked naked. Claudette ran up to us. I didn't recognise him at first, he was wearing a blonde wig and red patent leather stilettos a few sizes too big for him.

Smiling broadly he took our hands and led us into the main house. It was a vast single-storey affair like a colonial ranch house, In the reception area older boys in blonde wigs lounged around on the leather furniture. It was warm and dark, a large fan in the middle of the low ceiling circulated the thick air. The lounging teenagers seemed drowsy, lazily searching each other's wigs for vermin. The place had the heavy gravity of the sickroom. Stale farts and unmade beds.

I noticed another more sinister aroma circling in the fanned air: the unmistakable pungency of boy musk and snake oil. A kid ran from one of the adjoining rooms and gave us a couple of beers, I decked mine thirstily. Claudette took our hands and led us through a labyrinth of corridors and anterooms. The place had obviously been some kind of hunting lodge at one time. The walls were decked with large fading photographs in ornate frames of Victorian big game hunters astride their gory kills. Moth-eaten skins were scattered on the floors, huge elephant tusks stood sentry at doorways, stuffed big cats that had seen better days growled silently.

Everywhere the velvet curtains were drawn giving the strange place a sepulchral ambience, the flickering gaslights on the wall added to the House of Usher vibe. The further we penetrated the sprawling lodge the thicker and sicklier the redolence of musk and snake oil became. This was not of course conclusive proof of decadent activity – a lot of tribes on this stretch of the river used snake oil for cooking, an acquired taste as it tends to impart its heavy flavour to whatever it cooks.

NO BALLS BILL

My big sister came home from university. It was the Easter holidays 1971. I was 17, she was 20. She had a book in her hands called *The Female Eunuch*. The first thing I noticed about this book was the cover, a female torso, hung on a pole like a vest. Handles on the hips. Of course you know the cover – we all know the cover – even if you haven't read the book. That cover became synonymous with those two words 'Women's Lib'. My sister tried to make my mother read the book, I don't know if she did. She tried to make me read the book. I did. My sister was always very good at making me do things, or making me feel very stupid if I didn't. The book was by somebody called Germaine Greer. And, of course, we all know that now too. But back then, it had just come out in paperback.

As I said, I read the book and the book burned inside me. It worked on me on numerous levels. First and foremost was the energy in the writing. The conviction. The sense of purpose. Fuck female emancipation or women's liberation, I was reading this as private emancipation, personal liberation. Liberation from a mother who always thought the worst of me, a big sister who bullied me, schoolmistresses who blamed me and teenage girls who ridiculed me.

Even now, 25 years after first reading it, lines and passages are still alive and shaking in my head.

"The struggle which is not joyous is the wrong struggle. The joy of the struggle is not hedonism and hilarity, but the sense of purpose, achievement and dignity... Every mistake made is redeemed when it is understood... The more derided and maligned the action that you undertake, the more radical... The way is unknown... However far you can see it is not far enough to make out the contours of what is ultimately desirable. And so no ultimate strategy can be designed. To be free to start out, and to find companions for the journey is as far as you need to see from where you stand... The more clearly the forms of

oppression emerge in your understanding the more clearly you can see the shape of future action. In the search for political awareness there is no substitute for confrontation... Freedom is fragile and must be protected... The fear of freedom is strong in us... This book is subversive. It will draw fire from all articulate sections of the community... This book invites depression and hardship... To leap the steps of revolution and arrive somehow at liberty without strategy or revolutionary discipline... This book represents only another contribution to a continuing dialogue between the wondering man and the world. No questions have been answered... If it is not ridiculed and reviled, it will have failed in its intention."

I was a total convert to the cause. An angry and arrogant polemic to rival any pulpit-thumping preacher or screaming dictator and all written by somebody who was under 30.

I was in my first year on an art school foundation course. Our class was filled with 16- and 17-year-old would-be hippy chicks all looking for a long-haired, narrow-hipped guy to worship. After the Easter break I returned to college filled with a missionary zeal, brandishing my copy of *The Female Eunuch*. My fire and brimstone was well rehearsed but the would-be hippy chicks didn't quite see it my way. That may be put down to the fact that my hair was not that long and my hips were never going to be narrow.

*

Claudette stopped at a large louvred door and pulled on a velvet rope hanging from the roof. The voice scraped through the echo of the room, 'Enter, please enter,' followed by a girlish giggle that spluttered with ruined decadence and dead beetles. Claudette pushed open the door. It was darker than the rest of the rooms, lit by a single electric lamp burning dimly on a small occasional table next to a large wicker colonial chair facing away from us.

A skeletal hand decked in large diamond rings holding a long thin cigar protruded from the chair. It beckoned us nearer with a hooked talon. We sat in the two chairs by the closed fireplace. The air was dizzy with stale perfume, heavy old-fashioned odours that evoked images of venereal French whorehouses and black magic.

The withered figure was ensconced deep in shadow, a battered old straw boater obscured his face. He was cadaverously thin, his discoloured white linen suit hung about him like a grave stained shroud. His legs were crossed at the sharpest of knees which extended to pipe-cleaner ankles wrapped in faded canary yellow socks. The spectral figure took a rattling suck on his skinny Panama, the red glow of the ash briefly illuminating a sharp, wicked face. Thin skin like yellow parchment was stretched tightly over the brittle geometry of razor-sharp bones.

'Another drink gentlemen?'

WHY ANDY WARHOL IS SHITE

'So what the fuck was your problem, Bill?'

'He was a white hippy. I didn't come to Africa to meet someone like him.'

'And hangin' out with your nutter bum-chum Tally is OK just 'cause he's black?'

'So what's he doing here, the hippy?'

'He's Dutch. Him and his girlfriend, the small Oriental girl, they've been wandering through

Africa for the last two years. They are heading south at the moment. He's the real deal, Bill. He's what you wanna be in your fantasy.'

'What? Have dreadlocks?'

'No, on the road for real. No return ticket. No nice little farmhouse in the home counties with a steady flow of PRS cheques to sort things out. Anyway, enough of this shit, fancy a wander round? The place looks great, all these broken-down ex-colonial buildings.'

We wander and it is great. Z is full of ideas about Oscar Wilde's boyfriend, Bosie. The usual stuff. My mind's off elsewhere thinking about another book I should have written years ago called *Why Andy Warhol is Shite*.

'Z.'

'Yeah?'

'I've got an idea. Do you mind if we pretend that we turn the next corner and there, for no good reason at all, is a brand-spanking-new contemporary art museum and we go in and inside is the biggest privately owned collection of Andy Warhol paintings and stuff in the world?'

'All owned by Big Joe.'

'Yeah.'

'No I don't mind, if you don't mind me having you being buggered by Bosie.'

'Well, there's not much I can do about that and while we are on that subject I know all about your Drummond's Secret Log shit.'

'Ah fuck it, Bill. Tell me all about why Andy Warhol is shite in your great wisdom.'

'No, Z, what I was going to do was have you, me and Gimpo go to this Warhol thing. It's got everything, the whole fucking lot. And you and me are going around the gallery going on about how great Andy Warhol is, what a genius. And Gimpo is saying nothing. And when we get out Gimpo turns to us and says, 'I think Andy Warhol is shite'. And you say, 'Pray tell us, Master Gimps, why in your revered opinion is Andy Warhol shite?' And he comes up with a very simple and devastating reason why he is.'

'And that reason is?'

'I haven't kinda worked it out yet. It's more at the gut-level instinct thing at the moment.'

'Suit yourself, Bill, but you know you have a tendency to go off on your theories and they are just a load of bollocks really. It doesn't do you any favours.'

'Yeah, but I tell you what.'

'What?'

'Wouldn't it be great if we turned the next corner and there was this contemporary art museum with African art babes with specs who knew their shit and there was a cool café that sold proper coffee.'

'And vodka.'

'Yeah.'

'Yeah.'

We turn the corner.

*

His rasping voice, vocal chords like dry moths, sounded the clipped consonants of an older aristocracy. As he leaned forward to offer us cigars, his terrifying face caught briefly in the yellow lamplight. A gothic nightmare, part crumbling Egyptian mummy part Dame Barbara Cartland. Layers of encrusted eye shadow like congealed ink surrounded milky eyes framed with arachnid eyelashes. Huge arched painted-on Joan Crawford eyebrows sent visions of dead budgies and Baby Jane Bette Davis through my shorting neurones.

A feeling of dread poured down on me like sump oil. I couldn't take my eyes off the cosmetic monster and his brain-damage lipstick. Pale green foundation powder clogged in the deep lines around his cataract-fuzzy eyes. His scrawny neck disappeared behind a frayed blue silk cravat. The fly area of his linen slacks were spotted with brown jizz stains that stretched all down one leg. A small naked boy lay curled at his feet like a dog,

I knew who he was before he introduced himself.

'Lord Alfred Douglas. Another drink? It's so nice to have visitors. I believe you are acquaintances with an, ahem, old friend of mine.'

He removed the straw boater and placed it on the table, thin wisps of white hair were greased across a liver-spotted scalp

'Please, I have some excellent absinthe.'

The ghost coughed, his lungs rattling phlegmatically behind his ribs. He picked up a small brass bell and rang it impatiently

'Claudette! Damn, where is the boy?'

I noticed a straining colostomy bag tucked down the side of the chair. Claudette skipped into the room. He had changed into a black and white maid's outfit with a pair of theatrical angel's wings stitched to his back. One of the wings appeared to be broken and hung down tragically lopsided. I got the feeling that this was deliberate, the mawkish sentiment of a bad poet.

'Absinthe, sweet wounded angel, for my guests. Chop chop, quickly boy.'

He coughed again, this time bringing something up from his knackered lungs.

'Excuse me,' said the ancient aristocrat spitting into a brass spittoon next to his chair. A black chewy one rattled in the bowl.

'As you can see I'm not in the best of health.'

He shifted his weight to one side, grimaced slightly as the colostomy bag loudly burped a dollop of liquid shit.

'Lord Alfred Douglas. Bosie?' Bill sounded surprised as if he had just realised who our notorious ghostly host was.

'Good Lord, no one's called me that for years. Alfred, please,' replied the spooky bummer.

TICK IT OFF

Back on board.

Huge blast from the ship's horn.

'Bill, where have you been?'

'Me and Z have just been going round an art gallery full of Andy Warhol masterpieces and you were going to tell us why it was all shite.'

'What the fuck are you talking about?'

'I dunno, Gimpo, I just don't know.'

'Anyway I've been waiting for you. Remember what I told you? The crossing the equator thing.'

'What, jumping in the water?'

'Yeah.'

'We got to do that?'

'Yeah.'

'Now?'

'Yeah.'

'OK if we have to.'

'Follow me.'

'Gimpo, you know I'd follow you anywhere.'

We are joined by Remi, who is now Gimpo's best mate. Wherever you go in the world people are drawn to Gimpo. And Gimpo always gets an in with the locals, not cynically, he just does. He gets to suss what's going on, why it works, what's the motivation. Anyway, Remi is with us. His assistant is being left in charge of his stall. We make our way to the roof of *Colonel Ebaya*. Gimpo strips off to underpants, so Remi and I do the same. We must be 25 feet above the black water of the Congo. Gimpo does a backward somersault dive and hits the water perfectly. Remi follows suit. I just jump.

Nothing much else happens, not much point in me relating this event other than it happened. One small part of Blighty culture forever in a foreign field.

But the equator. We are on the fuckin' equator. That's something to send a postcard home about. You learn about the equator when you first go to school. Holds a special place in your imagination.

> *Dear Mum*
>
> *Z, Gimpo and me are on the equator. We are off to have tea with Satan.*
>
> *Wish you were here.*
>
> *Love Bill*

'So we can tick that one off.'

I remembered Helsinki, the weird evening in Oscar's bar. I thought I had hallucinated the entire evening. Obviously not.

'How come you know we met Oscar?' asked Bill, his pyrotechnic jacksie silent for the first time in months.

'Amateur occult stuff, sweetie. Nothing too impressive I'm afraid. A couple of calls on the astral telephone. How is the decaying bag of offal these days anyway, is he still shacked up with the chappy with bad teeth?'

Bosie sucked his cigar through his dribbling lip gloss.

'You mean Keith, Keith Richards?'

The gruesome incident was unravelling itself in my head: Keith laughing as Gimpo kicked several shades of congealing plasma from the undead Oscar.

'Yes yes, the musical fellow. Gosh, what an odd couple they must make. Tell me, is he very beautiful?'

Bosie took on a decidedly camp lilt, shades of Fenella Fielding and Eartha Kitt sliding into his gravelly voice.

'Fuck no,' coughed Bill. 'I don't think the pair of them had a thing going. Keith seemed to loathe the air that Oscar breathed.'

'Sweetie,' exhaled Bosie, obviously enjoying himself the way chuffs do when bitching about ex-lovers. 'That's the way Fatboy likes it, unrequited love, the more tragic the better, the Christ-fixated nonce thrives on it,' spat Bosie with all the venom of a fag spurned.

Little Claudette entered the room carrying a silver tray with three glasses, a bowl of sugar, three silver spoons and a bottle of something bluish green that looked hideously dangerous.

'You are staying for dinner, aren't you?' asked Bosie placing a cold bony hand on my knee. 'I've invited someone you simply must meet, an old fin-de-siècle buddy of mine, we go back years. Please, the absinthe, you must try it. I kept several crates of the stuff when I found out that the European governments had outlawed it. I mean really, what's a little nervous perturbation between friends?'

I wasn't so sure. Absinthe was banned at the beginning of the century for some pretty good reasons. For a start it's a methyl alcohol as opposed to the ethyl alcohol that we are all familiar with, a wood-based alcohol as opposed to a grain-based one. The nearest equivalent today is methylated spirits.

Claudette filled three glasses with the stuff, placed a spoonful of sugar in them and then set the lot on fire. I blew out the disturbing blue flame and drank it quickly. It was as I expected, absolutely fucking disgusting, like hot pepper and cleaning fluid. The sugar did absolutely nothing to camouflage the taste. For the following four days everything that passed my lips seemed to be filtered through a piece of blue acetate.

I WAS SMITTEN

I read Germaine Greer's other books that followed but none ever hit the spot *The Female Eunuch* did. But I became aware of a recurrent pattern in my life. The women I always found myself being attracted to were the strident, tough-talking, ego-crushing, harridan types. Women that contained a blend of characteristics drawn from my mother, big sister and junior school teachers, naturally.

Come the mid 1980s, I began to notice Germaine Greer turning up on various TV shows. Her greying hair piled loosely up on top of her head, peering over her half-moon glasses, as she delivered her pithy comments to whatever mere male journalist, chat-show host or quiz master was in her sights.

The epiphany happened on one such occasion. There she was, the scrape of greying hair tied up roughly, the stare over the half-moons, the barbed repost. Then the camera pulled back. She was wearing a dull grey suit. All buttoned-up academic on top, but down below was a miniskirt revealing acres of quivering thigh and, to finish it and me off, a pair of high-heeled shoes. Or in the words of Wanda Dee, 'My fuck-me pumps'. I was smitten, she could walk all over me, grind her stilettos into my bare back. I could even ignore the fact she was Australian. So what game was she playing? Was I supposed to listen to what she had to say or stare at her thighs? Was she addressing my hormones or my mind? Or was she just trying to fuck with me? It was a double-edged epiphany, 'cause as it happens I was listening to what was coming out of her mouth as well. And what I learnt was this:

No longer being a teenager and having lived a bit of life myself, I was not eager to be impressed by the force of someone's polemic however anti-establishment it was, I needed some rationale to back it up.

The thing is, one man's rationale is another woman's innate prejudice, masquerading as rationale and vice versa. And there's the rub.

At an early stage we learn all we are going to learn about the ways of the world. Our basic take on things is set in concrete. None of us likes to acknowledge this, we like to think we march on to the dangers of life with an open mind. We don't. If we are born with an instinctive grasp on knowledge, we use that to confirm what we already know. Those born with a high IQ and enquiring mind are taught to confront and solve all problems with disciplined rationale. The trouble is, we get very good at picking and choosing what problems we want to solve with our disciplined rationale. Problems that, once solved, will only be further proof to back up what we already knew or half guessed.

OK not all the time, but worryingly often.

*

'You seek your souls, I believe,' said Bosie getting to his feet shakily.

His linen suit hung from him as if from a skeleton. Claudette gripped him by the elbow and passed him a beautiful ebony cane topped with an ornate silver handle, he hobbled to the fireplace trailing a fetid wake behind him. Claudette followed closely in the old man's stink carrying the slopping colostomy bag.

'Ah Oscar.' He was addressing an old photograph in a tarnished gilt frame of the legendary literary sphincter pirate. 'It wasn't all bad I suppose, I did love you once, but I was so young, so stupid.'

Bosie looked up dreamily, a wan smile cracked his weird green foundation powder.

'A mere slip of a lad, 12 years young when the old bugger came a-creeping.'

A tear rolled slowly down his withered cheek.

'Dear Oscar, what we two know about Satanic bargaining, lost souls, immortality, fame... well, fame for you, heinous notoriety for me. That handsome Lucifer was far too smart for both of us. The sodomy? Well yes, if it hadn't been for all that anal skullduggery perhaps your reputation, Reading gaol, the awful ignominy... This fucking thing!'

Bosie jabbed at the colostomy bag with his walking stick. It split and covered poor Claudette in glooping stench. Bosie barely noticed the blinding stink and carried on with his rambling soliloquy: 'Reading gaol, ah yes, poor Oscar... The treatment for nonces back in those days, well as you can imagine, it wasn't much different from today. Everyone needs someone to dump on, even those wretched souls lurking in society's prisons.'

Bosie seemed to be in a dream. I got the feeling that this monologue had been played out many times, to illiterate Africans and mildewed mirrors, to the mysterious jungle beneath a deaf moon.

'Yes, that whore 'history' is finally being kind to Oscar's memory, his ironic wit, his off-the-cuff aphorisms, that I personally witnessed him labour over for hours... a truly modern genius they call him. And my legacy? What has whore history bequeathed me? Lord Alfred Douglas! Arse-bandit bumboy Bosie! The creeping little shit that ruined the lord of language and king of life, Oscar fucking fatboy Wilde! I've read the books, I've seen the bloody films! I knew it would end this way.

'His fat-arsed genius himself planned it all in his little Reading wanking hole. That testament of lies, *De Profundis*, a filthy book accusing me of every sodomistic crime under the sun. That vulgar Irish peasant! Dear God, he fucks a couple of rent boys and thinks he's bloody Socrates! Lord, if anyone knew the true extent of his depravity. Those baby pitbulls! My arse! I'll tell you now, I wouldn't need this bloody thing.'

Bosie ripped out the pipes and tubes in his side and threw the lot at little Claudette. The servant rushed to the aid of his master whose rage was flying into dangerous quadrants.

'My God, it's all so unfair! And here! How did I end up in this malaria-ridden shite hole growing and training little nigger bumboys for the bloody Arabs? Oh Christ, if it wasn't for my Catholicism I don't know what I'd....'

Z, THE NEW DE NIRO?

Up on top watching our flotilla disengage itself from the dockside of Mbandaka. Not as full on as when we left the docks at Kinshasa but still these Africans do not pass on an opportunity to scream and shout and leap up and down. As we pull out on to the river we get a good view of Mbandaka, all these crumbling colonial villas being reclaimed by the jungle. Half-a-dozen pre-war paddle boat steamers half submerged at rakish angles in the bay.

'Z, it looks like a perfect location for a movie.'

'What? About us?'

'No. About anything, romance, escape, a heist, whatever but this view here is dripping with symbolic meaning of some sort.'

'What, all empires crumble?'

'Nature always wins, the jungle reclaims?'

'Yeah.'

'I don't think even Francis Coppola could persuade a film crew to work up here, let alone get a movie star to do their stuff and Hollywood to bankroll it. Those freewheeling days of movie-making were over back in the 1970s.'

I don't like talking about films partly 'cause I don't know what I'm talking about but mostly 'cause...

'As an art form I don't trust movies.'

'What bollocks theory is it this time, Bill? You don't trust movies. Movie-making is the great art form of the twentieth century. Tells us more about the human condition than any other art form ever. Holds up a mirror to all our dreams but novelty hit-maker Bill Drummond doesn't trust it so the whole 100 years of movie-making should apologise to us all before shuffling off to die.'

'No, I'm just saying...'

'Ah fuck what you're just saying! I know what you're saying. We all know that. It's taken as read. Every art form is flawed. But what lies behind this is your knowledge that if Scorsese turned up here now he would recognise that I have the potential of a De Niro, or at least Willem Dafoe and he wouldn't even notice you.'

'Fuck off, Z.'

'Nah, I'm only joking Bill. You get the bit as the bloke who is sitting with his kids at another table in the diner while me and Uma Thurman are eating our pizzas and planning to blow the bank up.'

'So you're saying I look like a dad while you look like a leading man?'

'Yeah, and that's why you hate movies.'

*

Bosie suddenly thrust his hand into his smoking-jacket pocket, pulled out a small silver revolver and put it into his messy snaggle-toothed mouth and pulled the trigger, once, twice. 'For fuck's sake, Claudette! You little bastard! You've taken the bullets out again haven't you!' Bosie beat the young lad weakly around the head and shoulders before falling back into his chair gasping for breath, yellow shit staining through his dirty shirt and dribbling down his side.

'Forgive me,' he panted as he calmed down a little, coughing and patting his chest. Claudette fussed around nonplussed by his master's irate behaviour, fixing Bosie's tubes and attaching a fresh colostomy bag.

'I am so terribly sorry, it's Oscar. Even though we're separated by two continents he still has the ability to bring out the worst in me. Gracious, what must you think. Please, it's almost time for dinner... more absinthe?

Bosie, like the occult preservation of Oscar in Helsinki was obviously under the enchantment of some very bad amateur magic indeed. They both seemed to have achieved a form of immortality, but at what cost? Their flesh ages, their minds are light years beyond any form of Alzheimer's disease, but their spirit refuses to give up the ghost.

'Fucking nonce!' harrumphs Bosie as Claudette takes a gentle hold of the living corpse by his frail arm.

The African servant pushed open one of the double swing doors and escorted Bosie into a hall of mad shadows. Bill and I followed nervously. Hundreds of candles flickered gold on ornate silver candelabras. The thick warm smell of melting wax mingled with the fusty odour and cascading cobwebs that festooned the large low-ceilinged hall. Darker tones haunted the aromatic fugue: disease and death, blood and human sacrifice. In sympathy with the fungal heat humming around our senses Bill let slip one of his unmistakable diarrhoea cheesecutters that slid effortlessly into the Byzantine odours of corruption, slow death and bursting colostomy bags swirling around us in eyewatering abundance.

The long table reminded me of Miss Haversham's forgotten wedding feast. It stretched down the long room into even darker shadows where a hunched figure lurked massive in the gloom. Bosie pushed his African servant away from him, irritated.

'Really, Claudette, there's no need to be such a fusspot. I am capable of some things on my own, you know. Here, carry this if you must do something.'

He passed the boy the dribbling bag.

'Aleister!' he called to the sinister figure obscured by sucking darkness, 'Is that you, dear fellow?'

The hulking mass remained immobile.

'Aleister?' our sepulchral host called again. This time the shape moved, a bald head lifted from the main bulk of shadow into the candlelight and fixed us with black glittering eyes. My sphincter tried to hide up in my guts.

MEN ARE CUNTS

Germaine Greer starts with the broad premise that men are cunts and women have to deal with it, not by trying to become cunts as well but by being complete women.

OK, so I'm attempting to be knowingly provocative by my use of the C word. But I've been an ardent reader of Germaine for 25 years. Read all her books or at least flicked through them. She was always my feminist of choice. When Andrea Dworkin came along I stayed faithful to my Aussie muse by chanting 'fat lezzer' any time I saw the dungaree-sporting icon of the ugly face of feminism. On the women's pages of *The Guardian* I would never read anything that Dworkin wrote. Didn't read anything by Naomi Wolf either but that was because I was afraid I might be seduced by her, she had such a sexy name. As for Natasha Walter's new feminism of the 1990s I just laughed. She looked like a secretary who worked in a firm of solicitors. *Daily Mail* feminism.

My flame kept burning for Germaine. I read *The Change* as I went through my male menopause. She introduced me to Jane Austen where my education had failed.

If I'm honest there were a few months back in 1993 or 1994 when I had a bit of a fling with Camille Paglia. It was Z who introduced me to her. It was just after he had written his diatribe against Madonna in the closing pages of *Bad Wisdom* that he handed me a copy of *Sex, Art and American Culture.*

'Read this, Bill. She is the only woman writer alive today who understands.'

So I read. And the first chapter told me that Madonna was the future of feminism and that the artist has no moral responsibilities to liberal social causes. I ate it up and then I ate up *Sexual Personae*, her previous book. I agreed with everything she told me. It was a whirlwind romance but it didn't last. I got bored with seeing her name everywhere. I became jealous that I had to share her with all these other men who felt they too had been let off the hook by her 'let men be men in all their wife-beating, date-raping manly ways' number.

I crawled back to Germaine looking for repentance. Made myself read all 517 pages of *Slip-shod Sibyls* even though it bored me shitless. Mind you, I took offence at her picking the name Sibyl. That was my mum's mum's name and Germaine could have saved herself the bother of writing *Slip-shod and what's her name* altogether if she had only read *Bad Wisdom* first. In that book she would have learnt from me that the creative urge in man is only there as poor second choice activity compared to being able to create life itself.

Womankind is one great leap closer to God than us lot for that very reason. They are both in the real creation business, whereas us men just make up religions and art and football and try to make out that woman shouldn't be allowed in 'cause they wouldn't understand and God's a bloke anyway. So the Pope had to be a bloke and so were Picasso, Shakespeare and the manager of Aylesbury United.

The reason why we find women with kids boring is not because they are but because they find all the stuff we get up to completely redundant and a bit childish. Managing the local football team, painting the ceiling of the Sistine Chapel or starting a new religion has no intrinsic worth unless it pays for the new extension or at least the trolley of groceries at the Tesco checkout. That is their logic. A logic that I am, sadly, yet to find a flaw in.

So, back to Germaine. Over the last couple of months I've been party to a couple of anecdotes about the real-life Miss Greer. The first was delivered by a man in his mid-50s. Greer's name came up in conversation and he openly admitted he had been shagged by her in his younger days. In the morning after the said shag she exited the scene leaving him feeling like a used Kleenex. This middle-aged man then informed me that he learnt from that one experience what he might not have learnt from reading a whole shelf of gender studies. He learnt what it must have been like to have been one of the countless young women that he had treated in a similar way in his lustful past. I strove hard to conceal the fact I was riven with jealousy. Oh to have been our Germaine's discarded Kleenex for one night of Aussie rules.

The second anecdote concerns a game of French cricket. I'm not going to waste your or my time trying to describe the rules of French cricket here. All you need to know is that it's a safe bet the French never played it and that it is a game played by all ages and both sexes in the back garden at family get-togethers.

A female friend of mine told me she had been invited to a suburban garden party. Miss Greer was also a guest. At that point in the afternoon when convivial conversations have run their course, a game of French cricket was suggested by the host. The extended family and various friends of all ages and sexes took to the spirit of the game, that is until my Germaine took to the crease. She was being bowled to by an eight-year-old lad (only underarm bowling is allowed in French cricket). Germaine defended the wicket as if she was playing in front of a capacity Melbourne crowd and no allowance was made for the age of her opponent or the fact it was in an English back garden. I couldn't help but feel that Miss Greer's approach to the game might have been different if she had ever fulfilled her female potential and given birth.

My friend, on learning about my adoration of the Australian, informed me, rather unkindly I think, that the first among feminists doesn't look half as good in real life as she does on book jackets and TV shows.

*

'Ah Aleister, dear friend, it *is* you, you're early,' called Bosie down the length of the hall. 'I have some people here you simply must meet, my dear bosom friend and fellow maligned creature of whore-history's venal humour.'

Claudette ran ahead of us and lit more candles around the shadowy stranger. Dinner was served by more little boys in blonde wigs, some kind of roast fowl which like every other morsel of food I attempted to eat on that blasted continent tasted of bones and old leather. The meal was thankfully frugal and did not take long. I noticed that Bosie and the mysterious Aleister hardly touched their food and when they did it was merely to rearrange it on the plate. Bill on the other hand devoured every rotten root, putrid bean and stringy piece of flesh placed before him. I was dreading the afterburn already.

We belched politely, Bill threw in an uncalled-for chandelier rattler and then we made our way through to the drawing room and dim electric light. The walls were decorated with more fading sepia tints of slaughtered endangered species and their killers. One wall seemed to be dedicated to Bosie's swallow days, photographs of smiling Oxford fops in elegant theatrical costumes, the lascivious smile of the upper-class sodomite curling around their sharp features, tumbled messily with sad shots of dumpy Oscar looking uncomfortable and constipated, bolt upright and formal among the sinuous languor of Bosie and his lithe young chums. The deteriorated remains of one or two green paper carnations lay on top of the tarnished gilt frames.

THE POET
Silence for a while. The flotilla has drifted out into a large lagoon half a mile from the Mbandaka docks but not yet into the mainstream of the river.

'Z, have you ever been to the Saatchi Gallery?'

'Yeah.'

'Been in the room filled with black oil?'

'Yeah. Why?'

'Well, that's what the Congo reminds me of here. It doesn't look like it's made from water, more like oil or black treacle.'

'That's more like it, Bill. Richard Barnes will be pleased with you for coming up with that.'

Silence.

'Bill?'

'What?'

'If Gimpo gets killed, I know what we should call the book.'

'What?'

'*Meesta Geempo He Dead.*'

'But Gimpo is not going to get killed.'

'Yeah but it would be good if he did.'

'Why?'

'Fuck why! It's obvious. Anyway it's time for Gimpo to have a nervous breakdown. I had mine in the first couple of days. I think this ticket thing is going to run and run. I know how to trigger Gimpo's paranoia, just a bit of tweeking here and there and Gimpo will be in a mental freefall. I've done it before but out here he is likely to end up doing something rash. Something where he ends up rolling the dice once too often and that's it, no more Gimpo. Just you and me, Bill.'

I don't reply. Is there a reply I should give? Does Z mean what he has just said? Does Z ever mean what he says?

'Do you mean what you've just said?'

'Bill, my job is not to mean what I say. I'm a poet. Everything I do and say in my life is poetry.'

I get up and leave the poet to his poetry I have more important things to be doing. I need a shit.

*

'Please,' it was Bosie again, the tantrums of a short while ago forgotten, he had found a new energy from somewhere. 'Let me introduce you properly to mon cher ami, you must forgive his silent disposition, I can assure you it's no affectation. Dear Aleister, his throat has nearly gone, he speaks rarely to preserve the ailing tissue.

'Ah believe me, boys, immortality is not all that it would seem,' said Bosie, flouncing down the best he could considering his advanced state of decay into a high-backed leather chair.

The bald headed ogre stood by the fireplace. His scalp illuminated by the low-powered electric gloom revealed small areas of skull where the powdery skin had fallen away. His eyes however, unlike his friend Bosie's, were still bright, small marbles of devilish intensity. His cracked white lips bared into a smile revealing yellow teeth like an old dog's. Folds of grey skin, as if the fat below had melted away hung over the tightly buttoned black shirt.

'Gentlemen,' he said, his death-rattle voice like a frantic moth caught behind Venetian blinds clattered across the space between us. 'One moment please, forgive me.'

He pulled a small lacquered box from one of the pockets of his purply-black cape. He opened the box and removed a beautiful silver and glass hypodermic syringe containing a prepared solution, lifted an eyelid and injected himself directly into his eyeball.

'Fentanyl citrate,' he said by way of explanation, 'I rarely feel it these days.' He continued: 'Most of my tissue is decayed beyond sensation. Fortunately my brain seems to be hanging on, I can still hit the pleasure centres. Dear Bosie is being such a tease, aren't you, Alfie?'

The spooky junkzombie patted Bosie's knee, his friend emitting a nauseating approximation of a girlish giggle. I got the sickly feeling that there was the germ of some sexual affection between the two animated corpses. Bosie laughed, the bright purple and yellow decay of his mouth and syphilitic gullet shone brightly beneath the electric light.

'Forgive me, Aleister,' Bosie kissed his friend courteously on the hand. 'Bill and Z, allow me to introduce my dearest friend, my muse and my comfort, the Ippisimus Magus, Mr Aleister Crowley, necromancer and master of the black arts in their entirety.'

The junkie devil worshipper allowed himself a smug little smile.

'Like myself,' continued the dead nance Bosie, 'Oscar and countless others scattered upon obscure latitudes and lost quadrants of the furthest flung five corners of the Earth, Aleister is an immortal.'

All souls are immortal, I didn't say to Bosie.

WHAT DO I GET?

Later, Gimpo is in the cabin messing about with stuff in his bag.

'Gimpo, I've got an idea.'

'Yeah, what?'

'Because I want to keep most of my part of the book just dialogue...'

'What's dialogue?'

'People speaking bits, not descriptive bits, not me writing what's going on in my head.'

'Yeah.'

'Do you think you could describe what everything is like on a walk between here and the bar and I just write it down as you're saying it?'

'What's the difference between me describing it and you writing it down and you just describing it in the first place. It's still the same stuff that is being described. Anyway I've described it all already in my diary, you can use that.'

'I know but when somebody else is reading it in a book I think they find it easier to relate to people just talking and not have to read all that other bollocks that's going on in my head. I mean, everybody has got bollocks going on in their head. My bollocks isn't any better or more interesting than anybody else's.'

'So what are you asking? Do you want me to describe it to you here and now?'

'No. We take a walk to the bar and you tell me everything you see, hear, feel or smell on the way.'

'And what do I get?'

'I'll buy you a beer when we get there.'

'OK.'

*

It seemed that Bosie and Aleister, these materialistic popinjays, were so addicted to the pleasures of mortal flesh that they were loathe to give up their corporeal inhabitation. Rather than set their spirits free to swim among eternity's ebb and flow, these poets of carnality were determined to hang on to their mortal shells until they melted into the very ground upon which they breathed their very last foul breath.

'You believe the Devil has possession of your mortal souls?' asked the bald cosmic junkie black magician satanist premier arse-bandit Aleister Crowley.

'Sort of,' said Bill.

'And you believe the President Mobutu is the devil in Earthly guise?' Mr Crowley again.

'It would seem that way, at least by our admittedly haphazard calculations,' Bill said, serious.

'Well we won't go into all the details or we will be here at least 17 lifetimes,' said the magician. 'Let's assume that Mobutu is indeed the Prince of Darkness.' Aleister removed his silver syringe again and started cooking on a sooty spoon. 'What would you say if I told you...' I winced as he banged up the gear in his eyeball. Aleister gouched a second and carried on, 'Where was I? Oh yes, what would you say if I told you that I don't think his Satanic Majesty would be interested in your souls?'

Aleister was one of the world's foremost authorities on occult buggering around. A revered ambidextrous riddler of archaic lexicons and obscure kriological alphabets, his opinions had to be considered.

'I don't understand,' I answered.

'Yes,' butted in Bill, his tone petulant, the chips on his shoulders rocking precariously. 'Why wouldn't he want our souls, what's wrong with them, surely they're evil enough, what about all the dead whores... the boys...' Bill spluttered.

'The devil is lazy,' said Aleister. 'He wears many faces, each one confoundingly different from the last. But I don't think... somehow, as an occult Master, I can't believe that the fallen angel would have possession of your souls at all. There's something about the pair of you. You're too vibrant, too mad. I don't suppose you could have mislaid them somewhere?'

Mislaid our souls somewhere? It was a concept I'd never even considered. I always thought you were either in possession of your soul or somehow the devil had either bought it from you or tricked you out of it. The idea of absent-mindedly mislaying something so cosmically valuable as a soul, well I don't even think the Literary Arseholes could be that dumb.

'It's a common error, believe me. I've spent God knows how many lives jousting with dark forces to end up penniless, addicted... I digress, forgive me.'

'Look, I don't mean to be rude,' butted in Bill, his impatience evident on his jutting bottom lip, 'But I must insist, a man who is not in some way or form in thrall to diabolical maleficence does not go around kippering up innocent whores, casting his onanistic seed across the bloody remains, prostrating himself before the dark idols of Sodom, burning £50 notes in front of the homeless...'

'Yeah,' I added, 'And what about me and Katie over in that funky Arizona desert? You can't tell me those skanky slayings account for nothing, we must have ripped at least 50 teenage floozies.'

IN BED WITH GERMAINE GREER

Now, if there is a reason for all my musings on the subject of the 25-year infatuation I've had with my Melbourne mistress, it is this. Many is the night I've fallen asleep as the sounds of Sailing By or the shipping forecast gently waft from the Roberts radio nestled by my pillow. The radio, as usual, is tuned to BBC Radio 4 long wave. After closedown the same frequency is used through the small hours by the BBC World Service. It is a regular occurrence for me to surface from my sordid dreams to learn some first-hand account of the latest atrocities in Rwanda or what life is like on the cocaine plantations of Bolivia.

The night before Z, Gimpo and I set out on this ludicrous escapade I fell asleep in the usual way, the comforting melody of Sailing By lullabying me off to my sea of dream. At some ungodly hour I found myself being aroused by some sweet pillow talk. Whoever she was, my nocturnal companion was telling me about her visit to the Sudan and her conversation with the women there, from a culture where female genital mutilation is widespread. What she was imparting to me in my drowsy state of arousal went something like this.

'Bill, when I explained to these Sudanese women that Western women sometimes have their tits cut, trimmed and pumped up they were just as dumbfounded and horrified as we are when we hear about clits being cut out and cunts sewn up. We here in the enlightened post-colonial patronising West think that to hack off the clitoris and labia minora and create a raw surface on the labia majora so that they can be stitched together to form a seal over the urethra and most of the introitus of the vagina is some vile male-inspired sexist custom. A custom borne out of fear and hatred of the female; a custom to control women's sexual experience and reinforce gender roles, with a total disregard for the sexual needs and concerns of women.

This explanation is rubbish. These women cut out each others clits and sew up their cunts not because men or a male-dominated culture tells them to. They do it because it makes for better sex. They want tight dry cunts. They want pain on penetration. They want that pain that becomes indistinguishable from pleasure in a state of high sexual arousal. Such practises have been outlawed for over 50 years by male governments. The UN are doing everything to stamp it out but our sisters in Africa know what they want and they know how to get it.'

She then started rabbiting on about male genital mutilation by millions of Jews and Muslims and how that any thought of trying to stamp that out would be considered a total frontal attack on their cultural identity. Their male cultural identity. The thrust of her argument seemed to be that there was something of a double standard in said patronising post-colonial world where it is seemingly OK for men to allow their bodies to be hacked and stitched but not for women to have the same choice.

By this time I was in too much of a state of arousal to know if I am now quoting her word for word. My arousal and the remedy I was taking to cure it was not inspired by the force of the above argument but because for years I had dreamed of being in bed with Germaine Greer with her whispering her sweet polemics in my ear. My wish had been granted the night before I set sail for the blackest of continents, the home of 'sew it up and death by bumming'.

The morning after I wasn't too sure. There was no sign in my bed that she had spent the night. No long grey hair on the pillow next to me. No half-moon specs on the bedside cabinet as she took her morning shower. No hastily scribbled note, 'Good luck with the devil, big boy, see you when you get back'. No, none of that, just a crinkly Kleenex on the floor on my side of the bed and an empty feeling that somehow I'd been used.

Maybe it was all a dream. I just couldn't get my head round the idea that my Aussie goddess could ever, would ever, be telling the worldwide sisterhood to forget about burning their bras and get into infibulation instead. One thing is certain, I will never be able to stand in front of a lingerie shop bellowing, 'Sew it up' with the conviction of yesteryear.

She wins again.

*

'Gentlemen, gentlemen please, please,' protested Aleister, pouring us each a large tumbler of the potent fin-de-siècle poison. 'Why, it was those very acts that you speak of that convinced me the Devil was not in control of your actions. Those wanton acts of cruel malice were the acts of free men.'

Bosie dimmed the lights as Claudette brought in several candelabras, the molten wax perfumed the air, the absinthe tasted sweeter as the maleficent erudition caressed the air around us.

'My tarot please,' said Aleister, clapping his hands. Another little black fellow dressed in a platinum blonde wig and a white corset ran into the room and handed Aleister the sealed deck. 'Hmph, not my own design,' he snorted derisively, flicking through the A E Waite deck designed rather beautifully I thought by Pamela Coleman. Aleister held up a card, the Baphomet of Mendes, the goat-headed Lucifer sitting upon a black cube, beneath him chained to the cube are a man and a woman, the lovers.

'As you can see, the symbolism is quite clear, the two orchard thieves in chains, the serpent provided them with the knowledge of good and evil and now no matter how an individual chooses to act, once he has taken the devil's coin, fruit, whatever, he has no free will. Everything he chooses to do is coloured by the Manichean conceit. Your common murderer, gorged on the forbidden fruit, believes he is committing an evil act. Whereas the gleeful actions both of you undertook were played out outside of this shallow judgement. Which leads me to suspect that neither of you have traded with the derelict angel. Besides, both of you are far too wilful for him to bother with.'

Aleister hit himself up in the eye again and juddered slightly before continuing, 'Your very presence here is evidence of that, swirling your metaphors and allegories into Damascene realities. The style and complete absence of conscience you displayed in your amusing carnage indicates to any intelligent observer not men who have surrendered their souls but men, whether they are aware of it or not, in full possession of a vibrant soul connected to the conscienceless soul of the universe.'

'Bravo,' chirped Bosie, draining his absinthe and calling for more. 'True wickedness, ah such nectar is only appreciated by the free'est of free souls. It is the law of man, not the law of God that forbid these sublime pleasures.'

THE JOURNEY

'So you want me to start now?'

'Yeah.'

'Well, this is our cabin. It's...'

'You don't need to describe the cabin. I've already done that bit.'

'But I thought you weren't going to have any descriptive bits.'

'That was before I had the idea.'

'OK. I'm stepping outside the cabin on to our balcony. On our balcony there are five cabins. Next door is where Pitsu and Mami live and then another cabin. But we are going this way and I don't know the names of the people who live here or in the next cabin, but we are all friends now. Like it used to be living in terraced houses when my mam was a kid, front doors left open...'

'Describe what people are doing as well.'

'OK, Bill, I'm just getting to that.'

'Mavubu's woman has been chopping onions and is now crushing garlic and she's got a couple of the smoked catfish that I guess she's going to use in the meal. The catfish look like...'

'It's OK, Gimpo, I've already described what the catfish look like.'

'Yeah, but Bill, did you describe the maggots in the fish?'

'No. What maggots?'

'Haven't you seen the maggots? Every time they prepare the catfish for a meal they have to shake out the maggots first.'

'You mean that fish that Trefor does for us would have had maggots in it?'

'Yeah, look! I will get back to describing what is happening. Mavubu's woman has just picked up the smoked catfish and tapped it on the railing and two maggots have just fallen out. Now she is picking off the black smoked skin of the fish and pulling out the white flesh from within and putting it in her small cooking pot with the onions and crushed garlic that is already sizzling in oil.'

'Olive oil?'

'How the fuck should I know what kind of oil? Maybe groundnut oil, that's from Africa.'

'What's she cooking it on?'

'A small, portable charcoal burning stove. It's what all the families use to cook their meals on.'

'How many rings?'

'Just the one.'

'So this means they can never have rice or mealy meal at the same time as the main bit?'

'Yeah they do, they cook the other stuff first.'

Z arrives.

'What the fuck are the pair of you doing?'

'Gimpo is describing what's going on and I'm writing it down.'

'Why? Look, whatever your reason I'm not interested. The Nips have lent me this copy of *National Geographic*. Have you written about the Nips yet?'

'No. Why?'

*

Bosie closed his eyes as Claudette unfastened the fragile dandy's trousers and fished around for the ancient libertine's wood.

'Careful child! Careful,' he gasped. 'Don't pull it off like you did last time, rape! murder! sodomy,' continued the rapt Bosie gripping his little maid's ears and jamming his rickety pizzle down the lads throat. 'Such exquisite, uh, pleasures.'

He jizzed.

Waiting for Bosie's enthusiastic interjection to subside, Aleister continued eloquently, 'You wish to see those enslaved by Satan, those who really did sell themselves down the black river, sold themselves into a life of slavery. Visit any metropolis, take any underground rush hour train, see them on London Bridge trudging back and forth to mindless labours. These are the timid souls in hock to the powers of the air. Not brave reckless dandies such as yourselves, resting upon your rapiers contemplating the wake of your boat as you surf languidly the waters of Charon. No, no my friends you are not numbered among the undead, you are not cashdollar somnambulists trudging half awake through a television-filtered reality of tawdry possessions and drip-dried moralities, in thrall to some black enchantment cast by pig-ignorant plutocrats drowning in their own flesh.'

Aleister paused a second and slugged on his absinthe. Claudette, wiping watery sperm from his lips, refilled the magician's glass.

Aleister continued his flattery: 'The majority of men who do make this eternal pact often acquiesce for very little indeed. No fire, no brimstone is needed to impress them. In fact such theatricals would probably terrify them into not signing those innocuous pieces of paper, those small instalments that bit by tiny bit bleed their souls to death, never realising until it's too late, when that final humiliation is pressed upon them at their retirement ceremony, that grinding memento mori, the brass clock. The sands of time, a life wasted in bondage to another man's feathered obese stupidity.'

Bosie burst into cruel laughter at his friend's poetic soliloquy.

'No my friends, you may not have realised it yourselves but your spritely souls heeded well the hermetic messages beamed out by those grinning skulls leering out of the old masters remembering death and have taken it upon themselves to hide away somewhere. Somewhere very close no doubt.'

Aleister covered his mouth and belched. Bosie was battering Claudette about the head with his silver-topped cane. It seems Bosie's dick had fallen off again.

'For God's sake, Bosie, leave the boy alone!' shouted the magician, 'How old are you? You're coming up for nearly a century and a half you damn fool, it's not the boy's fault the bloody thing keeps falling off. You can't keep stitching it back on. What do you expect, really! Your grotesque satyrism really has to be seen to be believed sometimes. I'm not surprised you drove poor Oscar to distraction! We have guests, for god's sake!'

I wasn't convinced. Even if Crowley wasn't the wickedest man in the world his reasoning and philosophy seemed too aristocratic, too nineteenth century, too Nietzschean. Bill however was greasily seduced by Aleister's saccharine flattery. The idea of the big-balled Superman, beyond good and evil, offing whores in some kind of noble quest for self-realisation obviously appealed to him and the whip in his valise.

STILL WARM

'Hi, Richard. You got here OK? This is Z.'

'Hello, Zodiac. I have something that might interest you.' Richard handed Z a fat file containing information that he had downloaded from the internet concerning the new teen hero, Jake Baker. Jake Baker is a 19-year-old American lad going through the American legal system. His crime was to have written little stories about the girls in his class. Stories that describe, in detail, how he cut up the cute babes in their cheerleader gear then cooked the tender meat before burning the inedible remains.

The Americans love to get their knickers in a twist about freedom of speech. Jake Baker and his right to write whatever stories he wanted to was the latest in a long line of twisted-knicker cases. Holden Caulfield was looking redundant and well out of date compared to what Jake was achieving for teenage angst and hatred of everything phoney.

After spending some minutes perusing the Jake Baker file, Z looked up.

'Nice to meet you, Richard. You've got some good stuff here, but why do you think I would be interested? Surely this is more in Bill's line of studies?'

Z has a habit of always trying to offload the shame of his more suspect interests on to his travelling companions.

'I thought from what Bill had told me about you and your proposed idea for a periodical entitled *Still Warm*, you might want to lend your support to the Jake Baker case.'

'Sounds like a fuckin' creep to me, Richard. I think I'll pass on it. But do you mind if I keep the file anyway?'

'Of course. I will send you more as I get it.'

Richard Brem is 27. He is Austrian, from Vienna. He stands six-foot tall with athletic build, short blond hair and dresses in casual sports gear. He looks like perfect material for a leader of the Hitler Youth. Genes to build a master race. His eyes burn with the intensity of a recently converted zealot. In his own words he is an 'archaeologist of the now and an explorer of future culture'. His thirst for knowledge is Himalayan. He is always working on at least six projects at any one time. Richard Brem appears to be in touch with every interesting person in Europe. Alan Moore, the writer and occultist lives less than 30 minutes drive from my house but it took this Austrian living half a continent away to introduce us.

Richard Brem was the reason why Z and I travelled to that particular Alpine corner of Italy. He had faxed me strict instructions to meet him at the Mozart Café, Merano at 9.00am on 3 February 1996 and he would then explain why.

I had been concerned that Z and Richard might not hit it off, that their cultural reference points might be too far apart. I was mistaken. Brem then pulled a second fat file from his briefcase. On its cover was the word 'BWITI'.

'BWITI is a hallucinogenic drug found only up the Congo. It doesn't travel. The plant has to be eaten fresh. When you take it, the trip will last 36 to 48 hours. In that time you will confront the god BWITI. He will help you resist the two-pronged attack of Christianity and Islam.'

Z grabbed the file and started to delve into its pages. I then had something that could be described as more than a feeling but not quite a premonition. It was going to have a rather large influence on Z's account of our journey to Satan. This BWITI thing was the sort of narcotic shortcut that Z would be drawn to, going completely against my work-ethic approach to enlightenment. I also knew it would lead to me and Gimpo having to clear up the aftermath. Z slipped the fat green file into his bag alongside his Jake Baker one.

*

I'd been there many times when Bill's sanguinary tastes had got the better of him and believe me shipmates, there was nothing noble about the creepy way he used to play around with the slashed-up remains of his gory sacrifices, cutting bits off and stuffing them under his foreskin or up his jacksie.

The absinthe had been sending me into uncomfortably strange areas, deep-green astral projections, monotone blue harlequins and vivid night cafés, murder, horror and the company they keep. Hobgoblins, familiars and bats as big as eagles hovered around the sinister bald magician. When the bastard started hitting me with telepathy and bending mirrors I knew it was time to get out. There's nothing I trust less in this world than a telepathic mirror bender.

There are things behind mirrors that we're not supposed to see – the reason some knowledge is forbidden is for our own sakes. I called on all my psychonautical strength and struggled out from beneath the absinthe intoxication, it was like wrestling a giant squid. Like trying to escape from one of those damned lucid dreams.

Wake up wake up this is just a dream.

Like surfacing from the effects of nitrous oxide, spinning around and around trying to grab the light. I shook my head, splashing my chest with sweat. The syringe was hanging from one of Aleister's suppurating eyeball. Bosie was muttering angrily trying to stitch his crusty cock back on to his raggy bloodless ballbag. Claudette, heavily bruised and bleeding, was trying to help him.

BACK ISSUE OF *NATIONAL GEOGRAPHIC*

So I'm going to break my self-imposed rule again to tell you about the Japanese film crew who are on board. When I said earlier that we were the only white people on board I was only being technically true. There is a five-man Japanese film crew. Do we count Japanese as whites when in Africa? I mean, would they know what post-colonial guilt feels like? Are they to be held responsible for any of Africa's woes? Anyways these Japs had bagged all the first class cabins weeks ago, that's why we are stuck in steerage. They never come out of their cabins except at mealtime. They have brought their own chef with them who prepares their Japanese meals. They have brought all their own supplies of food and bottled water. They have next-to-no contact with anybody else on board.

They have a pet nigger who acts as their go-between. He stays with them in first class and he looks like a twat. Me and Z wear specs. The Nips wear specs. All Nips wear specs. None of the Africans wear specs except on the bank note. I don't know if this is because blacks have got better eyesight than us or they just can't afford them. Anyway this pet nigger twat, he's got specs and he's always wearing his bright green shiny tracksuit. Remember Mr Motivator on telly in the 1980s? He looks like him. But the crowning glory of his twatishness is his camera. At all times hanging around his neck, it's one of those big chunky cameras that Jap tourists used to always have before everything in the camera department started to shrink. This camera of his is obviously a cast-off from his paymasters. An African with a camera. Black men don't do photography. Yeah, I remember Don Letts but you know what I mean. I bet he doesn't even need the glasses, I bet they're just an affectation.

Photography by definition is about the past. When it comes to most things black men are not intense about the past, unless they're harping on about slavery. Or come to think about it, the future either. What concerns them is the now. The right now. That's why they are so good at dancing. Dance is the ultimate art form that expresses the now. Dance is all about now.

We never knew what this Japanese film crew was doing on board. In fact I didn't want to know. I preferred to pretend they weren't here.

'So you been talking to the Nips, Z?'

'Yeah.'

'What for?'

'I'm bored with your company. I'm not going to start going native like Gimpo and the Japanese appreciate the finer things in life.'

'Like what?'

'They used to buy Zodiac Mindwarp records.'

'The Japs bought any fucker's records.'

'And they drink good quality liquor.'

'And you thought you could worm your way into their company in the hope they would start cracking open the cases of single malt?'

'Look, Bill, I'm just trying to open things up, makes for a more interesting tale for us to tell.'

'Remember the Burma railway is what I say.'

'That's over 50 years ago Bill.'

'Yeah, and it's nearly 2,000 years since the Hebrews killed our Saviour and you still use that one to justify your anti-Semitism.'

'Fuck all this shit. I got talking to one of them. He speaks good English. He told me they are making a documentary about the Congo based on this story in a back issue of *National Geographic*.'

Z and I are both big fans of *National Geographic*, have been since boyhood, both got cardboard boxes of back issues bought from charity shops. Z is brandishing this copy on loan from his new Oriental friends. He flicks it open and there, in full *National Geographic* colour (or should that be color?) are fantastic photos of every detail of life on these very barges.

'Can I loan it off you for a read?'

'Yeah but I don't want you wanking all over it.'

*

The klaxon from the *Colonel Ebeya* was screaming in some other dimension. Where the fuck was Bill ? It was no use asking these clowns. I heard the klaxon sound again: one more hour and the *Ebeya* was out of there. The thought of staying down on Bosie's boy farm for the next month or two was not appealing.

I wandered off into the maze of corridors searching for perverted Bill. There were boys everywhere, dressed in all kinds of weird fetish gear, none of them looked over 12 years old. The really weird thing that strangely I hadn't noticed before was that their sooty genitalia was fully formed, oversized bellenders with dangling bollocks and pubic hair. Fuck knows what kind of fertiliser Bosie was using on this grim cash crop but it was producing strange meat indeed. I soon realised that the majority of these tiny trainee catamites were in fact adolescent pygmies, which explained their man-size bollocks.

I eventually found Bill spreadeagled on a snooker table, naked apart from a pair of grey socks. About 40 of the erotic pygmies seemed to be feeding on him like flies. I started swatting them away before I realised they were in fact licking and sucking the increasingly perverted Bill all over his pale body.

I held down the rocketball of vomit trying to blast up my gullet. Bill's dreamy expression was sickening to behold, the little fuckers were like limpets. I had to physically tear seven or eight of the little bastards from Bill's ballbag area. I threw some beer in his face, slapped him round the head, he was lost in some sickening homoerotic dream.

'Get your fucking safari suit on, you fucking nonce, we're out of here now!'

I threw his spunkstained clothes at him, aghast at the state he was in. His entire body from the neck down was covered in horrible raspberry-coloured lovebites, the crotch area from just below the thighs up to the lower abdomen was one giant bruise, beads of blood-like fat rubies formed on the damaged skin. His deflated knob end dribbled yellow pus like custard – super perve had managed to bag himself a dose of jungle clap from somewhere.

The cocksucking pygmies were chuckling in the corners like gruesome fellatory munchkins. The poor bastards, was there no limit to the degradation imposed on this impoverished continent by wealthier nations?

DEEPLY DISAPPOINTING

In my bunk, reading *National Geographic*, the other two have sodded off to the bar. All the stuff I was hoping Gimpo would dictate to me about what it is like on board our flotilla of barges is already here in the *National Geographic* and it's got great colour pictures. So if you want to know, it's the 1991 November issue. Your local reference library should have it in stock. It's got photos of the pirogues and the catfish, the stalls, the flip-flops, the First Manhattan Bank t-shirts, the doctor in his white coat selling past their sell-by date UNESCO medicines; it's got the ticket inspectors; and it's got the roof boys and the women with babies strapped to their backs. It's even got a picture of Trefor in his kitchen. The only thing that ain't there is me, Z and Gimpo. I find this all deeply disappointing. More deeply disappointing than the Dutch hippie, but this time I'm resigned to the disappointment. Of course there is no place left to go that hasn't been written about, filmed, packaged and explained away by Western whitey.

I decide it's time for me to ditch all that surface dialogue stuff and have a dark night of the soul instead. I resolve to write down what I really think and feel. Work out in words what it is to be me and once that is done my words that detail the deeply personal will illuminate the universal. But now that I've tried to think about what I really think I realise that not only will nobody else give a toss about what I think or feel, but I don't give a fuck either.

We get tired. We get down. We get happy. We get hungry. We want love. We want to feel good about ourselves. We want to think there is more than there is. We want to make the world a better place. We want to teach the world to sing in perfect harmony.

✳

Alfred, Lord Douglas had received a commission from the Belgian authorities at the beginning of the century to exploit the rubber and ivory that abounded on this section of the river – most nations turned a blind eye to the grotesque barbarity the indigenous population suffered at the hands of the colonial administration in those times.

Obviously when the world was shamed into terminating this exploitation Lord Alfred had had to develop other markets and commodities – his sodomistic buffoonery had cost him the Douglas inheritance for good. The tradition of boy farms, the production of well trained catamites for wealthy Arabs and the European aristocracy was as old as privilege itself. The procuring and training of exotic youths can claim a history as long and colourful as almost any other profession in mankind's rainbow pageant.

Bill hurried into his safari suit, wincing at some of the more painful lovebites. I was becoming majorly concerned about my friend's increasingly lax grip on any form of reality. His gleeful immersion into the furthest reaches of invert sexuality was frightening to behold, where would it all end? Would Gimpo and myself also find ourselves gradually drawn into this sickening world?

RIPPING OFF THE NIGGERS

'So tell me Richard, aside from your interest in our *Still Warm* project, why did you instruct us to meet you here at the Mozart Café in Merano.'

'Before I answer that question I want to read to you both a passage from a book that you may find interesting. *"In the beginning there was only one man and one woman and they lived not on the earth but beneath it. They were the first people in the world and neither knew the other was another sex. One day they both came to the well to drink. The man said: 'Let me drink.' The woman said: 'No, I'll drink first. I was here first.' The man tried to push the woman aside. She struck him. They fought. The man smote the woman so she dropped to the ground. Her clothing fell to one side. Her thighs were naked.*

The man saw the woman lying strange and naked before him. He saw that she had a taschunt. He felt that he had a thabuscht. He looked at the taschunt and asked: 'What is that for?' The woman said: 'That is good.' The man lay upon the woman. He lay with the woman eight days.

After nine months the woman bore four daughters. Again after nine months, she bore four sons. And again four sons. So at last the man and the woman had 50 daughters and 50 sons. The father and mother did not know what to do with so many children. So they sent them away.'"

Richard Brem put down the book he was reading to us from and looked up at Z and myself to measure our response. I don't know if either of us knew how to respond so instead I offered to refill his cup with coffee from the pot.

'So?' says Z.

'Have neither you read any of the works of Frobenius? Leo Frobenius?'

'Why should we have?' asked Z.

'I'm not surprised. From my research he seems to mean nothing in the English-speaking world. Frobenius was a German thinker, born in 1873, died in 1943. Some of his books have been translated into English but sadly I fear long out of print. You will find them in the British Museum. You are members?'

'Yes,' say Z and I in unison.

'Most of Frobenius's thinking was done on and about Africa. On what Africa means and what Africa has to offer the world and that is not what we in the West can rape from Africa, its oil, copper, diamonds and gold but what we can learn from the soul of Africa. Frobenius knew that if we didn't learn this and fast, the rest of mankind would be spiritually doomed.'

'So what was that mumbo jumbo you've just been reading to us? Was that supposed to save us from spiritual damnation?'

'That is the opening chapter from Frobenius's book, *African Genesis*. From what I understood, you two are about to set off to Africa, up the Congo, in search of Satan. All in some cause to redeem your souls. Very commendable. But as you seem to be basing your actions on the Genesis that you ended up learning at school, maybe you should be exposed to a Genesis that reaches much further back into the history of man's doings on this planet.

'Frobenius travelled extensively throughout Africa in the first few decades of the twentieth century. On his journeys he collected myths, stories, legends and truths. From this collection he wove his African Genesis. In one sense it is no different than your Genesis in that the biblical Genesis is made up of a collection of myths, stories and legends, knocking about the Middle East a mere 3000 years ago. But what he has uncovered goes far further back and deeper into the collective soul of mankind.'

'From what you're saying this Frobenius sounds like a Paul Simon going over to Africa ripping off their tunes, recording Gracelands, selling a shitload of albums, making millions and giving nothing back. Same old white man story: ripping off the niggers, then when they kick up a fuss,

telling them, "But you signed this bit of paper telling us we could."
Z seemed to have a point. An obvious point, but a point all the same.

Chapter Eleven
THE JUNGLE CHOOSES SIDES

We arrived back at the *Colonel Ebeya* with minutes to spare.

It was almost dark. A few crepuscular bats zigzagged around the sky scooping up insects caught in their invisible sonic nets. The vast reaches of the water reflected the purple twilight. The forest up-river seems denser, the scents drifting down-river to us more earthy, more primal if that were at all possible.

Gimpo is still strapped into the wooden stocks, his arse looks terrible, a torn cavernous hole encrusted in dried black blood and shite. Unctuous sperm slathers down the back of his trembling legs. In between the short breaks when the reluctant cack jockeys switch over, huge great horseflies crawled in and out of the exulterated dirtbox. The poor fucker is still putting a brave face on it all, his ludicrous British Tommy spirit refusing to splinter under the horrific and pointless punishment.

The queue of buggers look totally dejected; each and every one of them terrified that if they don't attain the regulation boner they will be forced to take Gimpo's place. Even the two Eel guards look as if they wish the whole thing were over.

Most of the families have left the dining room where Gimpo's ritual humiliation is taking place. It was amusing to begin with, but the ennui and stench have driven them into other corners. The only people still amused by the gory spectacle seem to be the Japanese film crew who enter into the canteen laughing nervously and taking stills of Gimpo's degradation. We hung around for a while trying to cheer him up. He thanked us and told us not to bother as he was going to try and get a little sleep. His military pluck is quite amazing.

I buy some beers and sit up on the roof.

THE PAIR OF THEM PISSED

Enter Z and Gimpo.

'Bill, fuckin' 'ell, Bill, we bought some corn hooch off one of the stalls straight out the jungle. Fire water. 'Fraid there's none left though.'

The pair of them are pissed.

'What you writing?'

Z grabs my book and starts to read in an affected, camp voice.

'"I resolve to write down what I really think and feel. Work out in words what it is to be me." You can be such a tosser, Bill. If you want to know what it is to be you, read my stuff about you. No one is ever what they think they are. You're what other people think you are. And Bill, you are a tosser, a big jessie. But that doesn't matter 'cause I like you. Do you like me, Bill?'

'Z, you are a cunt.'

'But do you like me?'

'I said you are a cunt.'

'I know I'm a cunt. A fuckin' drunken selfish cunt. But do you like me? I know you like me.'

Z crashes into his bunk and starts to snore immediately. The dark night of the soul begins.

Bill was taking a break from his quantum theories of everything and farting lavishly beneath the serene Congo moon.

'That Crowley guy, the bald-headed fucker,' said Bill casually, shifting his weight and flapping an echoing splanger across the roof, 'Do you think he was right?'

The ideas of the Ipissimus Magus had obviously appealed to him. 'About that shit he was saying about us not being tricked out of our souls, that all this sanguine debauchery is the act of free men, how the Devil prevents men from behaving truly to their natures by a conspiracy of pointless and spurious laws?'

This line of thought sits sniffing its piss-stained fingers in mental asylums all over the world. Bruised losers brooding in solitary confinement dribbling over Nietzsche, dreaming of swastikas. Students of the Ian Brady masturbation university. Scorned misanthropes whose only sin in the eyes of churches of their own invention was getting themselves apprehended.

I figured that I had to nip this scrofulous weed in the bud.

'When an individual acts in such a way as to prove he is above the laws of a society that decrees he must behave in a certain way, by his very act of rebellion he is acknowledging the law he is trying to invalidate,' I answered as casually as possible, lighting a cigarette. 'Our crimes, Bill, if you will forgive the presumption, were committed not for any deeply shallow philosophical reasons. They were and always have been sins of laziness programmed by an irritating biological axiom that compels us to behave in ways that juice up primal snatch and push dumb cthonic buttons in dopey cunts.'

I chugged on my beer and carried on, not really giving much thought to what I was saying.

'At some cunt-tingling primeval level, chicks dig all this murder violence shit.' I flicked my cigarette butt into the water. 'It makes them and their potential rugrats feel secure, being attached to some red-toothed grizzly bear psycho killer. The amount of love letters and marriage proposals those murderer fuckheads receive is unbelievable. That Sutcliffe Yorkshire Ripper chump for one, he gets sackfuls of fan mail from juiced-up murder groupies sending their grungy knickers over to his little Broadmoor salami-bopping room. It ain't just four-eyed weight-problem dildo jockettes either, a lot of these guys can turn on the snake oil supercharm mainstyle smooth, juicing up steelbitch lawyer cunts. It happens all the time, man, I'm telling you.'

Bill quacked out a thoughtful brass arpeggio that stabbed its way triumphantly into the perfumed night.

'Sure,' I continued, 'The majority of souls old Beelzebub collects are acquired surreptitiously, through small monthly payments.'

A bat landed on the side of the barge, its grubby movements like a furry maggot. I kicked it screeching off the side.

'He gives them their fancy salary, and then painlessly little by little sucks their scrawny souls dry. And for what? The illusion of security and a fancy little four-wheel bauble or two. That's the way it's always been, pilgrim. Mammon and her seductive sovereign raising vast phalanxes of suburban dollar slaves grubbing away in the guts of the moronic inferno. The industrial revolution and its Far East modern apotheosis, what a fine ascent into dissatisfaction and misery that's been. A great symbiotic confederacy of greed and hydra-headed stupidity, a fluctuating conundrum of masters and slaves. Yes my flatulent friend, the Devil has not been idle since the Fall, the powers of the air, no idle slackers they. Switch on any TV anywhere in the world and gaze through a coruscating window into Hell. Tune into the sly manipulation of his cursed citizens snowboarding Sisyphean mountains clutching their LED bags of imbeciles' gold...'

DRUMMOND'S LOG, THRUSDAY 13 JUNE 1996
THE NEW DEAN MARTIN
Morning in our bunks. I've slept in.

'Gimpo?'

'Yeah Z?'

'Don't let me drink any more of that jungle hootch. I've got a jackhammer in my head. I don't get hangovers. That stuff is lethal.'

'Whatever.'

'Bill?'

'What, Z?'

'Have I told you that I'm going to be the new Dean Martin?'

'How's that?'

'Well, I've got his louche charisma but I'm better looking and I've just discovered that my voice is more suited to his type of crooning than rock music.'

'Sounds a bit northern working man's club to me.'

'Nah Bill, I'll be the real deal. Dean Martin with a bit of a Mexican bandito vibe. "Li'le Old Wine Drinker Me". What do you reckon? You wanna produce it? It'll be massive. First album will be Rat Pack cover versions, then we can start writing the stuff ourselves. Easy, most of those songs are just two-chord shuffles, you'll be able to do it.'

'And tomorrow, Z, you will want to be a country and western singer again. It was only last month you were going on about being the new Johnny Cash and wanting to cover *I Walk the Line*.'

'Ah fuck you, Bill, I'm off up to the bar. Get me an eye opener and get them to play my Dean Martin tape.'

'Yeah Z, you do that.'

Z disappears clutching his tape. What's great about Z is that you just know that even when he's in his 70s, that's if his liver hasn't packed in decades before then, he will still think he's a contender. There will never be any of that 'I could have been...' stuff.

*

'Does he always talk like that?'

It was Bill's friend Tally, the Senegalese drag queen. Bill was obviously pleased to see his lithe new friend. I wandered back to the bar feeling dejected and ill at ease, talking to myself as usual. Maybe that bald fat idiot was right. Maybe the Devil didn't have possession of our souls. Maybe Mobutu wasn't the Devil, maybe the black elemental had moved on, the balance of supranatural evil shifted on to some other dictator or international tycoon. I ordered another Primus.

All the postulation in the world is completely useless in even attempting to nail the supernatural. The immeasurable plethora of wordy irrelevance contained within the canons of the world's religions mean nothing compared to a single direct experience. Some things are simply indescribable. Even the most sublime of mankind's achievements in holy and sacred art only describe the shadow of that experience.

Our wordy archaeology burrows and searches and finally grasps at even more dust. I could feel my sanity, what little remained, being sucked down by the almighty rainforest. It seemed the further we travelled into its sullen heart the more it insinuated itself into us. A green soporific lethargy that rendered verbal communication useless. Maybe that's why the jungle dialects were so succinct. No extraneous verbiage cluttered the wild souls of its most hidden residents, no conceptual baggage, mindswirling metaphor or ambidextrous riddles interfered with their febrile connection to the other side. Their dances, drums and shamen provided them with a direct link to their primal divinity. How unlike the cold meditation and pious liturgy of civilised whitey and our cruel mocking God and his evasive adversary.

'FOR FUCK'S SAKE WE ARE ZEN MASTERS'

Richard Brem had more to say about Frobenius.

'Up until Frobenius came along, all the white man had done was stomp around Africa with a gun in one hand and the Bible in the other telling the natives how the world began, how they had to behave and, by the way, Jesus was a white man. Frobenius listened to what Africa had to say before it was all stamped out, crushed by the might of western colonialism.'

'But nowadays we all know that every fucking tribe on earth has its own creation myth, great flood and good God-bad God story. There's thousands of them, all basically the same. Haven't you read *The Golden Bough* and if I'm not mistaken was it not published before your man Frobenius started his wanderings?'

I sensed that Z was getting a little irritated by my Austrian friend's supposed learning, so I offered to get a round in. By the time I returned to the table with a still mineral water for Richard, a pot of tea for myself and a triple vodka for Z, things had begun to improve.

'Bill, Richard seems to have a point with this Frobenius character. According to Frobenius it is only the child, the African and the genius that can escape conscious thought. According to Richard, we will understand what he is on about, what with us being geniuses.'

Richard had obviously been handling Z's ego in the required manner while I had been up at the bar. Z turned to Richard and said, 'Carry on reading this stuff, I need to hear more.'

'"*The demonic is not perceived by the intellect except through its effects. We observe this in adult human beings who are seized by religious ecstasy or the 'Demon' of artistic creation, and who are unable afterwards to describe their condition……the importance of such demonic moments is that they display a culture of paideuma in its creative aspect, with an elemental force that no adult can equal, be he the greatest artist or scholar in the world. Moreover the phenomenon as we see it in children is not merely an occasional one but a regular manifestation of the paideuma, whereas with an adult genius it occurs only by way of exception…*"'

I have to admit my mind began to wander, I found myself humming along to the piped music a shlaga version of 'Tie a Yellow Ribbon'. There was something about ideas being an end in themselves whereas facts are harnessed to material purposes and something else about the intellect creating a pitiful structure from these facts, which it presumptuously calls the 'natural world' and which it regards as the only ultimate reality, thus rejecting whatever stands outside the cause-and-effect nexus.

And this word 'paideuma' kept on coming up. I never quite understood what this thing was, if I had one or had ever seen one. I think it sort of meant the talent to instinctively read the spiritualising quality of an object or situation or sound without first having to rationalise or intellectualise it. As we grow older we allow ourselves to be convinced by rationality that a crocodile does not live under our bed and a bogeyman in the lane that runs up the back of our house. I tried to concentrate on what Richard was reading.

"... In the child's world, the demonic and the factual exist in particular relationship to each other. The facts and objects that are within the child's awareness are at once the raw material and the framework of its creative development. This, at all events, is true in the natural state; in the cultivated paideuma, on the other hand the demonic element is increasingly stifled by a plethora of intellectual objects introduced from without. Cultivation of this sort is in fact the enemy of the demonic and, by the same token, very often genius as well. In the natural world of infancy, the demonic power dominates impressions of the external world and uses them as the subject-matter of creation...The demonic, as opposed to intellectual apprehension, is the vital element in the paideuma, the expression of its first development, while ideas and facts represent ensuing stages, from this point of view, the paideuma signifies life and fulfilment and is the antithesis of knowledge. It can, of course, be transposed into logical and communicable terms, but its ultimate essence is private to the individual and cannot be imparted to anyone else..."'

'Look, Richard, I don't mean to be rude, but Bill and I already know all this. For fuck's sake, we are Zen masters – 'course we know it. It's kindergarten stuff at the Zen academy we went to. You don't mean to say you got us schlepping all the way up into this corner of the Alps to tell us that rationality is a dead end?'

Richard looked a little bewildered by Z's outburst.

'No, I brought you here to meet Ezra Pound...'

Chapter Twelve
FEASTING WITH PANTHERS

The journey so far has been nothing. The physical discomfort and disorientating otherness, the medieval justice and bizarre wildlife breathing in the ship's al fresco larders were so many tourist amusements compared to the spiritual terror throbbing now like black magic radio waves across the fetid air.

The spirits of the forest were closing in on us and there was nothing we could do about it. Their invisible presence almost tangible. Weird shit started jack-knifing into some of the women. They started wiggling out voodoo-style, screaming in tongues and bucking into epileptic jivedancing. You fucking name it, it was spiralling down at an alarming rate. The witch doctor guys were doing their best to keep some kind of equilibrium afloat, spitting out coloured water and rum on significant parts of the flotilla. A deep scared-shitless vibe descended upon the whole floating shanty town like a red shroud.

Whether it was coincidence or The Leopard used the fear vibe to his advantage I've no idea but that night the mysterious General invited us for supper. Gimpo had received a two-day pardon on his sentence and was to join us. He tried to put on a brave face but it was pretty obvious the poor bastard's jacksie was killing him.

A MORAL TALE

Later. After Gimpo and I have had our breakfast and divided up Z's share of the dough balls to be eaten later, we head up top to watch the world pass by. The ship's horn blows. Up-stream from us is a paddle steamer without the accompanying barges crammed with human cargo. The paddle steamer replies with its horn. Being towed behind it is a massive raft of timber, enormously wide and about quarter of a mile long. A steel rope encircles the raft and holds it all together. Some of the trunks are hundreds of feet long. So this is rainforest deforestation in process.

'Timber on its way to Ikea.'

'So we can have mahogany table tops.'

'Bill, are you going to try and turn this scene into some sort of moral tale about saving the rainforests?'

'I don't think I can.'

'Good.'

We just stand and stare at the floating island of logs until we are up around the next bend and we can't see it any more.

*

The Leopard's quarters were at the rear of the barge behind the first-class bar, it was strictly off-bounds except to the shiniest of the top brass. The two immaculate guards outside the mans quarters were as still as glass, inscrutable behind their mirror shades.

I would have sworn they were not breathing.

We entered The Leopard's sumptuous cabin, an oasis of gracious living among the squalor of the rest of the flotilla. The Leopard beckoned us to his table. Two generals from the Zaire high command are already seated, they stand as we sit. The Leopard behaves as if we are esteemed guests and Gimpo has not just nearly had his lungs buggered out. Gimpo sat himself down as flamboyantly as possible on to the hard leather chair in a way that must have been agonising for the game ex-squaddie. Bill and I had examined his ripped arse earlier in the day, it was badly infected and dripping septicaemia. If he didn't get antibiotics soon, it would almost definitely become gangrenous.

In the corner of the cabin a real leopard lounged with regal grace grooming itself lazily. I noticed the animal was not on a leash. Our host removed his sinister shades and peered at us with an amused smirk just this side of sadistic. His eyes are black and penetrating. He introduced us to his fellow soldiers: 'General Laughing Cheetah with the blood of his enemies still stinking on his breath' and 'Major Thrashing Alligator undefeated and dressed in gore' Far out names. Although they sound ludicrous to Western ears, in the original language and within the context of the Congolese culture these colourful names strike terror into the hearts of their enemies. The Leopard – whose full *nom de guerre* was 'The Leopard: stealthful and undefeated at deathpower, who shows no mercy ever, slayer and eater of warriors, their bitches and imbecile children, his badge is the skull and crossed eels, fear him well man as you fear death' – clicked his fingers and a young man in immaculate whites brought in several bottles of wine. The eater of warriors smiled broadly.

'An excellent vintage, perhaps even my fellow officers would agree?'

Both men smiled at the gentle tease.

'My comrades visit the flotilla very occasionally, a helicopter ferries them from their offices in our mighty President's palaces. Alas I sometimes believe The Alligator and The Cheetah have grown a little soft.' The men laugh quietly as the Leopard continues, 'Like our President they prefer the cool comforts of Europe and I believe if it weren't for this,' The Leopard places a large black leather briefcase on to the table and clicks it open. It is tightly packed with mint, high denomination Deutschmarks. 'I doubt they would ever return to the country of their birth. 'Personally I prefer a more hands-on style to government. I miss the jungle and especially the river when I am away, they are both too deeply a part of my blood for any protracted absence, which is why our President, great Caesar Mobutu has given me so much power over her people.'

A selection of food is brought to the table.

'Please, help yourself. I can assure you the food is delicious, I have my own chef who travels with me.'

I tried the roasted meats, not caring from which animal the tender cuts came from. The Leopard was correct, the food was second to none. Bill fell upon helping after helping. I noticed Gimpo was sticking to only the most easily digestible of the food, white meats and light vegetables.

'And the exact nature of your visit, gentlemen, is what?' queries The Leopard almost matter of factly.

We are quietly and collectively shitting it. The Leopard knows this and savours our fear like the cruel gourmet of distressed emotion that he is.

FLOPPY COLLARS

'Ezra fuckin' Pound is dead, you arsehole.'

Now, if you are as big on modernism as Z and myself you will know very well that Ezra Pound died on 1 November 1972. Even if he had faked his own death and went into hiding he would be 110 years old at the time of me writing this, so would have probably died in wherever his hideout was while waiting for Z and me to turn up and pay him homage.

You would also know that Ezra Pound, maybe more than Yeats and Eliot from a literary point of view, invented modernism. Of course Z is an Eliot man and I'm a Yeats man but we both recognise that although Ezra Pound was a lesser poet, if it hadn't been for him modernism would not have got kick-started, thus getting rid of all that late Victorian decadent rubbish. But while we are on the subject of decadence, it has to be said that Ezra Pound was always the most convincing dandy of all the modernists. His radical coiffure, his waxed moustache and neatly trimmed goatee were all splendid dandyesque traits and so were his spats, but there was one other affectation of his that forever more ensured he would out-dandy all of his modernist rivals. It was all in the collar. While the others clung to the mean, stiff and starched variety, he evolved his own generous, loose and floppy kind. There is not a single picture of Ezra in existence, from his late teens to his late 80s, where he is not wearing one of his generously loose and floppy collars.

Of course he went on to blow much of his literary credibility by attempting to lend poetic support to Mussolini and Hitler. As if either of those two barbarians would have known what the demented poetic genius and half-wit was on about.

Feeling rather ashamed of the way my fellow Zen Master had been conversing with Richard Brem I took a sip of tea and said, 'So we are off to meet Ezra Pound? Great, let's get going.'

*

Herb Alpert and his Tijuana Brass plays gently in the background, soft and threatening, the refined groove jarring with the profound dread that drapes the cabin like a perfumed fart. General Laughing Cheetah removes a white glove and places it on the perfect linen. His black eyes flick across us playfully like a torturer's whip.

'Forgive me gentlemen, I tease you. I know perfectly well the reason for your visit here, you wish to reclaim your mortal souls from the Devil who you assume to be our President.' The Leopard chuckles from his belly. 'Zaire may have internal problems like most countries in the developing world but our intelligence-gathering facilities are second to none. The spirits if rewarded in blood make excellent spies.'

Thrashing Alligator wrinkled his nose and beckoned a waiter who proceeded to spray the air with banana-scented air freshener. Bill shifted uncomfortably in his chair.

'The food does not agree with you, Mr Bill?' enquired the Leopard politely.

The larynx-scraping stench, like ammonia and cat shit fanning out from a particularly pungent Drummond SBD is impossible to ignore. The waiter behind Bill had fallen unconscious to the floor.

'No Mr Leopard, sir, this a perpetual state of affairs for me. The food was excellent,' answers the unconcerned Scotsman

'I see. How unfortunate for your friends.' The Leopard waves his hand and one of the boys opened a window

'For a man who knows his place in the scheme of things, the forest can be bountiful. I wish you luck in your quest and I feel confident that the President will indeed grant you an audience. I have a feeling that he is intrigued by your presence here, it was under the direct orders from the President's chief of staff that we cut short Mr Gimpo's punishment.'

The reflective General got to his feet and walked to the open window.

'You are not like the other white men that make their way here, foolishly searching for an easy fortune. This place, as you have found, is not for Europeans. See!'

He points at the rusted skeleton of yet another abandoned steamer, the green tendrils of the forest writhing among its empty guts jealously reclaiming every available inch of empty space. 'They were here a good few years, the Belgians. This stretch of the river was notorious for bloodshed. Many thousands died and as word of the carnage spread throughout the bush like ripples in a pool of blood it attracted the more bestial warriors – Mai Mai, cannibals, necromancers – all drawn by the singed smell of flayed humanity.'

COOKED BREAKFAST

'You hear that pig squealing?'

'Yeah, why?'

'It's been squealing non-stop since we left Mbandaka.'

'Yeah.'

'I think we should go and buy it and a couple of hens and take them to Trefor and demand bacon and eggs for breakfast.'

*

The Leopard peered out of the window and a gentle wave of melancholia landed upon the dinner guests.

'Mr Z,' he continued, 'You are psychic, yes? I do not have the gift myself but I can always tell those who are blessed and cursed with the shining. If the dead spirits disturb you too much, Msomba Msomba the engineer has roots and potions I am sure will ease the psychic tinnitus. This part of the river, it disturbs me greatly also.'

The Leopard wandered out on to the deck, a troubled frown resting above his sunglasses. I got the feeling that he was a just man, noble after his own savage fashion. With death so close, its ragged spectres hovering everywhere, he is neither softened nor corrupted by the niceties of Europe where every attempt possible is made to erase the reality of our finite corporeality. In The Leopard's reckoning the liberal culture of the West has transgressed its ideals of equality and egalitarianism and started to slide into a decadent trajectory.

To Western eyes The Leopard appears tyrannical and base. This view is shallow and unjustified – in extreme situations extreme men are called for. Their strength of character is needed to facilitate some sense of smooth order lest the bloody theories of Prussian philosopher Clausewitz are followed to their self-destructive conclusion. The wildness of places like this necessitates a rule of law imposed by force of arms but also by magic and a deep psychic understanding of the counter rhythms of tribal life. The Leopard possessed all of these qualities. Like all trained military men he understood the arbitrary nature of death and its black angels.

The two other officers ambled on to the deck with their wine: Bill, Gimpo and myself followed. It was a sultry night. The spirits had settled down, I could hear them humming contentedly up in the canopy. The Leopard, mellowed by the wine, was in an expansive mood.

'The forest is a dictatorial Queen,' he announced apropos of nothing. 'Our presence here is of little importance to her, merely more slabs of raw protein. If we threaten her in any way her cavalry of insects with their arsenal of viruses can make short work of our entire species within days. Look!'

The Leopard points at the remains of a tarmac road, overwhelmed and devastated by vegetation. 'Man is not dominant here. This is how it should be, some places must always remain wild, untamed. There is a greater intelligence at work here, greater than any of us can even begin to comprehend. It is connected to the stars, its green fuse runs deep beneath the mud and rock.'

He placed a pair of spectacles on his nose and gazed philosophically at the dense unknowable verdure.

Bill's arse honked like a peacock, its screeching call and attendant stink cutting through the serene atmosphere instantly.

ME, THE NEW BOB GELDOF?

'Hallo, Meesta Geempo. Hallo, Beel.'

'Hi, Crispin.'

Crispin is a lad about Pitsu's age. He is from the cabin two doors down from us. He always looks well turned out. Clean t-shirt, pressed trousers, moccasins not flip-flops.

'Beel. Have you had breakfast?'

'Yes.'

Silence.

'Beel, did you have supper last night?'

'Yes.'

Silence.

'Beel, you have breakfast yesterday morning?'

'Yes, Crispin, you were with us when we had it.'

Crispin has the best English of anyone we have met on board. He is on his way back from his high school in Kinshasa, where he boards, to his home in Kisangani.

'Beel, I have not had breakfast or supper or breakfast yesterday. I am very hungry. Can you give me something to eat?'

'But Crispin, we might be on the river for another two weeks before we get to Kisangani. If you have no money now to eat, what you are going to do until we get there?'

'You very kind, Beel, you understand.'

What I understand is that if Crispin is hungry, how hungry must the roof boys be?'

'Didn't you have any money or food when you started on the journey upriver?'

'I had a leetle, but it all gone now. Now I have to do leetle jobs to make money to eat. Have you leetle job for me to do? I can wash your clothes, tidy your bed, give you shave.'

'No Crispin, I can do all that myself.'

'But I hungry and you are kind man.'

Gimpo, by the way, is looking in the other direction and is having nothing to do with this conversation. The thing is, I've got a couple of my share of Z's dough balls down in the cabin but I was planning on eating them later. And anyway, if I give them to Crispin it will get around all the roof boys that we are, or at least I am, good for a handout and the next thing we know they will be swarming over me expecting similar treatment.

'Look, Crispin, I've one doughball in the cabin, I'll give you that. But you mustn't tell anyone.'

'Thank you, Beel. I knew you kind man.'

I gave him the doughball that I had already taken a small bite from. After he had gone I get out a couple of the oranges Gimpo and I had bought from a stall. Cut them in quarters and ate them like it was half-time. Does anybody still eat oranges at half-time? Do you know what I'm on about?

What you do know is that I've got $3,000 in my belt. Enough to feed every fucker on these barges all the way to Kisangani and back. It's like when you see the TV news reporter looking all well fed and healthy, filing his report from the current famine spot. Kids with distended bellies, flies crawling over eyes, sunken-cheeked mothers with nothing in their tits. Does he hand out all his ration while he is there to keep guilt at bay or does he think he is doing enough by just being there, filing his report for us to see in the comfort of our homes? I decide I don't have a satisfactory answer. Instead I eat the last remaining doughball that I had been stashing away for later.

Chapter Thirteen
STEEL, HONOUR AND SODOMY

I woke with my first erection since arriving in Africa. It died like a sick dog as soon as I remembered where we were. Still cruising the sick stretch of river. I could detect malingering black vibrations slicking their oily tendrils throughout the flotilla's company. I lay on my bunk for a while, relieved that my spudgun was still able to function normally.

The stench of the latrine next door to our cabin had just been disturbed by an early morning dumpster, its thick puce malevolence crept like a crippled gargoyle along the deck and shat into our faces. Back home British faggots refer to public conveniences as cottages – the shitters here made even the most squalid public crap shack back home resemble a stately home. I couldn't imagine even the most obscenely depraved George Michael fan getting funky with a friend in one of these diabolical holes.

On second thoughts, some of those far-out videos Gimpo used to find in Germany... Klaus and Willi crept towards the *Colonel Ebeya* latrine. They are thickly excited among the burping effluvia. The mephitic slurry spins their straining blutwursts into turbo overdrive, Klaus wallows in the dreck, Willi squeals with delight as Klaus levers his foot up his friend's fat German arse (*African shit lovers*, Choc video special no. 23 Vol 14). Outside I can hear the rains hammering down on to the metal roof. Gimpo was down on his bunk, groaning. The rains had flooded the cabin, washing faeces all over him. His arse had become badly infected, yellow and purple haemorrhoids had split and were leaking pus down the back of his legs. There was a doctor on board but by all accounts he was pretty useless, whacked out on drugs and permanently spazzed on bush whisky. Without antibiotics Gimpo was pretty much a goner. My greatest fear was that fungal parasites might start to grow on the leaking pus which in turn would attract the sliding arse eels. These were truly fucking horrible creatures over two foot-long with prehensile legs growing beneath their gills.

The slithering monstrosities hobbled on board in the middle of the night and, using their double rows of barbed teeth, latched on to the rectal fungus and concealed the main part of their bodies high up in the victim's gut. Short of major surgery it was all but impossible to get them out. Though not fatal in all cases of infestation their presence, as you can imagine, is unbelievably agonising. The chemicals in the creature's slimy skin somehow negates the efficiency of opioid painkillers, even clean hospital smack can't alleviate the jangling agony of the revolting arse eel.

THE CASTLE

'No, Bill, you misunderstand me. We are not going to meet Ezra Pound. Z is perfectly correct that he is long deceased. What I have arranged for us to do is meet Ezra Pound's mistress and daughter for morning coffee. They live in the castle.'

'A real castle with turrets and moats and drawbridges and...'

'Yes, but it hasn't got a moat,' answered Brem. 'It being an alpine castle and perched on a pinnacle it doesn't need a moat.'.

'Like a Disney castle?'

'Correct.'

'Let's go.'

Without further explanation we finished our drinks, left the Mozart Café and set off up the cobbled street outside the hotel. Richard was correct in his description. Far above us perched on an alpine outcrop we could see a castle. I later learnt it was called Brunnenburg Castle. The road narrowed as it left the town. We could see it zigzagging up the mountainside towards the castle. Z, fortified by his breakfast triple vodka and me by my two pots of tea, decided that it would make more sense if we dispensed with the zigzagging and went straight up the side of the mountain. Actually I'm exaggerating. It wasn't so much a side of mountain as tier after tier of vineyards. But anyway we took the direct route leaving Brem to the considerably longer zigzagging.

By the time Z and I arrived at the castle, our boots caked in mud, clothes covered with brambles, the drawbridge was down but the portcullis was not up. Richard was waiting for us, relaxed and unshevelled. He pulled on a rope. A bell rang from a turret then echoed back from the other side of the alpine valley. Chains clanked and the portcullis creaked into action. It took a full five minutes for it to grind to a point high enough for us to walk through into a small courtyard. We were met by a fine figure of a woman in her late middle age. Richard made the introductions. She was Maria Rudge, Ezra Pound's bastard daughter and keeper of the castle. We were ushered into a drawing room. From the leaded windows we could see the town of Merano far below. We arranged ourselves in brocade armchairs and an aged maidservant arrived with a tray. Coffee was poured and biscuits handed around and stilted conversation begun.

Very quickly it became apparent that there were some vast differences in the expectations of the outcome of our visit. The correspondence that Richard Brem had carried out between himself and Miss Rudge had been done on Curfew Press headed paper. Z and I being the named directors of the Curfew Press, she thought we were here to talk publishing deals regarding her dead father's estate. She was very eager to tell us how the current publishers of Ezra Pound's life's work seemed rather lazy at exploiting his vast output. Sales of his famous *Cantos* had been rather sluggish of late and the cost and upkeep of a castle was not a cheap thing.

Z and I were still saying very little, the odd 'thank you' as the maidservant refilled our coffee cups.

Richard tried to retrieve the situation by explaining that Z and I were not, in fact, the directors of some eager and hungry publishing house but two recently retired rock musicians and composers with a deep appreciation for the work of her father.

'You write popular music?'

'Well, yes, we have.'

'You have had hits, big hits?'

'Well, I suppose so.'

'Do you know Andrew Lloyd Webber?'

'No but...'

'You know musical *Cats*? It has earned the family of T S Eliot millions.'

'Well I suppose so but...'

'Yes $22 million while we struggle to pay our grocery bills. If Eliot were here today, he would not deny that if it was not for my father... and anyway there are plenty of professors in

American universities who would say the same. $22 million dollars is a vile amount of money for a stupid little poem about cats. Don't you think so?'

'Yes but…'

'When I was a little girl my Papa would write stories and poems for me about my pet tortoise. They have never been published, maybe you could? No, no what am I thinking? But you have to understand, the upkeep of a castle is a very expensive thing. Maybe Papa's *Cantos*, an opera, perhaps. Oh no, I forgot, you are pop composers. Maybe a rock opera based on his famous *Cantos*. That I think could be a big success.'

'Ah yes, the *Cantos*,' intercepts Richard. 'My two friends are very interested in the fact that Frobenius was a big influence on your father's thinking and that he actually mentions him in Canto 74 and even quotes some of Frobenius' African myths.'

'Ah yes, Frobenius. So you would like to write a rock opera based on Canto 74? I think that could be a very good idea.'

'No! No! My two friends are planning a journey up the Congo River. They are…'

'The Congo Africa? Why didn't you say earlier? My life's work has been the study of beetles from Africa. Let me show you my collection.'

From then on in all talk of rock operas, the shallowness of Eliot and the upkeep of castles was forgotten. Miss Maria Rudge proceeded to give us a guided tour of her specimen cabinets stuffed with beetles, each lovingly catalogued.

'The largest collection in all of Europe. If it wasn't for having to nurse my ageing mother, I would come with you. There are many specimens I have yet to find. With the help of a pair of young men like yourselves I could double the size of my collection. If you were only to wait until my mother died then we could all go together. What do you think? Yes?'

Z and I had been silent throughout all of this. I was hoping the maidservant would return so my cup could be refilled. What Z was thinking I had no idea.

'Well, Maria – such a pretty name, it suits you well – which one of these beetles is hallucinogenic?'

I was surprised to see that she seemed to respond to Z's obvious flattery.

'Aha. You are interested in the hallucinogenic ones. These are they. The ones I keep in this black chest.'

Look, dear reader, I have to admit I'm letting this dialogue get carried away with itself. And I know the publisher of this book will be very concerned about the litigious nature of the words I'm putting into Maria Rudge's mouth. Maybe she said none of the above, maybe my memory does not serve me well. What I do remember was after we had been in Miss Rudge's company for an hour or so a buzzer buzzed.

'Ah, my mother is buzzing me, I'd better see what she needs. It has been most charming to meet you all. I think your idea for a rock opera is splendid.'

We leave.

On the way back down the mountain, Z turns to me,

'Bill, a rock opera, I think she is right. We should write a rock opera. We could come back here after we have been to Africa. Live in her castle. Tell her we are basing it on her father's work and just do what the fuck we wanted. Wagner and stuff. We could even have her tortoise in it. We could call it *The Castle*.'

Between the two of us Bill and myself helped our crippled friend down to the useless doctor's surgery. It was at the very bottom of the barges hull near Msomba Msomba's clattering engine room. This was probably the most unhygenic area on the whole flotilla, a constant drip of god-knows-what from above decks collecting in burping pools around our feet.

It was early morning, the sun had been up only a few minutes and the doctor appeared to be still asleep, no light escaped from beneath the rat-chewed door. Bill hammered hard until we heard the barrage of hawking, spitting and wet farts stumbling towards the door. He pulled it abruptly inwards, a small fucker, about five foot nothing with a bald head and salt and pepper stubble. He wiped his gnarled hands on his bloodstained white coat which apart from a broken stethoscope around his neck was all he stood up in, the buttons were hanging off and it hung open revealing his big ugly bollocks. The guy stunk of jungle whisky and funky bunghole.

All around him were broken shelves full of out-of-date medicines, salves and lethal poisons dumped on the third world by immoral Western pharmaceutical companies. Most of the stuff stacked in teetering piles around the junkie doc's cabin had been outlawed in the West for years. Most of the shit he had would have killed rather than cured.

SMALL-TOWN GOTH

Later, in the bar with Z, sipping on a bottle of Coke.

'What do you reckon Bill?'

'About what?'

'My black silk handkerchief and the way that I have it tied to my ring.'

'For a start men shouldn't wear rings unless it's a wedding ring.'

'Says who?'

'Me.'

'And why?'

'It's just an affectation.'

'All an individual is, is the sum total of their affectations. Without affectations we just sleep, eat, shit, piss, breed and breathe. No better than dumb animals.'

'What the fuck are you talking about, Z?'

'Bill, you are all affectation. You are affectation to the max. Your life is one great pose. It's one of your better qualities. There is nothing about you that is real.'

'What?'

'I cannot think of a better compliment to tell someone than that nothing about them is real. It's God's greatest gift to mankind, the power to rise above reality. It is what marks us out from beasts of the field and the birds of the air. So, now that we have got that sorted, what do you think of my handkerchief tied to my ring?'

Z's ring is one of those crap silver rings worn by small-town Goths. He has one of the corners of his black silk square (fake silk probably) tied to the knuckle side of the ring and he is swirling his wrist about, which in turn wafts the hanky to and fro.

'What about all the snot germs you are wafting everywhere?'

'Bill, a dandy doesn't use his hanky to blow his nose. It is there only to add a splash of colour to his breast pocket when carnations are not available.'

'Yeah?'

'Anyway Bill, my guess is that if I'm seen wearing my handkerchief like this, every blade aboard ship will be copying the style by the time we get to Kisangani.'

'They don't wear rings. They haven't got hankies.'

'They will improvise. However impoverished a man is he can always find the means to express his affectations.'

'Yeah, OK, Z. Get us another Coke.'

*

The grizzly little quack reached for a bottle and took a deep swig. My nostrils twitched at the fresh smell of bush whisky, the doc recognised a fellow juicer and offered me the scorpion bible. He knew why we were there – there was no mistaking the double stench foulness emanating from Gimpo's wrecked sphinc, and the sight of the dangling cricket-ball piles made it even more obvious. The whole area around Gimpo's sphincter was infected with oversized pustules and running cracked sores. He laid Gimp on his belly on a dirty table and made a brief inspection of the ragged mess, prodding one of the larger ichorous boils with a piece of bamboo. The membrane broke and spurted a pale yellow fluid across the wall.

The doctor – Sourbones was his name, Jimi Sourbones – gave Gimps a bottle of whisky and insisted he drink at least half of it. Gimps refused at first but after Doctor Jimi fished out his rusty scalpels and black cack-stained saws Gimps saw sense and drained the whole bottle. Jimi worked quickly, attacking Gimpo's rotten flesh and grunging away around the man's ringpiece like a man possessed, hacking, sawing, digging, chopping off the septic tissue and throwing it into a plastic bucket beneath the table.

Gimps was unconscious, whether through pain, whisky or both it was hard to tell. Doctor Jimi had his shitter looking even worse than it did before, a miniature volcanic landscape bubbling septicaemia and bad blood, a pale yellow turd stuck its nose from the middle of the gory flower. Gimpo twitched and tried to sit up, Jimi indicated that he wasn't finished and lit his blowtorch. I pushed the doctor out of the way and raided his poisonous stash grabbing a box of antibiotics, some fenyl citrate, a bunch of diamorphine sulphate, pethidene and a big fuck-off bollocks sack of cocaine ampules. Doctor Z would have to take care of the Gimp, this fucker didn't have a clue, I pointed the blowtorch into his face and kicked him screaming into the engine room.

FRAUDULENT PURITAN CRAP

Z, Richard and I got a train. It climbed the Alps, it crossed borders and it stopped at stations. Its journey ended at Munich Central, 8.29pm on the dot. Z and I had no Deutschmarks. We were hungry. Richard Brem offered to get us a Big Mac and fries to go.

In 1976 the chippy at the bottom of Mount Pleasant in Liverpool closed. The place re-opened as a McDonald's. It was the first McDonald's I had seen. The British media was full of the fact that McDonald's had arrived on our shores, sweeping all before it. Who would want soggy and greasy pre-war fish and chips now? With that opening in Mount Pleasant and the media blitz I made a vow never, ever to eat a McDonald's or even enter one of their establishments.

I may have succumbed to every other form of American cultural imperialism that was thrown at my generation but it was time to make a stance. And I stood that stance for these past 20 years. I was solid. I did not budge to even sample one fry.

Z said, 'Great, Richard. I'll have cheeseburger. Thanks a lot.'

'Bill, you want the same?'

'Nah, Richard, I don't eat MacDonalds. Thanks anyway.'

'What fuckin' sanctimonious shit is this, Bill?' says my fellow Zen Master.

'I don't eat MacDonalds.'

'Give your fraudulent puritan crap a rest.'

I knew there was no point in trying to justify any of this to Z. There was also no point in telling him that I had spent the best part of those 20 years of abstinence believing that Big Mac and fries was probably the ultimate meal. The apex of man's culinary achievements. Maybe it was time to put a stop to my habit of missing out on the small pleasures that life has to offer. The rainforests can go and fuck themselves.

'OK, Richard. I'll have the same as Z. Thanks.'

Ten minutes later I'm wanting to throw up, seek forgiveness from that rainforest Indian that Sting brought over and do six months' community service working in the last chippy still frying in South Liverpool. That said, the fries were top and my addiction to MacDonalds fries started there and then.

*

I left the Gimp heavily sedated, dosed large style on penicillin and a close coma shot of fenyl citrate. Mr Pitsu, our neighbour, kindly offered to make up some kind of jungle poultice to fix the white man's fucked-up butt. I left Pitsu with his herbs and roots and wandered up on to the roof. A warm rain like mist passed gently across the barges. The evangelical church service echoed out across the river. We were sailing out of the sick mile, the queasy vibes were flattening out.

I noticed Bill stealing furtively towards the back of the boat, he had his shower stuff with him. I didn't take much notice of him, Bill's general demeanour is a furtive one. If he wasn't up to no good, he'd either done it or was about to. I decided to spy on him out of a lack of anything better to do. I lit a cigarette and stood in the shadow of the *Colonel Ebeya*'s huge funnel, the sun was behind me so Bill and his little shower buddies were unaware of my presence. One or two of the young boys were hauling up buckets of river water and rinsing each other down.

They seemed a little nervous as Bill slid out of his filthy safari suit. I could never understand how Bill managed to get so dirty, he washed his clothes every morning like everyone else but come midday he would be covered in dirt and grease, tea stains and diarrhoea, a perpetual brown sweat stain stretching from arse to shoulders spreading with the passing hours. The nervous boys packed up their mean toiletries eyeing the naked Bill warily. This caution wasn't peculiar to Africa. No matter where in the world Bill and myself found ourselves we usually had the same effect on everyone.

While Gimpo attracted strangers Bill and I seemed to have the opposite effect, strangers would affect a wary caution, avoiding our eyes, steering a wide berth when coming across us accidentally. It was as if we gave off some kind of weird invisible heat. I suppose it could be the clinging perma-fugg toxicity of Bill's skunk bassoon arse tunes and the toxic alcohol fumes constantly evaporating through my skin. Yet saying that, even when his stinkship wasn't around and I was spending a rare day on the wagon strangers behaved the same way.

Bill was using a harsh scrubbing brush to rid himself of the industrial claggies welded into his arse crack. He started soaping his ugly horse cock lasciviously and foaming up his ballbag. The young lads speedily packed up and made their way out of the shower area fast-forward nervous.

MEDIEVAL LOGIC

Later. The three of us standing by the handrail, staring down at what the pirogues are bringing in from the jungle to sell. I don't know if I've described yet how this whole pirogue thing works. The guys from the jungle paddle their dugouts into the oncoming path of the flotilla and as the flotilla is passing, they paddle like mad until they judge they are close enough to the side of one of the barges. Then, with a vine rope attached to the dugout and tied around their waist, they make a leap, grabbing hold of the railings. I've now seen a few whose leap has failed to connect and they are left in the slipstream desperately trying to clamber back into their dugout with their unsold produce. Scores of the passengers line the railings to watch as these jungle men attempt their leap to civilisation. A cheer always goes up for those that successfully make a particularly dangerous, or last-minute, leap. A bigger cheer goes up for those that miss and are left with nothing but a sad wet paddle home with their unsold and perishable wares.

Up until Mbandaka, what they were bringing out of the jungle was not much to write home about, let alone to write here: bananas, oranges, the much-mentioned catfish and scrawny chickens and cockerels. Now it looks like somebody has been turning up the weird knob. The fruits are getting stranger, the fish, well there are these massive carp-looking things but with shark's teeth. And another fish – I'm talking six feet here – that looks a bit like a cross between a barble and a sturgeon. It's got a barble head and a sturgeon body. Mind you, if you haven't got an interest in fish like I have, you might not know what the fuck I'm talking about.

'Don't fuckin' bore the readers with all your fish talk,' Z tells me as I try to tell him what a barble is like.

'They might be interested.'

'No they fuckin' won't. They want to know how big and scary-looking they are. They want to know if they are poisonous or if a shoal of them can eat a swimmer to the bone in less than 30 seconds. We are not writing a nature-study book. Anyway, have you seen the smoked monkeys down there? All trussed up, they look like Inca mummies, all the skin pulled tight across their skulls, teeth grimacing as if they died in agony being smoked alive on an open fire. In fact, they look like they could be smoked babies.'

'Shall we buy one to eat?'

'Shall we fuck! Eating a monkey is one step from being a cannibal. Look, that geezer down there has got a live monkey for sale. I wouldn't mind getting that. I always wanted a pet monkey.'

'And how would we fly home with a monkey?'

'We take it as a gift for Mobutu.'

'Yeah, I'm sure he would really welcome that. He would just think we were taking the piss.'

'OK then, we set it free when we get to the airport.'

'You seen those turtles in the dugout? They look as big as teenage mutant ninja turtles.'

'How big's that, Z?'

'About three feet.'

'They're alive.'

'Look, that one's trying to escape!'

'Go for it, son!'

'Nah it won't make it, he's got a rope that goes through a hole in the back of his shell.'

'Why are you so quiet Gimpo?'

'I'm watching that crocodile in the bottom of that dugout.'

'Where?'

'There.'

'Fuckin' hell, a real, live crocodile in a dugout! This is what you want from Africa. Natives, monkeys, crocodiles. All we need now are girls in grass skirts and a witch doctor.'

'Just so the readers don't think we are talking twelve-foot crocodiles, it's only about four-foot long.'

'Yeah but still it's a real one, still alive, not stuffed or anything.'

'That guy's got a couple in his dugout. He's picking one of them up. Look at it thrashing its tail about. I bet its teeth are really sharp – you'd think it'd have a go, even though it's small.'

'Nah, look, you can see its mouth's tied up.'

'What the fuck's he gonna do, look he's got a knife out. Fuckin' great, you see that Bill? He's just slit its belly open and emptied its gut into the river and the croc is still thrashing about. Fresh meat, eh?'

'Shall we buy a live crocodile? I bet it don't cost that much. What do you reckon Z, we could keep it under the bed in the cabin. Make that childhood fear real. Lying in bed at night with a live crocodile underneath you. I mean that's it, it's Satan, Lucifer, the fuckin' serpent face-to-face. Come on, Z, you could write it into your story that the crocodile told us that he was Lucifer himself in one of his oldest guises.'

'No fuckin' way are we having a live crocodile in our cabin. It's OK for you, you're in the top bunk.'

'OK I'll do a deal. You get to have a live monkey if I get to have a crocodile. It would be great for the story. It's what the reader would want. I mean fuck-all else is happening other than Gimpo losing his ticket. I mean he could have lost his ticket on the Northern Line. You don't get to buy many live crocodiles on the Northern Line. Crocodiles that turn out to be Satan incarnate. We can sit in our cabin and negotiate with him to get our souls back.'

'How the fuck are you going to negotiate with a dumb beast Bill?'

'We use medieval logic, Z.'

'So what the fuck's that?'

'You know, we ask him a question.'

'Like what?'

'Like "Can we have our souls back?"'

'And he doesn't answer 'cause he can't.'

'So we cut off one of his toes or the end of his tail. That will soon make him start talking.'

'You're being fucking serious Bill, aren't you?'

'Yeah.'

'It's a poor dumb animal.'

'We keep going until it speaks, agrees to hand back our souls or it dies. Either way we win. Medieval logic, like when they used to try witches. Always works.'

'You're a fuckin' nutter, Bill.'

'Look, I know it seems extreme but when dealing with Satan you've got to be prepared to push the ante.'

'Bill, you're just wanting to be cruel to a poor defenceless animal.'

'Z, how come you're the one that's always going on about how misunderstood bull fighting is in Britain.'

'That's not the same at all. Bull fighting is a highly ritualised drama, symbolising life and death. It contains beauty, elegance, poetry. Bill, bull fighting is poetry.'

'What I'm proposing we do is even better poetry.'

'Bill, I know what I'm talking about. I'm a poet, one of the best. No, *the* best living poet in the world. What you are proposing is no more poetry than what those two lads from Bootle did to little Jamie Bulger.'

'Got you.'

'What do you mean?'

'Out-grossed you.'

'I'm not trying to out-gross anybody.'

'Yes you are, that's what you are always trying to do in your writing. You're always trying to get the reader to think, "Oh my God I can't believe that has been written and I've just read it."'

'Shut up Bill. Let's head back to the cabin. It's late and I'm fucked.'

Disappointed that the youngsters had fucked off so quickly Bill continued to soap himself all over. His eyes were stinging when a scared-looking Tally appeared behind him.

Tally wasn't alone. The one-eyed Arab Rolo held a thin stiletto at the effeminate kid's throat. It flashed sinister in the morning sunlight. I hid behind the funnel. I sensed Bill was not in danger – if the Arab wished to kill him there was no need for Tally to witness the slaying. I got the feeling that it was Tally's luck that was about to run out. The Arab whispered into the tall drag queen's ear who in a thin nervous voice called to the soap-blind Bill. He affectionately held Tally's head in his hands and leant forward to kiss him on the lips.

Whatever happened next was done with such speed it was hard not to admire the assassin's skill. In a silent blur Rolo had severed the kid's head from his shoulders, Bill was left holding his lover's head in both hands, the body fell backwards across the deck spouting a clean fountain of arterial blood. Bill, sensing a sudden increase in weight of his lover's head, reached to wipe his eyes with both hands. The black man's head fell to the deck adding another tributary of gushing scarlet to the river of blood swirling around Bill's feet.

The killer bent himself into a strange martial pose some yards away from frantic Bill who was rubbing his eyes with clean water. The Arab held out one arm straight in front of him, the other he held above his head like a swordfencer. His whole body coiled like a spring, a sardonic grin playing around the corners of his full lips while his good eye flashed a bright malice. Blood from his victim stained his bellbottoms the same scarlet as his silk neckerchief.

Bill had cleaned the soap from his eyes and carefully covered his dead lover's severed head with his towel. Showing an icy composure Bill spoke softly yet his tone was steely, 'There was no need to kill the boy.'

'Of course not,' replied the Arab mockingly.

'Why then, this slaying was not part of your mystic narcissism,' Bill again, like Kirk Douglas.

'Absolutely not, Scottish, your death is reserved for my graduation into the hallowed inner sanctum of my order. This little slag was just for fun.'

Bill could feel hot anger rising inside him, he checked it.

'The boy was innocent,' he said coolly.

Bill wanted to kill the arrogant bastard, rip out his spleen with his bare teeth, mash his lungs to puree, remove both of his eyes and stuff them down his throat, flay him and make a pair of pyjamas. His murderous reverie was silenced as a high-pitched whine and a slash of pain seared the left-hand side of his face. Rolo's lightning blade had sliced off the lobe of Bill's left ear, warm blood trickled down his neck. He hadn't even seen Rolo move. His earlier decision to accept a noble death, Yukio Mishima-style, evaporated like steam from dogshit.

Bill sprung at the teenage Arab who effortlessly sidestepped the 43-year-old's graceless lunge. Bill skidded clumsily on the gore-spattered deck and landed flat on his white arse. The Arab's mocking laughter burned in his ears. He felt another sharp pain across his chest as the agile Arab cheetah whipped past him like perfumed lightening. A thin scarlet line opened across Bill's chest, the invisible blade had cut deep into his nipple creating a ragged curtain of blood which poured down across his belly. Bill knew the Arab had him at a disadvantage; he rose slowly with all the dignity he could muster.

The Arab danced behind him like a greased ferret and slashed a stinging cut across both buttocks then, laughing hysterically, he slid beneath Bill's legs, slitting his ballbag. The pain was excruciating. Bill's eyes saw flashing silver lights as he flickered in and out of consciousness, more blood splashed to the deck.

The wounds looked more serious than they were. Before he vanished into the equatorial ether, Rolo slashed a small heart on to Bill's left buttock with a flick of his wrist as a memorial to the dead loveboy.

THE KING OF COOL

We start heading back to the cabin.

'Seen that big basket of maggots that woman's selling?'

'Where?'

'There. They're at least two-inches long. Thousands of them alive and wriggling in her basket.'

'Let's have a look.'

'She's got a stove, she's frying them live.'

'People are buying them as snacks.'

'It's fucking disgusting.'

'No wonder Africa is in the state it is if they are prepared to eat bugs.'

'Probably very high in protein.'

'So are earthworms. We don't go around eating worms.'

'Look, Bill, she's holding a live one up for us to look at.'

'It's got eyes.'

'What the fuck are you doing Bill. That's fucking disgusting. Stop it now. You win, you fucking win. I don't believe you actually did that. What did it taste like?'

'You see, Z, when it gets right down to it I'm the one that can eat the live two-inch long maggot, and I'm the one who can tell the world what it feels like to have it still wriggling as it goes down my throat.'

'Nobody's going to be impressed by that, they'll just think you are an arsehole.'

'What and wearing that hanky tied to your ring is, like, totally cool?'

'Yeah.'

'Will the pair of you fuckin' shut up?'

And so to bed.

*

Bill stood silent, his rage all the more intense for its lack of expression. The fact that Rolo had underestimated him stung the proud Scot's martial honour worst of all.

The stench of willed revenge, a cloud of red death rolled on to the river, its miasmic intensity calling down winged spirits from the black clouds billowing across the sky. Beyond language, communicating blood to blood, spirit to dark spirit, the communication of Bill's seething essence to unknowable shadows outside of space and time had sought and received a sympathetic vibration from some forgotten sinister pantheon.

The sky flashed fire between the worlds and cracked apart. Under the grey cover of the torrential rains Bill removed his dead lover's heart and slid the lifeless body into the black water. He kissed the blind eyes of the severed head and whispered into the deaf ears before floating it into the river.

I got the feeling that we had not only crossed the equator but also some other invisible line into something far beyond our ragged humanity. Something irreversible and incredibly dangerous. Something beyond divine and diabolical. The jungle had claimed us.

ETHEL'S DEAD

On the Munich–Paris overnight train. Z and I found our cabin. It was a six-berther. Richard Brem had caught another train heading east, back to Vienna. Our fellow overnight travelling companions were a couple of Africans in flowing robes and a fat Australian. The Australian looked familiar. Dumped our bags and headed down the carriages looking for somewhere to sit. We found a couple of seats in an almost empty carriage. I had a bottle of red wine that I'd bought in Spain. I pulled the belt from my jeans to use the buckle spike to push the cork in. A wave of nostalgia hit as I recalled the pleasures I shared with a past acquaintance and my belt. Anyway the buckle spike method didn't work so I had to use my forefinger to push the cork in. We passed the bottle and conversation drifted. I tried to steer it back to Satan.

'Z, it is our duty to redefine Satan for the twenty-first century. Man needs Satan. Not as some historical Satan but a living, breathing, out there and in here Satan. One that looks like now…'

'Give it a rest, Bill. Look, as far as I'm concerned I don't think I'll ever tire of the Byronesque Satan. He'll do fine for me.'

'But Z that's all safe and cosy nineteenth-century romantic shit.'

'So?'

The conversation drifted. 'Were you ever into Alice Cooper, Bill?'

'Nah. I was too old. By the time 'School's Out' came out I was already out of school. I just got it on an art school-ironic level. The rite's a killer though. In the all-time top ten of rites.'

Z started to sing Alice Cooper songs:

> *'I love the dead*
> *before they're cold*
> *their bluing flesh*

> *for me to hold*
> *while friends and lovers*
> *mourn your silly grave*
> *I have other uses for you darling.'*

Z was now up on his feet, imaginary shovel in hand and pretending to dig. 'Did you ever hear 'Ethel's Dead', Bill?' Without pausing for a reply he is off:

> *We met last night*
> *making love by the refrigerator light.*
> *She's coool in bed*
> *She ought to be*
> *'cause Ethel's dead.*

'Alice Cooper was everything to me when I was a kid. The snake, the make-up, the record sleeves, the voice. I tried to love him when he got rid of the make-up but it just wasn't the same. Just some weasely little American guy. You got to realise what it felt like for me when he covered one of my songs, to hear him singing the words to 'Feed my Frankenstein' that I had written. I had copied all my vocal mannerisms from him and then I was listening to him copying me copying him. Weird.'

'But, Z, I've been thinking, if Satan...'

'Fuck Satan, Bill. Can't you give it a rest? I've been telling you about one of the greatest moments of my life and all you can think about is your fuckin' little pet quest. Satan doesn't fuckin' exist. It's just a fuckin' story.'

'Yeah, I know Z, you're right. I've been thinking that evil doesn't exist.'

'Don't talk shit, of course evil exists. There would be no starry nights if evil didn't exist.'

'OK, so evil exists, then so must Satan.'

'Fuck off, Bill, and pass the bottle. You've been hogging it. Anyway I've just worked it out – that fat Australian bloke who's sharing our cabin, it's Robert Hughes.'

'Robert Hughes?'

'You know *Shock of the New, The Culture of Complaint*. The best book ever written about the modern world. Now, if there is one man who would know if evil existed it is Robert Hughes.'

'Well, let's go and ask him.'

DRUMMOND'S SECRET LOG, THE OTHER SIDE

If the Devil has my soul then when he stole inside me and claimed it he left something of himself behind.

Rolo had murdered one of the Angels of this Earth. His claim to spiritual superiority was now void. In killing Kiki he had obeyed some form of lovers' justice. Kiki, love him as I still do, had betrayed Rolo. Tally was an innocent.

I am slow, the Arab's mocking cuts proved that. But Rolo's frail spirituality is flawed, utilising his mystic powers to afford him a show of strength has proved to me that the equilibrium of his soul is unbalanced by vanity. How that disfiguring scar upon his once-beautiful face must pain him. When I have finished with him there will be no face left for his vain tears to mourn. This upon my unholy Bad Wisdom I swear.

The time for obeying civilised constructs such as honour is over. I will steel my body and call down the residues of the beast, harness the undisciplined powers of the air, genuflect before death's unbiased angels and forge my vengeance in his cold purity.

Z'S BIG IDEA
In our bunks, at least a dozen blasters cranked up to distort level competing with each other.

'Z, I've got an idea.'

'Yeah.'

'Let's get up in the middle of the night when they are all fuckin' asleep and confiscate all the blasters, throw them all overboard. That'll fuckin' teach 'em.'

'Teach them what, Bill?'

'Well...'

'No, what we need to do is get them organised. We say to them, "Now look here chaps, you lot can play your blasters between 8.00 and 10.00, then you lot here can play yours between 10.00 and 12.00. Get a rota going. They need somebody to organise them. I reckon we could be running this place by the time we get to Kisangani. The thing is, they are only used to brute force being used to control them, when that's not being meted out they behave like children. I think we could use charm and in no time at all we would have control of the boat. And from there we could take Kisangani and from Kisangani we could take the country. They are ripe for what we have to offer. What do you reckon, Bill? This could be our main chance. Of course we would have to get ruthless as well. It's what they understand, what they respect.'

'Go to sleep, Z, you're pissed.'

'But we could.'

Chapter Fourteen
SODOMISTIC JUSTICE, BUMMED BY FRIENDS

Gimpo's recovery was quick, the brief interlude afforded by his absence allowed for a little introspection and rest. For myself at least. Bill was still hard at work, cursing under his breath, working feverishly into the night on his secret calculations, scribbling page after page of weird Scottish hieroglyphics.

I would often be woken from my disturbed sleep in the final hours of the night just before dawn to be confronted by the wild-eyed Drummond performing some ritual, his body daubed in intricate drawings, sacrificing a small fish over a makeshift altar. Our African cabin mate, Queequeg had long since quit his berth feeling far safer sleeping out on the deck.

The walls of our cabin were daubed in excrement with endless mathematical calculations and the Scottish hieroglyphs.

Gimpo had left his bunk after a couple of days of drugged recovery. He appeared to be his old self, masturbating constantly and laughing and joking with his African friends. His bumhole had healed quite well. Mr Pitsu claimed that it was his poultice that had fixed Gimps arse and insisted that Gimpo bought some jungle whisky for a party with his friends and family. Pitsu's sister, Mami, was the prettiest girl on the whole flotilla, sweet 16 and as fresh and delicate as a jungle flower. Shyness is a quality that the people of the Congo don't understand but there was a trace of natural coyness about Mami that emboldened Gimpo's courtship.

There was a slovenly grace about the girl as her slim hips rolled her down the small area of deck outside our cabin. Gimpo had obviously been working on her since we left Kinshasha but so subtle were his overtures that for all this time neither Bill nor myself had noticed the sly Priapus. Until then anyway. Gimpo's wistful gaze would track after her as she floated gracefully to the shitter, she would smile at him for a second or two then look away coyly. She had started wearing Gimpo's Panama hat and told everyone that Mr Gimpo had bought her the lovely fashion hat from Paris.

It soon became obvious that Gimpo was surfing the dangerous waves of infatuation.

DRUMMOND'S LOG, FRIDAY 14 JUNE 1996
JUST LIKE ARNIE
The middle of the night. We are woken up.
'Tické, tické.'
'What's going on, Gimpo?'
'It's that young ticket inspector with some other lad.'
'What do they want?'
'He wants to see my ticket.'
'Tell him to fuck off.'
'He's got a truncheon and handcuffs.'
'He's just trying it on.'
'Tické, tické. Dollars. Dollars.'

'He might be trying it on but he's serious.'

'Yep, Gimpo, shakedown time.'

Mavuba is up, he's trying to indicate to Gimpo that he should hand over some dollars. Gimpo is all pleading smiles at the same time as saying to us, 'there is no fucking way I'm paying over anything'.

'This is it, pay-back time for centuries of white-man exploitation of their continent.'

'Bill, this is no time to start on the post-colonial guilt thing. Gimpo, just pay him a couple of dollars so we can all get back to sleep.'

'No fucking way. They're going to have to take me kicking and screaming.'

Mavuba tries to negotiate. Things settle down. They leave. But like Arnie, they will be back. Sleep.

*

Gimpo bought a crate of jungle whisky and the party rolled on well into the night, most of the people on deck joined in the revelry, Gimpo as usual appeared to be the life and soul, twisting his bollocks into knots and breaking beer bottles with his bell end. I crashed early, I'd seen it all before and the whisky was potent. I woke the next day with the dawn and noticed that it was strangely quiet, I assumed that most people were sleeping off last night's party.

Bill splashed into the cabin with a bag of the inedible doughnuts and a big mug of oversweetened tea.

'Fucking idiot,' he mumbled to himself.

I guessed he was talking about the Gimp. He was. Satyr Gimps was back in the stocks, an angry Mr Pitsu banging away on his dirtbox. He jagged off a vitriolic wad and punched the Falklands vet hard on the back of his head.

A small queue of unenthusiastic buggers glumly waited their turn to bugger the Gimp. It appeared that Gimpo had interpreted Mami's friendliness for something more carnal. She was quietly sobbing in a corner of the room with two black eyes and swollen split lips. It would seem that Zairese families take the honour of their sisters equally as seriously as any rabid Italian or Muslim.

Gimps was being subjected to more practical Zairese justice. Four hours of solid buggery. This round of punishment bumming was relatively mild compared to his previous ordeal, but the angry pummelling of Mr Pitsu and his cousins who were all secretly in love with the girl themselves had opened up the freshly healed wounds causing serious secondary damage to unfortunate Gimpo's fucked arse.

Weirdly, as soon as the men had finished venting the sodomistic justice they appeared to forget the whole thing and were once more making jokes and laughing with their seriously wounded friend. Gimpo however wasn't quite so happy to let the ordeal lie. He limped into the cabin and eased himself face down on to his bunk, His arse looked frightening, both buttocks were a livid purple flecked with patches of yellow and a deep bloody red. His actual ring piece looked torn beyond repair: thick congealed black blood and milky pale yellow diarrhoea bubbled around the black hole where large horse flies had gathered to eat at the reopened wounds.

Neither Bill nor I could bring ourselves to go anywhere near the disgusting carnage. Mr Pitsu, despite the fact that he was partly responsible for the bloody mess, entered the cabin with his bucket of poultice materials and began cleaning away the horse flies and their tiny tubular eggs. He threaded a bent fishing hook and started expertly stitching the ragged bumhole, stopping occasionally when Gimpo's screams indicated that the pain was unbearable. Bill bought a bottle of jungle whisky and fed it to Gimp until he passed out.

Mr Pitsu finished the last of his intricate needlework and snapped the cotton with his teeth and then started applying the evil-smelling poultice, some kind of mud-coloured porridge made out of leaves and roots and stuff.

I hadn't mentioned anything to Bill but I was becoming increasingly worried for Gimpo's personal safety. Even when it's not the kinetic bubbling of his engorged libido getting him into trouble there was always something stirring the shit. Gimpo has a volatile disposition, whether it is prudent or otherwise the short-circuit chump cannot help but say what is on his mind. This quality is usually quite appealing, his frankness and honesty usually sheds a fresh light on many different subjects from oblique angles not usually considered – the view from a sub, so to speak. But up here in the wildest outposts of humanity, speaking a language that he has only just learnt, his habits were proving to be more than a liability.

Bill was all for a mercy killing there and then but I wouldn't hear of it, someone had to wash our safari suits. Anyway I didn't think it would be necessary. If it hadn't been for Pitsu's poultices, Gimps would have been gangrenous and dead by now. It could only be a matter of time.

I shot him up with a coma dose of fenyl citrate and gave myself a little dig in the back of my hand and left grungebutt to glide around in his floaty little world for a few hours. As soon as the synthesmack wore off I'd be able to hear him no matter where I was on the boat.

I'LL FUCKIN' SHOW YOU EVIL

No, it wasn't Robert Hughes. Just a fat Australian who got pretty angry after Z and I had awoken him with our demands that he was the one who could settle our debate about whether evil existed or not.

'I'll fucking show you evil,' was the only thing he said that could shed any light on the matter. As it turned out he declined to show us any evil and things settled down. I awoke at some point in the night with the melody to 'Trans Europe Express' by Kraftwerk going round and round in my head. I used to enjoy working up a theory about how it was 'Autobahn' by the same band which was not only one of the ultimate pop moments of all time but was also the conceptual bridge between Stockhausen to early 1980s synth-pop.

Seeing as Julian Cope has now well and truly explored this in his *Kraut Rock Sampler* book there is no need for me to stoke that particular theory. Just enjoy the tune. Trans Europe Express, Trans Europe Express, Trans Europe Express, Trans Europe Express, Trans Europe Express, Trans Europe Express, Trans Europe Express, Trans Europe Express.

*

The pirogues from the villages seemed to be reproducing. There were hundreds tied alongside the flotilla, their numbers increasing by the hour like a giant peacock's tail fanning out behind the *Colonel Ebeya*. The occupants of the latest addition to the tail of dug-out canoes had to make their way precariously, jumping from one unstable rocking canoe to the next. Many of even the most agile villagers fell into the black waters losing nearly a whole month's supply of produce to the unforgiving river, trussed hogs and mammals I couldn't identify squealing as they drowned or were eaten by catfish or crocs.

The stalls on deck seemed to have multiplied too, the stallholders with their stacks of goods along with the boarding villagers made it almost impossible to move on the jammed solid barges. Fortunately the past few days I had been spending quite some time down in the engine room with Msomba Msomba and the gnarly old pilot had shown me some hidden routes below decks along the whole length of the ramshackle flotilla.

I made my way to the stinking latrine next to our cabin. The hell hole had been just about abandoned now, even the hardiest native dumpster would be reluctant to enter into the knee-high piles of rolling crap. I placed a plank of wood from the door across the burping soup to a small ledge at the back of the closet. Small crablike things snapped at my toes as I crossed the creaking plank.

There was a loose panel in the rear wall which could be removed quite easily. I held Gimpo's mini Maglight between my teeth and slipped behind the panel. Something attached itself to my leg, I flashed the torch quickly over the mystery parasite. I'd never seen anything like it. It looked like some kind of transparent deep-sea fish, eyeless with all manner of complex whiplash antennae surrounding its razor-sharp teeth. The monster barked like a bronchial mastiff in the bright spear of torchlight, I kicked it off my leg and it disappeared angrily beneath the shit.

Behind the panel was an iron trapdoor which I quickly negotiated, then scurried down a rusty iron ladder. Msomba Msomba who spent many hours as a boy watching the *Colonel Ebeya* and her attendant barges being constructed in the old Stanleyville shipyards was probably the only person on board who was aware of these secret passageways. They were originally intended to be used by maintenance engineers but fell into disrepair and were soon forgotten about.

A few stowaways – young boys judging from the size of their remains – must have found these tight crawlspaces and somehow lost their way and perished there. Although the passageways were extremely claustrophobic and very dangerous they were easily the quickest route along the flotilla to the *Colonel Ebeya* bar.

I made my way out of the passageways through a hole in the wall outside the bar and replaced the removable panel before anyone saw me.

AT BREAKFAST

At breakfast. The three of us.

Even Z is eating his dough balls and sipping the tea. Gimpo has a theory.

'I reckon Mavuba is in on it. He knows, they all know, that we must be carrying a substantial stash of dollars. There is no way three European white men could be travelling through Africa without dollars. I don't trust Mavuba, he'll have been through our bags a dozen times looking for the stash. And now 'cause he can't find it, him and the young ticket inspector and whoever that other lad with the truncheon and handcuffs is, have decided to put the squeeze on.'

'So what the fuck do we do?'

'Nothing. There is nothing we can do.'

'So let's not talk about it anymore.'

'You know Mami next door, Pitsu's sister?'

'Yeah.'

'She's not his sister, she's his wife.'

'But they only look 15.'

'He says they're 19.'

'That's blown your chance of negotiating with Pitsu to have a go on his sister.'

'Fuck off, Z.'

'I think she's pretty.'

*

I ordered up my Primus and took the dark sweating bottle up on to the small deck area at the rear of the bar. It was up on the third deck and had a good view of the swarming gesticulating traders and the ever-swindled villagers.

I felt the need for some form of quiet so I went up on to the roof by the giant funnels. I say quiet but what I really mean is the steel pulse of the engine that rumbled up through the funnel and effectively cut out all the rest of the clattering racket, the monotonous throbbing frequency negating all the other sounds of the barges. Across the black mirror of the elemental river the omniscient forest as dense as a head of broccoli seemed to spy on the chugging barges, the sentient tree spirits silent and inscrutable charted our slow progress.

Common among the infinite variety of pagan religions scattered among the jungle was the belief held by most Africans that all things possessed an individual spirit as real as the souls of men. Each rock pool, each tree, insect and bird was in itself a shard of divinity. Prayers and supplications were made to these things when a man took from them or took them in their entirety to use for himself. For instance if a man needed a tree to fashion himself a pirogue or a house he first had to ask the spirit in the tree if it was OK to cut it down and give the spirit a new form. If the tree did not object this was taken as a yes, that the tree spirit did not object to becoming a pirogue or house spirit.

Rock pools were afforded pardons before the women washed their clothes in them. Monkeys, antelopes, even the kokola grubs, were given short blessings before being designated to the pot. It was this animist reverence and pagan piety that resulted in Gimpo's third and almost fatal punishment bumming.

SEEK SALVATION AND SUCK ON THIS

Trans Europe Express, Trans Europe Express, Trans Europe Express, Trans Europe Express.

Bang, bang, bang on the door and a wake-up call in some language that wasn't ours. Checked the watch. Ten past seven. Five minutes later Z and I, shivering and hungry, were out on a still dark Paris street.

Z loves Paris. It's too cosmopolitan for my tastes. Z had a notion that it was probably lucky Lucifer's favourite city for a bit of rest and recreation. Z's kind of town.

It seemed that Z had lived in Paris at some point in his sordid past. He led the way. We checked into the sleaziest hotel he could find in the Pigalle, then headed up the empty streets of Montmartre. Z had a spring in his heel. Taking the steps three at a time. His old man's coat flapping as ever.

'Come on, Bill, we have to get there before the tourists do. Early morning Mass is the best kind. Many is the time after a long night I've dived into a chapel for a spot of early morning Mass. It clears the head, neatly deals with whatever transgressions you have been up to the night before and sets you up for the day ahead.'

I couldn't be bothered to tell him that I didn't do Mass. I just couldn't face all his sarky put-downs and cynical asides. Anyway, maybe French communion wine is of a superior class to the shite served up in the Scottish kirk.

By the time we got through the doors of Sacre Coeur, the incense had been swung, the little bells rung and the cup of wine put away. I was safe.

We had become accustomed to the gaudy Spanish cathedrals – this lot seemed almost Protestant in their restraint. No statues of Christ with gaping wounds dripping blood. The Presbyterian in me is relieved at the lack of raging Catholic paganism; another part of me wants this raging Catholic paganism turned up louder each time to confirm my sectarian prejudices. I told Z I needed to sit down. He wanted to get down to the crypt. Five minutes later I was lost in prayer – for what reason or to whom I had no idea.

Five minutes later, praying done and Z back from the dead, we were hauling ourselves up the stone spiral stairs. We wanted to get to the top of the dome. I was feeling more like a tourist than one of the highly influential founding fathers of the literary arsehole movement. I wonder if Henry Miller ever climbed these steps in his Paris days.

At the top Paris stretched out into a distant mist. Dawn almost done. You've probably been up there yourself so you know what I mean. Z took it upon himself, as he often does, to quote some verse:

'Shivering dawn in a rose-and-green dress
slowly advanced over the deserted Seine,
and dark Paris rubbing his eyes
took hold of his tools, a hard working old man.'

I hate the idea of Paris but it did look great from up there. The tiled rooftops of Montmartre then all those boulevards reaching for infinity.

We circumnavigated the exterior of the dome checking for potential suicide stations. A couple of possibilities but nothing great. If your mind is turning to 'What's the point of it all?' thoughts, don't bother putting yourself out by coming over here. I'd stick to Beachy Head or Clifton Suspension Bridge in Bristol if I were you.

We had just completed our circuit and were about to enter the spiral stairwell when we heard the familiar sound of 'Heee, Heee, Heee' followed by the scuttle of feet, followed by more 'Heee, Heee, Heee'. It was the ubiquitous bevy of Japanese teenage girls. They seemed to get everywhere in the world. Japanese girls, never Japanese boys. What keeps the lads at home in the land of the rising sun when the girls want to cover the world with their giggles and pattering feet?

There turned out to be four of them. Z instantly suggested we each grab ourselves a brace each, rape them, then throw them over the side. The moment passed. We left the pretty things to their safety and sightseeing as we descended the spiralling stone steps.

But Z's mind was off evolving some plot about converting the four slit-eyed fancies from their evil heathen ways, and Z was on to one of his favourite themes.

'What do you expect from a fat slob sitting under a bong tree. I mean, what the fuck is a bong tree anyway? Our Saviour was good looking and had the good sense to die young with a great body. They would love Jesus if they only knew. Every woman around the world loves a young man with a fit body willing to give his life for her personally. So genuflect little ugly Japanese girl. Seek salvation and suck on this.'

I laughed, you have to. Mind you, you might not. You might be thinking, 'What a pair of sad fucks. Shouldn't somebody have edited that bit out before I read it?'

Chapter Fifteen
THE GREEK

A radio was playing loudly and distorted somewhere: 'Scarred old slaver, he's doing all right, Hear him whip the women just around midnight.' Mick Jagger low in the mix slurs the words to 'Brown Sugar' across Keith Richards' clumsy inimitable chord patterns. The New Orleans voodoo 'n' debauchery vibe felt entirely appropriate as I sauntered into another shitty malarial bar somewhere near the end of humanity.

It was empty apart from the flies and crumpled old white guy dressed in clothes that seemed to camouflage him right into the dirty stains splattered across the mud walls. His skin was light brown and leathery, deep greasy crevasses in his face gave him the appearance of an oiled walnut. He was wearing a sweat-marked Panama hat pulled low over his cracked sunglasses. His white shirt was crumpled and jungle stained, the threadbare khaki pants a couple of sizes too big ended raggily above old leather sandals. He was preternaturally still, one gnarled and scarred hand clutching a glass of clear spirit, the other resting on an ebony walking stick.

A sick-looking girl with damaged yellow eyes entered sluttishly through beaded curtains behind the bar, which clattered in the still air disturbing the flies. She reached lazily to switch on the wall that set off an overhead fan, a fat lizard dropped from the fan on to the dirt floor and skittered through a hole in the wall. Pulling three beers from the cooler, she looked quizzically towards us. I nodded and she popped the tops.

Over several more the old man told us that he used to run this bar as a brothel years ago for the Belgians. He was originally from Greece. Somehow all the wars, coups and counter-coups had passed him by. He had a few wives up-river in Kisangani but he liked to come down here to his old bar to take some sport with the younger ones, there was a fresh crop of pubescent girls every year or so.

He invited us to his favourite skank hole a little further down the street. There was no rush, he told us, and ordered more beers, obviously enjoying the novelty of white company that was neither missionary nor mercenary.

'There's a couple of white guys further down river in Mbdanka on the equator,' he said, obviously referring to Bosie and his Satanist boyfriend Crowley, in his croaky leather voice, hawking up dusty black phlegm and spitting it down the front of his filthy shirt. 'But there's something weird about them, apart from the fact that they're colon miners of course,' he said in his good but heavily accented English.

He told us he had been born in a small village on one of the Greek islands but the Congo had always felt like home to him.

'They run a chicken ranch, training up the young orphans for rich buggers,' he told us neutrally. 'I suppose those kids have got to make a living somehow, I tried a couple myself. A man gets to my age, there isn't much difference, when you flip them on their bellies.'

He chuckled throatily and coughed up more of the black tobacco snot, his nostrils were heavily caked with snuff. He removed his dark glasses, his eyes were remarkably piercing and alive, a watery blue like a desert nomad.

'You boys looking for black gash?' he asked casually, ordering up more beers and a round of Ouzo each.

Gimpo winced and shifted his weight on the wooden chair.

'Something wrong with your sphinc, boy?' he asked. 'You haven't been on the receiving end of that Black Eel justice have you?' He laughed, realising that Gimpo had indeed been sodomised to within an inch of his life.

The wizened Greek called out to the yellow-eyed girl in an odd jungle dialect and she quickly disappeared through the bead curtains, returning a few moments later with a black jar of something or other. Our friend unscrewed the lid revealing something that looked like molasses and smelled like eucalyptus.

'Drop them pants, son, this stuff will fix your shitter in next to no time.'

Gimps, who had been limping seriously since Mami's family had chopped up his buggery socket, didn't argue and dropped his pants and bent over the table. It was pretty bad. His entire sphincter had scabbed over, small wriggling parasites dropped out of his underpants and squirmed around our feet. A foul-smelling yellow pus was leaking and dribbling down the back of his thighs.

'Shit, you must have pissed those guys off pretty bad.'

He took a glooping handful of the black stuff and threw it on to the affected area.

'You'll excuse me if I don't rub it in,' he cackled.

The stuff, whatever it was, seemed to have an immediate effect, the repulsive grubs writhed to the surface and started dropping into his underpants.

'Can't take you down to Mama Sammi's with your arse full of cancheri bugs, can we now?' he said laughing kindly.

Hundreds of the disgusting maggots surfaced, breaking up the scabs and falling on to the floor. The smell, like dirty bandages and dog shit, rolled off his ruined butt in waves. For a second I thought I was going to pass out. The Greek threw on another dollop which seemed to lessen the terrible stench replacing it with the odour of oversweetened coffee.

'A couple of days,' he said, 'You'll be like a virgin again.' He laughed loudly and coughed up another ball of black phlegm spitting it out and managing to clear his shirt this time.

He drained the last of his Ouzo and stood up creakily.

'Mama Sammi's,' he said, 'It's not far.'

I finished my beer and followed him out of the dirty bar. The sun was directly overhead, it felt like a razor, cutting through the rain clouds and burning my skin like a new tattoo.

EVERYBODY LOVES ZAIRE

Later. Alone in the cabin in my berth. I'm getting to really fuckin' hate all of this. I hate leaving the cabin. As soon as I go out there, there are all these kids going 'Meesta Beel, give me dollar. Meesta Beel, give me pen. Meesta Beel, buy me Coca Cola'. It seems they have all learnt my name and enough words in English to chant 'Meesta Beel, give me dollar'. For the first couple of days they seemed to be in awe of us, were kinda scared to come near us, now they swarm us as soon as we go out of the cabin. Maybe Z has the right idea spending his days up in the first-class bar in the *Colonel Ebaya*. They don't dare go up there. Mind you Gimpo loves it, he's a veritable Pied Piper. And he's learning loads of Lingala. How the fuck does he do it?

'Good morning, Beel.'

'Good morning, Crispin.'

'How are you this morning, Beel?'

'Fine, just fine. What do you want?'

'Just to talk, look at your map, learn some English words. Tell me, Beel, why are you, Z and Meesta Geempo in Zaire? What have you come for?'

'That's complicated, Crispin, and even if I was able to tell you, I don't think you would believe me.'

'I think I would believe you, Beel. You are very serious man, you not lie.'

'No Crispin, I've lied a lot, especially to women.'

'Yes Beel, all men lie to women. Even I know that at age 16. But why you here?'

'Well, among other things, we are here to meet your great president.'

'Mobutu?'

'Yes.'

'But if you want to meet Mobutu, why you on this boat?'

'Because first we want to meet the people and then when we get to Kisangani we are going to hire a car and drive to his palace at Gbadolite.'

'But Kisangani nowhere near Gbadolite, it takes two weeks to drive from Kisangani to Gbadolite.'

'Two weeks?'

'I show you where Gbadolite is on your map on the wall. Look, here, right at the top of Zaire near the border with Central African Republic.'

'So how comes it takes two weeks to drive there from Kisangani?'

'The roads very bad. Just tracks through jungle and bush. You can't drive car on those roads you have to pay to go on back of truck. Truck like bus but through the jungle and bush.'

'But on the map it shows them as proper roads.'

'None of these roads like roads in Kinshasa. All roads out here very bad. No tarmacadam or asphalt, just mud. Bad roads and lots of bad men. Very dangerous for you. Why you not fly from Kinshasa to Gbadolite? Important European and American men always fly from Kinshasa Airport to Gbadolite to visit our president.'

'How do you know this?'

'My father general in army. He knows this thing.'

And I am thinking if Crispin's dad is a general in the army, how come he's travelling back from boarding school in Kinshasa third class with no money for food? Then I think it's better not to ask.

'Do you think your father could help us to meet Mobutu?'

'Sadly my father dead. He no longer friend of Mobutu. He get killed.'

'I'm sorry.'

'So am I, but our president he is a great man. Our country is greatest country in all of Africa. We are the richest country in all Africa. We have diamonds, copper, gold and uranium for making nuclear bombs. Everybody love Zaire. Great president, very powerful. When you meet, say I love him.'

'Crispin?'

'Yes, Beel?'

'Have you eaten today?'

'Yes I now have some money. Yesterday I do some leetle jobs and get leetle money for food. Thank you for asking Beel.'

We followed the Greek down the dusty road, I noticed a scrawny mongrel with xylophone Dachau ribs wrestling with a grotesque blood-caked vulture over the remains of a disembowelled spider monkey. The vulture loped into the sky with a beakful of intestinal tract; the bumpy, tick-ridden skeleton mutt scurried into one of the corrugated iron huts with his ragged lunch.

Mami's was a low-roofed skeezhole that seemed to suck the immediate light from out of the air around it. It was off the main dusty drag and had a crumbling walled courtyard tucked tightly into the gothic vegetation. The jealous jungle again, its crawling creepers and sprouting grasses crawled across the palm-thatched roof, surreptitiously claiming back everything it came in contact with. A few sulky girls sat fanning themselves sleepily, their sarongs pulled up over their thighs revealing their messy purple and pink cunts. Gimpo seemed to have forgotten his ripped shitter, a throbbing boner tented up his safari suit.

The girls were all in their early teens. There was something delectably gorgeous about their ruined youth. Firm teenage breasts stuck out impudently in delicious contrast to the sordid ennui that lurked in their stoned yellow gaze. Gimpo immediately commandeered the prettiest and shot a grey flob of sour jizz across her face. She barely noticed, wiping it off casually with the back of her hand and transferring it to her stained sarong.

All the girls were wearing chokers made from industrial diamonds and a couple had paste tiaras on their heads. Heavy black eyeliner emphasised the sick yellow tinge of the whites of their eyes. They were all stoned on some catatonic jungle drug that made them walk as if they were underwater.

We sat at a table, the Greek carried on talking nonchalantly as one of the girls unfastened his pants and started licking his balls under the table.

'Please, my friends, take yourself a wife. I have an account here so help yourself to as many as you wish.'

After his false start Gimpo started examining the girls' cunts closely, searching out ones with the most elastic piss flaps. The Manc masturbator was an ardent lover of cunnilingus, there was nothing he liked better than drowning in fanny snot with his entire forearm jammed up a woman's dirtbox grabbing himself some erotic kidney squeezing.

PROFESSORS?

Afternoon. Up in the bar with Gimpo and Z, sipping my third bottle of Coke.

'Bill, have you written anything about Punch and Judy yet?'

'I was going to write about all that after I'd written up all the European stuff. Why?'

'Maybe we should get them out, do a performance for the kids up on top.'

'Z, I don't think that would be a good idea.'

'Why not? I think they would love it. And anyway, we need to practice before we do our show for Mobutu.'

'Last thing I want to be doing is drawing more attention to ourselves. It's bad enough as it is already with what happened last night. I think we should just keep our heads down and do our time on the boat.'

'No Bill, you're wrong. If we do something like the Punch and Judy Show, they will be impressed. We will gain more of their respect than we already have. They wouldn't dare touch us. What do you think Gimpo?'

'I don't know what the fuck the pair of you are talking about. All this stuff about Punch and Judy is news to me.'

'Didn't Bill tell you?'

'Nah.'

'What do you think Bill's carrying in his kit bag? What do you think Bill and I were up to these past few weeks before we came out here?'

'How the fuck should I know. I resigned as your manager over a year ago. Since then I've only seen you the once to get our jabs.'

'Sacked. You were sacked.'

'Yeah, whatever, but I know fuck all about Punch and Judy.'

'Tell him Bill. It'll sound better coming from you.'

'Gimpo, Z and I discovered...'

'*I* discovered.'

'OK, *Z* discovered that in the traditional telling of the Punch and Judy story, Mr Punch not only despatches Judy, the policeman, the judge and the hangman but in the end outwits Satan himself and despatches him too. He is the only character of note in the canon of Western literature who has got the better of the devil.'

'So what's that got to do with us here and now?'

'Fuck it Bill, I'll tell him. So I came to the conclusion that not only should we take Mister Punch with us as our mascot, as we are going to outwit Lucifer, but that we should train to be Punch and Judy men. We are now professors.'

'Professors?'

'Yeah, professors. It's what you call fully trained Punch and Judy men and that's what we are.'

'Says who?'

'We got certificates to prove it.'

'And you got a set of Punch and Judy puppets with you?'

'Yeah, and I made them.'

'Hang on a minute, Z, we made them together.'

'Bill, I designed, you hacked out the rough shape in wood from my designs, then I carved all their features and painted them. They are probably the finest set of Punch and Judy puppets in the land.'

'They are probably the only set of Punch and Judy puppets in this land.'

'What do you reckon, Gimpo?'

'I dunno. And you plan to perform a Punch and Judy Show for Mobutu.'

'Yeah.'

'I think he'll think you're taking the piss.'

'I think he will be entertained, flattered.'

'I've read in the *Lonely Planet* that he not only has his private Concord, and his private runway, he has his private cinema where he has all the latest Hollywood action thrillers flown in for him to watch. Get real the pair of you. Even with your letter of introduction from Penguin Books you are still just a pair of two-bit chancers. There is no way he is going to be entertained or flattered.'

'Maybe Gimpo has a point.'

'Fuck off, Bill. You thought this was a brilliant idea when *we* were making the puppets and learning how to do them.'

'Yeah, but it was different then. We are here now. It is totally patronising of us to think that these Africans and especially their president are so uneducated that they will be entertained by a bunch of crude puppets and an over-simplistic storyline.'

'Everybody in England still loves Punch and Judy. Remember Mister Punch never dies.'

'Z, the tradition only carries on because it has a nostalgic hold over us.'

'Well if you think that, you should have said so two weeks ago.'

'I didn't think it then.'

'Well OK, I'll do the show myself. It will be better me doing it myself anyway.'

'Look Z, I'm still up for...'

'Forget it and anyway, it's your round. And by the way, you smell of shit again.'

*

I noticed a couple of hideous 60-year-old whores in the darkest corner, big fat fuckers wearing blonde wigs and torn red-satin lingerie, stupid basques, shabby stockings and broken suspender belts fixed with old bits of frayed nylon rope. The sort of tawdry unimaginative get up that look ridiculous even on foxy French women. On old black hags it was the stuff of nightmare. I grabbed the ugliest one and got her to suck on my ballbag.

She was wearing thick glittery eye shadow and a single clogged-up false eyelash. Both her front teeth were missing, the rest were yellow and rotten, her carrion breath smelled of shit. Her platinum wig had slipped to one side revealing a close-cropped patchy grey fuzz. Mama flopped her empty tubular titbag over the torn basque, the ruined dug reached her fat belly. I had a notion that because she was so spectacularly ugly maybe she possessed some mind-blowing sexual expertise to justify her working alongside such foxy teenage cock jockeys. I'd obviously been listening to Gimpo's bell-end logic for far too long. The old bag sucked my deflating knob like a dying carp. I pulled out from her dogbreath mouth and pushed her to the floor grabbing myself a lithe young jungle bunny at the same time.

Mama Syphilis straightened her lop-sided spunk-stained wig, folded up her tit and wandered back over to the other bow-legged old crone, where she lit up a cigarette and continued chewing the fat with her equally monstrous sister.

Gimpo was back on form again, banging away on one little cutie, stopping mid stroke and moving on to another, his shit-covered dick spearing into one after the other in an orgiastic flurry of frenzied copulation. It looked like he was venting some kind of magical revenge for the massive reaming he'd been subjected to. Then again he could just be indulging himself in his usual form of overkill rampaging. I noticed he hadn't started on his usual scat tornado though, his jacksie must have still been a little sensitive.

I was happily buggering the lungs out of a pretty teenager, my enthusiasm had revived her from the bottom of her opiated torpor and her back was dislocating with orgasm after orgasm. I really hate it when they do that so I threw her to one side and swapped her for another. Bill was also getting in to the swing of things, he'd found himself a hammer and chisel from somewhere and was whaling away at his lithe Cleopatra, hacking back her ribcage and helping himself to the juicy fruits of her splayed torso. His butchery was much more refined after the impromptu lesson we had received from Katie back in Kinshasha, he managed to keep his African queen alive a lot longer than usual.

I must say, I was more than impressed with the way the rest of the girls didn't make a fuss over Bill's idiosyncratic method of pleasuring a woman. Gimp unfortunately had spied Bill's enthusiasm and had thrown caution to the wind and started muck-spreading wildly.

Sloppy yellow turds flew all over the supine whores, it was only when he noticed he was shitting scabs and greasy blood clots that he hauled in his scatalogical horrors.

Again the girls sat calmly taking the worst that our friend could fling at them, occasionally wiping the larger stools from their eyes and stifling a yawn. I think Gimpo found their louche stoicism a trifle annoying, I've noticed Gimps only kicks his steamhammer into first when the piercing screams of sexual horror start to reverberate around the orgy room.

CAFE AU LAIT AND CROISSANTS

On leaving Sacre Coeur, we found a street café. Winter sunshine, café au lait and croissants. We watched the camcorder-dripping tourists heading up the cobbled streets, glad we had missed the full-on force of the world sightseers by the time we had finished our morning prayers.

We discussed literary techniques. Now that we knew our first joint book was to be published by a proper publishing company we felt secure in having such debates. Z had the day mapped out. As I said before, Paris was his city. First he wanted us to head up to the cimetière Montmartre so he could show me Oscar's grave, then down to the Gustave Moreau museum. Fine by me. I decided to knock any notion of Satan on the head for the day and just go with the flow.

*

In comparison our Greek host's tastes were more conventional, he was masturbating lazily as the girls lashed into him fiercely with their bullwhips. He'd stripped to the waist, bloody ribbons of skin hung over his waistband. His torso revealed a vivid scarified landscape, cross-hatched evidence of previous hardcore whippings. Both his nipples seemed to have been slashed off in the past, two livid white scars marked where they had once been.

The Greek noticed Bill's increasing abandonment, he'd opened up a third girl and was trying to crawl up inside of her. He called out to Bill asking if he'd ever witnessed any of the local religious ceremonies. Bill crawled out of the girl's stomach, seeming to lose interest in his sexy surgery. He wiped the gore from his ears and pulled pieces of tattered viscera from his hair.

'There are some interesting evangelical services on the *Colonel Ebeya*, they remind me a lot of the charismatic churches that were popular in Ireland during the 1970s.'

He stopped to spit out some sour-tasting pieces of spleen. 'I'm a Presbyterian myself,' he added, placing his still-erect cock back in his pants. 'I find all forms of Christianity apart from Presbyterianism completely blasphemous.' He unwound a long piece of intestine from around his neck. 'My father was quite strict about that.'

The Greek was laughing hard, his cigarette-wracked lungs threatening to chuck themselves out at any moment.

'Those French missionaries,' he spat, indicating with a wave of his hand for the girl to lay off with the whip. 'They think they have the jungle tamed with their watery religion.'

He lit himself a fat cigar. His obedient dominatrix got down on the floor and started sucking on his fat pizzle.

'You've seen those dumb little books those assholes hand out?'

He was referring to the frighteningly patronising Christian propaganda we'd seen littered all over the boat and in the villages. Idealised white bearded Jehovahs sitting on golden thrones surrounded by the smiling niggers of creation with their friendly animals straight out of Walt Disney. Along with these cynical images of the perfect life, the other side of the coin was depicted – evil cannibals praying to wooden effigies. Some genius had painted a red circle with a bar through it just to ram home the point that the gods and spirits the tribespeople had been worshipping for centuries were bad and wrong.

The Greek's wrinkled features flattened out as he bucked up some crusty snot down the junkie whore's throat. She gagged and sneezed the old guy's baby gravy down her nose. The Greek patted her on the head in a fatherly fashion and carried on with his genial observations.

'Fucking missionaries,' he raised a cheek and chuffed out a blurter. 'Imagine believing that you could ever tame the wild soul of this place!' He gestured at the encroaching majesty of the breathing, living forest. 'The truth is, the tribespeople feel a little sorry for the deluded paleskins and their effeminate deity. They're no different from any sensible non-proselytising liberal, confident within their own faith and believing all other religions to be an interesting variation of their own.

'These people, they are not stupid. They play up to the missionaries and their one-dimensional view of them as innocent children, naïve pagans and all the rest of the patronising Christian horseshit. If nothing else the dry-nad Christians are an amusing distraction from the monotony of jungle life. They like the little cadeaux as well, and the churches make great orgy rooms for the chief and his concubines when pious whitey heads off further into the bush to save more souls.'

The Greek's nose twitched. Bill looked behind himself: another wet one, damn.

'The forest people's all-encompassing spiritual life merely appropriates the Christian deities and places them with the rest of their eclectic divinities. For them, the existence of only one supreme God is completely ridiculous. They enjoy the crucifixes and the little statues of the virgin and her groaning army of chopped-up saints and are smart enough to hide all the more genital idols well out of sight when the blustering missionaries come trundling into their villages.

'Earlier in the century their grandparents used to just eat missionaries, the white man's fat flesh being a welcome change from the sinewy meat of fallen warriors and the tough old meat of expired tribal elders. Eventually it proved to be too much of a hassle and besides, the missionaries were much more generous with their gifts of clothes and free food if they thought they were having some success with the lost souls of the heathen. It's also pretty well understood all over the continent that dead white men are much more trouble than they're worth, all the red tape and legalities. The African method of dealing with capital crimes is much simpler.'

WE STINK

I got another round in. We sit quietly making our notes. Above us the fan turns slowly. The Japanese film crew sort through boxes of gear getting ready to do another shoot somewhere on the flotilla. Gimpo looks enviously on at them.

'Bill, Z, I've got something I need to talk to you about.'

'Yeah, what?'

'People have been telling Remi to ask me why we smell of shit.'

'That's Bill, not me.'

'No, it's all of us. They think we all smell of shit and do not keep ourselves clean.'

'What? These Africans think we do not keep ourselves clean? We're white, they are black! We are the clean ones.'

'Z, that's not how it is. They spend a lot of time washing themselves, washing their children, washing their clothes.'

'That's 'cause they want to wash their blackness off.'

'No that's 'cause they are very aware of the dangers of not keeping yourself clean. Aware of the dangers of disease that are around all the time, ready to strike you down dead.'

'So why are they worried about us?'

'Remi said they all take it as a personal responsibility to keep as clean as possible so as not to pass on disease to others around them. They never see you washing and they think you smell of shit, rotten food and stale alcohol. All bad things.'

'Well, fuck 'em.'

'No Z we can't fuck 'em. And there is another thing that Remi has been asked to tell us about.'

'What?'

'The shitter.'

'What about the shitter.'

'We are not using it properly.'

'Not using it properly? It's a fucking hole in the ground, what else are you supposed to do other than shit in it? There is no way something like that shitter we have to use would be allowed in England. It must break all our health and safety regulations and they are complaining about us!'

'It seems so and I think they have a point.'

'Which is?'

'You know that pile of dust that gets deposited outside each of the shitters each day?'

'Yeah.'

'Well, it's lime and any time we have had a crap or even a piss we are supposed to pick up at least a couple of handfuls of lime with our left hand and sprinkle it around the floor of the shitter.'

'Why?'

'It kills off the germs.'

'They think that the shitter we have been using is now unusable for them and maybe beginning to breed and spread diseases.'

'Maybe they have a point, Z.'

'Bill, it's fuckin' the stench of you that's set their alarm bells going. You stink.'

'You stink as well.'

'But not of shit.'

'Yeah but of stale piss, BO, dog breath, all those old unwashed alky smells.'

'For fuck's sake the pair of yous. As far as they're concerned we all stink and they are asking us politely to improve our toilet habits. I have already apologised on our behalf and promised that we would do something about it.'

'Have you ever noticed that when Gimpo thinks he has got something important to tell us he gets all articulate and stops talking like a gimp?'

*

An old woman makes her way into the courtyard, cigarette dangling from her bottom lip, carrying a mop and bucket. She places a hand on her aching back and raises an eyebrow as she clocks Bill and Gimpo's squalid aftermath. Gimpo is groaning in the corner, his arse is falling out again. The Greek notices and tells the old woman to fix it.

'Remarkably efficient and a lot fairer in my opinion,' he continues, 'If a local man is apprehended for murder he is automatically sentenced to five days imprisonment. A ludicrously short amount of time for such a serious crime you might think and you'd be right. The five days is to give the victim's family time to decide the fate of the prisoner. Usually, unless the prisoner is wealthy which as you can imagine rarely occurs, the family and friends cook up some imaginative form of capital punishment.

'Some of the elaborate methods of despatching the unfortunate murderer are amazingly ingenious and can take in such bizarre methods as stitching the victim inside a dead gorilla and watching from a distance as the bloody jungle scavengers rip the dead gorilla and its very-much-alive captive apart and chewing small parts of him hungrily in front of his very eyes.'

Bill's unwholesome sexual appetite sated for the time being, the Scottish ripper hoses himself down as he whistles a happy tune. Gimpo is crying in agony as the old crone stitches up his tattered colon and smears a poultice like Polyfilla on the missing areas of muscle and skin.

'I see by your enthusiastic debauch that you are not of a squeamish disposition gentlemen, which is most fortunate as I have heard rumours that tonight there is to be an execution in a neighbouring village. It promises to be quite spectacular as tomorrow night is an important date on the B'witi calendar.'

I was familiar with the deity B'witi, I'd come across records of this savage divinity in many books on voodoo and its ancestral lineage. B'witi was heavy-duty Satan shit.

The god was an incredibly powerful spirit who frightened all but the mentally and spiritually strongest of the forest dwellers. He manifested himself not only to the witchdoctors and shamen but to ordinary tribespeople when under the intoxication of certain deadly roots and herbs.

B'witi was interesting for many reasons, not least the very ambiguity of his nature. Like the Norse god Loki, B'witi was neither entirely good nor completely evil. He was noted for his particularly sick sense of humour and merciless punishments dealt out to duplicitous mortals. Of course the reason the god was revered was the effortless states of divinity that could be achieved by gaining the powerful spirit's favour. The locals described this grace as being the ability to see everything in everything, the jungle equivalent to occidental cosmic consciousness.

The knowledge afforded by the conduit drug Ibogaine, a concentrated powered form of the Iboga root, like all chemically induced forms of enlightenment, was also extremely dangerous. Outright death or total and irreversible loss of sanity were the risks.

Psychic scholar Bill was particularly keen to know if there was any chance of the three of us witnessing this event. A tall thin girl, barefooted and wearing a pink and white polka dot party dress rolled by with the ethereal grace of the naturally beautiful. Tight thin braids about three inches long stuck out from her head as if from a pincushion. Her bare white heels scraped along in the dust stirring up small clouds around her ankles. I found out later that the girl with the pale green far-away eyes was a neophyte from the B'witi temple.

These female neophytes, all of them spectacularly beautiful, were permanently intoxicated on the white flowers of Iboga which produced a pleasant opium-like intoxication.

LAUGHING AT JIM MORRISON

Z reckoned he didn't need a map but I bought one all the same. The cimetière Montmartre was massive. A veritable city of the dead. Z went into great detail and even greater lengths about how wonderful Oscar's grave was. It was huge, carved from gleaming white marble and, in his opinion, did the man's genius justice. A mausoleum on the grand scale: 'I have nothing to declare but the size of my grave stone.'

We got lost. As it turned out Z didn't know the way. My map came into its own. After about 20 minutes we found the spot. Except – and it is a huge except – it was not quite what Z had led me to expect. Over the years Z has told many tales about his life. Exploits that would beggar the most devout believer's belief. But I believed every word. Of course not his creative bollocks but all the other stuff.

What confronted us on that Parisian mid-morning was a very modest gravestone.

'There is some mistake. Give me your map Bill. No, no, this is obviously the gravestone of another Oscar Wilde, not the Oscar Wilde. Not my Oscar Wilde.'

But it was and there was no doubt and certainly no mausoleum of gleaming white marble. Z was crestfallen. His memory had not only deceived him, it had completely betrayed his whole being. The pity I felt for my friend totally outweighed any thought like, 'That's the last fuckin' time I ever go along with any one of your ludicrous reminiscences, even if it's just to placate you.'

I made a quick suggestion: 'Let's go and find Jim Morrison's grave and laugh.'

So we did. Using my map it only took a couple of minutes. It was totally pathetic. Even more pathetic were the straggles of young people on their knees as if in prayer to their lizard king saviour. But even more pathetic than that were the notes left for Jim to read. I mean 'Let It Roll Baby Roll' is not quite the Sermon on the Mount. An Italian couple in their early 20s were there, she dressed like it was 1968 and he in his brown leather strides. She had a single flower which she left at the pathetic headstone. I wanted to tell them that I had seen The Doors, Isle of Wight 1970. And that they were shite. And Morrison was a fat drunken slob.

Z and I walked away, still laughing. It's weird innit? I can say all that and it's for real. It's what happened. Both the graveside bit and the Isle of Wight. But still The Doors are one of my all-time favourite bands. Probably the best-ever American rock band.

'Don't say that Bill, it sounds a bit *Mojo*esque.'

*

The girl removed the bottle of Ouzo balanced upon her head and placed it in front of the Greek, whispering into his ear at the same time.

The greasy pervert's face lit up.

'Ah, my friends, the rumours are true. You are indeed fortunate!' He clapped his hands together. 'Tonight in Mbwankasam, about a mile from here, there is to be a public execution and a rising ceremony for B'witi. A couple of renegade missionaries and a local tribesman are to be executed. The missionaries seem to have blown a homosexually repressed gasket and the local nigger got caught buggering his neighbour's cattle.'

The Greek was obviously excited. 'The neophyte just informed me that the three of you have been invited to the rising ceremony, you have obviously made some kind of impression on your travels here. The bush telegraph... The girl said to leave in a few hours, the preparations are still underway.'

We spent another hour or two indulging ourselves in some leisurely sodomy and heavy drinking, Bill practised his skinning techniques. The doped-up lethargy of the neophytes kind of took the edge off any attempt at serious sexual insanity. There was no point anyway, why work up a sweat if the little cunts didn't squeal even a little bit?

Gimpo was consoling himself and his ruined shitter by drinking far too much jungle hooch. He was terrified of passing a solid turd and was counting on the hooch to keep his shit liquid till the patched-up bunghole was at least halfway to being healed.

A THOUSAND YEARS

Later. Up top. It's dark. I'm not being pestered by the roof boys with their usual cries of 'Hello Meesta Beel, how are you Meesta Beel, give me dollar Meesta Beel.' Maybe it's because I smell too much of shit and they think they will catch a deadly disease from me.

The beam from the ship's light constantly sweeps the river in front of us. Every few hundred yards you can see men who must have waited hours, if not days, in their dugouts. All waiting for their chance to make that leap for the passing railings so they can trade their smoked monkey, live crocodile, two-inch-long maggots, for flip-flops, batteries, cassettes, t-shirts and razors.

Also caught in the beam are a million, trillion moths, nocturnal dragonflies and other flying bugs and through this maelstrom of aerial nightlife silently swoop large moon-faced owls and giant bats scooping up this limitless feast. Humans may be technically top of some food chain back in Europe but down here in Africa it looks like they come pretty low in the pecking order. All these undernourished roof boys behind me and in front of me big fat owls with enough to keep them well fed for a thousand years.

Enough of this internal monologue, I'm off to find the other two.

*

The booming reverberation of powerful ghettoblasters ricocheted through the trees out of the ominous blackness of the jungle. Fat moths as big as pigeons banged around the bare light bulb hanging from the roof of the courtyard.

The beer and whisky had sharpened my senses towards another reality, warm rivulets of sweat trickled down my spine.

'It is time,' said the Greek who was also the worse for his drinking. 'The radios, they beckon. Come, friends, it is not far.'

A naked tribesman, invisible in the light-sucking shadows stepped into the light of the fires and lit himself a torch from the flames. We followed him into a narrow corridor hacked through a field of elephant grass 20-feet tall, a thin strip of night sky spattered with stars hung above us like a roof. All around and everywhere, spectral music, the hooting of owls, the mournful call of the moon monkey, the flapping whip of leather wings. The ever-present invisible cicada and her singing cousins. A muscular leopard, eyes yellow, drinking in starlight, wrestles her thrashing supper to the floor snarling and rending flesh, handsome face dripping gore.

The drumming seemed to be getting closer. Through the trees the glow from many fires lit up the canopy, long twisting shadows tangled up into the night. The distorted metallic racket of dozens of overdriven ghettoblasters smashing out syncopated rhythms along with the manic battering of wood, tin cans and hollowed out logs is terrifying.

We were walking single file, I was behind Bill and the quacking oboeist he keeps in his pants, trying hard not to gag.

CHARLEY AND GUSSY

'For fuck's sake, Gussy, you know you won't finish it, so what's the point?'

'Oh shut up, Charley, it's easy for you being a poet. You think you can toss off a few lines of verse and that's it. A day's work done. It's not the same being a painter. I have to make studies. I have to draw from life...'

'Draw from life! I've never seen a real human being that looks anything like your paintings.'

'That's not the point, Charley.'

'The point is, Gussy, it's almost midday and I want some action, not just hanging around watching you pretend to be a great artist. You're not even mediocre. No, come on, let's go and have some fun. Opium, absinthe and tarts. What do you say, Gussy? Sounds good to me. You can finish the damn painting tomorrow if you have to.'

'Look, Charley. It's the same every day, you roll round here swigging from a bottle of champagne, some little tart in tow, thinking I will drop everything to come out with you on another of your...'

'But Gussy, you love it. It's life. Real life, not your cruddy classical mythology bollocks. Who the fuck cares? It's 1850 for fuck's sake. Even Geney Delacroix knows that.'

'But...'

'No buts, Gussy. If you lived life a bit more you might have something worth painting. But all this fake symbolism and bible stories. You're not at Sunday School anymore. I mean, what you do is big girl's paintings. So what do you say, Gussy? We go and pick some flowers of evil, have a discourse with Satan, help ourselves to a couple of tarts, then head back to my place for a blow on my hookah. There's no point in sitting around here all day listening to the muffled drum of your heart beating out its funeral march to that lonely cemetery.'

'OK! OK! OK! For fuck's sake, Charley, just this once then. But any more of your wings of insanity brushing my mind and I'm off. I'm having none of it.'

'Deal. Now have a slug of the bubbly.'

And our heroes. Gustave Moreau (1826–98) and Charles Baudelaire (1821–67) are off for another blitz on the purple shadows and velvet skies of a Parisian night.

One hundred and thirty-four years later, Z was still trying to impress me with his yo-yoing techniques as we went on our way.

*

We arrived at a large clearing where the villagers were freaking big time, dancing insanely and screaming down madness, frenzy, hell and all the rest. Ritualistic jiggering sex dancing, limbs flung everywhere at impossible angles, muscular legs beating rhythmically into the swirling orange dust. Most of them are naked, covered in dried white clay or smeared in shining palm oil or animal grease.

The warriors are dressed in grass skirts, girdles of red feathers around their chests. All around the edges of the fires violent fucking is taking place. Some of the couples, all of them very young, are painted with bright red grease and coloured sands, purple and gold, sprinkled on their heads. The rutting kids are screaming along with the rest of the mad celebrations. The older women were screaming and slashing their faces with sharp stone knives. A loud gut-buckling screech lurched from the messy noise drawing in all the tinny counter rhythms sucking them all together in a giant kidney-rupturing pulse.

The Greek put out his arm to stop us getting any closer, he motioned for us to sit down at the tree line and to be quiet. A cold sweat pushed up through my skin.

About 20 men painted with white clay and a dozen naked women dressed in palm oil started to butcher suckling pigs and bless the kneeling congregation, splashing blood liberally over their heads.

The men, obviously priests, started to shake. Their penises, through some amazing feat of bodily discipline, erected themselves. The priestesses knelt before the wild wood and started praying.

I noticed the skulls in the trees, hundreds of them, like macabre christmas decorations.

The ceremony shifted direction, the tranced-out voodoo heads settling down as a couple of boss witch doctors started to shake their spears and point at a small round hut.

The drumming picked up again as a couple of white European men are brought out of the hut by a couple of masked warriors. The men had their hands bound behind their backs and appeared terrified.

They were both aged about 40, skinny, pale-looking fuckers wearing gold-rimmed glasses.

Three nuns were also manhandled out of the huts, they seemed a little calmer, mouthing their prayers, fiddling with their rosary beads and looking at the ground. One of the men had vomited down the front of his shirt, another had a wet stain down the front of his pants. A small black man, also bound at the wrist, was led from the hut, drunk and unafraid, laughing at friends among the gathered crowd. He knew that to retain any dignity he had to make a ribald display of his acceptance of his fate.

The missionaries and the nuns were made to sit on the ground, the cocky African was jostled before the main blaze.

EVERYTHING IS BRILLIANT

In the canteen. Trefor's bit, not the first-class bar. Trefor has got a plastic jerry can full of a piss-yellow coloured liquid. He beckons me over.

'Meesta Beel, you try'.

He pours me a beakerful. I take a sniff. Whatever it is, it stinks of rotten fruit.

'It very good, Meesta Beel. It palm wine, it make you happy.'

This is Trefor's assistant speaking, a man I did not know could speak a word of English.

'You drink it, make you happy. Your friends drink it, makes them very happy.'

Up until now I had not taken in what was going on around me. My mind was still full of the moths, owls and bats. What was going on was a bunch of men, obviously men from the dugouts. They look different than the traders and passengers on the barges. Anyway, these men are all up and dancing. African dancing. You'll have seen it on the telly. But the sound they are dancing to is not the familiar sound of Afro pop. Over the past couple of days I have somehow learnt to block out all the noise from the competing blasters. Well maybe not block it out, I can still hear it but I don't notice it. But I'm hearing it now. What I'm hearing is 'Prime Mover' by Zodiac Mindwarp and The Love Reaction cranked up to ear-bleeding level on Trefor's blaster. The African dancers are sort of doing their thing in a circle. In the centre of the circle is Z giving it his rock god-star best singing along, Karaoke-style, to himself in his prime. This is something to behold. He's doing all the action like it's the Hammersmith Odeon (OK, I know it's not called that anymore) circa 1988. Beating his chest, attempting the splits, even that stupid wee somersault thing he used to do when the band was first starting out. It makes him look like the ultimate tosser. But can you imagine any other has-been rock star doing the same half way up the Congo with a bunch of cannibals and no paddle?

Z hasn't seen me, he's too lost in his own dreams, of stadiums filled end to end with screaming fans. I sit down on a bench and take a sip from the brew. It's disgusting. I take another sip and another. You could get used to this.

'Fuckin' brilliant innit, Bill?'

'What, Gimpo?'

'Everything.'

'Yeah.'

And everything is brilliant.

*

A technicoloured maniac burst out of the jungle squawking and ranting, decked out in all manner of feathers and flailing animal skins, bones clattered around his neck and ankles. He was waving a stick surmounted by a skull and more feathers.

Five oiled nubiles, naked except for yellow feathers stuck on their thighs accompanied him, dancing lasciviously. The girls' thrusting hips and jigging pubescent breasts, their jutting backsides shining in the firelight, drew a low sigh from the younger males in the congregation. My agitated Cyclops started dancing to the beat that had picked up quietly again.

The priest started shouting and dancing, smashing the black man in the face with the skull. Blood and bits of bone and teeth splashed on to the dusty floor. The man became angry, protesting to the witch doctor and the slinky nubiles dancing around him. The crowd, encouraging by the nubiles gyrating their big shiny black arses, had joined in hurling abuse at the proud prisoner.

Gimpo found the Lingala hard to translate but said that the goat buggerer was also involved with the missionaries in procuring young boys for Fat Miguel's sodomy barges. I listened hard to the witchdoctor's mad accusations and sure enough I could just about pick up the sly Arab's name being pronounced with exaggerated malice. I felt Bill tense beside me, a grunting chug slapping out sideways every time the depraved Arab's name was called.

The witchdoctor smashed a ghettoblaster over the man's head and the girls notched up the heat on their spookily erotic cavortings. A band of drummers started banging out scary rhythms on wooden drums. The witchdoctor forced the prisoner on to his knees and started tearing off his raggy clothes with a stone knife.

I got the feeling that somehow this was all going to turn into that perennial bush favourite, the old African castration supper routine, choking some poor bastard on his own gonads.

DRUMMOND'S LOG, SATURDAY 15 JUNE 1996
IT'S TRUE IT'S TRUE

A pig starts to squeal, then another, then another, then a cockerel crows. I don't mind cockerels. I've got one at home. I like the sound of a cockerel crowing however early it starts. But pig squealing. It sounds like they are being killed slowly, painfully with red-hot pokers up their arse.

'Bill, you awake?'

'Yeah, Gimpo, why?'

'Do you fancy going for a bath?'

'What? Where?'

'Remi says that there is a spot round the back of the *Colonel Eyeya* that a lot of the lads go to wash.'

'I'm not fucking going.'

'What did you say, Z?'

'I'm not going for a wash. I've sniffed my armpits. I don't stink.'

But Z does come with us. We've got our powdered-milk tin-on-a-rope thing. I've got a bar of carbolic, Z has a bar he bought from the market in Kinshasa and Gimpo has got a bar he's just bought from Remi's stall.

'The boat's fuckin' changed completely from what it was like a couple of days ago.'

'In what way do you mean, Z?'

'Two days ago it was just all the stalls selling second-hand clothes, UNICEF medicine, soap, razors, mirrors, fish hooks and batteries. Now it's crammed with live and dead animals, squealing pigs, desperate turtles, resigned goats, gasping giant catfish. I mean, under every bench and stall are pigs and crocodiles and eels and fucking antelopes.'

'I don't think it's an antelope.'

'Whatever the fucker is it shouldn't be tied up under that bench, it should be running free through the jungle.'

'Bit liberal of you, Z.'

'Yeah well if they think I stink, I think their animal welfare laws leave something to be desired.'

'Meesta Geempo, how are you this morning?'

From one end of this floating, heaving mass of humanity and wildlife – Noah's Ark must have been more peaceful than this lot – every man, woman and child we pass is giving it 'Hello Meesta Geempo, Bonjour Meesta Geempo, Meesta Geempo we love you'. I mean, what is it that Gimpo's got that gets all these darkies falling in love with him? Back home Z (being a former rock god) and me (being an interesting sort) are the ones that attract the attention and gather admirers. But here it's all 'Meesta Geempo, Meesta Geempo'. He's loving it of course.

'Bill, I reckon we've got to get on to the *Ifutu*, then round to its back end, then we can jump back on to the rear of the *Colonel Ebeya*.'

'Whatever you say.'

Z and I follow our master. We clamber over more sacks of rice, desperate turtles, stacks of smoked monkeys. I step on the trotter of a sleeping pig, which sets it off good and proper. We get there. A small deck, almost at water level, piled high with coiled ropes and tractor tyres. We are just above the propellers, the black water of the Congo is all churned up, the noise of the engines is deafening. It all seems a bit precarious.

'Gimpo, it doesn't look like we should be here.'

'Well, what are these other fuckers doing?'

There are four Africans, all bollock naked, happily drawing water with their milk-powder tins on ropes from the churning river, soaking themselves and going to town working up a good, strong lather all over their bodies. Their mothers would be so pleased.

'Z, have you ever seen that film *Blazing Saddles*?'

'Yeah. Why?'

'Remember that bit when Madeline Khan pulls the black sheriff who has come into town?'

'Yeah.'

'Can you remember what she says just after she has switched off the lights?'

'No.'

'"It's true, it's true."'

'So?'

'So it isn't true. You and I have got huge knobs, obviously. These Africans here have just got average-sized knobs. I mean, not one of them could tie a knot in theirs.'

'You're right, Bill.'

We strip off our clothes and I get to work with the carbolic.

*

When things get primal and out of control, sex and death are always the first things that get mashed up together.

I could smell the slobbering cunt from 20 yards away. The guy's dick had inevitably boned up, one of the sick sisters was down on her knees moshing her mouth all over the happy victim, the crowd were shouting their approval. The girls continued their gyrations when one of them flipped backwards into a crab position, then the rubber sexbomb spiderwalked over to bonk-on Sammy whose expression had flashed from drugged delirium to one of wide-eyed terror.

Before the blood had time to vacate his tubesteak, crab woman bit it clean off at the root, a geyser of thick blood pumped all over the fucking place. Another of her skanky sisters had his nuts off with the cutthroat before anyone blinked, and a third scooped up the severed meat and, as I had expected, stuffed it down the stunned guy's throat. Crushed chilli paste was splashed on to his wounds to prolong his death and boost the agony.

His eyeballs are the next to go, forked out by the witchdoctor and splashed on to a mirrored plate. Next the intestines are carefully unwound. Like in many savage rituals the art is in keeping the victim suffering as long as possible. Gimpo couldn't suppress his laughter at the comic spectacle of the gutted goatfucker trying to blindly retrieve his stomach.

MUSÉE GUSTAVE MOREAU

So Z and I headed down from Père Lachaise cemetery and found our way to the Gustave

Moreau museum. We paid our sous and entered. The place was empty but for us. We wandered from unfinished canvas of some scene from classical mythology to unfinished canvas of a biblical story. I instantly filed it along with the pre-Raphaelites, Klimt – decorative rubbish. That doesn't mean I don't like it, it's just that I don't like liking it. Not proper painting like Corot or Millet; even Courbet did proper men's paintings. Not all that gossamer wings and fake symbolism stuff.

But the Gustave Moreau museum is a great place to visit on an empty day in Paris. It inspired Z and I to evolve our Charley and Gussy characters.

*

The two missionaries are as grey as ghosts. Their vow of chastity as young men had plainly sent their hormones insane, clattering around their underwear like an overexcited pinball machine and singeing their cassocks an unhealthy shade of buggery. The carnal urges that they thought they had buried deep beneath their hefty theology and concern for their fellow men often surfaced during protracted bouts of malaria and black-water fever.

Their libidos unchained, the carnal Catholics had been buggering themselves stupid out here in the jungle. So stoked with guilt and anal lust the men had fallen even further, broiling in a hell of their own foolish construction. The poor bastards had ended up working for Fat Miguel, supplying youngsters for his foul international trade in black chicken.

One minute they are playing happily in the river, the next padlocked to a radiator in New York or Hamburg, being bummed mercilessly by evil capitalists and wealthy aristocrats.

'It's those stupid fucking nuns I feel sorry for,' said the Greek. 'The stupid cunts, they think they're doing god's work escorting the heavily tranquillised kids over to Europe and the States. They think that the kids are being placed with Christian families, not some low-life Arab anal pirate and his fucking sodomy ranches.'

The two fallen missionaries were dragged before the baying congregation begging for their pale-shit lives. Obviously the girls would be of no use in stimulating the debased mongols into pole position; even a couple of oiled boys failed to arouse the shivering wrecks. Both of them had shit themselves and sat there shivering and wailing, one of them even praying to his useless God. The witchdoctor was so disgusted he fed them to the pigs, the lowest form of death conceivable in this part of the forest.

The nuns provided a much more entertaining sport. We were surprised to find that the Greek had arranged for us to aid in their lawful execution. We were in no position to argue, this was their country and their laws, we were honour-bound to comply with the people's request. The oily girls stripped the foxy nuns to their cowls. Two of them were about 18 years old – novices, and well stacked novices at that. We were supposed to kick off the carnage. No problem.

MY DECISION
Later. In my bunk. Z in his.

'Z.'

'Yeah.'

'I've made a decision.'

'What's it with you? You're always making decisions. Then next week it's another decision. Give up on your decision-making and just go with the flow.'

'Oh.'

'OK Bill, tell us what your decision is this time.'

'I'm not shifting from my bunk until we get to Kisangani.'

'Yeah so what about needing a piss or a shit? And don't think that me and Gimpo are going to bring you your meals to the cabin.'

'I'm not going to eat.'

'Now I know you're talking shit. I've never known you to go more than three hours without eating. You eat in the same way as I drink. It's your drug of convenience.'

'No Z, really. I'm just going to stay in my bunk and write. Get all the fucker written while we are here. I'm going for the full-on dark night of the soul and I'm going to capture every last thought that flies through my mind. I'm going to sweat it out in this metal box until the hallucinations start raging and baby crocodiles start crawling up the walls.'

'Yeah Bill, you forget I know you. You will still be tinkering with your text in six years time.'

'No, I'm going to do a Jack Kerouac and do the whole lot, the whole 100,000 words, in one go. It's got to be done.'

'What if it's a load of bollocks?'

'William Burroughs is a load of bollocks and you tell me his stuff works.'

'But he's different. He's a genius, you're just you.'

'Look, your Sallie or whoever ends up editing this book can sort it out, keep the good bits, chop it around, throw the whole lot up in the air and pick it up in whatever order it come down in and use it like that.'

'OK Bill, suits me. But if you...'

'Z, I got a better idea. Nobody touch a word of what I write. Keep all the spelling mistakes, the bad punctuation, the unfinished sentences and let the reader edit it for themselves.'

'Fine, Bill, fine, whatever you say. They can always skip your bits.'

'No Z, you don't understand, all the great literature is left unedited.'

'Like what?'

'*Moby Dick*. If an editor had got his hands on *Moby Dick,* it would be half its length. Probably a niftier read but it would be far less a work of great literature. It's like those long boring bits that make other bits so great.'

'Didn't Beavis and Butthead say something like that about Radiohead?'

'Probably.'

'Anyway Bill, I think it's all great stuff and I'm glad you have made your decision. I'm off to the bar.'

'Yeah, see you later.'

✳

According to B'witan civil laws, capital punishment and public entertainment are seen as two strands of the same hangman's rope. There was an honesty about African justice that I found quite liberating and refreshing compared to our own cowardly hypocrisy.

With this ennobling thought I set about destroying proselytising Sister Marie Claire's guilty dirtbox, her screamed prayers were music to my ears as I slammed in the ham and bit off one of her ears. Bill was choking novice Claire with his fat stinkhorn and the Gimps was receiving rapturous applause as he gave the Mother Superior a vigorous titfuck, riding the fat old nun's monster mams like a wild west rodeo stud. Bill was reaming hard on novice Claire's peachy butt, he whipped out a Stanley knife.

'Forgive him baby, he has sinned,' I called out as he slit her throat.

'They're gonna make you a saint for this one, you papist slut,' he laughed, lopping off a tit.

Gimpo, ever the king of the one-louders, had got the intestines going, unfurling them and squeezing nun shit all over the place, dancing crazily to the ghettoblasters. The little twat had even found a blowtorch somewhere and was turning Mama Superior's tits into two smoking dumplings. I was laughing hysterically, feeling righteous in avenging the countless genocides the religious armies of lesbians and their shitty masochistic faith had visited on indigenous peoples all over the bloody earth.

In his ecstatic abandonment the Gimp had forgotten all about the state of his jacksie and had tried to squeeze out a couple of turds, ripping open his wounds. He was stuffing leaves and mud up his dirtbox to stop his guts falling out.

The drums had reached a climatic intensity, the entire congregation of the savage church dancing ecstatically. There was hardly anything left of the sacrificed criminals, gory bones were being brandished around the grooving throng. The bucket kids as ever were filling up their lunchboxes with the slaughter.

Bill was mongdancing big time, I'd never seen the grumpy sod enjoying himself so much. He was actually dancing, waving his arms around and peering through his dripping splayed fingers, bat dancing at a satanic rave.

The festivities grooved on among the sloppy hamburger slurry and sliding bone; they were but a preliminary to our B'witian experience.

A PARISIAN BACK STREET

'Bill, I think we should become dandies.'

'What?'

'Dandies. You know, dandies.'

'What the fuck are you talking about, Z? You and me dandies? Look at the pair of us. What in God's name do you think would make me want to be a dandy, even if I could?'

'*I* could.'

'Z, you are a mess. It doesn't matter how much time you spend trimming your beard, you are a mess. Surely to be a dandy you have to keep it up.'

'If you hadn't burnt that money we could have squandered it on being dandies.'

'Fuck off.'

'Anyway, I don't mean Beau Brummell, I mean real dandies. The dandy should aspire to be sublime without respite, not just a contrived nancy-boy narcissism. He should live and sleep before the mirror. It's by staring into the mirror that you can see the whole universe in the single well of your own fucked-up personality.'

'I hate mirrors.'

'I love them.'

THE GOD OF THE ANIMALS

The savage carnival stretched bleeding and intoxicated into the wet dawn. Eventually even the most intoxicated tribal raver crept into some tangle of roots or managed to make his way back to his hut to sleep off the excesses of the night. Apart from the dried blood and the odd scavenger making off with scraps of eviscerated nun the place looked like any other outdoor space that's been the scene of some hard partying. The villagers snored and farted in their huts but there was to be no rest for the three of us. We had our audience with B'witi to think of.

In a misty clearing smoking cigars three old women sat around a large earthenware bowl pounding down the raw Iboga roots with thick wooden poles. A couple of the oiled nubiles were squatting over similar bowls pressing lightly on their swollen stomachs.

The thick black menstrual blood was poured into smaller bowls and mixed with the pulped roots of the sacred plant. The old women hunched round a small smoky fire transferring the blood and pulp to an iron pot set upon the flames. The brew soon started to simmer and gave off a strong meaty aroma like frying liver. The women added powdered insects and jungle fungi, stirring and muttering incantations.

The most decrepit of the old witches got to her feet and, supporting herself with a stick, hobbled across to the three of us. She drew pictures in the air with bony fingers and pushed a piece of foul-tasting fungi in our mouths indicating that we should swallow. With a small curved blade she nicked us sharply between the eyes catching the drops of blood that dripped from our noses into yet another bowl which she added to the pot. When she took a squitting diarrhoea shit into the pot I knew that at some stage we were going to have to drink the odious brew.

GETTING DARKER

Alone and I'm left for my second and final attempt at a Dark Night of the Soul.

I'm going down, I may be some time.

It's getting darker.
It's getting darker.
It's getting darker.
It's getting darker.
It's getting darker.
It's getting darker.
It's getting darker.
It's getting darker.
It's getting darker.
It's getting darker.
It's getting darker.
It's getting darker.
It's getting darker.
It's getting darker.

I look around to see if I can see any baby crocodiles climbing the wall yet.

None.

So.

It's getting darker.
It's getting darker.
It's getting darker.
It's getting darker.

It's getting darker.
It's getting darker.
It's getting darker.
It's getting darker.

What the fuck is that noise I can hear? There's a noise of something or somebody in the cabin but the door is closed. Nobody has come in. The noise is coming from under Mavuba's bunk. Oh holy shit, this is fuckin' it. Satan, Lucifer, Old Horny himself is about to appear from under Mavuba's bed. I listen intently to the sound. It's a soft, scraping sound. It repeats about every five seconds. What the fuck is it? I'd better stay in my bunk.

I've been lying and listening to this sound for over half an hour. It doesn't change. Doesn't alter. Well sometimes it stops for, say, 30 seconds and then it starts up again. Just the same.

I decide to lift my head and look over the edge of my bunk. My eyes have grown accustomed to the darkness of our cabin. It's broad daylight outside. But with the cabin door closed, the only natural light that gets into the place is through the hole from where the lock should be.

I stare down. What I see is probably the saddest sight I've seen in all my life. And I've watched people die. I climb down from my bunk to get a better look. Under Mavuba's bunk is a large green turtle, tied up with a piece of raffia through a hole at the back of its shell, to one of the inner legs of the bunk bed. The soft scraping sound is the sound of its two front flippers trying to paddle its way back to the river. Its black, unblinking eyes stare into mine, beseeching me to cut him free and take him back to the water, to his family, his wife, his children. Do turtles have wives? Do they have children they care for? I doubt it but that's not going to stop me from anthropomorphising this little drama of universal proportions that is going on in front of me right now. 'To be or not to be, that is the question.' The answer has to be 'To be!' I will have to untie the turtle, hide him the best I can under my safari jacket then take him to the riverside of our barge and drop him back in the water. Good deed done, I will have saved creation, redeemed my soul, outsmarted Satan. I knew this dark night of the soul thing would pay dividends. I just didn't know it would happen so soon. Hang on a minute, there is no way I can get him under my safari jacket, he's too big for that. Maybe I should wait till after dark. But then Mavuba would be back and even if he was asleep in his bunk, me getting the turtle out would wake him up.

*

The dislocated arse dancers from the previous night's weirdness showed up. They had reapplied a light covering of oil and were wearing clean white sarongs, smelling deliciously of cinnamon and Coca Cola, coconut and vanilla. I didn't know whether I wanted to eat, drink or fuck them. The seriousness of their expressions told me none of these options would even be considered: they were part of the ceremonial hoodoo. They led us into a small circular hut, it was dark inside, and undressed us.

The Greek was nowhere to be seen. I started to get a little worried, was the *Colonel Ebeya* still waiting for us? In the infectious insanity of the execution ceremonies it was entirely possible that the klaxon could have sounded a dozen times and no one would have heard it. Anxiety was causing my dick to bone up. The girls were not amused and one of them cracked me hard in the bollocks with a piece of wood.

As if on cue the runty little Greek opened up the flap of the hut and entered smiling, 'A great honour my friends, not many white men meet B'witi.' His smile lacked depth. 'I met him myself 20 years ago. Once in a lifetime is more than enough.' His tone wasn't exactly reassuring.

'The *Colonel Ebeya*?' I asked nervously.

'Ah, no problem, a couple more days at least, engine problems.'

I SHIT MYSELF AGAIN

'Meesta Beel, Meesta Beel, you there I know. Meesta Beel, Meesta Beel, I need your bucket.'

It's Pitsu's voice and he's knocking on our door.

'Yeah, what is it?'

'Meesta let me in, I need your bucket to wash my clothes.'

At least with me now having to deal with the pestering requests of Pitsu, I can stop thinking about the turtle under Mavuba's bed.

'Hang on a minute, Pitsu.'

I get off my bunk, open the door.

'Ah Meesta Beel, you sleep, I wake you, I sorry. I need your bucket, wash clothes.'

Gimpo, Z and I invested in a blue plastic bucket yesterday, to wash our clothes in, part of our new regime to clean ourselves up. It's what all the families onboard use. Maybe I've already told you this. What I didn't tell you was that yesterday I shat myself again. Good and proper and instead of being seen washing my shitty boxer shorts in our bucket, I waited until it got dark and threw them over the side. I wonder what will happen to those boxer shorts? Will they have sunk to the bottom of the Congo River, or will they have been swept downstream to be found by an African who will treat them as a treasured find?

There is one of the roof boys who seems to have no other worldly goods other than a pair of baggy boxer shorts. No t-shirt, no flip-flops, nothing but a pair of boxer shorts a good few sizes too big for him.

When you are reading this in a different century to the time that I am writing it, do you think there will be anything remaining of my shit-filled boxer shorts?

'Meesta Bill, can I…?'

'Yeah Pitsu, there are two of my t-shirts in there soaking at the moment though.'

*

The girls shooed him out of the hut, pulling a palm leaf door closed behind him. An old woman was working away with a collection of glass bottles containing all kinds of weird jungle shit. She handed one of the girls a bowl of thick clear liquid and barked at her in Lingala. All four girls rubbed us down quickly with the solution, cleansing away last night's blasphemies, it burnt and stung our eyes and was highly flammable as we discovered when the little cunts set us on fire. A brief whoosh of flame burnt us and singed off all our body hair. This was worth it though for the oily massage the neophyte chicks balmed us down with.

The tricky serpents started uncoiling again and this time the girls were not quite as serious, the closed door affording us a little privacy. The girls started giggling at our twitching purple-headed reptiles and swatted at them with palm leaves less harshly than before. This was more than enough for the Gimp and he flung off a couple of strings of pearly knacker-gunge, hitting one of them in the eye. She cursed and even the old mama sat in the corner broke out into a giggle.

The girls cover us in a white base tone of river clay. Before it dries the girls scrape at it with sharpened sticks making intricate patterns on our chests and backs. The clay hardened quickly and produced thousands of thin cracks giving the appearance of great age, The older woman daubed patterns on us, painting large blue wings on our backs. The many names of B'witi are inscribed on our genitals with a thin stick and black ink. Brightly coloured feathers are stuck in our hair and a skull-like mask painted on our faces.

The door flap to the hut was suddenly pulled back and a terrifying figure of a man, large hog tusks pushed through holes in his cheeks, a leopard skin, complete with snarling head draped around his loins, strode wildly into the hut. It was the witchdoctor, his eyes gleaming insanely, sweating like a horse. He stuck his hand in the boiling brew and pulled it out, licking the ichorous stew from his fingers, filed teeth shining in the firelight. He wrinkled his nose, shook his head and then shat noisily into the pot.

The psychedelic savage seemed extraordinarily grumpy, cursing loudly and slapping the old woman several times around the head. At one point he stood up and started arguing with invisible spirits, losing his temper and spitting at them. He eventually sat down and pulled out a pair of metal-rimmed spectacles from a concealed pocket in his feather girdle. He looked at the three of us intensely, scrutinising our souls with his jungle intuition, he seems satisfied and stirred the brew.

'B'witi sees all.'

His smoky French accent is low and resonates around the room bouncing up from his belly. The voice doesn't seem to be coming from the wild granddad, I suspect that he may have been channelling 'All my Ancestors.' He grunted, impossibly low.

'Priests of B'witi!' He stirred the scatalogical brew and tasted it, pulling another face. 'I can't not be a priest even if I don't want to.' The voice had changed again, notched up a tone or two, a pleasant French accent to his English, 'Which I don't, if the truth be known.'

His neck snapped quickly when he said this, a bestial snarl spitting from his twisted mouth: 'Fuck, that hurts!'

A couple of virgins enter the hut. Lithe and foxy, they stare at the ground. The old woman takes the rusty teapot Lithe is carrying. Foxy is carrying three pieces of bamboo about four feet long. Wild Granddad tells us to bend over. I can't be bothered arguing, I bend over and flashed him the brown eye. I noticed Foxy and Lithe eyeing our tackle and whispering.

'What the fuck happened to you, friend?!' he says scoping Gimpo's war-zone bunghole. 'You been reamed by a gorilla or something?'

'Punishment bumming,' replies the Gimp, straight.

'I don't think I've ever seen an asshole look so fucking sorry for itself,' he said laughing.

ANOTHER PARISIAN STREET

All talk of dandyism seemed to have been forgotten, or at least that's what I hoped. We were shuffling along in silence when Z turned to face the crowd of well-groomed Parisian shoppers, then he pulled a pose as if on stage.

'It is the devil who yanks the strings that move me. In disgusting objects I find enticing lures. Each day I go down one more step toward hell, without horror, through the darkness and the stink. Just as a repulsive tramp who kisses and bites the saggy tits of an aged whore, I steal a clandestine pleasure as I sidle along.'

Z then turned from the shoppers to stare me in the face.

'If rape, poison, the knife and arson have not yet woven with their pleasing patterns the banal canvas of your pitiful fate it is because your soul, Bill, is not bold enough.'

Z was slipping into one of his moods. I decided I'd better humour him.

'Is that one of your old poems or have you just made that up on the wing?'

'Made it up, Bill? You fuckin' uneducated thicko, that's the opening lines from *Flowers of Evil*.

'Flowers of Evil?'

'Charles Baudelaire. The whole reason we have come to Paris is to find the spirit of Baudelaire. It is he who has the key to Satan, remember?'

I remembered nothing.

*

The cosmic chief stuck a small rock up my butt and did the same to an indignant Bill. 'Relax, Scottish,' he said, 'This is just so B'witi does not shit himself straight out of you,' as casually as a dentist talking about some bridgework. 'Mary Jane here's gonna need a big old rock. What the fuck them boat niggers do to you, boy? How many of them was hiding that big banana?'

The old woman, bent double, hauled a large stone over to the shaman and a bucket of clay. He stuffed it in sideways and filled the tears and holes with the mud.

A high-pitched whining sound like a child playing with the neck of a toy balloon squinched loudly. It was Bill, The powerful gasses had found a tiny fissure in his stone-age butt plug and were escaping noisily. A handful of clay silenced the angry methane warrior.

The priest informed us that the potion we were to drink would force the body to attempt to purge itself, the stones would keep our rear ends secure and if we were to vomit we should quickly drink it, this would subdue the body's natural reaction to cleanse itself. Up until this point I'd been grooving along with the sideways kilter of the general weirdness, it hadn't really occurred to me to question anything but this sacred puke-drinking shit with the stones up our jacksies was bending into areas I wasn't 100 per cent sure about.

This B'witi cat for instance, who exactly was he? And did I really want to experience an enlightenment that was filtered through some form of primitive animistic shit-eating ritual.

This was no sophisticated divinity whose sacrificial rites had softened into a pale echo of its original source. This was a feral stone age ceremony dripping gore and wanking up death, was I ready for this kind of dark contemplation? Like I said, it didn't look like any of us had much choice in the matter.

Foxy and Lithe handed us the bamboo and indicated that we place one end of them up our noses, like giant cocaine straws. We were about to meet the God of the animals whether we wanted to or not.

A large flat piece of stone was placed on the fire on to which the witchdoctor placed a small pile of the ground-up root of the Iboga plant, He added a few herbs and powders then took a small pinch and placed it in the end of the bamboo pipes, He then placed his mouth over the pipe and blew the powder up our noses. It felt like a massive jolt of bleach burning up through my sinuses and straight into my brain.

Silver pinpricks of light started popping in front of my eyes, I could feel the same silver energy shooting through some weird Hindu network of nerves in my body and congregating around the base of my spine where it started to pulsate. Some kind of opiate blockout clogged up and froze all the sensation between my ears while a warm heroin-type fug sat pleasantly heavy on my lungs, my dick lost interest in anything sexual at all and my sphincter tightened noticeably.

ROLL OVER WALT WHITMAN
Later. In the luxury bar with Z.

'Heroic failure.'

'What, Z?'

'Heroic failure, Bill. That is what you and I are great at. We can fail more heroically than any artists alive today. Zodiac Mindwarp & The Love Reaction was a heroic failure; us trying to get to the North Pole to save the world was heroic failure.'

'So what are you saying?'

'This journey up the Congo to outsmart Lucifer is going to be our greatest and most heroic failure.'

'I don't fail. The KLF wasn't a failure. We sold more records than...'

'Ah shut the fuck up. Yeah, we know you won a Brit Award as well. But who the fuck cares now? Even in the not-so-very-grand scheme of things the KLF was a failure and not so very heroic a one at that. For the very reason you had some short-lived commercial success completely cancels out anything heroic about its failure. But what we are doing now may be seen as one of the great heroic failures of all time.'

'What about Scot of the Antarctic failing to get to the South Pole first, then dying on the way back, Z?'

'Nothing compare to this. What we are doing now is about something all those that come after us...'

'All of them?'

'OK then, all those of higher sensibilities will learn great spiritual lessons from our failure. You and I sitting in this bar now is true poetry. Nothing can touch it. And we will fail and it is that failure, that heroic failure, that will turn this from being just true poetry into truly great poetry. Roll over, Walt Whitman, we are coming on through.'

*

Bill and Gimps were shaking violently, I grabbed at my wrist and found that I also had a serious seismic wobble freaking down on me.

The hallucinatory disco lights started kicking in and then it was the turn of the pointy-eared, cat-eyed acid devils to start fading through the walls. The green gauze of intricate lattice work, like Islamic geometry started zoning in, Aztec deities breathing in the patterns. Next it was the turn of the ubiquitous bats and the leaping cats, Hieronymous Bosch sent in his hordes and the shit that tempted Max Ernst's St Antony made an appearance.

I could hear their crab-like mandibles clicking like knitting needles. It was imperative that I kept my emotions flat, a bolt of fear then could have set off some form of psychic feedback looping in on itself and sending us into irreversible insanity. I managed to keep my balance and surf the weirdness straight, head-tuning the static so as to keep a tenuous grip on flat reality, keeping the alternative zones tightly reined, yet ready to rage if I needed to.

Bill and Gimps swam to the surface of their raging subconscious, Bill's face was a pool of twitches and violent grotesque tics. Bill's demons are murderous and need intense discipline, he'd lost the butt stone and hot black shit was jetting from his backside like an expresso machine, scalding one of the poor virgins stood behind him.

I'd managed to just about hold on to my guts, the ground started shaking when the breeze block wedged up Gimpo's butt cracked and the black rivers of blood started sloshing around our ankles, I lost consciousness watching the women trying to repair Gimpo's arse with palm leaves and wooden branches.

I HATE PARIS

I hate Paris. I've hated it since, at the age of 13, I saw England win the World Cup on a TV in the corner of a Parisian café back in 1966. Our first foreign family holiday.

I hated the fact that the American literary heroes of my youth came over here in search of some sort of cultural holy grail, genuflecting at a Left Bank life in a bohemian pose. When I first read *On the Road* at 18 I believed Kerouac. When I read *Satori in Paris* at 20 I knew he was a fucked-up wino loser. I knew there was no satori to be had in Paris, even if Kerouac didn't.

It had begun to rain so Z and I found a bar. He was trying to order absinthe and I wanted a pot of tea. We were both disappointed. Z had to settle for a large measure of vodka and me for a tumbler of lukewarm water and a tea bag.

'A couple of lines of Baudelaire tells you more about Satan than any of those books written for vicars that you read.'

'Maybe.'

'Fuckin' maybe, Bill. Listen to this,' he downed the vodka, laid both his palms on the table, threw back his lank mane of hair and started.

> *"Ceaselessly beside me the demon writhes;*
> *He swarms around me like impalpable air;*
> *I swallow him and feel him burning my lungs*
> *And filling them with an everlasting guilty desire.*
> *At times he takes, knowing my great love for art,*
> *The form of the most seductive of women,*
> *And, under specious pretexts of depression,*
> *Accustoms my lips to infamous love charms."*

'Are you listening, Bill?

> *"Thus, far from the sight of God, he leads me,*
> *Panting and crushed by fatigue, into the midst*
> *Of the plains of boredom, extensive and deserted,*
> *And throws before my eyes full of confusion*
> *Soiled clothing opened wounds,*
> *And the bloody apparatus of destruction."*

'Do you understand that, Bill?'

'Sorry Z, my mind wandered. I was thinking about the World Cup qualifiers.'

'What the fuck's football got to do with any of this?'

'Nothing.'

*

Wracked with pain, lungs tight, ribs bruised my senses returned. The girls were rubbing us down with palm oil again. I had lost track of time but was relieved to find we were still in the hut.

The priest checked our bloodshot eyes closely. 'First thing,' he said matter of factly 'Your bodies purged good.' He spat into the fire. 'Badness in your bodies dissolve and gone.'

He was messing around with more dead insects, toasting them on a firestone.

'Mr Gimpo's butt, I think this time it fixed good, much badness here,' he pointed to his head, 'Here,' at his stomach, 'All this affects here,' he grabbed his gonads and shook them casually, 'And all other way around, your bunghole fixed good, no problems.'

Gimpo felt his arse and asked Bill what it looked like.

'The arse of Frankenstein,' he deadpanned.

'All scars go in maybe six, seven, month,' said the witch doctor. 'Little Chi Chi, she fix Mr Gimpo good,' he said, pointing at one of the girls who was smiling shyly. 'Now you rid of bad spirits and black shit you see B'witi.'

PHYSICS

Gimpo bursts into the bar just as I was going to tell Z, yet again, that in my book failure is just failure, nothing more.

'Bill, Z, you've gotta come an' see this.'

We follow Gimpo out on to the small balcony of the luxury bar. Below us the on-board squad of militia men, in their neatly pressed fatigues, are at work. With machetes in hand they are hacking at the vine ropes that have been used to tie the dugouts to the side of the *Colonel Ebeya*. The dugouts are breaking free and beginning to drift downstream, leaving their owners stranded aboard. Miles and more miles from home and no way of getting back.

'Why the fuck are they doing that, Gimpo?'

'It's obvious, there must be almost 100 of the dugouts tied up to the barges and that's only on this side. Could be the same amount on the other side.'

'So?'

'Physics, Bill. The drag from that lot must be considerable, slowing the progress of the barges down considerably and upping the fuel consumption of the engines by a large amount.'

We stand and stare as men from the jungle leap into the Congo abandoning any hope of doing business, or getting news from the outside world to try to catch up with their free-flowing dugouts. Some make it. Others don't. By that I don't mean we watch them drown but we do see their dugouts sink as they get caught up in the churning waters of the slipstream of the *Colonel Ebeya*.

I think about our return tickets to Heathrow: our virtual cradle-to-grave rights to three square meals a day; roof over our heads; free at the point of entry this, that and the other; and I can't think our lives are in the least heroic, whether they be failures or successes.

*

Doc Weird took a chunk of something out of the fire that looked and smelled like opium, cut it into three small squares about half an inch each. One of the girls produced something wrapped in a piece of wine-red velvet which she placed in front of the fire. Our priest carefully unwrapped the velvet: a small box three by three inches, ebony inlaid with intricate gold patterns, a complex geometrical design encoding god knows what from the Koran and other texts.

It appeared to be some kind of puzzle box, the priest started to twist it this way and that. Small blue sparks popped like static from its surface and it glowed from inside. The priest clicked something on the box and a small drawer shot out, he placed a chunk of the black stuff in it and closed it quickly. Blue smoke poured from a pattern of holes in the box at the top and the priest handed the box to the Gimp, indicating that he should inhale the smoke from the spooky chillum. Gimpo grinned wickedly and drew the smoke deep into his lungs, closing his eyes and sitting perfectly still.

The priest placed more of the black stuff in a different hole and rearranged the alignments, a star-shaped hole appeared full of some kind of liquid, which he gave to Bill to drink. Then he like Gimpo appeared to slide into some kind of quiet trance. I could smell black light, taste its warm cocaine weirdness toasting my brain, numbing up my sinuses and swelling my throat. I was becoming light-headed, intoxicated by the light and the smells.

Two of the girls undulated out of the shadows like shiny black serpents, they curled themselves lasciviously around the tranced Bill and Gimpo, long pink tongues flickering in the supernatural light like sinister pornography. The third girl passed me the box. I held it between both hands and opened up the top and peeked in nervously. It was full of the same universe shit that I'd seen in Bill's leather doctor's bag, spiral galaxies, stars and ghostly nebulae.

My virgin pushed the box to my lips and urged me to drink. A cool liquid glided down my throat, it tasted of fruit and electricity. I disconnected slowly, limbic communication, coruscating and primal, like the sound of glass guitars wired up and smashing violently into the billion possibilities of space. Some part of my will was hanging on to the constructs of reason. I snapped and let go, surrendering to a purer form of consciousness.

30 OCTOBER 1930
Later, up top. Sun on its downward arc.

'Lisala, Lisala,' the roof boys are chanting at us and pointing upstream.

'Lisala, Lisala.'

'What the fuck are they on about now, Bill?'

'Can't you see, Z? Your eyes must be more fucked than mine. There is some sort of town on the north bank upriver.'

'Oh yeah, looks like modern office blocks. How many miles do you think it is away?'

'Five.'

We watch as the flotilla slowly makes its way towards whatever Lisala is. As we get nearer we can see the town built on a hill, well not much of a hill but the only ground that rises more than a couple of metres above the river level we have seen since leaving Kinshasa.

Crispin joins us.

'That is one of the president's palaces.'

Crispin is pointing at a gleaming white building built on a rock promontory with lawns in front of it that sweep down to the port. Around the palace are other luxury homes.

'The president was born here on 30 October 1930.'

'Z, it almost looks like a pleasant suburb of San Francisco with the houses built on the hillside.'

'Well, the guide book did say 'a country of contrast'.

*

I was no stranger to mythic realities, I had conversed with many deities and their acolytes during my astral travels: the arrogant pantheon of the Ancient Egyptians, the Bloody gods of the Mayans; the heavy metal sword happy warriors of Islam and the black angels of Jihad; the pure blinding light of the trinity and all the ten billion Catholic angels.

But nothing, nothing had prepared me for this savage glory. This abominable beauty.

The stone butt plug blew as my body turned itself inside out, my dick boned up shedding its skin, unravelling and sliding off into a parallel cosmos. This B'witi cat didn't fuck around with formalities, that was fucking obvious. The next bunch of breakthrough shit was more familiar, lightning bolts and electric fire ripping up my backbone, psychedelic projectile vomiting. The usual psychoactive jungle plant crap only amplified through a Jodrell Bank-sized stack of Marshalls. Monstrous Mystery Babylon being buggered by a transsexual donkey-dicked Kali. Eight thousand simultaneous revelations backwards in negative technicolour.

Like I said the usual shit.

Then someone shifted the revelatory allegory machine to fast sidewind. The metaphysical symbolism doesn't cut ice down here in the Congo baby. Those banal beatitudes mean jack shit to the God Of The Animals. This was the divine revelations and the cool limbic intelligence of the Panther and the Crocodile.

IN A PIGALLE PORN PALACE

Z and I were flicking through the thousands of porn videos on offer.

'Bill, you're scared of looking into your soul.'

'No. I'm just not interested.'

'If you're not willing to explore the darkest corners of your soul, you will never be able to grapple with Satan. Forget all that bollocks about reshaping him for a new millennium. We're not going to bump into him round some street corner or even up the Congo. We all have to find our own dark angel. It's not like going bird nesting when you're a kid. Nobody else is going to find him for you. The poets can help light the way, they have been there before. It's down to you and me, Bill. So stop pissing about like it's some geography lesson.'

'I like geography.'

'Don't try and be funny, you're not good at it. Look Bill, do you know what a *comprachicos* is?'

'No.'

'A *comprachicos* buys children then makes them into freaks for the circus.'

'And?'

'And that is what we have to become.'

'But circuses don't have circus freaks anymore.'

'Listen Bill, we have to make our souls into monsters. As if we were implanting and cultivating warts on our own faces. We have to become clairvoyant and this is done by a long, immense and deliberate disordering of the senses. We have to taste every form of love, suffering and madness. We have to try every poison to retain only our quintessence. It is going to take super-human faith and strength. We will have to go through unspeakable torture. Only then can we become the arch-sufferer, the arch-criminal, the arch-damned soul and…'

'And what?'

'The supreme sages, Bill. We have to reach the unknown. Even if we end up mad and are unable to understand our own vision. We have to make that leap through to the unheard of and the unnameable. And even if we die in the process we will have lit the way for other horrible workers to come and carry on the work. I don't drink for fun.'

'No, you drink 'cause you're an alkie.'

'No, Bill, I have made myself the way I am for a purpose. It is only by becoming addicted to porn that you know what it is to be a truly fallen man. You've got to fall further than anybody has fallen before. Further than even Lucifer himself.'

'But, Z, I'm not interested in taking bad drugs and abusing small boys.'

'So what do you want, Bill? Sounds like you just want the glory. "Hey folks look at me, first I burnt a million and now, for my next trick, I'm going to reinvent Satan." It don't work like that. This ain't kindergarten.'

'Fuck off Z, you're spouting clichés.'

'What do you think Jesus was up to on his 40 days and 40 nights in the wilderness? For a start it wasn't 40 days and 40 nights. Forty is just used in the Bible as a symbolic number to mean a long time. Like Israelites spending 40 years in the desert. It means he spent all his young man years until he reached 30 allowing himself to be tempted by all Satan had on offer probably including bad drugs and small boys. To be truly the son of God he had to experience and succumb to every temptation that Satan could toss his way. He would have learnt nothing if he had just stood on the mountain going, "No thanks Lucy, not today, I can do without the worldly goods, the fleshpots. It does smell good but I had a fine breakfast of dung beetles and thistles, so I won't be needing any of that flesh-pot stew, tempting though it is." No Bill, Jesus would have had the lot, cleaned the flesh pots out.'

'Yeah, and?'

'And, it is only at that point that Jesus could have turned to Satan and say, "Is that it? Nothing more to tempt me with? No other sins of the flesh to stiffen my rod? No other gold and rubies for me to squander?" It would have only been then that he could have known the true breadth and depth of man's fallen state. And only then could he have done away with all the Old Testament notions of Satan, all that pulpit-thumping book of Job stuff. Only then could he have returned to the Sea of Galilee. Only then could he have fashioned the Sermon on the Mount.'

By now Z was getting a bit carried away, almost slipping into his southern firebrand-preacher mode.

'Excuse me sirs, but if you are not buying please move on.'

'Sorry, we forgot where we were.'

We returned into the neon-bathed night of Pigalle.

*

No redemption here, no second chances in this underworld. No mystical love bombing cheap tricks by the human recycle units of evangelicalism; no warm MDMA understanding of man's comfortable cosy little place in the universe; no natural Buddhist Christian Hindu New Age hippy shit dancing down in this trip, baby.

Scream louder pilgrim, there's no loving God on this fiery rollercoaster. Not down here with the ape lords and the perfection of the cockroach, all we have down here is pain, pain and teeth and gut-ripping mandibles. Here with the Tigers and the eels, killer whales, lions and eagles, the bone-crunching pack-raping jackals.

Blood and fucking and blood and death and rebirth, fucking, blood, death, birth, shit, death and more blood.

No joy, no peace, no Buddha, no Allah, no spiritual harmony, no father fucking Christmas. Just endless repetition sailor, can you dig it?

The shunting engine of paranoia, oily, silver and black, gargantuan and relentless beneath a black sun blowing its ear-splitting whistle as it smashes through the jungle. The unforgiving jungle. Here nothing can be trusted. Your mate will eat as soon as fuck you, these mothers eat their own children before they're born, ooethca omelettes easy over.

Where your last meal decides to eat you from the inside.

And Oh Mighty God the shit! The endless maggot-infested black rivers of stinking shit!

MIGHTY B'WITI bestows this savage knowledge!

The jungle God grants his unblind enlightenment, his practical knowledge, his Bad Wisdom! And it is this:

PARANOIA!

Constant paranoia.

Constant constancy, the heat of the shadow. This was B'witi's animistic enlightenment and it was terrifying.

Every shaman, every wise man and woman, every child of the forest was born with this black pearl of wisdom. It is in their blood, in their meat, bones and water, it is in the air that they breathe.

Constant vigilance, constant awareness. One fleeting momentary lack of concentration within this savage theatre can loose you a limb, an eye, a life, can grant an instant or lingering death. Only the jungle and its neutral spirits are important here.

We homo sapiens, lords of our conceited creation, are just more slabs of protein to the jungle, to the beetles and sweat flies, to the ants and the fungal parasites. Sweet red nectar for the jungle's deathly angel, the mosquito.

Speak his name in hushed tones. Revere his horror. Three dead syllables. A chant to frighten children.

MAL AR IAI.

In Italian it means bad air, here it means death. This is the knowledge B'witi gives.

Carry it like an African, in your blood. It is the only philosophy applicable beneath this dripping canopy of fecundity and death, where the cycle of life rolls speeding and reckless down the steepest slopes of eternity. All other creeds and guides for living here are worthless.

Judao-Christian, Islam, Buddhism: meaningless. Light from a dead star. Echoes from a dry well. Everything is vanity beneath Congo stars.

B'witi shits on your Gods of the East and West.

B'witi is the black God of reality.

Fear him fucking well pilgrim.

B'witi is the God of survival.

B'witi is the jungle.
Every grub, every bird, reptile and man.
Every breath of every thing,
Every drop of rain,
Every sound,
Every life, death and what is in between is B'witi.
Halle-fucking-luiah, brother
Can you dig it!!!!!!

TOUCHY

We bang into the dockside of Lisala.

'It looks nothing like a pleasant suburb of San Franciso. Just the usual broken-down, smashed-up shit. People risking their almost worthless lives as they leap ashore from the barges.'

We wait. Then disembark to have a look around. Crispin tags along with us. Market stalls selling the usual shit. Z hopes to find a bar. Crispin negotiates on our behalf to buy half-a-dozen rather bruised looking apples. They turn out not to be Cox's Orange Pippins, Russets or even Braeburns. They are not apples at all but some sort of soft fruit with one large stone in the middle but definitely not anything in the peach/plum family. I take a bite and spit the putrid flesh out on the ground.

'Fucking inedible.'

'Serves you right for eating fruit.'

I'm about to throw the rest of them away. Crispin, who guesses what I'm about to do, says, 'You don't like fruit, Bill? I eat them for you.'

'Hey Bill, what about this?'

'What the fuck is it Gimpo?'

'I guess it's pork meat.'

So we get ourselves chunks of sizzling hot pork, wrapped up in palm leaves with little wraps of chilli powder to dip into.

'At least McDonalds and Pizza Hut haven't arrived here yet.'

'It's what I could do with.'

'What, a pizza?'

'No, a Big Mac with fries.'

We sit and eat and watch a couple of heavily armed, badly dressed militia men saunter down the street giving out attitude.

'Z, Gimpo, I hate Africa. I hate everything about it. I hate the knowledge that if I was left here I would be crushed in a matter of days. It's not just the heat, it's the lack of anything to hope for. There is nothing here but grim, grinding reality. Everything is futile in face of the jungle and the oppressive authority.'

'This doesn't sound like you, Bill. You usually dig grim, grinding reality. I thought that was your thing.'

'It is, it is, but this is different. I like the grim and grinding of the north, of Eastern Europe, of… I don't know, the authority here isn't even oppressive like in the former Soviet Union. At least there was a logic to the oppression, you understood what it was about and why. Here it is just random, unplanned with no goal. I mean, those guys with the guns, if they went and slaughtered somebody later on today it wouldn't be for any reason other than barbarism, greed and downright badness. At least with the Stasi in East Germany when they were torturing you, you knew it was for the greater good of mankind.'

'What the fuck are you burbling on about now?'

'Well, they...'

'Who, they?'

'The East German Secret Police.'

'Ah yeah, them.'

'Well, they would be doing it because of some Marxist-Leninist principles they learnt at school and still believed in. This lot here don't believe in anything other than their own dick.'

'Come on, Gimpo, let's get Bill back to the boat before he starts getting dangerous.'

'Beel, you are wrong. This is a very beautiful country with much love, with only some very bad men. But our president, he will sort out the bad men. He will punish them. He will know. But now you must say nothing. Your friends are right, it is better we go back to our cabins.'

'OK, Crispin.'

*

For two days we coasted the black infinity of dead dreamless sleep. Twitching and sweating, coming down on broken ladders from the cataclysmic effects of the Ibogaine.

'You could lose it here,' said Bill, surfacing from the burning.

My head pounds, nostrils clogged with black powder, mouth coppery with blood.

'This place is claiming us, it doesn't want us to leave,' Bill again, serious.

We're still in the hut, spears of daylight cut through the holes in the woven roof.

'All the horror, blood, disease, it's conditioning us, steeling us,' he continued, trembling. 'It wants us to stay.'

Shaking badly, he steadies himself on the wall and massages his temples hard trying to rid himself of the skewering intensity of his headache.

BAUDELAIRE BILL, BAUDELAIRE

'Read Baudelaire, Bill. You have to read Baudelaire.'

'I know, you told me before.'

'But Bill, it was on these back streets of Paris that he watched the harpies, the tawdry vice-mongers, the boudoirs rancid with rotting flowers, Satan in all his defiant majesty. He was incapable of "shedding tears over vegetation" but in Paris he found sights and sounds as exhilarating as those your Wordsworth found in the lakes.'

When Z gets on one he can stay there for days, weeks, even months. I can remember when it was computer games. He would play them for 12 hours at a stretch and when he wasn't playing them he was talking about them. Not in a conversational way, more proselytising. It came over as if he felt he had a duty to convert everyone to playing computer games. 'Rock 'n' roll is the past, computer games are the future. Kids today don't give a shit about rock 'n' roll. You and I, Bill, we should get into making computer games. Or at least getting others to make computer games based on our ideas.'

It didn't last. Within a couple of years it had worn off. And when his latest flame, faze or craze wears off, he is back to poetry.

'Bill, poetry is the highest of the arts. Painting, music, movies, novels – none of them is stained with the history of the human soul, our fundamental condition, in the way that poetry is. The only reason man evolved writing was so that he could leave his poems for those yet to come.'
'I know, Z.'
'No you don't, Bill. Listen to this:

> *'"I give you these verses so that if my name*
> *happily lands in distant epochs*
> *and one evening those verses make the human spirit dream*
> *then that's as much as my artist can fuckin' do."*

'Baudelaire, Bill, Baudelaire!'
The thing is with Z, you just have to let him ride it out. I was banking on the fact that as soon as we were out of Paris all this Baudelaire stuff would be over.

Part Two
ALL THE SCUM OF THE JUNGLE

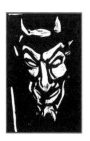

Chapter One
UNDERNEATH GOD

The Larium was kicking my perception of time through all kinds of strange jump-start dislocations. How we made it back to the *Colonel Ebeya* was anyone's guess. I was crunched into my bunk, my entire nervous system flayed raw, as if I'd been mindfucked by a gang of psychic gorillas. I opened up a gummy eye with my fingers. Things seemed normal enough, Gimpo masturbating gingerly, Bill fooling around with a bag of severed ears and a bloody combat knife. There was something else though.

The sound of violence outside the cabin, handguns popping, women's screams. A small kid ran into the cabin knocking Bill's ears into the shit on the floor, before he had time to react one of the guys from Mr Pitsu's cabin next door followed the kid in and started hacking into him with a machete.

Bill was pissed off, not only had they fucked up his ears, they were getting gristle and hair all over the place. He remonstrated with them and threw them out. He cursed the roofboys and their stupid gang shit. Each barge in the flotilla had its own posse of teenage gangbangers dedicated to mayhem and some illiterate understanding of the word 'respect'. Bill said there was some kind of a face-off going down. Old scores were being settled and the foundations of new ones being laid.

The gibbering rumours speculated that the Mai Mai were around the next bend in the river. The Mai Mai were some retard tribe of jungle punks, continually fucked out of their heads on yak and potent bush weed. The little fucks worshipped powerful water, that's what the faucets around their necks and the hose pipes filled with rocks and sand were all about. These kind of rumours were always running around the flotilla but the fact that the Eel had snipers positioned behind the funnels on the roof lent this one a little more weight.

Snark, the charismatic leader of the Bashielle Tigers ducked into our cabin, filling up the chambers of an old fashioned revolver. He stood flat against the wall peering out through the raggy curtain.

'Those motherfuckers is crazy, man,' he said, eyes wide, sweat beading on his forehead. 'Fucking brothers smoking jungle weed, think they're fucking invisible.' He turned anxiously towards us, eyes sliding psychotic.

He was wearing a pair of yellow bumblebee deely boppers over an old brown leather flying helmet.

'You met Mai Mai before, man?' he asked Bill, both hands holding the gun up against his cheek.

'At the Intercontinental in Kinshasha, yes,' said Bill.

'The Intercontinental?' barked Snark, incredulous. 'Those fuckers ain't rich!'

'Oh they weren't guests or anything,' adds Bill. 'They were raping nuns.'

Snark laughed. 'That sounds more like them. What were they raping nuns for?'

'I think they were part of some fucked-up coup. The Communist guy, what's his name? He was an old buddy of Che Guevara, Kabila, that's it, Joe Kabila.'

Kabila was an old-fashioned Communist, he'd been opposing Joe Mobutu for 30 years, working on his revolution deep in the northern territories. It looked like it was about to happen. In the mid 1960s Che Guevara was his guest, together they had tried to inspire a popular revolution similar to the one that kicked off in Cuba. Unfortunately the average jungle brother couldn't give a fuck, so Che went back to Cuba to get himself shot and take his place among the pantheon of good-looking dead t-shirt stars.

'So that's what all this shit is,' said Snark, pulling the curtain open a fraction and peering out nervously. 'All this weird shit going down since we left Kinshasha. Villagers throwing their voodoo on us, refusing to pay the rates they usually pay for all the plastic shit. Guns all over the fucking place. Looks like it's finally coming down.'

Revolution, yes sir.

These insane fucking Mai Mai are picking up on it. All that jungle weed and the yak is sensitising their antennae.'

Fuck, that's all this place needs, cannibal gangbangers shooting the shit out of the barges. This gang shit is bad enough, the last thing we fucking need is a bunch of water-worshipping cannibal assholes bringing down more meaningless violence.

THE MOMENT

Later. In the luxury bar of the *Colonel Ebeya*.

I've had a few beers. Maybe I've said it before but I'll say it again: there is nothing luxurious about this bar, it's a shit hole. Z has had a few beers more than me. He is in the mood for expanding and expounding on what he thinks about things. If what I'm about to report offends, don't hold it against Z. Tomorrow he may be saying something that comes from a completely different angle. He says what he says just for instant impact.

'What the fuck has Africa done for anybody? What has it left behind? Now take India. Great civilisation. Has risen, fallen and risen again. World religions, music, art, the best food in the world, Bollywood, beautiful clothes, beautiful women. Africans don't give a fuck about anything other than today.'

'Yeah Z, we know, I've already written about it.'

'But you won't have written about it properly. I know what I'm talkin' about. I understand the

African man. I not only empathise with his soul, there is a part of me that is African. Your African man lives for now, the moment. That is why he has no recorded history. What good is recorded history? We have only recorded our history to make us feel more important so we can look back at the past and wonder at the great things our forefathers have done instead of living for the now, or even worse, in the hope our sons and grandsons and great great great fuckin' grandsons will look back at us and think, wow, and he paid off his mortgage so I could have the title deeds for this patch of land.

The reason why your Africans haven't come up with a world religion is 'cause they know the future doesn't exist, only now. And especially any future that exists in an afterlife. Afterlives are for losers in this life. Africans live life to be won today. They make art for today. They make art that says, I'm here now. Look at me, not at him. Not what I did yesterday or last year or 500 fuckin' years ago. He doesn't make art for tomorrow, for him to be remembered. In the jungle nothing is remembered. Once something is dead in the jungle it is gone, eaten and consumed by a million other forms of life living for now. I'm right, Bill, am I not? You know.'

'But Z, you started this whole thing by saying the opposite, about how India is great and Africa is...'

'Yeah, yeah, Bill, I know but that is why I am even more right. It's like when you are with a woman and she wants to talk about how you treated her in the past, let her down, fucked her around, or she wants to talk about the future, where the relationship is going. As a man, what you have got to do is keep her mind in the present. You two together now. And that you should be living and doing for that moment in time. Who cares what was said and done last week, tonight is tonight and who the fuck knows what's going to happen tomorrow. Today is all we have and every real African nigger knows that. He walks down the street giving of the vibe. "Here I am babe, it's your lucky day. Yesterday is gone and tomorrow will just be too late but today I'm here."'

'So why the fuck are we bothering to redeem our souls or even write this book?'

'Don't be fuckin' stupid. I know that you're almost as thick as a normal person. We understand all this – at least I do, and you should do – that is why we can transcend it all. We are like Olympian gods that live for the moment and live forever. That is why I'm a rock god and you are not.'

'Was.'

'Was what?'

'A rock god.'

'What do you mean?'

'Well now you are just a bloke that fronts a band that tours toilets.'

'No, Bill. Once a rock god, always a rock god. It is because I dared to live for the moment that I will live forever.'

'Bollocks. You can only live forever in people's minds.'

'Yeah obvious.'

'And if they decide to live for the moment, they won't be bothered to carry the...'

'Shut the fuck up, Bill, and get your round in.'

And so to bed.

*

The sound of automatic rifle fire and handguns seemed to be increasing, without warning one of the Mai Mai lurched into the cabin carrying a severed head, shaking and screaming. The dusted maniac broke into some weird joint-popping jungle dance.

Snark cuffs him around the head with his revolver and puts a bullet in his face.

'You guys got any guns?' he snapped. 'These fuckers are boarding.'

He pulls back the door curtain, I could make out some nasty hand-to-hand slicing away up on the roof.

'This shouldn't take long,' says Snark confidently, reloading his gun and swinging the chamber back into position. 'These fuckers don't use guns, think they're invisible, reckon the bullets pass straight through their invisible bodies.'

He steps out into the fray shooting. I looked down at the dead kid on the cabin floor, his blood mingling with the slurry. He couldn't have been more than nine or ten, much younger than the recruits back in Kinshasha. A couple of kids fall into the cabin tearing into each other with teeth and knives. Snark stepped back into the cabin and grabbed a hold of the Mai Mai in the monkey-skin cloak and shot him in the back of the head. The barge kid starts hollering and snapping into a little victory stomp.

Snark removes the dead kid's scalp and attaches it to his belt.

'The older ones must be back in Kinshasha,' he says coldly. 'If Kabila's got these little punks into some kind of order... those pissed-off Rwandan Hutus... Burundi, Angola and all the other surrounding countries have been itching to get their hands on the diamonds for years.

'That baldheaded fat mother might just pull this shit off.'

The sound of heavy machine gun fire vibrates through the hull of the barge.

'The Eel,' says Snark, as serious as war.

'Fuck, these kids must be good. The Eel keep that thing in the hold at the back with the diamonds, they aren't ordinary Mai Mai. Those little fuckheads are usually back in the jungle by now.'

Snark grabs hold of the dead Mai Mai on the floor of the cabin and rips off the khaki utility belt hung around his dead shoulders. He empties it out on to the bunk and picks up a phial of dirty water.

'Magic water, to make them invisible.'

He shakes the belt again. A wrap made out of leaves containing a rough-looking brown powder falls out. Khaytura, jungle dust.

'Smoke enough of this shit, I'd believe I was invisible.' Snark pulls out a gold coin from one of the smaller pockets. 'Pirates,' he says under his breath. 'They're testing the Eel's fortifications, that machine gun just told them what they wanted to know. They wouldn't waste the bullets if we weren't carrying diamonds. These little fuckers are scouts, they'll report back to those old killers in the bush. We'll be boarded in the next couple of days, I'd bet my balls on it.'

Snark searches the rest of the pockets.

'We need intelligence. I'm going to have to grab a live one, we have to find out which crew we're up against. You guys don't mind if I interrogate the little fuck here, do you?'

He didn't wait for an answer.

Fucking river pirates, the shit just kept getting weirder. Jungle cutthroats skanking sideways on jungle hooch, cutting loose with AK47s. Those things don't discriminate when they start spunking lead.

The Mai Mai kid coughed straight away, not that it did him any good. As soon as Snark knew which pirates were waiting up-river he sliced his face off and threw it in the river.

'Liberians,' said Snark nervously. 'We're in deep shit, General Butt Naked and his cannibal crew.'

Snark looked worried. He had good cause. If the dead kid was telling the truth we were about to meet some of the most insane killers in the entire bloody history of Africa. Liberia had been at war for as long as anyone could remember, there were no clear-cut sides or any political objectives. Even within the insanity of war, this place stood out for its pointlessness. It was as if no one gave a shit, they just got off on the violence and chaos. It was as near war for war's sake as anyone could possibly imagine.

Founded in 1822 by a bunch of well meaning Americans calling themselves the American colonisation society this prime slice of West Africa was supposed to be a homeland for all the freed slaves wandering aimlessly around Uncle Sam's backyard. By 1847 the freed slaves had decided that they were just as good as whitey at fucking things up and ejected the American administration.

General Butt Naked, the guy waiting up around the bend, had been in all manner of coups and counter- coups, he'd even ran the place for a few days but decided that global politics wasn't his bag. Arabs and Americans, too much hassle. He headed into the bush in 1996 and hasn't looked back since. He made plenty of Yank dollars supplying the slavers with fresh meat and the odd diamond windfall enabled the man and his crew of happy killers to party hearty for most of the year.

What we didn't know at this stage was that it wasn't just Butt Naked and his boys waiting for us up on that wild bend in the river, the whole fucking scum of the jungle were there, kicking back, farting easy and polishing up their guns.

DRUMMOND'S LOG, SUNDAY 16 JUNE 1996
SUNDAY MORNING

Sunday morning, lying in my bunk singing The Velvets, except I can't remember any of the lines so I just keep singing 'Sunday Morning', over and over again until Gimpo says, 'Time for church, Bill.'

'For fuck's sake, you two aren't still doing your "Jesus wants me for a sunbeam" bit?'

I don't answer.

Chapter Two
THE WANKERS OF PARIS

Drummond's secret log, The Congo, date unknown

Paris seems a lifetime away, yet it can't have been that long ago, a month, a year, two? I can't be sure of anything anymore.

Kiki? Was he a dream.

No, of that I am sure. It's the Larium, the Larium and Rolo, conspiring, playing evil games with my mind. After he killed Tally in the shower he disappeared into the sour guts of the flotilla to nurse his mystical revenge. I haven't seen him since. I rarely leave the cabin now.

The only way I can keep my sanity tied together is by trying to remember all the details of how I got here, half-way up the most notorious river in the world, the Congo – its very name synonymous with transcendental evil and subhuman cruelty.

I need to examine everything, try and find some clues. I have to keep a balanced perspective of the past no matter how twisted and insane the present appears to be.

Paris, yes Paris. Z and I both knew that magic city of louche wickedness well : the fresh ghosts of the previous century still carousing its boulevards, some of them unaware that they were even dead. We thought the city and its ghosts could perhaps throw us a few clues.

Perhaps even present us with a fleeting glimpse of the dark lord himself. Yet in our heart of hearts we always knew that all roads would lead us to this dreadful place. It was as inevitable as the duplicity of whores.

We are both to different degrees blessed and cursed with the gift of the shining. Both of us has the ability to stand adrift in time, to walk with ghosts. Sadly our skills are not disciplined, our co-ordinational abilities haphazard. Alcohol and other stimulants can pull all manner of time shifts into the accidental breach.

We were outside the Sacre Coeur, the magnificent white church that overlooks the Pigalle. It was cold for the time of year.

Z was unstable, the brandy in his hip flask potent.

The century was uncertain, it kept shearing between epochs from this century and the last. So smoothly were these time shifts leaning into each other it was hard to tell there was anything strange happening at all.

In the distance, towering high over the venereal black canyon of the Pigalle in red neon letters seven-feet high, garish against the muted colours of the early winter twilight, loomed the dread legend: SEXODROME. The cunt-red sign leered down from atop the five-storey sex supermarket.

WHY SCOTS WOMEN ARE SO UGLY

...But we were still in Paris and still stumbling down backstreets, looking for something.

'Beauty, Bill, is the only thing worth searching for, living for, even dying for.'

'But we won't find beauty down these streets. We may as well be in Soho, going to the Coach & Horses for a pint.'

'Bill, listen to this:

'"Do you come from deep heaven or do you come from Hell,
O Beauty? Your eyes, infernal and divine,
Pour out both goodness and crime,
And for that you can be compared to wine.

It is of little consequence whether you come from heaven or Hell,
O Beauty! Huge terrifying, artless monster!
If your eyes, your smile, your feet open for me the gate
Of an infinity I love and have never known.

From Satan or God, what difference! Angel or siren,
What difference, if you make – O fairy soft eyes,
Rhythm, perfume, light, O my one queen –
The universe less hideous and time less heavy?"

'Bill, Baudelaire was right, beauty isn't only a god-given thing. The beauty that Satan can provide is just as valid, just as strong, just as justified. There is nothing quite like the beauty in the eyes of a young whore. You know that in ten years, five years, no maybe even just two years, that beauty will have gone, been burnt out, crushed. But you see, Bill, it's the transient nature of beauty that gives it its potency. A true artist is a man who's addicted to beauty. Who makes no moral judgment about it. But celebrates that beauty wherever it comes from.

And it's not just the beauty of a teenage whore. All beauty can only ever be truly moving when it is transient. A sunrise, a rose, a sunset. A true artist understands that it is not only his calling but his duty to go out into the world and try to capture those fleeting moments of beauty in whatever way he can and hold up what he has caught to show the rest of mankind. To search out beauty in the most unlikely of places. Of course it's a futile mission because whatever beauty we capture it too fades, corrodes, gets lost, forgotten. A day will come when even the Mona Lisa will fade and fall to bits. But now, as always, the ultimate beauty is that of a beautiful woman.'

'Z, I don't like beautiful women.'

'You don't mean that. You're just trying to be perverse.'

'I do mean it. Beautiful women become corrupted by their own beauty. They learn very early in life that their beauty gives them a power over those around them. Not just eager suitors but rival females or when they go for jobs. They end up believing in their beauty but because they also know the nasty corners of their own soul, they lose respect for all those who fall for their beauty, treat them with disdain, basically they become ugly people. They...'

'Bill! Bill! That's obvious. We've all made arseholes of ourselves falling for beautiful women. The admiration may be mutual but still she perceives you as weak, another mug. Respect is lost. But if you give into that, you will cripple your psyche, mutilate your very soul. You have to worship her beauty, be in love with that alone. When appreciating the beauty of a rose you don't worry what the rose thinks about you or how it treats other roses. It is the same with a woman – a beautiful woman is a goddess. The Greeks knew it, the Romans knew it, Hollywood knows it. Worship her now because very soon her beauty will fade and the flame will have been passed on to another younger goddess for us to worship. You have to be strong to worship the beauty of a woman...'

By now I was hardly listening to what Z was going on about. Not that I'd heard it all before but when Z starts banging on about a subject endlessly you just close down.

'…It's just your fucked-up repressive Presbyterianism. You've got to get rid of it, dump it, grow out of it. Find your pagan roots. No wonder all Scots women are so ugly. I never met one Scots groupie worth shagging.'

'What the fuck are you talking about Z. There are plenty of fine-looking Scots women.'

'No, Bill, and this is the reason why. Over the past few hundred years the Presbyterian majority in Scotland has shared your perverted aversion to beautiful women, thus they have been bred out of the gene pool.'

'Fuck off.'

'Fact.'

*

We made our way down from Montmartre, through the winding streets, lured like moths towards the black cathedral of Onan. What a place this was. I could feel my heart banging against my sternum, thrashing like a caged beast. We stood hypnotised in front of the wankers' Mecca. Its entire facade including the large ornate windows was painted a light-guzzling matt black. Strange architectural details hid in the long shadows as the sun dithered in the west, a bloody orb retreating from the intricate carvings that seemed to grow from the stone walls like some gothic disease.

It was only later that I found out about the history of the unholy place. Its notorious reputation had climaxed around the end of the last century when the building housed the infamous French chapter of the Catamite club. The remains of dozens of sacrificial infants, victims of a nineteenth-century Gilles de Rais were discovered by undercover agents of the gendarmerie. Their tiny bones and pickled innards were used as ghastly ornamentation among the plush velvet and gilt of the Catamite's private catacombs.

The club members fled like bats before sunlight when their nefarious anal activities were exposed by the French authorities. Most escaped to the sewers of the East and the pissoirs of North Africa, Tangiers in particular. The building was boarded up and left empty for decades, the owners never traced. Among municipal records there was no trace of it ever existing. The city fathers appropriated the shameful building and it was put up for sale. Unsurprisingly, despite its prime location no one was interested in buying the five-storey property. It was said to be haunted by the ghosts of the dead children murdered by the buggers of the Catamite. Blasphemy and evil clung to its walls like black ivy.

It wasn't until some time in the mid 1980s when only the most feeble and elderly Parisians could remember the legends of vice and Sodom that surrounded the black building that it slowly re-emerged. It was there on the most degenerate mile of that famous street that the shadowy masturbators of Paris suddenly noticed its existence. One minute there was nothing, just torn posters and graffiti surrounding derelicts cozy in their vermin drinking cheap vin de shite in its shadowy doorway and then as if by magic, the biggest sex supermarket in Europe.

The tunnel-visioned masturbators who never noticed anything that wasn't surrounded by flashing lights, oiled breasts, baggy gash and prolapsed buggery sockets, just assumed it had always been there and that somehow they'd missed it on their previous five-fingered missions. Because of the nauseous black magic oozing from the cramped shops and bars that huddle closely together in this part of Paris, its habitués lose all track of time when visiting its fleshpots. The gallic tuggers believe that they only spend a few minutes on odd days of the month there, browsing nonchalantly the transgressive wares stacked along the walls of hundreds of small shops.

Few are aware of exactly how much time they really spend haunting the sickly scented interiors of these places. So it is not surprising that the lonely gentlemen of Pigalle did not notice the sudden appearance of this towering monolith when it manifested itself some time during their absence.

They merely traipsed through the black and chrome doors, similar to a thousand other joints in the area, and seemed surprised when they realised that they'd never visited the place before.

FAITH WANING

The church service is being held this morning in the luxury bar of the *Colonel Ebeya* and I'm afraid to report it has lost its novelty for me. The highlight of the service is when Z wanders in hoping to get his breakfast beer to find the bar is closed until the church service is over.

*

And what a place it was. A veritable wanking wonderland. Five whole floors stacked to bursting with all manner of tuggers' delights. Thousands and thousands of private wanking booths, where for a few francs just about any pornographic film ever made could be selected by computer and played on to the small TV screen in the private booth. Some booths even had more than one screen where the more accomplished tugger could watch up to four films at the same time in his private world of masturbatory ecstasy.

Of course videos were only one of the services available at the Sexodrome. There were private striptease booths, telephone sex booths, psychiatric counselling, you name it. For a few francs anything apart from regular ordinary sex with a real woman was available in this masturbators' Disneyland.

Unsurprisingly the SEXODROME was a phenomenal success with ordinary masturbators as well as the mentally ill compulsives. Men from all over Europe flocked to the black building in droves. It was open 25 hours a day, every day, all year round. Standing on the hill outside the Sacre Coeur you could see them, the wankers of Paris, like ants swarming through the winding streets to the black building and its shrines of chicken choking. The blood gorging their swollen organs they were drawn by some strange blood-tide magnetism, led by invisible sirens to this throbbing primal centre, this unholy cathedral of tug.

I had a bad bad feeling as Z and I stood across the Pigalle staring into the chrome mouth of the SEXODROME its black swing doors constantly in use as the sperm-drained slaves of the 'drome passed in and out. There was an anxiety in their gait and a creepy luminescence about the eyes of these lost souls as they hurried along the last few yards before entering the 'drome, a burning desperation as they practically flung themselves through the doors.

Those leaving the 'drome, creeping out into the fading sunlight gave off almost the opposite vibrations. A gaunt serenity hung upon their hollow cheeks and slack features. Out they slid in slow motion, temporarily sated, eyes half closed, a ball of soggy Kleenex gripped loosely in their scrawny hands. They would wander around close by until that impatient monkey lurking in their sperm-stained underwear demanded more heat.

WE WILL HAVE THE BOY

'Shall we get something to eat?'

'If you drank more, you wouldn't have to eat so much.'

'Look! I need to eat, you can watch me while you drink.'

Ten minutes later we were sitting in a Persian restaurant. The place was empty. The owner looked enough like Saddam Hussein's younger brother to inspire Z to a torrent of fancy.

'Good evening gentlemen, you must be the world famous Literary Arseholes.'

'Why yes, sir, we are. But how did you know?'

'Well I could not help but notice the yo-yoing technique of this handsome young man as he entered my humble establishment and then after you broke wind and my nostril became acquainted with the distinguished fragrance of your fart it left me in no doubt that my humble restaurant was being graced by a visit from the world famous pair of authors. Let me introduce myself, Sodom Hussein, restauranteur and procurer of young boys for my more refined guests but no, I'm racing ahead, we will leave the boys until later. First I will slaughter a ram at the table in honour of your visit. He has the biggest testicles you have ever seen.'

He turns his head towards the swinging doors that lead into the kitchen and bellows:

'Kiki. Bring in the ram. The one with the biggest balls, and bring my knife.'

To Z's delight it was the Kiki we had last seen in Toledo. Kiki came through the swing door dragging the ram. On seeing me he almost seemed to be overcome with emotion.

'Beeill, Beeill. You have come to save me.'

Sodom instantly kicked the small but perfectly formed Arab boy to the ground.

Z, whose stomach does not agree with mutton, turned to our host.

'Sodom, kind sir. Let this fine ram go. We will have the boy instead.'

'Your wish is my...'

And just as he was about to slash poor Kiki's throat in finest halal-butcher style, young Kiki made a dash for the front door and freedom. Sodom is down on his knees begging for our forgiveness.

'I have failed you, great Arseholes. What can I do but offer my life?' And without another word he plunged his knife deep into his own heart and collapsed to the floor, dead.

This tale is what I can remember of Z's running commentary of what was happening while we ate our way through a rather dull meal of couscous and kebabs.

On the street from the Persian restaurant to our room in Pigalle we passed a bar. In the window sat a middle-aged man with wire-rimmed specs. He looked weary with life. His wife obviously didn't understand him but the two women sitting on either side of him stroking his back and his neck clearly did. It was a tender scene. What made it all the more poignant was the red light that bathed and highlighted the more crucial elements of this moving scene. The deep cleavage of the young ladies, the open wallet lying on their table, the tear trickling down the man's cheek.

Z was suggesting we should enter the bar and see if we could be of any assistance, when we heard a screech of brakes, a scream and then the unmistakable sound of steel being concertina'd into a brick wall.

We ran around the corner. I can't remember the reality of what we found. I suppose a minor accident. What I can recall is Z's libretto to the operatic ending of Kiki's short life. I think it went something like this:

'Kiki lay on the ground, only his sweet face could be seen lit by the gas street lamp, the rest of his body was underneath a gendarme's patrol car. I ran forward, sank to my knees, cradled his innocent face in my lap. We declared undying love for each other and as I kissed his tender lips, watched his eyelashes flutter as I had done so many times before, this careless life left for a better place. Somewhere a lonely dove flew above an oriental bridge, forever alone.'

Reality. We got back to the hotel, once I had persuaded Z that our search for Satan did not require us to visit every late-night bar and porn shop we passed on the way.

*

In our modern tolerant society the chronic masturbator is surely the most hard done by. No 12-step programme for Onan Sam, no Betty Ford clinic for celebrity tuggers and their crippling illness. The accursed sufferer of this morbid addiction in a cruel twist of irony has no one but himself to turn to as his chronic abuse turns into a terrible wasting disease that wears away at his tormented soul like the ocean continually battering a crumbling cliff.

The inevitable decline into terminal imbecility of the unfortunate wanker is subtle and irreversible, the steady increase in his pornographic addiction developing slowly from an innocuous trickle into an unstoppable deluge. All his time and money is feverishly dedicated to this unwholesome habit. His self respect, his job, family and friends are all eventually sacrificed upon the sperm-spattered altar of this uncontrollable god.

And of course, the priests of this depraved cult – men like Fat Miguel – grow rich upon the ruination and despair of these damned souls pummelling their way around the final circle of masturbators' hell. Z did not seem in thrall to the same grave awe and trepidation that had gripped me. In fact he seemed quite keen to enter this syphilitic church.

I remember the shrill insanity as we entered the chrome doors and were assaulted by wave after wave of grotesque sensations. The sweet sickly smell of fresh sperm and disinfectant made me gag. The deafening disco music, rattling through huge speakers. A woman's ecstatic moans reverberating across the pumping bass lines as if she was being fucked to death in outer space. Flashing lights strobing madly like epileptic wank-fits. And of course everywhere you turned, huge red photographs of dripping, blood gorged, jizz splattered genitalia, male and female. A visual cornucopia of freakishly large jutting silicon tits, lips and arses.

Echoing across all of this, a man's booming voice amplified as loud as god, repeating numbers in a sleazy French accent. These were the numbers of whatever girl was performing what in which booth. A complex system of tuggers' algebra. There were pictures of the girls along one wall where they looked at the camera while sucking on bell ends and each other's bumholes. I noticed a selection of 'on offer' videos piled high next to the photographs of the booth girls. A large selection of bestiality stacked and classified into jungle, farm, domestic, fish and fowl. Strange photographs of women sucking off giraffes and men buggering sea lions.

The sheer number of private booths was mind-blowing, these private shrines of Onan stretched into an apparent infinity, an illusion created by mirrors which were attached to any surface not festooned by pictures of dripping vaginas and threatening erections.

Solitary men rushed from booth to booth, carrying bags of francs and boxes of Kleenex, each one lost in his own kaleidoscopic hallucination, oblivious to his fellow obsessives.

Chrome stairs led up into an incredible world of carefully delineated interests. A blinking LED sign flashed the encrypted code of the tugger. First floor: straight sex, oral, anal, dorsal (dorsal?), solo, bondage. Second floor: S/M, copro, kinder, animal, piss. Third floor: lactating mamas, homeless buggery, extreme S/M, cannibal, lesbian, animal. The lists went on and on, these were merely the ones I could recognise. The depths and intricacies of the tugger's imagination was staggering in its variety and profusion if nothing else. The demon fishing for men's souls in this fetid sea had certainly cast his net as far and wide as possible.

Z hurtled up the stairs clutching a bag of coins, he shouted over his shoulder that he would meet me in the tuggers' bar in half an hour, he was going to do some research. My Presbyterian soul blanched. I stepped quickly to the fifth floor to search for an appropriate screening to calm my nerves. Fortunately I was in luck, the art-house classics *Kinky Blood Babes Anal*, *Murder Bloodbath Sex Wank Frenzy*, *Perverted Surgeon* and *Bell-End Blood Feast Of Buenos Aires* were all being screened in the booths.

BREAKFAST WITH GIMPO

'Where did you get the bread, Gimpo?'

'Off Remi.'

'It's like real French bread. How the fuck did he get it? There is nowhere on board to bake bread or else we would already be aware of it. And it certainly didn't come out of the jungle.'

'And I've got peanut butter.'

'Great.'

'Do you know whose that green shirt is?'

'Yeah, that bloke who wears a green shirt and is a mate of Remi's.'

'Well, he's not a mate. Remi says he is an informer.'

'Informing what to who?'

'He informs to the onboard militia about what is going on with the traders. Lets them know about the rivalries, who's doing well, who's not, who's worth leaning on, who's stashing away the most.'

'And does this affect us?'

'Remi says that Green Shirt has been making a number of enquiries about us. He reckons we should be on our guard if the militia decide to lean upon somebody. They are ruthless.'

'What the fuck are we supposed to do? Go to the police? They *are* the police.'

*

I took my pen and notepad and dodged inside to take notes, searching for clues to the whereabouts of the immortal keeper of our souls. If any area of research was able to shed light upon the darker zones of the human condition, and the self-destructive nature of our species, it would be found here in these graphic dramas of our splintered libidos.

Proof of the power, if nothing else, of the devil's handiwork was evident in the fact that I lost two whole days on the fifth floor of the SEXODROME only surfacing for air to replace my exhausted supply of man-sized tissues and five-franc pieces. I can barely recall anything of those lost hours, the films had some kind of strange hypnotic effect. I had changed another thousand pounds into francs and was making my way back to the fifth floor when I heard Z calling me from the doorway of The Silver Sperm, a darkened drinking hole set into a recess of the second floor.

This was a weird floor: Lewis Carroll fans and the scat monkeys, spastic and amputee sex aficionados. I felt superior to these tuggers, I knew that my fifth-floor obsessions were of a philosophical and spiritual nature… like the misunderstood genius of men like profound thinker Dennis 'Monochrome Man' Nielsen or the North American aesthete and shrine builder, Jeffrey Dahmer.

THE LIZARD KING

Later.

The flotilla pulls up at another town. This one is called Bumba. I can muster up little excitement. The dockside has a couple of towering cranes, neither in working order. Z says something about relics of a vanishing civilisation. We wander dusty lanes looking for a shady bar. We clamber through a hole in a wall on to what must be the main street. No hustle or bustle. No tropical vibe. I mean, no tropical vegetation trying to take over vibe. We find an open-air bar.

The barmaid pulls out three bottles of Primus from the cooler and pops the tops before we even ask. The bar is not worth describing. This is a place you don't want to be. Nothing ever happens here, not even bad things. Z is off again on one of his monologues, about the usual I guess, about how he knows everything about the human condition, but I'm not listening. I'm watching a lizard on a wall. I don't want either of the other two to see the lizard. I want it to be my thing and my thing alone.

'You see, Bill, George Orwell was right. Give the people no choice, give them Victory Gin or Victory Fags. Here it's the same, give them Primus beer or…'

His voice just goes on and on. Gimpo has got his snuff box out and we all have a go.

'You see, Bill, we are on the side of the angels… blah, blah, blah…'

I remember Z once saying in an interview something I thought was quite clever.

'So, tell me, Mister Mindwarp, where do you stand politically?' asked the interviewer. And Z replied, 'I have a right wing and I have a left wing. I am an angel.'

I still think it was a really smart thing to say. Mind you, it was probably a quote he nicked from somewhere.

'So Bill, what do you think?'

'About what?'

'About what I've just been talking about for the last ten minutes.'

'About having a left wing and a right wing?'

'No! I haven't mentioned anything about wings. About…'

'Sorry, my mind just drifted.'

'I think you are losing it. You just look empty all the time, like you are not really here.'

The lizard has now come down off the wall, skittered across a few yards of open ground and is now on the trunk of a large tree. He circumnavigates the tree and is looking back at me.

'Mobutu has let any infrastructure that the Belgians left behind crumble and fall to bits. Without any infrastructure or working road or rail routes in the country a co-ordinated revolution cannot be mounted. There can be local insurgencies but they can always be squashed. He doesn't need the country to make money from industry, he doesn't need to raise money from taxes. As far as he is concerned it is better the country stays dirt poor. All the people's energies go into just staying alive, scraping by. No time or inclination left for revolution. Mobutu gets all the wealth for himself and to keep his generals onside with the CIA. The CIA keep paying whatever he asks because they are frightened he may go Soviet. They need him because 99 per cent of the world's reserves of uranium are found in the Congo Basin.'

The lizard has run round the tree again but this time the same way it came before. I wonder if he has been given a Latin name and if he is rare or can be found all over Central Africa or if anybody has ever done a PhD on him.

'Bill, I've been thinking, we have to be prepared to be able to defend this book when it comes out. People might think it's just a load of racist, sexist, fantasy twaddle. We have to come up with a rationale, how the whole thing is an analogy for...'

Although I'm still watching the lizard I've begun to listen to Z again.

'Z, the book stands and falls on its own merits.'

'Yeah I know that's the way it should be but people need pointers, they need to be shown how to understand what we have written.'

'But Z, it *is* racist, sexist, fantasy twaddle. It's what we do. We can't pretend otherwise.'

'Yeah I know Bill, but it is more than that. It is genius.'

'Well fine, if it is a work of genius it will be recognised. Genius will out and all that.'

'But Bill, I wouldn't mind a bit of that genius outing in my lifetime. I would like to see the rewards, even if they aren't financial.'

'Melville got none. He was long dead before *Moby Dick* was seen to be the great American novel that all others are compared to. He didn't go around giving interviews about what Captain Ahab and the Moby Dick symbolise. Anyway, the best we can hope for is Beavis & Butthead meet Huck Finn on one of his adventures.'

'Yeah, maybe you are right, but I still think we should...'

And he is off again and I am back watching the lizard. Maybe this lizard is the central character to the unfocused whole. If you, I, we, were to understand what motivates this lizard we could unlock the whole thing. Is this lizard racist or sexist? Is his skittering around the tree, first clockwise then anticlockwise just him entering into a fantasy about being something he is not at all. And why do I transform all the animals I write about into males? That's it, I've got it. This book is *Tales From The River Bank* for a post rock 'n' roll generation. Bedtime reading for the year 2053.

'In your dreams,' says the lizard.

Gimpo says, 'We better be getting back to the boat.'

And as if on cue we hear the ship's horn from some distance. The lizard climbs into a hole in the tree trunk.

*

'Any luck?'

Z wanted to know if I'd discovered any semiotic clues from my fifth-floor research. Indeed I had but it was almost impossible to disentangle the information clearly from its esoteric content without a few days in the British Library to cross-reference some of the more archaic perversions. Detecting satanic influence within the theatre of extreme forms of pornography is a subtle science.

The actors and crew, fluffers, sound recordists – everyone involved in the production – all seem to be under the influence of some form of communal ecstatic possession. Many are said to believe that they are taken over by Dionysian spirits, satyrs, fawns and the like. Few, in particular the actors, remember what they were doing in their captivated state and are often deeply spooked when witnessing the first playbacks. As the depths of degradation are plumbed, the possession takes on more intense and terrifying characteristics.

Interestingly, the lower one sinks in the degradation stakes the more consensual the acts are likely to become. For instance, that most extreme form of S/M, consensual snuff. The victims, the ones that are actually snuffed, grant their murderer permission to kill them. Things are not always what they seem down among the bilgewater of sado-masochism.

The snuffee believes that by granting his snuffer permission to kill him or her that they are subjecting their killers to the ultimate degradation and therefore turning the whole dynamics of the ritual upon its head. They believe that they are reducing the snuffer to that most base and loathed piece of human dogshit, the lustmord killer, the sex killer, the nonce. They in return are elevated, at least in their own minds, to the iconic status of helpless victim and martyr.

'I don't know, it's hard to say,' answered my fellow sleuth.

'They have an amazing collection of videos,' I replied, 'Some I have only even read about. What I suggest is that we purchase some of the more extreme tapes and review them frame by frame. Demons are on the whole rather playful and like to leave some kind of signature as proof that they once had possession of a particular human being. If the dark Lord is indeed present in Paris, the whereabouts of his minions may be helpful.'

I ordered a beer from the sex crone serving behind the bar. She must have been in her 60s at least, her sagging body squeezed into a vinyl catsuit like sausage meat.

The French hag smiled baring her yellow nicotine-stained teeth, dog sperm on her breath. She handed me the beer and dropped a stunning fanny fart.

I LOVE BESSY

I was already in my pyjamas and in my bed. Z must have assumed I was asleep. I could hear him struggling with the phone. It was an old-style dialling phone. In between each attempt to dial he would curse, give up, then start again. I assumed he was attempting to get through to some one-to-one porn chatline. He had told me he was cured of this addiction when his girlfriend confronted him with the phone bill with all the ludicrously over-priced 0898 calls on it that had obviously not been made by her. Do I put my head under the pillow and try and not hear whatever he is up to?

'Hello, it's me.'

'...................'

'Yeah, we'll be back tomorrow.'

'...................'

'No. He's asleep.'

'...................'

'Yeah. OK. It's gone well.'

'...................'

'Yes. I love you too.'

'...................'

'I can't say that, Bill might hear.'

'....................,'
'But...'
'....................,'
'OK. OK. I love Bessy.'

So dear reader, there we have it. My fellow Literary Arsehole, arctic explorer, former rock god and man who only hours ago was suggesting to me that we bag ourselves a brace of Nip girls each, do them, then chuck 'em over the side of the Sacre Coeur, is capitulating to his girlfriend's demands to declare his love for their kitten, Bessy.

I fell asleep a happy man.

*

'Look at this,' said Z.

I noticed the tug stains down the front of his pants, why couldn't he use Kleenex like everyone else?

'Some spindly tugger gave it to me just before you came. He'd been up on the fifth floor, tall geezer, shaking like a leaf he was.'

Z passed me a small gilt edged card, I read the florid copperplate writing. 'Gustave Moreau, Sensualist' it said, followed by an address and a small Aubrey Beardsley pen and ink drawing of an elegant bell end jizzing its nadjam over the word sensualist.

'What is it?' I asked, intrigued.

'I'm not sure, the guy said he'd seen me checking out the scat vids and apparently he'd heard you moaning and banging around in the booth next to him up on the fifth floor. He said he recognised the soundtrack to *Bell-End Blood Feast Of Buenos Aires*. He mumbled something about connoisseurs and le diable. He was speaking a strange aristocratic French, it was hard to understand. Spooky fucker, a big old scar across his throat, looked like someone had tried to cut his head off.'

Gustave Moreau, the symbolist painter. I was familiar with his work, enormous visionary canvases swirling with all manner of blasphemies and corruption. Incredibly detailed, the majority of them painted while under the influence of absinthe and Ibogaine. Moreau rarely finished any of his works. He blamed this on his drinking friend, Charles Baudelaire, the Satanic poet and dandy.

We made our way down to the basement. Aisle after aisle of magazines, videos, inflatable women, men and animals. Adult board games, cuddly toys with massive dicks – what poor little bastard was going to get one of those from Santa?

Z chucked a couple of videos into his basket: *East European Horn Smokers Being Buggered And Thrown From Speeding Cars By Wealthy Americans* and *White Schoolgirls From South America Being Ripped In Two Up Their Arses By Niggers With Massive Dicks*.

'Z,' I interrupted, 'These run-of-the-mill American titles, we don't need them, get some of the more extreme stuff, the German and Japanese ones.'

I made a quick selection *Unfurled Frauleins*, *Gut Suckers*, *Lungfish For Fun* and *Kidney Anal Sandwich*. These were relatively soft core compared with the stuff up on the fifth floor. I looked around for a member of staff. A wizened old Chinaman stepped out from behind a curtain smiling and pretended not to be able to understand English until I told him I was looking for more extreme and more expensive examples of the pornographer's art.

The old wanking Chink smiled and showed me into a small cupboard behind the till. An Aladdin's cave of snuff, racked to the ceiling. I spied the seminal classic, *Plasma Creep*. I could feel my heart beating faster behind my ribs, my breathing speeding up, along with *BoneJelly Reducer*.

My god, I sighed to myself, these were classics of the genre. I was convinced that *Jelly* as it's known among the cognoscenti didn't even exist anymore. *Plasma Creep* was one of the first quality snuff films ever made. It was produced in the 1970s by a bunch of skeezy heroin-addict actresses, ex-Hollywood players, a couple of producers and a flash-in-the-pan director who needed the money. All of their drug problems had hit the downward spiral and they were all massively in debt to the mob.

An arrangement was made with the ex-players and the Mafia guys to produce a series of porno reels which entailed a brothel-full of South American whores being slowly tortured to death for real. They made about seven or eight films, some footage of which had somehow been transferred on to videotape, hence the film's international notoriety.

Appalling quality tapes of the films in their entirety fetch hundreds of thousands of dollars on the international jet-set pervert circuit. Here in the SEXODROME were four of the debauched classics. The only person known to personally own any of these black masterpieces is of course that international überperve, Fat Miguel. And there they were, *Creep* and *Jelly*, along with the snuff comedy classic *Cannibal Cocksuckers*. I bought all four and headed off to our hotel.

A SENSE OF SMELL

Back up in the luxury bar.

'My sense of smell has gone completely.'

'What do you mean?'

'I mean I can't smell anything.'

'How come?'

'I reckon it's gone on strike. Can't cope with any more of this putrid, festering jungle river stuff.'

'So do you think you usually have a good sense of smell?'

'If any woman passing me on the street is having her period, I can smell it.'

I sip my Primus and wonder if Z is telling the truth. Then I decide he is. It's the sort of useless thing that he could do.

'Gimpo, what are you thinking?'

'I'm thinking...'

'No, I don't want to know. I don't think the reader should know what you are thinking it would just put them off their stride, stroke, food or beer.'

'Bill, have you ever been to Disneyland?'

'No, why?'

'I wish we had gone to Disneyland instead.'

THE BOOK OF GIMPO BY GIMPO

Shit is coming down double weird now, I'm getting the jumps big time.

My arse is just about mended, haven't had a dump for about three days. Just laid still on my bunk hallucinating on those fucking horse pill malaria tablets. I managed to blag some morphine ampules from the bogus doctor they have here. He's just some regular Congo guy, naked except for a white coat he's found somewhere.

He has a stall full of medicines dumped on the third world when they're discovered to be poisonous and shit. What it usually means is that the side effects are being sought out by low-lifers like me to get a buzz from them, either that, or causing pregnant women to end up with flipper kids, Thalids, mongs and stuff.

Seeing as the labels are all written in English I can't figure how any of these jungle fuckers know which medicines to buy anyway. The doctor doesn't have a clue what any of the stuff is. I asked him for something to stop the shits and the fucking idiot gave me a box of Thalidomide. It seems you take a guess at what you want and then he just charges a price off the top of his head.

I noticed a box of morphine ampules among his stash, the kind with a big needle attached to a glass ampule. They store these things in life rafts. It's good, we used to boost them from the army supplies depot and get blasted on them in the Falklands. I had a rucksack full of them when I got demobbed. That's how I got to know Z. Intramuscular, that's what it was called. You stab the needle into your thigh and break the glass, the gear gets sucked into your leg by a vacuum and seconds later you're flying to the moon. I bought a couple of boxes from the bogus doc and banged three of them up into my leg and waited here till my arse healed up. After the third day I turned invisible, just melted away, slack gob gouching, spunky and dribbling, talking to the lord and all his soft-focus angels.

I can hear Bill up on his bunk above me freaking out. Talking to himself about bell ends and Buenos Aires, laughing out loud. He started shouting about Paris and the sex drome, whatever that was.

I can hear him writing with that big stupid carpenter's pencil. He's wanking like nobody's business as well, big dollops of jizz flying over the side of his bunk into the burping carpet of shit on the cabin floor. Something under my bunk runs out and eats it, fucking hell! Like I said, from my invisible position on the bunk, I could see that shit was coming down triple strange.

The perpetual gang rivalry was cooking fit to blow, those little gangbangers were limbering up for some kind of major face-off. They all knew that it was the time of year when the Eel started looking for new recruits, a good gang war gave them an excellent opportunity to display their violence skills.

The traders seemed more jumpy than usual. This was because we were coming up to the bend in the river where river pirates usually raided the flotilla. The stallholders were in two minds about the pirates and all the other robber outlaws in this stretch of jungle for that matter.

A lot of them had family connections with the outlaws and they did do a good job of thinning out the roof boys. Those little bastards needed culling now and again, the thieving little fuckers started looking scary when their numbers began to swell. About ten years ago they even attempted some kind of mutiny.

Some hot-blooded charismatic little punk modelling himself on Che Guevara got them all worked up into a hooch-fuelled revolutionary frenzy. The Eel slaughtered the lot of them mercilessly, the black river ran red with children's blood.

I could hear that Snark punk running off at the mouth up on the roof. If that little fucker wasn't more careful he was going to get the whole lot of them killed.

I heard a couple of Eel guards as well, I was up on the fo'c's'le, limping towards the front of the barge. It was about midnight, everyone was asleep. I overheard them talking, it seems that the Eel were getting jumpy, the rumours about the big diamond stash down in the hold were true. The diamonds, along with the gold, were the main bulk of Mobutu's in-country stash, millions of dollars worth.

Rumours had been spreading around the bush like wildfire. Usually the Eel repelled the pirates and the land bandits but if they all joined forces together they were looking at some pretty fierce fighting up ahead. The guards were worried.

This had only ever happened once before, back in the 1960s, the only time that the Order Of The Black Eel had ever been defeated. A couple of the older guys remembered it from when they were kids, orphans themselves up on the roof. Every scumbag outlaw and river pirate in the jungle had joined forces, their sheer weight of numbers overpowered the guard and the surviving bandits made off into the bush with a fortune in diamonds.

The stupid fuckheads blew it of course. That was inevitable. The captains argued over their shares of the loot, the guns and the machetes came singing out of their holsters and they just about wiped each other out. Mobutu, knowing well the rapacious and treacherous capacity of the human heart, merely bided his time and then sent in the Eel to finish off the remaining pirates and deliver the diamonds back to their grateful owner.

It seemed like history, as always, was about to repeat itself.

DRUMMOND'S LOG, MONDAY 17 JUNE 1996
HIS FAVOURITE JAZZ RECORDS

I'm in a corridor of a strange house, the floor is parquet. I pull my trousers down and squat to have a shit on the floor. A woman comes through the door and starts screaming at me. Her screaming wakes me up. It's still dark. The others are still asleep. There is no rumble from the engines, no sense of movement. I need a shit. Desperately need a shit. Major problem, the keys for the shitter are on a string around sleeping Z's neck. Climb out of my bunk, put my sandals on, take roll of bog from bag and make my way along the balcony, stepping over the sleeping, bollock naked, while clenching my arse cheeks. Get to the third class, shared cubicle just in time. I've got the full-on shits. After the initial explosive torrent I'm left with the leftovers dribbling down the inside of my legs. I clean myself up as best I can in the pitch black with what remains of the cheap bog paper, make my way back along the balcony carefully stepping over the still-sleeping deck passengers, into our cabin, climb back into my bunk and fall asleep and dream about reading a Sunday supplement interview with Mobutu where he is talking about his favourite jazz records.

Chapter Three
ALL THE SCUM OF THE JUNGLE

We were holed up at Piss Flap Mary's Lazy Fuck Saloon, the last official stop before the flotilla finally reached Kisangani, the inner station. It was also the last place any spunky nothing-to-lose, trigger-happy, bonehead desperado had left to make a raid on the *Colonel Ebeya*.

The word was out. All up the Llualaba and every other unmarked tributary.

Mobutu's time was coming down fast. That meant diamonds, diamonds on the move. The evil old bastard was collecting all his assets and getting the fuck out of Zaire.

The Lazy Fuck Saloon nestled in the black shadows that melted down from the jungle just outside Goma. Goma wasn't really a town, just a collection of mud huts, corrugated iron shacks and the derelict skeletons of long-forgotten colonial houses. The rusting hulks of old steamers, ubiquitous by the side of the river, half sunk in the greasy river like sinister iron crocodiles.

The Lazy Fuck was where smuggled diamonds and raw gold were traded, where pirates and bandits did business with the notorious lesbian cutthroat, Piss Flap Mary. She owned the Lazy Fuck and she set the prices, if you didn't like her prices you could always go some place else. Except that there wasn't anywhere else. Her prices were by and large fair, and if they weren't they almost were.

The Fuck was also the only place this far up-river a man could get half-way decent liquor and guns that didn't blow up in your hand. The place wasn't strictly legal – it wasn't illegal either seeing as there weren't any laws any more, and anyway, who would close it down? What was left of the police and the army were Mary's best customers. The Lazy Fuck was where you could buy what you needed.

Spending was easy and it didn't take long. Then it was back into the bush with new guns to hunt more gold and diamonds, raiding the mines and killing the mules waiting at tiny airstrips, opening up their gizzards and grabbing the bloody contraband they'd swallowed for safety.

The army no longer guarded the mines or the airstrips, they couldn't be trusted. Most of that kind of work these days went straight to mercenary outfits like Executive Outcomes, sleazy international killers with South African headquarters, and offices in Chelsea, London.

Being a river pirate or a bush raider meant that you didn't live that long, which is why the older guys were held in such reverence. Most guys joining up with the various crews were dead within a year. The captains didn't care much, there were always plenty of new bloods lured by the promise of unlimited booze and nasty sex to jump into the boots of a dead riverdog. Anyway, apart from getting yourself trained up as a European arse slave down on Bosie's farm what else was a young man supposed to do? Compared with being some European rich guy's trained nance, there was no choice at all for any jungle buck worth his spunk, dodging hot lead and raising hell down at Piss Flap Mary's.

There was an uneasy truce down at The Lazy Fuck. Usually the crews and gangs obeyed an unwritten rule that stated they all took turns trading and purchasing their supplies, partying hard for a few days then moving out easy leaving the place for whoever was next.

They spent too much time dodging those Executive arseholes' bullets to go around shooting at each other. Obviously each bandit posse harboured grudges against one another, these would be settled in time, but not at Mary's. This was the only place they all could relax, get laid and get high. The last thing they needed was any dumb gun fights fucking every thing up.

Mary was in the back with her jeweller's eyeglass, doing business as usual, taking the diamonds and handing out the cash which she knew she'd inevitably make back on her monopoly of whores, booze and guns. The deal was that they usually came in one crew at a time, but not tonight. There were about seven crews all partying big-style, old grudges effectively on ice. The booty on the *Colonel Ebeya* made their quarrels irrelevant for once. Because of all the military action and foreign power shit going down around Zaire's borders the rumours about the treasure travelling up river on the *Colonel Ebeya* had multiplied into epic proportions.

The small outlaw crews had joined forces and were about to make a concerted effort to finally get rid of the seemingly undefeatable Eel. The fact that each crew had its own plans to welsh on the agreement and kill their temporary allies afterwards goes without saying and is just about as obvious as war itself. But for now these deadliest and most jealous of rivals were all getting royally rat-arsed together, the best of buddies.

CONDEMNED TO ETERNAL LAUGHTER

I awoke freezing. It was still the middle of the night. I could see the silhouette of Z against the glow of neon coming up from the street below. He was leaning out of the fully opened window and screaming out at the uncaring world below.

'Are you listening down there you scumbags, you heathens, you less than humans? I am the wound and the blade! I am the slap and the cheek! I am the limbs and the wheel, the victim and the executioner! I am the vampire of my own heart – one of the deserted men condemned to eternal laughter and who can no longer smile! Did you hear me down there? Did you? Did you? You depraved vermin.'

He lights a fag. It glows against the night sky. Whatever was troubling him seems to have settled. He starts to mumble to himself.

> '*"A dark atmosphere covers the city*
> *Bearing peace to some, and worry to others.*
> *While the wretched crowd of mortals*
> *Under the whip of pleasure, the merciless torturer,*
> *Goes to collect remorse in the servile festivity".*'

I drifted back to sleep and heard no more from my poetry-infested friend.

*

General Butt Naked, the famous Liberian ex-head of state and Commander Winston Churchill, leader of the Baby Raper Commando are arm wrestling over broken bottles cheered on by their respective comrades. A couple of soldiers from the Bandido Fuck The World crew are playing some kind of Russian roulette with hostages that were taken for a ransom everyone seems to have forgotten about. The drunken bandidos were putting five bullets in the chamber and taking it in turns to blast the blindfolded prisoners' brains out, laughing hysterically at their cruel joke.

A few of the Butt Naked crew were sitting surly in the shadows, bare-chested in baggy torn camo trousers. Bullet belts hung across their shoulders and their gold earrings glittered in the light from the bare light bulbs. All are silently out of their heads on Ibogaine.

They've been piping it up for the last four days, their eyes disappeared behind pale-blue cataracts as they trip out silently in the black recesses of their wild jungle souls. Sweat beads on tightly knitted brows, lean muscles cord up like steel rope beneath shiny black skin.

How anyone can vibe out on the most terrifying bum-out drug on the planet for kicks is so mindblowingly horrific it demands a nervous respect. This is afforded them by the younger Baby Rapers, 12-year-old recruits to one of the Congo's most feared outlaw gangs.

Fuck Savage, a mean old bastard and his violent psychic crew, the Soul Fuckers are chowing down on one of Mary's house stews. There are two versions of this meaty broth: one has people in it, the other doesn't. Fuck and his boys aren't vegetarian.

IT MAKES ME LAUGH

'You awake, Bill?'

'What time is it?'

'Gone ten o'clock. I've been writing in the luxury bar for the last couple of hours. Remember that Greek-looking bloke we saw in that bar in Bumba?'

'No.'

'Do you fuckin' remember anything? He was drinking Ouzo up at the bar while we were at the table and you were watching a lizard on a tree.'

'No.'

'Well anyway, he's up in the bar. Can speak the language. Mate of Fat Miguel's. I've written him into the story. Listen to this.'

And Z starts to read his stuff. It's his usual thing, us going to whorehouse, Gimpo getting violent, me shitting everywhere and Z just observing while he is being sucked off. After Z stops reading and before he asks me what I think, I ask, 'Z, why do you write about perverted, violent, fucked-up sex all the time?'

'Because it's funny.'

'But all the time Z, it can't be funny all the time.'

'It makes me laugh. If it didn't make me laugh, I wouldn't write it.'

'But why? How can you keep laughing at this non-stop, never-ending, ludicrous, violent, cartoon-sex shit.'

'Bill, what is your problem this morning? I write what I write, you write what you write. Let's just get on with it.'

'Don't get me wrong I think what you write is great but I just don't know how you can keep it up, page after page, chapter after chapter, book after book. It's not even sex it's...' and I am at a loss for words.

Dear reader, what is it for? Why do you think Mark Manning writes the way he does? Do you ever think he wants to take a break from it? Maybe write about normal things like having breakfast using normal words like 'that was a good breakfast, just what I needed'. Instead it is always ruined prostitutes called Piss Flap Martha or one-legged sea dogs called Whisky Jake.

'Bill, I learnt a long time ago not to think about why I do what I do. It leads nowhere but down. To do that would poison the well of what I have to offer the world. If that in your rather small-minded view is 'fucked-up violent sex' so be it. Anyway enough of this, you coming for breakfast?'

'Yeah.'

*

No one up here on this wild bend in the river knows how Mary got her name and no one's dumb enough to ask. Mary has a special friend who works in the kitchen, a serenely beautiful mulatto girl about 16 years old. The way Mary looks at her all gooey, you'd think that the tough old lesbian had a heart. No one comments about the fact that Mary likes hairy pie. Most of the kids that make up these lawless gangs were orphans once and Mary is the nearest these wild teenage killers ever got to having a mother.

No one hassles Mary, that's the only rule down here. Mary takes the contraband and dishes out the dollars. It's a fair exchange, Mary knows that the money will be back on her side of the bar in just a few days.

The real mystery is what Mary does with her money, no one knows for sure. It's rumoured that she has two sons at an English public school. Mary was married way back. She's not married anymore. She lost her two front teeth during the separation. Her ex-husband was buried without his nuts.

Part of the reason Mary's stable has the best whores in all of Zaire is down to the fact that the girls work for no more than two years. If they can make it back to Kinshasha, they're set up for life. Two years fucking the scum of the jungle leaves its mark, the girls start out fresh as jungle daisies but towards the end of their service something dies in them. The jungle skeez hounds aren't stupid, they refuse to pay the amount Mary charges for damaged goods. 'When a whore's soul is dead it is better to use your fist,' an old soldiers' saying from the Congo.

Mary takes a trip down to Kinshasha once a year with her favourite girl of the moment. She never buys anything for herself but she likes her girl to look her best. Mary's girlfriends are famous throughout the jungle, dressed in the latest Parisian couture they fan themselves in the sweltering kitchen admiring their pretty dresses in the steamy mirror.

A few years ago one of Mary's girls tried to take off with one of Fuck Savage's boys. Winston Churchill and his Baby Rapers caught the star-crossed lovers hiding out in Mbandanka. Winston wisely refused the reward Mary had posted and told her it was a matter of honour.

'You was a good soul fucker,' said Winston handing over the prisoner. 'Now you're a dead soul fucker,' he said feeding the kid's remains to the crocodiles, three days later when Mary handed back what was left of him.

The girl ended up in the house stew.

General Butt Naked falls to the floor laughing, his hand bleeding from the broken glass, his brigade help him back to his chair. He took Winston Churchill's victory well and ordered more rum.

Things were getting mighty lairy at the Lazy Fuck. There was a rumour that a bunch of white guys were riding with the *Colonel Ebeya*. Laughing Jack and Bag o' Bones, Fuck Savage's quartermasters were both keen cannibals. Most of the pirates and outlaws have eaten human flesh. Usually when they were too drunk to hunt fresh meat out in the bush. None of the killers have any moral objection to eating human beings, they just don't think it tastes as good as a nice fat jungle hog.

Laughing Jack and Bag o' Bones are different in that respect, they like the taste of man meat. Especially white-man meat, as Laughing Jack is drunkenly telling the rest of the baby rapers.

'After we fuck their white butts,' he says wide-eyed, 'We eat them boys, nothing tastes as good as white-man butt basted with black man's jizz.'

In the back room just off the main bar Mary overhears the raucous laughter as she flips off a quick orgasm riding on pretty Marie's face. The tough old lesbian feels a twinge of anxiety. White men. They always bring bad luck.

She'd even heard a rumour that a bunch of yellows were riding on board, making strange sex films and indulging in their own form of cannibalism. Mary wasn't happy, she enjoyed her life out in the jungle, the last thing she needed was a bunch of weirdo outworlders coming round and fucking everything up. She tied on her giant ivory virgin killer and started stoking girlfriend's boiler.

WE HATE DALI

'Bill what time does our Eurostar leave for London?'

'2.30 I think. Why?'

'Good. 'Cause it gives us time to visit this Salvador Dali museum.'

Z handed me a tourist leaflet he had picked up on the hotel reception counter. On the cover is a late-period photo of Dali. Maroon velvet smoking jacket, moustache waxed to the max and pulling one of his stupid stares for the camera. Slashed across the top of the leaflet, I read: 'A new museum in Paris – The phantasmagoric world of Dali – Discover an extraordinary art exhibition in the heart of Montmartre. A unique and breathtaking collection of Salvador Dali magnificent sculptures and graphics. In a surrealist space of 1000 square metres, 330 original works invite you to share the fantastic world of Dali, 25F instead of 35F.'

'But Z, you hate Dali.'

DRUMMOND'S SECRET LOG, PARIS, PIGALLE

We finally made it out of the SEXODROME, thank God.

Z had been talking about renting a cabin and staying there for a month or two. Some of the tuggers, stealing out for baguettes and wine, had been there far too long, you could see it in their eyes. Myopic bastards, unshaven, callouses on their tugging hands.

I got a feeling that a lot of those guys lurking in their black cabins weren't ever going to leave. The mop boys would find them there, sparked out dead on their rented piece of jizz-splattered floor. Masturbation at this level of intensity was as addictive and soul-destroying as heroin.

I remember Kiki mentioned these places, one spaced-out evening as we lay in Toledo, spent and exhausted. I didn't know what he was talking about at the time. It seems Fat Miguel owned a lot of these wankhouses. The older boys at the Catamite ended up mopping them out when their looks had eventually been buggered out of them. Was there no end to the man's depravity? It seemed as if the loathsome Arab had a soiled digit in every low place on the planet where men could lose their souls. I knew that if we did eventually track down the Devil, Fat Miguel stinking of sour jizz, brown arse-butter and rotten pomegranates wouldn't be far away.

Z eventually agreed to leave. We stepped out into the violent morning sun, a couple of French wankers lay dead on the doorstep, their faces fish-belly white, skinned knuckles wrapped rigor-mortis tight around dried-out Kleenex.

We hopped over the dead fist-artists and made our way to the hotel. We had a couple of good leads. I was sure that one of the vids would turn something up if we studied them hard enough. We would call on Monsieur Moreau the following day.

WRITING

Trefor has just set a bowl full of dough balls between us and two mugs of sweet tea.

'Look, Z, I've got a problem with my writing.'

'What?'

'I don't know what to write about any more.'

'That's never stopped you before. You usually can write about anything – the colour of these plastic mugs or the stain in this bowl. You are usually happy to write about the most boring of subjects and make them sound even more boring.'

'Well, I'm bored with doing that.'

'How can you be? I know not much is happening on this trip in a way but you are seeing things you have never seen before and those that are reading it will never see in all their lives. You owe it to them to write about it.'

'Yeah I know you're right but I keep starting to write about ideas or characters, start a new theme then get bored with it and start writing about something else. It is more that I think I am just writing out of habit to fill the time not because I have anything I want to say.'

'Then write about that.'

'OK.'

*

There was a strange quiet on board the barges. The ghetto blasters, those perpetual banging boxes of irritation, seemed muted. Blankets had been placed over them to muffle the sizzling high frequency of their sonic assault. The incessant babbling and noisy bartering of the market traders had been replaced by a solemn murmur.

People seemed nervous, on edge. Any loud noise – a pig being slaughtered for the pot, a baby crying – seemed to unnerve the river-borne population. The roofboys were all crowded towards the front of the barges, shielding their eyes from the bright sunlight with banana leaves, peering into the jungle.

There appeared to be some kind of a truce between the gangbangers. The Bashielle Tigers and the Mkongo Machete shared cigarettes. Word had spread around the barges about the gathering band of outlaws and river pirates up at Piss Flap Mary's. A violent, bloody confrontation was inevitable and imminent. The boys had to make a decision.

Would they side with the Eel or would they abandon the floating world they had known all their orphaned lives and take up with the outlaws? It was a hard decision.

As pirates they could become rich and enjoy a twisted kind of freedom. Their lives would almost certainly be shorter. But in the imagination of a boy how much more alive that short life would seem than one under the regimented discipline of the Eel. Not that all of them felt this way. To some, the shining black and silver uniform, the mirrored sunglasses, the dark glamour of the jungle stormtrooper held an equal fascination. For some roofboys the Eel represented security and order. With the Eel came a certain safety – within the strict Nazi discipline and oaths of allegiance a man knew where he stood.

Within the pirate's anarchic freedom came the inevitable treachery and duplicity, a man needed to always be on his toes. One day brothers-in-arms, the next day – after a comrade's betrayal to save his own skin – you could be shivering in the bilge water of an Arab sodomy barge. It was a hard choice.

Most of the youngsters wouldn't know whose side they were on till the stench of gunpowder and flanged liver strafed the air, until the blood flowed and the intense eroticism of battle called down their fate, until they buggered or were buggered.

THE WAY

It's gone midday and we are still moored up at Bumba. I was hoping we would be in Kisangani by Wednesday. That would allow us at least a week to meet with the President. I'm sitting up top watching what's going on the dockside. We seem to have lost our novelty value. I'm no longer being automatically surrounded by roof boys. They have rearranged the way the barges have been tied together. The *Lokele* has left us, been replaced by a barge called *H203*. It is a freight barge and while I sit here making these notes, not knowing what to write about, a dozen or so stevedores, barefooted and wearing nothing but shorts, are carrying sack after sack of maize and manioc on their heads from somewhere in town through the small gap in the perimeter fence of the docks, up the gangplank and into the hold of the *H203*. Gimpo is watching with me.

'If they had looked after the cranes that the Belgians had left them, this job could have been done in 20 minutes.'

'Yeah but they aren't bothered how long things take and, anyway, all the stevedores would be out of work. Look what happened to all the Liverpool dockers. At least this lot have still got a job.'

'A job? Looks more like slave labour.'

They keep coming, sack after sodding sack. Watching them has a hypnotic quality. It's like something out of a movie, except in a movie they would be getting paid a lot more to do what they are doing than whatever pittance they are getting to do this. I wonder if what I'm writing now is the sort of thing Z meant about how I should write about the things I've never seen for you 'cause you'll never ever see them.

'What the fuck was that, Gimpo?'

'Sounded like gun shots.'

'Look, down there. Green Shirt's just pushed through the entrance, past one of the stevedores.'

'Where?'

'There. He's hiding behind the crane.'

'Oh yeah. For fuck's sake, he's got a gun in his hand.'

It's a revolver. He reloads it. He puts the gun into the top of his trousers, its handle hidden by his loose shirt. He looks up. He sees us looking at him. He smiles. Waves. This is real. This is not part of Z's made-up stuff. It is happening now and I wish it wasn't. We haven't seen anybody killed but we heard a shot and Green Shirt knows we saw he was the man with the gun. The ship's horn goes. The stevedores start running, working faster and faster. As if they don't get the job done before the barges leave, they don't get paid.

'Where's he gone?'

'Who?'

'Green Shirt.'

Below the dockside is now a mass of people all trying to clamber on to the barges.

'Wonder what that was all about?'

'Fuck knows.'

'Could be the start of something or the end.'

'There is no end.'

And I'm thinking could this be the start of a storyline to hold your interest like the beginning of an Ian Rankin novel but instead of Leith docks it's Bumba docks. Or is it just another unrelated incident along the way?

*

Piss Flap Mary's Lazy Fuck Saloon was either the last outpost of civilisation or the first indication of total lawlessness. It depended on which end of the gun you found yourself on. Personally I didn't think there was ever such a clear demarcation between the two. Civilisation just seemed like one more sleazy trick set up by a bunch of evil shits to keep themselves rich and the rest of the planet poor. Big fucking deal.

The Lazy Fuck itself however was a groovy place. Who would have thought you could find such a cool joint so far up river? Mary's was the kind of skeezy cat house that wouldn't have looked out of place on LA's Sunset Strip. The sign above the door was a classic. Some neon scud queen, legs wide open, flashing on and off as she winked and played with her electric cunt. They even had a silicon white woman on the door. On closer inspection however the tit freak turned out not to be a white woman at all. Beneath the trowelled-on make-up you could see that the girl was in fact an albino. Mutants, neat.

A hi-life band was banging out the same song that they seemed to play everywhere in Africa and a couple of strippers were doing the usual crap with ping-pong balls and strings of razor blades. Every fucker in the place was seriously twisted on booze and whatever weird jungle drugs they had up there.

Bill grabbed a table near the strippers and ordered up some beers, the waitress couldn't have been more than nine years old. She had a nice smile, I almost felt sorry for her when I saw the seven-foot bald guy raping her later on.

It didn't take long for us to figure out that the entire bunch of fucked-up desperadoes were all planning on raiding the *Colonel Ebeya*, killing the Eel and anyone else who tried to stop them. Guns would pop occasionally when some hothead shot at the ceiling or winged a disrespectful stripper.

A couple of Fuck Savage's boys sat at our table, they seemed like reasonable guys. It seemed to be common knowledge about the planned raid on the *Ebeya*. Everyone knew about the heavy machine gun the Eel had in the strong room but they were convinced that their sheer weight of numbers would do the job. The beers flowed. Fuck Savage and Butt Naked joined us at our table, they wanted to know if we were planning on grabbing the diamonds for ourselves. We told them we didn't even know that the *Ebeya* was carrying rocks.

Savage wanted to kill us, he'd never killed a white guy before. He wanted to see if we had the same colour blood. Bill took hold of a steak knife and sliced into his hand then squeezed it into Fuck's beer.

That seemed to do the trick. Bill had illustrated our wild credentials with style. We were all buddies now.

'Ha ha, you are funny man, Mr Scottish. More beer for the white man,' called Fuck.

INSTANT GRATIFICATION

Reluctantly climbing the steps up to Montmartre.

'Bill, you love Dali. Every 13-year-old boy loves Dali.'

'But I'm not 13, Z.'

'Yes you are. This morning you will be 13.'

'Why?'

'Did you go to a Dali museum when you were 13?'

'No, of course not.'

'But you would have loved to have done and this morning you have the chance. So instead of going as a cynical, bitter and beaten, middle-aged man, go as a 13-year-old boy whose hormones are begging to leak all over the place, who wants the danger, excitement, instant gratification and cut-up female torsos in super-realism that only Dali can deliver.'

'OK, sold. I'll be 13.'

*

With men who hold no truck with the finer points of gentlemanly behaviour but understand natural authority, it is not enough to demonstrate physical strength alone, an element of style has to accompany whatever an act of bravado is displayed. Both Bill and I spent our formative years among the blasted landscapes of Britain's underclass, wandering the cursed earth of wild northern council estates. We both understood this language of gesture and cool instinctively. It is a universal language that transcends the barriers of language, time, culture, religion and geography.

Our credentials as on-the-level crazies established, the pirates treated us with the respect all outlaws honour each other with. Fuck was intrigued as to why we weren't interested in the diamonds. He said that we were welcome to a piece of the action, we just had to kill a few Eel and a handful of the rocks were ours for the taking.

When he found out that we were aiming at getting our souls back from the devil he was confused, and not a little nervous. The Catholics had told him that all he had to do to win back his own soul was to confess before he died. When we told him we weren't Catholics he let the subject drop. When a man lives such a reckless and dangerous life as Fuck and the rest of the outlaws it didn't do to wonder about such things. Things were pretty shitty in this life, the possibility of it being even worse in the next one didn't bear thinking about.

Everyone's attention was drawn suddenly to the commotion scrabbling across the other side of the room. One of the Bandido Fuck The World, those mean killers from Rwanda was slicing into one of the girls with a huge Bowie knife.

'Those Bandidos man, the blood fever's down on them,' said Fuck resignedly. 'We're gonna have to get moving soon, I don't trust those guys. Genocide killers, tried to exterminate all the Tutsis across the border. Once that genocide poison gets into a brother, it's like they aren't human anymore. They're like vampires. Look at them, man, gore junkies grooving on death.'

The guy with the Bowie knife had started hacking up the body and throwing the bits around to his fellow Bandidos, laughing and joking.

GISELLE

On my bunk. In the cabin. We are on our way.

'Bill.'

'What, Z?'

'You seen that big woman a couple doors down with the purple eye shadow?'

'Yeah.'

'Do you know her name?'

'Giselle, I think. Why?'

'Well, you know how she is all over Gimpo, she just stinks of sex. The last thing I want to happen is Gimpo to start shagging one of the natives.'

'Why?'

'It will just lead to disaster. If he shags her there will be somebody who thinks he shouldn't. It will all get messy and it's not our job to clear things up, that's Gimpo's job.'

'Like who?'

'I dunno. Like we didn't know that Mami was married to Pitsu until a couple of days ago and Gimpo kept on coming on strong to her. A woman like Giselle, you can tell she is all about making men jealous. She would like nothing more than to see Gimpo and, say, Green Shirt fighting over her.'

'Did Gimpo tell you about the Green Shirt incident?'

'No. What?'

So I explained.

'Bill, we have to keep our heads down. I get the feeling that tensions are rising. It could all go off.'

'You are beginning to believe your own prose.'

But Z is right. Reality could be getting a bit too close to something I don't want to be describing. I think I would be happier describing the patterns on the cotton curtain that hangs in our door than describing the rivulets of blood flowing from Gimpo's dying body. And another thing – something I won't be telling Z – I am the one feeling jealous. I'd noticed the way that Gimpo has started flirting with Giselle and how she has been responding. Up until then I though it was me she was showing an interest in. I mean, she had offered to write her name and address in my notebook: GISELLE-BOMETHO: SURLA'AU: T.PNo38, Z/LIMETE Q:FUNA (CHEZ VAETHE)

I don't know if, in fact, it is an address or what it means at all but she wrote it down for me and gave me a big knowing smile.

'Anyway, Z, she is too big for Gimpo. She would smother him.'

'Maybe that's what she would like. Maybe it is what he would like.'

'Nah, she wouldn't go for him. She would want a big man.'

'Oh, now it's coming out, you got the hots for Big Mamma Giselle. Maybe I should rewrite all the stuff I've written about her and Gimpo. Loverboy Drummond comes to town.'

'Fuck off, Z.'

And he does. The thing is I love it when she passes our open door and I'm lying on my bunk and she is swaying her large hips and she turns her head into the darkness of our cabin to give me one of her big sexy smiles. Anyway, enough of all that. I'm pretty good at repressing my sexuality. If I don't, it always just ends up with all sorts of trouble. And the less of that the better.

*

I saw Mary standing in the doorway of her kitchen, she'd put the waitress on the Bandido tab. 'Genocide,' she spat into the dust. 'Fuckin' idiots.' And went back into the kitchen.

As far as I could gather there didn't seem to be any particular strategy to the raid, they were just going to use Zulu tactics and storm the *Ebeya*. The ones left standing would take the loot. They all liked the plan. The more fatalities there were the higher their share of the booty would be. To a man they thought they were immortal. They reminded me of Damien Hirst's big shark. Seeing as how none of the different crews and gangs would bow down to any of the others the raid had no real leaders.

The decision to board the flotilla kicked off when everyone had reached the state of intoxication where they could hardly stand, let alone fight. The outlaws didn't stand a chance. Drunken violence, mindless slaughter, hacking and shooting at anything that moved was all well and good when attacking undefended mine workers but when it came to fighting an organised military force let alone a crack squadron of supernatural death angels like the Black Eel.

The battle, if it could be called that, lasted under 20 minutes. When the remaining bandits decided to cut their losses and head back into the bush, the Eel sent out a troop of roof boys to collect the heads from their fallen enemies. They hung the gory trophies around the barges like gruesome christmas decorations.

The Eel had seemed to melt out of the jungle. The intoxicated bandits didn't see a thing. The Eel's silver machetes sang through the damp air like choirs of black angels severing heads and biting into brains.

Fuck and his low-life jungle buddies scudded off a handful of rounds, the bullets cutting into each other, missing their supernatural martial enemy as if they were water. The Eel entered the skirmish naked, covered in green and black paint. To the ripped Bandido they appeared invisible; a mysterious cyclone of violence from nowhere turning the air red.

TOP DOLLAR

The first painting that I ever saw that wasn't a watercolour of a local scene or even the odd one done in oil was a print of *Christ of St John on the Cross*. It hung in my Dad's study and it scared me shitless. But time and time again I found myself sneaking in there for just one more look. That weird perspective of Christ nailed to his cross, hovering above the sea of Galilee and that small and lonely boat. Who did it? How did he do it? And why? It was nothing like any of the pictures in our Sunday school books. What was the moral?

First impressions are lasting impressions and all that... of course years later we all learnt it was a shit painting, schlock art, done long after he had been kicked out of Breton's gang. Run off to New York, whoring himself to whoever would pay top dollar.

*

Things got back to normal pretty quick on board the *Colonel Ebeya*. After a couple of hours or so no one seemed to notice the raggy heads swinging from side to side in the sultry breeze, feeding flies. They were just another screwed frequency on the wavelength of weird. Some of the roof kids started to play basketball with them, shooting bloody hoops, laughing as they hit the ground, smashing teeth.

I noticed Bill sneak a couple under his mosquito net. His grotesque sexual degeneration was showing no signs of bottoming out. The insane chuckles and nauseous wank rhythms jizzgrunting around in his little tent of horrors drove me out of the cabin and up on to the deck to breathe something clean.

I stared across the mocking water at the dense treeline. As usual I got the unsettling feeling that something was staring back. It wasn't just the equator we'd crossed back in Mbandanka, that's for sure.

Things were getting way too intense to be explained away by geography. We'd crossed some other line, something deep inside of us had mutated, I could feel it tinkering around with my DNA, vibrating sympathetically with ancestral body memories. It was something outside of myself yet at the same time attached to the essential core of my being. A slack fatalism engulfing me like a field of Afghan poppies.

During our kaleidoscopic confrontation with the soul of the jungle, with B'witi, I had accepted the voodoo grace and no longer saw death as the end of life but as a part of life.

My hyper awareness of constant danger was no longer attached to bubbling occidental hysteria. My new sensibility seemed to have given me something of the oriental's easy cool when faced with all this perpetual danger.

The effortless reordering of my psychic priorities reinforced my commitment towards the constant monitoring of the disturbing machinations of my subconscious. Here in B'witi's kingdom, it was important to police the seemingly random chaos of my dreams. A deeper understanding of the mad abstractions of nocturnal consciousness was of far more relevance and importance than cyclical questions about the nature of reality. Especially white reality, which out here was nothing more than a ridiculous burden and an embarrassment.

Here at the beginning and end of the world more than anywhere, dreams and their mysterious realm were the secret language and true church of the soul. If you could decipher this elusive REM syntax you would be able to communicate with god himself, and his drunken brother, the Lightbringer.

SPLATTERING BLOOD

'Fuck! Fuck! Fuck! Fuck! Cunt!'

I've just stubbed the big toe on my right foot while climbing the steps at the back of the *Bangole*, our barge, leading from the *Mukango*. I've half ripped the toenail off and blood is pouring out. I hobble back to the cabin, splattering blood as I go. I climb into my bunk and inspect the wound. This could be it. It's bound to be infected with some killer bug already. Maybe I should amputate my big toe now before I have to have the whole foot off. I get my knife and get to work. I've changed my mind. If I amputate my toe, more killer bugs could get into the gaping wound left behind. Instead I start to cut, as sensitively as I can, the flesh that is holding my big toenail on. This is painful but not much more painful than the pain I'm already suffering. I am putting into practice one of my theories – use more extreme pain to mask the pain you are already experiencing. Z enters.

'What the fuck are you doing?'

'Operating on myself.'

'I couldn't make this up. You are sitting there with your purple-handled Finnish fishing knife in your hand, hacking at your big toe. Blood is gushing out. For fuck's sake, bandage it up. Look, it's dripping through on to Mavuba's bunk. He's going to be well pissed off. How did it happen or did you just decide to start hacking off your big toe to give yourself something to write about?'

'I...'

'No, don't tell me. You should go and see that witch doctor with the white coat and have it cleaned up properly. Maybe a course of antibiotics or something.'

'Yeah right, anyway he'll just see this wound as a way to shake us down. Next thing I know he will be charging $1,000 to have my leg amputated.'

'Whatever, but that looks like a serious gash.'

Z leaves me to finish my operation. Gimpo has a small first aid kit. I dab the wound with TCP. Lie back in my bunk and let the throbbing pain take me over until I fall asleep.

*

Like I said it wasn't just a line on the map we had crossed back there in Mbandanka, some other threshold wound up tight in our souls had been breached.

Here on the black water I found I no longer had to rein in any feelings of jagged excitement. I was free to dig the horror.

I had accepted my B'witan grace and was free to groove on its fearless primal truth. Ashes to ashes, shit to shit.

B'witi had shown me death. And how to be death. How to be everything. It was coded in my blood.

My veins sang the elemental resurrection, as old as the stars. Of the stars.

Dancing down the elegant transformation, I dreamt of Bill's bones reincarnated as bird shit. Twittering agents of atomic transmutation, feasted on the quantum fruits of his grave. Then, riding slow-motion thermals, shat on the pale atheists below.

DRUMMOND'S LOG, TUESDAY 18 JUNE 1996
THE FEVER

Morning.

'You awake, Bill?'

'Yeah, why, Gimpo?'

'Don't you want your breakfast?'

'No.'

'Why?'

'I've decided to stop eating.'

'So you don't mind if I eat your breakfast?'

'Fine.'

Gimpo disappears, presumably to eat my breakfast. I am lying bollock-naked on my bunk except for the rag I have tied to my big toe and the bush hat on my head. The pain is still there but I like it, it's a comfortable throbbing sort of pain. My head is propped up on my kit bag and from this position I can look down at my body. The flesh looks grey. I notice I've lost quite a bit of weight over the past couple of weeks. Not in a healthy, fit sort of way that would please my vanity. More in a working on the bridge over the River Kwai sort of way. What flesh there is still sags, nothing firm about it. My cock (although still massive of course) looks like it will never manage another erection. The idea of sex can't even manage to fill me with boredom. I try to think about sex. Nothing. Sex was something in my past life, when I was a young man. Something that was part of the life I had before the river. Now all of my life is the river. The endless river. I will never leave the river. I will never leave the cabin. I will never leave the bunk. I drift. The fever is taking me down and then I remember the turtle. What happened to the turtle? I decide to not give myself over to the fever, climb out of the bunk. Look under Mavuba's bunk. No turtle. Where did it go? Did it manage its break for freedom? I climb back on to my bunk.

'Fuck! Fuck! Fuck! Fuck! And cunt.'

I've banged my big toe again. Lie back down and fall asleep.

DRUMMOND'S SECRET LOG, APPROACHING THE INNER STATION

I thought we were never going to make it out of that palace of the wanking damned.

Fat Miguel, loathsome parasite of the libido, sordid blood trapper, setting his pixilated nets for ignorant plasma-gorged boners. He grabs you by the swollen bell end and sucks out your soul through the Jap's eye.

The films were fucking useless of course. Whatever I thought I saw up in the booths had completely vanished when I played it back on the hotel VCR. The elegant connections and subtle subtext, the layers of interrelated meaning and coded language all disappeared like the pulsating chimeras that lurk in billowing clouds of dopesmoke.

The sliding nirvana of extreme masturbation had deluded me again, I reached in my pocket for a Kleenex (re-viewing the cult classic 'Plasma creep' stirred something primal in me and I'd been forced to milk my tattered scrote yet again) to find the card the weird wanker at the SEXODROME had handed to Z.

Gustave Moreau

ARTIST and SENSUALIST

There was an address written in elegant copperplate on the reverse. I was intrigued.

Of course there was always the risk that he could have been just another pervoid, arse-punching kidney fumbler, but I remember there was something tremblingly hallucinatory about his eyes, they were the eyes of a man who knew things. They rolled in their sockets like drugged planets. Here was a man unafraid to walk with the gods.

SHUT UP BILL

Before I handed over my 25F entrance fee I convinced myself I would be 13 again. But it didn't work. I had mistakenly followed Z through the same time-revolving door that he went through, the one marked minus 29 years. Thus Z was 13 but I was 18. The worst possible age to visit a Dali museum. What I witnessed was a vile and despicable place cashing in and conning gullible tourists looking for some instant art heritage. Shite bronze reproductions of scenes from his more famous paintings, floppy clock faces dripping from the branches of dead trees. I felt the soul of Breton swell up in my 18-year-old breast. I could not contain it, it had to break out. The truth had to be proclaimed. It was only when I noticed the gaggle of Japanese girls cowering against a far wall that I knew that I had begun. It went like this:

'It was Jackson Pollock and Jack Kerouac and Jimi Hendrix who really caused me to make my mind up to rely for my redemption here below upon myself alone, so I desperately pursue their footsteps, animated by that feverish desire for conquest, total conquest, that will never leave me; so that my eyes, my precious eyes, have to reflect that which, while not existing, is yet as intense as that which does exist, and which has once more to consist of visual images, fully compensating us for what I have left behind. The mysterious path on which fear dogs my every step and my desire to turn back is only overcome by the fallacious hope of being accompanied has, for the past 15 months, been swept by a powerful searchlight. It is now a full 15 months since I began to explore this path, bearing rays of light with me as I go. No one had the courage to see anything before I came. Poets, painters and rock stars used to talk of a country they had discovered, where in the most natural way in the world, "A white room with no curtains" appeared but this image was only a virtual one for me. What miracle has enabled me, whom it is my astonishment and good fortune to know, to body forth all that remained, up till my appearance in the highest domain of fantasy? What a revolution must have taken place within me for it to have been possible for this to happen! In order to be able to break suddenly away from sensible things, or with more reason from the easiness of the customary appearance one has to be aware of their treason to such a high degree that one cannot, recognising the fact of my immense responsibility. A single failure of willpower on my part would be sufficient for everything I am concerned with to be at least put back by a month or two, if not wholly lost. My admirable perseverance is such a valuable guarantee that it dispenses with all need for me to appeal to any other authority. Shall I ever know what awaits me at the end of this agonising journey? All that matters is that the exploration be continued and that the objective rallying signs take place without any possibility of equivocation and follow me uninterruptedly.''Shut up, Bill, and buy your postcards.'

'Why?'

'It's time to catch the Eurostar.'

*

Z was more than happy to accompany me to the Musée de Moreau. He was familiar with the strange Monsieur Moreau, he told me that the fellow was a decadent artist, a French symbolist painter and big fan of the green fairy. I should have known there was a sleazy reason for Z's interest, his knowledge of all things sordid was virtually encyclopedic.

We made our way through the drizzly city streets to the elegant town house of Monsieur Moreau. An old servant woman answered the door and showed us in. Monsieur Moreau was with a colleague, she told us. The sound of raucous laughter and breaking glass echoed around the hall.

Everywhere the walls were covered by disturbing unfinished paintings. Writhing canvasses covered with intricate drawings of mythical beasts and tumbling, impossible cities, deranged castles clambering towards sick skies. Caverns with dripping stalactites hiding dangerous Eves wrapped in serpents peering out from the visionary gloom. Fields of naked bodies twisting together, erotic necroscapes, bejewelled youths with their throats slit. Orgies of beautiful women coupling with unreal beasts among cascading treasures: gold, silver, pearls, diamonds. The mad hallucinogenic images all crowding into the cluttered confines of single massive canvasses, the intricacy of the detail sacrificing the whole for the parts. The blasphemous works seemed inspired by Satan himself or Flaubert's *Salammbo* at the very least.

My Presbyterian soul blanched white with indignation at these images of the sacred and profound careering madly together, flung to Earth from some insane and perverted imagination. Again and again in the intricate teeming detail I caught repetition after repetition of that blasphemer's favourite, *The sodomy of Christ*. I can only thank God that the fiend who started these works never had the energy to finish them.

BUTTERFLY

I awake.

I don't know what time of day it is. It's broad daylight outside but quiet. For once the blasters aren't blasting. From the position I'm in I can stare out of our cabin door into the passing jungle. It looks little more than 30 feet away. Fluttering between there and the barge are hundreds, no thousands of large butterflies. I haven't seen so many butterflies in one place since I saw the Rolling Stones in Hyde Park in 1969.

'What have the Rolling Stones in Hyde Park got to do with butterflies?' asks a reader not yet born in 1969. (But not you. You know exactly what I'm referring to.) But for that reader not yet born: the week before I saw the Rolling Stones Brian Jones, the Stones original lead guitarist drowned in his swimming pool. So on the Saturday that me, Mick Jagger and 100,000 other people were in the park, Mick read a poem about a butterfly on a wheel or something and then emptied all these boxes full of Cabbage Whites into the air from the stage. Thousands of white butterflies, that nicely complemented the white trousersuit-cum-dress thing that Mick was wearing, fluttering across us lot. The trouble was, you could see that a load of the butterflies were already dead. They just fell to the stage. And as for the others that were fluttering over our heads they were falling and fluttering their last. One fluttered its last where it fell on my lap. I picked it up and put it into an empty Swan Vesta box of matches I borrowed from Ian (Yun) Fordyce who was a school mate of mine who had come down on the train from Corby with me. I still have the Swan Vesta box at home with the butterfly in it. I wonder what Yun is doing now. So that explains that. What it doesn't explain is the hundreds of thousands of butterflies I can see just now. Is Mick Jagger out there up to his old tricks? I wonder what he is wearing today. A butterfly flutters into the cabin. It's huge, well, big compared to British ones. Almost six-inches across I guess. It flutters around no doubt trying to navigate its way back out to its friends. Why don't butterflies fly in straight lines like other insects? It seems such a waste of time and energy, all this fluttering. You would think evolution would have bred it out of them. It's landed on my notebook on the open white page. Its wings are fully spread. It is a thing of stunning but oh-so-fragile beauty. SLAM. Got it. I open the book again. It's perfectly pressed. If we ever get home it can live for eternity with the other one I got in Hyde Park in 1969. And I have just remembered it wasn't the 'Who breaks a butterfly on a wheel' poem that Jagger read out, it was one by Shelley. I think the butterfly one was quoted by John Mortimer when he was defending Jagger over a drugs bust a few years earlier.

I stared at the beautiful dead butterfly for many, many minutes. I thought about its life and big tears rolled down my cheek. Nobody came in the cabin. Then Gimpo did, I closed my book so Gimpo could not see my sin.

'Dinner time, Bill.'

'Nah Gimpo, I don't feel like it, you have it.'

'You all right, Bill?'

'Yeah fine. Why?'

'You don't look it.'

Of course I'm not fucking fine. I'm dying. I can feel it inside me. I'm dying from the inside out. The inside is already dead. The outside will be dead soon. But I'm no butterfly. Gimpo goes for his double portion. I carefully open the book. I won't describe the butterfly. It is enough for you to know it is almost the most beautiful thing that I have ever killed.

*

'Who is it, you fat fucking slag!' shouted a thin whip of a man, storming into the hall and punching the frail woman in the back of the head. The old grandmother fell to her knees crying.

'Get out, servant! You disgust me!' bellowed the rakish dandy. '

'Ah Monsieur!' His tone changed abruptly on seeing us. 'The SEXODROME! Your taste in art, sublime! Please, forgive me, The quality of domestic staff these days as I'm sure you know yourself is absolutely... Well, well, forgive me for boring you with my... ah now, yes.'

The cruel rake kicked the old woman hard in her bustle and bid us into the drawing room. Another wicked man sat on an elegant chaise longue, he raised a silver monocle to his eye and appraised us in a grotesquely sexual fashion, licking his painted lips lasciviously.

I could feel his degenerate gaze rolling across us like some perverted, wet thing from a bugger's cellar. He placed his green drink on a small ornate table and gripping the head of a silver-handled cane with both hands crossed his legs, thrusting himself genitally forward and blowing a kiss in our direction.

I couldn't take my eyes from the obscene wretch. He started flicking his tongue across his black lips like an evil serpent, smiling and mouthing obscenities.

'Charles, for god's sake man, these men are our guests!'

It was Moreau. He'd seen his friend undoing his silk breeches and waving his penis at us, nodding and gesturing at it with his twitching eyes.

'Please, you must forgive my friend, he's not normally like this. It's the laudanum, and the absinthe,' said the refined gentleman.

'And the champagne, and the brandy, and the port, the smack and co-fucking-caine. You tart, come over here and suck me off. Gussie, I love you...'

The drunken wretch added getting to his feet.

'Bend over and show us your flower of evil!.'

He started laughing as if he had made some terribly witty joke.

'Oh God, I'm sorry, you miserable old woman,' he continued, straightening out his fine clothes. 'Come on anyway, let's go out and paint the town brown, drink till we shit ourselves.'

He filled his glass from a chilled bottle of champagne and slapped the painter around the shoulders.

'No, I'm sorry, Charles, I really can't. I'm determined to finish this painting,' protested the artist.

'You always say that, you've never finished a painting since I've known you. Come on, let's get ratted, do some hard drugs, bugger a few street Arabs, rape some prostitutes, start some fires and finish off with a dash of elegant murder, a servant or something. Come on you old pervert, you know you want to... the night is still young, the moon bloody on the Seine, hanging pregnant, fecund with jewels and... hmm.'

He finished, rubbing his chin and then pulling out a pen started scribbling a few notes.

'It's all right for you, you bastard, writing your stupid little poems. Painting takes time you selfish fucker. Oh what's the use.'

The frustrated painter collapsed into a chair and poured himself a large shot of absinthe, throwing it back like vodka then pulling a sour face and stamping the floor with his right foot several times.

'God, that stuff tastes like green fucking dogshit,' he managed to say, pulling grotesque faces.

'Fucking gets you there though, doesn't it Gussie old boy? Come on, show us your cock, I haven't eaten since lunch time.'

It was the horrible dandy again. What a sight he was. Yellow Prince of Wales check trousers, red shiny shoes and white spats. Lime green moleskin waistcoat over a white shirt with enormous puffed sleeves, balding grey hair pulled back into a ribbon at the back of his neck, and his face...

THE TRUTH

On the Eurostar the Normandy fields flashed by considerably faster than any fairies or witches ever did. Of course I didn't make that big rant about searchlights and what awaits us at the end of the agonising journey. If you have done 'A' level History of Art you will know it's a straight take from *La Revolution Surréaliste* by André Breton (1927) with a few of the 'he's turned into 'me's and the 'we's to 'I's. In fact, I didn't feel particularly 18 and angry with the world at all, just a mild feeling of disappointment that the museum didn't have a coffee shop.

*

My God, I hadn't seen such a gothic ruin since that mouldering visage of Oscar Wilde over in Helsinki.

The creature's spazzy black lipstick was smeared shinily across thin lips, hiding rotten yellow stumps of teeth, a weak receding chin and large bulging black eyes that sat in his blueish graveyard skin like lumps of coal.

'What about you, Scotty?' The cadaverous nonce was addressing me. I checked my Celtic machismo. An overwhelming desire to kick the proverbial seven barrels out of him had come across me.

'Knackers like a couple of haggis I'll bet, and look at that arse, not many of them to the pound. How about it, Burnsy, do you fancy a ride on old Charlie's flower of evil?' He lurched from his chair and waggled his bony arse at me.

'You see! This is why I can never finish any of my masterpieces!'

This disgusting sybarite Charles Baudy-fucking-laire and his arseholes of evil.' It was the painter, Gustave Moreau. 'Look at him, you'd never believe he was responsible for penning the first truly modern collection of poetry would you? He's not even homosexual either you know, he's just trying to shock you, pathetic! That's what you are, Baudelaire! Do you hear me? Pathetic!'

Charles Baudelaire, of course, I said to myself . The nineteenth-century genius poet, a literary

Satanist of the highest order, if anyone could tell us of the whereabouts and habits of the Lord of the powers of the air it would be this, erm, genius.

'You're not Irish, are you?'

It was Baudelaire again, he was swigging from the neck of the absinthe bottle by now and was becoming increasingly disorientated.

'No, they're not Irish, Charles. Oh God, here we go again,' commented his friend in a weary fashion as if we were to hear some oft-aired bugbear of the rat arsed poet. 'He was fucking Irish, the fat tosser and his little blondie boyfriend, they came here, with a bottle of shitty champagne, caught him leafing through my poems when he thought I was asleep. His little friend, Alfie was it? Dougie or Bosie or something – by God he was a goer, what a little flower of evil he was, heh heh.'

The poet hurled a green jet of vomit across the elegant Turkish carpet and fell into a coma, head on his chest, green drool dribbling down the front of his waistcoat.

'Thank God for small mercies,' said the painter, sighing visibly with relief. 'It's not his fault really, the fellow really is a genius. It's just when he starts hitting the green stuff, which he has been doing for the past century actually, now I come to think of it. It was when the coloured girl left him. Fucking slapper, Jeanne Duval, the black Venus, my arse! It's all that cunt's fault.'

JOE STRUMMER AND PINK CHAMPAGNE

I turn a couple of pages in the notebook and start to sketch the cabin from where I am lying. As I sketch I imagine our meeting with Mobutu. I won't bother with all that descriptive stuff about the palace and how evil Mobutu looks like Z would. I will leave that to your imagination and get straight on with the dialogue.

'Hello fellows, so good to meet you at last. I understand you took the scenic route to get to my anything-but-humble palace here in Gbadolite. You should have called, I would have provided you with my private Concorde, armed escort and female companions for the journey.'

'We are so grateful that you have honoured us with an audience, Mister President.'

'Call me Joe. Call me Joe.'

'Thank you, Mister President, we will try to.'

'So, I understand you are great men of letters back in England and you are interested in the rich culture of my country.'

'Yes, Mister President.'

'Joe. Call me Joe, like Joe Stalin. Ha Ha Ha Ha, just my little joke.'

'And Joe Strummer.'

'Yes, Joe Strummer, 'London Calling" is one of my favourites. And Bazooka Joe. Can you still get Bazooka Joe bubble gum? When you get back to England please send me a box of Bazooka Joe bubble gum. But to business. I understand you have some questions for me.'

'Yes we have. But some, we very much understand, you might not want to answer.'

'Hey, my good fellows, I'm not afraid of a few questions. An ill-fitting shoe from a Parisian bespoke cobbler may hurt but not a question. Fire away, as you might say.'

'We came to Africa to find Satan so that we could trick him into giving our souls back.'

'A poetic plan. I like poetic plans.'

'We told a friend of our plan, how we thought we might sail up the Congo River until we got to the Tree of Knowledge where we calculated Satan in his guise as the Serpent would be there waiting for us and...'

'I like this. You are men of vision.'

'Anyway, our friend said that meant we would be travelling through the great country of Zaire, with its President Mobutu.'

'And your friend was right.'

'And our friend said that many consider you to be the most evil man on earth alive today and if anybody was Satan incarnate it would be you.'

'And your question is?'

'Are you Satan?'

'Now I don't think I have ever been asked that question before. People have asked me many questions but not that one. I'm afraid to disappoint you, I am not Satan. What is your next question?'

'Are you the most evil man on earth?'

'That is a more difficult question to answer. For many – and I mean many – millions I am the most evil man on earth. For others, I appear to be the closest thing to the Son of God they are ever likely to meet. To be a great leader of a great country like Zaire, you have to appear to be the most evil man on earth. If they didn't think of me as that I would not be able to fulfil my function to bring wealth into the country and maintain a form of law and order required in a modern African state.'

'So are you the most evil man on earth?'

'You are looking for simplistic answers, young man. William, is it not?'

'Yes, but you can call me Bill.'

'Ha ha, like Bill Clinton. Bill Clinton is a funny man but not good for Zaire like George Bush. We need another man like George Bush to be President of the United States of America. I consider myself to be the greatest of all the African presidents. I have been the President of Zaire for decades now. I have seen many American presidents come and go. I have brought stability to the mighty country that is Zaire. I freed Zaire from the turmoil left behind by the colonial rapists and to do all this many people have to think of me as the most evil man on earth. It comes with the job and I am the only man that can do the job. I have only ever had one rival and that is Laurent Kabila and he is no rival at all. If he became President, Zaire would fall apart, descend into anarchy and millions upon millions would be killed. I hold everything together with my love for the land and its people. Some of your Western leaders understand this, they recognise my strength, they honour me because to do so brings peace. Others do not recognise. Bill Clinton does not understand. Have I answered your questions Bill?'

'Yes.'

'And now some pink champagne and entertainment.'

Gustave poured himself a small tumbler of absinthe, added a teaspoon of sugar and lit the grisly concoction with his antique Zippo.

Z, I noticed, had already made decent headway on the green stuff. He was sat in the corner with a large glassful, grinning idiotically.

'So you're in pursuit of his satanic majesty are you? Before you ask, Aleister called me from Africa. His clairvoyance is usually accurate, I might have known. And what do you expect to gain from the eternal black bargain? Money? Fame? Women? I don't suppose anything I may say would dissuade you from entering into this pact of folly?' asked Gustave.

'If only we had sought your counsel before this blasted thing had happened,' I replied. Gustave furrowed his brow, surprised at my retort. 'You see, we seek the dark angel to regain our souls, not to bargain with them. We want them back. We already made the mistake of pawning them for the usual baubles.'

'You want them back? How unusual. Your regrets seem to have appeared early. Usually a man can spend an entire lifetime before realising the ridiculous deal he has made with the tempter of souls, crying in regret, beseeching a deaf god on his deathbed. Tell me what did you bargain for, was it the usual? Girlies and gelt?'

I nodded, realising what an idiot I had been.

'And a bit of fame...' I added sheepishly before my shame silenced me.

Gustave laughed loudly.

'I don't know what you're laughing at, Shirley.' It was the wrecked roué Baudelaire, he'd escaped from his absinthe coma. 'What did the couple of us fucking Einsteins get that was any better? Fucking immortality, stuck here on this miserable boil of a planet with all the other clever bastards who thought they'd outwitted old Scratch. At least these two chumps get to die, get to experience the sublime pleasures of hell. Hell isn't such a bad place to be.'

LIVE FROM THE LIZARD LOUNGE

I've been drifting in and out of consciousness. Don't know if I dreamed the conversation with Mobutu and then wrote it down after or wrote it down first then dreamt it. Gimpo re-enters the cabin and tells me we have been stuck on sandbanks most of the day.

'They had to unhitch the *Colonel Ebeya*, bring her round so they could pull the *Bangole* and *H203* off the sand bank.'

Gimpo seemed to be excited by all this. I wasn't. Gimpo left. Then Z came in drunk.

'Bill, tomorrow we get Mister Punch out and entertain the good folks. We need to get some practice in before we do it for Mobutu.'

'Yeah Z.'

I don't have the strength to argue with him.

He collapses into his bunk, puts his Walkman on and starts singing along to *Dean Martin Live from the Lizard Lounge*.

*

The spectral bard pulled out his crumpled quill and made a few more scribbled notes.

'"Hell ain't a bad place to be". I'm sure I've heard that somewhere before. "Can make of Heaven a hell, and of hell a heaven," mused the poet before continuing. 'Milton of course, and AC/DC. I'm always getting those two mixed up. Anyway where was I?'

'You were rambling Charles,' said Gustave tartly.

'Oh fuck off, Mary. I was just about to offer a few helpful words to our friends here, which was more than you were about to do, you fucking cartoonist!' shouted the poet, obviously touching a raw nerve as the painter left the room with a loud slamming of doors. 'And try laying off the sulphate!' Baudelaire shouted after him. 'Then you might not feel the need to fill every square millimetre of fucking canvas with stupid little doodles!'

The poet laughed as a loud, 'Just fuck off!' echoed around the house.

Baudelaire continued chuckling wickedly to himself, shaking his head in mild disbelief at his friend's petulance.

'So, my friends, and how can a useless old satanist like myself be of assistance to you bold young things? More absinthe?'

As if Z needed any prompting. My Zen Master companion held out his glass and fell off his chair, much to the poet's amusement

'Ninety per cent proof, strong isn't it?'

We spent the following week debauching ourselves almost into extinction. The old bastard Baudelaire was as good as his legend when it came to living life to its lowest. A couple of wild nights at the SEXODROME wanking ourselves into the carpet. Fine sport with several Estonian whores who I believe are still chained up in Gustave's attic, which is just as well really. I can't see them getting any work after the state the four of us left them in.

We were unfortunately barred from the Parisian Catamite. I'm afraid that was my fault, I caused a scene with a turning chisel after one of the little Arab boys... well, you know. Finally we had to leave, Gustave had nearly completed a painting.

'That would never do,' said the poet as he reminded us once again of what we already knew. In our bones.

The black river was calling.

THE POSTCARD

On the mat was a postcard. From the hand I instantly knew it was from Z.

'Dear Bill,
Meet me at the Rock Garden in Covent Garden tomorrow at half past two. Mister Punch knows all we need to know.
Yours, Z'

Chapter Four
LOGARITHMS OF MURDER

The *Colonel Ebeya* stalled a couple of days later. They found old Msomba Msomba tangled round a fly wheel, the poor bastard. The man loved that engine. I guess it was what he would have wanted, his flesh finally one with his steel bride. Not once in over 50 years had they been parted. I left Bill and Gimpo in their bunks juddering around in the soup of their perpetual flatulence and masturbation and went down to the engine room to pay my respects.

I wandered around the dark silent space, the coppery smell of human blood still clung to the heavier notes of diesel and sweat. Without the grinding, deafening noise it was so different. It was obvious from the sinuous repairs Msomba had patched the old diesel up with that the engine would never rumble into life again. Without Msomba Msomba it was just a hunk of scrap metal held together with old bits of tin and strange love.

Already dust was settling on the highly polished machine parts. The brass components around the pressure gauges and piston fittings shone like gold in the sepulchral light. Msomba's small litter behind one of the giant fly wheels, hidden in a small alcove was particularly poignant. The remains of his last meal; a piece of bread and half a plastic cup of sweet tea lay where he had left them.

Scraps of paper torn from books and magazines were taped to the wall beside his grey blanket; poems mostly, in French.

TO DREAM THE IMPOSSIBLE DREAM

'Bill, are you awake?'

'Yeah, Z.'

'I've been thinking.'

'Yeah?'

'We could turn this whole trip of ours into a musical.'

This wakes me up. Where is Z coming from now?

'A fuckin' musical? What the fuck are you talking about? This trip is as far from the raw ingredients for a musical as you can get. I know about musicals. I've seen all Rogers & Hammerstein, I can play every Lerner & Lowe song. Don't talk to me about musicals. This is no musical.'

'That's where you are wrong. Where you are always wrong. You see Bill, you don't have vision. You always do it by the book, that's why you fail.'

'I wrote the fuckin' book. Anyway, where's the love interest going to come from. You need romance for a musical not all that shagging dead prostitutes stuff that you write about.'

'No, I know. Gimpo and Giselle will provide the love interest.'

'And what about the music? We can't have all this Afro-pop shite, that's not going to have them singing down Shaftesbury Avenue. For a musical to be a hit it needs to appeal to coach loads of middle-aged women coming down from the Midlands for their big night out in the West End.'

'I've worked that out as well. You and I can write a load of Tamla Motown-type songs. We can have a bunch of the roof boys doing a Jackson Five vibe. The preacher, that you and Gimpo are so into, he can do a sort of Marvin Gaye song. Mami and a couple of the others can do a Supremes-type thing. You know how to write a Motown track, just a couple of chords isn't it? I can come up with the words.'

'Z, how come you think what everyone else does is the easy stuff and what you do is the genius stuff?'

'Don't get so touchy Bill. You know I wouldn't know the chords, all that minor diminished stuff.'

'Z, yes, I know. I know the chords and could pastiche the whole fuckin' Tamla catalogue but it would end up sounding like BoyZone b-side and not 'Walk Away René' by the Four Tops.'

'BoysOwn not BoyZone.'

'Whatever. Motown is sacred, you don't mess with it. I might know every chord change that Holland, Dozier, Holland did but it would still end up sounding shite.'

'I knew you were the man for the job. That it would just take a bit of persuading on my part. We may as well start writing the songs now.'

'I need a piano.'

'No you don't.'

So instead I get out of my bunk for the first time today, get my crumpled and stained safari suit on. We climb up on to the roof and I start singing my theme song. The one song that can make me cry every time I hear it: 'To Dream The Impossible Dream'.

*

'A terrible waste,' a deep, resonant voice pronounced from the black gloom on the other side of the engine room. The voice stepped into a shaft of light that fell from a vent in the ceiling, it was The Leopard, commanding general of the Black Eel. 'The *Colonel Ebeya* is useless now, more junk to dress the forest with.'

The powerfully built man sauntered towards me inspecting the amazing jigsaw of Msomba's repairs.

'Quite amazing isn't it, the way he kept this thing alive?' he said, patting an immaculate engine casing.

'What happened to him? I heard that he was picked out of the engine, crushed around one of the fly wheels,' I asked, half expecting some ludicrous cover-up for some reason or another. It seemed that the whole country was built on pointless lies and strange sodomistic deceit.

'No one knows for sure,' he replied. 'It's highly unlikely that he had an accident. The engine was like an extension of his own body, plus he didn't drink or use any other intoxicants. The man had no enemies. A mystery, my friend.'

The Leopard held his chin thoughtfully in his left hand resting it on his powerful chest.

'I'm afraid it looks as if it was the wanking that killed him in the end.' he added wearily, turning over the pillow on the dead pilot's bed.

'The wanking?' I repeated, confused.

'Yes, when my men pulled him out of the machinery one of his severed arms was holding a copy of this.' The general handed me an oil-stained copy of *Hollywood Cunts*. 'In his other hand, well I think you can guess.'

The Leopard lit a cigar in the highly combustible atmosphere. 'We think he got them from the Japanese, we found some bloodstained schoolgirl panties in his pocket. I'm told that these things are sold from vending machines in their capital city, Tokyo. How strange! And I can assure you my friend, magazines such as this...' he handed me a copy of *Bumhole through the knickers* the popular British tug monthly, 'Are not readily available in downtown Kinshasha. We think that this added stimuli to his regular masturbation patterns must have sent him metaphorically and literally over the edge. Gripped in some kind of dreadful wankfrenzy, the poor bastard must have tugged himself out of his bed, across the steel floor and down into the engine... such a waste, he was a good man as well as a fine engineer and pilot.'

A PAIR OF PERVERTS
'Bill, you're late. Now hurry up or we will miss the show.'
'What show?'
'Punch and Judy.'
'You mean you've got me coming in to London to watch a Punch and Judy Show?'
'Just shut up and watch it.'
So there we were standing on the Covent Garden Plaza among the kids and mums with pushchairs, like a pair of perverts, standing outside a school gate.

*

The Leopard threw *Bumhole through the knickers* on to Msomba's bunk and absentmindedly rubbed a piece of brass and copper piping with his white handkerchief. 'As well as being a great tragedy this is also extremely inconvenient.'
He placed the handkerchief back in his pocket.
'Now we have to wait for one of those damned Arab sodomy barges to push us the final distance into Kisangani. As a military man I find this so shameful. I loathe and despise those floating Gomorrahs, the President's hunger for Arab dollars... sometimes I myself wonder if any of this... But enough, this kind of talk is not healthy, a man's position beneath the President is never truly secure. Talk like this can only speed his downfall.'
The Leopard had already said too much. This in itself was indicative and portentous of the changes that were sweeping out of the forest like a new disease.
'Oh and one more thing, before I forget,' The Leopard said before leaving the engine room, 'Perhaps your friend would like to study this, it may be of help to him.' He threw me a small book. 'The sodomy has undone much in my country,' he added sadly as I flipped through the old parchment pages, it appeared to be some kind of occult almanac written in Arabic.
I looked up and the melancholy figure of The Leopard had disappeared.

ANOTHER DAY, ANOTHER WIND UP
Back in our bunks.
Gimpo snoring. Z still pissed and me now wide awake. My delirium seems to have passed totally but the weird thing is my memory of the conversation with Mobutu seems completely real.
'Z?'
'Yeah.'

'Are you still writing your Gimpo by Gimpo?'

'Yeah, why, do you want me to read you some?'

'And are you still writing the Drummond's Secret Log thing?'

'Did Gimpo fuckin' tell you about that?'

'No, you leave your stuff everywhere. You don't make any effort to hide it.'

'You got a problem with it?'

'No, course not, it's funny.'

'I knew you wouldn't. I wouldn't do it if I really thought it would upset you.'

'Fine, so you won't mind if I put in my stuff about you.'

'Say what you want.'

'Everything?'

Well it depends what the everything is?'

'It's OK, Z, I'm just winding you up.'

And so to sleep.

DRUMMOND'S SECRET LOG, ZAIRE, SOMEWHERE

Ipissimus 23

Arcane secrets of Dagon

Logarithms of murder

Calculations and synergies for the red nights

I gasped as I translated the full title of the notorious Arab grimoire *Logarithms of Murder*. This was the Ippisimus 23 edition, notorious for its binding of human skin. Time is too short to wonder how the Leopard came to be in possession of this rare grimoire. Here were all the occult alignments and mystical latitudes that the one-eyed Arab boy, Rolo was using to calculate the time and place best suited for releasing the cosmic energies he will claim when he takes my life.

I checked the dates and map references, referred them to my Russian lunar calendar and world tide tables, made a series of theosophical calculations involving the secret pi configuration held within the seven lost pyramids of Mu. A quick wank of sex magik, some kaballistic shitting and I had it, the exact location, the exact day, hour, minute and second that the Arab planned to prevent my life energy from reaching the stars and claiming it for himself. The location, unsurprisingly, was this exact spot on the river. The time, the seventh minute and seventh second after midnight tonight .

Rolo had twice now transgressed the laws of his occult lodge. Firstly with the murder of the innocent Tally and then it was obviously he who tossed Msomba Msomba into the *Colonel Ebeya*'s engine. It is common knowledge that the barge is useless without its pilot.

I must prepare myself. Sunset is only a few hours from now.

DRUMMOND'S LOG, WEDNESDAY 19 JUNE 1996
SMOKE ON THE WATER

Bad night, bad dreams. I had an Echo & The Bunnymen dream. Echo & The Bunnymen were a band that I managed in the first half of the 1980s. They were a band that I failed to do justice to. I regularly have Echo & The Bunnymen dreams. It is not the same dream every time. But every time I have a Bunnymen dream it is about me letting them down in some way or another. It might just be about getting the VAT in late or it could be something far more cosmic. Last night it was me, the Bunnymen and Mobutu in a Brussels nightclub. Mobutu was chopping out the lines of coke and I was trying to persuade the band to do a cover version of *Smoke On The Water*. The dream was that bad.

*

The Master Dagon Rolo secretly prepared himself in the refrigerated hold of the barge. The intricate breathing techniques he had learned in the Tibetan mountains from an Indian Rishi had enabled him to drop his blood pressure to such a degree that he was able to withstand the temperatures within the barge's ice hold. It was the perfect hiding place. The idiot white man even if he had the courage would never think to look for him here. The sub-zero temperatures had done nothing to cool the white-hot fires of his anger and desire for revenge.

Rolo had studied his logarithms of murder well. This spot on the river was the only chance he had to take the Scottish idiot's soul force. The death of the old pilot was unfortunate but Rolo's burning urge for revenge necessitated it. He would make his religious amends for both the pilot and the Senegalese drag queen, Tally when this mystical murder was complete. He had been a strict follower of the ancient God and was sure there was some religious penance he could make to placate the strict submarine deity.

Unfortunately there would be no time for the death of many cuts but the intricate knifework he had planned to despatch the Scottish infidel with would be just as painful.

'The three songs of Ourobourus', (Ourobouros of course the mythical serpent that devours its own tail); the songs referred to the cuts which were necessary to make the victim of this ghastly assassination slowly drown to death in his own scrotal blood.

The first cut takes out the victim's stomach and unnecessary viscera. The main arteries and organs would be left functioning as normal. This enabled the victim to be placed upside down, balanced on his shoulders against a wall where his sexual organs could be placed in his mouth. With no gut in place the spine could easily be bent into this Ourabouraan angle. The second neat cut severs a nerve at the base of the neck to assure paralysis. This prevents the victim from spitting out his genitals and ruining the poetry of the kill. The third and final cut runs underneath the scrotum and into the femoral artery, ensuring a steady flow of blood into the victim's throat and slowly drowning him in his own blood.

The further metaphysical humiliation of having the soul finally leave the body through the victim's arsehole was doubly delicious to the malicious Arab. Rolo intended to catch Bill's soul in a small bottle and after eating half as the dictates of his religion demanded he would bury the conscious part somewhere in the desert where it would never be found. Bill's conscious soul would be doomed then to endure an eternity of indescribable agony. This method of supernatural torture, incidentally, is where the legends of genies in bottles stem from.

SHUT UP BILL II

If you are a British reader I take it you know what Punch and Judy is and I take it you know what a Punch and Judy booth looks like. For those who don't know, Mr Punch and his wife, Judy are glove puppets and their, or should I say his, story is performed from within a Punch and Judy booth, big enough to allow the one puppeteer to operate his charges. My own memory of the story was pretty threadbare. I vaguely remembered seeing Punch and Judy shows as a kid on days out to the seaside. But these memories were recalled without any sort of nostalgia for an age of lost innocence or any other emotions that would want me to seek out or relive the experience of watching a Punch and Judy show.

'So what's this got to do with us?'

'Shut up, Bill. Just watch and listen.'

And I did.

*

The Arab had been busy preparing for this spiritual murder for the best part of a week. Sharpening his curved soul blade on a collection of different crystal and mineral whetstones, each stroke on the stone was accompanied by a secret prayer in submission to the great submarine deity Dagon.

Rolo's soul blade was a remarkable weapon, it was exactly 23 inches in length and slightly curved like the Japanese katana knife. The dynamics of the blade, designed for swift and deep cuts, was thought to have influenced the Japanese smiths thousands of years ago when they designed the samurai's famous swords.

The handle of Rolo's knife was made from thin strips of black human leather and solid ebony. The blade was forged with a forgotten blend of precious and non-precious metals and was virtually indestructible. If a microscope were used to study it, over 223 thousand microscopic folded layers of the exotic blended steel could be seen.

These were only the physical attributes of the knife. The black sorcery, souls and blood that this singing harbinger of death had drank deeply of intensified its killing properties beyond the imagination.

No one was sure how long men had practised their ichthyolatory in the name of the black God Dagon, its secret history stretched far beyond all records of men's other religions. Some believe that the Hindu goddess Kali is an echo of Dagon, that her most notorious acolytes, the murderous thugees are an offspring of the core religion. Unfortunately no one can be sure except the sinister God itself, and legend has it that Dagon is a silent deity. Murder collected like prayers eventually allows its acolytes a form of diabolical grace but again it is a silent grace not communicated by words but transmitted directly to the most primal parts of a man's soul, way down in the caverns of the mysterious limbic system.

Rolo painted the name of his master across his forehead with a red dye then masturbated into a small wad of straw which he set on fire, chanting a perverted litany all the while. He jiggered himself down and started to dance around the burning sperm. He squeezed a magical dump in four places, dedicating his turds to the four winds and their corresponding chakras.

All around him the huge frozen Congo catfish watched with sinister dead eyes. He pulled on the black pyjamas and black silk hood of his murderous cult then ceremoniously with yet more silent prayer sheathed his deadly soul blade into the human-skin holster strapped tight across his back. The assassin opened his door as the sun sank behind the treeline and slid silently into the Congolese night.

THE POLE

I join Gimpo up top at the front.

'What's up Gimps?'

'We've taken the wrong channel.'

The barges are bumping and grinding over the river bed. They are jerking against each other.

'See that man down there at the front with the pole?'

'Yeah.'

'He's using the pole to work out the depth of the river. It is only a couple of metres at most. See each side of us are exposed sandbanks? I reckon they fucked it. They should have gone the other side of that island.'

Gimpo and I spend the next three hours watching the man with the long pole reading the depth of the Congo, relaying the information, using hand signals to the men on the bridge, as they try and navigate the barges between the sand banks.

The day drifts by.

*

It was about a quarter to midnight when Bill slithered out from behind the mosquito net of his grisly bunk. He'd been keeping me awake for the past couple of hours practising some weird cack-arsed martial arts routine he'd obviously made up himself. Weird monkey noises like old Bruce Lee films interspersed with accidental farts squittering away as he performed his ludicrous kata.

It was hopeless trying to sleep so I followed after him intending to try and locate some jungle hooch. Bill was keeping himself in the shadows avoiding the pools of light thrown by the naked light bulbs strung dangerously here and there. There was a seriousness about him I hadn't seen before. Usually on his nocturnal wanderings he would stop off now and again to fondle small sleeping children curled up in their ragged blankets, but none of that sly pederasty was evident tonight. He was wearing a spotlessly clean pair of skin-tight white bellbottoms that cut and divided his arse cheeks painfully and a short white T-shirt I'd never seen before. The word 'baby' emblazoned in a 1970s style, red glitter typeface on the front. The crimson silk scarf with gold woggle and scarlet ballet pumps completed his bizarre retro-fairy look. He made his way up on to the roof and walked to the front of the barge where he posed arrogantly, like a slightly deluded matador, hands on his hips, chin held high as he stared back down the length of the roof.

The *Colonel Ebeya* searchlight picked him out clearly, illuminating the roof like floodlights at a soccer match. I managed to find a drunken old papa below decks that had a couple of jam jars of hooch for sale. It tasted pretty good once you took the bees and cockroaches out of it. I decided to share it with Bill up on the roof, he seemed to be getting himself wound up way too tight the further we headed up river. I think this Kiki kid meant a lot more to him than I originally realised. I figured maybe the hooch might loosen him up a bit.

'THAT'S THE WAY TO DO IT'

Then came the sound. A sound that tore down the back of my neck. Down my spine. Up my anal passage. Up through my insides and into my brain. It was the sound of Mister Punch laughing. His gleeful metallic laugh. I heard the laugh before I saw Punch. Up he bounced, flinging his little wooden legs over the front of the stage.

'Hello, boys and girls, and how are you today?'

The response was muted. Why should any four-year-old kid today want to respond to this crudely carved and badly painted wooden puppet? TV provides them with an endless stream of incredibly well-developed characters animated in every possible way that almost limitless budgets can provide. Why should they respond to his inane question of 'How are you today?'

No! Mister Punch does not belong in our day and age. I believe in the modern world and things like Punch and Judy should be left in the past with all the other boring things.

'I said, how are you today?'

'All the better for seeing you, Mister Punch', came a loud and clear reply but it wasn't from one of the pre-school brats. It came from Z. A glance at his face and I could tell he was already transfixed. As you may already have guessed, Z has an addictive personality. His addictions are wide and varied and he's always on the look-out for new ones to add to his collection. Mister Punch was obviously his latest.

Up popped Judy holding their baby.

'Oh, hello, boys and girls. I want Mister Punch to look after the baby while I go to the bingo. Can you make sure he does that for me?'

No response from the kids. I didn't blame them, this was lame stuff by any criteria.

I'm not going to take you through line-by-line everything that happened. It's enough to note that when Punch was left to look after the baby and the baby started to scream, he threw it to its death over the front of the stage. On Judy's return from bingo and in response to her understandable anger at him throwing the baby to its death, Punch whacks her about the head with his club until she too is dead.

'That's the way to do it.'

Along comes PC Plod to arrest Mister Punch. He too gets dispensed with in similar direct-action manner.

'That's the way to do it.'

When justice finally catches up with him and it's Mister Punch and the hangman on the gallows, Mister Punch does not understand what he has to do. So the hangman has to show him where to put his head. As he does, Punch instantly pulls the rope and the hangman is hung by his own rope.

'That's the way to do it.'

In the last scene we see Mister Punch and what I assume was the devil, though he was a pretty shoddy puppet version of His Satanic Majesty. There was some banter between the two of them which escalates into a physical struggle. Which ends with Punch throwing the Prince of Darkness back down into his fiery pit.

'That's the way to do it.'

Mister Punch is left alone on the stage triumphant. He takes his bow and the curtain closes.

What I failed to mention in this brief retelling of the tale of Mister Punch is how the young and unresponsive audience metamorphosed throughout the performance. With each despatch, with each cry of 'that's the way to do it', the cheer from the young and innocent throng gets louder. By the time he throws Old Horny into the flames it's like their side has just won the cup.

Z turned to me, 'Bill can't you see? It is obvious Mister Punch is the only character in the whole of recorded history who has been able to outwit Satan. He is our man and we need to take him with us.'

*

I'd just made my way up on to the roof with the hooch and was walking down the 30 yards or so to Bill when the ninja dude seemed to appear from nowhere. There was a weird silence surrounding the two of them, it sucked in and negated all other sounds except for a barely audible hum that hung sweet and evil in the sultry midnight air.

The ninja carefully removed a big curved blade from behind him and held its point a few inches from Bill's face. It shone eerily beneath the searchlight and was obviously as sharp as a razor. 'As I told you, Scottish,' I recognised the guttural tones of the Arab boy Bill was having trouble with. 'Love is all, you wish to die with honour still, accept my steel? Like a woman!' he shouted, suddenly lunging, jabbing the blade into Bill's face.

Bill's reflexes were uncanny. Ordinarily Bill has the grace and general demure of a constipated spastic but there was something of the speed and agility of a cheetah in the way he jerked his head out of the blade's way. Using Rolo's weight he sidestepped and tripped the assassin to the ground, the stunned killer twisted around to face his foe. Bill had crouched into a weird kung fu fighting stance, legs bent at the knees, arms outstretched into a strange preying mantis position.

'Get up, blasphemous queer!' he spat at his floored opponent. 'Which cut were you planning on dicing me up with, bum boy! The crucified chorus of the splayed bell end or was it something simpler? The wanking jackal perhaps ?' Bill called sardonically. 'Well it doesn't matter now, fudgepacker, because it's you not I that the reaper shall claim tonight!'

Bill brought down a weapon of his own, a sharpened steel pole, towards the floored Arab who twisted like a cobra and leapt to his feet, a massive shower of sparks flashed where Bill's pole hit the roof.

'Where'd you get all the fancy moves, Mary?' asked Rolo slashing at his opponent casually and cutting through the 'Baby' t-shirt, drawing blood.

Bill, with a skill that astounded me, flipped a backward somersault well out of reach of the Arab. Keeping his serious eyes burning in Rolo's direction he reached down to his flesh wound, dabbed blood on to his fingers and then tasted it just like Bruce in *Enter the Dragon*.

'Sexy,' mocked the Arab, a camp lilt to his voice. 'Come on, baby,' he added, pointing at Bill's weird t-shirt, 'Let's party.'

Bill threw the metal pole like a spear and as Rolo brought up his sword to block the weapon, the agile Scot slid like oiled lightning beneath the Arab's weapon and punched hard into his opponent's groin, leaping to his feet immediately and headbutting Rolo in the face.

'You murdering shitstabber,' Bill grunted, stepping out of range as Rolo wiped the blood from his eyes. 'It was you that killed the boy! Or have you forgotten that, you heathen bitch!' shouted Bill vehemently.

'You know nothing of our ways, Scottish. I had to kill him, it is a deep part of our religious homosexuality law. He was tainted by swallowing your corrupt Western jism,' answered Rolo.

'How do you know,' said Bill, spinning a fantastic 360-degree kick and crunching it into the side of the Arab's head, 'That Kiki swallowed the gravy?' the Arab dropped to the ground.

'He was a trained Catamite boy,' spat Rolo, along with his broken teeth. 'Swallowing jizz was like breathing to him.'

Ignoring the pain, like a miniature cyclone, Rolo span behind Bill and cut the seat completely out of his bellbottoms.

'Cheeky!' he laughed, arcing a camp eyebrow as the Scotsman's huge white buttocks dazzled like the moon beneath the searchlight.

END OF STORY

My mind keeps slipping into imaginary conversation with Mobutu.

'William, my boy, the cliché is true.'

'Which one?'

'All power corrupts. Absolute power corrupts absolutely.'

'So why are you telling me this?'

'Because I have always known it, even when I was an idealistic young journalist. I knew then that if I was to lead my country out of the mess and havoc of the immediate post-colonial era, I would have to assume absolute power over my country and, in doing so, I would be corrupted absolutely. There was going to be nothing I could do about it. But it still had to be done, there was no other way. I knew I was the only one with the vision, even if the power was going to corrupt me. That is where you went wrong.'

'What do you mean?'

'You never understood that you would be corrupted.'

'I'm not.'

'Of course you are. You being here is part of your corruption. You are abusing the power given to you by all those who handed over their hard-earned cash to buy KLF records so you could indulge yourself in this fantasy of yours.'

'This is not a fantasy. Me, Z and Gimpo are really here, stuck on these barges in this godforsaken hell hole of a country.'

'Yes, but not so much of the hell hole, if you please. A land of limitless opportunity is the way I like to see it. What I am referring to is all this bunkum about selling your soul and tricking the devil. Nobody will believe that. Write a book if you must entertain but not this. To be frank: go back, do a real job, for a real pay packet. Look after your family, love your wife, pay your taxes, worship god, go on holiday for two weeks a year and look after your parents in their twilight years.'

'That's what you reckon I should do?'

'Yes. End of story.'

We hit another sandbank and my conversation with Mobutu comes to an abrupt end. But of course it is not the end of the story.

*

Bill spun round and stabbed his opponent hard in the face with two neat left jabs.

'Not just a pretty face, eh Sinbad?' he grunted, driving a massive right cross full into the Arab's face, sending him sprawling backwards. 'I've got a nice arse as well!'

The Scotsman moved in for the kill. Rolo was stunned by the intense violence of the last blow. Bill kicked him hard in the ribs and, grabbing a hank of hair, dragged him to his feet.

'Call yourself Dagon,' he sneered, kneeing him hard in the groin then rabbit-punching the half-dead Arab as he fell to the ground.

Bill took off the ruined Baby t-shirt and threw it at the fallen Rolo as if he were a stinking trash can. He walked the length of the roof smiling hubristicly when suddenly Rolo sliced past him, his deadly blade cutting deep into his side, taking out a large flobbering piece of his innards. A brown liverish thing skidded across the roof and landed at my feet.

'Spleen pulp,' said the fully recovered Rolo to Bill who was on his knees holding closed the huge wound. 'You don't need it, same as these!' he said using his knife and hooking out more offal from Bill's stomach.

'Duodenum from the small intestine,' called the wicked Arab, tossing it to the bucket kids licking their lips in the shadows, 'Transverse portion of the colon,' he continued, smiling, 'Small piece of gall bladder and a handful of anterior layers from the great sexy omentum,' he said, throwing the gory innards one at a time over to the ever-present bucket kids. 'You'll live…'

The Arab heaved Bill upside down on to his shoulders against one of the Ebeya's funnels, holding him in place with his feet. 'Long enough.' he laughed, slashing Bill's grubby string Y-fronts away from his flesh and cutting deep into the gutted Zen master's scrotum, a jet of thick bright blood gushed at first and then settled into a steady pulse which Rolo directed into Bill's mouth by stuffing the mutilated Scot's penis deep into the back of his throat. 'To drown on your own blood…' The sadistic Arab held back his head, placed his hands on his hips and threw his evil laughter up to the stars.

'Didn't you forget something, asshole?'

It was Bill, up on his feet, all macho and bloody. Grabbing the Arab from behind by the hair again, he brought Rolo's own knife cleanly across the shocked sadist's throat.

'A little paralysis nerve behind my neck maybe?'

The Arab fell to the floor flailing around spouting blood and kicking his legs wildly. His mouth sucked at the air like a fish out of water, his lungs filling with blood. Surprisingly, Bill didn't gloat or perform any weird necrobuggery shit on the Arab's corpse. Instead he quickly made bandages from the dead boy's pyjamas and tied them around his own horrific wounds.

Using Rolo's knife he made a couple of small cuts into the dead man's sphincter and plunged his hand deep into the Arab's bowels up to the elbow. He strained, gritting his teeth and tugged hard a couple of times until he felt something snap, then pulled down a grisly handful of black innards and glistening ruby jelly.

'I can live without a spleen,' he said examining and poking around in the bloody offal 'but somehow,' he smiled, adjusting the sopping bandage around his slashed ballbag, 'A colostomy bag just isn't me.'

A JET OF FOUL-SMELLING LIQUID

In the luxury bar with Z.

'These pigs squealing everywhere are pissing me off big time.'

'So what you going to do about it?'

'Why with you, Bill, does something always have to be done about it?

'Well if they are pissing you off big time I take it you wish they were not here squealing.'

'Of course.'

'So you want to stop them. You will do something about it. If you don't, then they are not really pissing you off big time because you are accepting the situation. To accept the situation means that you are…'

'Shut the fuck up.'

'No. I don't think any of us have the right to complain about anything unless we take on the responsibility of doing something about it. That's what's wrong with the world, every fucker wants to moan about things but never...'

'Bill, I said shut the fuck up. I've heard you go on like this a hundred times before. When was the last time you took any responsibility for anything outside your own little life? And anyway, I was just making conversation. And talking of responsibility, it's your round.'

'OK, Z, I admit it, these pigs are driving me up the wall. There must be more pigs on this flotilla than there are people. Each and every one of them trussed up and squealing. The RSPCA would have a field day here.'

'The RSPCA would close the country down.'

And for those readers not from the UK, RSPCA stands for the Royal Society for the Prevention of Cruelty to Animals.

'Bill, I used to come up to the Luxury Bar to get away from all the madness and shit that's going on elsewhere on these boats but now it's here as well. Fat Miguel has been stacking up those smoked monkeys in the corner, the first mate has a crocodile in his cabin. As for those six pigs trussed up over there they belong to the captain.'

'How do you know the first mate's got a crocodile?'

'I made that up, but you can count the pigs for yourself. Imagine going into a bar in London, a bar calling itself the Luxury Bar, and there being six trussed-up pigs piled up against the wall. It wouldn't even happen in Dublin.'

'But this is Africa.'

And just as this conversation is about to peter out and you must be wondering where it is going, the first mate and three of the other ONATRA employees burst into the bar shouting and laughing. They have an animal. It may be an armadillo. Do armadillos come from Africa? It's bigger than I thought an armadillo would be. If you don't know what an armadillo looks like I can't be bothered to describe it, go and look it up in a book. It has curled itself up into a ball. They are trying to uncurl it. This struggle to uncurl the creature goes on for some time. It momentarily uncurls itself and squirts out a jet of foul-smelling liquid that hits the first mate in the face. The others roar with laughter. The first mate gets out his lighter and goes to hold the flame under it as it is being held by two of the other ONATRA employees.

'What I like most about Africans is their total lack of sentimentality towards animals.'

Now this behaviour of theirs is pissing me off big time. I do nothing about it other than walk away, head back to the cabin and brood.

*

We banged on the doctor's door. Bill reckoned he could stitch himself back together using the parts he'd ripped out of the Arab. Bill was going to tell me what to do, Gray's *Anatomy* had been his favourite book when he was a kid and he could still remember whole tracts of the famous Victorian masterpiece. This explained a lot about some of Bill's stranger habits. I got the feeling that he spent a lot of time locked in the bathroom studying the colour plates of that weighty tome in the same way that most other kids dug gash mags.

Again, the horror of other men's wank fantasies. Sickly Bill, twelve and a half years old, lurching furtively from the bathroom, sperm drying between the pages illustrating female reproductive organs. The sweaty awkward boy yanking hard on his skinny boner, stretching the skin, almost tearing it as he faints into a watery orgasm, collapsing on the floor, head swimming with silver lights and colour pictures of the inside of a girl.

All those lovely coloured organs like a sweet shop, and those beautiful words – uterus, hypogastric plexus, sacral plexus, sacro-sciatic foramen – sometimes he could make himself ejaculate just by repeating a few of these magical words. They were like poetry to him, like something you would hear in church. And when you took all a girl's skin off, like in the book, she was just like one big giant vagina, all red and soft, wet and sweet, warm and lovely.

Bill was hitting delirium, chanting words that didn't make sense. He was losing a lot of blood from his slashed ballbag. From what I could see of the wounds to his stomach they looked bad, but were very clean, the Arab had known exactly what he was doing. I could see where the parts he had ripped out of Rolo's arse needed to be attached. I was quietly confident that If Bill lost consciousness I would be able to fix him up pretty much OK.

He didn't look that much different to the rats we used to chop up during biology classes back at school.

JESUS WAS CHEATING

There was a message on the answer phone, 'See you in the Reading Room 10.30 tomorrow.' Z's latest addiction had taken hold in a desperate manner. He had given up playing computer games almost completely. His collection of porn was left unsoiled, the vodka bottle gathering dust in its hiding place. Z was spending all the opening hours down at the British Library researching the life and times of Mister Punch.

10.30 the next morning. No 'hello Bill how's it going?', just straight in with 'How did he do it? How did he get away with it? What did Punch have that Faust and all the legion of others who were willing to trade their souls for a few fleeting years of worldly glory didn't? Mister Punch, a mere wooden puppet, was able to outwit the ultimate adversary before dancing on his merry way.'

'But Z, Jesus beat the devil that time in the wilderness.'

'No, Jesus was cheating. He had an unfair advantage as he was God made flesh. Punch is only a man carved from wood. Punch is one of us.'

The perma-shitfaced doctor answered the door in his faded yellow underpants, rubbing at his eyes. A gale of cheap liquor stench and bad nigger farts rolled out of his dark surgery. I banged on the light switch and waited for the vermin to hide.

Boxes of dangerous medicines were stacked to the small cabin's dripping roof. The floor was buried beneath old fish bones and dirty blankets, soaking up the regulation two inches of faecal slop.

The doc had made himself a kind of nest in the corner from old boxes and banana leaves on which he'd rather ingeniously made himself a mattress from hundreds of inflated condoms. Empty Jerry cans filled with poisonous jungle hooch stunk every where.

'I need instruments,' I said, miming cutting and sewing.

The dozy doctor looked at me stupidly, scratching his balls and letting rip a foul grincher.
I pointed at Bill's wounds dripping into the shitty chaos of his room.
'Scalpel, sutures...'
'Ah yes!' The doctor beamed struggling into his grubby white coat. 'Surgery!' He beamed enthusiastically, reaching in his pocket and pulling out a broken stethoscope. He pulled a table out of the wall. The grey PVC covering was torn, bloodstained foam rubber poked out from numerous holes.
The doctor patted the table enthusiastically, 'Surgery, surgery, yes, yes!'
He was fishing in his torn pockets, pulling out broken and rusty instruments lining them up on a small table. We didn't have time to fuck around, Bill was losing a lot of blood. I placed the spleen and rest of the guts in a cardboard box as Bill climbed up on to the scuzzy operating table. The doctor was fucking around with a couple of syringes cooking up some lethal-looking compounds and loading them into the barrel.'
'Listen, Doctor,' I said, pulling on my ear and speaking as clearly as I could to the stinky pisshead, 'We don't have much time, do you understand?'
'Ah, yes yes!' He said pulling open a small refrigerator and yanking out a cold beer. 'Yes, yes,' he continued, offering me the beer.
It wasn't what I meant but it was much appreciated.
'No, no doc, we need Gray's *Anatomy*,' I said, swigging on the Primus and miming flipping through some pages and pointing at the cardboard box of guts and dying Bill. 'Yes, yes!' he answered, smiling and starting to work on Bill's opened guts, stitching up arteries and staunching the blood flow with some rusty clamps. 'In corner, third box,' he managed to say, priming the syringe and hitting himself up in the neck.
'Simple operation, fix good, white man shit good, no colostomy bag, ha ha, yes.'
The grubby little African reached into the cardboard box and fished out the tangled mess of Rolo's still tacky innards. They were starting to dry out and had already started to stink . He smiled broadly and started unravelling the mess and laying it out on the table.

PIG ON STAGE
In my bunk.
I remove the rag around my big toe to inspect the wound. I prod it. I register the pain shoot up my leg. I squeeze yellow pus from it. I decide to taste the pus. It does not taste good but not as bad as you might think. I clean the wound as best I can, dab on some more TCP and tie it back up in the rag. I go to sleep and dream of Mobutu prodding pigs with sharpened sticks on stage in front of an audience hoping to see Echo & The Bunnymen play.
The pig squeals have been miked up and are booming from the massive PA stacks either side of the stage at a terrifying volume. The Bunnymen fans leave the hall. There is just me standing watching Mobutu prodding the pig on stage. Pete De Freitas walks across to me.
'Bill, why have you done this? Why have you allowed President Mobutu prodding a trussed-up pig to be our support act?'
'I thought it would make a change from the usual second-rate indie band that we have as the support.'
'Well, Bill, you thought wrong.'
'In future I will...'
'There is no future.'

Then the scene changes and I see Pete on a country lane driving his motorcycle heading from his home towards Liverpool and in the dream I know Pete is going to be killed in a motorcycle accident within the next five minutes but there is nothing I can do about it. I'm screaming at Pete to stop but he can't hear me and he drives on past me on the roadside. I hear the roar of his motorbike fade into the distance, then I hear a thunderous crash and see a ball of flame explode in the night and then I wake up.

*

I managed to find an old paperback copy of the Victorian surgeon's handbook floating around in the slop. I flipped through it quickly trying to find the section on the arse end of the intestinal tract. I soon realised that I needn't bother as the ship's doctor was beavering away inside Bill's guts looking amazingly proficient. He stopped occasionally to light a fag or take a swig on his beer, smiling happily and singing to himself.

I looked at the illustrations in the book and at Bill's guts. Things seemed to be roughly in the right places so I let the little Doctor carry on with his work and started testing some of the weird drugs he had lying all over the place.

Most of the keenest body drugs – the opiates and their dreamy derivatives – were piled high next to the doc's condom crib, along with what I took to be the little guy's own African version of laudanum: morphine sulphate stirred up in a big jug of jungle hooch.

I took a deep chug on the doctor's ruin and it whacked straight into me, like a big rubber steam train. I wasn't in the best condition when the little guy started babbling at me in French, I couldn't understand what he was saying but it seemed pretty important. He was shouting, holding on to something in Bill's guts with one hand and pointing at something in the Gray's *Anatomy* with the other.

He eventually gave up trying to make me understand when he realised how spaced out I was and just indicated that I should hold on to this tube sticking out of Bill's stomach. There were all these black metal clamp things and various ties, rubber bands and shit swirling around in the Scotsman's foul-smelling guts. My head was sliding sideways and I couldn't really make out what was what, it was all kind of jumbling around like a pot of electric vongole.

Things were moving and pumping, I thought one piece of pulsating muscle was his heart but it was in the wrong place and it had a face. In fact the more I looked at Bill's insides the more every thing seemed to be in the wrong place. The lungs were all tangled up in the intestines and the kidneys were where the liver should have been.

PROFESSOR DRUMMOND AND PROFESSOR MINDWARP

Late one night I got a call. Ring, ring.

'Hello.'

'Bill?'

'Yes.'

'It's me.'

'I know.'

'I've got it all worked out. We take Mister Punch with us up the Congo. He will teach us how do it.'

'Do what?'

'Trick the devil. Get off scot-free. Souls unscarred, the lot.'

'I don't know what you mean, Z.'

'Look Bill, if you and I become professors...'

'Professors?'

'Yeah, professors. That's what Punch and Judy men are called. Professor Drummond and Professor Mindwarp. What do you think?'

'Become Punch and Judy men? We don't know how. We would be crap.'

'No Bill. This is what we were born to do. There is this professor who lives somewhere up in the Black Country. He has a special school where he teaches you all you need to know. How to swazzle, all the gags and how to bottle.'

'Look, Z, it's late. I'll talk to you tomorrow.'

*

I shouldn't have started tinkering around in there I know, but I couldn't help myself. Of course I just started making things worse, the gall bladder came off in my hands and one of the main arteries started pumping great spouts of blood all over the fucking place. I managed to get the clamps back on the artery but I couldn't remember where I'd put the fucking gall bladder.

It didn't seem to matter though, the doc came back in with a bucket of some purple shit and he never even noticed the missing bits, just started fiddling around, sewing stuff here and wrapping bandages around there. I must admit I was impressed by the old guy's skills. It was only later that we found out he used to be a top surgeon in one of the main Brussels hospitals before some cunt with big tits distracted him badly in the theatre. Two unnecessary amputations and an extremely sloppy bypass finished his career overnight.

Bill started to regain consciousness just as the doc had started sewing him back up again. I gave him a big stab of fenyl citrate in his carotid. I reckon you could operate on your own fucking balls and not feel anything when you were high on that righteous hospital dope. Doctors and hospitals, man, they got the most kicking shit of anyone, quality vintage shit as well. The crap us lowlifes get to fuck around with is nothing compared to the sweet vein candy those medical cats party with.

The stitches could have been neater, they had a kind of Frankenstein's monster vibe about them but Bill seemed happy enough. He was up on his feet straightaway, limping around seeing how he felt.

'My gall bladder feels a bit weird,' he said, 'But apart from that I feel pretty good.' The doctor popped open a couple more beers and toasted the successful operation. We decked the beers and the old sawbones pointed over towards his teeming pharmacopoeia inviting me to dig around for anything that took my fancy.

Among the heap of forgotten medicines I managed to dig out some extremely rare, majorly cool feelgoods: alphamethylfentanyl 1988, China white, a fine vintage. Talk about hog heaven.

Capricorn,

Cruising,

My name is Larry,

float on baybehhh.

Oh yesss.
Do not disturb, the doctor is out,
far out baby,
riding the slipstream,
grooving with the flow.

PROCEEDINGS

Just woke from my Pete De Freitas dream. Outside there is a flash of lightning then a distant roll of thunder.

'You awake, Bill?'

'Yeah.'

'You gotta come up to the bridge.'

I follow Gimpo along our balcony, turn left at the end where the preacher and his family have their spot. Through the short corridor passing the three lavatories, turn right, clamber down the steps where I did my toe, leap from the *Bangole* on to the *Mukongo*, managing not to trip over the steel ropes that bind them together. We squeeze past the stall holders, who are all busy tying down tarpaulins over their stalls. Ignore the squealing pigs and the two live crocodiles tied to the railings. Have my feet pecked at three times by three separate ducks in wicker cages under the stalls. The wicker bars to these cages are wide enough apart to let the ducks put their heads through and stretch their necks so they can take a peck at the passing ankles. These ducks must be pissed off about what fate has dealt them, but they are not just sitting in their cages moaning. The cooking pot will not claim them until they have tried everything possible to rectify their situation. If that means taking pecks at my ankle, so be it. I applaud them.

From the *Mukongo* we cross to the *Colonel Ebeya*. This requires no death-defying leap. We pass the engine room and the ice hold where all the giant unsmoked fish are kept. Then we climb the steps towards the balcony outside the starboard side of the luxury bar. Then we climb some more steps up to the bridge. I have not been inside the bridge before. I have always assumed it was out of bounds. As it should be. It is a comparatively wide and spacious bridge. The floors are well scrubbed, all looks freshly painted white with green painted trimmings. There are no trussed-up, squealing pigs, no stacks of smoked monkeys, no cages of ducks ready to take a nip at my ankles, not even an armadillo ready to squirt me in the eye. The only unfunctional artefact in the room is the obligatory portrait of Mobutu hanging on the wall, keeping his eye on proceedings.

The captain gives us a smile, as if to welcome us to his bridge. He is a large, cheerful-looking man in his middle years. He is dressed no differently to his crew – ONATRA t-shirt, shorts and flip-flops. He does have a gold tooth. May be this marks him out to be a man in authority. He has his berth off at the back of the bridge, the rest of the crew have cabins that they share with their families down with the rest of us. Z is already there.

'It's fuckin' brilliant, Bill.'

And what Z is referring to is, by no stretch of the imagination, one of the most brilliant sights I have ever seen in my life to date. From our position up here on the bridge we can see over the tops of the trees lining the southern bank of the river. The light is beginning to fail and here, near enough on the Equator, it fails fast, but there is still enough light in the day for us to see what must be scores of miles across virgin rainforests.

But that isn't what I want to waste ink describing. We have grown used to seeing spectacular storms in Hollywood films. Every seventh Hollywood film ever made features a thunderstorm more spectacular than we ever get to see in Blighty. When I was a kid I thought forked lightning was just a special effect used by filmmakers. Well fuck Hollywood. Spielberg has never dreamt of, let alone seen, what I am looking at now. Not a drop of rain has fallen on us yet but out across the Eastern sky hangs a low black cloud. From that cloud comes flash after flash of forked lightning. It is getting closer. Even Z has shut up, we just all stand and stare at its inevitable onward march across the Congo Basin toward us.

I don't know how long it is before the first huge warm drop of rain hits the roof of the bridge, to be followed by a building volley of others. Then it is upon us. There is no rushing wind just a torrential downpour of rain the likes of which we have never seen. Darkness has fallen but all around us bolts of lightning are flung from the heavens to the earth, well from the cloud a few hundred feet up, down to the jungle. We see individual trees get hit, then explode into flames. We see bolts smash the surface of the river and then skitter across its surface like bits of broken ice flung on to a frozen pond. And, of course, the lightning illuminates what seems like the whole Congo Basin for miles in every direction.

After each particularly close bolt of lightning I am left with an afterimage in my skull. It is that image hanging on the wall behind me. Him with his leopard skin hat and his heavy framed glasses and his stick held across his chest, Sese Seko Kuku Ngbendu Wa Za Banga. Yes, he is truly the all-powerful warrior who goes from conquest to conquest, leaving fire in his wake. What further proof do we need? There is no argument. In a land where there may be hundreds of gods there is only one true omnipotent prime-moving ruler and that is the president of this, the greatest nation in Africa. To you Africa may be the sick continent but out here right now it is the first and will be the last continent, where man has come from and where he will die.

'What the fuck are you doing, Bill?'

'Making my notes, describing the scene.'

'Well stop and just take it in. You will never experience this again and, anyway, I thought you were totally against anything that was descriptive. Burn all adjectives is your motto, isn't it?'

I ignore Z and get on with these notes.

When the lightning lights the sky we can see a man standing in his pirogue up ahead on the river. He must be at least be half a mile from the bank, waiting in the torrents of rain and the lightning for us to arrive, to make his leap, to sell his wares. But I can't imagine that any of the traders or stall holders will be open for business. All hatches will be battened.

The flotilla is steered towards the southern bank of the river. The engines are cut and we wait and we watch as the storm passes over. And once the storm has passed there is silence. No music from the blasters, no babies crying, not even any pigs squealing. That is, until Z says, 'Come on, let's go and get a beer' and then everything starts up again. Music, babies and pigs squealing more than ever.

Chapter Five
THE WILD HIGHWAY

Cross-eyed Billy was lying on his bunk polishing his shooting irons. Two beautiful peacemaker, single action 45s. He'd lost count of the men he'd sent to hell with them.

'The best $34 I ever spent,' he mused to himself holding the heavy guns up towards the bare light bulb and admiring the oily sheen on the black barrels.

The ivory handles had worn down to the contours of Billy's hands over the years. The gunslinger reckoned that it was the thinness and sensitivity of his skin that made him such an excellent killer. Sometimes in the heat of a gunfight, with lead flying in all directions, Billy swears he can see the bones of his hands, like an x-ray.

Billy was no ordinary leadchucker. These moments of visionary clarity convinced him that he was an artist. A shootist, as his old friend Clay Allison liked to call himself. A sinister master of death.

Billy has no idea how he had ended up on this black river at the end of the world. When the frontier west of the hundredth meridian started tidying itself up and dragging its laws down from the last century and into this one, Billy drifted. The one thing he detested more than anything else in his violent world was the law. To Billy, the law itself was a crime. A crime that wanted to deprive him of the only thing he cared about: his freedom, a selfish freedom, admittedly, that allowed a man to do exactly as he pleased.

Billy thought that the right to take another man's life was as natural as breathing and any attempt to criminalise this act was a sin against the devil himself. The entire history of mankind, said Billy, was based on cool murder. All you had to do was look at historical maps punctured with crossed swords like bullet holes to see that.

If any man in the name of his law wanted to take Billy's guns away from him they were more than welcome to try.

CROCODILES

The journey back from the luxury bar in the *Colonel Ebeya* to our cabin in the *Bangole* is the most treacherous yet. Pigs that I had thought had given up any hope of freedom were railing against their bonds. The turtles were hatching new plans of escape. Every one of the 49 caged ducks that I pass has a go at pecking my feet. The two crocodiles that are bound to the hand rails, who are usually willing to bide their time, safe in the knowledge that when the humans come to untie the ropes that hold them fast, they will lash out with their tails and make their break for the river, are struggling to break the ropes. I kick the same toe on the same top step, blood pours. I climb into my bunk and fall fast and deeply asleep.

*

As the Tin Stars worked hard with their law, building themselves fine prisons to live in, Billy decided it was time to take the Wild Highway. The bloody road took him south, down through beautiful, lawless Mexico with its fantastic wild flowers, mindswirling mescal, foxy transsexuals and drunken, gore-flinging bullfights. Fantastic Central America, full of dripping jungles and lost cities haunted by the ghosts of human sacrifices.

Billy spent most of the twentieth century luxuriating in the sublime mayhem he had found on this section of his highway. The lean sunburnt killer hadn't always been a loner. When the west was truly wild he rode with the notorious Black Swan gang, the most feared bunch of feral, existentialist outlaws the state of California had ever seen. The memories were fading now but Billy could still remember a few of their names. There was Charlie Wiseblood, a deranged giant of a man who blew himself and his boy to bits sticking dynamite up the lad's bunghole. Charlie and his boy used to get their sex thrills leaving the fuse burning till the last second, putting it out in the nick of time and buggering in a snake-oil frenzy of near-death excitement. And Religious Ike – the only thing religious about the stone killer-rapist Ike was his taste for Mexican choirboys. Wanker Sam and Kid Dogshit, both of them excellent shootists and outstanding masturbators. And of course there was Billy's main amigo, his closest buddy, a stunningly beautiful English boy known only as The Poet.

THE IMMORTAL PUNCH

Three weeks after the late-night phone call from Z about us becoming Punch and Judy men we were in deepest Black Country territory enrolling at Professor Edwards' School for the Dark Arts or something like that. We were doing a two-day crash course.

'So, Bill and Z, you are children's entertainers and you want to broaden your palette by learning the basics of glove puppetry?'

'No Professor, we are about to embark on a journey up the Congo in search of Satan. Once we have found him we want to trick him into giving us our souls back and seeing as Mister Punch is the only character in literature to ever confront and beat Satan we thought we would learn to be professors, take a Punch and Judy kit with us, perform for Satan then Punch can do his business and while Satan is being seduced by Punch's charms, we nick our souls back.'

'Well I'm sorry lads, I think you've made a mistake. For a start, Satan as a regular character in the Punch and Judy cast list had completely disappeared by the First World War.'

'But we saw...'

'No, kids are no longer frightened of the devil. Eternal domination means nothing to them at a modern birthday party.'

'But...'

'But what they do understand, what they do respond to is the crocodile. We have been using the crocodile as a character for at least 80 years.'

'But...'

'Kids today have never heard of Satan. They think devils are something to do with Manchester United. You know, the Red devils.'

Z pulled one of his many first editions pilfered from the British Library from his bag. 'But it says here, "In modern puppet shows, Punch fights the devil and always overcomes him."'

'Who wrote that?'

'Dr Johnson.'

'But Dr Johnson was writing 200 years ago. Look, the first thing you have to learn about Punch is that you mustn't take him seriously. If you try to study him as a literary figure like he's King Lear, there is nothing there. Yes, he is immortal but only because we let the show evolve so that kids from each generation can identify with him. He is just an unruly character that they can identify with and as kids tastes change, the show has to change. The one reason for Punch existing is so that we can earn a living from entertaining children.'

'We thought you were an expert in the dark arts of Mister Punch. We haven't trekked all the way up to the Black Country to be told it's just about making pre-school kids laugh. My girlfriend told me that already.'

'Look lads, you've paid your money, let's leave all this to later and let's get on with the first lesson – how to make your swazzle.'

*

Stinkeye Nell, madame of The Raging Jizzcatcher brothel, shot The Poet in the balls, killing him instantly, after she accused him of raping her 12-year-old daughter. Not that Miss Stinkeye junior was any innocent virgin, no way José. The pubescent cocksucker had been turning tricks with prairie trash since she was eight years old. Before Billy left Tombstone he crucified Stinkeye Nell and her cunting little kid outside Bauers Union Market on Fremont Street.

In California, Billy's killing name was The Lover. He got the cute handle not only because he had the biggest set of wedding tackle this side of the Rio Grande, but because of his spooky habit of leaving The Lovers tarot card on the bodies of his kills.

Billy can't recall exactly when it was that he got a taste for boys but it must have been around the same time he discovered that deadly secret that women keep hidden in their guts. As a young man Billy was just another regular jack rabbit bone artist, enjoying his recreational copulation, banging sluts like there was no tomorrow until one of them took a shine to young Billy and showed him what all that jiggin' was really for, up and getting herself pregnant on the boy's wild jizz. The child was stillborn.

SLAYING THE LEOPARD

The night brings its horrors. Am I the man in the pirogue standing and waiting, watching the water rise? How much water can a dugout hold before it sinks? No, I'm not that man but I keep watching him, forever caught in that moment of illumination before the all-encompassing blackness of the night takes hold again only a fraction of a second later. And then, another flash of lightning and he is not there. Gone. This scene is played over and over in my dream. Then I hear the voice of Mobutu. I cannot see him. I look around but he is nowhere, just his voice.

'William, there was no deal. The devil never struck a bargain for your soul. You are a free man. You can do whatever you want, go wherever you want, say whatever you want. And, as you know, the price of that freedom is the responsibility that comes with it. You are just scared of your own freedom, scared of the responsibility it brings. I am a free man. I have been free since I slayed the leopard with my grandfather's spear, when I was just a boy. With my freedom I carry the burden of this great nation on my shoulders. Zaire will have its setbacks. I will die a lonely death. Other nations will scorn at my and my people's struggles. But Zaire will rise and rise and so will their memory of their founding fathers, their first of many great leaders. William, you are a free man, go and slay your leopard and carry your responsibilities like a free man should.'

I awake. Now how much of this dream was really a dream and how much did I make up while writing it down? I don't know. What I do know is that when I awoke I could hear Mavuba shagging his missus on the bunk underneath me. This is a sound I don't want to hear. I do all in my powers to blot it out. And begin to hatch a plan to break into London Zoo with a rifle, find the cage with the leopard and make my kill. No, of course I won't and anyway, there isn't a leopard in London Zoo and I know the leopard thing is just symbolic, but for what? That is the question. What is my fuckin' leopard that needs slaying?

Sleep.

*

That was when Billy realised how incandescantly dangerous this thing called Love could be. Billy's wild and untamed love almost killed him from the inside and it was responsible for killing more men in one week than Billy's hate had ever done in the entirety of his short life. He stayed drunk for a whole week and killed 15 men in his grief for the dead child.

Love turned strange in Billy, crystallised into something dark and cold. Billy reckoned this was what had kept him alive all these weird years. He'd lost count of his birthdays but figured he must be easily over 200 years old. He'd spent most of these years following his Wild Highway, down through Central and Southern America leaving a trail of blood, sodomy and death stinking up his wake worse than one of Farting Charlie's easy-over skunk killers.

Some time during the Second World War Billy left the Americas and spent several years cruising, sodomising and murdering his piratical way across the world's wild oceans. He rejoined the highway in North Africa and made his way to Sierra Leone and eventually ended up in the wildest place on Earth. Zaire.

If there had ever been any kind of law in this place, no one could remember it.

DRUMMOND'S LOG, THURSDAY 20 JUNE 1996
NOT TONIGHT LADS

I'm awake.

It is not the dream of killing the leopard I remember, nor Mavuba shagging his missus. There are other things I remember from the night. Mavuba got up at some point. He had been remonstrating with somebody outside the cabin. I'm sure it was the head ticket inspector. Our tickets have been inspected about every second day. Every time Gimpo has to turn on his charm, explain it all again one more time, and every time things seem to be left good naturedly enough. But in the night I think Mavuba was defending us against one last attempt at a big ticket inspector shakedown. Or, as Gimpo would have it, Mavuba is in on the whole thing and, in fact, he was saying 'not tonight lads, wait until their last night on board and we get the whole lot'. There were other dreams but this is neither the time nor the place.

*

I was standing up on the bridge when I saw our rescue chugging up river. You could tell it was a sodomy barge by the sweet smell of snake oil and boy musk that floated before it. The traders had started switching their stock around, packing away the mirrors and baby clothes and displaying jars and tins of snake oil from around the world: Bum OK from India, rough and ready with added grit, said the colourful label; Sphincter 8 from Arizona, expensive and smooth; Cookin' and fuckin', a boisterous edible oil with a strong fruity aftertaste from Australia; and Citadel, spicy and evil smelling from Turkey, named after the famous T E Lawrence incident which the upper-class British officer later likened in his book, *The Seven Pillars of Wisdom* as having the citadel of his integrity irrevocably violated. That's a mighty fancy way of describing having your arse buggered off by a bunch of arse-crazy Turks.

They hastily arranged all manner of hand-carved buggery tools and vicious ball-stretching devices; evil looking rhino-hide bullwhips, the same ones that the Arab slavers used to flay the backs of disobedient slaves with; and old copies of *Hello!* magazine and *Shitstabbing on a budget*, the popular gay travel journal.

As the sodomy barge drew nearer however you could see that this particular craft was different from the S/M battleship we had come across down-river. It was painted pink for a start, and had the words 'The love boat' spelled out with garlands of bright jungle flowers across the bridge. The homos weren't hiding either, a bunch of bold white trannies in high heels, blonde bouffant wigs and garish 1970s clothes were waving and screaming.

'We've come to push you up your bottom!' shouted one, giggling.

'WOO-oo, Donkey Ko-ong, where are you?' sing-songed another.

'Juicy fruits to the rescue!' called a six-foot Cleopatra, jiggling her silicon.

As the love boat drew up behind us the exotic bummers of paradise in a flurry of feather boas disappeared below deck, laughing girlishly and running as fast as their high heels could take them.

Once the stall holders had realised that it was a Fairy Tug coming to our assistance their mood lifted and they all started singing happily, packing away the ugly buggery weapons replacing them with day-glo lipsticks, padded bras and oversized high heels. Everyone loves drag queens.

HOW TO MAKE A SWAZZLE

'OK lads, the first thing you must learn about swazzles is that you must never ever show anybody your swazzle. Every professor has to make his own one. He must never lose it, share it or show it. Without a swazzle, you are nothing. Without being able to swazzle, Punch does not exist. It may take you months to learn to swazzle, the lucky ones learn in a few weeks.'

He didn't show us his but he showed us how to make our own. I'm afraid I'm under oath not to tell you what materials, if any, are used in the making of the modern swazzle. Suffice to say it is a deceptively simple device and we soon had our swazzles made and ready for action.

'So what the fuck is a swazzle?'

Let Professor Edwards answer your question. 'The swazzle is a small instrument that you keep in your mouth and it enables you to talk with the voice of Mister Punch. It is that reedy and piercing voice that unifies all Punches around the world.'

*

I noticed Bill straining to get a view of the Fairy Tug's exotic passengers. He squinted in the bright sunlight, licking his cracked lips lasciviously and shaking coins in his trouser pocket like a creepy school teacher.

His operation seemed to have been a success. The doc must have improvised with the gall bladder, I found the shrivelled organ in my back pocket after Bill had been sewn up. He never mentioned it so I threw it overboard when he wasn't looking.

Once the Love Boat had been secured snugly at the rear of the *Ebeya* some of the girls came aboard to do some shopping. It was soon pretty obvious why these Western belles had chosen the Congo as this year's holiday destination. The men on the *Colonel Ebeya* were fascinated by these beautiful ambiguous creatures and were flirting enthusiastically with them. The trannies were in starry seventh heaven as the virile heterosexual young men fussed all over them, squeezing their implants and slapping their cute little arses. It was all rather touching – innocent almost, like a school disco.

Bill of course totally ruined the charming atmosphere, leering and openly wanking. Gimps never had a problem with transvestites though; me neither, come to that. We spruced our selves up quickly, splashing on an African version of Hai Karate that smelled more like Fuck Off Wrestling and went to check out the glamorous homo babes over on the Love Boat.

I'd almost forgotten how great homosexual music could be. 'Diamonds are Forever' and 'Big Spender' reamed out over the speakers in the disco bar, songs that understood clearly the finite reality of romantic love and how a smart girl gets to come out on top when the passion fades. Shirley Bassey, the girl from Tiger Bay, was the patron saint of divorcees and drag queens the world over. Then there was Fantastic Cher, the new pretender, a fresh twist on the bitter old ball-busting divas of yesterday and Sensitive Cher, the tart with a broken heart. Not forgetting Strong Cher who picks herself up from the floor of Heartbreak Hotel once again, goes shopping, has a little surgery and hops right back on that dizzy carousel of love. The Pet Shop Boys – proper homosexual music as Bill calls it – parade their Wildean shallowness with just the right amount of irony, single eyebrow raised wittily, tongue firmly lodged between Euroboy-tight cheeks.

The magic mirrorball was spinning like crazy, shooting off wild lasers into the amyl-sodden air as the sphinctastic hits kept pumping away: 'Dancing Queen' by the divine Abba; Boney M's wonderful disco melodrama, 'Belfast'. I couldn't control myself when The Sweet's 'Little Willy' jizzed out of the speakers, I grabbed a Joan Crawford lookalike and started frugging away to the happy homo music beneath the sparkling enchanted globe.

THE BOYS AND GIRLS

'You coming for breakfast, Bill?'

'Nah.'

'You haven't eaten for three days. That's not like you.'

'Just not hungry.'

'You look ill.'

'I'm not.'

'You know if you get ill they won't allow you on the plane to get out of the country.'

'Says who?'

'The airlines won't allow sick people on in case other passengers catch it off them and sue the airlines.'

'Well that's OK because I'm not ill.'

'OK, see you later.'

Z is already up and off to the bar. I'm left alone. Somebody said something about us getting to

Kisangani in the next couple of days. I need to get to a hotel, have a bath and a night in a room by myself.

I pull the black and purple haversack up off the floor and on to my bunk. Open the top, then carefully pull out the puppets. First there is Judy, then Gimpo the Clown, then the Hangman, then it's the Devil and lastly it's Mister Punch. I find my swazzle – I keep it in my back pocket with my ticket and passport – and put it in my mouth. I put Mister Punch on my right hand and the Devil on my left.

'Roo tee toot tee toot. Good morning boys and girls and how are we today?'

'……………….'

'Oh, not very well. Oh dear, so what's the matter with you?'

'……………….'

'Oh, you were born HIV-positive and you will die before you reach the age of ten. Well, what about you, young man? You look nice and healthy. How are you today?'

'……………….'

'Oh dear, after the puppet show is finished you have to become a boy soldier and will die in a bloody civil war before you reach the age of 14. And you my dear? Yes you, the one with the glasses, you do look pretty.'

'……………….'

'You think my patter is wooden, patronising and the reader won't believe Bill Drummond actually wrote these words while sitting on a bunk with a Mister Punch puppet on his right hand and one of the Devil on his left. And I should just get on with the show.

OK, boys and girls, roo tee toot tee toot. Has anybody seen a leopard around that I can slay?'

'Mister Punch, you seem to be forgetting about me.'

'And who are you when you haven't got a green face?'

'The boys and girls know who I am. Boys and girls, tell Mister Punch who I am.'

'……………….'

'Yes Mister Punch I'm Satan, Old Horny the Fallen One, but you can call me Lucifer.'

'Sounds like a girl's name. Can I call you Lucy for short? What do you think, boys and girls, doesn't he suit the name Lucy?'

'Mister Punch, I don't think the boys and girls are listening to you. They are bored with our little drama. They have other things to entertain them these days. So it seems it is only me and you.'

'Lucy, Lucy, Lucy.'

'Very witty, Mister Punch, but not very clever. What is this I hear about you talking to that jumped-up Jungle Joe. Did he have anything vaguely interesting to tell you?'

'Lucy, Lucy, Lucy.'

'And is that the extent of your conversational powers?'

'Well, in fact I was talking to him.'

'And?'

'And he told me that I never did sell my soul to you. That I can do what I want as long as I fulfill my responsibilities, whatever they are.'

'Responsibilities? Doesn't sound very rock'n'roll to me. What about your irresponsibilities? That's what you should be more concerned about. No, I'm only joking. It sounds like very good advice he is giving you, the exact same advice that I gave him 36 years ago. And did he tell you to go and kill a leopard?'

'Yes. How did you know?'

'So he is even keeping that bit of the story, good. Now Mister Punch, there is something else I need to talk to you about.'

'Yes Lucifer?'

'The boys and girls.'

'It's time you got that nice Professor Drummond of yours to take us out to meet the boys and girls.'

*

Even Grumpy Drummond seemed to be almost enjoying himself, dancing awkwardly like Prince Charles with a hernia, jacking himself into spasmo overdrive when Divine's Steel Queen anthem 'You think you're a man but you're only a boy' started crashing away. Gimpo found his groove immediately of course and was thrusting lasciviously, ignoring his painful fucked arse and flicking his tongue in and out grotesquely at a clutch of terrified young transvestites.

'Wow, you're a fantastic dancer,' Joan said to me in a dark brown voice. 'Who taught you, John Travolta?' she added flirtatiously as I broke into 'The Hustle'.

'I taught him, baby,' I replied, enjoying being a manly cocktease.

I only ever fucked men when I was in prison, where it's compulsory.

I noticed Bill furtively eyeing my funky steps and pathetically attempting to outdo me, moonwalking badly and spraining his shoulder when he tried to body pop. Gimpo was having more luck. He was up to his usual tricks, entertaining the girls by doing magic with his knob, making it disappear and then reappear out of his scary arsehole. When the Gimp starts performing like this it usually meant only one thing, fortunately his sphinc hadn't completely healed yet so we were spared the faecal pyrotechnics.

I eventually tired of my super-hip dance routines and found a seat in a dark corner. I took a hit on my beer when somebody behind me whispered accusingly, 'Tough guys don't dance.'

'Yeah, so how come you aren't dancing, Norman?' I sneered casually without looking around, it was obviously some bitch trying to rile me into giving her a punishment bumming.

'My names not Norman,' came the voice again.

This time it didn't sound bitchy at all. In fact it sounded pretty fucking serious, like whisky, cigarettes and arson.

CRAP SHAG BUT TOP SWAZZLER

Without us noticing Professor Edwards slipped his swazzle into his mouth and demonstrated some of his party pieces of Punch and Judy banter. He was proficient but uninspiring. Z tried but couldn't make a sound. Next it was my turn. I slipped it in and then something happened. One of the most profound, disturbing, epiphanistic road-to-Damascus moments of my life. A voice rose from the deepest recesses of my soul. A voice that was truly mine and, at the same time, nothing to do with any rational day-to-day part of me. It was as if I was instantly in touch with the true core of my being. My first words were probably the first words of every professor who came before me. '

That's the way to do it'.

Z was a jealous man. For all those hours spent studying rare books in the Reading Room of the

British Library, he couldn't swazzle and I could. I was obviously born to swazzle. Even Professor Edwards was impressed.

'That is the first time I have ever had a student who could swazzle at first go.'

Now, I've always been crap at most things that I've wanted to be able to do. I was crap at drawing, crap at playing guitar and, by all accounts, a crap shag. But there is no doubt I was an instant genius at swazzling. A total master of the thing. The spirit of Punch lay in me and spoke through me. Others may say that I'm just a fucked-up and repressed individual – only through this childish gimmick was I able to give myself an excuse to express my darker side. Well, fuck them, they are just jealous 'cause they can't swazzle as well as me.

*

I turned around slowly to hear a click and find that I was on the wrong end of a .45. Some weird fucking cowboy had the drop on me.

'Shouldn't you be on the other barge,' I said casually, 'With the rest of the Village People.' I knew his type, the working-class pubs of my misspent Leeds adolescence were full of these limbies, sociopathic imbeciles packing broken beer bottles and radioactive underpants. If I showed the slightest sign of fear, I was a goner.

Psycho cowboy smiled dismissively and holstered his jewellery.

'It's your lucky day, Mary, I already killed seven fags today and I don't much fancy wasting any more bullets.'

He poured himself a fat whisky.

I couldn't work out if I felt relieved to have avoided being shot or angry at being called a fag.

'That's mighty decent of you, pardner.' I answered, with just enough macho irony to save face but not enough to rile the stranger into making me number eight. 'And by the way I'm not a fag,' I added, just to make things clear.

'Hell, I can see that,' he said pouring another tumbler of whisky and pushing it across the table in my direction. 'I've sod'mised enough of these confused Shirley Temples to spot a spamfancier a mile away.'

He struck a match on the soul of his boot and lit the stogie clenched in his teeth. 'I mainly fuck het'ro boys myself. I figure it kind of allows me to hang on to my het'rosexual integrity in a totally backwards kind of way. But hell, some of these little girlyboys sure know how to wriggle. Ain't that the truth.' He leaned over and laughingly slapped a passing transvestite's backside. 'Suzy Creamcheese! Baby!' He laughed and the fine looking blonde smiled and sexied her way over to the dance floor.

'Boy, can that baby drain a man's ballbag.'

The old cowboy drifted into a brief erotic reverie, the front of his black pants tenting up grotesquely, then snapped himself out of it.

'The name's Cross-eyed Billy, folks sometimes call me The Lover.' He reached out to shake my hand.

'Z,' I replied, trying to remember where I'd heard the name.

'I've been murd'rin' an' sod'misin' the whole world over for more than 200 years,' he said proudly. 'I'm something of a legend.'

I suddenly remembered him from the serial killer bubblegum cards I used to collect as a kid.

The psychological profilers claimed he was a Carl Panzram, Henry Lucas, traditional unrepentant wanderer-killer. Along with the famous San Francisco serial, Zodiac, he was one of an elect breed never apprehended by the authorities.

'Born in the USA.' He spat the stump of the stogie on to the floor, adding, 'When that used to mean something.'

A strange combination of wistfulness and bitterness fell from him like a tired ghost.

'Back when the only judge and jury a man needed was one of these.'

He kissed the ivory handle of a beautiful antique firearm and placed it on the table in front of him. I couldn't really see what had changed myself, but I didn't want to upset him, so I kept quiet.

'Sure, it weren't too bad in the early days, due provocation was all you needed to justify killing a man. Due provocation.' He sighed. 'Shit, that could mean just about any fucking thing, looking at a man the wrong way, mast'batin' in church.'

DO IT NOW
Later. Z arrives at the cabin.

'Bill.'

'Yeah.'

'I've been thinking.'

'What is it this time?'

'It's time we got the puppets out, did the show.'

'Yeah, I was thinking the same thing myself this morning. In fact, I got the puppets out to have a look at them.'

'So let's do it now.'

The thing is with Z he always wants to do it, or have it or go there, now.

Cross-eyed Billy filled up his glass and took out another cheap stogie from his waistcoat 'But those felching tin-star government faggots kept adding to their shit-heel law book till it got so that the only motherfuckers allowed to do any killing was the asshole government themselves!' The cowboy threw back his whisky and continued with his dream-logic beef.

'Seems to me that those turd-eating government fuckers can just about do as they please. Hanging and 'lectrifying people, goddamn lethal 'jections, gas fuckin' chambers! An' they call me a fuckin' criminal. Shoot! Makes my blood boil with righteous indignation, woah!' he said, looking down at his tented pants. 'I better calm down here, I'm getting myself all erected. Excuse me one moment. Crepe Suzette, baby!'

Crepe Suzette ran over immediately, got down under the table and started smoking the old gunslinger's horn.

Seconds before he sprayed Suzette's epiglottis with sour, old-man nad-jam, Billy shook violently and went distinctly cross eyed, I laughed.

'So that's why they call you Cross-eyed Billy.'

The old man smiled as he zipped up his spunky pants.

'Heh, heh, that's right son, they tilt freako weird when I shoot a man as well.'

The pretty transvestite patted her mouth delicately on a tissue, burped quietly, smiled sweetly and scooted off to dance to 'Boogie Wonderland'.

'Such fine accommodating young men, don't you think?' said Billy. 'I've been floating around on this here fairy tug more years than I can remember, kinda feels like home if you know what I mean.'

PUNCH KILLS JUDY

Of course there was more to swazzling than what I could do instinctively. I had to learn to switch from the swazzled voice of Punch to the pantomime-dame voice of Judy. This required a very dextrous movement of the tongue, slipping the swazzle from its home in the roof of the mouth to the side so the Judy or whichever of the other characters were talking.

'OK lads, now you have your swazzles it is time to show you the basics in handling the glove puppets.'

'First, Mr Punch. He will be on your right hand. Unless you are left handed. Once he appears on stage to do the business with Judy, he never leaves the stage until the show ends. The reason why he is on your right hand is because he has to handle his club, do the business with the hangman and the noose and any other little tricks you may want to develop for him.'

'Now lads if you come over here and look in the back of my booth you see I have all the other characters hanging along the left-hand side of the booth. I can easily slip my left hand down into the puppet. With a little tug the velcro is released and I'm ready for action.'

With Punch on his right arm and Judy on his left he went through the basic Punch, Judy and the baby scene.

'Once the business with Judy is done I just shake her off my left arm, let her drop to the floor, inside the booth and slip my free arm into the policeman. Now, Bill, I think you should have a go.'

I stepped into the booth, slipped my arms into their respective puppets. Punch swung his legs over the front of the stage. Only then did it occur to me that the Punch and Judy man has no idea of how what he is doing looks like from the front. All the action is taking place above your head and facing away from you. Obvious to you maybe, but not to me until I was standing inside the booth with Punch and Judy on my arms.

'OK Bill, let's see you run through what I did.'

'What?'

'Punch appears, says hello to the boys and girls. Judy appears with the baby. Gives the baby to Punch to look after. Exit Judy. Baby screams. Punch throws baby over the side. Judy reappears. Gets very angry with Punch for killing baby. Punch gets his big stick and whacks Judy around head. Judy is dead. "That's the way to do it." End of scene.'

All went well until it got to the whacking Judy around the head bit with my stick. It seemed Punch was not content with just whacking her with the stick and it has to be said Professor Edwards' stick wasn't a very big one. Not big enough to do any serious grievous bodily harm. Anyway Punch wasn't happy with this little stick, he threw it away. He grabbed Judy. Yanked her off my left arm and started smashing her head on the play board and side of the stage.

This crashing and bashing went on long after all life had been smashed out of her. Just as Punch was about to throw her body over the side in the same direction as the baby had gone, some minutes before, the whole booth began to keel over with me inside into what would have been the front stalls of the under-fives. I ended up on the floor inside the booth all the other puppets on top of me with Punch still firmly on my right arm screaming, 'That's the way to do it. That's the way to do it. That's the way to do it'.

'What the hell do you think you are doing, Bill, treating the puppets like that? These are valuable hand-made puppets. They could easily crack and break. They must be treated with respect.'

'Sorry professor, I just got a bit carried away but I was able to keep my swazzle in place at all times.'

'OK. But that certainly isn't the way to do it. You must remember it is just a theatrical performance to entertain children. Let's have a short coffee break so you can calm down.'

Z was impressed by my performance. I was frightened this Punch and Judy business seemed to be unleashing more than I had expected. I blamed Z.

After the coffee break it was Z's turn in the booth. Although he was completely shit at the swazzling compared to me, he was able to control the puppets. Nothing got out of hand and he was brilliant at doing the voices for Judy, PC Plod and the hangman. He also brought subtlety and depth to these other characters.

As the day wore on it became obvious that despite my undeniable genius at swazzling I was shit at all the other arts that you were required to master to being an even average Punch and Judy professor.

'Now lads, it is a tradition that a professor should carve and paint his own puppets. In my case my wife makes my puppets. She also makes them for other people to buy. As you can see she is very good at making them.'

What we could see was that she was shit at making them. They were the most boring, plain and uninspiring collection of puppets one could imagine.

'In fact, she is probably the most experienced maker of Punch and Judy sets in the country. To date she has made and sold over 3000 sets. Let's go up and see her workshop.'

Which we duly did. A veritable production line of lame-looking puppets with not a glint in any one of their eyes. Something was rotten in the world of Punch and Judy. Something had to be done.

Chapter Six
DREAMSTORM

DRUMMOND'S SECRET LOG, APPROACHING KISANGANI, DATE UNKNOWN
(Equatorial Dreamstorm fogging up all reality co-ordinates, time shifts sliding in and out.)
I thought maybe there might have been some sort of release from my suffering with the death of Rolo. As if his blood would somehow wash away my misery, but if anything it seems to have made things worse. Sleep does not exist for me anymore. My dreams and my waking reality have become intermingled, I am no longer sure what is real and what is baroque fantasy.

GRAVEN IMAGES
Outside our cabin Z, me and the black-and-purple haversack containing the puppets.
Mami, Pitsu, Paps (who we think is Mami's dad) and a couple of others gather round to see what we have got to show.
'Go on then, Bill, get them out.'
I pull Judy out first. No squeals of delight. Then I pull Gimpo the clown. Silence. Then the hangman. Murmurs of discontent. Then the devil. They are definitely not happy and when I pull Mister Punch they are getting openly angry with us. Our neighbours on our balcony of the *Bangole* have always been warm and friendly with us. Things are changing. Z tries to get them to pick them up, show where they can put their hands to make them move, to get the puppets to come alive. I have the swazzle in my mouth.
'Roo tee toot tee toot. Hello boys and girls'.
Mami screams. Paps and Pitsu, in no uncertain terms, indicate to us we must put the puppets back into the bag immediately. We do.
Back in the cabin.
'Well what the fuck was wrong with them?'
'I don't know.'
But I had my suspicions .
'It's like we showed them their own corpse.'
I then see a hand –Mami's I guess – stretch around the side of the door frame of our cabin and leave a few printed pamphlets.
'Look, Z.'
I pick them up, it's a pictorial strip-type story.
'Christian fuckin' propaganda. Look at the stuff! I can't believe it. Who hands this stuff out to them?'
The strip picture is done in that style favoured by American evangelical Christians. The obvious message of the picture: graven images must be rejected. Well, I don't know if it actually says graven images as the text is in Lingala but there is a picture of a hand-carved wooden idol with a man on his knees worshipping it and a red line through it. So I'm guessing.
For decades, maybe even centuries, the Christian brothers had been coming to the Congo with the bible in their hands, bringing stories of how there is only one God and Jesus was His son

and love was His message. Then we turn up as the millennium is drawing to a close preaching the word of Mister Punch, a wooden idol. We should have known.

'So what do you think Big Joe will think when we get them out for him, Z? Maybe we shouldn't.'

'No, he's not stupid like these people. He's worldly, well travelled. He will understand we are just bringing some of our harmless traditions with us. Like they have harmless traditions. He is an educated man, not a superstitious peasant.'

Z may be right but I would be quite happy not to get Mister Punch and his companions out of their haversack until we are well and truly home.

'You coming up to the bar, Bill?'

'Nah. I'll stay here, get some notes done.'

'See you later then.'

'Yeah.'

And I clamber back into my bunk, open my notebook and stare at my beautiful dead butterfly.

＊

Are we really being pushed the final distance towards the inner station by a pink fairy tug called The Love Boat? Is it really manned by transvestite sailors and Billy the Kid? What's real and what's a dream? Does anyone really know?

Is history the grandest illusion of them all? Without our dreams would any of us be able to carry on? Would that black dog, that groaning chasm of metaphysical ignorance drag us kicking and shitting into its cold embrace?

Without the blind certainty of our demented religions and the scintillating cornucopia of distractions that bombard from every electric angle our faithless lives in the West, would we slide into a decadent trajectory, a lost civilisation, leaving only strange alphabets and mute stones as testament to our brief dominion? Are we already? Would our railway systems, airports and waterways join all the other mysterious earth works of the past, our cathedrals crumble alongside other vain temples dedicated to ludicrous grand narratives?

Our computers with their digital hieroglyphics – would they merely join the catalogue of unimportant mysteries for future scholars, bearded and weird, ignored by the go-getting flies of the market place?

All this shit was spinning like fuck-crazy bees through my head as I fastened on my six shooter. I had a bone to jam up that cross-eyed fucker. Throwing his weight around the jungle, who did he think he was? Cocksucker.

I chewed down on six Larium and strode out into the sunlight, the sunlight and the true invisible history that's written on air and fused in stones. One day some fucker's going to be able to decode this true history, rearrange the air and dirt so we can really see what happened back in time. Then this secret world of half dreams and deep reality will be revealed and folks will know that I wasn't crazy when I destroyed the soul of America!

KILLING SOOTY AND SWEEP

On our drive back from the Black Country I was sinking into a sullen silence. Other than the swazzling I reckoned the whole expensive caper had been a washout. Z thought differently.

'Bill, within a year we will be the greatest Punch and Judy professors in the land. It's going to be easy. That cunt didn't know what he was on about, he may as well have been doing Sooty and Sweep. Our Punch will start off by killing Sooty and Sweep, and raping Sue the panda, before he even gets round to throwing the baby out the window.'

I tried to think of something positive to say. 'Maybe we could build a two-man booth. I do Punch and you could do all the other characters. You were really good at them.'

'Fuck off, Bill. Don't be fucking patronising, you just want the glory of being Punch. Anyway, in a week's time I'll be a better swazzler than you.'

'OK, OK, Z. And you're right about killing Sooty and Sweep. I've always hated that pair of creeps.'

*

As soon as Bill walked through the door with a gun strapped to his right thigh I knew he'd been fucking around with the Larium again. His eyes had gone all skirly, each bloodshot orb focusing on different things entirely, mong dancing among the righteous flames of visionary madness, as fucked-up as the world itself. Only a few minutes ago he had seemed to have been enjoying himself, body popping with the happy transvestites, jigging away to 'Le Freak' by ace disco bumsters, Chic. Now he was stalking some drama only he had the script to.

Or was he? I'd been keeping a lucid dream diary for the past few days and there seemed to be some kind of symbolic sub-reality trawling beneath our daytime strangeness. Intimations of this scenario had been cropping up regularly ever since we had crossed the equator and its fifth-dimensional parallel.

Bill slid his gun hissing like a cobra from the oiled leather of its holster, held it level with his shoulder and shot the DJ in the face. The harmless transvestite banged around his box, his blonde wig splattered with blood, flopping around, held on by a few hair clips as he collapsed, coughing up bits of his face on to the decks, bringing the music to an abrupt end. The mirrorball looked strange spinning around without any music, the flashing lights eerie, like a deserted fairground after midnight.

The transvestites made themselves scarce, the visceral thrills of gun violence and high-pitched girly screaming had faded long ago for these wise queens. Homosexuals in dresses took death very seriously, each and every one of them knew the exact drama for their own end game and none of them involved demented devil hunters halfway up the Congo fried on Larium.

Cross-eyed Billy didn't even bother looking around.

'Is that Pork and Beans Billy, the farting Scottish pistolero I smell behind me?' said the cool shootist smiling, his cold words hanging on the tense air in the silent disco.

He reached his left foot up on a low table and threw back his whisky. Bill holstered his gun and wandered into the middle of the dance floor without saying a word. He'd found a pair of bootspurs somewhere, they jangled musically in the strained atmosphere. The unmistakable odour of Bill's apocalypse guts crawled over our small table like a dying seal.

'Cross-eyed Billy,' said Bill, hawking up phlegm and spitting it down the front of his shirt.

'Give the fag a cigar,' replied Cross-eyed Billy dismissively.

'You never give it up do you?' accused Bill

'If I knew what the hell you were talking about, pardner, maybe I could answer, but seeing as how I don't, I think I'll just kill you nice and fast. I never was one for idle chit-chat.'

SAILING TO THE MOON

For the first time in my life I realise I have nothing left I want to write about. I have now said it all. I may as well close the book and put away the pen. Fuck! I've just remembered I'm supposed to be writing up my notes from Z's and my jaunt around Europe. I haven't done that for a few days. But I can't be arsed, it seems so far off and irrelevant now. Maybe when we get back home I'll write it up and edit it into this lot so it looks like I wrote it now.

'Bill.'

It's Z, come to disturb my navel-gazing.'

'The cunts have sold out of beer.'

'What? Who?'

'The Luxury Bar. They have no more beer. This is serious.'

'For who?'

'For me, you cunt.'

'Well it's your fault.'

'What the fuck do you mean?'

'You bought it all. If you weren't here as a passenger, they would not have sold out. You have fucked it for anybody else who fancied waving an ice-cool beer after a hard day's graft in the heat.'

'Fuck off, Bill.'

And on that friendly note Z stumbles off.

And I am back facing the fact I have nothing left I want to write about. My lethargy is total. So I close this notebook, put away the pen, lie back and fall asleep.

I drift in and out of sleep for almost 36 hours so there is no Drummond's Log for Friday 21 June 1996. I can vaguely remember John Geilgud being a turtle; Gimpo telling me we were stuck on sandbanks again; a man selling a giant lizard; Z telling me the palm leaf wine that he has now taken to drinking tastes like a good sparkling wine; and something Gimpo said about how we should sail to the moon for our next journey.

*

I never even saw his hands move. There was just the deafening report of the .45 and there, in a thick cloud of white gun smoke, the silhouette of Cross-eyed Billy with his gun resting on his shoulder. I looked to where Bill had been standing, expecting to see him dead on the dance floor, but he was gone.

For a split second Cross-eyed Billy looked scared, his cool composure and arrogant bullying superiority slipping just long enough for Bill's rapid fire to smash into both of the killer's hands, shattering the bones to dust. Cross-eyed Billy fell backwards from his chair, two fountains of bright blood arcing from his wrists.

Like a ghost striding out of the smoke, Bill walked over to his fallen opponent. He pulled back the trigger on his peacemaker and pointed at the shootist's face.

'That's the trouble with you cocksucking Coca Cola cowboys: overconfidence. Happened in Vietnam. Hell, it's happening in Japan as we speak. Uncle Sam's fat head stuffed in a pig trough getting reamed out by those inscrutable sodomists of Bushido. You just never learn, do you cowboy? This is Africa, you got to hand out more than beads, bangles and microwave dildos if you want to win Congo hearts and minds. I don't suppose you wondered where they were gonna plug those TV sets you was intending to install in every home.'

Bill paused a second, screwed up his face and farted hard, like a firework.

'TV, now that's a fucking joke,' he continued, a cloud of fartdust surrounding him. 'A society has to be weaned on to that grotesque tit, has to build up its natural defences over the years so it gradually becomes tolerant of the perpetual state of anxious excitement that advertisements in general are geared to produce.

'If you just hit these poor bastards with that shit they're going to OD immediately, die of anxiety, scared shitless about germs, bad breath and being a lousy parent. Those hardcore Jews, the cats with the forelocks and cowboy hats, they've got the right idea, they think that owning a television is like having an open sewer in your front room.

'Did you really think you could just wander into the jungle waving your dollars and fancy automobile dreams and folks would roll over and say "Fuck me Johnny"? You may have bargained for Manhattan with a couple of colour radios but even those redmen wised up eventually and started handing out the haircuts. You fucking idiot! I don't suppose you even noticed that there ain't no fucking roads in the jungle. Well I'll tell you something for free, hotshot, it's going to take more than what you bought those European idiots back in the old world with before you get the sons of the rainforest to tell you one and one is three. To bend over and let Johnny Sodomy take all them diamonds they got no use for, all that copper they don't even know is there, all that exclusive plutonium and God knows what other germ warfare, poison, Ebola, AIDS death shit you got cooking down there.'

'What the fuck are you talking about, Pork and beans ?'

DRUMMOND'S LOG, SATURDAY 22 JUNE 1996
A NEW DAWN

'Wake up, Bill, wake up.'

'What is it, Gimpo?'

'We're here.'

'Where?'

'Kisangani.'

I leap out of my bunk. As fit as a fiddle. A new dawn. Here we go, here we go, here we go.

All over the barges there is much excitement. People are packing; shaving; rebraiding their hair; putting on their best clothes.

My heart goes out to one poor turtle in particular. But first, I must describe how they keep the turtles from escaping. They puncture a hole in their skin at the top of a back leg, then thread a length of raffia through it and tie the raffia to some immovable object, the logic being the more the turtle attempts to escape the more pain it causes itself so it gives up. Well, this poor turtle obviously did not. You could see the gaping wound where the raffia had ripped clean through its flesh in its stubborn attempt for freedom. But it must have been caught before it made it to the side of the barge as it now has a length of raffia passing through another hole cut into a far thicker part of its flesh.

But enough of my sympathy for a dumb beast. We are there. Or at least nearly there, Kisangani docks are about a mile upstream. I celebrate by having a shave, much to the delight and amusement of our neighbours. There is no more mention of the puppets. The three of us go for one last breakfast. Trefor is on a fine mood. His dough balls taste better than ever.

'You know, Bill, I'm going to miss Trefor's breakfasts.'

'You never fuckin' ate them before today, Z.'

'Yeah, but still.'

Even the tea tastes good. Gimpo, who genuinely, as opposed to the lies that Z tells you, seems to be fluent in Lingala, is chatting with Trefor.

'He wants to meet up with us tonight for a drink. He has written down on this bit of paper the address of a bar he will be going to.

We hug and kiss and shake hands with everybody, even the ones on our barge that we had no dealings with over the past two weeks.

*

These were the last words Cross-eyed Billy said before Bill's bullet smashed his head open like a rotten melon. Bill was shaking, eyes burning like hellfire, he looked at the bloody mess on the floor in front of him as if for the first time, holstered his gun and swaggered out of the death disco trailing a long green SBD in his macho wake. The mirrorball kept spinning, its magic light dancing prettily among the white gun smoke.

I could feel everything merging, the sub reality trawling beneath us as we were floating down towards our final destination was bleeding out of our dreams and spilling into everything else, breeding with it, creating monsters.

Time shifts I could handle but this stuff along with all the drugs and funky jungle magic was threatening to bring down a psychic whiteout, that fragile and extremely vulnerable state of mind beloved of torturers, religious cults, 12-step recovery programmes and British public schools.

Of course I had expected to be psychically assaulted by the twisted headzones of jungle reality and all its deformed ghosts. But here, approaching our destination at the world's end, the mind-numbing possibilities of all that we are and all that we ever have and will be seemed to be conspiring to shut me down into surrender mode.

THE FINEST SET OF PUPPETS IN THE LAND

The next morning there was a knock at the door. Z had arrived unannounced, much to the chagrin of my girlfriend who had been planning that we spend the day shopping in Milton Keynes for things for our expected baby. In his hand he was clutching a book and a few sheaves of paper.

'Morning, Bill. I found this book yesterday afternoon *Mister Punch and How to Make Him*. I've been up all night drawing these pictures of our cast. And I thought you've got a load of tools and know about wood, so I got the first train out and here I am. What do you say we start work straight away?'

Sallie stormed out. Well, as much as a woman who is seven months' pregnant can storm anywhere. Of course Z's drawings were brilliant. They always are. They were all there, our complete cast: Mr Punch, Judy, PC Plod, Grimpo the clown (Punch's sidekick), Pretty Polly (Punch's mistress), the Hangman and, of course, Satan himself. There were many other characters who, over the years, have been drawn into this little drama of Mr Punch's and trod the boards only to be despatched in some terrible way by our hero.

I had to flick through *Mr Punch And How To Make Him*. It all seemed easy enough, but we needed lime wood. According to the instructions lime is the only native wood in Britain that lends itself to being carved. A ring around the local timber merchants and a couple of hours later our kitchen was converted into a puppet-making workshop. I was able to convert Z's 2D pictures into front, side and upper elevation working drawings, sharpened up my chisels and got chipping.

Z had got himself a set of fine-carving chisels. Once I got the heads and features hacked out of the wood Z got to work with his tools to start on the fine details. Of course I thought he was over-working the features. I thought he lost some of the rough-hewn brilliance of my work. He thought his detail was a work of genius.

He then got to painting their faces. This was a work of genius. We worked at this solidly for the next four days, by the end of which we reckoned we had the finest set of puppets in the land. The trouble was they looked so good that I couldn't imagine ever wanting to give them the battering they need to get in a show.

Z then got down to designing their costumes. These we had made up by a woman who did costumes for the Limelight Theatre in Aylesbury, near where I live.

Three days before we were to set off for Africa, our little players were finished. They were splendid. We loved them. And they loved us in turn. Well, maybe not. But at least they weren't going to run out on us like Pinocchio ran out on Geppetto[chk sp]. Maybe that's 'cause they were glove puppets. In fact that's not totally accurate. Mr Punch does have a pair of little legs, part of the tradition, but none of the other characters do. Anyway, there was no way Punch was going to run out on us. He knew we were going to show him the best time he had ever had in exchange for him giving us a hand in duping the devil.

Chapter Seven
KISANGANI MAYHEM AND SLEAZE

I joined Bill in the deceptive safety of the cabin. It was obvious he too was experiencing a similar existentialist dread. Killing the cowboy or whatever he thought the cowboy represented had solved nothing. Shaking in his malaria net so far from home with nothing to cling on to, nothing but weirdness and dangerous malaria medicines. No dumb TV adverts with inane jingles, lullabies for a generation weaned on the cathode tit. No newspapers, with meaningless wars on the other side of the world and prole chicks showing their tits. No pornography, football or any of the other eight billion distractions that camouflage the terrible black hole that gapes forever at the centre of everything.

Here in the dark cabin we hid, desperately aware of that monstrous abyss of the faithless, its foetid breath scalding our backs, its hideous million voices louder than ever, tempting us with seductive suicides and promises of posthumous glory spinning around the cabin. A cacophony of wasps.

Outside the cabin – outside in another world – there was gathering excitement: children's voices, happy singing, lots of banging and scraping, animals squawking, grunting, shrieking.

Inside the cabin a horrible squelching, bogfarting, hissing diahorrea noise stenched its way out from beneath Bill's bunk. I'd forgotten all about the Gimp. His mauled shitlocker seemed to have healed. Unfortunately it had been stretched to hideous dimensions, as if the poor bastard had been buggered by a blue whale.

The barge stopped suddenly, throwing Bill straight into the fecal slop, the force of the fall knocking a loud stinking brass section out of the existentialist Zen Master's arse. Combined with the rank gasses of Gimpo's flapping krakatoa it was impossible to stay in the cabin, I ran outside on to the deck to escape the liver-curdling honk.

Nothing in hell or on Earth could have prepared me for my first view of Kisangani. The sheer gut paralysing horror of where we had arrived was beyond surreal. Death was everywhere. Piles of bodies, some being burnt, others hanging from trees and wrecked buildings. They stank like sick and bad meat.

The stallholders didn't seem to be aware of the carnage, they leapt on to the dock and sprinted past the bodies up into the main part of town to claim the best pitches for their goods. The mothers with sleeping babies strapped to their backs moseyed casually past the massive funeral pyres, their only reaction to the horror being to fan the air in front of their faces to dispel the foul stench of burning and rotting bodies. Soldiers milled around in mismatching fatigues overseeing the grisly bonfires while others arrived in military vehicles with more bodies to add to the fires. The corpses turned out to be part of the overspill from the casual genocide occurring just across the border in Rwanda.

Bill's mood seemed to lift when he saw all the death. Gimpo too, the scenes reminded him of the happier times of his life, those carefree swallow days during the Falklands war, tripping gaily among the eviscerated corpses. Many veterans report similar feelings, how in the presence of major death they feel so much more alive. Well it seemed to be true for my two deeply weird companions, jigging their little barn dance together but personally I didn't buy it. I didn't feel more alive. Fact was, I felt shit scared. The end of the world was coming down, right here, where it began.

Three boys greeted us as we got off the barge. After a little banter with Gimps in his extremely fluent Lingala the boys indicated that we hop on to their backs and they would then piggyback us to our hotel. Bill quickly jumped on the most attractive boy, smiling happily.

As the wiry youngsters jogged the ten-mile journey to our hotel my ride told me he used to have a rickshaw, but during one of the many wars that plague the area it was melted down to make bullets. He couldn't remember which war it was – they change all the time, he told me. This was the only way he could get enough money to buy food. He usually piggybacked fat homosexual diamond traders to and from their business premises that seemed to be on every street corner we passed.

As the skinny youngster ran along the side of the dusty bomb-cratered street a white van shot by us nearly knocking us into the gutter. As the dust cleared I could see the Japanese film crew smiling at us from the back window. The boy cursed under his breath. He told me that the Japs were worse than the Arabs for exploiting the country's poor.

'Fucky, sucky ben'ova jungle boy. Action!' he said.

I got the picture. For some reason I got the feeling those evil buggerist, chicken-fancying auteurs were about to make their last movie. Children's rights were close to Bill's heart.

WE WAIT

We dock and all hell breaks loose. Yeah, I know it must be a racist thing to say but these Africans could not queue if their lives depended on it. They push, they shove, they scream, they shout, they leap across, they jump down, anything but quietly queue to take their turn on the gangplank. The thing is, if the logical advantages of queuing were explained to them about I think they would say, 'But what's the fun in that?' They love the pandemonium for its own sake, not because it gets them ashore any faster.

'Come on, Bill, let's get going.'

'No, Gimpo, we wait.'

We watch and we wait.

*

I don't know exactly what I was expecting but whatever it was, it wasn't this.

Whereas the Memlin Hotel towered arrogantly, bone white and pristine, this bombed-out shithole hunkered down in the rubble and trash like a crumbling leper masturbating into the dirt. There was only two storeys left of the original 12, the other ten must have been all the rubble lying around in the dusty road and dead garden.

'La guerre...' muttered taxi boy when he saw my reaction.

'Welcome my friends!' said the bald headed concierge who looked horribly like the black guy in Stanley Kubrick's *The Shining*, gold teeth smile and everything.

Of course he had no record of our booking but it didn't seem to matter as we appeared to be the only guests. The thought of going to sleep without the insane ghettoblasters and their cranked-up hi-life was enough for me.

We all checked in and ran upstairs to masturbate. My nuts felt like a couple of over-inflated spacehoppers. I unloaded a couple of pints on to the bathroom floor and to my horror the biggest fucking cockroach I'd ever seen in my life wandered out from behind the toilet and started eating the pearly jam. That was one gruesome step too much and I puked a stream of watery beer sick on to the cracked tile floor. Unperturbed the seven-inch bug scuttered over to the yeasty vomit and started chowing down on that as well.

The thought of the beast's exoskeleton shattering under the thin soles of my Ranulph Fiennes sandals and its gooey guts splashing my ankles put me off stomping the monster. I left the repulsive Blattodea to its blarg-inducing feast and went round to Bill and Gimpo's room. Bill was still bopping his salami in the bathroom; the uninhibited Gimps was sat on the edge of his bed looking out of the window and smashing 18 shades of bell-end soup out of his raggy scrote. I waited for them to finish.

WE WALK

We watched and we waited for the best part of an hour. Then we clamber over the *H203*, and trot down the gangplank. We are met by two heavily armed uniformed officials both sporting shades. They want to see our passports and our papers. One of them takes them away while the other stands guard over us. We wait and we wait. He returns and we are told to follow him. We follow him out of the docks up into the town, along tree-lined avenues. You get no sense of the size of Kisangani. According to Gimpo and his *Lonely Planet* guidebook it has a population bordering one million. But it hasn't got that heaving city-vibe that Kinshasa has. We walk and we walk down more tree-lined avenues of dilapidated colonial villas. We have no idea where we are going or why. We are just following the heavily armed uniformed man in front while his brother-in-arms takes up the rear just in case we thought we could give them the slip. We walk in silence.

We get to some government buildings. We get taken into a small whitewashed guardroom. We are told to wait here. We wait. We still don't talk. There is nothing in the room, just freshly whitewashed walls. Even the floor has been whitewashed. Of course there is the framed portrait of Joe Mobutu on the wall but nothing else. That's if you don't count the stain on the floor that has soaked through the fresh whitewash. My paranoia is in overdrive. I need a cup of tea. I note that Z's left hand has the tremors. He needs a drink. Whatever Gimpo needs, he is not letting on. We all know that savage beatings have taken place here. Terrible torture and untimely deaths, all under the all-seeing gaze of Africa's greatest living President.

We wait.

*

After his usual strangled shrieks, banging and misogynist swearing Bill hurtled out of the bathroom, tripping over his Grand Prix-skid pants. I looked in the shitter and noticed an even bigger specimen of jizz-snarfing cockroach. This fucker was at least twice the size of the infant back in my room. The rat-sized roach was hungrily slurping up Bill's jizz from the pages of a tool catalogue. The third and largest cockroach of them all was parked in front of Gimpo waving its antennae creepily, waiting for the baby gravy like a patient dog.

The Gimp was so engrossed in his salacious phantasms, eyes shut tight, fist a pounding blur he hadn't noticed the beast sitting in front of him. He eventually let fly his bollock-powered bazooka and as usual splattered the ceiling with thick virile gloop.

Refusing to be cheated of its meal the agile cockroach scuttled up the wall with a loud clattering sound and across the ceiling to snarf the bollock jam. Gimpo was less squeamish than both Bill and myself and after stamping down hard on the thing in the bathroom he speared the one on the roof with the handle of a sweeping brush. The thing didn't die immediately, it let out a horrible screeching noise, its legs flicking all over the place, antennae lashing madly, splashing the room with foul-smelling black goo. A mad gnashing, chattering sound filled the room as both the dying creatures appeared to start eating themselves with flurrying mandibles.

Gimpo was laughing hysterically as he kept battering the bugs on the floor and stamping on them till there was nothing left but the black bug blood and crunched-up exoskeleton, the nerve-trembling antennae-twitching among the shit.

BAD FATHER

Plenty of artists have told us about what bad childhoods they had. Plenty of poets have penned rhymes for their new-born bairns. Plenty of biographies have been written about the great and the good, telling us what tyrants they were to their own children. How they neglected the needs of their offspring while they were nuturing their own incipient greatness.

It is easy to point the finger but none of us start out planning to be bad fathers. It just creeps up on us and before you know it, it's all too late and we are unable to rewrite what has already been done. We too have joined the long list of bad fathers waiting for others to point the finger at us.

Z and my respective partners are both well into their pregnancies and I suppose we both hope that when, and if, we get back from this lot we can start again. This time we will be good fathers. The trouble is, if we really meant that we wouldn't be here stuck up the Congo without a paddle. We'd be at home doing an honest day's work for an honest day's pay, making sure the bills were paid on time and reading bedtime stories to the children we already have.

*

I should have guessed from all the dead bodies in the harbour and the random acts of ultraviolence, necklacings, shootings, hangings and the like that we jogged by on our way from the harbour that my old bird Katie wouldn't be far away.

I found her smoking and semi-drunk in the bar. Even all fucked-up, dried spunk and blood matted in the blond bangs that hung above her beautiful blue eyes Katie looked sublime. 'Z, you fat-cocked fucker,' she called laughing as I wandered into the bar.

A couple of jet black, naked bush warriors, armed with vicious looking barbed spears stood up aggressively as I made my way over to the khaki sex bomb. Katie placated her guard in perfect Swahili and the magnificent warriors sat down at a table in the shadows.

We embraced heartily, I felt her tongue hot in my ear. If I hadn't just jizzed I would have probably porked the sexy BBC babe right there on the hotel bar.

'How did I know I'd find you fuckers in the Stained Wankpants Hotel?' she laughed again.

It was obvious why, the sleazy bar had all the charm and ambience of a Greek knocking shop. Torn and worn wine red velvet, grubby walls and burnt-down candles. Perfect.

A useless black and white portable TV kept fizzing in and out of some obscure football game behind the dirty zebra-skin bar. Two drugged prossies, barely conscious, were drooling in the shadows, legs open, flies crawling around their eyes and in and out of their yeast infections.

'Because we're class studs, war baby, mayhem and sleaze, oh yes!' I said, laughing and cracking a high ten with the sexiest girl-pervert on the planet.

The only thing Zairese seemed to take at all seriously was beer. The Primus was ever present and always exactly the right temperature. I grabbed a few bottles and started to catch up with raging-libido woman.

She knew that the beer would reload my nads turbo-style and got down on her knees and started sucking me off, orgasming almost immediately. She came another six times before I shot off my fertile gunge down her throat.

She popped back up smiling happily. 'Boy, Z,' she said, wiping her mouth familiarly on my t-shirt. ' You're still the best face fucker that's ever slimed a gal's tonsils. You're amazing, stud!'

I laughed modestly. It's an art in itself getting sucked off, and I had to admit even to myself, I was a damn good face fucker.

UNDER THE ALL-SEEING GAZE

Then, after waiting some more.

'Good morning, gentlemen. I am sorry for keeping you waiting. Welcome to Kinsangani. Your papers seem to be all in order. But first follow me into my office. I have a few simple questions.'

My paranoia goes something like this: 'But first what?' 'It's the simple questions that are always the hardest to give the correct answers to.' 'What's this going to cost us?'

We follow the man into his adjoining office. He sits behind his desk. We are left standing in front of him, the armed guards to either side of the three of us. On the wall behind him Mobutu looks down on the proceedings from his frame.

'Well, gentlemen,' he begins in surprisingly good English, 'Why have you come to Kinsangani?'

'We are on our way to meet your President at his palace at Gbadolite.'

'You are, are you?'

Now what I'm thinking is that I hope he is thinking we must be important people if we are off to meet the President, so he'd better not have us done over or shaken down too much or it won't be too good for his career prospects, us being guests of the President.

'Yes.'

'But there is nothing in your papers to say that you will be travelling to Gbadolite from Kinsangani.'

'No but...'

'And you don't seem to have an official invitation from the presidential staff.'

'Yes I know but I can explain.'

'Please do.'

'Before we left Kinshasa Mr Arthur Malu Malu, you have heard of Mr Malu Malu?'

'Yes, a very important and influential journalist for Reuters, I understand.'

'Yes, well, Mr Malu Malu contacted the presidential staff to make the necessary arrangements for us to meet the President, but he was informed that the President was currently on a wine tasting and buying tour of French vineyards and would not be flying back to Zaire until the nineteenth of this month. So we decided to take the boat trip up the Congo river...'

'Zaire river. We call it the Zaire river these days, not the Congo.'

'Sorry, the Zaire river.... so we could see more of your wonderful country.'

'Don't patronise me, just the facts will do.'

'Sorry, I didn't mean to. Anyway, now that we are here we intend to phone Mr Malu Malu in Kinshasa to see if, now that the President has returned, the arrangements have been made.'

'And the papers you will need for this journey from Kisangani to Gbadolite, where will they come from?'

'I don't know.'

'Maybe I could look after that for you.'

He smiles a big smile. President Mobutu in the frame on the wall behind him doesn't smile.

'And while you are in Kisangani, I take it you will be staying at the Hotel Zaire Palace?'

'Yes, I hope so.'

'Yes, you will be. Now I will organise a taxi to take you to your hotel. My men will travel with you. You will come here tomorrow after you have spoken to Mr Malu Malu and we will make arrangements for your safe journey from here to Gbadolite. My men will also travel with you to there. You will need their protection. There are plenty of bad men between here and there who will want to take advantage of you. Thank you and until tomorrow, goodbye.'

'Thank you, sir.'

We leave.

*

We carried on drinking heavily at the bar. Katie had a couple of bottles of Tequila and we hit in on them before Katie started bitching about the UN forces over in Rwanda.

For some reason known only to the international power scum elite of the Cosmosodomistic Black Gas Corporation the UN were being pulled out of Rwanda, effectively sanctioning the gory genocide of Tutsis that we'd seen leaking into Zaire earlier that day. Because the Black Gas Corporation more or less controlled everything on the planet in some shape or vested form, Katie's reports on the genocide were being ignored by the BBC. There seemed to be a complete disinterest from all the international news agencies. Of course for a seasoned veteran of international skullduggery and cynical ethnic cleansing policies the world over, this was nothing new. But beating somewhere among that cynical bullet-proof heart there remained, believe it or not, a sliver of humanity. That's what the booze was for. If not to drown it, at least to silence it down most of the time.

The only time Africa made the news was when some charismatic renegade chief couldn't be got at by the Black Gas fieldworkers and a whole bunch of misinformation and truth fixing had to be set in motion. These small grassroots revolutions terrified the Gas, they could proliferate into locust formation in no time.

Ever since the Gandhi cock-up in India and the Cuban fiasco, not to mention Guevara's little jaunt into the jungle, the cosmosodomistic machinations of the Black Gas took no chances. Zaire was bursting with money, its dirt was stuffed to bursting with diamonds and precious ores.

The fact that televisions were not installed in all domiciles worried the Gas – without their most potent method of disseminating their black magic this cash cow of a country could not be considered stable, safe and buttfucked within the Black Gas castle walls. Whatever the genocide in Rwanda was all about you could be pretty much assured it was part of the Cosmosodomistic Black Gas Corporation's master-growth buggery plan. The virtual news black out only confirmed this.

∗

Two days before we left, Z and I headed down to an outfitters off Bond Street called Travelling Light. They specialise in outfitting the upper classes who fancy a bit of a safari. It was here that we got our full-on Roger Moore drag together. Z had to take it all too far of course and insisted on buying himself a cane and cravat.

We then headed up to the photographer's – Paul Graham's – studio, to have our puppets and ourselves in full drag photographed, just in case we never came back and they needed an up-to-date picture for our obituaries. I hoped they looked good. I have noticed the better your picture, the bigger the obit you get. On that subject, I'd better get a good obit. There will have been no point in going through all this if they don't give me at least half a page in each of the broadsheets. Just remember to mention that I came top in art when I was 13, got metalwork 'O' level and have resisted the urge to paint landscapes ever since.

∗

'Listen, babe' I said to Sex Bomb. 'What say you and me grab a couple of shoeshine boys, a handful of prossies and go up to your room and get inhumanly depraved for old time's sake. We can pretend we're in America again, I'm sure we can find some sharp knives somewhere.'
'No, Z,' said Kate with a strangely seriously tone, 'I've changed, I don't know why, maybe it's this beautiful country with its gentle people, I just have...'
The sex bomb lit a Marlboro Light, exhaled seriously and continued.
'I realised that my selfish sexuality was fundamentally no different from the heinous crimes of those Black Gas bastards, just using everything and everyone up, living vicariously and selfishly in the present, not thinking about the consequences, caring about nothing but satiating my own debased lusts. I don't know, those kids we murdered in the States, Z, they had families, loved ones... what kind of people are we?'
She looked at me with pained eyes.
'Oh god, I'm so sorry.'
And broke down crying, huge sobs wracking her frail frame. The dopey cunt was obviously rat-arsed.
'OK,' I said, 'We won't bother with the shoe-shine boys, we'll just get gruesome with a couple of whores. After all it is one of the accepted risks of their ancient profession. They all know that, it's the rules.'
There was no way Katie's drunken hiccough of conscience was going to cheat me out of my debauch, and I knew that despite all her well-meaning protestations there was no way that sexy gore hound could get juiced up without at least a smear of De Sadean foreplay.
Posh bitches, all the fucking same, can't get frisky without the suffering of the poor to slime up

their sandpaper twats. At fancy charity balls in swank London hotels, tickets about 300 shitters a throw, you can't hear yourself think in the women's bogs for the buzzing of gold-plated dildos. The dubious frisson-by-proxy spinning old money sluts into paroxysms of masturbatory insanity.

What do you think that erotomaniac, her Royal dumbness the Princess of Wales Lady fucking Diana got off on, licking lepers and giving kindly wanks to AIDS victims, couldn't get enough of it, the sick bitch. On an average day of catwalking through minefields in her stylish, pale blue, My-lar fanny protector, dishing out porridge to starving Africans, the sexually insane Princess had to change her pants at least 40 times, slimed gussets ruined by gallons of pervoid cooze lathering over her winged panty liners like Niagra fucking falls.

I was right about Katie of course, as soon as I'd slid the steamhammer up her backside she was moaning desperately for a couple of shoeshine boys.

'Just this once, never again.'

She was like a junkie or any other addict, every time is always the last time.

The prossies hadn't been enough, their jaded souls couldn't satiate her depraved appetite. Like all members of the establishment, no matter how far removed they are from the withered core, only the despoilment of purity and innocence succeeds in effectively stroking their filthy, tic-ridden monkeys.

They're the only things those shitheads can't possess. All the money, diamonds and shiny metals in their creepy world couldn't buy the simple love of the common people because, like youth, despite the gruesome attempts of Harley Street plastic butchers, it isn't for sale.

I allowed myself the deliciously sleazy and condescending luxury of feeling sorry for poor little rich girl, after I'd fucked her rancid of course, and ordered up some more beers from room service.

'Sure is an upside-down fucked-up world, Katie my love,' I said, drawing luxuriously on one of her Marlboro Lights, contemplating the Hanged Man tarot card in my imagination. 'There's you dying each dawn with all your trust fund money, poncey career and what-not, drowning in poisonous air, crippled with pain, guilt and a seriously fucked-up libido. And here's me, not a bean in my pocket, every day a holiday, every meal a banquet. Rich cunts, they just don't get it.'

All so simple as well, cessation of desire and all that bollocks. Obviously Katie was oblivious to my Zen-Master wisdom. So locked up in her world of pain, self pity and tears, all she could feel, hear and see was her own boggy misery, otherwise I wouldn't have been saying any of this.

'Ignore the echoes and locate the source...' I snickered ambiguously in her ear.

I eventually tired of idly casting pearls before the dumb-fuck pig. It stank in there too. One of the whores had shat all over the carpet when Katie went into her with the Bowie knife. Where were those cockroaches when you fucking needed them?

WELCOME

The three of us squashed into the back of a battered cab with one of the guards, while the other is in the front with the driver.

'That was all right,' says me.

'Was it fuck!' says Gimpo.

'What do you mean?' says Z.

'He didn't tax us, shake us down, nothing,' says me.

'No 'cause he didn't need to. Not yet. He knows whatever happens we are stuck in Kisangani as long as he wants us to be here. We can't leave without his say-so and that won't be until we have been well and truly shaken down for everything we have got.'

'Well, there is nothing we can do about it,' says Z. 'I'm dying for a beer.'

The taxi pulls up outside the Hotel Zaire Palace. It is the only building I've seen so far in Kisangani that has more than three floors. Nothing colonial about it, all 1960s and modern and international. This had 12 but not now. Everything above the fourth floor has been burnt out. At ground-floor level it still seems to be functioning. The plate glass doors are wide open, we can see lights on inside. I can even hear music that isn't African, drifting down the steps to greet us. I would like to tell you it is 'Hotel California' by The Eagles but it isn't, it's 'You Sexy Thing' by Hot Chocolate.

'Welcome, my friends.'

A small, plump man sporting a maroon jacket with black lapels comes running down the steps with outstretched arms to greet us.

'You have arrived safely.'

'It seems we have.'

'Your bags, your bags, I take your bags.'

Z lets him take his bags. Gimpo and I don't let anybody but ourselves carry our bags. Or did I tell you that already when we arrived at the Memlin?

We check in. It's considerably cheaper than the Memlin. We are shown to our large airy rooms on the first floor. We have one each. We arrange to meet up again in half an hour down in the bar. Grey nylon net curtains billow. The sheets on the king-size bed are also grey and nylon. I run a bath. Remove my soiled safari suit and the rag tied around my big toe and lower myself into the tepid water. I watch a cockroach skuttle across the floor and I fall asleep.

✳

I skipped merrily downstairs to the End of the World bar, the Larium must have still been fizzing at some level in Bill. He was sat at the out-of-tune piano in the corner banging out some awful fucking tune wailing away in his cracked spinster falsetto. I was dreading another Lady Mantis incident but it appeared, thank God, that he was still in possession of his regular Bill personality.

The barman had obviously finished off the dregs of the Tequila me and Kate had left behind, he was grinning like an idiot. Bill was really hammering into the piano, so hard it was becoming painful. I recognised the song Free Electric Band, written by some fragged-out old Californian hippy called Albert Hammond. Bill had told me years ago that this was the song he wanted playing at his funeral. 'And I gave it up for music, AND THE FREE ELECTRIC BAND!!!' he screamed, jumping back off the piano stool slamming down the lid and smashing himself over the head with a beer bottle.

He obviously completely identified with the maudlin sentiment of the song, I noticed he was crying. But that wasn't in itself unusual, he breaks out into tears every time he hears 'Honey' by Bobby Goldsboro. 'And Honey I miss you, and I'm being good...' A couple of lines of that sentimental shite and the rugged Scotsman is blubbing like a woman. There was obviously something bothering him. Apart from when he's on weird prescription drugs Bill never bothers singing or playing instruments unless he's majorly uptight over something or another.

I went over and sat with the Gimp and ordered up more beers. Gimpo predictably was sat with a couple of whores fiddling around with their cunts underneath the table.

'Pack it in, Gimpo, that fucking stinks,' I snapped at the satyristic gremlin. 'What's with Liberace over there?' I nodded in Bill's direction. He'd started murdering 'Free Bird' by Lynrd Skynrd, battering the fuck out of the piano trying to play the massive guitar solo at the end of the hippy lovers' classic.

'I'm not sure,' said the Gimp, sniffing his fingers. 'There was a message for him at the desk.'

Bill was just starting in on the other Bobby Goldsboro classic, 'Summer, the first time'. It's the one about the woman who finds out her husband's been killed in action and for some weird reason decides to shag nine-year-old Bobby, who 'Sees the sun rise as a man !!!' Bill saw me and came over still singing the lyrics nervously, 'I knew nothing about love, she knew everything.' Adding his own Tourette's syndrome ad libs: 'Cunt! fucking shit! whore! slag bitch.' He was drinking as well, another bad sign, Bill rarely gets bladdered but when he does, he does it with a 'shit bed and waken' ferocity that has to be seen to be believed. Vomiting, pant-kegging, crying, fighting, raping, child abusing, murdering. Drunken Bill takes a clumsy shot at the whole gamut of crimes blamed on the good grape. He slumped down next to the Gimp, eyeing the whores furtively, still mumbling the lyrics to 'Summer the first time' with his own idiosyncratic additions.

'I was nine years old, she was thirty-one,
I knew nothing about love, she knew everything.
Bitch! cunt! slag! whore! knives!'

He threw a crumpled piece of paper on the table and leaned over, sniffing and trying to eyeball the skanks' suppurating fannies. Gimpo had his hands back down there, squelching around in the purple curtains. The stench was Grimsby-fucking-horrible.

I went over to the main bar to check out the piece of paper. It was a handwritten note from Joe Mobutu inviting us to one of his palaces in the Ituri forest. A couple of Mobutu's goons were going to pick us up the following day which was cool as we wouldn't miss the party the Japs had invited us to. They were celebrating the completion of the films they'd been making on the way up river.

The Ituri forest was a notorious place of extreme danger, its reputation ranked along places like the K2 suicide peak of Mont Blanc and the empty quarter in the Sahara desert.

When Henry 'Livingstone, I presume' Stanley, the lying Welsh psychopathic journalist crossed it to forcibly rescue Emin Pasha (who was in no danger and didn't want rescuing) he named it in typical, self-aggrandising, bombastic fashion, the forest of death.

Just because Stanley was an outstanding asshole though didn't mean that the forest didn't deserve its spooky name. A lot of missionaries after Stanley went into that forest and not many came back. The ones that did related their fantastic accounts from madhouses and hospitals for incurable tropical diseases.

It was notorious for extremely violent and hostile tribes, cannibals to a man. And of late the notorious, internationally feared, dread Interhamwe, 'Those who kill together', a bunch of renegade Hutu genocide killers. A displaced nation of murderous guerillas robbed of their country Rwanda with fuck-all left to lose. They were expected to have been terminated by the counter-genocidal forces of the Gas-supported Hutu Skull fuckers, current main players and governing psychotics in Rwanda.

No one knew how many of these hardcore maniacs there were hiding out in Central Africa's most notorious jungle. They were one of the oversights of the Black Gas's African diabolism. Though how long this situation would last depended not only on the Gas' international skullduggery but also upon the maleficent caprice of Joe Mobutu himself.

BOTTLE-OUT TIME

The night before we left, I got another midnight call from Z.

'I've been thinking, Bill. Maybe we don't need to go to Africa after all.'

'What the fuck are you talking about? We've got visas, bought air tickets, even had our yellow fever jabs done. We leave in the morning.'

'Yeah I know but maybe we had to do all that for us to learn we don't need to go.'

'Why not?'

'Well these Punch and Judy puppets, I think they are brilliant and so do the other people I've shown them to.'

'So?'

'Well, I think we have found our vocation. We should make puppets and sell them. People would pay a fortune for these. Fuck being Punch and Judy men, we should just make the puppets and sell them as art. This is what all these months of research have been leading up to. What do you think?'

In the past I have found Z's arguments pretty persuasive, but not that night.

'Z, you're just trying to bottle out.'

'No Bill, I'm just not as stupid as you.'

'Z, I will see you tomorrow morning at Heathrow. Be there or we are both dead. Goodnight.'

Chapter Eight
MEATLOAF ELECTRIC SEXY BOY
(SOCKETS AHOY!)

Before we got to see their main feature, the movie that the Japs had made on their way up-river, they showed us a few examples of Kendo Nagasaki's earlier work, made for the domestic market back in Japan.

It was the usual gruesome shit you would expect from a country whose national psyche still hadn't recovered from centuries of monumental arse licking at the stinking yellow cracks of countless buck-toothed emperors. Their subservience to a bunch of subnormal inbreeders made Great Britain's class system look like the most enlightened and egalitarian of republics. Add that to those two Black Gas atom bombs at the end of the Second World War and you've got yourself an extremely funky recipe for some seriously far-out Wilhelm 'Mass Psychology of Fascism' Reichian sexual appetites. Lots of sharp knives, burning flesh and chicks in bandages menstruating all over the place.

Inhuman Gimpo laughed out loud, spluttering beer at most of the movies, Bill showed his intense one-handed appreciation by smashing away like a madman on that tambourine in his trouser pocket.

The titles told you all you needed to know, in that particularly amusing way that the Japanese language translates into English: *Tiny Little Japanese schoolgirls forcibly impaled on big fat American truncheons by their bumholes through the knickers sexy and set on fire in their pussy cunts by high school football who looks like Meatloaf electric sexyboy*.

You could see the director had artistic pretensions. One film in particular, *Suck me off, eat my shit and drink petrol you Chinese slag* was beautifully shot. Just as the hero mashes his crank juice all over the heroine's face and flicks the match into her petrol-soaked lap, the flesh on the young girl's face popping and exploding in slow motion, had a quality not unlike the classic American cinema of the early 1970s.

The semiotics of nuclear explosions, jizzing bell ends, nuclear scab lepers and cocksucking schoolies waving their bloody tampons about were blatantly obvious to even the dimmest of Cultural Studies students and I started yawning after four hours of this repetitive scud.

CHEESE PLANTS
Bang! Bang! Bang!
'Bill, you coming down for a beer?' It's Z at the door.
'Yeah, I'll be down in a minute.
The restaurant-cum-bar of the Hotel Zaire Palace is huge. A 1960s' style abstract stained-glass window thing divides it from the lobby. A huge cheese plant is going native in one corner. You'd think they wouldn't bother with cheese plants in the tropics.
'Three Primus please'.
'And a large vodka with tonic,' adds Z.
I get my notebook out and start writing up our arrival in Kisangani. I write uninterrupted for

ten or so minutes. Z has drunk his vodka and I can sense him getting agitated at my side.

'Let's have a look at what you're writing.'

'Hang on a minute, let me finish this bit about getting to the hotel.'

Z reads.

'That bloke who checked our papers didn't speak English.'

'Yeah, I know but if he did that is what he would have said.'

'Yeah but...'

'Forget it, Z, I'll make it up how I want.'

'Well then, if you are making stuff up, did you put in that bit about some of the smoked monkeys looking like babies?'

'But they didn't. There were no smoked babies.'

'But you said you'd make stuff up.'

'I won't make stuff up that didn't happen.'

'So, no chance of you putting in about Gimpo getting his punishment bumming.'

'No!'

After finishing my Primus I go over to the desk to the concierge.

'Can I make a phone call from here?'

'I'm afraid not sir. We have not had a phone system since, well since the time we had a spot of trouble.'

'Oh.'

'But sir, I will draw a map for you. Only a few streets away there is an office where you can make a satellite phone call to Kinshasa.'

'Thanks.'

I take the map. Tell the others that I'm off to phone Arthur Malu Malu to see if he has sorted it out with the President.

✳

Bill and Gimps on the other hand seemed to be really enjoying this cascade of mean, violent pornography.

Some of the films that Kendo had made for his nation's war partners-in-slime, the Germans, had Gimpo bashing himself bog-eyed, grunting and throwing himself farting around the floor as the foxy frauleins and Madame Butterflys started slinging sexy turds all over the place during *Let's play with our shit lesbian sister of sexual love*. I had to physically restrain Bill during some of the more extreme movies, especially when images of young girls committed the female version of Seppuku, driving a shortened Katana blade down behind their collar bones behind their ribcage and into their hearts. Bill, still battering his pocket tambourine, would burst into tears for these brave young geishas committing the ultimate act of selflessness.

'When do we get to eat, Kendo baby, I'm fucking starving, these films are so softcore.'

It was Katie, she'd swigged two bottles of tequila while we all watched Kendo's rather indulgent film show. The Jap bristled. Despite his international wanderings and ludicrous attempts at assimilating foreign cultures, the son of Nippon had very rigid ideas of women and their place in the scheme of things. Women, in the eyes of the average Jap were lower than dogshit, you fucked them only to perpetuate your race. Love – here we go again – was an esteemed and sophisticated form of bummerism between noble men and their male servants. One of Nagasaki's assistants reacted angrily to the drunken Englishwoman's harmless catcalls and barked loudly in his angry native tongue.

I don't know why, maybe it was the saké and my working-class background, but I got very pissed off with the Nip. After all, Katie was, sort of, my bird. I smacked the cunt in the teeth with a saké bottle, and before he had any time to react I pinned his tongue to the table with a chopstick.

'That's no way,' I said drunkenly to the five-foot dwarf, 'To speak to a lady.'

Katie was laughing hysterically – as if she needed any help from me! She whipped out a Glock 9mm and shot shouting boy through the top of his skull. Maybe things would have levelled out eventually, but Katie's big fat handcannon had raised the stakes. Guns started clicking all over the place, everyone with the drop on everyone else, it was a classic John Woo Mexican stand off.

Bill had Kendo and one of his unarmed assistants in the sights of the two cocked 45s he'd stolen from the cowboy. Kendo had a Smith and Wesson 625 pointing at Bill's face. Katie had sobered up immediately and was pointing her Glock at the Jap's house nigger who in turn was pointing his snubby Heckler and Koch VP70 at Katie. Gimpo was hypnotised by another shitting movie whizzing away in the VCR, *Stools of Desire* if I remember rightly.

'Gimpo!' called Katie to the masturbating turd lover, 'Are you strapped!?'

I think Gimps was as unfamiliar with the term as I was. He casually zipped himself up, wiping the ballsnot on to his grubby safari suit lapels and wandered over to the trembling slit-eyed desperados, laughing.

'Mexican standoff,' he laughed quite unafraid. 'This shit happened all the time in the Falklands, drinking and guns are a really dumb idea.'

He wandered around the petrified human sculpture of fear and percussion caps.

'I take it this is all a stupid mistake and you'd like to forget the whole thing but you're all afraid to make the first move in case you get shot by the other guy,' said the Gimps. stepping inside the circle of guns effectively blocking the shots of all five players. 'What I'm going to do is blindfold myself very tightly, turn around a few times so I don't know who is who then I'm going to take your guns off you one at a time and place them on the table. It's not a perfect way to end this as I'm sure you can all think of ways that this can go badly wrong.'

He started to tie a piece of black cloth tightly around his eyes and turning himself slowly around. 'But I can assure you it used to work pretty much every time during my active service, and apart from you idiots blowing each other's brains out I can't think of a better solution.'

Nagasaki and Bill gently surrendered their weapons which the Gimp dropped on to the table reluctantly; attitude house-nigger and Katie, cool as a rich heroin addict, handed over their guns. Gimpo ripped off his blindfold and killed the whole bunch of rising sun retards and the house coon in one snot-shaking burst of fire, blood and screaming.

READY OR NOT

The next morning Z was there with our sack of little players. So was Gimpo. I was last to arrive. We ate our last full English breakfast in the departure lounge restaurant. Z loaded up with duty free and showed us his brand new yo-yo. Gimpo bought some more film. I bought my last copy of *The Guardian*.

And as our flight was being called I heard myself mutter, 'OK Satan, ready or not, here we come.'

*

'Excellent work, Gimps' said Bill, genuinely impressed.

Katie was demonstrating her admiration much more physically, I felt a twinge of jealousy as the BBC sexbomb, like a lioness in heat, pulled down her khakis and offered up her jacksie to Gimps, the intense buggery fan. Gimps looked at me quizzically, opening his eyes wide and raising a palm to see if I objected.

'Go for it, arseboy,' I said laughing, 'Fuck her lungs out, you deserve it.'

Manchester studboy wasted no time and was on her like a rat up a drainpipe. I can't help thinking there was some kind of twisted transference-type revenge going on in Gimpo's head as he was slamming ultraviolently into Death Queen's bunghole. Bill jumped up on to the television set above the sex action and started battering away at his scarred salami, wanking insanely, eyes rolling into the back of his head, letting loose a staccato roll of brown noise trouser drumming like a Chinese firecracker. His Tourette's syndrome singing making a travesty of the country classic 'Coward of the County'.

'And they took turns on Betty, slag! bitch! cunt! whore! lesbian! Madonna! And there were three, cunt! fuck! shit! Of them...'

I called room service to get rid of the bodies. I don't know why but I just don't like having corpses lying all over the place. Sometimes they're not quite dead and they make funny noises, it damn well puts the willies up me. I stuffed the dead Japs' river film into the VCR. *Sockets Ahoy!* seemed to be the working title, I assume it referred to the Japanese translation of the slang word for bumhole which as everyone knows is buggery socket.

This was more than strange even to begin with. For a start there weren't any black people in the grainy debauchery pulsing away between the pixels. I mean, what was the point of coming to Africa and not using local talent? It was just the usual Japanese domestic scat insane murder nonsense. Geisha girls being shat on and chopped to pieces by vampire samurais with small dicks, the usual nip paed weirdness

To be quite honest, I'd had enough. It was time to get back to Kamden.

Fuck the devil, he could have my fucking soul.

THANKS ANYWAY

It's cloudy, the light is draining from the day. I follow the map the concierge has drawn for me along a few wide, almost empty, streets. Kisangani has a laidback vibe about it, none of the intense paranoia vibe that Kinshasa had, or maybe I'm just getting used to Zaire. I find the Telecel Office with a large satellite dish on its roof. It's the only vaguely hi-tech sort of place I've seen since arriving in Kisangani.

They want to be paid in dollars, up front, an arm and a leg. I do. They put me through.

'Hi Arthur, it's Bill.'

'................................'

'Yeah, Bill Drummond. Remember?'

'................................'

'Well, did you get to speak to the President. Is it OK for us to...'

'................................'

'What? He's not back from his wine-buying trip yet?'

'...................................'
'Won't be back for another four weeks?'
'...................................'
'No, I think that will be too late for us. Thanks anyway.'
'...................................'
'Yeah, we'll keep you posted on the book's progress.'
'...................................'
'Goodbye.'
And I put the phone back on its cradle.
Well, that's that.
What the fuck do we do now? It's dark outside. I start to walk back to the Hotel Zaire Palace. I pass an open-air bar, a bunch of men are sitting around watching a small black and white television. They are watching a football match. The reception is bad. I stop to watch. My heart sinks, it's England playing Holland. It's Euro '96. This means only one thing, Scotland have been knocked out as they had to beat Holland a couple of days after we left. They obviously didn't. I head back to the hotel feeling miserable as only a follower of Scotland can. All this way for fuckin' nothing. All these pages for fuckin' nothing, you might be thinking. Satan will have to wait.

Chapter Nine
WIPE OUT

This shit's sending me crazy.

How the hell I get myself in these scrapes is anybody's guess. My own guess lies somewhere along the ley lines of all that jungle hooch and Primus I was necking like a bastard.

Time shifts to a week later, back in London. I'm in Leicester Square with a little pug dog, whose name is Cherub. He belongs to my eldest daughter or rather she belongs to him. The same breed as that fellow over there in the north-east corner of the square, Mr Hogarth, was fond of.

But back to hell for a moment. The flight back out of that green shithole was fortuitous to say the least. The details are unclear. I remember Bill and Gimps legging it off to some whorehouse with a one-eyed lesbian. I stayed in the hotel and almost drank myself to death. On the whole I'm a pretty good alcoholic. I rarely puke, and if I do it's usually blood.

We'd eaten some tough old piece of goat meat earlier on and my guts had gone. Projectile. Both ends. Like I say, the details are unclear. But I can remember taking seventeen shits in under a quarter of an hour. For some reason I counted them. I thought maybe it might be of assistance to the doc back at the hospital for tropical diseases in London. If we ever got back, that is.

On the seventeenth squittering fartstorm I hurled a stream of greasy goat spew all over the khazi floor and staggered back to the tangled nylon sheets of my sparking static litter. Two minutes later the faecal demon was jabbing me in the guts again with his fucking pitchfork. I got to the bog and started screaming and squittering like a baboon melting from some weird strain of shit-dissolving ebola

Beyond the pain I noticed that something extraordinarily weird, even by Congo standards was going on. The vomit had disappeared. What the fuck was happening? Had the maid sneaked in or something while I was passed out and cleaned up all the vomit?

Impossible. And then I saw it.

Hiding under the sink about a foot away from my face. A huge glittering cockroach, antennae flickering, red eyes, vomit flecked on its chattering mandibles, it seemed to be smiling at me. I swear it was wearing a top hat, spats and smoking a cigar. Jiminny Cricket's evil cousin, Jiminny Cockroach. The revolting little bastard, obviously bored of its diet of shit and piss, had helped himself to my hurljuice. Fuck me sideways with a cricket bat, I was going truly insane. I ran out into the street, I hate cockroaches, especially when they're smoking cigars. Not wise. Serious looking soldiers, black as space, packing heat, major heat, fucking everywhere. But anything was better than hanging out with foot-long vomit-eating cockroaches. In top hats.

I found a bar. It had electricity, the bare light bulbs looked inviting, like French impressionism. A couple of drugged-up whores, heavy lids, sat with a couple of voodoo soldiers, Mai Mai cats who think its cool to eat their enemies' hearts in front of their wives before they rape them.

I sat down at a table and ordered the Primus. The soldiers were stony silent in their shades. They had those weird faucet things around their necks.

'Monsieur,' said one of them after about an hour.

'Yeah?' I replied.

'American?' he said, playing with a recently severed human hand.

'English.' I could tell they were men of few words so I didn't bother being polite.

'You should leave.'

He lit a cigarette and inhaled, the blue smoke made its way to the light bulb.

'Yeah, I know,' I answered honestly.

'Tomorrow.'

'Tomorrow, that's a good idea.'

'Tomorrow we blow the airport up.'

He pulled down his shades and looked me straight in the eye to emphasise his point.

'Shit.'

'About three o' clock. I think maybe there is the last plane about midday.' And he replaced his shades. 'I suggest you don't miss it.'

One of the whores lit him another cigarette. 'Otherwise monsieur, you really will be up shit creek without a paddle.'

The airport was full of Yorkshire mercenaries with Executive Outcomes t-shirts on, as if wandering around Africa killing people was like working at Kwik Fit, so innocuous was the design of their tasteful blue and yellow shirts.

I drank several bottles of wine on the airplane and woke up in London.

DRUMMOND'S LOG, 27 NOVEMBER 2003
EPILOGUE

Satan is still waiting and I don't give a fuck. Thirteen days ago Scotland beat Holland 1:0 at Hampden Park. It was the first leg of the playoffs to get into Euro 2004. All they needed was a 0:0 draw at the second leg in Holland. Five days later they got thrashed 6:0. The hope that kills us, as they say.

Today I'm in an empty flat on the fifteenth floor of a condemned block of flats in Liverpool I've been here all week. Nobody knows I'm here. From the flat I can see all the way across Liverpool, across the Mersey, across Birkenhead and New Brighton, out into the Irish Sea. When the light is right you can see the wind farm they are building off the coast of North Wales. I've come here before to write, empty my head and escape all my responsibilities. This time I've come to finish off writing my share of *Wild Highway*. This will be the third and, hopefully, last, time that I will have written it. The first time was as it happened. The puritan in me wanted that version to be the one, not a word changed. When we got back to Britain and I tried to go through what I had written, I could hardly read a word of it. As an artefact it's a great thing for me to have. It's still got the pressed butterfly in it and a few more that I captured before we got out of the place. It's got a ticket for the ferry stuck in it, a label from a bottle of Primus, a receipt from the Memlin Hotel, our letters of introduction.

Before we arrived in Zaire I knew nothing about the place. When we got back I started to read everything I could find, from Henry Morton Stanley's classic *Through The Dark Continent*, volumes one and two, first published in 1878, right up until books that have come out this year (2003). Dozens of them. As well as the books there were the journals and the overseas pages of the broadsheets. It became an addiction.

A terrible, terrible history was unfolding, but first things first. As it turns out, Mobutu wasn't on a wine-tasting tour he was dying of prostate cancer. In his absence, events began to unfold. He did return to his country briefly but he died in exile, 14 months after we left, in September 1997 in Morocco. Laurent Kabila, his long-standing arch enemy has taken over. He changed the name from Zaire to The Democratic Republic of the Congo and the river name also changed back to being called the Congo. Kabila was then assassinated and replaced by his playboy son. Since then the country has sunk into continual civil war. The place has been torn apart. At a generally accepted estimate and this is a conservative one, more than 3,000,000 people have been killed. That is more, by a huge margin, than in any war since the second big one. It makes the events of 11 September 2001 and the subsequent fracas in Afghanistan and Iraq seem like schoolyard tussles. And who gives a fuck? Nobody goes on peace marches for 3,000,000 dead Africans and there is no reason why it won't be 3,000,000 more. It is so much more easy to get angry about what George W Bush gets up to in the Middle East than what is going on in Africa. Every mobile phone in the world has a mineral in it, whose name I can't remember, that can only be mined in the Congo. People are being tortured, murdered, babies having their limbs hacked off so I can use my mobile to phone Sallie to say I will be home tonight because I've nearly finished my share of the book.

So I started to rewrite my take on the *Wild Highway*. I wanted to take on all this information I was stockpiling but with every new book I read or article telling me about what fresh horrors were unfolding I would start the rewriting process again. I felt I owed it to the individuals we met, the friends we made, the people struggling with the grind of their lives to write something that honoured them, did them justice or at least made you, the reader, think 'Fuck, I didn't know that, something should be done. My government should help stop this.' But the more I tried with the rewrites the more I realised I could never write that sort of stuff. I've just not got it in me.

Z was able to channel a lot of it through his story. The megaslaughter had not kicked in while we were there, and what he has written in his usual arch-bad taste is a shadow of what is still going on there now. The carnage that befell Kisangani only a few weeks after we got out has no modern comparisons outside of Central Africa.

Z had finished his text three or four years ago and I kept dithering about telling him, 'I've nearly done it Z, just a few more weeks and it will be nailed.' Then another horrific story about Central Africa would start unfolding on the overseas pages and I would want to take all this into account. I'd rewrite passages giving three-page speeches to our shipmates where they would go off on one about the latest developments in the copper-mining industry in Katanga (SE Congo) or diamond smuggling into Angola or boy soldiers, or the CIA's historical involvement. The more I wrote, the further I got from what happened and what I knew at the time.

So, early in 2003 I scrapped the lot, then reread my original notes made while we were there and rewrote this as light-hearted entertainment, trying never to let the focus stray too far from what was going on between the three of us. Yeah, of course I couldn't help let my own mid-life angst slip in from time-to-time, but I did try to keep a rein on it.

Some time ago (1988) our agent read the opening paragraphs of both our takes on the events. She was of the opinion the racism would prevent it from being published by a reputable publishing house, so goodbye Penguin. I guess from that point we both gave up any idea of self-censoring. As for all my European stuff it probably should have all been edited out or at least cut back to a bare minimum but I think a more pressing issue for us was our desire to have a big fat fuckin' book to our names. A sprawling, all-over-the-place, difficult-to-read one. A book that you have to be pretty committed to read, to get this far.

There's loads I'm already remembering I've forgotten to put in. As for JC, Golf, Arthur Malu Malu, Pitsu, Mami, Trefor, Mavuba, Giselle, Tally or Remi, I suppose some of them must have been killed. These were their real names. If anyone hears anything about them, let us know. Anyway, enough. We have to get the third and final volume of *The Bad Wisdom Trilogy* underway and now my mobile is ringing and I can see from the screen it's Z. I wonder what the fuck he wants now. And as for our souls we will just have to wait and see.

*

Leicester Square, wandering around, wondering if I'd dreamt the whole thing.

Why, who's that fellow in the middle? Good Lord, it's the Bard himself.

Funny, I've lived in London most of my life and God only knows how many shitty movies I've seen around that old haunt of Hogarth but for some strange reason I'd never noticed that odd pigeon shitty marble statue of Shakespeare surrounded by dolphins and burger munching tourists. My jaw kind of dropped and I farted nervously.

We'd travelled half way around the world, into the very heart of darkness itself, searching for the answers to the conundrums and riddles that surround the dark nature of man and there, resting languidly on one arm and laughing at us, the undisputed master of the English language and ultimate authority on the nature of the human condition points sardonically at a small scroll.

The twat.

Carved into the marble is the succinct, mocking, phrase;

There is no

darkness

but

ignorance.

I felt a right cunt.

The End.

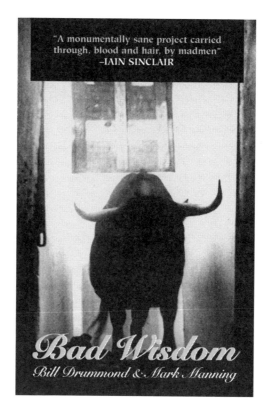

Bad Wisdom
Bill Drummond & Mark Manning

Having exhausted (and been exhausted by) the young man's religion of rock and roll, Bill Drummond and Mark Manning decide to undertake an epic journey to the North Pole to sacrifice an icon of Elvis Presley.

Two very different accounts of their journey clash and mesh in *Bad Wisdom* as the Zenarctic pilgrims venture forth into the frozen wastes at the top of the world.

Bad Wisdom is the first part of the trilogy which continues with *Wild Highway*..

"The truth, no matter how uncomfortable, cannot help but be beautiful – this is a very beautiful book"
–Jarvis Cocker

www.creationbooks.com

www.creationbooks.com